**The
Gold
of the
River
Sea**

Other Books by Charlton Ogburn, Jr.

THE WHITE FALCON
THE BRIDGE
BIG CAESAR
THE MARAUDERS
co-author of SHAKE-SPEARE—*The Man Behind the Name*

The Gold of the River Sea

by

Charlton Ogburn, Jr.

William Morrow
and Company
New York 1965

Copyright © 1965 by Charlton Ogburn, Jr.
All rights reserved.
Published simultaneously in the Dominion of
Canada by George J. McLeod Limited, Toronto.
Printed in the United States of America by H. Wolff, N.Y.
Designed by Adrianne Onderdonk

Library of Congress Catalog Card Number 65-11330

for **D. S. O.**

The
Gold
of the
River
Sea

1

In Czarist Russia serfs were called "souls," whereas in the United States today employees of the Government are called "bodies," at least by their fellows in the administrative divisions; an office is said to have "slots" for so many "bodies."

I was reminded of that by the sight of the building for which I was headed. It is a new building and a huge one, extending over so vast an area that its quite considerable height is scarcely apparent. Stark in form, unadorned, its bleak walls of limestone punctured by rows of aluminum-framed windows fixed in position, it resembles a model penitentiary. The inside is in keeping with the out. The offices open like cells off interminable corridors, and since each corridor is identical in appearance with every other and no provision exists for a glimpse of the outside world, floor-plans have to be posted at intersections with an arrow showing where you are, or would be if you were there, so that you may find your way.

I worked for many years in the organization housed in that building—before the building itself was erected—but why I was returning now I did not know. The head of the bureau in which I had served for most of those years had said only, when he telephoned, "Julian, I have something interesting to show you. You must come over. . . . Yes, the sooner the better." Odd and demanding as the summons was, I was close to forgetting it the moment I put the receiver down, I was so preoccupied. I often worry about my absent-mindedness. There is almost nothing I cannot forget—no current obligation, that is. But I know how fortunate anyone is whose work can fill his mind for hours at a time to the exclusion of virtually all else.

I am a painter. When I speak of the rewards of work in connection with my own, I do not mean to suggest that I live in a mood of self-congratulation. I am grateful enough to be able to make a livelihood and support a most deserving wife and children by painting, even though this has meant doing a fair amount of commercial work—less as time has gone on. (I teach a little, too, though the money it brings in is inconsiderable and I probably get more out of it than the students do.) One has to pay one's way in the world, and the necessity may as well be accepted with a good grace. But thankful as I am that my life permits me to go straight to a canvas in the mornings, I know what it is—none better!—to turn away from one in despair at my ineffectuality, to look up at the hypothesized abode of the gods and, burning and choked with gall over my limitations, cry, "Why? Why? Why am I trying to do this?" It is too hard!

Yet I cannot resist it. It takes me out of the house in all weathers, at all hours—out at dawn on the estuary of the river beside which we live, when the sun first burnishes the tops of the pines—to a logging road through a forest lost in fog, when the trees recede into a whiteness without sound or motion—to upland meadows murmurous with insects, tangled underfoot, fragrant with summer grasses in the heat. I drift about among the landings of the fishing-boats down the river, wander along the beach where the line of flotsam skirts the grass-crested dunes and gulls take wing ahead of one into the wind, stand blowing my hands in the cold of a winter's day on a hilltop from which the city may be seen mantled under a cover of snow freshly fallen from the still yellow-grey clouds. And I paint. Perhaps like all painters, I am tempted to cry,

2

"If only I could paint what I see!—what I see and therefore what I feel!" But I know better. I have learned the vanity of that wish, with its comforting premise that technique is what counts. It is not technique but seeing that counts. If you can see, the rest follows. The great painters have seen what others have failed to see. That is why they are great.

To see—that is the problem: to empty the mind of habit, of preconceptions, of thumbed-over impressions so that one may be receptive to the essential nature of things, so that one may perceive and hold in the eye the crowness of a crow, the blossomness of the first crocus in spring, the rainfulness of a squall coming in over the water, what is implicit in the bulk and texture of a rock, of a bird in repose, of the elemental human figure. In what is there before your eyes is that Truth we all seek —but fleetingly, tantalizingly, just beyond the edge of your vision! You catch the stir of its movement, can almost feel for an instant that it has looked out upon you like a woman unseen behind a shuttered window; and then it is gone. But once you persuade yourself that you have mirrored some suggestion of it in what you have brought into being, nothing will serve but that you must go on and try to do better, try to be more open, more accessible to it.

I know what I am trying to do, but I have to learn from others what I have done. On the whole, critics have dealt with me sympathetically. I read that I awaken in the beholder those associations of the past that cause the picture to have for him the intensely-realized character of the remembered. It is gratifying to be told that and to learn that one's paintings remind the viewer of those instances, familiar to all, when we feel with overwhelming conviction that we have been through this before, that we are reliving precisely that which once happened to us, or of which we had some miraculous precognition in a dream.

Said a literary critic half a century ago: *All great art is like a ghost seeking to express more than it can utter and beckoning to regions beyond*. That is true. By God, it is!

I am not a great painter. Yet I have seen that which the greatest artists have given us no more than an inkling of, and I am sure there are others who will recognize what I mean, who will have known times when, for no more than an instant, it may be, their awareness was prodigiously enhanced, as if blinders had been struck from their eyes and they saw, as it were, to the heart of things—the heart of the rose and the heart of the thunderhead—grasping the ineluctable, understanding in a flood of il-

3

lumination how it all is and must be. It seemed to me, at the moment when *I* knew what it was, that there was revealed to me, as there could have been to no one before me, that which is within and behind all we see. I say this in no spirit of vainglory—God knows. It came not from within me but from another. Through her I had a surpassing sense of ultimate recognition and fulfillment, of confirmation, of discovery and homecoming. Then I lost her, and it, and the desire to live, and there followed days of which it was not possible to think for a long time afterward. When, in the end, I came to life again, miraculously, as it seemed to me, it was with the belief that I could regain, in some sense anyway, that which had been taken from me. I had an incentive that has not failed since then.

In the years when I worked for the Government, I painted after hours, whenever I could and as long as I could, but I was only waiting until I should be able to give all my time to it—until I had put by enough money and acquired confidence enough in my ability to make a go of it. When I went to work for the Government, I was not looking for a career. I was looking for a means of subsistence. You have to meet the world on its own terms, my father had insisted while I was growing up—a point well taken in my case—and looking back on it, I realize that the injunction acquired force from the distaste for the encounter he had had to overcome in himself. The necessity was undeniable, of course. I had not much to offer the market but a smattering of Portuguese and some acquaintance with north Brazil, and a government flushed with enthusiasm for being a good neighbor of the countries to the south seemed a logical employer to which to offer them. I had not expected my application to be accepted, and when it was I entered upon my employment with a nervous dread, anticipating that my first piece of work would be instantly spotted as spurious, the product of an impostor. Instead, it was astonishingly accepted at face value. In time I learned that my colleagues were human in much the ways I was and that they got along by refraining from overclose scrutinies of their own qualifications—and, it is only fair to add, by working long hours. I worked long hours, too, and before many months I was rewarded with a commendation, marvelous to relate, followed in time by a rise in grade. The long hours became long years. Responsibilities grew, and with them authority. I played my part in promoting the good and constructive purposes of the United States Government from ever higher levels, over ever larger areas. I never lost

4

sight of my aim, but the fact that I *had* met the world on its own terms made the decision to quit the Government when the time came a bigger one to make. There could, however, be but one decision, and I never regretted deciding as I did.

I had a long distance to go to turn out paintings that, even for what they were, satisfied me, and have had a longer still, by far, to work my way back to where I stood so briefly when I was a young man, far away and long ago. The practice of an art is not easy. I have been beset by that particular devil of those who work at any art or, I suppose, at any solitary pursuit. It is a more dangerous devil than the one who tempted our Lord. That one had no more imagination than to try to subvert the Son of God with offers of wealth and power. Even I would be resistant to that. The devil I am talking about would seem innocuous enough. He has only one simple taunt—a question. But, standing always at your shoulder, he never tires of voicing it: "What makes you think *you* can do it?"

Still, I have made progress. I have consistently, if unevenly and sometimes unbelievingly, gained ground. And the farther I have traveled, the nearer I have come to knowing what I knew when I was with *her,* and, for that reason, the nearer to her herself. I believe I am getting there, "there" being where every artist hopes to be, "there" being above all, for me, where she is, and though I do not know exactly what I mean by that—only that it is beyond definition—the belief suffices.

These things were in my mind as I walked the seeming mile of corridor to the office of my friend, the bureau chief; the familiar atmosphere, as of the court of some unsleeping, inexhaustibly demanding, inconceivably rich but penurious tyrant, never yet seen by anyone, making his ukases known to each rank of his servants through the one above, anxiously served by all, tolerating no competing interest on the part on those closest to him, made me aware of the gap between my former life and my present. If the past had not been in my mind before I arrived at my friend's office, it would have been so directly afterward.

"Look there. Do you recognize any of it?"

I looked first instead at the bureau chief for an indication of what I might expect to find on the table to which he beckoned me. All I could discern, apart from his rather smug smile, was confirmation of my first impression that, in the distressing fashion of my other contemporaries, he appeared to have aged. Parker Willis and I had grown up together in

5

the service, but I had not seen him for several years. High officials of an overworked department of the Government have little life outside it.

So I gave my attention to what lay about on the table—old-looking papers, some yellowed around the edges, handwritten and typewritten; a few sketched maps; small bottles of what resembled gold. Recognition came first as incredulity. It was not possible.

"I didn't mean to give you a shock," Parker interposed quickly; his smile vanished.

"It's all right. Where . . . where did these come from?"

"From the Brazilian Government. Do they upset you?"

I turned away from them. "It's been a long time. How do they happen to be here?"

"They came with a mass of supporting documentation, in connection with a request for a developmental loan. The scheme would be to develop the economy of a sub-basin of the Amazon River from scratch, as a unit—a kind of Tennessee Valley Authority. The river playing the role of the Tennessee would be the—" He glanced down among the papers.

"The Massaranduba."

"Yes, that's it. We call it the M.V.A. Well, you can imagine our astonishment to find from the material the Brazilian Government sent us that one of the early intrepid explorers was—Julian Tate. I was sure it was you—from your handwriting and from remembering your having once mentioned that you'd been in that part of the world before you came to work for Uncle Sugar. What on earth were you doing there?"

I explained that I had been working for a man who was trying to interest a syndicate of New Yorkers in a gold-mining concession in the area. He said he would like very much to hear all I could tell him about it. Accordingly, we had lunch together.

I had never been in the staff dining-room, and reverting to the status I had had when I had eaten in the mere executive cafeteria, I felt a certain awe, as if in entering it I were breasting a denser medium than ordinary air. The Supremo himself was at a table with half a dozen others, smiling and chatting and looking no larger than life. He nodded to me with a generalized friendliness, remembering my face but not whom it belonged to, for we had known each other ten years before. When I looked around and recognized half of those present as contemporaries of mine in the service—some of whom greeted me in a way to make me suspect they did not know I had left it—I felt more at home.

6

I told Parker as much about the Massaranduba as I thought would interest him, and he explained the importance it had in current planning in terms of its wealth of resources—gold, silver, manganese, bauxite, timber, water power, probably oil and probably also uranium ore—and, given a significant amount of highway construction, its accessibility via navigable waterways to world markets. What excited Parker and others who were close to the project was the prospect that with an initial "infusion of capital" from without, the Massaranduba could "spark" a "self-generating economic development." Commerce, industry and agriculture would spread outward from the Massaranduba, nurtured on their own proceeds. The "reclamation" of the immense Amazon basin would be on its way. The day could be foreseen when it would support a population of several hundred million persons, more than the entire present population of Latin America. Long before that—within a few years—it would be an example for all South and Central America, a "showcase" of cooperation between the United States and the other American republics. . . . I remembered vividly a time when the picture Parker portrayed had presented itself to me with an overwhelming plausibility. I felt sick.

"There's a tremendous job to be done," he said. "I suppose you're too famous to consider coming back with us. Getting back into harness, getting your teeth into things again."

"The image is of a refractory horse."

"Exactly how I think of you!" he exclaimed. "Come, what about it?"

"The Department's already overstaffed. And well you know it."

"Nonsense! How could it be? As the staff increases by arithmetical progression, the work of administering it increases by geometrical progression. The more we expand, the farther we fall in arrears of our needs. And well *you* know that. No, but seriously," he declared, "there's always a dearth of good men with experience. We've got an enormous problem in Latin America. And it does mean something to serve your country."

"Conjugation: *I* serve my country, *you* are a Government employee, *he* has his snout in the public trough. . . . Yes, I agree with you. But I did my stint—eighteen years of it, including the war. Before I quit I was having a recurrent dream in which I suffered the delusion that my nervous system, the channels of command in the Department and the wiring of the building were all one. There it would be, laid out before me, a combination of anatomical diagram, plan of electrical circuits and or-

7

ganizational flow-chart. I shouldn't have done any good if I'd stayed on."

After a silence, during which we left the table and started back to his office, he said, "When I'm tempted to leave the Government—and God knows it would be nice to be able to count on three or four evenings a week at home—I worry that I'd have a feeling of letdown. I've seen it happen with others. I'm afraid that nothing I could do for myself would seem to be of much consequence after I'd been working on problems affecting the lives of millions and having a sense of helping make history—even if that's an illusion. I think I'd want to come back. That's why I should think you would."

We had arrived at the elevator, for which several others were waiting. It was nearly a full minute before we reached Parker's floor and were alone again. I said then, "I'd better render my contribution to your history-making by staying away. I'd be a negative influence—a ghost at the banquet."

"Why do you say that?"

It was high time for me to be going. I reflected on his question, seeing in memory as I did so a remarkable man I had met in Manáos, to whom I owed much of what I might have said in reply—were there time. "I'm having a show next month," I said. "Perhaps you could find a chance to come see it. It might speak for me better than I could."

"I shall," he replied, standing aside for me to precede him into his office. Following me in, he said, "But whatever your notions are, don't forget what I've said. If you'd give it a chance you'd soon see the value of what's waiting to be done in Brazil. The job's one you began as a youngster. And now you have an opportunity to pick it up and carry it through to something far bigger than you could ever have imagined then. Who ever has a chance for such a satisfaction as that? You could get in on the ground floor and on the top rung of the ladder—a remarkable trick, surely." He had moved over to the table on which the articles from the Massaranduba were spread. It was uncanny that after such a span of years they should retain for me such a powerful odor of death.

He continued. "I don't think one of these nuggets would be missed— if you'd like one as a souvenir or talisman—a touchstone!"

"No, let them all go back with the supporting documentation," I replied. "They were ill-omened. They put a curse on those who were led

8

on by them. I shouldn't count on their having lost their power. Perhaps you ought to be warned."

After observing that I was not joking, he gazed at me while sifting in his mind what I had said. "Yes, I suppose being led on by cupidity is always a danger," he observed, speaking slowly, without taking his eyes from mine. He smiled a little. "There's something about gold, I grant." I could tell that he was prepared to make allowances for the childishness on my part that he had stumbled upon; I had not for some years had the benefit of the Department's schooling in realism. "But mind you, in this case it's not a matter of individuals seeking their own gain. What we're concerned with is the good of a great number—the whole New World, actually."

As I said nothing, his voice when he spoke again had a slight edge. "You apparently did well enough. Considering how few weeks you were there—if I read your reports correctly—you brought an astonishing amount of booty back with you. And evidently with impunity."

"That's true," I said. I paused to ensure my control over my voice, to be able to speak casually, with an effect of indifference. "And you can expect to achieve the same kind of success for your beneficiaries." The surprise in his eyes told me I had failed in my aim. "The whole New World, is it?" Despite myself, my voice was tense and harsh. "I wish you all the satisfaction of it!"

9

2

I had been several years out of college when my father asked me if I should like to take a trip to north Brazil—to Pará. "It would be on business, of course," he added. "In connection with the Massaranduba Concession."

I had heard of that enterprise. It was one in which my father's associate —they were not quite law-partners—Oliver Willet, was interested. But that any outgrowth of New York's financial district could have the potentiality of transporting me to the Amazon River was more than I could credit.

"How would I fit into it?" I had asked warily, fearful lest a single exploratory poke of the finger might cause this vision to explode like a bubble.

"There seems to be a failure of communication between Oliver's client in Brazil, Mr. Monteiro, and the syndicate here in New York. An extra effort appears to be needed to bring matters to a head. Perhaps the syndicate requires more reassurance about the attitude of the local government before it acts to acquire the Concession. Or perhaps it requires more reassurance of a kind less easy to put your finger on. After all, no one on either side has ever actually seen the mines or been to the area." A shade of worry puckered his brow for an instant. "It's a part of the world you might enjoy visiting."

Another parent than mine might have put it differently, viz.: "There's an opportunity here for someone with application and drive. If there is any possibility of your ever being inspired to display either in a constructive cause, it would probably be in such a place. At least it is something to try."

So far I had given no indication of a purpose in life. The trouble was that everything I should have liked to do—especially anything in the field of art—seemed impractical, an evasion of the demands the world makes on one. I had worked in an insurance office and in an advertising agency with equally unsatisfactory results. The latter—a small organization, operating in hard times—had just gone out of business. If I could not be charged with having made its collapse inevitable, neither could I be credited with having delayed it.

I did not feel hopeful and never had. Most adolescents doubtless have times of feeling lost and impotent in an oversized world of invulnerable competence. I was brought to New York at the age of ten. Until that event I could remember no unhappiness, only the normal unpleasantnesses of cold, hunger, sickness and arbitrary parental rule. New York was crushing. It was, and it was not, the city itself that was so overbearing: its interminable vistas of grey and massive stonework. In the very act of running from its monstrous presence, riding its elevated railroads and subways and walking its streets, I acquired that kind of backhand affection for it that a private and intimate knowledge of almost anything will foster. I was like a mouse whose fugitive existence makes it more at home in a house than the master it flees, who owns the place. I trod the broad, gaping avenues of uptown Manhattan, where grocery, hardware, cigar and drug stores and Chinese hand-laundries—all barely making a go of it—formed a repeated pattern, where streetcars stood with a meditative *chung-chung-chung* of their air brakes and went complaining off, growling and lurching, where the ice-wagons were pursued by bands of pallid youngsters, for whom the world was a few blocks square. It must have been dreary enough, but I did not know it. I rode

11

the subways, thrilling to the black, swaying faces of the incoming trains, jeweled with red, green and yellow lights. I knew the waterfront along Riverside Park, where the waves from the Fort Lee ferries heaved onions, fruit crates and a dead dog languidly against the rocks. I was adept at eluding the gangs of young toughs in Central Park, who were always hungering for a chance to strip a solitary boy of any valuables he possessed. The adaptation was nearly perfect. Yet there remained the master of the house, against whom I should someday have to measure up, with whom I should someday have to contend. The world was a place in which you had to make your way.

I had been accustomed to a yellow clapboard schoolhouse with fewer rooms than classes, set in a grove of water-oaks just back from a salt river on the coast of Georgia. There I had known not only every other pupil as a matter of course but also, if he were a boy anywhere near my own age, his pocketknife, marbles, bicycle and what he was collecting at the moment. The institution I attended in New York was as big and handsome in my eyes as a state capitol, and as intimidating. I escaped to the American Museum of Natural History and made drawings of birds and mammals. On weekends I had confederates, three other boys as unreconciled to confinement as I. Meeting before dawn, we would travel as far out of the city as our finances would allow, which, straitened though they were, was far in those days of five-cent fares. We despised the Boy Scouts with their grown-up leaders, organized troops and paraphernalia. With only a lunch in a bag, which we had generally eaten by ten o'clock to free ourselves of the encumbrance, we would strike out from the end of the line without even a canteen, so that when we got back to the outposts of civilization at the end of the day we were prepared to down a full quart of cream-soda each. I wonder if any of the others still remembers the old squatter with crazy eyes in the Overpek marsh who charged us with having tried to set fire to his shack the night before and threatened us with a shotgun, or the fuselage of the airplane half buried in the sand at Long Beach and the gulls that wheeled around it in the winter wind, dropping clams on the hard shingle to break their shells.

During the summers I worked in a country boardinghouse, what today might venture to call itself a resort hotel, modest as it was. I worked in the stables and vegetable-gardens, first for room and keep, then for wages, always for the chance when the work was done to tramp the meandering back roads of Connecticut, the hill-pastures, the bottomlands dense with alder, and the dry, forested ridges which were too steep and rocky ever to have been tilled. They were not high, but they stood as islands above seas of change, their hours measured in the life-span of oak trees and granite.

Gazing upon a valley from a mountaintop, you can understand how a Supreme Being from a far loftier point of vantage could look down upon the world, static as a painting from that elevation, with benign composure and be puzzled to account for the torrent of excited invocations forever rising from below. But it was to a different order of things, to an earlier day, that the open, sunlit woods of those unvisited ridges took you. They gave you a hint at least of the age of folklore and myth, when the gods still came to earth, frequenting hilltop and meadow, before they and men and animals had moved so far apart.

I had set myself to learn all that could be learned of plants and animals—to make their kingdoms mine. I cannot remember ever feeling lonely, except with that formless, all-pervasive loneliness of youth which nothing but the fantasy of youth can reach. Of that I had my share, and it was never more active than in those groves of oaks not altogether unlike some others in which hamadryads were glimpsed in days gone by. I did not believe in the nymphs of Attica, at least as being subject to appearance in the woods I knew, but at times I was not far from believing in a nymph native to them who would advance from a glade where a ruffed grouse trod its drumming log untroubled by her presence and a tanager pursued its lilting, buzzy song a few feet away. She was most plausible where the black birch grew, with its cool, flesh-smooth trunk and sap tasting of wintergreen. Idealized in figure and not fully personified in feature, she was nonetheless all but real to me as I sat, still breathing heavily from the climb up the hot, airless slope, arms and legs smarting from the scratches left by blackberry-canes and cat-briar, into which the perspiration had trickled, gazing in the direction from which she might come, bringing an understanding of what I could not explain in myself.

It was in the tropics that those things that exerted the strongest pull on me would be at their grandest, their most exuberant, their most formidable. The thought of them helped me bear the drab, frigid wasteland of a New England city where I went to college. I read books on tropical countries and fell further under their fascination, under the spell of an idea embodied in a tumult of impressions—of images of sluggish rivers

13

that slipped between banks of mud over which crocodiles waddled in hasty flight, of forests of enormous trees with buttressed trunks and limbs saddled with ferns and hung with lianas, of the fall of darkness upon a last outpost of trade, the swarming of strange insects around the lamp and sudden, weird cries that made my flesh tingle with anticipation, of the intoxicating profusion and variety of life crowned for me by the figure of a harpy eagle, such as I knew from the Museum of Natural History in New York, with monkey-slaying talons the size of a gryphon's and eyes burning in a face like an Indian war-mask. All of it, I thought, must reach its most prodigious in that place where the world's mightiest river, fed by melting snows from two thousand miles of Andean mountainside, flowed through the world's greatest forest to meet the ocean squarely upon the equator and push it back out of sight of its shores with the volume of water of a dozen Mississippis. The conjunction of such superlatives was to me beyond explaining as mere coincidence. A religious mystic or a lover might understand the feelings that sprang up in me at the name *Amazon*.

How, I asked my father when it appeared that the abruptly thrown-out suggestion of my journeying to the Massaranduba Concession might actually bear my weight, was I to begin? It was in my mind that the project should be nailed in place, invulnerable to second thought, without a moment's unnecessary delay. "I suppose I should see Mr. Willet as soon as possible?"

"I think you should. There's a great deal of background for you to acquire."

I was deeply anxious about the impression I might give Mr. Willet. I had to pass muster as a likely, or possible, catalyst in an international gold-mining deal. It was a large order. The strain I was on may have communicated itself to him. Our initial interview was a rather formal one. My father had told me I should find his associate on the sober side. "He's not a flashy type or the kind to twist a jury around his little finger, but he's a profound student of the law and very highly thought of at N.Y.U. He has an evening course there, you know. He's a deadly strategist: never overlooks any possible contingency." He was, I judged, in his late forties, as humorless in demeanor as I had been led to expect, with a glistening dome of forehead and grey eyes heavy with thought. These settled upon the middle of my chest, not, I discovered, because I had a spot on my tie, but because that was his way. He conducted himself, I thought later in reviewing the proceedings, as if he were a glass of milk in danger of spilling over; but that was probably also the way I struck him. He expressed his gratification at the prospect of having my father's son as a collaborator. He trusted that I should find the connection not without interest . . . the word "reward" figured in what followed, but his voice was indistinct and in tone sounded more as if he were commiserating with than congratulating me. But that, I decided, reflected a trait of personality rather than an appraisal of prospects.

Before we parted with renewed mutual embarrassment, Mr. Willet recommended that my first step be to acquaint myself with the files on the proposed Concession. A small table was set up for me in the reception room, and to this I repaired daily.

When I saw those bulging folders, which stood between me and the forests of the Amazon, my heart sank. It remained at a low level while I forced my way through the mass and tried to take in what the problem of the Massaranduba Concession was all about. One difficulty I had was with the language. I do not mean that what I was reading was in Portuguese (though much of the printed matter was). What I was up against was the terminology of finance and financial law. I did not understand it, and what was just as bad, it took me back to one of the worst weeks of my life, when my father had suggested that the most promising opening the business world offered to one of my bent (I had a fair head for figures) might be the field of accountancy. I actually enrolled in and commenced a course, though the outcome was pretty clearly foreshadowed the first day when it transpired—and a never-to-be-forgotten sensation it created, too—that I believed double-entry bookkeeping to be a nefarious device to conceal peculations.

It was not only the quality of the words that gave me trouble; it was also the quantity. I feared that any enterprise which produced such reams of paper was, like a plant that runs to foliage, apt to produce little else—little fruit. It was not the prospect of profits for future stockholders that concerned me; I hardly thought in such terms yet. It was that I looked to the business, frantically, to get me to Brazil. I reminded myself that the streets I walked, the subways I rode, the buildings I inhabited had sprung originally from just such unpromising piles of typed-over sheets, unaccountably and mysteriously it might be, by my lights, but demonstrably nonetheless, as mushrooms pop up overnight out of fallen leaves. There was no doubt that was right. It seemed unlikely, however,

15

that the business enterprises that made America synonymous with progress, or soon would again, it was hoped—the country being then in the
depths of the Great Depression—did not normally, as ours did, revolve
about the person of a seventy-five-year-old Levantine Greek. But it was
only my inexperience that found anything odd in that either. Mr. Willet
acknowledged that Dr. Xenides was perhaps past the physical meridian of
life, but that, he said, did not mean he was out of the running. Oh no!
Indeed it did not! Alekos Xenides was solid as rock—in more than one
way, as it sometimes appeared, alas. He was a keen geologist, a petroleum
engineer, and reputedly a very wealthy man, whose advice carried great
weight. As for his being Greek, some of the world's leading businessmen
were that. Anyone who could locate in times such as these the capital
that would be required to put the Concession on a paying basis was entitled to respect in Willet's view—as in mine; the element of the Depression had greatly contributed to my doubts about the enterprise.

The correspondence consisted of heavy white sheets with blocks of
print in the large letters of an old-fashioned typewriter, generally short,
obstinate and to the point, signed roundly by the Greek, alternating with
flurries of featherweight airmail-paper from Brazil covered to the margin
with purple type, the sheets bitten deep by the lettering, the punctuation-
marks gone clean through them, voluble, passionate, caustic, signed
with a careful flourish of the pen intersected by two neat little vertical
strokes under the name *J. R. de Monteiro*. The argument, or plot, seemed
to be a simple one. Mr. Willet's Brazilian client, Dr. João Raimundo de
Monteiro, had undertaken to obtain from his Government a mining
concession covering an immense tract of land on the Rio Massaranduba
on behalf of an American syndicate represented by Dr. Xenides. The
only trouble was that the principals, the correspondents, appeared to be
at odds on almost every particular.

Mr. Willet, whose opinion I hesitantly sought, conceded that there had
been considerable sparring and said he thought it was time to bring matters to a head. He reminded me that there, of course, was where I came
in, which was a consideration I had almost forgotten and recalled only
with a cold tremor. "What you might bear in mind meanwhile," he pursued, his eyes glancing off mine, "is that Mr. Monteiro and Dr. Xenides
are not tyros. The Pôrto Alegre Concession, which they engineered, was
a history-making enterprise—or could have been. I believe it would repay

your looking into." He instructed his secretary to supply me with the necessary materials.

I had come upon references to the Portalegre Corporation in my reading. "His syndicate!" a missive from South America had exploded. "Who are these great men? They have a million dollars, he says. Well. But I must know who they are. I will not have them do with this concession as that other was done with—that is, nothing. Because of that I am a man to be laughed at by my Government." (The identities of the men behind him Alekos Xenides steadfastly refused to divulge. "Let Mr. Monteiro worry about the persons on whom the issue depends on his side, the officials whom my syndicate know to be inefficient, unreliable, arrogant and corrupt.")

I spent two days piecing together the story of the Pôrto Alegre Concession from what fragments I was able to understand, and I must say I found it illuminating, in an oblique sort of way. Dr. Xenides had caught wind of petroleum on the breezes emanating from the central Amazon basin. He had interested a New York investment house in the possibilities. Geologists had been sent out and had spent two years exploring the area. Their report was a glowing one. Senhor Monteiro obtained a concession for the exploitation of the oil-fields—a concession covering a territory the size of Germany, one of the biggest in history, it must have been. The Portalegre Corporation was created under the laws of the State of Delaware, and stock was offered for sale. (I have today five thousand shares of it bearing in facsimile the seal of the Corporation and the signatures of the President and Treasurer.) This brought those on the inside, I judged, a mint of money.

"What happened after that?" I asked Mr. Willet, for the exegesis I had been given was silent on the aftermath. My question awakened an echo in my memory, and it was a moment before I could place it: "And what happened to Br'er Rabbit then, Uncle Remus?"

"I'm afraid that was about the end. The Concession was allowed to lapse."

"Without any drilling? One well would have held the Concession until . . . well, until now, anyway, I gather."

"Without a well," Mr. Willet replied with his usual economy of emotion. "The interest of the financial community had begun to alight upon the Venezuelan fields. They are, of course, the ones being developed

17

now. Your father believes—and I concur—that we had grounds for a stockholders' suit against the officers of the Corporation. There is a possibility, though, that the Portalegre Corporation could become the instrument for exploiting the Massaranduba Concession, which could make a great difference to the stockholders."

I went back to my files with little more confidence in my ever emerging from the realm of negotiations, prospectuses and legerdemain. It was at this stage, however, that the name Braga began to appear in the correspondence. The Braga family, it transpired, owned a parcel of land along the border of the intended Concession and on the Iguarapé Urubu two young men of the family were actually engaged in mining gold. That was a reality to cling to.

Concurrently I was brought back to earth in a rather more immediate fashion. Mr. Willet sent for me and, confirming the fact of my presence in his office with a cautious look, stated, "Mr. Monteiro wishes you to—" Breaking off, he focused more studiously upon the letter he was holding.

"—to buy him a ship."

"To do *what?*"

"The details are all here." He extended the letter to me. "He thinks it may take a little time to find a vessel fully meeting his requirements. And if Mr. Monteiro anticipates difficulties, you may be sure they will not be lacking."

I read my name in the familiar purple print with a queer sensation. Senhor Monteiro expressed great gratification over the news that the young American was coming to Belém and wondered if before he left he might have a chance to look into the availability of a cargo vessel suitable for both river and coastal navigation, specifications enclosed.

I expected that when I called at a steamship-broker's office to inquire if there were any such thing to be had as a secondhand freighter with a displacement of fifteen hundred tons and a twelve-foot draft the staff would be sent staggering backward in helpless hilarity, so I was surprised when my interest appeared to be viewed as perfectly normal and plans were produced. "Now here's one at present in a Baltimore berth. . . ."

I made the rounds of the brokers with growing aplomb. "Ten knots is sufficient for our client. Fuel consumption should not be over . . ." I kept sending the information I gathered on to Monteiro.

Having come up to the present in my reading on the Concession, I was now waiting to see Dr. Xenides. He had vanished without warning into

Canada and wrote from there with a calm that I found alarming. He would let us know when he would be back. Meanwhile, he asserted, if I left any time soon I should probably find the area to be explored under several feet of water because of the season of the rains, which was then beginning.

I did not worry about the requirements of the part I should be expected to enact in Brazil; in the shadow of the equatorial rain-forest everything would be different. There was room in my mind for only the one anxiety it contained—the fear of my never getting embarked. There was nothing untoward in what was delaying it, I am sure. The world could not be expected to drop everything it was doing to get me off to Brazil. Yet its failure to do so made me suspect a dark design on its part to hold off my departure forever.

At all events, Monteiro was not part of it. "When are you coming?" the fountain of purple typing in Belém demanded to know. "I tell you, if any more time is thrown away all is lost. You write me of annual floods in the Concession! I wonder if you know what they say of me in the Ministry of Labor. They say I am the useful fool of Americans who want money without work or responsibility. You must be here before the end of the month."

A biting cold had settled upon the city. On the streets and sidewalks an unusually heavy fall of snow had been beaten to a superstratum of fused quartz as indestructible as the chasm-walls that rose, tomblike, above it. When the winds finally died they left in their wake a ceiling of snow-cloud, a wearisome expanse of tarnished silver. The prisoners of the metropolis shuffled along on the icy footing, unsmiling, heads bent, resembling a stunted race from underground newly ventured forth into a city built by giants and abandoned to the cold. There seemed to be no possibility that things could ever be different.

While awaiting the return of Dr. Xenides, I continued to run down small cargo-ships and send their specifications to Brazil. I became familiar with every vessel approaching the desired type that was up for sale from the Mediterranean to Montreal, where the vessel most favored by Monteiro was frozen in for the winter. While exploring for new offerings I found a ship called *Boadicea* listed for early departure for north Brazilian ports. The next mail brought word that Dr. Xenides was on his way back to New York and would see me in his office in two days.

Alekos Xenides turned out to look not at all like the Patriarch of

19

Constantinople, but rather like a substantial businessman of the kind you might have met in the lobby of an hotel on the Mississippi around the turn of the century. My first thought was of Mark Twain. Dr. Xenides was a great deal heavier, however, and his nose was bulbous, as if it had been stung all over by bees, but he had the same disheveled eyebrows, doggy look about the cheeks, and large moustache that bristled under the nose only to droop resignedly at the corners of the mouth. At the moment he was hanging the same plantation-hat of tan felt on a hook on the wall, disclosing the same old-fashioned coiffure, the hair in disordered waves about the ears but sparse on top.

"I am a hundred years old, Mr. Tate, but you would never know it, would you?" These were his first words. He cocked his massive head inquiringly, and I rallied sufficiently to assure him that he looked hardly half of that. He chuckled. "One of my countrymen has lived to the age of one hundred and forty-two and has just taken another wife—his eighth. You may have read. For myself, I shall be satisfied if I do only as well. What do you think? I can say that my organs are in perfect condition," he pursued placidly. Only what he really said was, "I gan zay dat my organss are in berfegt gondition." His speech was guttural, the result of several youthful years spent in Germany. He added, "Off gourse, I am no longer zo attragdive to de girlss—de beoodiful girlss— but I gan blease dem. I tink I gan zay dat I blease dem."

"I'm sure you do," I responded. The unintended effect was decorous, even demure. It was not easy to rearrange the expectations I had brought with me.

He came close to laughing aloud, his eyes nearly disappearing between his rising cheeks and the puffs beneath his eyebrows. "You hear? De boy hass a gude understanding." It was difficult to guess to whom this remark was addressed.

Bringing his eyes back into line with mine, he regarded me inquiringly, his arms crossed—they could hardly have been folded—across his very considerable torso. I had the horrible feeling that he was going to ask me what had brought me here.

"Mr. Willet told me—" I began, but he held up his hand and I stopped.

"*Tête de veau à la reine dérangé* is heavy for lunch, would you not agree? I cannot always account for my tastes. Possibly it was my companion at table—one of your leading engineers in my field. From him I heard much of the good works that our profession can do. And many has he done. He has made himself ill, in unhealthful countries, and all the while he is bringing health to others. Especially by public water supply. And public sewage. Mother of God, the sewage pipes that man has laid! And all this is only an incident to the sinking of oil-wells. His reward is to be martyred—to indigestion. Surely this is a strange world! I am afraid he was very disapproving of my lunch. Even more when I finish with a Tokay. But there is worse to come! I am reminded of the first time I have had Tokay, and I hear myself telling him of it. It is served by a young woman who is blonde and of the utmost beauty of form. She is veiled. This is arranged by my schoolmates, for I am a student in Berlin. It is in respect for the sensibilities that are attributed to a youth from a Moslem country. Veiled she is, but otherwise completely nude. Allow yourself to imagine. I am gripping the edge of the table. It is for me an education, just by itself.

"It is on the tip of my tongue to say to George, 'At that moment I am without thought of self.' It is a favorite phrase of his: 'without any thought of self.' But I do not. I am a charitable man, at heart I am a charitable man. Yes, you must understand that all he has done has been 'without thought of self.' This to me is very curious. I have never done anything without thought of self. Have you?"

"I—"

"Your American businessmen surprise me. They are always surprising me. Their chief object is never the making of money. In all their working they are thinking first of service. That is the word I am hearing. The money that comes is almost an accident, a pleasant accident. With me it is quite different. I am thinking of money, as I am also thinking of self. One is told that money will not buy everything. And that is obvious. It is only too true! It is my great regret that money will not buy everything. But I have never known money to be an encumbrance. I do not sleep less well when I am making money. Now, Mister— Did I tell you his name, the man I have had lunch with? No? He would like very much to meet you, I think—when you have come back from where you are going. He has insomnia. Yet he has achieved peace of mind. This has come from being an official of the Church. No, he is more than that. An official of the *national organization* of his Church. He is wondering if I am a practicing member of the Orthodox Church and whether if I am he can talk to me man-to-man about the problems of a vestryman. While he is looking at me in this certain way, I say to him, 'George, do you

21

know that my middle name is Costas—that's from Constantinos—and that the nickname for Costas in America is *Gus?* I am unable to imagine why.' The question is, will George call me 'Gus' the next time we meet? I am betting no." He paused, looking at me benignly. "Perhaps it would be better if I had a little insomnia too, and not such good digestion. What do you think? I can say that when I am leaving Toronto I can obtain only an upper berth. But for me it is out of the question to take off my clothes and put them on again in an upper berth. I have to threaten the conductor to undress in the aisle if he does not provide me with a lower. Fortunately, this threat is productive."

It is usual when speaking reflectively or in a reminiscent vein to let the gaze wander or attach itself to space, but in all his rambling discourse Dr. Xenides kept his eyes fixed upon my face, still questioningly. Not surprisingly, it made me self-conscious.

He had gone on to bring up the business he had had in Canada, which had to do with the evidence he had of hitherto undetected oil deposits in Alberta. I lost the thread of it. Being under scrutiny, I could not let my attention wander, but I had become more conscious of his physical presence than of what he was saying. His eyes, which rested comfortably in beds of fat, had a bluish sheen over the brown iris, much as if they had picked up a film of the oil he had ferreted out in such great quantities.

I was feeling heavy, partly from hopelessness, partly from a kind of torpor that had settled over me. As I was wondering, not without impatience, why it was that old people seem to have so much time when that is precisely what they haven't got, I heard him say, "Time is, of course, one of the goods we cannot buy with money—above all others." I may have started a little at the coincidence. His eyes slid off to the side. "It is altogether the other way around," he resumed. "In youth we are rich in time and poor in money, and if we are diligent we become rich in money as we become poor in time. An inferior bargain, you will say, Mr. Tate, and that is so. Yet it is better than being poor in both. Or is it better to be poor in both and rich in the retrospect of a full life? When I speak of memories of living you will be leaping to certain conclusions, and these will be well justified. Yes, there are no memories like the memories of the knowledge of attractive women. And when one has had them unexpectedly—that is the best of all! I have in my mind the wife of a professor of geology when I am studying in Berlin, where I learned English. I have gone to the house of the professor for discussion,

22

but he is away, and the wife, whom I have met, asks me to come in for shelter from the rain—which it is doing. Very heavily. Simply, while we are sitting there having some refreshment, the idea presents itself to me. Fantastic! Yet there is this instinct which is speaking in me. And, as we have been told, nothing ventured . . . eh? You may believe me, she is greatly surprised at my advance. This air of surprise continues as I proceed. Every step: most unexpected! Yet she seems powerless to stop me. She is too surprised, perhaps. . . . There are memories and memories. At the time of which I am speaking I have memories which I am seeking to drown."

He unfolded a tale of revolutionary activity in the Ottoman Empire in which he was involved. It was rather difficult for me to follow. Finally it came to the point that Alekos was captured and imprisoned, along with a number of his fellows. "There we were in the stone keep, all implicated beyond the shadow of a doubt." The locale was Iskenderon. They were to be cast alive into the sea at dawn, done up in sacks. He wagged his head at that, evidently without rancor. It was for this death, he went on, that they had prepared their hearts when, at the very last moment, there galloped into the courtyard of the prison a figure on horseback whose uniform of a cavalry officer did not conceal from the young Alekos the identity of the girl with whom he was then deeply in love, he said. She was waving a reprieve purporting to come from the Sultan's own hand. Grudgingly released by the guards, Alekos, the girl and the other conspirators made their way down to the harbor, where there lay, on the point of departure, a steamship flying the flag of "my friends the British." Alekos Xenides was the first to leap aboard. While he was in the very act of extending his hand to assist his rescuer to the deck, the prison-troops, who had by now discovered the deception, appeared suddenly and fell upon the remainder of the party. Alekos alone was saved. He escaped because the ship had at once cast off.

"I never knew what happened to the girl," he concluded, dropping his eyes for the first time and letting them rest upon his hands. These were clasped in his lap beneath the bulge of his abdomen, for which his vest served as a sling. "We were very madly in love and had planned to run away to Paris together. But I think she must have been killed."

This was evidently the end. We sat in silence.

Mr. Willet's counsel had never been altogether out of my mind while I had sat listening, and now I bethought myself of it anxiously. "I am only

23

stating," he had said, "what you well know when I point out that every-thing depends upon Dr. Xenides. Unless he moves, nothing moves. The aim of all we do must be to move him. I should certainly not say that he moves readily. It is easy to despair of his ever moving. But the Porto-alegre affair showed that he can move when he judges the moment to have come—and move fast." I had nodded, resolving upon a forceful presentation of the circumstances calling for quick action. In the presence of the venerable figure, however, and in the teeth of his apparent indif-ference to our business, it did not seem quite as natural a thing for me to attempt as it had in Mr. Willet's office. All the same, I had to make my pitch, not because any good would come of it but because I had to be able to report to Mr. Willet that I had done so. I waited long enough after the end of his recital to give his emotion its due but not so long as to let him suppose me completely taken in by the implausible narrative, and then, in a voice I expected to sound rusty from disuse, and which did, re-minded him of his observation about the importance of time. Clearing my throat, I set myself to review what Monteiro had been hammering away at to spur the syndicate to apply immediately for the Concession on the terms that offered, and after the first few sentences it began to come more easily. There was the local political situation, which should be taken advantage of while it was as propitious as it was. There was the growing interest in the Massaranduba, which was sure to encourage rivals. There was Monteiro's position; his *bona fides* was likely to come into question if time went on and still nothing happened. There were the latest assay reports, which were even more promising than the early ones.

Dr. Xenides sat thoughtfully throughout, but the performance, I was only too well aware, sounded far more forced than forceful, and in the end it was left hanging in midair, on a rising inflection. "Well, that's what I wanted to say," I added, bringing it down like a dead duck.

"I think she was killed," he said. "My inquiries revealed nothing, and I never heard from her again." He fetched a great sigh, like a hippopot-amus coming up for a breather. With difficulty he got a hand into his pocket, beneath the taut trouser-leg, and extracting it, held up between his thumb and forefinger a lump of gold the size of a kernel of a walnut. "A nugget from your Amazonas. Beautiful, is it not? Always slick to the touch, always sure of its power—is gold." He had turned half from me to hold it in a shaft of sunlight from the window, and in the brighter light there was also a brighter glint in his eye.

24

"You are not greatly interested in geology?" he asked.

It took me an instant to grasp what he had said. Then I felt my face grow warm. My resentment at the treatment I had been put off with broke through the surface, and I am sure it was in a sharp voice that I said I did not know what made him think that.

"Let us say," he replied agreeably, "because while I was talking of the evidence of a productive anticline in Alberta you were watching a bird from the window. What was it? A pigeon [a bigeon]?"

I suppose I colored again. I should never have suspected that he had noticed my surreptitious glance, let alone the object of it.

"Actually, it was a falcon."

"Oh? A special kind of falcon?"

I hesitated. "A peregrine."

"Have I not heard of this bird, perhaps?"

"Probably," I said. "The peregrine was the mainstay of the sport of falconry in the Middle Ages." The sentence, complete, had bobbed up in my mind doubtless from a book I had read years before.

"The mainstay of the sport of falconry in the Middle Ages! Is it often that you see one of these birds in the city?"

"As a matter of fact, I've been seeing a young female regularly down around the shipping-offices—a young female peregrine, that is."

"And how do you know it is a young female?"

"Well," I replied, wondering how far this was likely to go, "the female is considerably larger than the male and the young are brown above instead of grey-blue and they're streaked with brown beneath."

"And have you a reason why this young female peregrine chooses of all places this city to inhabit?"

"It's the pigeons that chiefly bring peregrines here. Also, oddly enough, the craggier skyscrapers have attractions. We have at least two pairs nesting on them."

"Is it possible? How wonderful! Amid all the great buildings and depravities of New York—falcons nesting! I must remember to speak of this at the Bankers Club and ask what interpretation is to be made of it. They will think it very like the Old Doc, and that will give them amusement. My associates are very tolerant of me—the old man. It is altogether behind the times to have been almost sewn up in a sack on the orders of the Sublime Porte and thrown into the sea. It is necessary that they explain their great plans to me in simple terms, within my understanding,

25

lest my reason be overcome by the marvel of it all. If only I am not talking so much nonsense and drinking so much! They think they must keep up with me, in both, you understand—for politeness. I have some value to them. Not because I have degrees from the best universities in Europe—although that is an unusual trick for the son of a Alexandrian merchant to have done—but for other reasons.

"Your Mr. Monteiro observes that I do not tell him their names—the men I am dealing with. He makes much of it. He has found my weakness. I am afraid he will go direct to them and leave me out of the deal! As if they would take a step without me!" His heavy sarcasm broke like a wave into giggles. "No, that is not likely—not a step into the dark. I have an instinct for valuables hidden in the earth. Perhaps you have heard? It is uncanny, like the condition of my organs. Do you think it possible there is some connection? The ancient Incas had cities greater than any their conquerors had ever known, but they had little feeling for gold. They fabricated fishhooks from it, and had no passion for women, either, though of course they multiplied.

"And what about the great empire of the New World today? Of all the gold that has been mined since the beginning of history, half is in the United States of America. I would think to find here a splendor beyond the dreams of Alexander, Akbar, Nadir Shah and Suleiman the Magnificent—golden rings on every finger, chains of gold around every neck, golden table-services and chalices, urns, lamps, fountains of gold. But what do I find? All the gold in subterranean chambers, guarded from sight. Where is the grandeur that goes with gold?" He shrugged. "And the passion for women? Well, well. There is sex. Perhaps we should be content with that." He looked at me cheerfully, placed his hands on his elephantine thighs and rose monumentally to his feet. The interview was over.

I was shocked. Rebuffed once as I had been, I still found it in me to murmur a word of remonstrance about our neglect of the subject that had brought me there. His answer was to place his hand on my shoulder and look down at me—or so it seemed, though he was a good three inches shorter than I—benevolently. "Of course, of course. But later, when we meet again—now that we have come to know each other."

I came away in a state of despondency if not fright. This, however, I felt I must conceal from Mr. Willet; it would not do to have *him* disheartened. "It was mostly a feeling-out process," I said of the meeting.

26

I added, "He doesn't strike me as the kind of man who'd have invested all this time if he didn't expect to be compensated." It was true, and the thought was reassuring. Nevertheless, I was not convinced that I should ever hear from Dr. Xenides again, and when I received a message from him the next evening asking me to call again the following day, I was prepared for the worst.

My expectations could not have been more mistaken. Dr. Xenides was businesslike, even impersonal, from start to finish—to, but not quite including. One would have supposed the prosecution of our enterprise to be the absorbing interest of his life. From his first observation, which expressed doubt as to whether I was aware of all that was involved in an undertaking of this magnitude ("Von ting I'll zay for dat Mr. Monteiro, he's not a berson of betty fision"), the conversation progressed in the atmosphere of an examination. I was quizzed on all I could have been expected to know. As for what I could not, he had prepared for that, too, and presented me with several sheets of foolscap (as I thought of them without knowing what the term meant), which he had covered in his own hand with questions that were to concern me in Brazil. ("Does the Brazilian Government concede the right of an explorer to take out a concession for exploitation, regardless of soil-ownership, in every case conditional only upon failure of the owner to exploit?") Next, maps— "De only vuns of deir kind in de entire vorld"—were spread out upon the table and only with difficulty prevented from curling up again. Evidently I had been accepted.

"Are these from Monteiro?" I asked.

"No, no!" he scoffed. "Nothing so precise from *him*."

The maps covered the area of the Concession in fairly large scale. Dr. Xenides had yielded to the human impulse to color the fields of alluvial gold with actual gilt. He was a shade embarrassed about the weakness, I thought; he made un unconvincing remark about the draftsmanship of his secretary.

"They do look detailed," I murmured. "I had no idea so much information was available."

"More is needed," he replied with an effect of shortness. "Much more." Meticulously he rolled his maps up again.

"So!" he declared in an altered voice. "Now we have our bearings. Let us hope that our zeal is pleasing to the Almighty and will receive its reward." He gave a little heave of amusement resembling a hiccup.

"Certainly to be young is pleasing to the Almighty, though His attentions are not always those we would choose for ourselves, eh?" Since this question was addressed not to me but off to the side, I did not offer to answer it. Looking back at me, he added that on no account was I to let him outlive me. Those were his final words, and with them, wagging his head, he waved me out.

Mr. Willet was gratified by what I was able to tell him of the interview, and he passed word of his gratification on to my father. (He was able to follow it later with a report that Alekos Xenides himself had expressed his pleasure at my enlistment in the cause.) "I think," he stated, "that we have the eminent geologist by his cupidity."

"He's rather an elderly cupid," I said doubtfully.

Mr. Willet gave a laugh, if a sound like the stirring of dry leaves could be so termed. "I see nothing to prevent your leaving at once for Belém, Pará."

Neither did I, certainly, yet hearing the idea openly verbalized rocked me, as if the wall of the building had fallen away, leaving me looking off into space.

I had made up my mind some days before that I must get away in *Boadicea,* and no mistake. I had a passage reserved in her, having brushed aside the agents' uncertainty that accommodations could be found for me. Now when I appeared at the shipping agency three days before the scheduled date of the vessel's sailing and inquired if the 13th were still the day, the clerk at the counter did not conceal his puzzlement. "The thirteenth?" he repeated as if he had never heard of such a day. "Oh, that," he laughed when I pointed to the bulletin-board. "Oh, *that!* That's just to hurry the shippers along. But for a fact, she might quite possibly sail on the seventeenth."

The agency overlooked the one avenue of egress from the port. The Upper Bay presented a scene of desolation. It could have been a vast dump laid out between slum districts and buried under shattered sheets of dirty glass. You could imagine that the ugly grey firmament, like the roof of a greenhouse, had crashed to earth there. You would have thought it the last place in the world in which to look for a ship, but ships from all quarters of the globe plowed across its expanse through the icy shale that stood on end before their bows and slid back across their wakes. There were liners glowering from beneath their brows and bellowing in the helplessness of their immensity, heavy-laden

28

tankers that seemed just to have nosed up out of the ocean's depths, tow-boats spouting tall plumes of vapor as they cockily made off with collections of railway barges and garbage scows. There were war-vessels and patrol-boats, grey, lean and aloof, hankering after trouble, and cargo-ships of all descriptions coming and going without hail or farewell, patient, matter-of-fact and romantic, some of them empty, blind-looking and dirty, thrashing the water like wounded sea-monsters, their listing hulls exposed, rusted and red-gashed. They all went their ways with the stubborn independence of steamships. All but *Boadicea*.

"*Is* there such a ship?" I asked at the offices one day.

The clerk, a soft, plump young man with small eyes, pale to the tips of his fingernails and the ends of his hair, which was more than half gone, looked startled. "Of course!" he declared. "I've seen her out the window here." He laughed a little nervously.

I had fallen into the habit of dropping in almost every day. And day by day *Boadicea*'s departure was put off. Once it was in the hope that a Brazilian trade commission in Washington would give rise to more cargo. Another time the expectation was that holding off a bit would make it worth while to call at Savannah. I knew my father would be pleased by that change of plan, much as my grandmother would have been by the news that I was attending church. "Of course you'll go see your aunt Lucy?" he said, and I promised to do my best.

This went on for two weeks. Then one morning I had a call telling me that I had really better get over to Hoboken right away.

A month on the New Jersey waterfront had left its mark on *Boadicea*. Fixed in a sheet of ice onto which you stepped from the gangplank was an accumulation of ashes, coal-dust, fruit-rinds and newspapers. The rest of the deck was littered with hawsers, chains, crates, canvas and metal buckets, ashcans, hatch-covers, tarpaulins and other odds and ends of nautical gear, while above the debris the grey spars stood like tree-trunks denuded by a hurricane, some still upright, others nearly toppled. *Boadicea* was dwarfed by the pier, dwarfed by the great cube of a building at her stern upon which LIPTON'S TEA was spelled out for readers across the river. Seen from her center hatch, she was dwarfed even by her own funnel. Such as she was, she was frozen fast in her berth.

A few other parties of three or four, each cowering inside his over-coat, stood about disconsolately. A knot of seamen, obviously Brazilian

29

and nearly frozen to death, was gathered about the machinery of number three hatch. The ship seemed to be doing the job of loading by herself, however. Quietly and absently, like a shoplifter, she was extending her derrick-arm and feeling over the pile of merchandise on the dock, all the while looking disingenuously ahead. When she had hooked what she wanted, she would swing it aboard and before you knew it had let it slip down into her bosom.

A man in a baggy navy blue uniform with an unnaturally red complexion and a roving and uneasy gaze came up, spoke my name questioningly, and when I acknowledged it greeted me with effusion and the breath of a still. He had come to show me to my stateroom, which, he had the effrontery to inform me, he had had great trouble securing for me "at the last minute." The little cubicle was located in the officers' quarters amidships, just aft of the galley.

"Whatever misgivings I had about this vessel," said one of the two exceptionally hardy friends of mine who had come to see me off, "have been more than allayed by the confidence the Captain inspires."

"I think he's probably the steward," I said.

"Come," said the other. "In all nuptials there arrives a time when the lucky groom should be left alone with his bride and his ecstasies."

In fact, I had been completely won over by *Boadicea*. It had happened when with a hand raw and swollen from the cold the steward had pulled open the door of the stateroom to reveal an inner door of screening—to shut out the insects of the Amazon!

There is always a hollow feeling when you are going away and you see the last familiar back receding in the distance. It is death in miniature. I was not immune. But, above all, expectation filled my heart like a sunrise, as it might a novitiate's when the curtain is at last to be drawn back from the divine mysteries, from the vistas of paradise.

On deck the air was bitter and the cold of the steel plates cut through the shoes with a razor edge. The hour for departure came and went like any other. The Brazilians stood by like men abandoned on the moon. Occasionally an officer in a blue uniform with features concealed in a white muffler and visored cap would appear upon the boat-deck for a brief, inaudible exchange with an expectorating Irishman who, with a felt hat on the back of his head, seemed to be in charge of the loading. The buildings of Manhattan, resembling stalagmites formed by the drippings of the cloud-roof overhead, began to merge with the chill grey sky

30

and river. A few lights appeared among them, shivered like matches struck among mountain crags and burned twinkling.

I had ducked back into the cabin for a minute to unfreeze when somewhere in the ship a bell tinkled. Putting my ear to the bulkhead, I could detect a faint pulsing like the feeble throbbing of a heart, a rheumatic groan, some suppressed squeaking. I went back on deck and saw that the pier had moved away from *Boadicea*'s bow and that the shoreline was askew. The Irishman had gone. The ship had broken clear of the ice. Through the iron mask of the bridge the illuminated portholes seemed to peer like eyes past the rapt helmsman, fixed upon the remote unseeable. The ship held onto the pier only by a last hawser. They had some trouble detaching it, as if, not sure of herself yet, she were afraid to let go. But finally it came free and fell with a nerveless plop upon the ice. Voices spoke softly on the bridge. As she felt her way to the open water, the bell tinkled once more, encouraging, peremptory. *Boadicea*'s engines responded with a stronger, more masterful beat.

A towboat doing its good turn for the day but anxious to get on with it helped us out beyond the end of the pier, then surged off. We headed toward the bay. The low-roofed cavern of the world was turning blue. Across the river the great city rose like hollow rock newly erupted from the bowels of the earth, still blazing with internal fires through its perforated shell. The failing light might have been filtered through ice, ourselves inclosed in a glacial cave. Footfalls on deck rang out loud and clear. *Boadicea* gave three blasts of her whistle, as is expected of departing ships, and seemed to shrink from the sound. She glided forward in watchful stealth, an escaping phantom. To the commuters going home to Bayonne, Elizabeth, Newark, Roselle Park, Linden and Plainfield in the ferryboat ablaze with light that dropped us astern, *Boadicea, Liverpool,* bound for Belém, Manáos, Ceará, Pernambuco and Bahia, must have been all but invisible. From her blue-green shadowy form light shone over the side, silhouetting the black streaks of ice drifting seaward, and one port threw a beam on a detachment of the crew hammering the wedges into the cover of the center hatch. When they had finished, I found myself alone on the deck, and determined to see the end of it, I remained until the furnaces ashore had been swallowed up in the cloudy darkness and even the last pinpricks of light had flickered out astern.

31

3

There were half a dozen passengers altogether. Among them was a young married couple in whose romance, as we sat with the off-duty officers around a long table athwart the dining-saloon swung portentously through the winter grimness of the North Atlantic, we were evidently to be regarded as basking, at least in the eyes of the bride. It was from her that we learned they were newlyweds. The confession was tendered with a blushing, eye-batting confusion implying that it had been wrung from her by force though in fact she had volunteered it with almost her first words and never thereafter let us forget it. She was blonde and pretty in a shallow way, and her interests, insofar as they were separable from herself, ranged from popular music to motion pictures and back again. Her husband combed his longish hair straight back from his forehead, and he seemed to approach life with just such uncomplicated directness—admirably enough, I thought. He was going to

Belém to work for an American motorcar agency. His world was built so completely upon the internal combustion engine—like an aardvark's upon an ant-economy—that you wondered what he would have become had he been born before its invention. The demonstration that the device could inspire and continue to reward such devotion made you, I must say, regard it with new respect. Ted Lumkins, it seemed to me, deserved a better matrimonial deal than he was likely to find he had got, but so far he evidently took his Marge at her own valuation and was content. He was, I imagine, still bemused by the incredible translation of the forbidden fantasies of youthful singleness into the day-to-day fare of marriage.

Another married couple was Peruvian. Both husband and wife had a manner gentle and resigned, for reasons which did not have to be sought very far. The little boy who sat between them had obviously been not quite right from birth. He had a slightly Japanese look and a remoteness in his eyes that sometimes seemed almost Christlike and at others mentally deficient. A metal valve was set in his neck, and through this he breathed with a whistling sound audible when a speaker had halted, and then sometimes having an appropriateness as a commentary which, inherently funny, intensified our collective distress and embarrassment.

Mrs. Alice Mann, on the strength of her widowhood, her inherited means and her generous endowment with that female force which produces indefatigable patronesses of causes and matriarchs of society, had set out to know the world. She had so far succeeded that few places could be mentioned that she had not visited. Inflexible in outlook, she was built on the lines of a cylinder, like the ship's funnel, so that on both counts you wondered how she ever bent sufficiently to get into one of *Boadicea*'s chairs, which had an uncommonly snug embrace and were bolted in place. (It took you a week to stop trying to push back when you got up from the table.) *Boadicea,* for which Mrs. Mann had been led to sign up by the vogue for tramp-steamer cruises, was her first mistake. Boarding her in Hoboken under the impression that she was boarding the tender that would take her to the ship she would sail in, she was to quit and take passage home on the first northbound vessel after discovering in Belém what the sun can do to a small iron cargo-ship laying over in an equatorial port. To begin with she was upset because in Savannah another passenger was to be installed in her stateroom, and she declined to be mollified by the ameliorating circumstance brought out by Señor Augusto, the Peruvian: "But surely it will be another woman, yes?"

33

The last was Mr. Watson, a septuagenarian who was being sent to Brazil by the Ford Motor Company to drill wells in its great holdings on the Tapajós River. With his single-minded faith in the virtues of honesty and hard work, his obsession with inculcating them, his querulous conviction that others were deficient in them, his idolization of Mr. Henry Ford for exemplifying them in supreme degree, he was a bore made bearable only by his inability to come abreast of any conversation before it was too late; his lips would move, but the subject would be changed before he could relate it to his creed.

Boadicea's officers, having a job to do, and thus a reason for being, had a validity and substance that were denied the rest of us. Perhaps that was why they seemed more alive, too. I grew very fond of them. As I did so, though, I seemed to detect a certain forlornness behind their good humor. In the case of the Captain, it was much more. He was unmistakably a tormented man.

Captain Byram in full-face had a physiognomy that was open and mild, overshadowed by eyebrows as bushy and perky as an Italian organ-grinder's moustaches. In profile it was dominated by a lower jaw out-thrust like a bulldog's, and was severe. Seated at the head of the table, he talked almost without cessation or reference to his audience, indiscriminately, as if he were trying to fill a void with words. His special themes were modern women, for whom he could not say much, Latin Americans, for whom he could say even less, and the "barbarians" or "Afghans," for whom he could say nothing at all. These last, it developed, were the Irish. Inasmuch as we had representatives of all three categories among us, meals did not pass without a certain ruffling of feelings, but we understood that the Captain's onslaughts were on a plane of abstraction, delivered without personal malice in response to obscure and possibly quite unrelated inner goadings. Moreover, as he would explain, clinching the diatribe, "And I'm half Afghan myself, so you'll see . . . !"

The chief officer was a Welshman of fair complexion, powerful build, the slow manner of dependability, and a laugh that came out in great, slow whoops, from the bottom of his chest, like someone beating a carpet. The second was a lanky, bony Englishman with the nose of a proboscis monkey between a wrinkled, receding forehead and wrinkled, receding chin which were mirror images of each other, and with a bent for snatching subjects of innocent witticism from the rather meager materials the daily round afforded. The third, a plump, dark Scotsman with a shining face, was initially too devastated by embarrassment to give out anything.

I tried not to fall asleep too soon at night so that I could listen to the sounds of the ship: the sighing of the steam in the engine-room, the wash of the seas outside, the rattle of a small, round object rolling back and forth through a ventilator-pipe overhead, the creaking of the wood-work like two voices of different pitch in a muted dialogue, and above all, the purposeful plowing of the engines. The engines beat throughout the day with a determined vehemence, and at night with a wrathful thrust, as if the fall of darkness called forth a fiercer defiance. *"Chug-a-rum,"* they called in a sort of booming hum, *"chug-a-rum, chug-a-rum, chug-a-rum!"* I lay and listened, and I felt that everything that had happened to me for the past ten years, or the past thousand, had fallen away.

Then there was the satisfaction, fathomless and indescribable, of awakening in a ship that had tirelessly ridden out the night. Aloft on the boat-deck the air was alive and damp, from the east. It inflated the lungs in great draughts, and it struck the ship in racing, bouncing billows, severing our smoke neatly at the funnel-top and whisking it away. On the hoary North Atlantic, beneath a sky the color of aluminum from which there emanated a dawn-light, curiously pallid, clear without intensity, luminous and shadowless, *Boadicea* conveyed irresistibly the thrill of her power and exultation. Never would you have known her for the cornered waif of Hoboken. In her forward surge she would tower at the bow, hesitate, then plunge, rearing at the stern, at once joyously buoyant as she rose upon a swell and vengefully heavy when she fell in all her dead weight upon its successor in a long-drawn hiss of surf and a deep, reverberating *boom* that echoed through her hull. Off North Carolina her water-pipes thawed out, rendering life pleasanter for all and making it possible to wash down her decks for the first time in weeks.

"The clergy!" the Captain exclaimed, pitching heedless into a conversation about Hollywood, where Marge Lumkins had spent a week of rapture among gods and goddesses. His head was set low upon his massive shoulders. "They're . . . they're like . . . D'you know what I mean by the clergy?" he demanded, his grey eyes sweeping the assemblage. The officers dropped their gaze innocently to their plates. "I recall when I was a lad in Liverpool—and it's a place you'll do well to avoid: gangs of louts out after dark every night, and half the population Afghan to boot," he began. He followed this with some reminiscences throwing little perceptible light upon his estimate of churchmen, but, "There you are!" he summed up, glowering. "Sniveling around, all in black! Remind you of the grave. And mean to, by heavens! Can't wait to shove you in. 'Consider your immortal soul.' Immortal soul! Better you keep an eye on the seams of your boilers!"

Another time it was democracy. Why didn't they say what they meant? he asked. They meant pulling everything down—government, manners, morality—so low the common man could feel as good as the best, the cock of the walk, as if he'd invented all that was marvelous in the modern world. "Talk to him of duty or honor! Hah!" He was no gentleman himself, he declared, but even he was too good for Parliament. "I don't shove my cap on the back of my head and talk like a collier. And that's what you must do to show your constituents you're no better than they are, that there's none better in the world." He was in a cold grey fury.

The American contingent was perturbed. Mrs. Mann had drawn herself up to the full height of Bunker Hill and Cemetery Ridge, but for the moment was at a loss for an adequate retort. It had got through to Mr. Watson that the meaning of Dearborn had been held up to question, and his lips worked, like the spinning wheels of an overloaded locomotive, but as usual, in vain.

The Captain, his eyes passing over the company again and finding no comfort in what he saw, had gone on, "D'you know what a seaman's hardest task is? Do you? It's writing letters to his wife. Once you've told her what a flying-fish looks like, there's nothing left but the weather. It's fine or it's thick. And there you have a sailor's life! If she's a seaman's daughter she knows it all to begin with anyway. Still, I'd best get to it."

Mr. Watson, with gaze set, had already preceded the Captain out of the saloon. He was off to hunt down Mr. Gibbons, the steward. It was not Mr. Gibbons's place to run out on him. Whenever Mr. Watson was absent from the table we would hear, during lulls in our talk, his persistent, argumentative voice issuing from the steward's quarters; and then, sooner or later, Mr. Gibbons himself would hurry through the saloon, muttering in a shamed manner, "There's nothing now I don't know about Detroit, I'm sure. Nothing."

I asked the third officer why Mr. Gibbons had so miserable, self-

36

deprecatory an air about him and was told that he had once been chief steward in one of the crack liners of the South American trade but drank excessively. After repeated warnings he had been cashiered. On her next voyage the ship turned turtle in a storm with very great loss of life; she was S.S. *Vestris*. Mr. Gibbons was left with the knowledge that he probably owed his life to his incorrigible vice, of which he was at that very time most abjectly repentant after a protracted drunk. "He still gets plahstered," the young Scotsman added, speaking in all seriousness, "but with his moral code turned upside down, the heart's gone out of him. Well, he's not alone in his predicament," he finished enigmatically, retreating into a study in pink.

I asked about the Captain, too. Was it possible that he had ever been marooned and had never recovered from it—imagined, indeed, that he was still marooned?

Mr. Evans, the first officer, let loose a couple of small thunderclaps of laughter, deep down. "He'll be all right once we're well out of Savannah."

"What's he got against Savannah?"

"Nothing—except that it's a port."

I had a perch in the stern, up on the housing of the rudder gear, where I was as solitary as a castaway, alone with the sea and the gulls. A flotilla of these birds lay constantly overhead, their wings bent at identical angles, acutely in a stout wind, nearly straight out in comparative calm. From time to time, apparently under a collective impulse, the ranks would carry forward to the bridge without a discernible motion of pinions. Then, tilting in turn ever so slightly, they would swerve out individually to windward in a breathtaking rush, each bird skimming the water a hundred yards from the vessel, and completing the tremendous circle all in one movement, as if whirled on a cord, would rejoin us from astern. "Ugly brutes!" the Captain called them, with venom. With the ship making heavy going of it, every rise of the stern would carry you to a dizzy height right up into the flock. At close quarters the ice-grey, heedless eyes of those wind-sculptured birds flapping with batlike purpose beside you seemed to bring to a focus the vastness of the grey-lit wastes, of the eternity of waves that leaped and fell back with no human eye to see them save by rare chance.

"The ghouls nearly got their wish the last time—coming up," the Captain said. "It was a proper blow. It looked as if the old girl's time had

37

come. Not that we got off scot-free. Two of the boats were smashed. It would have been less bother if we'd gone down. No reports to write about it then!" You could see, you could even feel in your stomach, the kind of waves it would take to reach the boats, and it was not pleasant.

"Look at them now!" the Captain exclaimed with satisfaction. A bucketful of scraps had been heaved over the side from the galley, and the gulls, with all their flawless grace abandoned in a medley of anxious cackling, had simply tumbled down from the sky, wings back-beating awkwardly, legs dangling, like so many chickens dumped out of a sack. "That's putting them in their place!"

It was dark when we arrived off the mouth of the Savannah River, and a little foggy, too, so we anchored. In a silence that seemed deathly we came around into the wind. At least that was the presumption from the manner in which the buoy lights of Tybee Roads, flashing their cryptic communications to one another through the gauzy void, moved evenly around to the other side of the ship. It was expected that we should lie there until the next day, but when I waked during the night I heard the engines surging again and a bell-buoy clanging its despairing warning as it passed beneath my port. In the morning I was up, shaved and dressed before daylight and launched on a day as queer as any I had ever spent. On deck, in a strange silence upon which distant city-noises intruded incongruously, I found we were tied up to a wharf covered with barrels—acres of them. They were full of Georgia crackers, averred Mr. Willcox, the second officer, whom, before taking off, I joined on the bridge for a cup of the hot, deep brown tannic acid that *Boadicea*'s galley served as tea and that puckered the entire digestive tract in its passage. I could see the ground covered with crumbs, couldn't I? The ground was, in fact, frosty white even in the dim light of wharf lamps with resin dust. On our other side, in the darkness, the river was as black as an asphalt highway on a rainy night. It was in a ship tied up alongside here that Captain Flint had died, calling to Darby McGraw to fetch aft the rum.

Walking down Bay Street, where the crunch of grit beneath my feet echoed against the brick fronts of the old shipping-offices, I began to know how a departed spirit would feel in returning to the mortal world. The feeling grew after I had turned southward on Whitaker and under a lightening sky pursued my way past the imposing houses of a century ago where in the yards the pale trumpets of jonquils already showed, past Forsyth Park with its live-oaks and banked shrubs, every-thing in the mild air of the dawning spring day having a freshly-laundered air. I bore on my hand the scar of a cut I had received on the path that encircled the fountain of Neptune as a five-year-old visiting a cousin. The Negroes on their way to work with whom I exchanged grave good mornings looked much as I remembered them, with a quality of un-self-consciousness, of accepting life, of immutability, that made one think of them not as detached individuals but as outcroppings of a submerged human bedrock.

I felt disembodied. I was lighter than air, a creature of fiction. It was enchanting, even while I was devouring an order of eggs, bacon and grits in a café on West Broad inspired in decor by the men's room of the Central of Georgia railroad depot.

Hitchhiking promised the quickest means of getting where I was go-ing. At a service station I came upon a truck stacked with the kind of baskets in which Sheldon Bluff sent its vegetables to market, and Sheldon Bluff, it turned out, was where it was going.

"Your home there?" the driver asked after motioning me into the seat beside him.

"Yes. No. I was born there."

When he learned I had not been back in four years he promised I should find some changes, among them the diggings for the new paper-mill, which was to be the biggest on the Eastern Seaboard. "Jacksonville turned it down, on account of the smell of the pulp. Sure the pulp smells bad. But as Mayor Pender said, with the fragrance of the money you won't hardly notice it."

The driver was a scrawny young man but had the negligent bearing of a physically formidable one, probably because of disposing of so much power in the form of the truck. When we had turned off the Ogeechee Road—the coastal highway to Florida, as it had become—we had a con-crete straightaway almost to ourselves. It led across a country resembling a luminous green plate under an inverted luminous blue bowl margined with dark green pine forests. As we lapped up the miles toward the coast, the plate was increasingly fissured by salt rivers reflecting the blue and bordered by marshes—the reeds still brown—from which occasional grey herons sprang up with legs dangling and were left behind before their panic had done a fraction of justice to the emergency. With far more to fear than the herons, the mule wagons crawled along on the shoulders of the highway, their left wheels barely on the concrete. Replacing the gravel road I had known, the highway entered Sheldon Bluff over a causeway and steel-girder bridge. Of the wooden trestle that used to rumble under passing wheels, only a few barnacle-encrusted pilings remained. I was a relic at twenty-three.

Sheldon Bluff, from what I saw of it from the truck, looked much the same, if a little meaner, as places will when you have been away from them. But when I had been set down and had started walking, I noticed more that was altered. Where I vaguely remembered trees there were new gas stations with broad concrete aprons, two of which were at the moment being hosed-down by uniformed attendants. There was the incredible new hotel at the end of the bluff, The Hermitage, Spanish in architecture, Floridian in impact, acres in extent, its parking-lot crowded with cars bearing license plates from all the states in the East; their owners were presumably still in bed or at breakfast. There was the new marina where sportscraft played daintily with their painters and the sparkle of sun on varnished mahogany and polished brass was like nothing ever seen on the local fishing boats. I wondered how the vacationers were going to like the smell an offshore breeze would bring from the paper-mill.

The old houses of the historic quarter appeared also at first sight unchanged. They ranged from small white clapboard structures, like boxes, rising straight up from the sidewalks, to mansions of aged dark brick with deep verandas, secluded behind mattresses of ivy or wisteria, magnolias and camphor trees and hedges of red-fruited cassena-berry and fleshy-leaved pittosporum, which grew with surprising profusion from the white-sandy soil. But a closer look showed that most of them were going downhill. There was flaking paint, crumbling mortar, splintered lattice, dulled windows. Some of the houses were empty. Some had "Tourists" signs hung in front of them.

An elderly man looked back sharply as he was about to pass me, in what is known as a double take. So did the shrewd, well-fed-looking proprietor (as I judged him to be) of Sister Mandy's Grill, formerly the Habersham Restaurant, who was kicking a wedge under the front door of the place to hold it open. It made me know how it must have been to be Rip van Winkle on his return, though it was not me they recognized, only the narrow, slightly bent nose and wide mouth of the Tates, familiar so long in Sheldon Bluff.

40

The feeling of being a ghost grew on me—only it was not a tomb to which I would be summoned back, not the cold stone chasms of New York, but, I thanked God, a living ship with the sea and South America before her. It seemed both fitting and inevitable and yet against the nature of things for me to be here.

I kept up a fast clip until I reached the other side of town, where my road ran between two cemeteries. One, surrounded by a brick wall topped by iron pickets with a couple of fat little cannon at the gate and the Stars and Stripes drooping at the head of a tall pole, had the appearance of a fortified outpost on a forgotten frontier and was the last resting-place of the Union soldiers who had met their end here in '64 while putting the country to the torch. The natives were buried across the way, beneath spreading oaks which soon, hung with clusters of lavender wisteria blossoms, would resemble a celestial vineyard. The older graves were sarcophagi topped by slabs of brown stone dimly incised with the elongate script of a hundred and fifty or more years ago. I was reminding myself, I suppose, that I was in no whit different from those to whom death had inevitably come, and not really believing it, when my eye fell upon an object that made me, in my turn, do a double take: a grey headstone marked with my own name, JULIAN TATE. What jolted me was the unexpectedness; I could not recall having seen it before.

I went in for a closer look, instinctively reverting to barefoot boyhood and picking my way carefully among the cockleburs. The grave was not yawning open, awaiting me. Neither had it opened to permit my egress; this was not a century hence. It was covered by sparsely sandy soil indistinguishable from that surrounding it. Buried beneath it was my great-grandfather, whose dates the stone recorded as 1838 to 1867. As I remembered the family history, he had come through the war only to die of a fever. *In Final Settlement* was the curious inscription. What, I wondered, could a bereaved wife have intended by that? I wandered about for a bit among the graves. Of the older ones, I recognized most of the family names. They were the stuff of the reminiscences of my father and grandparents. Today few of them were living names locally, most of their inheritors having long since departed for Atlanta, Texas and New York, as had indeed all the Tates but my aunt. If you went as far back as 1865 you would even find some who, rather than suffer Yankee rule, had cut their ties to their homeland altogether and set sail for Mexico and countries even farther to the south. The notion I had of

41

having heard that a number had gone to Brazil I thought probably the product of my current obsession.

I was on my way out to the road again when my eye was caught by the inscription on a small stone of the same rough grey composition as my great-grandfather's, and near it: *Not One Heart Alone Lies Buried Here.* Above it was the name ELLEN JANDREY and the dates Aug. 14, 1845 to June 21, 1864. She had been only eighteen when she died. She and Julian—the original Julian—would have known each other well. They would have ridden down this very road together, their horses stretched to the limit, the girl in the lead with her hair flying— past the cemetery, which meant nothing to them. Of course, that was only supposition. But I felt a weakness, like the onset of a sickness when you know suddenly you are coming down with it. Only eighteen! And nothing realized. Nothing, nothing!

I sat down on a nearby stone. The reality of that early extinction enfolded me, and I felt horror. I pictured her as brown-haired, slim of body and of face, quick with life, unequipped to deal with death, like a young girl left alone in an ancient, lightless house to face, out of reach of help, the terrors of the night, and a creeping coldness. . . . In that relentless war with the Union leaves from the battlefield must have been cruelly infrequent and short, maybe worse than no leaves at all.

I took a deep draught of the cigarette I had lighted. As if I were one of those long-stalked sea-creatures, I could feel my base of attachment far from where my organs of consciousness now were, back with *Boadicea,* lying alongside at Savannah. Before nightfall we should be at sea and with every beat of the screw nearer the Amazon.

Meanwhile there was my aunt. A widow in her early forties, she lived by herself in the old Tate house at the south end of the bluff. Her income must have been small. Of the original holdings of the family there were fifteen hundred acres left, twenty miles inland of Sheldon Bluff, and although of good farmland they brought in much less than they should have, farm prices being at rock bottom at that time and share-cropping the poorest way to get value out of land, though in this case it was about the only way that availed to get anything from it. My aunt supplemented the farm-earnings with a small plant-nursery, growing ornamental shrubs, and, I am sure, stretched out her groceries with fish and oysters; she was out on the water a good deal of the time. She looked, I can see now, as if she belonged to a later era. As far as I know, she was the first woman east of the Great Plains to wear blue jeans. Her dark brown hair looked as if it had been cropped with a pair of hedge shears. She had the outdoor look—honestly gained, surely—that goes with a deep, chronic tan and no make-up, and this brought out the brightness of her blue eyes, which seldom rested long on anyone, as far as my experience went. She was talkative and animated, but rather impersonal. She smoked cigarettes constantly and had, probably in consequence, a masculine huskiness about her voice. I had a great deal of admiration for her and felt complimented that she seemed as glad to see me as she did.

"I don't know why you want to go to the Amazon River," she said. "You can be just as uncomfortable on the Talahoosaw. The woods are just as tangled, there are just as many mosquitoes and the natives are just about as primitive."

"Are there sands and rocks of gold here?"

"Heavens! Oh, I see what you mean. If we had them we'd lose them. Or the price of gold would fall, so they'd be worthless. Let me tell you what Charlie's been doing. . . ." Charlie was the bent, deaf colored man who worked for her.

"Aunt Lucy," I said when I had a chance, "what did your grandmother mean by putting 'In Final Settlement' on her husband's gravestone?"

"On his gravestone? O-o-o-o-oh. . . . You came through the cemetery, did you? That does seem a strange thing, doesn't it? Hmm. You know, I think I heard he asked to have it put on it. That would *have* to have been it, wouldn't it?"

She did not know why he had wanted such an inscription, except that the war had changed him, she had been told. It was said that after the war he seldom smiled again.

I asked how long he had been married when he died. She thought it had been only a few months.

Did she know anything about an Ellen Jandrey; who she was? She did not and had never noticed the stone, but she thought she remembered having heard of Jandreys who had moved away from Sheldon Bluff many years before. She said, "You know, you ought to talk to Emily McIlheny if you're interested in the old families. Would you like me to get her over here? She'd be thrilled to have someone who'd listen, especially a good-looking young man."

But I assured her quickly that that would not be necessary.

43

We had as the main dish for midday dinner a perfect raft of deviled crabs which my aunt had caught off the end of the wharf in expectation of my arrival and which Nellie, the colored cook, had spent the morning preparing. In New York the meal would have cost twenty dollars, if it could have been had at all. Afterward, Aunt Lucy lighting one cigarette from another as we left the table, we took a turn around the place. Built nearly a hundred years before, with porches running around the major part of both its floors, its roof of sheet metal (on which acorns fell with the crack of rifle shots) sloping very gently from a central ridgeline and largely concealed by a balustrade encircling it, the house had a presence, together with an imposing weight upon the ground, that only complete collapse could have taken from it, and it was still far from that. It had an air, shared by other old waterside houses of its kind, of looking into the distance for the ship it still had faith would someday come in.

"We've put in a lot of cassena-berry, as you see," said my aunt as we paused before the small plantation of shrubs. "It goes well with the Easterners at Christmas, which is very discerning of them. There are more and more of them here. Old Mr. Reardon—he's from Pennsylvania ["Pennsa'vania," as my aunt pronounced it], he's spending the winter at The Hermitage—says we ought to boost it by calling it Sea Island holly. It *is* a holly, though I don't know how he knew that. *Ilex vomitoria.*"

"I think that would recommend it only to the *very* discerning Christmas shopper."

"You're being funny," she commented amiably. "It was called that because of a mistake by the botanists."

Going alone up to the room that had been mine as a boy, I gazed out the window upon the vista which the house contemplated with deathless expectation—or perhaps it was retrospection after all. The eye was led across the tidal waters and the marshes smooth as velvet to other forested islands which appeared to be lightly, if motionlessly, afloat, just touching the water. The tide could be heard running out under the wharf. How many nights had I fallen asleep to that sound and to the bumping of a boat against the piles? As with the house, the lines of that country were predominantly horizontal. The configuration of the land itself, the bottoms of the cumulus clouds, even the boughs of the oaks, were level, and that, I supposed, together with the questioning cries of the shorebirds and the terns and gulls that came in to hunt along the mudflats,

44

and the hanging grey moss that reduced even the stalwart pines to a melting softness, was what gave my native land its air of sadness.

"I'm going to have to go now," I said when I came down again, "I'm sorry to say. You think Tom Hardee really wouldn't mind driving me?"

"Oh dear. Do you think you must? Yes, he said just let him know. I wish you didn't have to go. I was hoping to drive you over to the plantation. Ed Williams keeps complaining that their well is filling up with leaves. I don't know what he expects—"

"I'll stay longer than you want me the next time. But it wouldn't do to miss the boat."

It was a two-hour drive to Savannah in Tom's Model A roadster. On the way I remarked that I wondered if I could make a living in Sheldon Bluff if I came back.

"Don't try," he said.

"No?"

"If you want to come back, don't come back as a native. Be sure it's out of your system before you come back. Then come back as just anybody. Anybody with money."

I looked curiously at him. He was gazing with set face over the steering wheel. There was a hint of a wild look in his eyes. I said I was surprised, hearing this from him, since he was one of us who had stayed.

"I ain't stayin' much longer. I'm goin' north with the ducks."

When we drove up to the wharf, Tom gave a brisk whistle. "What a beauty!"

"I'm afraid she's the other one."

In the foreground was a grey-and-white vision of a ship, long and elegant. *Djambi, Rotterdam,* was loading barrels stenciled *Sourabaya* and *Padang.* In the berth beyond, half her size, sooty, rust-streaked little *Boadicea* could not be recognized as the proud sea-steed which had towered so massively in the open ocean. After a tour of her appointments Tom Hardee raised the heavy black eyebrows I remembered best as lowered over a challenging marbles-shot. "Well, Jaybird," he said, holding out his hand, "I'm glad your years in New York haven't addicted you to senseless and ostentatious luxury."

From the wharfside he called back, "Someday, eh, boy?"

"Someday, Tom!"

Before we could get away we had to wait for a vessel to make fast below us. Filling the river, *Albert J. Wheelock, Philadelphia,* black of

45

hull with mustard-colored superstructure, looked as if it could swing us aboard with one of its forest of derricks and fit us comfortably in one of its half dozen holds.

"What a fright," said Mr. Evans, looking up at the enormous ship from beside me on the foredeck. "Not one graceful line. Not even any sheer. She'd bury her ends in a heavy sea, I'll be bound. Except I suppose she's too bloody big." He spoke with uncharacteristic animus. "Take a good look at her, because she's what we see ahead of us. She's the future." With a twitch of his capable shoulders he strode off.

The late afternoon was still and luminous as we descended the river. Past the lifted forecastle, past the boats in their davits, past the poop where the Red Ensign hung unruffled, the South slipped astern. It took with it an abstracted Negro standing in a rowboat and pushing it across the river with short and easy jabs of the oars, tawny-breasted cormorants in stiff groups on the numbered channel-markers, the far-reaching, closed world of the marshes, and behind them isolated houses that had seen better days but retained the pride of giant mounded oaks no parvenue could duplicate, no money buy. The tufted pines were grey-green ahead of us, black against the setting sun behind. I went aft to see the last of it and was looking up at the few remaining small harbor gulls—ring-billed and laughing gulls—which had been following us in diminishing numbers when I was startled by a controlled and ironic feminine voice behind me: "*I've* been told never to look behind. Always ahead."

I turned and beheld with surprise a girl, hatless, with straw-yellow hair forming a froth of curls around her face. She was wearing grey flannel slacks under a topcoat drawn tight by a belt around a slim waist. My mouth was open to speak, for I had expected to know her, and from her half-teasing, half-appraising expression and her pursed smile it might have been thought that she shared my expectation. But her heart-shaped, even triangular face connected with nothing in my memory. The grey eyes, seeming especially wide-set because her small nose was low-bridged, formed her most prominent feature. I could see that she was older than I had first thought—in the neighborhood of thirty.

"No, we don't know each other. I'm Cora Almeida," she declared, and added, "Cora *Braun* [as I somehow knew it would be spelled] Almeida," as if to account for her quite ordinary American speech.

I remembered to come forth with my own name, at which she nodded as if she were already aware of it. She had removed her

46

hands from her pockets and I expected her to offer one of them, but instead, crossing her arms, she tucked them into her armpits and hunched her shoulders. One would have thought she had suddenly felt the chill air.

Because, from her questioning look, she seemed to expect me to say something, I asked if she always followed the advice she had been given.

"Well, now that I come to think of it, I guess I don't look behind very much. As for looking ahead, I close my eyes and jump. . . . Tell me something about our fellow passengers. There's a very homey sort of girl who clings to her husband's arm like a sort of *question*-mark. She seemed to be *gloating* at me, as if she'd just *won* him from me. . . ."

In the days that followed I was very much aware of Senhora Almeida, as I started to call her but was told not to. ("I'm Cora, size ten, weight one hundred and eight pounds, not the embodiment of South American matronhood.") She had a way of flowing out and ebbing back.

Married to a "Paraense," as a resident of Pará seemed to be called, she was herself a native of New Jersey, and had come as far as Savannah by train to shorten the ocean voyage. But whether she was glad to be returning to her acquired home after three months of doing as she pleased —with the city of inexhaustible resources just across the river—I could not tell. It seemed to be one of those matters about which her feelings would go only so far in one direction before being reversed by a kind of recoil mechanism.

The same alternating currents governed her routine aboard *Boadicea*. There were days when she did not appear at all after breakfast or before dinner and was reported by Mrs. Mann, her unwilling cabin-mate, to be reposing in her bunk reading or simply looking up at the ceiling, smoking, in a state of— Here Mrs. Mann clamped shut her lips; there was no need to incite objectionable imagery in the minds of the men. On other days she would linger in the dining-saloon to the last, content to listen— noncommittally—but prepared, if the conversation lapsed, to supply anecdotes and accounts of experiences she had had. "I guess she was one of those who'll do anything for you if they don't kill you," she had ended, with amiable ennui, a recital of how she had emerged with a valuable gold clock from an inherently horrifying involvement with a homicidally-inclined fellow-lodger in one of those narrow four-story houses converted to apartments of which Manhattan was full; and the conclusion,

47

with its suggestion that that was how life was—ambivalent, I suppose the term would be—was typical. Her manner of speaking implied a curious disengagement from what she was saying, as one might relate the testimony of another without warranting its credentials, or casting doubt upon them either. The key bits especially sounded as if they were in quotation-marks.

Wearing a very feminine blouse with lace jabot, as I learned from her that it was called, conspicuously dressier than anything the other women wore, she would sit with one forearm and one elbow on the table, supporting her pointed little chin in her hand, her shoulders rounded. Or, conversely, she would be clad in a mannish shirt and slacks and be leaning back in the corner, her leg drawn up on the bench beside her and one arm on her knee. Thus, smoking, she would regard the Captain with grey eyes empty of opinion as he inveighed against modern women with their unwomanly ways. She handled a cigarette in a manner that made you very conscious of it, as if it were an art only just introduced to the Western world, and formed her lips into an O when exhaling, making of it an experience in sensuous living.

Never quick in such matters, I nonetheless could not help perceiving that Cora Almeida was not greatly welcome to the other three females. They gave the impression of closing ranks in her presence and holding high the banner of woman's mission. We learned that Mrs. Mann had seven grandchildren and heard much of the care and thought she expended on them. Señora Augusto all but ruffled up and clucked with solicitude over her poor piping gosling, and though Marge Lumkins, unavoidably so far childless, was at a disadvantage, she managed to convey a sense of her spiritual readiness for her function. As Cora Almeida expressed it privately, "I have this feeling that she is 'gestating before our very eyes.'" In respect of her own lack of issue after three years of marriage she remarked candidly to the company, "I simply don't know what I'd do if I had a 'wee one.' I probably wouldn't get any further than putting it in the middle of the table and 'standing around it.' Or maybe nature has her ways with cases like mine, such as with 'hormones.'" Turning to Mrs. Mann, she continued in a spent voice. "Did you feel yourself 'rising above your girlish frivolity and indolence' at your first parturition? As if a mysterious yeast had been *released* in your system?" Mrs. Mann colored. She replied shortly, "I was brought up on a farm. There was precious little opportunity to indulge in either frivolity *or* indolence."

48

The gulls, birds of the cold seas, gave us up with the first of the flying-fish, a few degrees above the tropics. After dark that day we ran through phosphorescence. From the boat-deck the ship seemed to have no headway on her at all. Her motions were those of a pendulum swung upon a pivot somewhere below your feet in the bottomless darkness. The heavens sidled past the masthead as if they meant to roll slowly down into the watery blackness, each time returning only after a momentous hesitation and a suspiration of surf from beneath our hull. The sea, so oily it was, reflected Venus on its swell and a low star in the Great Bear, which stood on its tail and pointed to a now depressed Polaris. At our bow there flickered the magical phenomenon. The phosphorescence was itself not unlike twinkling stars, or like rockets that flared up, cold white, and expired in the firmament of waters below us. Some of it was even more spectacular, illuminating the waves rolled up at our bow as if with floodlights, though these, too, were instantly extinguished. By day golden rafts of seaweed drifted by and porpoises rode our bow-wave and leaped for what seemed pure joy.

By the time we had crossed Latitude 24°, these had left us. It is difficult to accept the apparent lifelessness of tropic seas. We pitched our way in the perpetual center of a disk of untenanted ocean, its blue reflected darkly by a featureless sky. Once we came upon two tropic-birds resting on the water. They watched us pass, no more than twenty paces off, without fear, as if so monstrous a form as ours could only have been a mirage. But for the two long pin-quills in their tails, delicately elevated, they might have been white pigeons and have been provided to accent the solemn emptiness of that ocean. Apart from them there was nothing, only the momentary whitecaps on the lacquer finish of the water. Pools of cobalt and streaks of lapis, like oils, succeeded one another on the surface with the flowing of the wavelets. The sun had grown daily in power, had diffused its brilliance over the zenith of the heavens. You expected to see shafts of sunlight slanting into the ocean's awesome depths, but except where the foam of our wake showed grey-green a foot or so down, the water appeared as impenetrable as marble. The ocean was quiet as a lake, and the exaggerated rolling of *Boadicea* was unaccountable until you noticed that what seemed to be the curvature of the earth was an oncoming swell, one of the endless succession pushed up by the trades in their unimpeded course across the Atlantic. Between the darkened, sharp rim of the sea and the azure declination of the sky, far beyond it, the very memory of land seemed to have vanished. *Boadicea* ambled along without haste. Having outlived her day—as her officers averred she had—she had come through time's province, you might believe, and could go on forever. You forgot you had had any other life or other home.

The Captain, not one to let down his guard impulsively, was the last to shift from the winter uniform of navy blue to tropic cottons. An unaccustomed smile occasionally hovered upon his lips, but the necessity to talk drove him as hard as ever.

"We were in India, and the first officer and I—I was third officer then —took it in our heads to go turtle-hunting. *So* we loaded ourselves down with cartridges. I thought you got turtles—you know what turtles are? —by shooting them. But not a bit of it. They were coming up onshore to lay their eggs. You know how they lay their eggs? They dig a hole in the ground and—"

"And cover the eggs over," interposed Mrs. Mann.

"Ye-e-e-e-e-e-s." The Captain drew it out to forestall any other interruptions while he oriented himself. "Yes, we found dozens of them. Oh, heaps of them. And do you know how we got the turtles?" He hurried on. "By thrusting an oar out on the sand, like this. Then when a turtle came along we turned it over." These motions were duly reproduced. "We got eight of them. Oh, but we bitterly regretted that night's work. We paid for it, right enough. A proper mess it was."

"How was that?" I asked after a pause, dutifully; but I was always afraid the Captain would not be able to remember. He looked as if he might not, but he always did.

"Why?" he asked. *Tsk*—sucking a morsel of food from between his teeth. "We took them all on board. *And* we had turtle to eat. We had turtle soup. We had stewed turtle, steamed turtle, fried turtle, boiled turtle, and we had turtle. We had turtle for dinner, supper, breakfast and tea. We had turtle flakes and turtle steaks. We had turtle chops—*tsk*— turtle gravy, broiled turtle and roast turtle."

"How long did it last?" asked Marge Lumkins, businesslike.

"Months," the Captain replied. "Months." *Tsk*.

"My gosh, how big were they?" Marge had no compunction about putting the Captain on the spot.

"Oh," said he, "they were proper monsters, about so big." He outlined one of the monsters with spread arms. Marge was unbelieving, but the

50

rest of us rushed to the Captain's support. Yes, these sea-turtles were enormous. Every bit as large as that.

When not directly engaged in the conversation the Captain would be wrestling in oblivion with his own burden of thought. At the end of the meal he was likely to burst forth abruptly. "You'll excuse me if I leave you. I mustn't bore you too long. What's more, I've got no end of writing waiting for me. A master, you know—has to do it. The owners . . . they expect . . ." His voice trailed off, his eyes going hard as glass. It was with these words that, when he was finally able to bring himself to do so, he left us every evening. A few moments after he had gone we were apt to hear, of all things, the strumming of a banjo overhead, accompanied by an energetic thumping on the ceiling—if ceilings are what ships have. Mr. Evans had leaned toward me the first time and whispered, "Don't let on to the Old Man that you heard him beating time. He's given out that he never does it."

Often while we sat in the saloon I had the sensation of Cora's eyes being on me, but invariably when I looked around I found them elsewhere. I might have put the sensation down to vanity had I not observed that her eyes rested frequently upon Mr. Evans but always managed to slide away just before he turned his own upon her—not that my vanity received much encouragement from the observation.

One morning when she had failed to appear at breakfast and I had repaired to my perch above the rudder-gear housing to sit freed of all things, including myself, by the emptiness of the sea, the rhythm of the ship's sway and the wash of the waters, I had the sensation I knew from the saloon, and glancing over my shoulder, found her standing behind me. She had a way of being there when you were not expecting it and of not being there when you most—to be honest—wished she were. I was glad I had not yet taken up the sketching pad I had beside me.

She was wearing a pale blue cotton dress with a full skirt which, the breeze being behind her, she was holding down against her legs. The bodice had a square neck which, with her shoulders bent forward, had a little slack in it, provocatively enough. She was wearing high heels and no stockings.

Never given to banalities like "Do you mind if I join you?" she sat down with an abrupt movement on the deck next to the housing, settling her skirt around her and leaving me to drop down beside her.

"I felt this 'irresistible something' willing me to come back here," she

51

explained, "and lo! the something is you! You must have great *magnetism* to have drawn me past the galley. I thought I might be going to be sick there. But I think I have now separated out the main ingredients of this boat's smell. Would you like to hear them?" I said I should, very much, and she enumerated them, ticking them off on her fingers, bending each back in turn almost to her wrist, without strain, her narrow hands were so limber: "Coal smoke . . . fish . . . tar . . . paint . . . wet rope . . . brine . . . stewing cabbage . . . greasy meat . . . fetid icebox. Then there's the nauseous flavor a cigarette has when you smoke it in the wind. Have you got one, by the way?"

When she had tapped the one I gave her—ineffectually—and put it between her lips with her hands cupped around it, she extended her little finger for me to steady my hand against while I lighted it. I felt I had taken part in a sacrament.

"Doesn't your stomach ever feel queasy?"

I assured her that it did, especially in the morning, when that sensitive organ felt as if it had been awake all night, describing slow spirals in space.

She nodded. "All day, too. And at the top and bottom of the spiral there is this feeling that something big and heavy is being pulled out of you. Like the pudding we had for dessert, I mean. I hope it won't be. I suppose I must be a good sailor. I told Mrs. Mann that though I was very grateful for that my usual sentiment was that I'd rather see than be one. That was meant to amuse her. There was no sign that it did, though. She was working her way out of her girdle at the time. I am not supposed to look, of course, but out of the corner of my eye I can't always help it. It's like a birch tree trying to pull its bark down to its feet—'a veritable forest monarch.' . . . Another thing that made it hard for me to get back here is these high heels." She held her foot out, twisting it this way and that and studying it impersonally. "I'm always vowing not to wear them any more."

I asked her why she did.

"I have some very nice saddle-shoes, but they make me feel like Marge Lumkins. When I wear them I see myself standing flat-footed and unafraid on the threshold of something or other. . . . What brings you back to this lonely spot?"

I could have said it was excitement. The thought of what lay ahead was so vast it could not be confined for long to a cabin or to a corner of my mind while I read or talked; it had to have scope. However, from the example of an earlier conversation I had had with her I doubted my ability to convey this. When I had sought to find out from her how it felt to live in the world's most dramatically situated city, I gathered that the question had little relevance to what she had seen of life as it was actually lived in Belém. Her view was that life was pretty much the same everywhere. She summed up in her flattest tones, "When you've been pawed by a man in Manhattan, you've been pawed by men in— Oh, I don't know. You name the towns. Same look in the eyes. It's just as hard to get up in the morning in one place as another and just as nice to have someone else do the housework; in Belém someone else always does. And when I have a headache I don't care where I am. I don't even know."

I answered her by saying I liked to watch the waves. When *Boadicea,* having reared up like a Minotaur, came down upon a swell, the waters would rush from beneath her bows in a tide of milk. The waves she created would dash up at the next swell like onrushing white cavalry. The snowy chargers would surge madly up the passionless blue marble flank, hold their ground for an instant, then rear on their haunches before falling backward with a last despairing leap of foam to be borne —flattened ghosts—over the shoulder of the next mountainous sea. The sea would then heave *Boadicea* up and slip her, too, over its back. The ship, having slowed up on the grade, would gather momentum as she glided down into the sickeningly deep valley on the other side, cleaving the next roller for another charge of foam. Describing it as I saw it, I was a little self-conscious. I said I didn't think I'd ever seen it mentioned but there seemed to be a regular pattern in the way a ship rode the waves: she rode up on one swell and came crashing down upon the next; then up on the one after, and so on.

"Do you see God in the waves?" she asked.

My startled glance detected neither derision nor any special earnestness in her composed expression. Evidently it was just a question, such as "How do you like your eggs?" There was only mild inquiry in her eyes as she turned toward me to see what had delayed my reply.

"I've never thought about it that way."

"I don't believe you ever told me what you are going to Brazil for," she said.

" 'Study and travel' is what my visa application says." Had I not rehearsed myself in dissimulation I should certainly have told her about the Massaranduba Concession. This would have been counter to my instructions. A point was made of our moving in secret—out of deference, it was explained to me, to the sensibilities of several members of the Congress who had a connection with it they did not care to have publicized.

"Do you know anyone in Belém to stay with?"

I replied that I expected to be living with Senhor João Raimundo de Monteiro, although I had never met him. I asked if she had ever heard of him, though the question seemed unnecessary in view of her visible recognition of the name.

"I've lived in Belém for three years," she said by way of reply. "I can't say I ever thought of Monty as a patron of students and travelers, though. How do you know of him, if I'm not being too inquisitive?"

She had drawn her foot up uncomfortably to extinguish her cigarette against the sole of her shoe. The spark did not succumb readily to her tentative jabbings. Her awkward yet feminine posture and the disclosure resulting from the low cut of her dress as she leaned forward made devastating the picture I had of her as appealing, helpless and in a not-readily-definable way essentially *alone*. This picture, and the protective instinct it fired in me, would be recognizable, I suppose, to any man who has been exposed to an unaccompanied pretty woman. It occurred to me in an uncouth recess of my mind that she was not compelled to wear a dress with that kind of neckline, but I put the unworthy thought out of my mind, along with the vulgar cavil from the same quarter: "And you don't have to be so gimlet-eyed for that matter, Sir Galahad."

"A friend of my father's has a business connection with him. I gather he's a shipowner. Also that he's a graduate of California University. What's he like?" Given the state of my feelings about her, I could not have prevaricated so lightly had not the Concession seemed just then a matter of singular remoteness.

With a strenuous overhand throw she cast the dead cigarette over the side. "Well, he's not much like *you*." It appeared, briefly, that this estimate, requiring me to divine her impression of me and cast it in its antithesis, was all she was going to contribute, but she resumed. "He has eyes the color of Palmolive soap. You can't help being reminded of it. Once I saw a picture of an Egyptian statue with a cat's head, and I said, 'That's it! There he is! That's Monty!' He sits there with his teeth just

54

showing through that permanent little smile of his, and you wonder what 'nameless practices' he has been indulging in by moonlight. But that's not it. Nope. Those 'nameless practices' are business dealings. I haven't the faintest understanding of business, including my husband's, but . . . You know those fish they have in Brazilian rivers—piranhas —that can reduce the carcass of a big fat cow to a pile of bones in a matter of minutes? Whoever said the Latins don't make good businessmen never knew Monty. Speaking of soap, I took a nasty fall in that gruesome tub yesterday. I nearly poked a hole in my thigh." She looked at me with eyes that had taken on the blue of the sea and the sky and were wide as if in surprise at something I had said. It was a way she had that made you feel you had missed something. You felt that her awareness and nonawareness of you were out of phase with the occasion and nonoccasion for it.

My response must have been anxiously solicitous, for she said, readjusting her skirt and tucking it under her legs, that, oh well, it hadn't been as bad as that. "He has a cute little wife, Sophia. You'd hardly believe how warlike she can become if she thinks Monty is being injured. She makes a 'holy cause' of him. Some men are very lucky. Which reminds me that we haven't heard much about you. You're not married, I know. But you must have a *namorada* at home who's desolated by your leaving. Do you love her very much?"

I said I was afraid there was no *namorada*.

"*None?*"

"None!"

"American girlhood must be losing its grip. Doesn't Marge Lumkins make you yearn for a mate?"

"Marge Lumkins?" I repeated in astonishment.

"The way she makes everyone so much aware of her and Ted's going to bed together. Doesn't it drive you mad with desire—the picture of Marge scrubbed, honestly and understandingly accepting her role, just the way the girls in college and the doctor and the minister and the books on sex all said it was going to be? You may not know it, but in addition to the performances at night there are matinees occasionally. Yes, sometimes in the afternoon when clothes are being changed the unveiling of the form divine is too much for the young husband, and nothing will do *but*. This was hinted to me. I was very obtuse, and Marge became more and more impatient and explicit. She couldn't let me go on not

55

realizing how she inflames the senses of a man of the world like Ted Lumkins." She pressed her skirt farther, and supererogatively, down around her legs. "I don't think she likes me very much. I'm afraid the other two women don't either."

The words feeling like foreign substances in my mouth, I made some graceless rejoinder about their resentment at the notice she attracted from the men.

"You're too-too, too kind," she remarked in a way that put a great distance between my observation and herself. "My offense is more serious than attracting attention. I can eat half a pound of candy a day and never gain an ounce—and if I know my cabin-mate, that's what she reports I do eat. . . ." She raised her arms, her hands at her shoulders, and stretched and twisted, yawning, like one waking up in the morning. "If you'd just pop up, you could help me to my unsteady feet," she said when she had finished. "It's time for bouillon, and I am the hungry one, *a esfomeada."*

That night, not for the last time, sleep was rather a long time in coming. I lay in my bunk, and I went over in my mind a disquisition delivered in a harsh, self-pitiless voice one time by my roommate in college, a Bostonian, an historic Bostonian, as I thought of him, in respect, partly, of his seeming to me about a hundred years older than I. He had a straight, severe mouth drawn across a square jaw altogether at variance with the large, quick-seeing, unhappy grey eyes, as in retrospect I am aware that they were. Life was a jiu-jitsu artist, he had propounded. It used your own strength to throw you: not your physical strength, but your strength of imagination. The livelier your imagination, the more certain you were to be smacked down, and the oftener, and the harder you would hit. "If you hurl yourself with enough power against a master of jiu-jitsu, he can send you flying head over heels with his little finger. I give you an example. I offer it in my own person." It was then two o'clock in the morning. I had waked to see a light under the door and to find my roommate in our common living-room holding a half-filled glass drawn from our common store of rye whiskey and standing in front of an open window. He was drawing deep breaths as if he had been near asphyxiation. "The instrumentality in this case, the master's pinky, is a girl, a little girl, a daughter of man whom anyone might look upon and find fair."

I acknowledged having heard him speak of some such person before.

"Quite so. I forget that your faculties are not impaired by drink. The point to be made is that the jiu-jitsu artist would not find her a ready victim for his japes. She is not easily tumbled. No *sous-entendu* intended, but a *sous-entendu* warranted. Yes, by cracky, it is. I do not mean that lack of imagination is a special characteristic of hers. I only mean—and here I recognize that I am repeating myself—she is a girl." He took a draft of the whiskey, not looking at it. "I once read in a book of counsel for growing boys," he went on, "an inspired bit of advice on how to deal with 'impure thoughts.' It said, 'We cannot prevent birds from flying over our heads, but we can keep them from building nests in our hair.' Birds! *'Driven to It by Birds' Says Undergrad Held in Rape of Coed.* But let us not quibble. Let us allow the sage his image. Birds, so be it. But there are birds and birds. There's the kind Prometheus had his trouble with. 'We can prevent eagles from nesting in our hair, but we cannot keep them from sinking their talons in our vitals.'

"I put the question to myself: have the dainty creatures who look their charming best for us any comprehension of the ravening monster which does their work for them? We may be sure they're far from unaware that they have a dependable ally in the camp of the enemy. Do we not see them prettily toss it bon-bons? They live in a pastel-tinted world, and the picture they have—you may take it from me—is of a unicorn, a unicorn with melting brown eyes and no other urge than to lay its head gently in the lap of a virgin. How could such a mild and temperate beast get any wrong ideas and become restive? No, no, it would not be in its nature! You, sir, you would never be such a brute, so abandoned to depravity as to let on to an innocent young thing that you are disturbed— shall we say—by the forms of her breasts so unmistakably revealed by her dress. No, perish the thought! You must suppose that when she tried on the dress in the store she quite failed to perceive this feature. When she bought her bra, it was to restrain nature's exuberance, from dictates of modesty. It escaped her observation that the garment's design would emphasize the separation. And if, because she was too guileless to think of such things, there are telltale outlines that catch the unicorn's eye— how astonishing! But, if that's the way it is, why begrudge the attentive creature a few small liberties? There is no harm in that. Current convention authorizes considerable latitude. Thanks to a comparing of notes within the sorority—if my sources are reliable—a nice girl knows how much give there is to the condition of niceness—how far she may go, in

57

short. It is figured in specific gradations, steps on the way to the *grand prix*. Having properly allowed you to proceed to, but no farther than, Zone Three in a parked car after the theater, the girl of your dreams is blithe and unbothered when you deposit her at her door; it has been a *lovely* evening and absolutely *the* most enjoyable musical! You can be sure she's dropped placidly off to sleep before you've even got the car back to the U-Driv-It.

"As for you, there's your little trundle-bed awaiting, and there you may lie with cramps in your viscera and your imagination as feverishly awake as a Mad Scientist. What's the longing of a man perishing of thirst for a cup of water? What's the longing of the oppressed believer for salvation? You've had a glimpse of a drink and a salvation they've never dreamed of—within your grasp! Ecstasy, fulfillment, the end of pain, the merging of the soul with the infinite—all but yours! Your imagination makes it realer than real—just beyond your reach. It all looms before that inward eye which is the bliss of solitude, that great, bloodshot, staring orb. There's her scent, not the perfume she wears, but her natural scent as a girl. And her figure, all that the fit of her skirt burns into your mind, the hollows behind her knees, the certain fact of bare flesh above the stockingtops. There it is, God damn you. It's only a matter of a couple of shoulder-straps, a skirt that's open around her legs, a bit of silken-sheer fabric—and what's it designed for but to titillate on one side and tantalize on the other? There's nothing else between you and what you'd damn near give your life for, you're such a fool."

He drained his glass. "This is the last of this stuff I am going to have." He eyed me with a grin. "Don't look so anxious, Julian. It's all in fun! All in fun, lad! Breasts spring eternal in the human hope; man always is and will remain a dope. You New Yorkers are such earnest bastards. It's part of belonging to a society that's on the make, I guess."

Yes, I thought, sitting up in the bunk and lighting a cigarette, such a fool! I was a fool to torture myself and lose sleep. For there was nothing doing, nothing doing. The voice of reason told me that. The trouble was that the imagination is never bound by plausibility, never acknowledges the relevance of lack of grounds. As for the repeated admonition of judgment, Not your kind! Not your kind! I refused to hear it, I defended her against it, I saw her sitting in repose in the sunset looking afar, and the reality of the image guaranteed for me the existence of a deep accord between us. And besides, if she was not my kind, there was the corollary, inadmissible but slyly insinuated nonetheless, that when only physical interest is present that interest must by its nakedness acquire a sharper intensity. She would be detachedly cooperative, speculatively daring, observer and participant. . . . The mind recoiled from its own vapors. Was there not a fabled monster whose aspect was fatal to all who beheld it and finally to itself when a mirror was held up to it?

A cigarette smoked in the dark, as I have never known why, is not very satisfying, but I was not going to turn on a light. After all, there was a mirror over the washstand. There was the remaining week of the voyage during which we should be together, and beyond that Belém. Yet I could not see any opportunities developing in the very small world of the ship, and as for Belém, it was a city of several hundred thousand, among whom I might well never see Cora again, except casually, inasmuch as she had, and presumably was glad she had, a husband. Between the envisioned theoretical possibilities and the clearly perceived improbabilities, I felt myself between two carding combs, hardly knowing which set of teeth was the sharper.

Pulling on a pair of trousers, I went out on deck with my cigarette. A gibbous moon was nearing its setting a few points to starboard off our stern, and around it the strangely grey-dark sky was half masked by monstrous clouds rising to appalling altitudes. They were pale as death, but when they moved across the moon they turned black and solid-seeming as land-masses in a sea of air. The clouds were both the curtains and the most majestic actors in a mute and stupendous drama. Their slow drift made the whole heavens, stars and moon, appear to be in motion, unalterably, irresistibly. It was childhood's dream of the witching-hour, at which the trees, hills and houses come to life in a ponderous ritual dance, only here it was the cosmos. The moon, white as frost, spectral, sepulchral, was the central figure and called the pace for the clouds, and as we plowed our way along, linked with it by a path of warmthless white fire kindled upon the waves, it seemed to track us. I thought how the lifeless orb of the moon—the risen dead—must appear to one who had fallen overboard and been brought at length to know the futility of screaming any longer at the contracting light-studded shadow of the receding ship. I leaned against the side of the cabin and could well have embraced and clung to those staunch iron plates, faintly throbbing to the vessel's steady heartbeat. Her bows rose black against the sky, blotting out the lower constellations. In her lift was the soul's aspiration, as there was the spirit's resolution in her crashing lunge upon the uprearing seas looming out of the darkness.

59

4

The night, however disturbed, had its antidote. In the morning there was the sensation of having been resurrected in a world cleansed of its residues, a world all luminosity, bathed in light from a divine source. All around us the horizons were banked with clouds, but not like the night's ghosts of dead lands rising from the sea. These were lands yet unborn, magical, aerial mountain ranges, cloud masses ascending from flat, lavender bases to rounded, snowy contours, swollen with light, immense, awesome. Stupefied with wonder, the last survivor of a world that had been shed, blinking before the inconceivable whiteness of the peaks and crags, our ship steamed through the heavenly fjord. The alpine summits were pure, compressed light, enthralling light, and the enfolded valleys below them were not shadowy but filled with a soft, clear brightness. They were the enchanted homelands, remembered before their creation in the legends of a race in its infancy, crowned by Olympian castles, inhabited by ever-youthful immortals and the innocent-hearted creatures of man's dawning view of his earthly surroundings.

As the sun rose, the clouds grew thinner, faded and disappeared, leaving us alone on the platter of the sea beneath a sky that was deep blue overhead and paled as it curved to the horizon. Then, as the afternoon wore on, clouds, though of a different kind, ascended again from beneath the rim of the sea, ships riding upon an ocean of air. They concentrated around the sun, dark-centered but fleeced with silver and gold. They seemed to be waiting. They could have been the spirits of departed days gathered for the passing of the day that was ending.

The portholes, open to the sea, were black when we finished the evening meal. Cigarettes were lighted. Cora leaned forward, elbow on table, chin on her knuckles, singling out Mr. Evans. "Did they treat you very badly when you were a prisoner in the war?" she asked. Her characteristic pose brought out the line of her throat. "Did you suffer greatly?" Her tone of voice made the question personal, as if there were no one else in the saloon.

The first mate's reply was short. "They treated us very well."

"Did you get enough to eat?" I asked after a silence that seemed to me constrained, though Cora evidently did not find it so; she remained contemplating the aloof Welshman without change of expression, as if she were still awaiting his response.

"Why, considering how close the German civil population was to starvation, we did very well," he replied more discursively. "Baskets of food sent to prisoners were usually received intact. Those that disappeared would have been just as likely to have disappeared in Britain."

The young Scots third officer spoke up—daringly, you could tell he felt. "Anyone caught stealing from a prisoner-of-war basket at home was put to death." The way his black hair grew up in tufts from the sides of his prematurely balding scalp gave him, what with his color, the appearance of a cherubic imp from Hades.

Mr. Evans raised his brows. "Well, I can't say the Germans were as scrupulous in all cases as we would have been." He went on to cite the case of two British fellow prisoners of his with an uncanny knack for escaping. Though caught each time, they had got away so often that their captors became infuriated. When brought to Mr. Evans's camp they had recently escaped from another, for the third or fourth time. They were put in solitary confinement, each in a windowless cell. They were

61

taken out for exercise separately. They had no possible opportunity to exchange a word. One morning two weeks later they were gone—both of them. They were recaptured together. The prison commandant declared that the next time they would not be brought back alive. Two days later they had vanished once more. The day afterward they were returned to camp, dead. "They had been 'shot while resisting arrest,'" Mr. Evans finished sarcastically.

"You can't blame the Germans for having shot them," said Señor Augusto. "If they kept on escaping, they were entitled to shoot them."

"No!" exclaimed Mr. Evans, leaning over the table toward the Peruvian. "No!" he repeated as if correcting a child. "It is contrary to the conventions on the treatment of prisoners. It is not fair play. No one with a vestige of honor would have done what that German commandant did."

Sailing in from some conversational antipodes with an expression he used to prepare a listener for the worst, the Captain said, "You'll pardon my candor, I know, but in your country, in Spain, ever since the time during the Peninsula War in 1806 when the British commander carried out a difficult promise he'd made, the Spanish have said 'word of an Englishman' as we say 'word of honor.'" The distinction between the Spanish and the Peruvians was rather an esoteric one for the Captain.

"I'm afraid, Vicente," said Cora, "that the rectitude of the British is something the rest of us just have to get used to."

Señor Augusto was rueful but a good sport. "He is right, you know. I don't know how it is in Brazil, but in Peru we say, for instance, 'I'll meet you at two o'clock *para inglés.*' That means two o'clock. If we don't say '*para inglés,*' it means four or five. I have been educated in England, and I like the English. There is only one thing. I do not understand how they make coffee to taste like this." He elevated his cup and eyed it curiously. "It is inexcusable to criticize the customs of other peoples, but I cannot help wondering. The making of coffee is so simple. You would think everywhere it would be as good as everywhere else. Yet there is this. How can it be?"

"It comes from never throwing the grounds away," said Mr. Willcox, the second mate. He had just been relieved by the third and was hunched in a vulturine but appealing and affection-hungry way over a mug of the brew. "We just add a pinch of fresh to the old every day. A speck of the sludge at the bottom of your cup may have started in H.M.S. *Victory.*"

62

"Maybe you are exaggerating a little, eh? But it would explain. Yes, that is how the coffee tastes. Only why do you not throw away the grounds?"

"We believe in tradition. Haven't you heard?"

"It's like honor with them," said Cora. "It's something to punish themselves with."

The Captain thrust his napkin from him like a desperate gambler putting his last possession on the table. "If I'd a better hand for writing I shouldn't put it off so long, but there it is. I must ask you to excuse me. . . ."

That was one of the few nights when I managed to be alone with Cora. She left the saloon earlier than usual, and following her out, I joined her where she stood a little forward of the bridge, her forearms on the railing, looking down into the water.

"If I fell overboard, would you jump in after me, Julian?" she asked without looking up. Evidently she assumed it was I.

"There's only one way to know for sure," I replied.

She straightened up, resting her fingertips on the railing and still looking seaward. "I believe you would. You haven't known me long. It would be different with a lover. The more reason a man has to save a woman's life, the more relieved he'd be if she just disappeared. Secretly relieved, of course. It's a fact!" she stated as I demurred. "Even if he wouldn't come within a mile of admitting it to himself, it's true. It's true as day, true as gold, true as a tale that's ne'er been told."

"I'd hate to think so."

For all answer she put her hand on my shoulder—it was only to steady herself—and with the other reached down and settled her foot in her shoe, from which it apparently had been dislodged.

"You find Mr. Evans very attractive, I think," I said when she had righted herself.

She was standing apart, but in the moonlight I could see her tilt her head and purse her lips as she considered the proposition. I had expected her to be startled and perhaps vexed, but she gave no sign of being either. It was possible to imagine her a prospective bidder and David Evans on the block in front of her. "Don't you?" she asked.

"Yes, I suppose he's the kind that men admire as much as women do."

She remained unfazed, despite what my tone must have been. "He thinks I'm trying to seduce you."

63

The silence was in my ears, stunned and echoing. I hardly knew how I responded. It was probably with something artificial-sounding about wishing it were true.

"He hasn't said so, of course. If he had, I'd have told him you consider me much too old to be interesting. I have designs on you, though," she added quickly. "When we get to Belém, I'm going to find a little girl for you. A soul mate. You'd never believe how good I am at matchmaking. I can't pretend it's always the old business of And-then-they-lived-happily-ever-after. Sometimes they're already living ever after with somebody else—their husband or wife—*un*happily. But a little affair does stir things up for a while. And if you're a confidante of both sides it can be quite fascinating. Now let's see. . . ." She drew back and examined me in the same fashion as she had the conjured-up image of Mr. Evans.

"The question is, what is your type of girl? You don't have to tell me what you think it is. You think it's the 'passionate' type. That's what any man thinks. But what is this 'passionate' type? Men picture some black-haired *moreninha* with carmine lips. Spilling over the top of her bodice. The kind you'd find dancing in a cabaret, with taunting eyes and weaving hips. I suppose if I were a man I'd find that kind of maraschino beauty a dish. They say men are boys at heart, and I remember how my little brother used to drool at the sight of a hot fudge sundae."

She drew an arabesque on the railing with her finger, then made a quick motion of crossing it out. "Talk about sour grapes! Maybe that's what it is. I certainly used to be jealous. By the time I had reached physical maturity, as they say, I had to face the fact that I didn't look as if I had and never would. I kept telling myself how those voluptuous females look by the age of thirty-five, what with their robust biologies and all the french bread and spaghetti they've eaten. But waiting till thirty-five to have it made up to me was waiting till senility, the way I looked at it then. I was a discouraged gal. Then I read a story in one of those magazines printed on coarse paper—*Paris Scandals,* or something—I found under my brother's pillow, and it said about the girl in it that she was one of those slim-limbed, small-bosomed, sexy types. I'm not shocking you, am I? I didn't see how being small that way made you sexy, but I began to think of myself in a different way. Did you bring your cigarettes? Why don't you just light mine, too, it's so windy."

I turned away, ostensibly to leeward, to conceal whatever the illumina· tion of the match might disclose in my face. Handing her one of the cig·

arettes I had lighted, I kept silent. I had a feeling she had not finished with the subject she had been talking about.

The light of the coal as she drew on the cigarette glowed warmly on her face, which would not have been out of place in a rendering of an angel. With her eyes large and dark in the night, she looked too young to be smoking. A spasm of that recurrent protective feeling struck me. "Possessive" would doubtless be a more accurate term for it.

She exhaled the draught toward the sky and removed a shred of tobacco from the tip of her tongue. "Then there was *the* most delightful book, called *The Wellsprings of Love,* by this *doctor."* Her face was still lifted to the sky, her hand at her throat. "It said that a musician would never write love music for a big"—her hands outlined large rotundities in the air—"bass viol. The instrument of love music is the violin. 'The violin is trim, light and refined. It has taut strings. It is sensitive and responsive. It attracts musicians of imagination.' I thought I knew what the book meant by 'taut strings'—even by 'musicians of imagination.' The book said you might not think so to look at it, but the fragile, chaste violin has a much greater *range* than its more generously proportioned sister. Goodness, I thought! *Range!* I hardly dared consider what that might mean. The only thing a bass viol can handle better, it said, are primitive, tribal rhythms. . . . Aren't you going to smoke your cigarette?"

Obediently I took a drag on the thing.

"Anyway, that's what *I* think we should find for you. A trim, chaste little nymph—and high-strung. You won't be put off if she has a little-girl figure, like mine? Just remember: she's what the doctor prescribed. You know, an instrument with *range,* to challenge the imagination. . . . I don't think Monty's going to like it when he discovers we've been on the same boat."

"Who?"

"Senhor Monteiro. Your friend. Hold this for me, will you, please?" She presented me with her cigarette, and while I stood there, a cigarette in each hand, she picked up a white silk stole from a deck chair behind her and adjusted it around her shoulders, talking the while in her languid, offhand fashion. I did not follow what she was saying. It was about Monteiro and some governor. All I could take in was that the moment had passed. The moment, which a few seconds before had held the universe in debilitating expectancy, was gone, utterly. In the mood she had now created there was nothing left of it.

65

"You can give me back my cigarette now," she was saying, her hand extended. "You're holding two of them. One's mine." She took it and without drawing further on it snuffed it out on the underside of the railing and threw it down into the water. "Well, you can't study and travel in the state of Pará very long without hearing a *lot* about him, believe me. Or him about you, for that matter. I'm surprised Monty hasn't—what's it called?—*acquainted* you with the situation. Or am I? Of course, *I* don't pretend to understand it. You might as well try to explain politics to a canary. Still, if I were in your place I don't think I'd let some kind of relationship with Monty—and you've never even seen him, have you? —give Colonel Durondo the idea that I was necessarily to be counted among his enemies."

"Who did you say Colonel Durondo was?"

"Haven't you been *listening?* He's the *Interventor*—the Governor of the state. My advice is not to complicate things needlessly. That's Mother Almeida's recipe for a bearable life. Keep it simple. His Excellency is complicated enough himself, and very touchy—and please don't go around saying I said so. With what men have done with the world, it's practically impossible to keep *anything* simple. They're always charging off with banners flying. And have you ever seen a book on algebra? Of course you have. Or geometry? That's what men have thought up out of *nothing*. And for *no* reason. So you can imagine what they do when they're given half a chance. But then you're a man yourself. *And* you've got that book about the Naturalist on the River Amazon waiting for you. I mustn't keep you from it any longer. And I've got to get back to my cabin myself."

"Don't go!"

"I have to. Mrs. Mann will already be waiting to see if my lipstick is smeared. And she doesn't like it when I have the lights on after she's gone to bed. Have a good night!"

The clouds that had congregated in the late afternoon still lingered in the sky, only now they were black, with an unaccountable aureole of silver mist. A patient and meditative herd, they waited.

No enlightenment, no comfort could be looked for in that quarter, no relief from the sensation of having been wrung out like a washed garment. What it was that kept me, like an iron harness, from responding to her provocation, as I was sure it was, I did not know. I could not tell, and I am not sure even now. Was it the morality or prudery of youth, less celebrated but no less genuine than its prurience and hunger, strengthened in this case by the fact that the inciteress was older and married? Was it simple, discreditable timidity with its physical accompaniments of enervating weakness and a quaking emptiness within? Or was it a coldly calculating inner censor that warned of a rebuff if seeming invitations were put to the test? One thing was certain: it would be another night when sleep would wait upon those siren scenes that played themselves out in the mind.

It struck me that I could do worse than take a cue from the source of my turmoil and submit myself to the flow of Henry Walter Bates's methodical and wholesome observation. It would perhaps serve me as saintlier persons had been served by the mumbled repetition of Latin prayers when assailed by phantasmagorias of the senses. Having installed myself in my bunk for the night, I opened *The Naturalist on the River Amazon* at the marker and began, "Fowls, eggs, fresh fish, turtles, vegetables, and fruit were excessively scarce and dear in 1859, when I again visited the place; for instance, six or seven shillings were asked for a poor, lean fowl, and eggs were two pence halfpenny a piece." Bates was an informative writer with superior technical equipment, but as a reader I was easily distracted from his prose and consequently reserved his book for times when I was alone in my stateroom.

When I came to think of it, I could not remember ever having had it out of the stateroom. Indeed, I was quite sure I had not. That made it a little odd that Cora should have known about it. Doubtless a simple explanation would soon occur to me, I reflected, and I resolutely set about to partake of Bates's concern that an egg should have cost as much as five cents in 1859.

Passengers, opined the Captain, often refused to adapt themselves to the ship or even "carried on amongst themselves." Having them aboard ("You'll pardon my candor") was not much to his liking. I was the more surprised, therefore, when one evening while I was leaning over the rail outside his cabin he asked if I should care to come in for a bit, "though heaven knows there's nothing of any consequence in here," he warned gruffly.

His quarters were of two small rooms, one more than half filled by a bed, the other by a desk almost too wide to be reached across and covered by a neat stack of charts. A large mahogany box trimmed in brass,

67

which had a table all to itself, doubtless contained navigating instruments. All the paraphernalia in the little rooms was of a considerable size—large contrivances to cope with momentous problems in a big world. Of trophies he might have collected in a lifetime spent plying among romantic ports there were none. The walls were bare but for a large telescope and beside it a massive binocular. Captain Byram suggested I take the latter out on deck and have a look through it. But in the darkness there was nothing on which to focus. Even the seam of sky and ocean was invisible.

"It's very fine," I said on my return. But I could see that the Captain was not to be mollified.

"Turn it on another ship and they throw it into your lap. Enough to scare the wits out of a man," he growled. All the same he watched me closely from under the eaves of his eyebrows to see that, with the ship rolling as she was, I did not lurch into anything with it. When I had restored it to its place, he reached, with an awkward casualness, for two titanic tomes bound in red buckram on a shelf above the desk.

"They tell me you've taken a turn at the wheel and even been below and done a bit of stoking," he hazarded.

I said I was afraid I had not been much good at either. The helm, while I had it, seemed to have only a distant relationship with the vessel, messages taking a long time to go from one to the other, so that when she went off course on one side my overanxious efforts to bring her back would send her even farther off on the other before I could undo them. And then in the stokehold the heat that leaped out at you like a battering-ram when you opened the furnace door and the piston shafts the size of treetrunks that shot up and down as weightless as beams of light put me into such a frenzy of excitement that I kept missing my aim with the coal and hitting the edge of the door, turning the lip of the shovel. I saw that he was not listening, though.

"It's no good showing these around to everyone," he remarked indifferently, handing me one of the volumes. "However . . ."

I opened it and found it to be filled with handwriting. The giant leaves were inscribed from top to bottom with columns of figures in red and blue ink alternating with columns of verbal text. The Captain ceased scrutinizing my face long enough to glance at the page I had turned to. "Week of April seventh, nineteen twenty-one," he commented. *"Ben Dearg*—off Madagascar." He followed my progress through many more

68

pages with other brief identifications and the same close attention. I finally understood that these two volumes contained the particulars of every day's run of every ship he had served in as an officer for over thirty years, a record scrupulously maintained in fair weather and foul, as an end in itself. I could not tell what the verbal portions were about, let alone the columns of figures, but the style—"I should venture a guess that . . ." "It appears that . . ." or "My opinion would be . . ."—evoked a picture of a dedicated craftsman addressing with respectful formality a distinguished assemblage of his peers existing only as an illusion of his solitude. There were pages, too, of calculations worked out with precise geometrical drawings. I heard later from the third officer that Captain Byram had a genius for the mathematics of navigation. "Why," declared the young Scotsman in awe, "he even computes the critical depth—that is, the depth of water in which the best speed is possible—for every ship he's in. And of course the knowledge is absolutely useless!"

The Captain ostensibly shared his junior's view on that point. "Silly waste of time, really, I suppose," he interjected diffidently. I had given up the effort to communicate my appreciation of what was entailed in this work. The figures traced meticulously in those volumes by that heavy fist might have come from the hand of an engraver. There were no smudges; only, pressed flat among the leaves, were occasional shreds of tobacco from pipes smoked in ships of which these books were possibly the last remaining trace upon the seas. They were all pictured, too, each at the head of its section, in lusterless old photographs—ships that had vanished. "Lost, or broken up and made into razor blades," the Captain would comment flippantly, turning the page. "I was first officer in this one when she was mined—during the war." A few pages farther on he paused over the photograph of a deep-sheered old vessel with scarcely any freeboard, I think the term is. "This one was captured by a German. *Moewe,* the German's name was. Her commander came aboard and asked me to have a drink with him while they took my crew off," he explained briefly. "So we had a few from the ship's lockers. He *would* have it that I let him pay for them, though of course the entire stock was to go to the bottom in half an hour. A damned decent chap—and as young as I was. I shan't forget how he brought his men to attention and dipped his colors as my ship went down. My first command."

At the end of these obituaries was a picture that in such a company was somewhat chilling. "Yes, *Boadicea,* still afloat though most of her betters have gone to the bottom," he commented, apparently not unaware of my feeling. "You know, she was built in wartime, knocked together without much care for style, so you mustn't think too harshly of her fittings. They thought she'd be torpedoed before anyone could object very much to them. *War Merlin* was the name she bore then. You wouldn't think of her as anything so grand, but I could show you some of the letters still visible on her bow. And if her luck holds, you may shave with her someday. . . . Now for those figures I took off the Guianas which will give you an idea of the current and why we couldn't go southward through the islands." He turned back through a sheaf of pages, and again I wondered about the flags he had drawn neatly in the margins. They were done in red and blue inks, usually singly but sometimes three or four together. They were representations of the striped house flag of the company and were invariably rippling defiantly —that was the word that sprang to mind—from their rakish staves.

Our course, as posted on a chart in the saloon, lay almost straight southeast for nearly three thousand miles, then, directly above our destination, broke sharply and turned due south. The day came when *Boadicea,* rather surprising me with the literalness of her navigation, described the identical angle in a listing swerve to starboard.

That night the Captain, setting his fork down beside his mutton, snapped out the word "Pilots!" like an imprecation. "Nothing's ever right for them!" he declared in a voice of outrage. "Ship's not handy, quarters are bad, food's worse and they've got to have it any hour of the day or night. You'd think there was no such thing as a ship's routine." He launched with vehemence upon the story of a master he had known who had been ordered off the bridge by a Hooghly River pilot. *"His own bridge!"* He looked at me aghast, as if he expected me to faint with amazement. "But do you know what the Captain did?" he crowed. "He told that pilot he could march off the ship back to his boat in an orderly manner that instant or be heaved bodily over the side. So the pilot went —with his hands in his pockets and his face on the grin. It took years of apprenticeship before you could take a vessel up the Hooghly, and then you stranded her, like as not. But the Captain did it! Yes, by the Lord Harry, he put his ship through it and never touched a thing. The tale went all over India. The owners gave him a dressing-down in public —oh, a proper one!—but in private it was another matter, you may believe; the office never heard such laughter.

"One thing I'll say for the Brazilians. Those Amazon River pilots of theirs are as good as any in the world, and maybe a little bit better. Enough to make your hair stand on end, the cool way they take a ship up that river. A couple of thousand miles, too."

It was no good, however. You could see the storm regather on the Captain's brow. "But all those dock officials! What do these wretched South American countries want with so many officials? I can tell you what the officials want, right enough. They'd make off with the binnacle if they could. 'A leetle bottle wheesky, eh, Capitán?'" He leered. "'Or a leetle ham? Come, you got ham!' There's a port on the River Plate where I'm fined every time I show my face. All because I once refused a customs man 'a leetle cognac for the estomac.' I'm in the wrong berth, or my hawsers aren't right, or my rat-guards aren't on properly. And I've seen a dockhand *take my rat-guards off*—and then been fined for not having them!" he raged.

"They come aboard in droves, these Latino officials. They spit on the bridge and picnic on the decks. You'd think the ship was a blasted tramcar. And all the documents they want! A passenger of mine once had a canary, and would you believe it, they wanted a document for the canary!" He dug into his mutton.

"Have you ever been in a shipwreck, Captain Byram?" Cora interjected the question casually, as if she were making small talk, but it had quite a different effect. Perhaps that was because the officers seemed suddenly attentive.

The Captain himself came slowly around much as his ship had come around earlier in the day to her change in course. I was astonished to see the color leave his face. "Yes," he said, absolutely grey. "Yes, a bad one. Many years ago. We collided with a schooner one night off Hatteras. A five-master. One of the last of her kind, and nearly as big as we were."

"How did it happen?" Ted Lumkins asked. "Was it stormy?"

"Not for Hatteras. But it was thick. The schooner appeared out of the fog like a ghost ship, dead ahead. For a moment I think every man-jack of us who saw her believed that's what she was." You could tell from the Captain's eyes that he was seeing her again as plain as ever. "I don't know how long we stood paralyzed. It couldn't have been but a second or two, but it seemed much longer. Then I threw myself on the wheel—I was third officer and it was my watch. I sent the helmsman flying, but I got the helm over—too late, of course. Too late. We lowered away to take her men off, but she went down before we could get to her."

"And were you able to rescue any of them?" asked Cora.

The Captain looked at her as if the question puzzled him. "Most of the schooner's men were lost." I thought he was going to stop with that, and I believe he meant to. But it became apparent that the memory was of the kind that, once evoked, has to be rehearsed, even if for the hundredth time. "It was a very singular circumstance. The seas were not unduly high, but the schooner was loaded in watermelons, and when she broke open the sea was filled with them. There were thousands of black objects in the water—for us in the boats to choose among."

"Good Lord," someone murmured.

"The waves tossed them up," the Captain went on. "You couldn't rightly tell which were men and which were watermelons. You know what watermelons are? We'd hear the screams, and no mistake, but they were hard to follow in the dark, and when we rowed up to one of the black objects, twelve times to the dozen it wasn't a drowning man at all but another melon. Pretty soon the fog lifted—you'd have thought its only purpose had been to send those two ships into collision. We had a moon, at least intermittently, but the wind had come up too, and the melons kept drifting farther apart, so there was more and more sea to cover. And all that time the shouts went on, though fainter and fewer. When daybreak came, nothing was left but the melons and the grey water off Hatteras, and not a sound but the wind and the smashing of the seas against our hull."

There was not much sound in *Boadicea* either, except for the incorruptible beat of her engines and the wild surge of the waves thrown back from her bows.

"It was one of those things," he went on. "But in court we were at a disadvantage. A steamship against a sailing ship! The court found against us on a technicality: the master's books were not in order, it appeared. And why was he not on the bridge? Well, he had been, he'd gone below only for a moment, and he was back just as we struck. But there you are! One of those things. He was elderly, you know, and took it hard. It very nearly broke him. But he apologized to me! Fancy! He said he wished he had been there, not because he could have prevented it either, but so I'd have no cause to blame myself. 'I haven't as long to live with it as you'll have,' he said."

All the next day we tunneled beneath a brown mist that shrouded the horizon. The sea, which had been the whole world for us, days without number, was receding. The land, and the great river system of the Amazon, was reaching out for us. We had left the trades and the fair weather they gave us. Small rain-squalls chased one another like sand-storms across a desert-colored sea of choppy, aimless little waves. From the deck, smelling warmly of oil and wet rust, the vista was a sepia tint animated by schools of flying-fish that took off like flocks of goldfinches.

Then the sun came out again. It blazed fiercely in the zenith, but the cobalt-blue ocean on which it had last shone had gone. The waters that slipped sluggishly by us were like thin green-pea soup, from sediment, though we were still two hundred miles from land. The ocean was turning browner by the hour. Soon, as you could tell by the thinness of the foam, it was hardly salt at all. A night and most of another day still lay between us and a landfall, but already we were sailing, with a slow rocking motion and a steady hissing from the bow waves, through the discharge of the world's mightiest river.

During the night I woke off and on. I heard the plowing of the engines and thought how they would have driven us into the Valhalla of those morning cloud ranges or to our doom on a reef without a fault in their rhythm; even the imminence of the stupendous rain-forest with its shadows echoing to the abrupt cries startled from its wild depths, the thought of which caused my heart to skip a beat, affected them not. I woke up fitfully and by degrees, very early, not with a sudden completeness out of an unfathomable stupor.

I spent the day pacing the decks, though we were not due to raise Brazil till late afternoon. The sea was as deserted as ever, but there was no mistaking the nearness of land; you could feel it at the roots of your hair.

After lunch, as I was strolling aft past the officers' quarters, a voice called out my name through a door standing ajar and Mr. Willcox declared I must join him and the third for a last round of beers. "You can cheer us up," he said.

"You don't look as if you needed it."

"A pair of jolly tars."

"Like the Old Man," commented Mr. McLeod, fishing in his pockets and coming up with a pack of cigarettes.

"It was a dreadful thing that happened to him," I said. I had not been able to keep it long out of my mind: the mists, the implacable grey waters, the mute and ponderous vessels heeling awkwardly from the mortal impact, the clutch of mindless death, the ultimate cold extremity at which to be human counts for nothing.

"You'd best be prepared for some pretty nasty experiences if you follow the sea." Mr. Willcox, raising his glass, met it halfway with his hungry, beaked face. He had once passed a night aboard an ammunition ship in a harbor where others around him were being blasted sky-high by U-boats. "I'll be blowed if I know why anyone does—today," he continued. "That's what we were talking about."

"Not for the first time," the Scotsman put in.

"*Or* for the last. What's gone today is the satisfaction of doing a job." The second mate set his glass down with a bang. "We're not in demand. Not any more. A place has to be found for the likes of us. I've a master's certificate, but by the company's lights I should be on my ruddy knees with gratitude for a second officer's berth. I'm to forget the stitches on my cuffs where the third stripe used to be. It's not just the hard times that have fallen on the merchant marine. That'll pass, I daresay. It's what's happening to ships. You recall the monster we had to wait for in Savannah? The thing with the yellow superstructure and no sheer that filled the blooming river? They're not building ships any more. They're building floating warehouses. With the same staff of officers one cargo vessel will carry what once filled a whole fleet. Men, you say? They're unimportant! And mind you, we've seen only the beginning."

"The pride in ships is gone too," said the third, looking at me with the momentousness that the overcoming of shyness produced in him. "The time was when a shipowner would put everything he could into his vessels. When one of them was in he'd take his wife and youngsters and his relatives down to see her, to show off her brass and all the polished mahogany in her saloon. The best was none too good for a ship that carried the house flag across the seas."

"Today the company's only pride's in what a column of figures shows."

"And it made a difference to a master, though I can't explain why—and to all hands—when it was you and she against the sea." The speaker's color had flared up, and he was staring into his glass with the intensity of a crystal-gazer.

"Entries in a ledger, that's what ships are to your modern corporation," Mr. Willcox summed up, divested of his customary forlorn dogginess. "Not a penny to be spent upon them above the bare essentials."

74

We took up, severally, our beers and the burden of our thoughts. In mine the running swells of the cold and sullen sea were mingled with the rectilinear grey masses of the city I had left, looking as they had from *Boadicea*'s deck in the bitter chill of the winter evening. Only I had not left it. I was beholden to it for being here. Its will be done! Its requirements must be met, and what it required of me was a concession for the mining of gold, and the day of reckoning was at hand.

Startled by Mr. McLeod, who advised me to have a look out of the port—I realized he had just referred to his watch—I sprang up. Leaning across the upper bunk, I put my face to the opening.

Already, along the edge of the sea, lay a white chalk-drawn line, and above it, barely visible, an irregular, dusky green fringe.

"Go on, you fool," said the junior with a grin as I hesitated.

From the deck it was unmistakably there, the last thing, as I suddenly knew, that I had really expected, the last thing I could credit: the faint and broken margins of South America.

I had been staring at it for I do not know how long when I abruptly had the sensation of something enormous taking place in the universe. I thought my heart had ceased beating and for an instant expected to topple over head-foremost . . . But it was the engines; they had stopped. The silence had struck like an immense and soundless gong. I guessed at the explanation and looked around. Not far off was a little red boat with a high poop and bow, a diminutive galleon—the pilot-boat—toddling toward us over the murky water like a baby that has been left behind, while we waited.

We were shortly under way again. We kept our same distance from the coast until we had entered the estuary. The detached threads of shoreline seemed to suggest that only the spatulate extremities of the land were able to insert themselves between the mighty dome of the sky and the sky's oceanic pedestal. It was to the sky that your gaze was drawn, and a fabulous spectacle it offered. You could not take your eyes away for long. In its prodigal and immeasurable sweep around the rim of the earth it included all the varieties of weather you could expect to find in the whole circumglobal expanse of the tropics, as if here were the breeding-ground of them all. Astern, a coffee-brown ocean lay in the reflection of a cliff of cloud as solid and ominous as the cold rock precipices of an Antarctic promontory, while on the other side our bow pointed to a number of narrow rainstorms that sheered earthward as sheet-iron parallelograms.

75

There must have been half a dozen of these squalls in view, all neatly delimited. Their angle of declination indicated that they were traveling rapidly, but in these great distances they appeared static. Overhead, two atmospheric creations were in Olympian combat, ill-defined, dour grey clouds enwrapped in convolutions with clouds white and bulbous that were slowly turning themselves inside out upon the foe. Being below them, we were in shadow, but in other places the sun was shining brilliantly, aiming straight bars of silver at the earth. To port, the water led away in a plane of platinum to meet a sky of the purest milky white in a fine black line that might have been ruled off in India ink. To starboard, a chocolate-dark expanse of the bay paled gradually to white at the edge of the horizon, where a drapery of mist fell below the brink of the sea like a curtain.

Although our course lay up the lesser estuary of the river, hardly to be considered a mouth of the Amazon at all beside the main outpouring far to the north, the shores, parted at intervals by vast gaps, drew no closer as long as there was light enough to see them. After dark, however, the fires that sprang into flame and subsided to yellow sparks on the line of the invisible banks indicated that we were beating our way along fairly close inshore. *Boadicea* advanced without motion, the silence a sounding-board to the throbbing of the engines, which could be heard and felt the length of the ship.

During the evening meal, for which Cora did not appear, a moth came aboard and attacked the dining-table lamp. I caught it and detected a flash of blue from its eye. I examined it closely and with wonder. There was no doubt of it; its eyes were blue as sapphires.

A beaded chain of lights brought us even with some island village. An hour later a much longer series at the base of a low and extensive galaxy moved mysteriously out from behind a bank of denser blackness. Slowly it drifted toward us on our port side until it had come abreast of us. Then again came that terrible assault of silence following the shutting off of the engines. You could feel everyone on board holding his breath.

"Let go." An unknown voice spoke perfunctorily out of the night.

Boadicea responded with a deep rattle in her throat, like the sound said to accompany the departure of the spirit. Instantly the red and green lamps on the bridge went out and the anchor lights flashed on at the mastheads. In a quiet as profound as if the universe had exhaled a sigh

76

inaudibly and then gone still, the lights of Belém swung with infinite slowness around our stern until, on the other side of the ship, they came to rest, a dense constellation on the equator of the sphere of darkness that enclosed us.

It became evident after I had turned in that I was not going to sleep any time soon. At one o'clock I went out on deck. There was no moon, and apart from the diminished number of lights off our beam, nothing was to be seen but the water gliding by the hull where an illuminated port gave the blackness the translucency of obsidian. I was in a state of exalted tranquillity, beyond sleep, and I was thinking how different that was from lying wakeful in nerve-wracked response to only-too-obedient images of Cora when—and I should not have been surprised—there was Cora herself.

She waited for me to speak, standing a few paces off, but I only made a motion of recognition with my hand.

"I could see the whites of your eyes as soon as I came around the corner," she offered.

"How do you happen to be still up?" I asked.

"I'm a prowler." She must have wondered at my impersonality. I did myself. It was unpremeditated and uncalled for—but there it was.

"You haven't been to bed yet," I observed.

She looked down at her dress, smoothing the skirt against her legs. "I was in bed for hours. But I finally got up. I took off my pajamas and just pulled this on."

Far off, barely audibly, a cock crowed.

She came forward to where I stood by the rail and I remarked that in a few hours she would be back with her husband. I saw no change in her expression.

"I don't know," she said. "He may not be here. He disappears and re-appears. I don't mean to make it sound mysterious. It's probably just or-dinary business—if you don't call *that* mysterious."

"I don't believe you've ever mentioned what his business is."

"Search *me*." The then-current colloquialism made me blink a little. "He buys and sells, I think. Like everyone here. Things like hides and trees—lumber. I should take more wifely interest. He goes up and down the river a good deal. You'll hear about this kind of thing from your friend Monty. It's all very exciting, and mixed up with politics. It's not

77

unheard-of for people to get killed in the excitement. You won't have been long with Monty before you know more about Jorge's business than I do."

"Are they friends?"

"No, they're not friends." Resting with her forearms on the rail, she seemed rapt in contemplation of the invisible shore.

"Look, you stay right where you are," she said, straightening up. "I want to show you something. Don't go moving around." Turning her back to me, she raised her hands to her throat. Busy, evidently, at the front of her dress, they moved by quick stages to her waist, plainly undoing buttons. "Light your lighter and look at my back," she said, slipping the dress down over her arms.

In speechless amazement at the proceedings, I did as she told me. Her back, under the wavering flame, was thin-skinned, the back of a slight and fragile girl, and showed the little knobs at the top of the shoulders.

"Do you see anything like the kind of marks being lashed with a dog leash would leave?"

There were several faint scars extending across her back. My hand went out to them. From the stiffening start of the muscle beneath my fingertips I might have thought the wounds still fresh.

"Your *husband?*" I had dropped my hand as she began to pull her dress back on.

"No, my husband's mother."

"His *mother?* You can't mean it. How could she?"

She finished buttoning her dress and gave it a little tug at the waist as she turned back toward me. "Probably a good thing nobody came by just then. . . . If you had ever seen her! She's crazy. I suppose I could have fought her off, and if I'd been a *fee*-male defending her brood I guess I would have. But just for myself . . . to tussle around, probably on the floor. Can you imagine anything more repulsive? *Toujours la dignité,* that's Cora. I bled, though, and Mama Almeida collapsed."

The picture of her enduring those lashes without struggle turned me to stone, cold stone.

"The reason why I'm exposing my humiliating secret is just so you'll know something right away that took me quite a while to find out. You'd think you were in the doldrums here, and mostly you are, but all the time, underfoot, there's a kind of thin crust, and underneath, things smoldering. You don't have to try very hard to go through, and even if

78

you're careful they may erupt right under you. Nothing is safe from politics."

"Politics?"

"She accused me of having been unfaithful to her son with the *Interventor*. What made her suspicious was that the Government had suddenly seemed to be very well disposed to Jorge—and other things. The point is that she didn't regard Colonel Durondo as the right kind of politico for her son's wife to bestow her favors on. What she'd have thought if he'd been of her own class and faction, I'm not sure. It had got so she couldn't think of anything but Palace intrigue, and she never considered me good for much. It's a funny phrase, isn't it—to bestow one's favors. It sounds like a hostess at a party handing out trinkets."

"Is that what you're going back to? Does she live with you?"

"No, she went completely out of her head and had to be put away. By the way, in case you're wondering, she was wrong. I gave out no trinkets to Colonel Durondo." She clasped her arms across her breast and held herself tightly; I could tell she was not breathing. There were several things I started to say, but I caught myself each time. None of them sounded right. "We'll be running into each other, despite Monty, so I won't say good-bye," she declared, holding out her hand with a quick movement and as suddenly reclaiming it when I had taken it.

I stayed behind on deck until I felt there was some chance of sleeping.

As I first saw the Amazon at dawn from *Boadicea*'s deck I shall see it always, as I knew then that I should, as I knew also that however long I might live and however far travel nothing could ever in my eyes come up to that stupendous scene. In the months ahead I came to know, as well as I had expected I could, the face of that forest upon which I now gaped, which led the unbelieving gaze all around the length and breadth of that crowning plain of creation, spanning the farthermost extremities of the river at an inconceivable distance in a wire of burnished green, advancing along the nearer shores like a thundercloud, a mighty palisade of foliage, static and brilliant as if its sprays had fixed forever in a measureless wealth of emeralds all the pristine green in the kingdom of the earth. When the chance came, I was to follow with the eyes of an acolyte all the variations in its character for a thousand miles of its westward range to the Andes, trying to fix in mind every expression of an ocean of trees that a lifetime could not encompass. I was to awaken before dawn many mornings to the spectacle of its tumultuous contours, of its leafy pinnacles that resembled tongues of green flame shot out of the rolling waves of the forest-top, high above the ponderous breakers of foliage that cascaded down over the river, as if in this display of wild abandon there were caught and crystallized the supreme effort and mighty failure of earth-bound life to fling itself to the sky.

And that sky! Nothing I had ever seen before that morning could give any comprehension of it. In time, too, I even became accustomed to —no, I never became accustomed to them, however often I saw them— the clouds that every morning after sunrise ascended in sheets blue as burning gas, tier upon tier, toward the topless reaches of infinity, listing perilously, motionless, incandescent, illuminating rather than shadowing the world below, which they dwarfed beneath their pediments. But the impression made upon me by that first morning was always to stand apart, as if up to that moment I had dwelt in a cave and had then, for the first time, come out into the open. I felt that I could see, and perhaps live, forever.

The estuary, measured by the unsettling bulk of the clouds which extended even beyond the unnatural distances to which the meandering ribbon of forested shore led the eyes, appeared far to outreach any vista of the unbounded ocean, and over all its expanse it glowed with the hot pinks and blues of a sea of molten minerals. A few terns were hovering over its opaline waters, and their black-and-white pattern was conspicuous at distances that reduced the birds themselves to motes, for the air had the limpidity of a lens that intensifies the light it transmits. In its unearthly purity every fragment of that jeweled panorama seemed to have been cut to a finish of perfection, every bough and leaf, the red roofs of the city, the stone slabs of the wharfsides, the four-legged derricks on the quays, like red toy animals. Behind them the blocks of buildings along the waterfront looked to one's startled gaze as if they had been gutted by fire. I learned that this was the ordinary appearance of houses under the equatorial sun, with their unglazed windows, but to begin with I found it hard to believe that they were anything but four-story shells, burned out within.

The city of Nossa Senhora de Belém—Our Lady of Bethlehem—was set back from the river on a low slope. At this distance you saw it as if through the wrong end of a telescope. The houses might have been miniatures of colored wax, buried to their roofs in dark masses of foliage. Alone, dominant and unobstructed, was a monster trilobed baroque structure supported on stilts. It was evidently the municipal watertank. Above the quiet prettiness of that urban scene it towered as sternly imposing as the symbol of a faith, in design a small mechanical utensil, an eggbeater, exalted to the dimensions of a cathedral. Nothing came close to it in height but the palms standing single or clustered, lofty and erect, like the feather-tufted standards of a primitive and barbaric empire.

An effect produced by a person on first sight may never yield altogether to subsequent knowledge, but stand tenaciously in the background of an acquaintanceship with him, coloring it and perhaps in the end having the last word. So it may be with a city, too. What struck me about that harbor at the hour of dawn, next only to the flawlessness and radiance of its forms, was that nothing in it betrayed to the eye the presence of human life. There were three oceangoing freighters alongside the docks and a dozen or more little river-steamers tethered in a compact herd offshore, all facing in the same direction, like grazing cows, but nothing visible stirred aboard them. Out in the river, the scattered fishing-boats riding seaward with the tide, resembling quarter-moons afloat, each under a single, unjointed wing like a seabird's, appeared as ephemeral as the light they reflected from the shimmering waves, as insubstantial. They were like wraiths gliding through a world that stood still, imperishable, hiding nothing, revealing nothing, a world in which a mysterious doom had befallen mankind.

The illusion that a fatal visitation upon man's works had taken place embraced the stricken, bloated carcass of a wooden schooner lying on its side on the muddy shore, the shell of a stranded river-steamer red with rust under the tentacles of the advancing vegetation, the crowd of coffin-shaped lighters off the quays and the coaling hulk in its final mortuary berth in the roads—all black as if burned to charcoal in the sheer luminosity of the air, like the interior of the buildings along the waterfront, with their windows charred black rectangles in dazzling plaster walls. Above these buildings columns of wheeling vultures reminded you of the flakes of soot raised by a fire under a summer sky, when the smoke is invisible in the glare.

As the sun made its presence felt, the scene began to lose its sharpness and color. I had to go back in to make myself presentable.

81

I had just washed my face after shaving and was straightening up when in the mirror over the basin I met a pair of jade-green eyes in a somewhat catlike face of darkish complexion. Turning around, I thought in a flash that Cora had been right. Here was Sekmet, the Egyptian deity, in a cream-colored business suit.

We pronounced each other's names in unison and with an interrogatory inflection, and confirmed in unison the correctness of the other's identification.

"I never expected you to come out to meet me," I said. "It was very good of you. You must have got up in the dark."

Senhor Monteiro gave me his hand and smiled irresolutely. While looking me in the face his eyes seemed to rest at a point just below mine—on my mouth, perhaps. His own was distinctive. It closed in a line at once sensuously curved and discriminating. The tips of the two front teeth were just visible, resting upon the lower lip. In conjunction with the small chin the effect was certainly feline. He had a little the appearance of a puma, but a nice-looking, not fierce, even shy puma. I dropped his hand, which he seemed to have forgotten.

"So here you are in Brazil at last," he observed, raising his eyes.

"Yes, here I am at last," I said with an effect of *bonhommie* that did not feel natural. It was hard for me to connect this demure person with the passionate author of that purple typing. He seemed to be embarrassed and at a loss. The last thing I had anticipated of any meeting with Monteiro was having to take an initiative in it. "I've looked forward to this more than I can tell you. I've read a great deal about Brazil and the Amazon River—but never enough. I'm very keen to learn more—all I can." His regard was attentive, he expected me to go on. "And of course I've also read all your letters—from the beginning. They . . . they were very instructive." It struck me that the experience lost a great deal in the telling.

"Dze English: was it *all* right?" he asked anxiously. "I have no trouble *wiss* English, when I can take time." I assured him that he wrote the language very well indeed. His way of speaking it was all his own. The words issued from directly behind his teeth, where he kept the tip of his tongue, which made his accent light and rustling.

"I attended the University *of* California, where I learned English, where I met my wife, though she *is* from Brazil too," he went on conversationally. "Also I traveled in the States. I wished to acquaint myself with the kind of people. Here in the north we must enlarge our connections with other nations, for our future—the United States and England. In the northern provinces are many English. I have been much associated with Anglo-Saxons, you see. It has enabled me to understand them, and that has been an advantage to me—very much. A quarter of the earth in the ownership of this race—and most of the commerce! The port here is a British concession, and also at Manáos is British."

Through the screen-door came the aroma of frying meat and toast. I had not even had coffee, and I missed the sense of what Monteiro said next. It required concentration to follow him.

"I do not suspect this idealism, like many South Americans," he was saying when I caught up with him again. "I understand it. I share it. That is why I say we—we two—must have no policy with *each* other. Only good understanding, true friendship between *our*selves. . . . This ship brings a good cargo *with* her?"

When I had come around to the shift in our course, my feeling was that of picking up an examination paper and finding that the first question related to a text I had not read. "I haven't, er, had a chance to see the manifest," I replied, and recalling the look of the Plimsoll line in Savannah, added somewhat recklessly, "but she's fairly well down in the water. You probably noticed." It was Julian Tate the shipping expert who had spoken.

Again, I observed anxiously, he looked as if he expected me to go on. Nothing further being forthcoming, he said, "I ask because I am thinking to enter partnership with the agent of the line here. I only wished to see you before interviewing the Captain. It is unfortunate I have not had time to shave myself."

My apologies for the inconvenience to which my untimely arrival had put him were unheeded. I could not stop thinking of how badly I wanted breakfast. Monteiro was examining himself in the mirror over the washstand with un-self-conscious objectivity. His head, set low upon a broad neck between thick, sloping shoulders, was larger when seen in profile than would have been expected. His features, confined to the lower half of his face, were overshadowed by his forehead, which was not especially high but protruding. He stroked his chin. "I look nicer without [*wissout*] this growth here." His hair, when he ran his hand over it, was springy. It was black but lightly silvered, presumably prematurely, above the ears; he could not have been more than ten years older than I. "Perhaps I could shave here?"

In surprise I replied, "By all means." It occurred to me that of course he would be without equipment. "You'll find everything there."

So while he divested himself of coat and shirt I finished dressing. I asked him if he'd had breakfast. He had. "I might just pick up a bite," I said in apprehension of his bringing up the subject of the Concession before I had eaten.

"By the way, were you able to get the dolls for the little girls? I hope with not too much trouble?" He had asked me to bring two dolls of a special kind—especially large, for one thing. I told him it had been no trouble and that the dolls were in the big fiber suitcase if he'd like to see them.

"Thank you, but when you are unpacking will be time enough." Lathered, his face in the mirror looked as if it had been made up as an old farmer's. Our eyes meeting in the mirror, he stayed his hand holding the razor halfway to his chin and remarked, "I am thinking it would be better if we do not see each other until we are on land. I will meet you at the customs. When the reasons why you are here are being kept secret, we would be foolish to let be known that I have come specially out to meet you. That would make too much of it, you see?"

I was not sure that I did, but the preposterous cottony beard, striking the note of an amateur theatrical, made it seem unnecessary for me to. I nodded. "There's one trouble, though. One of the passengers who is an acquaintance of yours knows that we know each other, so if she sees you—"

"Who is this?"

"She is Mrs. Cora Almeida." I spoke with an unreasonable feeling of guilt. With eyes dilated Monteiro froze and remained so, rapt, unseeing. Not yet familiar with these spells of his, I did not realize that while looking as if he were hearing the voice of doom he could perfectly well be wondering, because of something you had said, what he had done with his fountain-pen—though you could not count on anything of the sort. "She was bound to find out that I knew you. I thought it would only make it worse if I pretended I didn't."

"Did you tell her why you are coming here?"

"I spoke only of study and travel."

84

"And did she believe this?"

"She thought it would be rather surprising if you were much interested in a mere student traveler."

Monteiro brooded on this. "She is very dangerous." There was no diminution of his gravity as his eyes met mine again in the mirror, but I could not escape the suspicion that it concealed a certain satisfaction. "I will make a particular effort to keep out of sight."

5

Within an hour *Boadicea* was under way again and headed for the landing. Making a majestic turn in mid-channel, bellowing at the unobtrusive riverboats, she was unrecognizable as the craft that had slunk out of New York. The miraculous aspect of the morning had gone. The clouds had dissolved, the farther banks of the forest all but faded away, the river become a chalky brown and the sky suffused with a haze desiccating in its brilliance. I descended from the ship into a blast of sunshine that seemed to soar out of the very cobblestones. Of Monteiro, I had seen nothing. The Captain had thought it likely that he had accompanied the launch back to shore, adding that my friend had struck him as a "very pleasant-spoken gentleman" with "a proper sense of the British way of doing things." He hoped I would not be knifed in the back before I managed to get away from this country. Good-bye. . . . Good-bye.

I looked with curiosity upon my first foreign people. The crowd around the row of sheet-iron freight depots gave the odd impression of having been collected here in the wake of some disaster, of a kind that leaves everyone homeless. It was not that it was dolorous. On the contrary, you could not mistake its good humor. Only it was the good humor of those who are bearing up under calamity, compounded of mutual sympathy and understanding. The prevailing attire of trousers and shirt, or Chinese jacket buttoned up to the neck, of a once-blue material bleached and patched out of recognition and donned clean that morning, was like the standardized garb issued to the victims of a flood or earthquake. A small number were clad in superior suits of linen or black alpaca and in twos and threes were conversing from under the lowered brims of stiff straw hats—addressing themselves solemnly to the crisis, one judged. These presumably were of Portuguese stock. The rest were of Latin, Negro and aboriginal Indian strains mixed in every possible combination and proportion; at least I took it that the liquid, narrow, intense eyes and smooth, hungry muzzle were Indian. The women, who ran to weight, seemed indolent and disgruntled as they shuffled by with loaded baskets or stood aimlessly, but the men were all keyed up to the exigency, alert and expectant. Voluble groups of them were continually dissolving amid handclasps and assembling with ejaculations of "Psst! Psst!" Some were engaged at various waterfront jobs and others, with jaunty cylindrical caps, were evidently sailors. But all were waiting. Moreover, they had a queer air of being as new to the country as I.

In the interior of the customs warehouse, before my eyes had adjusted to the darkness, Monteiro rushed up and embraced me heartily. The body I clasped in response had no feline softness about it. The somewhat thickset figure was taut with the vitality compressed in it. His coat fitted his shoulders like peeling; I had observed that his trousers tended to spiral up his legs. The nearest thing to Monteiro I have ever had my arm around was a tapir that wandered at large in the *Jardim Botânico,* a kind of trusty that was safe to handle, you were persuaded, only because its spirit was a thousand miles away. Monteiro's, of course, was not. We were two solicitous friends reunited after years. Everyone around us, I saw, was charmed and gratified.

I was mildly puzzled by Monteiro's behavior during the inspection of my luggage. His loquacity was extraordinary—and it distracted me. I was possessed by a thirst for the country I had dreamed about so long, I wanted to take it all in at once, though I must confess I was wondering about Cora, too. Monteiro kept dropping into Portuguese, though I did not see how he could have forgotten that I did not understand it. Emeralds and diamonds up the Tocantins! And he had information on sources nearer to here. He lapsed into his own language, then appeared to bethink himself. The products of the forest, without end, and the prodigious oil-field up the river—as I had good cause to know. The enormous river itself, an inland sea, *o Rio Mar,* as it was called here— the River Sea. Could not it be made to serve the development of the country with hydroelectric power, as well as by the navigation it afforded? The inspector, who looked monkish even in his military type of uniform, cut a menacing figure. His head was skull-shaped, his eyes were at once sunken and protruding and by his pallor he might have come out of a crypt. I felt a vague and unreasoning trepidation as the ecclesiastical hands fingered their way disdainfully through my belongings. He did not so much as glance at either of us, but it became apparent to me that his attention was absorbed in the bilingual exegesis that flowed without hiatus from Monteiro.

All around us, attuned to the murmur of conversation, could be heard the clacking of wooden-soled sandals on concrete and the whisper of bare feet. Cora was not to be seen. *Boadicea*'s other passengers were clustered about their belongings. They had a slightly shoddy look, as have one's indulgently-regarded possessions when they are huddled on the sidewalk beside the moving van. Marge Lumkins clung with both hands to her husband's arm, and her posture of draped dependence, and the smaller size of the Brazilians, made her look enormous.

The destiny of north Brazil was evident, Monteiro was saying. Here was another and greater Mississippi Valley of the future. (It was the first but not the last time I heard that.) I, with my connections in the United States (dze *U*nited States), would find much of interest. There followed more Portuguese.

The Inquisitor had just finished with me when a dilation of Monteiro's eyes and a tight little smile encircling his incisors, aimed at someone behind us, put a period to his flow of speech and caused me to turn. Cora was standing there. She was wearing an unbelted frock which stood out very white in the dim light, and she carried a furled blue parasol. Pretty as a princess in the dingy warehouse, daintily groomed but barelegged, she looked as if she should have had a chorus line behind her. The husband was evidently not present. She was accompanied by a couple who stood facing her a little stiffly. The woman was, I could be sure, an acknowledged beauty, ripe and with dark tresses gathered behind the head, a type seen on cigar-boxes. She was Cora's sister-in-law, I learned. Monteiro's smile never seemed easy or natural, but he and Cora, coming forward to meet each other, appeared rather surprisingly to be on cordial terms. Their greetings were in Portuguese, but I could not mistake the bantering, sardonic tone. The other two, however, had grown more distant at our approach, if one may put it so. The man, whose bolster of a moustache would have been comical at home, acknowledged my introduction in a dead-eyed fashion: it is a queer experience to be met with undisguised unfriendliness.

Monteiro did not seem to be disconcerted. In English he said to Cora, "You would not know the city while you are away. The spark of life has been missing! The husbands have been of necessity to have eyes for their wives again." "Unh-hunh," said Cora. She turned to me. Her first look at me had been one that I should recognize today as inventory-taking. (Was everything as she had left it? Yes, it was.) It was doubtless so recognized at the time by Monteiro. "Your friend," she observed to me, "has the highest regard for the truth. He treasures it. He's a miser about it. He only doles it out when he has to, and only in little driblets. You'll see. But he carries around a nice little bag of goodies to draw from."

With his having-bitten-into-a-lemon smile, strained but apparently genuine, Monteiro drew in his breath appreciatively. Cora bent to adjust the strap of her shoe. "I'm going to be lectured all the way home for being friendly with you," she said to Monteiro, speaking rapidly, virtually making one long word of it. "But why?" Monteiro demanded, his eyes round. "Surely you are going to explain you are being friendly to learn whatever is to be learned from your young *compatriota* here, as a good wife to your husband." Flushed when she straightened up, she regarded Monteiro with a raised-eyebrow, lowered-eyelid expression, sarcastic and quizzical.

When we had executed the punctilio of leave-taking and were following the porter out with my bags, Monteiro said, "It is very true what I said. She would be a very good spy for Jorge." I observed that she had never tried to pry any information out of me. "No. She doesn't really care. That is why she is dangerous."

Well, I thought, let him have it as he would. Emerging from the warehouse, I raised my hand to my eyes as one would to ward off a blow, and I kept them shaded as I followed him to his motorcar. The glare was unbelievable. While he disposed the bags in the rear of the car, I gazed out between my fingers across the plaza. There were triangular plots of grass bordered by calla lilies and rows of little spherically-sheared trees resembling the globes of lighting fixtures, of green glass, inverted on their rods, with the light full on. I wondered how anything could live in the sunlight with which that plaza blazed. If I had sought a land of absolutes, I thought, by heaven I had found it. I supposed we should be setting off for my host's residence, to get me settled, but there was to be a long morning before he turned homeward.

From the start Belém had for me an utter delightfulness, the air of a city enchanted by the novelty of its own existence, by the sheer unlikelihood of it. I was astounded to learn later that it could be found a dull place, third-rate; such was the opinion of the local agent of a number of American exporters for whom Ted Lumkins had come to work, a cynical but apparently prospering fellow-countryman of ours with bags under his eyes and a way of prefacing a reply to a question with a deep sigh, as if he despaired of being able to make you understand.

Along the avenues down which we drove or walked on our round of calls the buildings rose in an unbroken wall of plaster, in all the pastel shades, sheer from the sidewalks, with white pilasters ascending to the cornices. They returned your stare from very tall windows as black close at hand as they had been from across the harbor. They seemed just to have drawn themselves up to their full height, with an engaging self-importance, like dollhouses blown up to full size. The names of the establishments were printed in thin Roman capitals above the doorless entrances through which you could look in upon counters overflowing with slightly shopworn merchandise, cotton goods, shoes, trays of trinkets and of things to eat, a confusion often extending to tables out on the sidewalk. All this was transparently a cover, a front for secret activities in keeping with the character of an *ultima Thule,* whatever unimaginable form these might take; you had a hint of them in shops specializing in hides of deer and alligator and skins, incredibly wide, of boa constrictors, or in articles of native woods—lamps, tables, cabinets, walking-sticks—mostly of the color of freshly butchered beef.

I kept looking for the inhabitants to betray a consciousness of living in so stunning a situation, and was continually struck by their unexcited-ness. At the coffee shop which was our first stop, the other patrons, at the far end from the table Monteiro selected, raised tiny cups to lips with a calm that went beyond calm, that was portentous. And was that in itself, I wondered, perhaps significant? I watched intently but in vain for an exchange of glances that would give the show away, that would confirm my certainty that masks of indifference were being worn to throw the stranger from the North off the scent.

The demitasses they were sipping were here, said Monteiro, called *cafèzinhos* (Splendid! I thought), and it was over one of these, sweet-ened with a coarse golden sugar, that I had my first instruction in what was to concern me in this land. Of this, the most vivid impression I was to retain actually derived from the next time I saw the coffee shop, in the company of Monteiro's little boy, who pictured for me a scene in the last political contest when one of its victims lay on the sidewalk out-side with blood issuing from a hole in his temple "like water from a faucet." Monteiro spoke in a low voice, which made it necessary to pay even closer attention than usual if one was not to be lost. Also baffling terms cropped up, like "French eunucha," which held the key to what he was talking about at one stage. I finally comprehended that the *Frente Única,* more properly, was a United Front of political parties and that in it were enlisted the men I was to be meeting. Monteiro had a good deal to say about these, their acumen in business, their strength of character, their probity of soul—as I should see for myself—and rather less, I thought, about the figure who was the present power in the state, and between whom and the *Frente Única* the lines were drawn, Colonel Achille Durondo. He did, however, speak of the *Interventor*'s extor-tions and how hard they bore upon the businessmen, who were, as it happened, just now suffering from a twenty-five-year-old depression in trade, resulting from the collapse of the rubber boom. I asked how the prospects of the Concession were affected by what he had told me.

"The Concession?" The term struck him dumb. He waited for an explanation.

"The Massaranduba Concession," I reminded him anxiously. For an incredible moment I thought he was going to disclaim ever having heard of it. He sprinkled some coins on the tabletop.

"Come," he said. He ushered me out, and when we had reached the street observed that he had been "coming to that." The Concession,

91

I inferred, was not a topic you casually dropped into the conversation, like the weather.

"The Colonel," he began, then, letting a few paces separate the predicate from the subject, resumed, "is mad, he is crazy. He will be removed in the next election. But that is several months from now. In the meantime [inza mean*time*] the situation can be handled. It is by the Federal Government that concessions for mining are granted. I will take you to a man who will explain the laws. What we must work on is *New* York. That is where is all the delay." With this he embarked upon an expostulation upon the need for haste, "if all is not to be lost," of the kind I had come to know from his letters, and this took us to our first place of call.

I did not at all grasp the point, at this time, of the succession of visits we paid to the members of the business community, but that was only because I was incurious, too distracted by the extraneous. That I had misjudged Monteiro did become apparent to me, however. Among his gentle, austere and evidently harassed compatriots he stood out as a redoubtable if not intimidating figure, impatient and intense or playful and evasive, as the occasion seemed to demand. The apparition I had beheld in the mirror that morning recurred to me. I kept visualizing that mythological being transubstantiated to present reality to lend its sharp, realistic wits and animal force to a party of Christian worthies seeking a way through the forest. Dealing with his peers in his own tongue, there was about him none of the uncertainty he seemed to feel in speaking to me in mine.

The firms to which I was presented were, said Monteiro, "of the highest standing." The head, or senior partner, would greet us with alert but reserved interest of the kind, I thought, that a bearer of important news might expect to encounter in a household which had just suffered a bereavement. Upon the sedate quiet of the darkened chambers only the clatter of elderly typewriters jarred—like the voices of the deaf raised in oblivious indecorum. Our host would open a gate for us in the railing which divided the office into sections, his own on one side, his scribes' on the other. He and Monteiro would engage in a half embrace, both looking uncomfortably at the floor. Mostly I had to conduct myself in pantomime since Monteiro lacked the patience to do much translating. "Senhor Fuentes hopes your visit here will not be disappointing to you, and he says you must come to him when you are in need," he might explain, and I would say that Senhor Fuentes was very kind and that I was sure it would be impossible to suffer disappointment of any kind in Brazil, and that was about as far as it went. A point was made of handclasping at start and finish.

I found it a strain. To preserve a nonparticularized expression while seeming to be responsive to the unintelligible dialogue and the looks directed at me was exhausting. Everyone seemed already to know who I was, but I was not on that account spared a close examination. Monteiro, whose attitude toward me became deferential when we entered the portal of one of these offices, would take hold of my lapel—respectfully enough—and while the other divided his engrossed attention between us would express himself in crisp phrases interspersed with pregnant pauses. Our host's outgivings would be mainly questioning, but sometimes one would speak at length, reflectively, dispassionately and with a barrel-roll motion of his hands. Monteiro would stand by like a hot engine, his nostrils dilating, his eyes very alive in the shadow of his brows. Eventually the tension would be relaxed and we would all smile at one another, Monteiro throwing an arm affectionately around my shoulders. Outside in the street again the breath of the city would be wafted over one like a wand. Its scent was delicious, a cool and clayey odor, as of a cave, mingled with a sweet and herblike fragrance. It opened the very pores of the skin to the tranquil sounds of midday, to the soaring spaciousness of the sky.

What, I asked Monteiro, had Senhor Goẽs (which I visualized as Go-ish) meant by addressing me as the *salva-vida?* A great gentleman, as they all were, with close-cropped, grizzled hair, a dark, creased visage and searching brown eyes, he had accompanied this welcoming remark with a whimsical smile.

"It is an expression," he replied, then, apparently deciding something more was required, added, "You understand, there is a feeling of much hope that from Wall Street would come all the way down here one of your position." I gave him a sidelong glance: I was sitting beside him in his car. From his place behind its wheel he was regarding the controls, hands clasped, like a concert pianist about to perform. The vehicle seemed always to require an inordinate amount of managing. It gave the impression of trying constantly to escape his authority, and the unremitting duel between them kept one on the edge of one's seat. The cramped streets downtown—the old city—were thronged with incautious strollers who appeared always to be looking for something and seeing nothing, while every minute a trolley-car would heave around a corner, filling the street and driving every other movable, human and mechanical, to the wall.

The only word for my feeling about the city was infatuation. If I could not, like a lover in the conventional sense, pretend that my enchantress held a secret for me alone, I could at least determine to be first among all others in receptivity to the tantalizing intimations vouchsafed of her special character: the ferny growths and dagger-leaved saprophytes that sprouted from the wicker-trunked palms and the bell towers of a clay-white church; the procession of leaf-carrying ants that trickled through the gutter below the window of Monteiro's office, resembling a miniature fleet hurrying interminably along under shaky green sails; the advertisements for cigarettes and malaria-remedies advancing their faded claims from rain-streaked painted tiles and from wattle walls blotched with moss and fungus; the black vultures—*urubus*—that flapped and circled overhead or hobbled about in the street, quarreling and hissing with inarticulate spite. The palm-fronds jostled one another with a dry whisper, and the wheels of the bullock carts struck the cobblestones with the rumble of distant cannonading. From the harbor there arose now and again the wail of a river-steamer, like the cry of a solitary animal moved by the inexpressible. In dying it would leave a listening hush, leave you thinking of the endless solemn corridors of the forest through which the little vessel had come.

Yes, I loved Brazil, with excitement and with wonder. In that, at least, I lived up to the character I discovered Monteiro had constructed for me; indeed, surpassed it. Sophia Monteiro was quickly satisfied on this point, this all-important point, as it was to her. It was her uncertainty about it, I concluded at once, that accounted for the interrogation in her face for the first several moments of our acquaintance.

"João was cruel not to bring you here immediately from the ship. You have seen everyone in the city? He is tireless. But you, you, too, have the vitality of youth? Yes?" Her face upturned—she was rather small— and transparent as a child's, her scrutinizing gaze darted from one of my eyes to the other: it was like her not to be content with what one of them alone might tell her. "The heat did not fatigue you? Many North Americans coming here find the sun too strong. To be here is an exile to them—at the end of the earth. Of course, anyone coming here from the States must believe that that is where he is—at the end of the earth?" Having been ardently reassured by me on these various points, she turned to her husband and, the question now being safe, asked, "And does he like Brazil?"

Monteiro transferred his pensive and abstracted stare from her to me. His eyes, as was their wont, dilated as he rejoined us from wherever he had been. "I think he likes *cafèzinho*. How many have we had?"

"Seven—at least." It was part of the hospitality of the offices we had visited.

"And *rapadura*? Even *rapadura*?" she demanded.

"Especially *rapadura!*" That was the unrefined sugar.

Cora had said she was pretty, and that is what she was. Her brown eyes were quick with life. Her nose was small and the rounded tip was delicately indented, like a rabbit's; it moved perceptibly up and down when she spoke. When she listened, her attentiveness seemed to engage her entire being. Her figure had no suggestion of Latin fullness: it had the trimness that comes from physical activity, and her movement was impulsive, especially when, in a gesture of quick understanding, she would put out her hand to your arm. She was not as young as she seemed; a bright light brought out the fine lines in her face; but being responsive and much in motion, she would convey a quality of youthfulness when she was half again her present age.

"He will never leave, *I* think," Monteiro had said, now entirely on location. "The Concession is only the beginning. I will arrange to make him agent for the richest American corporations with a Brazilian market."

"Oh, he will, too!" she cried with gay enthusiasm. "So if you do not want it you had better stop him now."

It was a delightful joke, but as she watched her husband follow the houseboy upstairs with my bags the merriment in her face gave place to anxiety. She had held me back by surreptitiously tugging at my sleeve, and by this same means she now drew me off down the hallway, to the interior of the house. I could not imagine what was coming. "You will do me a favor?" The ceiling of the hall was high, the light dim, and looking at her, I remembered a childish confession I had once received or perhaps read about involving a lost or broken doll. "Please, when you are talking business with João, not to say anything just now that would disturb him? Today he has been given much to worry him. There has come bad news." We were facing each other like friends of years' standing, and my distress that anything should so trouble her must have been fully apparent in my face, for she gave my arm a reassuring pat. "Oh, it is nothing *fatal*. It is the kind of thing that happens. I am sure he did not tell you, but one of his ships has had an accident. It is on the Madeira—above Manicoré. She struck a floating tree. They had to run her onshore to save her from sinking. We heard only last night."

I expressed my dismay and asked what could be done. She replied quickly that it was not as bad as it sounded. "The vessel can be repaired and floated. But there will now be a defaulting on the delivery of the cargoes. They will be late. The six weeks' trip will be a total loss." She raised her hand and tucked some wisps of hair beneath a strand fastened at the back of her neck: the gesture was one I soon came to know well.

I confessed that I should never have known anything was the matter; her husband, I said, certainly did not show it. "Oh no!" she exclaimed. "He would never show his feelings—about anything that matters." Her voice had been pitched to continue, and I waited. "I was going to ask you. If João has reverses—you will see, he is very daring, he risks much for his country—not to . . . to make it sound very bad, any worse than it is, when you write back to New York. This is not wrong of me, is it?" I reminded her that after all, I was on her husband's side; we represented him, not Dr. Xenides. I observed that if I could do nothing else I could keep silent when I was trusted to do so.

"Then we may count you as a friend?"

"Altogether." My hunch that Monteiro would not have approved of her openness lent warmth to my declaration.

"I was sure of it!" She led the way back to the front of the house, explaining that I should find the interior "very Brazilian." Her laugh was mostly one of amusement, but was edged, I thought, with protectiveness.

At our approach two children scurried from behind the door of the living-room only to be trapped in their flight by our inescapable advent. Their mother presented them with the bright formality and peculiar em-

phasis that women adopt—the world over, I do not doubt—on such occasions: Alfr*E*do, who was *ten,* and Lou*I*za, who was *six.* The two little
forest-creatures wilted in turn. "You may go," their mother said in-
dulgently, and transformed, off they shot.

I saw what my hostess meant about the interior. The floor of the
living-room was of alternating black and white boards, and down it
the gaze skidded to be brought up by a sideboard reminding me of
the cathedral I had seen that morning. If smaller, it was far more
colorful, the wood of which it was carved having the character of con-
gealed flame.

I recalled to her the things they had asked me to bring from New
York and suggested that I might go get them. I asked if the dolls were
to be a surprise.

"The dolls?"

"The dolls Mr. Monteiro asked me to bring."

"João!" she called without taking her eyes from my own. Her husband could already be heard upon the stairs. "João!" she repeated when
he appeared at the door. "What are these dolls you have asked the
kind Mr. Tate to bring with him?"

Her voice had a certain sharpness, and rather uncomfortably I said I
hoped I had not given away what was to have been a pleasant surprise
for her as well as for the children.

"Alfredo does not play with dolls. And I do not either," she observed.

"There's Maria," said her husband, without strong conviction, still
from the doorway, where he had stopped short. "I was coming to this,"
he went on, "but there has not been time. There have been very many
people to see!" He paused, the set of his mouth like a chipmunk's. He
might have been smiling, or might not. "First I had to explain about the
political situation, and this I was not able to finish." So saying, and with
an air of patience, he took off again upon the subject. He explained
again that the *Interventor* had come up through the ranks of the state
militia, which he could now command, of course—"the state militias
being very strong in Brazil, unfortunately." In himself the Colonel represented an evil but dying tradition, one that was dying hard, though, it
appeared. What was at issue in the struggle had implications for all
Brazil, for all South America, thus for the whole New World. As I
had reason to know, having been introduced to some of them, there

97

would be no disposition to back down from their responsibilities on the part of the leaders of that principal element in the *Frente Única,* the Constitutionalist Party.

His wife, who had been listening with growing admiration, interposed in an aside to me, "It is the repository of our hopes, and it depends so much on João!"

"So, with the elections coming and events moving to the crisis, it is good to make every preparation," Monteiro continued, suddenly being brief about it. "These tear-gas shells would provide only for defense—not like other ammunition—and this, you may be sure—"

"These *what?*" his wife interjected.

"Well, I was going to explain," he said, frowning. "I arranged to have a Brazilian seaman of the *Boadicea* deliver them to me on board. With myself under scrutiny by the regime, to attempt to bring anything of contraband nature, and of such size, past the guard would be highly dangerous. So with Julian away from his stateroom, I took advantage to place the shells in the dolls which I had forethought to ask him to bring. A visitor to Brazil would not be an object of suspicion. I have thought of all this. The stuffing from the dolls, this I put out of the porthole." The recollection unmistakably afforded him pleasure. "Then I sewed them up—just in the time it would have taken another man only to shave."

"But, João dear, why did you not ask his permission? What will he think, to have had you do this without telling him?"

"It was for his own protection that I said nothing! The inspection at the customs is not thorough for tourists, but for a tourist who betrayed nervousness I could not answer. You remember how I diverted the inspector's attention?" he asked of me.

"Yes, but suppose he had just happened to find something not quite right about those dolls?"

"Oh, I had plans about that. You were in no danger."

"He's impossible," Sophia Monteiro declared brightly, inviting me to share her cheerful despair about him. "I never know what is next." She turned to her husband. "You are not fooling me. You have many ways of bringing objects to shore, except under the nose of the officials." Speaking to me once more, she said, "He cannot resist this kind of playing. He is like the most skillful musician, who must try the most difficult parts. But you are not to be blamed for feeling provoked. I myself in your place would be very angry."

I looked at the floor. Whatever I might have said was lost to the record by my hesitation. After giving me a moment my hostess announced that the meal was waiting for us. "But first I must explain about the maid. . . ."

The smoothness with which we had got over this awkward matter could have been the result of collusion between the Monteiros, but Sophia Monteiro being what she was, I am sure there was none. As for the dolls themselves, it is altogether certain that they formed Exhibit A at the conspiratorial meeting held that evening at the Monteiros' house.

This was the first of four or five such meetings at which I was present for an initial round of compliments and subsequently made my excuses and departed, relieving Monteiro of what I took to be a constraining presence and myself of a good deal of tedium and tension. A dozen, sometimes more, prominent *Constitucionalistas* would be ranged around the table of *macacaúba* wood, a companion-piece in hue and amplitude to the sideboard. The staunch, reposeful figures would be illuminated from behind by two standard lamps with shades seeming to rest upon the apex of a cone of light in the smoky air.

I occupied, on this first as on the following occasions, a hidden corner of the veranda, sipping coffee and munching buttered buns. For a companion I had a kind of spiritual dependent of the Monteiros', an individual so undemanding, so resigned, as to make but limited inroads upon one's solitude. We had picked him up on a street-corner that afternoon during our continued round of calls. Installed in the rear seat of the car, he had leaned forward with his arms resting on the back of the front seat between our shoulders and with little preliminary, speaking in English and in doleful accents, commenced a narration of what he had been suffering as a result of a tooth-extraction. At the first sight of his tall, angular figure, narrow face and blond coloring I had taken him for an Anglo-Saxon, but he was, it transpired, a genuine offspring of Brazil and of the old provincial aristocracy. His blue eyes had perhaps come down to him from the distant French ancestor whose name he bore—Beaupérie—growing paler and more disconsolate through the generations.

That tooth! From the first, according to Emile—as I was to call him—

it had plainly been against nature to have it drawn. Nature had meant him to have it. That could not be doubted. The valiant molar had defeated every effort to dislodge it, until—all at once—it had given up. It had crumbled. That had been a week ago. Yet even now he was unable to stay the flow of his saliva. It filled his mouth. He could hardly talk. He was always swallowing, but to no avail. Indelicate as it was to speak of it, he must say that he was all the time desiring to spit. For days his alarm about himself had been growing.

Monteiro, who treated Emile like a child, ignored his litany of woe. I fear I gave it little heed myself. I was having my first full introduction to the city's residential quarter, like which, I was soon convinced, there could be nothing else on earth. The houses of the well-to-do astonished the eye with an extravagance of colors surpassing those of a flower garden, even the kind depicted in seed catalogues. The background surfaces were of relatively subdued pastel tints—cerulean, aquamarine, lavender, pale pink and lemon, indiscriminately assorted, but for the ornamentation the palette was ransacked. Cornices, window-frames, balconies, beams, exposed uprights, frills and protuberances without name or function were emblazoned in carmine, emerald, magenta, plum, cobalt, canary, violet, with the doorways set off in bands of geometrical patterns formed by squares or triangles in alternating colors—blue and yellow, pink and green. Customarily the upper and lower floors were divided by a band of tiles each with a snowflake design also in vibrant colors. Otherwise—apart from the uniform, barrel-tiled terra-cotta roofs —no other convention was recognized. A half-timbered structure with all the beams of oxblood would be cheek-by-jowl with one in which, as in a watercolor, the deep blue of the upper floor melted into the azure of the lower. One outstanding mansion, which Monteiro pointed out to me not because of any eccentricity of taste he detected in it but as the residence of his supreme antagonist, Colonel Durondo, presented a checkerboard surface of alternating green and white building blocks. Homeowners who felt that the house itself gave insufficient scope for self-expression added borders of liver-colored plants or flagpoles spirally striped in green and gold.

I asked my escort what inspired this explosion of pigmentation. The two men looked reflectively up and down the avenue. I do not think they knew what I meant. Monteiro averred that "in this damp the surfaces must be protected." Emile added that the unhealthful climate was as ruinous to houses as to human beings, maybe even more: the houses were of miserable construction to begin with. Monteiro overruled his friend with a flash of irritation. The climate, while not the driest, was the most salubrious in the world, the air the cleanest. The inside of the nostrils never grew dirty, and if you wore a shirt for a week the lining of the collar and cuffs would be less soiled than after a single day in a North American city (which was true enough, so well rain-washed was the smokeless air). As for the houses—they were built to endure for centuries.

I asked the same question of Sophia Monteiro. I mentioned the fountain in the front yard of a house we had visited which was nothing more or less than an open umbrella wrought in metal and painted red, with water bubbling up out of the ferrule. I mentioned also the artificial tree-stumps cast in concrete that decorated the Praça da República, the park where, from a bandstand, Colonel Durondo had so often worked upon the emotions of the crowd in a voice that carried as a reedy, staccato whisper, ejaculated with puppetlike flailings of the arms, to the patrons of the café in front of the Grande Hotel. Sophia Monteiro saw the absurdity of the fountain and the tree-stumps and laughed about the embellishments of the houses, referring to her own, descriptively enough, as "the strawberry sundae," but to her these represented merely endearing foibles on the part of her compatriots. My question as to whether they were to be construed as a response to the city's peculiar situation, pressed upon by the great river and its attendant forest, and if so what the response signified, did not get across to her.

Whatever purpose or compulsion underlay the chromatic extravaganza of the residential sections, the impression a stranger to the city received was above all else one of a vitality that was not of man, that everywhere proclaimed itself in the tumultuous and pervasive manifestations of the sovereignty the city had incompletely displaced. Vegetation welled up from the dooryards in a surf of foliage star-leaved and elephant-eared, in every texture and every shade of green, blue-green and yellow-green. It climbed the sides of the houses and perched great clumps of vines above doors and windows. It smothered the ditches, buried the rubbish heaps, forced the stockade fences of the by-streets and poured through the breaches. It trickled up the trunks of trees in a tracery of tiny leaflets and found a lodging for frilly shoots and humps of moss in every crevice of garden walls. It stood between the city and the sky,

101

unchallenged in the airy region above the flat expanse of roofs where the palms held up their savage headdresses and the *sumaúmas* spread canopies of foliage over entire city blocks.

I had soon learned what Monteiro's object was in giving me "a background of business acquaintance in the city," as he phrased it. His wife, after lunch, had read me an item in the *Estado do Norte* announcing my arrival. It described me as a brilliant junior member of a firm among the most prominent in New York in the field of corporation law. The firm had handled some of the biggest reorganizations, receiverships and mergers in the history of American industry. It served as counsel for leading American investment houses and had been retained by several foreign governments seeking to place their internal economies on a basis to invite the participation of foreign capital in the exploitation of indigenous resources. Persons acquainted with the history of the development of oil in Venezuela and the Mosul fields, copper in Chile, timber in Canada, bananas in Honduras, rubber in Liberia and of the effect, approaching the miraculous, upon the total prosperity of these countries could appreciate the prestige of the firm both in American financial circles and among the governments of countries deficient in material means but alert to the meaning of progress. (The report was a little vague on the connection between the firm and the specific cases it had cited.) " 'Dr. Julian Tate himself [*"Zhulian Ta-te,"* she pronounced it, giving it local color and reading in a happily affected, declamatory style], who is the first to introduce to Brazil the illustrious name he bears, brings with him the results of an exhaustive study he has made of certain aspects of the world shipping situation for Dr. João Raimundo de Monteiro, steamship-owner and business leader of this city, with whom Dr. Tate will be residing. Drawn to northern Brazil by a deep and lifelong interest in the country and its incomparable promise, Dr. Tate may be expected as a matter of course to acquaint himself with the opportunities offered here for the investor and on return to place his special knowledge at the disposal of Wall Street, which is accustomed to looking to his firm for guidance beyond that ordinarily expected of legal counsel.' "

With the reading of this clipping I grew ever more embarrassed and confused. With the caution of a man picking his way among breakables I asked Monteiro where this information had come from. He had been standing by looking demure. That he had not at the outset apprised me of this incredible statement was owing not to any desire to dissemble, I judged, but to the reticence of modesty, handmaiden to pride of authorship.

"From Dr. Xenides. From letters he has written about you." Nothing was to be learned from Monteiro's tone of voice. It was that of one being negligently matter-of-fact about that which was by no means a matter of fact—but then that was the way he was about matters which really were matters of fact.

"You've been a client of Mr. Willet's for quite a while. You don't think the reader would get a mistaken idea of the extent of . . . er—"

"Wait! You have not heard all. There is the end here." He took the clipping from his wife and read from it. " 'Dr. Tate is in Brazil only for . . . *divertimento,* divertisement, and the . . . familiarizing of himself with the country in general. Any rumor which would assign a more material interest is to be denied.' That is the best part. Those who would make difficulties have it in printing here that there are no grounds for their suspicions, and at the same time those who are knowing will say, 'Ah-ha!' " Upon my trying once more to speak he rushed on. "Always it is what men *think,* it is the *picture* they have in the mind that makes them act this way or that way."

I sought counsel of Sophia Monteiro, meeting her expectant eyes. Her expression was poised, as it were, on the verge, ready to mirror my smile, my gratification. I was thinking of those tar-gas shells. It was quite evident, as she had pointed out, that her husband could have found some other means of bringing them into the country. I wondered if he wished to present me as a supporter of the Constitutionalist Party as well as a harbinger of profits for those who played it right. I looked away again, back at Monteiro, who was amplifying his previous statement.

"And where the *substance* is lacking, or is not easy to obtain in much quantity—as here, since we lose the markets for our rubber—then the *appearance* is counting for very much."

He had already, while we were at the table, lifted the veil upon an application of this principle. Senhora Monteiro had confessed to telling me about the misadventure of *Santa Sophia.* "That is the ship," she interpolated to me. "João named her after me and made her a saint. Wasn't that a lovely compliment? Of course there was not really a Saint Sophia. It means 'Holy Wisdom.' You must call me Dona Sophia, like a

Brazilian." Had there, she asked, been any news of her? Her husband's negative movement of the head was barely perceptible. I said I had been deeply distressed to hear about the accident and asked if the penalties for failure to meet the terms of the contracts would be serious. He had filled his fork, but having raised it nearly to his mouth, set it down again. While he had not been pleased, I had thought, by his wife's disclosure, he remarked casually enough that he had covered himself —early in the morning, while I was waiting in the *armazém*. "I went to the bank, to be there the first thing, before they could hear of what has happened to the ship. I tease them and amuse them with jokes. It is evident I have no worry in the world. Then just before I am leaving I say I must have some money; I am extending my service up the Tapajós. I have with me the contracts on the *Santa Sophia*'s cargo, and with these to show I am able to borrow enough to satisfy the charges against me."

After turning it over in my mind I ventured to say that I could see how this would *postpone* the day of reckoning, and hesitated.

His mouth full, he nodded vigorously. I awaited the fuller explanation that presumably would follow when he had finished chewing, but when he had swallowed he only reiterated his assent. "Yes! For three months!"

That seemed to settle it. There was another question I appraised as one a man with any experience at all in commercial practice would raise at this point, and so I raised it: what would happen to his credit when his bankers discovered how they had been taken in?

"It will be improved, I think. They will see at the bank what a sharp fellow they have for a customer, what a good businessman. Then, you see, they cannot be sure I myself have heard about the accident to the ship when I am there this morning, so there can be no complaint."

His wife, who had awaited his reply with undisguised interest, said, "Are you trying to say they do not yet know what kind of fellow they have for a customer?" There was a dryness about her tone that drew a sidelong glance from her husband and a smile that mingled bravado, affection and cunning. She held out against it as long as she could, and when she returned it, it was with wry resignation. Turning to me, she displayed the palms of her hands in an exaggerated gesture of helplessness. What would I do? Was there ever such a bird as her husband?

Catching sight of my plate, she exclaimed, "You are having trouble with your *farinha!*"

"He has not buttered it," Monteiro declared, putting down his knife and fork to scrutinize it.

"Even with butter *farinha* is to many North Americans and Europeans absolutely sawdust," Dona Sophia pronounced, leaning forward toward me in eager inquiry, her face shining.

I professed myself shocked to hear it. *Farinha,* was it? I vowed I hoped never to eat another meal without it.

Of the proceedings of the Faction—as Monteiro termed it—at the meeting that evening, little was to be heard above the creaking of furniture from where I sat with Emile in the obscurity without. The measured accents of voices speaking in turn, never interrupting, were faintly audible. It was otherwise when the host of the meeting finally spoke. His emphatic tones came through quite plainly, and though they told me no more than the others, I heard my name several times, also that of the Concession. Each time "Massaranduba" was uttered it stood out because of the pause that followed, in which the shuffling of feet and clearing of throats and the scrape of a chair sounded very close by.

"Do you see this butter?" Emile demanded, poking with a knife at the runny mound on the little table in front of us. "Observe the yellow color. It is from the dye of a plant known to the Indians for being a poison. The cows eat the plant, and now here is the dye in the butter. The cows are not injured, but in human beings it is poison. It . . . it produces sterility." Fatalistically he helped himself to a portion. *"Infelizmente,* our swarming lower class have not the money to buy it, enough to do any good," he averred.

While scarcely a ray of light escaped between the shutters behind us, we were not entirely in the dark. From the wide-open windows of the servants' quarters at the back of the house there poured, along with snatches of uninhibited chatter and humming, a steady yellow illumination. It fell upon the broad leaves of the plants beside the veranda, frosted and trickling with dew, and upon the ceiling above us, where gecko lizards, upside down, appeared to be inked upon the boards until a little lunge by one of them upon an insect would send the lot of them scampering in every direction, like mechanical toys animated by a charge of electric current. There was something peculiarly disarming about them. They alone would have endeared the place to me.

Raising his liberally buttered bun to the level of his eyes, Emile turned it this way and that, then with deliberateness approached it to his mouth and took a generous bite—quaffing the hemlock, I could not forbear to think.

"Do you know Senhora Cora Almeida?" I asked.

A small but bitter explosion of breath by way of answer expressed the futility of comment. Then, with an effect of being startled out of a reverie, Emile very surprisingly took the lobe of his ear between thumb and forefinger and shook it, in a gesture that by local convention conveyed unqualified approval. "Yes, yes. She is a charming woman. And very good company. She is most satisfying to the eyes, not altogether for most Brazilians, who like a little more fullness, but for me. My tastes are for refinement, always for refinement. And that is how it is with her conversation. To many here it is disconcerting. She is outspoken, realistic. That is for cultivated tastes. It is unusual here, where all is provincial. But to me it is very enjoyable. I am a cosmopolitan at heart, as you know. Dona Cora can understand how I find this country so limited." Ever since his travels as a young man, perhaps before, Emile had considered himself an exile from Europe. "But now I remember. She was a passenger with you in your voyage from the States. Did you not find her as I say?"

Very much, I replied, and asked if he knew her husband.

"She is always very kind to me. Every year she remembers my birthday." The light of his cigarette, as he drew upon it, revealed a face candid and serene. "Her husband? I have seen him often, but never to know. He is away much. He and that dog are very close. Some say he has a power over Durondo because of something he knows, some say he is the creature of Durondo because he is in debt to Durondo, or because Durondo knows something against *him*. He grew up in the States—but maybe in the wrong places. I do not like him. He is always smiling and laughing, with much show of many white teeth. I think he would not mind sinking them in the throat of another. There is no love between him and Dona Cora. He has probably women up and down the river. He is always traveling, either for trading or on the business of that dog. It is because of him, it could only be because of him, that Sophia does not like Dona Cora." A sigh broke from him.

Actually, when she heard that Cora had been one of *Boadicea*'s passengers, Dona Sophia had disavowed holding her husband's connections against her. "She cannot help what her husband does, and I think she has no interest in politics." This was after having first fixed me with a look of inquiry so transparent in its purpose that, being guiltless (for whatever reason) of what she was prepared to find, I could not help smiling a little. She averted her face, and when she looked around again, any trace of self-consciousness it might have betrayed had vanished. "All the same," she had finished, "she *is* the wife of Jorge Almeida. And, too, things around her do not seem to go well. She brings bad luck, in some way. Even to her husband. You remember, João, how once he was so well regarded, how he stood so high?" Said Monteiro, "Not for long. Only until he could lose all he has inherited from his father. He is a damn fool. He rushes to buy, he rushes to sell. That is the way to ruin. And now he is reduced to what he may obtain by favor from Durondo. And maybe there would be no favors except that his sister is the mistress of Durondo." Dona Sophia, coloring up, protested that this was only rumor. "Why don't you ask her?" said Monteiro, who liked to tease his wife.

"But," Emile had gone on, "she would not expect us—you or me—to be unfriendly to Dona Cora. If Dona Cora were Brazilian it would be a different matter. But being American, she is not implicated in our struggles. And there is no worry now about you." He had dropped his voice with this last sentence. With a jerk of his head at the room behind us he continued in the same low tones. "It is known that you have committed yourself to the side of justice and honest government. There has been great admiration that you have accepted the risks." He put his hand on my knee. "Everyone takes heart."

6

Never since then have I found it easy to put myself into the routine of those days. I did not find it easy at the time, even in the beginning, when I had only acute mental discomfort to contend with. A growing sense of need to see Cora Almeida, if only for the sake of her disabused unfancifulness, to partake of the familiar and uninflated values of her world, did not lessen the tensions of the impostor's role that now was mine, however it had come about. The desire only added to my frustrations, for there seemed to be no way of satisfying it. I had found out from Emile where she lived, a block off the main thoroughfare, which bisected the city, and not far from the green-and-white checkerboard gubernatorial residence, but I could scarcely present myself at the door of a married woman and announce that I had come to call. I often walked down the Avenida da Independência. Lined with white-trunked mangoes dark and somber in their towering masses of compact, leathery foliage, it invited the stroller with its restful aspect of a country lane. However, hang back and dawdle as I might in passing the Passagem Dr. Borbão in the hope of a chance encounter, haunting the neighborhood was clearly out of the question.

I had frequent meetings with Monteiro about the business of the Concession. What we did mostly was go over current developments that I could enlarge upon in my reports to Mr. Willet for his use in prodding Dr. Xenides into action or work up more material responsive to the list of questions the latter had given me as being of primary concern. In a drawer that extended the length of a largish table Monteiro kept a *Mapa da Concessão de Massaranduba e as suas cercaduras (Obra de João Raimundo de Monteiro)*, which I regarded with a glum fascination. In addition to the known terrain features and the boundaries of the (proposed) Concession it gave distances from various Brazilian cities, New York and London and showed the steamship routes, roads and a railroad giving access to the Concession and providing transportation within it, linking nameless towns located at strategic points. All these were of course matters of the future and at present entirely imaginary.

The map nicely complemented Dr. Xenides's, which dealt with what existed, even when it represented gold-fields with actual gilt. I once mentioned to Monteiro this map of Dr. Xenides's and its data on the depth of waterways and on alluvial gold-deposits. I caught a glint of the white of his eye and thought of the edginess of a horse at a glimpse of an unfamiliar object. "He has made up all this," he pronounced, and with that uninterested-sounding retort I supposed he had done with the subject. On visible second thought, however, he went on to declare in a livelier voice, "It is just what I would have expected! He is not stupid, and all this information would have an effect upon this syndicate he is always talking about. They would not know it is all out of his head. It is good psychology to paint the gold-fields with gilt." He cast a regretful glance at his own map. "I am glad he is taking all this trouble. It shows he is in earnest."

As day by day the scope of what we were aiming at in the Concession seemed to grow greater and the sway of the Massaranduba over the imagination, the credulity and the avarice of those around us to be extended, I became more oppressed by the notion that my projected expedition to the interior partook of the character (as it struck me) of the propositions (as businessmen call them) on Monteiro's desk—i.e., that it

109

was a kind of bookkeeping device, or symbol to move about, like a chess-man. This was unreasonable of me, since the delay could not be helped —for one thing, much of the area was still under water, just as Dr. Xenides had said it would be—but still my impatience grew. There was some consolation in knowing that it was not unshared. Every ship from Manáos brought a letter from Senhora Braga, the mother of the two young men immured in the vastness of the Massaranduba forest actually engaged in the production of gold, asking when I was going to set forth. It was hard to understand what her hurry was, for her conviction that the mines were very rich sounded genuine, and in the light of it, it seemed unlikely that she would be anxious to see the property (which she owned jointly with her sons) sold to other interests. Anyway, she continually urged that I set forth without delay—for Manáos and Topacindo, the jumping-off place for that lodestar of my thoughts, the Massaranduba.

I had the impression that Monteiro had managed to weave around himself a web of liens spreading all through the commercial community and over much of the Mississippi-Valley-to-be. In the litter on his desk, held down by paperweights of *pau-santo,* a wood so heavy I first mistook it for marble, were certainly documents pertaining to a galaxy of busi-ness ventures: sawmills, sugar-refineries, plants for shelling and pressing Brazil nuts, rum-distilleries and deals in rubber, hides and cocoa, all in addition to his primary occupation, which was operating a fleet of four vessels on the Amazon River. From what I could tell, he borrowed and invested right and left, counting on sheer force of personality and repu-tation, rather than upon a controlling financial interest, to enable him to steer the course of any enterprise he participated in. He did not deny that he had his own methods of getting his way. His flair for the presence of unemployed capital must have been remarkable. His creditors were many and were apt to remain his creditors indefinitely. Or, as he expressed it modestly, he had acquired some skill at renewing notes.

Having a half dozen times run into friends on his way to the office and stopped for a talk, Monteiro as often as not would burst in an hour or two after the time he had set for me to be there. I would have been thinking how I could have been exploring the city's environs or, from the quayside, surveying the harbor for new arrivals from the remote fast-nesses of the continent. There would be *gaiolas* of two decks, shaped like boxcars, down to discharge their cargoes once a fortnight or once every several months, or perhaps putting in an annual appearance for drydocking down at the Valley of Dogs, from the upper Amazon and the headwaters of its titanic tributaries, weeks away. One might see *Victoria* or *Cuiabá,* great, grey, Government-owned triple-deckers making the three-week run to Iquitos, Peru, or an odd, squat stern-wheeler, drawing no more water than a saucepan afloat whose normal beat lay on some lonely, shallow stream a thousand miles inland. There would be launches from heaven-knew-where belonging to prospectors or missionaries.

While waiting I would also note the other callers who collected in the anteroom and would have to be disposed of before Monteiro and I could get down to our affairs. They were mostly substantial-looking citizens with heavy gold rings and heavy gold watch-chains and the monumental deliberateness and impassivity of the north Brazilian merchant class. With scarcely a glance at the assemblage when he arrived, Monteiro could tell which few actually brought business. These received his first, and special, attention. The others, the favor-seekers and complainants, were processed with dispatch when their turn came. The timid petitioner would be suffered to speak his piece to the end while the addressee of his importunities examined his fingernails, opened and shut the drawers of his desk in some recondite quest, frowned out of the window and, at the expiration, crossed the room to converse with a secretary. When the visitor would find courage once more to intrude his presence and his plea upon the busy executive, Monteiro would regard him without expression or recognition. Then—ah, yes. He would remember. It would all come back to him. *Mas amanhã.* Tomorrow. *Amanhã.* The other category, of those emboldened by grievances, fared no better though it doubtless took them longer to realize the fact. Never had they found such an interested listener to their troubles. Their hands were clasped, their shoulders embraced. By gentle raillery and a flattering responsiveness to their every word that actually anticipated with sympathetic concurrence what they were about to say, Monteiro nursed them into a pleasant glow of self-satisfaction, a philosophical view of life and its vicissitudes. What a gratification it was to have this mutual understanding! But the upshot was the same. *Amanhã. Hoje,* today, it was on its face impossible. No one would expect today, least of all one with such knowledge of the world as our visitor. But tomorrow! Ah, tomorrow! Yes, *amanhã, amanhã!*

The most trying times were those I spent with Monteiro and others of the merchant fraternity when they forgathered at the outdoor tables of

111

the Grande Hotel or in the dim white rooms, still smelling damply of freshly set concrete, of the new Commercial Club to discuss the be-all and end-all of life in the province: the purchase and sale of commodities. Perhaps it was the undifferentiation of the seasons, the isolation of the city behind the buffer of hundreds or thousands of miles of ocean and impassable forest, the disarming warmth and sweetness of the air with its mysterious incense, subterranean and herbal, all conspiring together, that anesthetized the sense of time. It was certain that the talk rolled on without reference to its passage, despite all I heard of the grip of the political emergency. The possibility of establishing a direct shipping service between north Brazil and Canada, expedients for meeting the competition of Mexican cedar in North American markets, the feasibility of transporting lumber overseas in locally-built wooden sailing ships, outlets for the aluminum which was to be mined in the state (we had a whole hill of bauxite in the Concession), opportunities for opening up new areas of trade by bypassing the falls and rapids of distant rivers with railroad construction—these were among the many absorbing projects of the future I heard examined by a succession of speakers in sober and expressionless tones and by the hour, over *cafèzinhos* and glasses of the thick violet juice pressed from the berries of the assaï palm. These were, it is true, the very men who by all accounts were threatened with imminent ruin by the harassments, the confiscatorial and punitive measures, of the Tyrant. Yet there was the illimitable scope of the country at their backs to taunt the imagination, to leave it far behind. How could you disbelieve in the future, when it was all there, shaming the niggardly resources of Europe itself, how not build upon it?

Too nebulous, you say? Too far off? Ah, but there was the Massaranduba Concession, which was to bring American dollars pouring into the area. Gold-mining had ceased to be the sole inducement offered, and bauxite was not the only addition. There was manganese, and perhaps cobalt and nickel. And pitchblende? Did I hear pitchblende? No matter. There was the likelihood (who knew?) of petroleum, accessible (almost) by oceangoing tankers. And timber ("enough to run all the sawmills of north Brazil indefinitely"), and virgin lands to be opened up ("for colonization, special decrees must be issued, and application is already being made of the appropriate ministries"). There was the Concession—and I was the Concession. In the flesh. Large as life. The American capitalist that walked like a bear. At least I felt like a bear, a trained

112

bear. Was the bear required to look intelligent and interested? Enigmatic and narrowly speculative? Expressive of encouragement, implying confirmations? The bear did. Was the bear tempted to suggest that elephants be imported for snaking valuable logs out of the depths of the forest, and did the bear heroically resist the temptation? The bear was and did.

More than anything else there was the fact of the bear's presence. Wall Street had sent its begotten son, and this could not be doubted. If you were incredulous you could go feel the lapel of his jacket, look him in the eyes. (I had confidence in what my eyes conveyed from the first time I saw myself in the glass after coming in from a spell in the open. With all the respect I had for the luminosity of the equatorial sky, I was not prepared for what I beheld. The pupils had contracted to the vanishing point in irides that were radiant green gems. Monteiro's eyes were not in it. Mine were those of a man who could not sleep for visions.)

Why did I countenance the pretense that was made of me? Was it that having failed at the outset to say no—a monosyllable over which the diffident are prone to hesitate—I thereafter told myself the chance had passed, it was too late? Did I, despite what I thought I felt, find a sneaking satisfaction in the deference paid me, in being of consequence? Was it that I judged the Monteiros to be asking me not to contradict a fiction they had deliberately perpetrated for worthy ends and that I went along with out of affection for them and their kind and gentle compatriots? It may have been all of these, and one thing more. Whatever was likely to discomfit Colonel Achille Durondo automatically commended itself to anyone of ordinary sensibilities.

More than once I had seen him returning to the *Palácio do Govêrno* from an official inspection trip in the gubernatorial blue touring-car. Planted on the rear seat between two officers whose bulk shielded him from whatever bullets might chance to fly, he gave the impression of a loser in a *coup d'état* being sped off to a reckoning with justice. He sat erect and rigid in an always spotless white linen suit with wide lapels, a figure on the small side, his hands clasped upon the handle of a walking-stick (in which a sword-blade was known to be concealed) upright between his thighs. He managed to convey the impression of being in uniform, in which, it was said, he alone felt at ease. His face beneath the panama hat that was too large for him combined the feminine, petulant lips and short falconiform nose of a certain Portuguese type with pro-

113

tuberant cheekbones and receding forehead, which could have come from an Indian ancestor. His complexion was yellow. Driven always at high speed, he stared straight ahead until arriving at his destination. Descending then, still clutching his sword-stick, he would make for the shelter of the building with an unbecoming precipitancy, forcing his bodyguard to hurry to keep up.

The world since those days has grown accustomed to diabolism beside which the transgressions of Achille Durondo were small-time indeed, the crudities and grasping usurpations of a military strongman ruling an obscure province—though the State of Pará, which Durondo governed from the capital at Belém, under the loose reins of the Federal Government in Rio, was not a small fief; a map on the wall of Monteiro's office listed alphabetically twenty nations which were smaller, from Abyssinia through France (only half the size) to Venezuela. Of this constituency he had come into control pretty much by a fluke, on the death of his predecessor.

By diverse exactions Durondo milked the state for his personal enrichment, he browbeat and circumvented the legislature, he intimidated and threatened the press, he collected mistresses. ("He is building schools only to have more young lady schoolteachers to . . . to—you have heard of the *droit de seigneur?*" Emile said.) These and other practices charged against him, not excepting the elimination of several of his enemies, shot down in confused circumstances by unknown gunmen, were all time-honored. However, I myself had never before come up at first hand against such deep-died, premeditated wrongdoing, and it greatly shocked me. Moreover, Durondo had his unconventional side, and I think his peculiar technique of dealing with political opponents short of inflicting bodily harm would have struck anyone as not only novel but suggestive. Oswaldo da Lima, upon whom I had been taken to call in his house of dark red stone, before which two domesticated white egrets perched in the shrubbery, like ancestral ghosts of the place, had been only one of a number subjected to it; he had sat during our visit like a big doll with round face and wondering eyes, his feet barely touching the floor, and seemed not to comprehend what Monteiro was telling him, though at the end Monteiro's treatment had produced results, and he had become flushed and animated, seizing my hand between his on our departure and leaving it scented with toilet water. Dr. da Lima, it appeared, had offended the *Interventor* by an obtuse faith in parliamentary procedure, which had led him to be tiresomely outspoken in the *Câmara dos Deputados,* to the detriment of the Colonel's nervous organism. The *"carapanã"*—the mosquito—Durondo called him. One night he was pulled out of bed by some armed rapscallions and paraded barefoot and in pajamas to a waiting motorcar. He had a very good idea, soon to be corroborated, of what was in store for him. He would be taken by launch up one of the many waterways and, put ashore, be marched into the forest, there to be abandoned. Still barefoot and without light, he would have to wait in darkness, amid all the terrors with which Durondo's imagination must have peopled it, for hours, until day broke. Then he would be able to pick his painful way to the riverside, if he knew its direction, there to await transportation back to the city in a passing *montaria*. . . . He had had a very bad time.

Incidental political killings seemed to be regarded as inevitable in this country. An event which would have been reported in the United States in a shocked headline as FIVE KILLED IN UP-COUNTRY RIOT, ominous because of the implications for society, was treated here as a simple human event. BLOODY END OF CARNIVAL IN MANÁOS! the *Estado do Norte* announced with the pleasantly scandalized gusto with which a newspaper at home would have reported a shooting affray at a love tryst. I had an illustration of the attitude from Monteiro's little boy. Alfredo enjoyed serving as guide to an adult who had to be instructed on the simplest matters. On one of our tours he had pointed to some holes in the wall of the telephone and telegraph building where a few shots had gone wild in the most recent political fracas. "It was very lucky that no cables were cut," he said. "And that no one was hit," I moralized. "Oh, but two men *were* hit and one of them died," chirped the childish innocent, puzzled by the way the North American mind leaped to conclusions. It could be taken for granted, apparently, that the showdown to which the *Frente Única* and the *Interventor* were moving would involve bloodshed.

It seemed to me that to fulfill my obligations to Mr. Willet I ought to learn more about Colonel Durondo than I was likely to from the denunciatory epithets with which the *Constitucionalistas* dismissed him. In the *Gazeta do Pará* I kept up with the *Interventor*'s pronouncements and from its offices obtained copies of speeches he had made in the past. After breakfast, upstairs in the Monteiros' house, I would labor through them with a dictionary. Much of what exercised the *Interventor* was that

115

which exercised Monteiro and his tribe: plans, projects, dreams, hopes for the exploitation of the Amazon Valley's fabled riches. "I tell you, my friends, this wilderness—this *selvagem*—is the bounteous patrimony of our people and the guarantee of our greatness!"

Having heard him speak on one occasion, I could supply the gestures, the gargoyle-like forward thrust of the torso over the balustrade of the bandstand in the Praça da República, toward the passive, possibly spellbound, certainly unstirring crowd, the backward fling of the arm at the continent behind him. "Here is the treasure of nature, of which destiny says, 'It is yours.' And without reservation it is ours. Here spread before us are the boundless blessings of the Deity, waiting only for our determination to reap them for the redemption of our deprivation and the succor of our children. Here is a new world unborn, complete in every material endowment, waiting to be called into being, waiting only for our resolution to banish want from our lives! Yes, our resolution, compatriots! And this resolution you shall not seek in vain. I who have known your poverty and your hunger, I who have known the indignities that are heaped upon you by those of privilege, I in whom you yourselves have arisen to claim as your own the office of the Governor . . ."

The Colonel, like most orators, was prone to stay with a theme, ringing all the changes on it, but in time another would assert itself, soon to be sounded in dominant chords. "Courage, self-sacrifice, tireless toil: these are what are required of your chosen leader, and of you, patience and faith, incorruptible faith in the principles to which that leader has pledged himself. That which is our birthright has excited the envy of those with desperate hearts. Yes, those with hearts made desperate by greed for that which is ours."

With Monteiro and the business community it was lack of capital that blocked the way to a realization of the country's promise, with Durondo the "enemies of the people," *os inimigos do povo.* Invoked in a voice trembling with passion by the "idol of street-sweepers," as the speaker was called by his opponents, these enemies were seen to be everywhere. They strangled the small tradesman with usury, stole the wages of the laborer, depressed the price paid the farmer for the manioc and cane he grew, corrupted the public servant, defrauded the state of the revenues it required for the exploration and exploitation of the resources of the country, and if they did not actually send the *paludismo* that struck down the child and the blights and pests that destroyed the plantations, they looked with satisfaction upon the people's afflictions and diabolically withheld the remedies. "They," the people's enemies, were the ubiquitous tentacles of a single loathesome body, single in its will and direction, plotting its evil machinations sleeplessly in concealment and darkness. Durondo's voice would grow hollow, I was told. "Everywhere it is lurking. Nothing escapes its attention." Those nearby would be afforded the sight of his eyes rolling. "In the Palace of the Governor itself I can detect its presence, and behind me, even when I inspect the formation of the *Milícia Estadual.*" He had, evidently, a talent for creating an atmosphere of fear and inciting to fear's offspring, anger. The crowd would grow murmurous. You would think a great wind was gathering. Yet afterward, it appeared, the performance at an end, the crowd would go its way. Families, father, mother and four or five children all abreast ("There is the real enemy of the people," said Emile, "the numbers of children."), would promenade, as I often saw them, along the curving paths of the park (among the concrete tree-stumps) in a mood of mild expectancy, the older son in one group silently seeking in passing the eyes of an older daughter of another. A musical background would be provided by the squealing brasses of the military band, until a rendition of the stirring overture to *Il Guarany* concluded the concert and sent the strollers drifting homeward.

Durondo's psychology, no one could doubt, would have repaid study, but my interest was fixed upon what he was likely to do. It was to be surmised that in his estimate the *inimigos do povo* would lose in potency as a symbol if too closely defined. Or perhaps in his mind the chimera that frustrated his ambitions and haunted his solitude could not by its nature be particularized. It was nonetheless to be noted that whenever he was inveighing against his *encarnação do mal,* the terms *Partido Constitucional, possuidores da riqueza* (the rich), *acionistas estrangeiros* (foreign bondholders), *capitalismo internacional* and *Americanos ávidos* were spoken, as it were, in the same breath.

Laboring over the Colonel's speeches or working on reports to New York, I sat at a table in my bedroom with my forearm resting on a sheet of blotting paper, my back and limbs crawling with perspiration, my eyelids damp and sticky. From the window I looked out across the backyards of the neighborhood, over the lines of washing, the terra-cotta roofs and the bladed crests of the palms. The leafy foliage and the drooping banana-plants appeared weighted down, like the spirit of the city

117

itself. It was very quiet. Plugging away as I did through the siesta hour, I had the reputation of being indefatigable. What drove me on was of course the horrible knowledge of my lack of equipment for the business I was engaged in. Little as I enjoyed pretending to be what I was not, I should have enjoyed even less being seen for what I was. The decline of the sun from its zenith would bring the first sounds of singing from the Protestant meetinghouse and sharp, reiterated cries from a kiskadee flycatcher with a butter-yellow breast and a regular beat extending between the telephone wires and the orange trees behind the house. I would shut my ears to the die-away *wooooooooooo* of a riverboat bringing home to me the intoxicating fact of where I was and try to think only of the letter I was writing.

What was I to say to Mr. Willet? Or was it a question of what tone I was to take? In the course of the letter I observed:

> The most respected American organization known here is the Rockefeller Foundation. It has contributed a great deal of money to ridding the city of yellow fever. Agents of the local organization are constantly searching everywhere, in every alley and backyard, for breeding-places of mosquitoes; their khaki uniforms with green armbands are a feature of the city. My presence here, given the report of it by your client, explains to the more impressionable the reason for this extraordinary outlay by foreigners. The purpose has been to make the city safe for American investors. Now that this has been done, I have been sent here to conduct a preliminary survey of investment opportunities and investigate sites suitable for necessary facilities.

When I had typed this bit, the Monteiros' playful little puma-kitten of a daughter came dashing into my room scattering a cascade of shrieking laughter. She spun around my chair and clamped onto me, as if for protection—which, it instantly developed, was her object. Her mother was in pursuit, come to prevent the little girl from bothering me while I was working. The two children had ceased to be intimidated by me the moment they discovered I could not speak their language. Fluent in mine because their parents made a point of speaking it at home and read them stories in English, they found themselves for the first time at an advantage with a grownup. The little girl was thrilled. She had a life-sized father-doll that walked and talked—or could be made to. She would sit on my lap, studying my expression with face so close to mine that

118

her grey, kitten's eyes were—just as kittens' eyes are—slightly crossed and prodding my cheek with her finger to urge me on to the memorizing of Portuguese phrases she would feed me. "Here is what you say to the conductor of the *bonde* when you want to get off at Father's office," she would say, then when I was able to recite the sentence she had given me she would tell me that what I had said was "Please take me to the policeman with the purple nose sitting on a wooden horse." The law of diminishing returns does not work with children. If her delight was any less the twentieth time than the first, I could not tell it.

Dona Sophia, when she had succeeded in dispatching the mutinous child to the kitchen with instructions for tea to be brought, remained to sit, with legs straight out before her, on the arm of a chair of solid Victorian style—one much favored locally. She could not quite keep her eyes from the sheets of paper I had been filling. She knew that in addition to the reports meant to be passed on to Dr. Xenides, which I prepared under the scrutiny of her husband, I wrote letters to her husband's counsel which were meant to go no farther and which he did not see. Observing her slight confusion as she realized she had betrayed her curiosity about what I was writing, I asked what I should tell Mr. Willet about Colonel Durondo.

Startled, she said quickly, "Why tell him anything?"

When, after hesitating, she joined me in laughing, I pointed out that Mr. Willet would not go to Alekos Xenides with what I wrote unless it would serve her husband's interests, of which he was a very good judge. What puzzled me, I said, was how her husband expected to carry through with his plans in the face of the *Interventor*'s animosity.

"But the Massaranduba Concession will be a Federal concession!" Her face revealed her relief that my concern arose over a question to which she had an answer. She was leaning forward, supporting her weight on her arms, held stiffly at her sides; she still lapsed into the American-girl boyishness of posture she had picked up years before. "You have talked with . . . what is his name? The representative of the Ministry in Rio that grants concessions, when he was here. Da Costa—of the Ministry of Labor. You know of the favorable interest of the Federal Government in the development of the Massaranduba. It is the Federal Government that holds in trust for the Brazilian people the subsoil wealth of the country."

It was all I could do to keep from smiling—ruefully, it would have been. She was in scarcely better case than I, when you came down to it.

Exculpating myself from seeming to take advantage of her on the grounds that I had no advantage over her to take, I pushed on, stating that I was thinking not only of the Colonel's legal position but of what he might do *ex officio*. I did not know what *ex officio* implied, and she must not have either.

"João will have allowed for all that," she averred. She spoke with confidence, but her eyes did not appear quite as sharply focused on mine as they had been. "Ah, here is your tea. . . . And a cup for me also! *Et encore une tasse pour moi,*" she pronounced heartily. The maid was from French Guiana, somehow, a colored girl who seemed to regard her servitude as essentially ludicrous; her honks of laughter from the kitchen could be heard at the other end of the house.

Not to seem afraid of the subject, as I took it, Dona Sophia resumed, stirring the sugar into her tea with vigor and decision. "When the elections take place, it will be the finish for Mister Durondo. He is failing, and he is much afraid. As you know, there are no more speeches before a big public. He has promised so much and he has done so little. Even for himself! The money he steals from the honest people he must give to the crooked to keep himself in power."

That the note of desperation had been growing stronger in his speeches before he curtailed them was what I had very much in mind. There had been less about "the dawn to which we are marching together, arm in arm," and more about "the conspiracy that like a serpent seeks to constrict us in its toils." It was, I said, just the sense of impotence he must have that made me fear his striking out recklessly.

"Oh, but he is not impotent! Not at *all.*" The spontaneous words hardly voiced, she threw me an anguished and beseeching glance, turned red and fixed brimming eyes upon a corner of the ceiling.

With none of the aplomb of sophistication that would have savored the intimacy in which the inadvertent frankness willy-nilly conjoined us, I filled in hastily, and in embarrassment, with an observation about desperate men resorting to desperate expedients. That was what was behind my concern, I said. After all, he commanded the *Milícia Estadual*. Would he tamely accept an electoral defeat?

She shook her head, rejecting my reasoning. "No. He cannot count on the support of the *Milícia*. And he knows that in ten or twelve days Federal troops could be here. You have yourself seen Dr. Moura. Did he not give you encouragement for the future?" she went on.

120

Dr. Moura was the *Frente Única*'s candidate for Governor, a man of squarish head and squared-off build, whose scrutinizing gaze, which he was able to keep fixed upon his interlocutor without self-consciousness, could have belonged to a being concealed behind a mask. Monteiro, who was very attentive to him, stood beside me and made a little speech with the air of being my proxy, the gist of which was that American interests for whom I was an informal observer were following with close attention the intensifying struggle of political forces in the state, the issue of which, in their view, could advance or retard by many years the opportunity for foreign capital to perform in north Brazil its historic function, indispensable to the advancement and welfare of mankind.

As we made ready to leave, the candidate's visage was creased by a manly, leathern and not unaffecting smile, which made the unchanging eyes appear grave, even melancholy, and he gave my hand the only hard grasp it ever had in the countless handshakes it exchanged in that country.

It was perhaps the discomfort I carried away from that interview that made me reply to Dona Sophia's question by saying that I had thought the purpose of the meeting was for me to give Dr. Moura encouragement. I was instantly sorry I had done so, even though I had spoken half facetiously. To imply that she and I knew that a deception was being put over in the person of myself was to strike a foul blow. When I had let that notice of my arrival in the *Estado do Norte* pass without objection, I had in effect renounced the right subsequently to open to question the matter of what exactly I was.

Dona Sophia would perhaps have liked to be somewhere else, but to have got up and left would have made an issue of it. She raised her hand haltingly to her head and, in a seemingly involuntary action, gave a few desultory pokes to the hairpins above the nape of her neck. "What I was *really* thinking," I said, "was that the one who gives encouragement everywhere is your husband. He makes everyone believe that he can carry off anything, anything at all." Emboldened by the relaxation of her guard I read in her face, I added, "Just as he once carried you off."

She was pleased. Her smile grew as she studied her toes. "Did I ever tell you about the time I first met him?" It had been, she went on, at a dinner her father had given to introduce him to some Americans. "João was only twenty-one. He had just come from Brazil to enter the School of Business Administration. He had been studying English devotedly, but with Americans it turned out he could hardly understand a word that was said to him. But was he admitting it? No indeed! Not João. He had to sit there all evening and pretend he was missing nothing. And of course none of the Americans could understand *his* English, so they did not know. Only I could read the signs of his torment, the glazed eyes, the tight little smile that did not change. My brave country—in this big, indifferent world! And the way we can understand one another, we Brazilians! We know what it is to be Brazilian. No one else can know this. No one who has not lived our history with us, as one of us, sharing the same struggle, knowing the same suffering, the same love, the same honor. Foreigners make fun of our 'Order and Progress'—as if that mattered beside what we feel here!" she said, placing her fist upon her breast. "Of course we will have order and progress, too," she corrected herself. "That is very important. But what I was going to say: that night, when João had gone, I was seeing the stars and I thought they were also in the sky above Brazil. I knew where my place was. I knew I must be a Brazilian and could be nothing else. . . . I don't think I am making very good sense. I am only keeping you from writing your letter." With the comfortable smile of an established friendship she stood up.

I found it no easier to go on with it when she had left. Lighting a cigarette, I stared at the paper for some time before resuming.

> It is taken for granted here that I am serving your client's political as well as business purposes. I am rumored to have smuggled tear-gas shells into the country, and these are reported to be now in the hands of the leading opposition newspaper, against the contingency of its attempted suppression by the Government. Resistance to suppression, I should add, is not so much a matter of legal battles as of standing off an armed attack from behind barricaded doors and shuttered windows while a devoted staff keeps the presses whirring.
>
> Actually, your client's political and business interests seem to me mutually inextricable. He has confided to me that the regime is determined to ruin him financially. The confidence, it is only fair to say, was, however, imparted with equanimity, even with what sounded like pride.

The scene was the waterfront. We had hastened down to the docks to witness and, as it turned out, audit an historic event. A telegram had come with the information that one of Monteiro's *gaiolas* was nearing port, bringing not only a prize cargo but the blue ribbon of the river as well. On her way down from Manáos, *Águia* had overtaken the title-holder and dropped her astern. We arrived in time to see her swing into view around the tip of the Ilha dos Macacos, across the harbor. Bluff in the bow like all her fellows, she had, as most of them also had, a perky and jaunty air. She gleamed white as a seabird, and the big brass **M** on her blue-banded funnel reflected the play of light with a mirror polish. With his vessels as with his wife and children, Monteiro was a quite different person. All were objects of affection and pride with him, and when he was engaged with them he was quite unguarded and his delight was charming. He had grasped my arm when *Águia* hove into view, and as she approached he gripped it harder. "See! She is feeling the tide. She is taking hold. Now you will see her fly!" She came on, sidling, carried forward by the current as well as by the full force of her engines. She cut a tall, trim figure out beyond the oceangoing freighters and coastal steamers along the wharves. Her head up, the waves curling away like streamers from either side of her high bows, she grew steadily larger. "Feel how the propellers are digging into the water!" said Monteiro tensely. I could certainly feel his fingers digging into my arm. "She is giving it every—"

He got no further. The harbor's canopy of silence, resting oppressively upon the crowd of lethargic dock *môços,* idle khaki-clad policemen and umbrella-bearing, deliberate-mannered office functionaries, was whipped off, blown to nothing, like a tarpaulin before the onslaught of a gale by the most appalling, most terrible sounds that can ever have struck the human ear. Wail upon wail, mounting in volume and despair, filled the void, like cries of agony torn from the wracked soul of the earth itself. Everone on the waterfront, whatever he had been doing, had stopped it, and all were frozen in a general tableau, too stunned even to register stupefaction. The sounds could have had but one origin. Beaming upon the vessel that was now plunging past us, kicking like a muskrat, Monteiro bawled in a thrilled voice, "It is the new sireen!"

With the dying away of the last wail the tension of the crowd could be felt to subside, as if an approaching disaster had been averted. *Águia* had not done, however. Coming around under reduced speed to nose into her mooring, she lifted her voice once more. The death-dealing paeans of triumph lost nothing in repetition. Waiting until it was over, her owner, releasing my arm at last, said, "Jose, the engineer, promised he would give the engines a complete overhauling, he would put them

123

in the best condition since the ship has left Scotland, if I would buy this sireen. What do you think? It was a good bargain, no? The sireen brings attention and the improvement to the engines gives the extra speed. . . . But—" His face clouded over a little. "Perhaps, for the present, you will say nothing to Sophia? It is to spare her anxiety."

"Good Lord, Mr. Monteiro!" I exclaimed, unable to keep my irritation out of my voice and not half trying; being assaulted by those infernal yowls was in all truth a nerve-shattering experience. "You surely can't imagine she failed to hear the thing!"

"No, no. I do not mean the sireen. I mean the defeat of the *Boa Vista*. It will make her fear for reprisals."

He explained that Colonel Durondo had been subsidizing a rival fleet —one with which Jorge Almeida worked—to enable it to cut its rates. This example, together with the Colonel's influence with local officials of the organization, had caused the Government-owned Amazon Steamship Navigation Company to cut rates also. The object was to drive Monteiro's boats, and those of another, off the river and bring ruin to him personally. But, said Monteiro, Durondo had no understanding of business. It was a time of year when freight was most plentiful. In thousands of miles of forest the *castanha* crop was maturing. Moreover, the rivers were full and the ranches and trading posts of remote locations were enjoying their annual season of accessibility to steamships. There were cargoes for all, at the old rate. *O Coronel* was throwing away his money. But of course, he was not in a position to wait for the dry season. When it came, he must anticipate that the American syndicate would have taken up the Concession and he himself would be out of office.

I refrained from mentioning in my correspondence that the only things of a tangible nature I had seen coming from the direction of the Massaranduba were flocks of parakeets. They arrived with a rush and a jingling of rusty squeaks, raking across the heavens at dawn over the outskirts of the city. It was also in that quarter that there originated in midafternoon the rumbling march of the black thunderheads that rose over the city capped in sickly and sinister white. During the hours between these two occurrences the sky from my window was a sheet of shimmering blue, so like heated steel that one imagined the *urubus* at the summit of their soaring must fall scorched to earth. Their spiraling numbers in the rising pillar of air ascended with the heat of the day as human energies failed. From where I sat writing I could see them at full noon coasting down the sky on bent wings with prodigious speed in a single maneuver impelled by a mysterious common impulse.

I counted on the Carnival to give me a chance to see Cora Almeida again, and not in vain.

In growing older I have lost most of the superstitions to which youth is prone, but there is one which with experience has acquired a firmer hold on me. I have come to believe that the more certain one is of a specific eventuality, the more one sees it in complete and convincing detail, the greater is the likelihood that it will not come to pass, or if it does, that it will be given a twist such as to make it altogether different in flavor and meaning from what one anticipated.

One thing I was sure of was the urgency of my feeling about Cora. Heaven knows I had had enough experience of it. I had plotted the future course of our relationship so minutely and been over it so many times that I could scarcely doubt that reality would follow the grooves I had worn deep ahead of it. At the very least there could be no question but that once in her presence again I should hardly be conscious of anything else. And then, when I was with her once more, it was not merely a matter of seeing and talking with her. I even, such being the convention of dancing, held her in an embrace. My consciousness of her was every bit as acute as I had thought it would be. Admonish myself as I would that I was indecently taking advantage of her, that she would turn scarlet with shame and outrage if she suspected what I was about, I was at the mercy of the mutual pressures of our bodies, my imagination transformed into an agitated sculptor. And then something happened—something, nothing, everything—that put it all out of my mind.

The Carnival was the towering event of the year, in the anticipation and memory of which, it was plain to see, the city lived for the rest of the time.

All during the afternoon the population collected along the Avenida de Nazareth and the Travessa 15 de Agôsto, the main artery of the commercial district. I was amazed to find how many inhabitants the city had. Many came in costume. There were men made up as women, throwing their hips about beneath voluminous skirts of their grandmothers' time; children dragging along in their fathers' trousers; boys with bare chests and skins dyed red to resemble savages; maskers in blackface, in beggars' rags, in foppish finery in fashion when Dom Pedro ruled the

125

Empire of Brazil, in every conceivable assortment of garments. All mingled amicably with those in street clothes.

At the corner to which Emile and I had come down to watch, a young man in a white jacket turned up around the neck suddenly broke into song all my himself: *"Você me pareceu sincera; mas não era, mas não era."* We all knew by heart the music of the Carnival, or soon would. He sang at the top of his voice, staring dreamily ahead, then stopped abruptly to sidle hurriedly off through the crowd, possessed of another impulse. Two mimes—young boys in ankle-length petticoats with scarlet-daubed cheeks—at once went into action, commencing a jogging dance step. The example was infectious. Others joined in, one falling in behind another, costumed revelers and spectators alike, all instantly lost to everything but the measures of the jig. At length the leader of the now considerable line joined the end of it to form a circle. A sizable body of homeward-bound pedestrians was thus impounded. They awaited without protest the end of their confinement. It came in a sudden dissolution of the surrounding circle. The two boys in petticoats minced away with affected, girlish gestures, talking rapidly in falsetto voices, and the others melted back into the crowd. The throng flowed gently along. At any exceptional noise or outcry it turned instantly with one accord and mild, questioning eyes. Any trivial contretemps or bit of horseplay might be the sign that that for which crowds in this country gathered and waited was going to happen. Yes, even from such a small beginning that great and ultimate resolution might start to take form.

"Are they waiting for something in particular?" Emile repeated. "Yes. Without doubt. They are waiting for the pageant to begin."

This, at least, was not long in coming. Bands recruited from the *Milícia Estadual* had taken their places on wooden stands erected at important intersections. After they had begun to play, trucks filled with celebrants plied slowly up and down the avenue. Each truckload of youths or girls had its own special costume. Some were dressed as cowboys, some as harlequins, others as pirates or Portuguese peasants. They accompanied in song whichever band happened to be within earshot. Sometimes they carried the tune of one band deep into the stronghold of another, but the resulting cacophony made little difference; the din was too terrific for it to matter. One had chiefly the impression, as the trucks rolled by, of mouths exercising silently in grave young faces. By catching a few notes, however, it was possible to know what they were singing. *"Deixe a lua sossegada, e olha para mim"*—"Leave the moon alone and look at me"—one truckload would finish in a whispered scream, then throw off the rapt solemnity, like that of a choir, in which the songs were delivered, and leap wildly about hurling bagfuls of confetti at the heads below in a babble of shrieks and laughter only faintly audible even at close hand. Girls, wide-eyed, their faces rosy, their bare arms rosy too, their figures even more nymphlike for the generally masculine attire that set them off, shot quick expectant glances in every direction, as if seeking a visible source of the exuberance that possessed them. Nothing daunted by finding none, they clutched one another in seizures of irrational mirth and fell to hurling more handfuls of confetti with awkward overhand pitches.

The throng, forming a solid palisade along the curb, made feeble gestures to protect itself from the dry deluge pelting down from the passing vehicles and was enchanted. Glances of sheepish excitement were exchanged. What would happen next? Where would it all end? Mothers, all aglow and entranced themselves, had to find means to control their stamping, screaming children, transported by excitement almost past the point of no return. A few onlookers, marking me as a visitor from northern climes, smiled timidly at me by way of reassurance, patently concerned lest I misconstrue the funmaking of the passionate Brazilian temperament for unbridled license and depravity. Feeling a gentle pressure on my arm, I looked around and observed that Emile's normally pallid countenance was suffused with pink; his eyes were bright. I was touched to notice that his hand on my arm was shaking.

The inner core of the Carnival, the pearly nucleus, was in the Grande Hotel. Or perhaps it may be said to have been in the highly select Assembleia. A ballroom in the former, which had been converted into a motion-picture theater, was reconverted for a week by the removal of the seats. Tables were placed around the walls, the center of the room being left open for dancing. To one acquainted only with the workaday city, the air of sumptuous elegance created in the Assembleia especially by the crystal, the sterling, the linen, the masses of flowers, the platters of elaborate and decorative refreshments, the gowns of the women and the dinner clothes of the men—both expensive—was unexpected. Pretty girls abounded. Almost all were of brunette coloring, among them being some who, brunette in other respects, had naturally golden hair, and these especially, with faces full of life, had a quality that seemed to me Paris-

127

ian. All were electric with excitement, and what made their excitement more fetching, I thought, was the way in which they combined an outgoing, trim-figured, short-skirted modernity with a suggestion of nineteenth-century protected background, of never having been out unchaperoned. I chafed at the disadvantage at which I was placed by my inadequate Portuguese, scarcely more adequate French (which they all spoke well) and ignorance of the *samba*—then unheard of in the United States—which the band preferred to all other dances. Most of the guests, at least of the younger ones, came in costume as members of a *bloco,* a group of friends, young men and girls, all costumed alike as Zouaves or sailors, or something. They would come onto the floor in long lines, single file, singing with all the power of human lungs and waving their arms about ecstatically.

From the table at which I sat with the Monteiros and Emile, I saw Cora come in. She was with the haughty couple who had attended her at the customs warehouse and a man I should have known as her husband without being told: there was the row of teeth bared in the overwide smile Emile had prepared me for, and a rubbery limberness of movement as he insinuated himself among the tables in advance of the others that somehow conformed to my preconception of him. From the ugly thoughts that crossed my mind, I took sanctuary in Emile's assertion that there was no love between him and Cora.

When, upon looking around as everybody always does upon being seated at a table in a public place, she saw me and her face seemed to brighten spontaneously, I was buoyed up with gladness. She was stunningly turned out. Her hair, with its tight ringlets, seemed to be sculptured, and its soft gloss was richer even than that of her satin dress, which could have been fabricated of gold churned with cream. Pinned below her right shoulder, two small green-and-brown orchids were like little wicked, beautiful sea-creatures.

"You will have to dance with her," said Dona Sophia. She spoke with a touch of severity, but I could not tell whether the tone was one of assigning an unattractive duty to a protégé or of accepting the disagreeable inevitability of his self-indulgence. "And you, too, João," she added, clamping her lips tight upon an irrepressible smile as she looked at him with ironic eyes—eyes which had at bottom a complete trust.

"And I?" Emile demanded anxiously, not to be held at naught.

"I don't know. I think you are in love with her."

128

Emile, shocked and pained, was only partly mollified when she gave his hand a pat, actually a smack, with a laugh. "You should not joke about such things," he said, offended.

"You are all safe enough," she said, reaching for a *petit four*.

I realized with inner confusion that these words, which she would not explain, had affected me with an obscure feeling of relief. This I instantly rejected, putting it down to the perversity of human nature, as devoid of significance as the hypothetical possibility of jumping that presents itself to a person on a high ledge. I determined to seek a dance with her without delay.

"Yes," said Monteiro, "she will remain faithful to that *urubu* she is married to until there is some kind of finish between them."

Senhor Almeida did not take his eyes off me as I crossed the floor toward the table he occupied with his party although he was talking all the while out of the side of his flexible mouth to his dour, heavily-moustached brother-in-law. He had a slender but broad-shouldered build, a prominent nose, eyes that were large and in another face would have been attractive, but a protruding, almost wolfish mouth.

"Hallo, Mr. Tate," he said in a familiar voice, rising with a slightly exaggerated effort as soon as I had greeted his wife and before she had a chance to present me. "Sit down." After handshakes were exchanged, he himself dropped back into his chair.

I explained, stifling my repugnance, that I had come to beg of Senhora Almeida the favor of a dance, if he would permit, on the strength of our shipboard acquaintance.

Before I had finished, he had thrust out his leg, hooked his foot under the rung of an empty chair at the adjoining table, and pushing his own back against that of his sister, drew it up between himself and Cora. "Yes, sure. But first sit down." When I had done so, having no choice, he resumed, just before Cora made another—and last—attempt to speak. "You're staying with Raimo Monteiro. That's nice." He had thrown himself back in his chair sideways, to study me, though in doing so he turned his back squarely and rudely upon his sister. She bore no resemblance to him except that her eyes, under their dark brows, were identical with his. She was looking with a sleepy indifference directly ahead of her and twirling a heavy gold bracelet slowly on her wrist. Her and her husband's response to my acknowledgment of our previous meeting had been perceptible, no more. "Yes, that's nice. That way you

129

get to know the place. Makes you feel at home, too. To be taken into a good Christian, happy family. He's a good man. A heart of gold."

It being impossible to reply to assertions of this kind, I merely assumed a vaguely agreeable, affirmative expression, nodded and said to Cora that I was glad to see her looking so well. But he again broke in. "You want to get around while you're here. It's a big country. There's lots to see." His speech was that of Brooklyn. He seemed entirely un-Brazilian. "If I were a young man, coming here for the first time, I'd travel. I'd go around. I'd see the country. A man's only young once, and so's a country. How long you going to be here?"

I said I did not know. A few months, anyhow. With his sister's succeeding admirably in being unaware of my existence and Cora's succeeding equally in hearing not a word her husband said, the conversation was not one I was eager to protract.

"Only a few months? We'll have to get busy if you're not going to miss a lot. You'll be going up-country, no doubt. See the river, the jungle—parrots and monkeys. Maybe what the natives do for a living. Yes, that's nice. That's very nice. Of course, Raimo Monteiro can tell you just about anything you might want to know. But one man can't be expected to know everything, even Raimo, can he? Now you take the Palace. Come to think of it, you might want to go up there with me someday. Maybe it could be arranged for you to meet his Excellency Colonel Durondo."

His sister and her husband appeared startled at the sound of the name. I could tell by the look in Senhor Almeida's own eyes that he had rattled on a little further than he had meant to. Presumably invoking the name for effect within general hearing (the tables were very close) was not an ordinary thing to do. Bravado sat on the speaker's face, but not very securely. I stared at him uncomprehendingly, with rare presence of mind, then apologized for my thoughts having been distracted—"I suddenly remembered something I'd forgotten"—and asked mildly what he had said. A shifting of his gaze and an unpleasant smile told me I had made an enemy, or confirmed one. "I guess you remembered you wanted to dance with my wife," he said, recovering very well, I thought. "Well, go ahead. And if there's anyone you want to meet around here outside Raimo's circle, you let me know." He grinned in the manner described by Emile. "Or if I'm not here, tell Corazinha. If there's anybody around here she doesn't know, I don't know who it could be." Before we could rise he had turned to his disgruntled, Sicilian-looking brother-in-law—who, incidentally, bore the extraordinary name of Paradiso—and commenced to address him with copious gestures.

"I was afraid I was never going to see you again," Cora said when we reached the dance floor and stepped, in a somewhat gingerly way, into each other's arms. I replied, feeling as if I had taken hold of a flower that could be bruised by a touch, that that was exactly what I had been afraid of. I explained about my fruitless peregrinations of her neighborhood. "You're not very ingenious," she observed, not coquettishly but not critically either. She sounded a little listless, not like herself—which was certainly not hard to understand. I admitted ruefully that I knew it. I asked what she would have done in my place. She shrugged. "I'm not Madame Ingénuité myself, if it comes to that." She looked, I said, like Mademoiselle Ingénue. "Goodness," she said, "this sounds like a play." Evidently dissatisfied with the remark, she added quickly, "As a matter of fact, you look as if you were gotten up for a part in a drawing-room drama. I guess a man always does the first time you see him in dinner clothes. They're very becoming to you, by the way."

"I wish I could tell you how wonderful you look!" I exclaimed.

Her lack of response as we danced on seemed to impute an over-forwardness to my declaration, left hanging in the air. But in a moment she relieved my mind by remarking conversationally, "In half an hour it won't be fair to look at us gals at all. This place turns into a steam bath."

I felt light-headed. Cora had the gift of making her dancing partner feel that he was performing well; that, at least, I was sure, was why I felt I was doing so. With Dona Sophia—although I enjoyed dancing with her, she had such spirit for it—one was conscious of the need for coordination. There were little resistances one met that were simply the other side of her impulsiveness, and one had to lead with decision and avoid the unpredictable. Cora, no matter what one did, anticipated it. She was like a shadow, though tangible enough to my hand on her back. There was the touch of her hand on my shoulder, the ever-so-gentle pressure of her breast, the glancing contact of her thigh, but she was weightless. I asked her what she had been doing.

"More nothing than you ever saw done in such a short time. And keeping servants busy. Also having intimate chats with women who don't really like me. But they think I must be up to something sinful, if

131

they could just worm it out of me, or trap me into giving it away. I seem to give that impression. Some of them are watching us right now and thinking they've got a lead." I meant to say something, but before I knew what it was she had gone on. "I spent all day yesterday looking for a spool of thread to match a piece of material. You have no idea how satisfying it is to a woman to be able to spend a day that way and have it crowned with success. Women don't like confusion and turmoil and all the things that come from men going around turning the world upside down for the sake of some phraseology. I suppose you'd be appalled if you knew how much time I put into making myself look presentable. But it's like a farmer with his fields. They're what he's got to work with, and I'm what I've got to work with. It's part of the job. Everyone has duties, and I've got mine. I must look my best at Palace functions— dinners, receptions. . . . Tell me how you like Brazil."

I replied with enthusiasm. I talked about the spectacle of the dawn sky, the great *sumaúmas,* the astonishing appearance of the houses, the way the crowds with their wildly assorted human types reminded me of supernumeraries in the wings of a theater awaiting their cue to go on. She seemed attentive, twice backing away to look up at me, apparently with interest. Yet what I was saying seemed to lose everything in the telling. I did not see how it could matter to her. I stopped.

"I thought you'd like it here," she said when it was clear I was not going to add anything. "How about the girls? Don't you think there's an enticing assortment here tonight? Of course, girls of this class you wouldn't have much opportunity to entice very far in return. What have you been doing in the girl department?"

"I told you," I said, swallowing. "Hanging around the street where Cora Almeida lives."

"It's a good thing I don't take you seriously. I might get the wrong impression. I had a bet with myself whether you'd even dance with me tonight—I knew the Monteiros had a table. I made myself up as invitingly as I could."

"If you knew how I've been thinking about you—"

I had automatically drawn her closer, and with a slight pressure of her hand on my shoulder she separated us. Disengaging her right hand from mine, she turned sideways away from me and adjusted her corsage. "I have to be careful of these. It's not just on account of what people would say if I came back with them crushed. It's what they might do to you. They looked poisonous and evil to me when I saw them. I couldn't resist them. Do you like them? Orchids like these bring out the Cleopatra in a woman or else accentuate her innocent girlishness, depending on her type. Either way it's a gain." She restored her hand to mine. "At home I'd probably be wearing black. But here that's out of the question. In this heat the least you can do is try to *look* cool. That's the price you pay for never having to go around with sniffles and a red nose: being restricted to pastels. It does something to your idea of yourself. I'm very different when I can wear black. In a black gown I feel like a sword in a scabbard."

The music had stopped. We stood apart, though not very far in the press of couples on the floor. There was violent applause and a surge of voices. I must have been looking at her somewhat heavily. I felt heavy—quite hopeless. Yet again there was that trickle of relief, relief at having been let off, at being free. I castigated myself for it. What a poltroon I was! What an ignominious history the human race would have had if every aspiring lover were put off by the evasions of the quarry—designed, for all one knew, to spur pursuit—thankful to be escaping complications! Between her and her husband, I reminded myself, there was no affection. . . . The husband was away most of the time. . . .

She might—I do not know—have seen in my eyes a hint of what *I* was seeing: the house in which she lived, no one else at home, the shutters drawn against the glare of afternoon, she and I alone. As I looked at her I deliberately saw her in that setting. But she had not stopped talking. "We were speaking of girls, though, weren't we? I remember I was going to find you a little *moreninha,* wasn't I?"

The band struck up, and there impinged upon the turpidity of my thoughts the trivial hope that it would not be a *samba*. It was not. It was *"Você me pareceu sincera."*

"One thing we have to decide right at the beginning is about your intentions," she went on as the music brought us together again. "This isn't like the States, where different kinds of girls sort of merge and you can make up your mind as you go along. Here you could be just as sorry —though for different reasons—if you fell into honorable intentions about one sort of female as you surely would be if you tried to pursue *dis*honorable intentions with proper young ladies. Like the ones here tonight." Along with the other couples, we had pushed off to the side of the floor, close to the tables, to make room for one of those snake-

133

dancing *blocos*—the one attired in sailor suits. "It wouldn't do to be misled by these carryings-on. They may act for a week as if the sky were the limit, but as a rule there's nothing doing—at least until they've been married for a spell. Unless, of course, you're thinking in terms of marriage yourself." She chatted on, and it dawned upon me that she was talking not to hold me off but to quell her own agitation and that—radical as the notion must be to a man preoccupied with a woman—her agitation might spring from a source with which I had nothing to do. There was her husband. The luxury I was allowed of eradicating his figure from the situation by turning my back on him was not given to her. I was overwhelmed by the realization of what it would mean to have to live with that reptile, even if only *pro forma.*

"Maybe you've already fallen in love with Dona Sophia," she said, not very seriously, I could be sure. Though she leaned back to look at me, it was merely a matter of going through the routine of seeing what my expression might betray. The incidental and very real effect was to press her leg against mine. It would be, I said, like falling in love with an older sister. "Yes, I suppose I can see that," she said. "She's un-self-conscious and uncontriving . . . aboveboard, frank, friendly . . . with enlightened ideals. She's very modern—or for here, certainly."

"That's just what she said about you—that you were very modern, for here especially."

"She finds something to say about me? That's interesting to think about."

While she apparently thought about it, the slow revolution of the wheel of dancers brought us opposite the main entrance to the ballroom. The opening was nearly blocked by spectators who had evidently dropped in without having reserved a table. Glancing at them over Cora's shoulder, my eye fell upon a young girl with a sensation I was afterward to try with all my heart to reinvoke, to recapture. What was it I had felt at that first instant? What was it that set the ferment to working? That had caused me to build construction on top of construction upon the existence of that girl, working it over and over, so that getting back to the original impetus was beyond possibility?

She was at the edge of the little crowd, standing against the wall near a window, her soul in her eyes as she watched the dancers. The play of emotions in her face as she watched the couples move to the

134

rhythm of the music—and I express it this way unashamedly—was like the movement of sunbeams in the shade of a leafy branch.

She is the most beautiful girl I have ever seen. The sentence formed itself in my mind: there was no doubt of that. I kept reverting to it later —that much at least I knew—when I could not to save my life recall her features, as one may be saturated, haunted, by a strain of music and not be able to think how it went. While I watched, she turned and smiled up at a man standing behind her—presumably her father. Him at least I was to remember clearly enough. He was middle-aged though young in build, with a deeply seamed face and close-cropped hair turning grey, with character in his wide, straight mouth and reserve in his narrowed eyes, perhaps more in the way he stood, with a kind of withdrawn erectness, head back. His response to the girl was a softening of the features as he looked down at her; it could not have been called a smile.

She turned back, and in doing so her eyes brushed mine.

"Is everything all right?" Cora asked from a long way off.

The girl had resumed the position in which I had first seen her, but the intense mobility of expression had left her and, perhaps conscious of my eyes upon her, she regarded the dancers with a steady and, I thought—though this was probably the result of later imagining— slightly troubled gaze. Beyond her I was aware that lightning was now flickering in the black rectangle framed by the window, and I could see the dark shapes of the trees, and as if a breath of air had come through the window—though none stirred—or as if the lights in the room had dimmed, I felt the closeness of the soft, unfathomable tropic night.

I bent toward Cora and murmured, "There's a girl behind you, standing by the wall between the entrance and the window. When I turn around, see if you know who she is."

"What does she look like?"

I had swung us around so that Cora was facing her. "She has brown hair reaching almost to her shoulders and . . . and a slim, rather delicate face. She's very pretty. There's something about her." As Cora unaccountably said nothing, I went on, speaking urgently. "Her dress is about the color of yours—no, more ivory. It's . . . it's just slit for the arms to come through. I think it's a little too full for her. It was probably her mother's."

Cora backed off and turned a frowning, puzzled look upon me—not very surprisingly. It was a queer thing for me to have said.

135

"Look, you can't miss her!" I was in a hurry. "Don't you know who she is?"

"I don't see her. No one at all like what you've described."

In great impatience, but moving a few paces farther away so as not to be too pointed, I commenced to wheel partway around so that by turning our heads we could both face her at once. "With the man who—"

But they were not there. The wall against which they had been standing was empty.

7

Did any native of Belém, I came to wonder, know it as well as I? On the east was the only part I slighted: the recent outgrowths, away from the river, which held nothing for me. *She* certainly would not be found there! Here was the railroad station, the terminus of the narrow-gauge line that ran a hundred and fifty miles down the coast, the only railroad in the entire Amazon Valley, apart from that line of dreadful memory, built at a cost of thousands of human lives along the unnavigable stretches of the Mamoré and Madeira rivers to give Bolivia an outlet to the Amazon. Train service in and out of the city was infrequent, but little wood-burning locomotives with distended, cinder-trap funnels, of a breed I had supposed long extinct, were always busy about the yards. Nearby was a cemetery with acres upon acres of white wooden crosses carved with scrollwork and lettered in black script, from a distance resembling fields of stubble. The new purlieus, bald and vacant, had that peculiarly modern sordidness of flat, hard surfaces, bone-bare, sun-blanched buildings massively naked beside big shadeless expanses—parade grounds, recreation fields and huge, empty thoroughfares. They did not belong to the living city of the unpaved alleys, the *passagems,* that led off the avenues into the intimacy of precarious wattle abodes as indigenous as the nests of mud-dauber wasps, where women sat in the windows talking to friends on the sidewalk, resting their weight on the sills, while their naked progeny played in the gutters, self-absorbed, in the company of chickens and vultures. There were miles of such roads. The rains poured upon them, washing them clean and transforming the casual rubbish heaps into verdant pyres from which tongues of vegetation licked upward.

I had set about to comb the city and its outskirts for her.

On the south the roads were flooded twice a day by tides that backed the water up the river's subsidiary streams and the rough, boarded houses were set up on pilings and connected by platforms that served as sidewalks, while every doorstep had its dugout canoe: one had met the scene before in engraved illustrations in old volumes on tropical travel. But away from the river's province the city was bordered by farm-land. Traversing its outskirts in the heat of the day—the time when I was best able to get away and less likely than later to be drowned in a cloudburst—I would meet few other wayfarers. Sometimes, though, there would be a woman advancing regally under a basket, looking half hostile and wholly independent, or a man strolling by in meditation after the manner of the solitary Brazilian and inclined to linger thoughtfully at the corner of a fence. The road passed makeshift cabins, each with a yard enclosed by a stake fence. Inside, in the blue darkness, the family would have made itself comfortable, the children stretched out on the floor or sitting on the worn doorstep picking at the soles of their feet, the father showing only a bare leg over the side of his hammock, and the mother, thin-limbed but heavy-bodied, with a half-breed's features, sitting by the window, breathing visibly. They would all stare in polite astonishment as I passed, and a yellow-faced parrot on a perch by the door would throw its head back and try to disgorge the cry of amazement that had lodged in its throat. A starved, scabby mongrel dog would scurry forth obliquely to investigate, but would trip over its forelegs and fall if I so much as turned and looked at it. I walked on. My tan linen suit was regularly chocolate-colored in big blotches where the perspiration had come through.

I would pass from the realm of the black vultures to that of their red-headed congeners, the turkey vultures, which with their rangier build were apparently less adept at flying up from city streets and more at gliding tirelessly just above the treetops. In the transition zone, where the road ran between small fields of corn and forage and plantations of manioc forming shoulder-high canopies of leaves above the crooked stalks, slim grey asturinas—"goshawklets"—dashed between the crowns of trees screaming plaintively. Anis with drab black garb and blade-thin beaks swarmed in the brush and little ground doves sprang up underfoot with a whir of wings to zigzag off across the cultivated fields. Tanagers swept low among the bushes with flashes of claret-red or cerulean-blue, orioles burnt-orange in color frolicked in their treetop colonies, kiskadees shrieked aggressively from commanding perches, then looked around inquiringly. I could believe that the powerful compulsion of light and sky, earth and verdure that made the atmosphere alive worked on the birds as it did on me, seeming to liberate the portion of life I contained to a boundless expansiveness. Occasionally, out where habitations were few and second-growth woods stood by the wayside, a toucan alarmed by my appearance would drop headforemost from an overhanging limb into the lower underbrush, its long bill pendant like a tail, giving the impression of a bird flying in the opposite direction in a motion picture run backward. The woods of these cut-over areas were unimpressive in stature but so dense and matted they could scarcely be entered except where a stream clove a passage through them. Golden and clear the stream water was, like the water of cypress rivers, like tea, and if I were lucky I might espy a morpho butterfly flitting over the sun-flecked banks. It was worth waiting years, as I had, to see one of those creatures dancing on the air on wings the size of one's hands, fragments, you would have thought them, of the luminous twilight blue sky.

The end of every road was the same, though the end might take an hour or more to reach, or a few minutes. Out where the farmland was broadest you could stand with your back to the city's two low eminences, crowned respectively by the skeletonesque municipal watertank and the towers of the Cathedral of Nossa Senhora, partially hidden behind the *sumaúmas* of the cathedral square, and looking across the flat vista lying clear and quiet in the limpid, dustless atmosphere, see it a mile away, imposing even at that distance: the front of the rain-forest. You could meet it also within two blocks of the Avenida da Independência by turning off onto one of the fashionable side-streets, like the Travessa Dr. da Cunha. In this neighborhood the mansions maintained so profound a reserve behind their fences of iron palings or earthenwork walls that they might have had no occupants at all, though there was one from which, several times, as from the spellbound palace of a sleeping princess, I heard piano music so beautiful it fell upon the heart like raindrops upon thirsty earth: such—it must have been—were the circumstances. From the abrupt end of the Travessa Dr. da Cunha a muddy lane led past half a dozen palm-thatched hovels to peter out in a swamp a few paces farther on. A cow, startled by the crunch of my footsteps, raised her head above the rank grass at my shoulder and a swallow-tailed kite, performing evolutions overhead, shied off in a sidelong glide. And there, with the notes of a compositon of Chopin's still audible, rose the wall of the forest. The boles ascended white and sheer to the soaring branches, weighted by hanging creepers and the overflowing fall of sheets of leaves, standing like mighty works of statuary bearing enormous stresses in effortless immobility and repose.

I told myself that the chance of finding the girl again in any of the outlying areas through which I walked so many miles was negligible. What did I imagine? That she, too, would be drawn to the countryside and to the margins of the continental empire of the forest, as I was? Well, yes, that is what I did imagine. In an inexplicable way the impulse to go on, to leave the town behind, along with the business of the Concession, was associated with the picture of her that stood just outside my line of vision and defeated my every effort to catch it by surprise with a quick sidewise glance and pin it down. Not being able to call up her image, should I recognize her if I saw her again in different circumstances, in different dress? This was a traitorous doubt indeed, and I put it resolutely from me.

Besides its environs, I quartered the city itself systematically. I would begin at the upper end of the waterfront, site of the municipal market—a medieval guildhall of wrought-iron housing a solid block of fish- and fruit-stalls—and of the basin where the fishing fleet tied up, the fat hulls of the boats propped up at low tide on sticks above a compost in which the *urubus* sank deep at every step. From there I would skirt the harbor

140

plaza, past the trading establishments and the consular offices flying the flags of the half dozen chief maritime powers, thence walking along the streets where the shops were and on up through the residential district. I looked into every automobile, every streetcar, every window. I did not see her. However, when I heard the pianist in the Travessa Dr. da Cunha, I convinced myself it was she. Not knowing how many hours I might have to wait outside before I could expect to see her, or whether I should be picked up by the police on suspicion in the meantime, I contrived the clumsy expedient of buying a pair of earrings and, presenting myself at the door with one of them in my hand, asking the servant who answered my knock if there were a *môça* living there who might have lost it while dancing at the Grande Hotel. The answer was no. *Não há!* No had! No had a *môça na casa*. The maid spoke with a surly emphasis. I carried away not only a crushing sense of ignominy but some dark thoughts about a conspiracy to keep me from knowledge of the girl, a conspiracy of which the maid was a part, and also the Monteiros. It was true that I had not been able to describe the girl, but I had done pretty well with the father, I thought, and they had professed not to know him. . . . I drew a deep breath and decided I had better take hold of myself.

I do not know whether the Monteiros found anything out of the ordinary about me, more than was out of the ordinary with everyone during the Carnival. Doubtless they could tell that I was groggy from lack of sleep. In a week I had scarcely enough for two nights. Of course I went with them every evening to the Grande Hotel or the Assembleia; I thought my best chance was that she would appear again at one of these—which she did not. The dances did not hit their stride until two in the morning, and there was no flagging until much later, and even if the Monteiros left early I stayed on.

You would have to have been through one of those affairs to believe them. Cora had given me no idea of the heat generated by two or three hundred active bodies in a stifling ballroom. The soft shirts worn by most of the men with their dinner jackets would be plastered to their skins, literally without a dry thread in them. I found it cooler and less horrible to wear a stiff-bosomed shirt that stood out from my chest, but beneath it the perspiration trickled like insects crawling, and my starched winged collar soon had no more shape or body than if it had been parboiled. Whatever you wore, you were drenched, and your partner was in like condition. You might both have as well been garmented in steamed towels, and while you held each other apart the girl's bare back was slippery beneath your hand.

None of this oppressed the spirits of the Carnivalists. Far from being put off by the suffocating heat, the universal liquefaction and the racket of the band, which seemed to grow worse along with the pandemonium of voices, they had come equipped to top it all. Incredible as it may seem, everybody cavorted around squirting ether at everybody else—and so did you, since not to have done so would have been carrying Anglo-Saxon standoffishness to a supercilious extremity. Yes, everyone had his phial of perfumed ether, like a miniature Seltzer siphon. You depressed the lever and out zipped a jet of the liquid. Being highly volatile, evaporating on contact, it hit the flesh like an icicle shot from a rifle. Catching it full in the face for the first time was an experience to carry through life, for in the gaiety of the season no one would have thought to tell you that the effect of having had your eyes put out by fire was not lasting. The reigning confusion reached its peaks in the continual leaping and shrieking of those—especially girls—blasted by the icy squirts. It was my conviction that the only thing that brought these dances to an end was that sometime before dawn the air became so full of ether, rose-scented and violet-scented, that the revelers had either to get out or succumb to anesthetization.

At sunup the city was on its feet again. The theory was that the sleep you lost at night you made up in the afternoon. It was a trick I could not learn. The blaze of sunlight that stabbed through the chinks in the shutters left the room shadowless. It made one's eyes smart and revived in one's temples the pounding beat of the dance band. There was even less hope of sleeping late in the morning. The sun had only to clear the horizon for the whole dome of the sky to burst with light. There was no refuge. It did no good to keep one's eyes closed. With the shutters having been left open in the hope of letting in some cool air on a body still radiating heat from the dance, the glare was nearly as great through closed eyelids as with the eyes open. The city came awake with the rumbling of streetcars and, precisely as the first full beams of the sun struck the houses, with the passage beneath one's windows of the massed brasses of the *Milícia Estadual*. The band, in uniforms of olive-drab, striding smartly in tight ranks, marched the length of the Avenida da Independência, an infernal heavenly host of heralds blowing their brains out through trumpets ten feet long, or so it sounded. By the end of the

142

week I was in poor condition to reflect rationally upon the succession of unpleasant surprises in store.

Monteiro had learned through a highly-placed informant that the *Interventor* possessed a complete copy of the questionnaire Dr. Xenides had given me. He said he kept the document locked up and no one could have seen it since I had given it to him but Oliveira, in whom he had complete confidence. I asked if he were quite sure of him. Oliveira, his clerk, had a face that with almost stupefying exactness suggested the sole of a foot to which, as an afterthought, facial features had been added: the chin, or heel, entirely hid the knot of his tie, while his damp-combed locks stood up in very much the form of curled toes. He evidently disliked me, though whether for any other reason than jealousy of my privileged position in the office, I could not say. Monteiro declared that Oliveira had been with him for years without giving the slightest cause for questioning his loyalty. He then asked, what about Cora Almeida? Could she not have arranged to see my papers during the voyage?

Not at all pleased by the suggestion, I replied that even if she were not above snooping in such a fashion she would scarcely have risked being seen slipping into or out of my stateroom. But, Monteiro persisted, there was a steward, a Brazilian—he had seen him—who could have been paid to bring her my papers, perhaps one at a time. Yes, there had been a steward, overworked and of yellowish complexion. And there the matter had been left. It was only later that I remembered how Cora had known about the book I kept in my stateroom.

It could hardly be doubted that Monteiro had guessed the explanation. Looking back, I could see myself responding with fatuous complacency to an interest on Cora's part that was put on for ulterior motives, and even though I did not fully believe that that was altogether how it had been, even though the focus of my life had changed so that it made far less difference to me than it would have before the first dance at the Grande Hotel, I was bitter. I had not meant to let it show, but at the next dance at which we met it was obviously apparent to her that I had changed.

"Sometimes," she said, "I think maybe there's something to that story of Adam and Eve and the apple. Except that I don't think Eve had anything to do with their eating that lousy forbidden fruit. From what I've seen of humankind, I'm pretty sure it was Adam that got Eve to eat it,

143

by keeping at her until she gave in just out of weariness with the subject. Anyhow, with a man and a woman there always comes a time sooner or later when the man becomes very cold. You feel that if he isn't absolutely cruel you're lucky; it's only because he's self-controlled. What is it? Is it that he remembers being expelled from the Garden of Eden and feels he has to punish the woman? Or is it that the spectacle of a weaker being automatically brings out the sadism of the noble male? Which do you think it is in your case?"

In my case, I said, it was mystification. Something had happened to make me wonder how, back on shipboard, she had known that I was reading Bates's *The Naturalist on the River Amazon* when I had never mentioned the book or had it out of my stateroom.

For a moment she was plainly puzzled. I had time to come to a different feeling about what had passed, to consider how in her position I might be driven to the most distasteful lengths. Contrition began to set in. Then I felt her stiffen briefly, as one will when threatened with a loss of balance. We danced on. I waited for her to offer an explanation, to say something, but at length it became evident that she was not going to, and I marveled.

I steered us away from a *bloco* that was making a great hullabaloo, and she remarked that the Brazilians were like mayflies, with just a few days in the spring in which to live. "Only don't press me for information about insects." The effort to sound casual must have cost her something, I thought. "I'm just quoting an American who used to live here and who was rather fat and very philosophical about everything until he died of cirrhosis of the liver." A moment later the music stopped and she said she had better go back to her table, where her husband was sitting with half a dozen others.

On the way back she said, "I heard something good about a gentleman once. I guess it was a definition of a gentleman: a woman's only dependable refuge."

Shortly afterward she and her husband left, and I did not see her again during the Carnival.

A repellent-looking man had taken up a position against the wall near the Monteiros' table. I noticed him only when Dona Sophia said to her husband in a low, even a sepulchral voice, "*Olha p'ra lá!*" With head bent she directed his attention, by a surreptitious glance over her shoul-

144

der, to the bystander, who stood with arms folded across his chest. It was surprising what villainous-appearing types one frequently met with among the gentle, soft-eyed Brazilians. This sallow example, with black moustache and protuberant cheekbones, looked like Edgar Allan Poe caricatured as a border badman, or John Wilkes Booth, and would have been overdone if cast in an old-time melodrama. Monteiro sized him up indifferently.

"*Êste país maldito!*" Dona Sophia said in a harsh whisper, most astonishingly, raising to the ceiling, eyes closed, a face transformed into a mask of weariness.

"Every country is in some ways a country *maldito,*" said her husband.

Dona Sophia stared at the crowded dance floor. "And our curse is politics," she said with a glance at me. "It is our intoxication. We do not drink, like the North Americans. You may go all around here even at Carnival time and you will see no drunk person. You will see only good nature, and compassion. We do not drink alcohol to excess. What we drink is politics. It brings us to the level of savages. In politics we are alcoholics." She turned to her husband. "We must go. I will not be in the room with that man."

"We cannot go yet. We cannot let him drive us away."

"I will not be in the room with that man. You see how his coat is standing out on the side? Even here he brings his gun." She looked at me as if for support, in her agitation evidently overlooking the fact that I had not been apprized of what they were talking about.

"Let us dance. Then we think of going," said Monteiro, rising and holding out his hand.

When they had moved off, I asked Emile if he could explain the meaning of Dona Sophia's disturbance, but he replied by expressing a desire for some air. "You will go with me?" On the way out he confessed that he could not breathe happily in the neighborhood of "that Filipo." It was not that he was afraid—only that the presence of coarseness and brutality deeply upset him. But he did indeed feel the need of air, too. And halting as we stepped out of the door, he filled his lungs. "Air, air," he said, like the dying Goethe calling for light, but more vaguely. We took a table at the edge of the sidewalk and put on it the glasses we had brought with us. Like everyone else, we were drinking *guaraná,* which tastes a little of both beer and ginger ale, with the astringency of quinine water, and is possibly the most refreshing bottled soft drink in the world.

"What it is about that ruffian—in the last election, he has come up to João in the street and pushed his pistol in his stomach. He would have killed João if he had showed fear. But João is a very cool man, and very courageous. He looks this Filipo in the eyes, and Filipo is not equal to the engagement of eyes. He has to look down, and then he cannot shoot."

"That must indeed have taken nerve," I said.

"Yes. That I can tell you. I have reason to know. I have myself had a similar experience. Did you know? I . . . I have refused to move from the pavement for a gunman of that dog's. Yes, that is what happened. The fellow would have me step into the street. Undoubtedly he was armed. But I proceeded on my course, and it was he who gave way." He appeared to have no interest in the effect the recital might have had on me. His pale eyes moved in a homeless sort of way. Finally they came to rest on me. "Dona Sophia is right, you know. This country is cursed. To be here is a martyrdom. I feel it so. Politics, politics!" He raised his eyes in an ultimate supplication of the indifferent heavens. "I could not endure if I were unable to escape to Chapeu Virado." Chapeu Virado was a resort of the well-to-do down the river, facing the sealike vastness of the estuary. "If only we could be there now! I could show you life, then, amigo! Not this." He waved away the hotel, the avenue, the park. "Not this . . . this—" Words failed him. "In Chapeu Virado, I could show you the life of men. There I have a boat, you know. In an iguarapé behind the house. She is a boat that is much admired, for beauty and for strength—name' Felicidade. She is kept always prepared for my service." One could listen to Emile or not, as one preferred. He looked for no special response. I found I generally did listen, even when my own thoughts were most demanding. I do not know why, but his speech had a slightly magnetic, and lulling, effect upon me.

"Felicidade, she is called, And she is my felicidade. I think that I shall never experience a greater felicidade than my boat. To me she is alive. She obeys what is in my mind. She is like a living creature which has the intuition of love. I have trained my servants in delicacy of handling. And my orders are that she is to be always prepared for my service. Day or night. Without exception. She is to be ready. For the times when the desire seizes me to . . . to be on the water. Or to be fishing. My

146

great zeal for fishing is well known." He turned a gaze of mild inquiry upon me, and I nodded. A photograph was extant of Emile in Norfolk jacket and knickerbockers, holding a fly-rod, taken in England during his Grand Tour. "To me it is a challenge. And the river when it is rough is a challenge too. This is to know truly what is life—to experience the force of the wind and the savagery of the waves. My servants when they see the storm gathering would hold back. It is not from fear for themselves. Their devotion to me is very great. It is fear for me. They will not go until I say I will then take the boat by myself. Then they will refuse to be left behind."

"What kind of fish do you catch?" I asked.

"Big ones. Of a size to amaze you. You will see when you visit my house and we go together out into the bay. *Bacalhau*—Amazon cod-fish. And others. Some perhaps unknown to science."

As it happened, I was to visit Emile's island retreat before a week was out, but not to go fishing with him. All he could think of then was to return to the city as soon as possible. It was not the time to be at Chapeu Virado; the island was deserted, the emptiness of the houses oppressive, and the mosquitoes were at their worst—there was a plague of them. I did, however, prevail upon him to show me his fishing tackle. He kept it in a large drawer, neatly stowed away. There were barbarous hooks the size of ice tongs, flaking with rust, and coil upon coil of line as thick as one's little finger, quietly falling into dust. I did not have the heart to ask to see *Felicidade*.

Nervous at being away from my post in the ballroom, I suggested that we go back. The Monteiros had finished dancing and, though the gunman named Filipo was nowhere to be seen, were preparing to leave anyway, Dona Sophia having ruled that her husband and I get to bed. I begged the favor of a last dance with her: I had to explain why I could not go yet, and the only explanation that would serve was the true one. So I told her about seeing the girl. I was as brief as I could be, merely touching upon the episode as upon a trivial incident of interest chiefly for the amusement it would afford her, but I did not get away with it. Dona Sophia built the matter right back up again. She was delighted and congratulatory, and I was to understand that the necessity I had come under to find the girl again was testamentary of my deserts, the vouchsafement of such a vocation being a mark of grace. Of course I must remain behind at the dance! It was only a pity I could not depict the

147

girl in more detail and that she could recall no one answering to my description of the father. "You see what a wonderful country this is!" she exclaimed, her vehemence harking back, I was certain, to that utterance of despair about her native land so unfortunately wrung from her in my hearing. "I truly believe, only here in Brazil would romance be so quick and so certain. It is like metals that carry electricity. Here the air carries feeling. It carries love."

Was she not, I asked, reading a lot into a fifteen-second, wordless acquaintance? "Perhaps," I said, "I didn't see the girl at all!"

She gave me a surprised look. "It is just like an Anglo-Saxon to try to talk himself out of it!" The formula seemed to reassure her. With a syllable of laughter she gave my shoulder a firm nudge, as if to shake me out of it. "You must accept what has happened," she said gaily. "It is Brazil! It is the Carnival!"

In leaving she wished me success in my quest, but the only results of my persistence were further arrears of sleep and a sensation in the morning of being top-heavy and unable to focus my faculties. I had to put in an hour with Monteiro at his office, after which I was free until lunch. I spent the time walking. After lunch I retired to my room to finish up a report to Dr. Xenides. I found it hard to concentrate, however. About an hour after Monteiro had finished his nap and departed, there came a scratching on the door and Dona Sophia's whisper: "Are you awake?"

"Yes, yes," I said, springing up.

She opened the door. "I didn't hear your typewriter, so . . ." She was wearing a dress of pink and white vertical stripes, like a stick of peppermint candy.

I explained that I had been doing a preliminary draft by hand. "What's the matter?" I asked after seeing her face.

"The *Estado do Norte* has telephoned. They have tried to reach João at the office, but he is not there. They say there is a charge that his ships have carried cargo without the proper clearance papers—that is to say, contraband. They say an order has been issued to intern all four of them. I think João is with the *Águia*. Do you think it might be well if you went to the office? I am terribly worried."

The taxicab got me there just as the first heavy drops of the afternoon shower were splashing on the sidewalk. Monteiro had already arrived. The tableau upon which I entered recalled one I had seen before, perhaps a painting of Napoleon after Waterloo. Monteiro was sitting, knees apart, his white trousers as tight as the Corsican's satin knee-breeches, a dark look on his swarthy face, in his hand a long green envelope of the kind used by the *Estado do Norte,* the leading newspaper, which supported the *Frente Única.* Standing around him, in the place of the loyal marshals, were Oliveira, a junior clerk, a tall stranger who turned out to be from the *Estado* and, to my surprise, two nuns. Anything less likely than that Monteiro had sought spiritual solace at this juncture could hardly be imagined, yet that possibility did cross my mind. After a glance at me he addressed the sisters briefly in Portuguese. In the depths of their hoods the diminutive faces of the two were of a pure, creamy pallor and wore expressions of strained eagerness, probably accounted for by the tight bindings under their chins. They replied to Monteiro softly in unison, then, bowing their heads, disappeared within the tents of black material that housed them, seeming in doing so to gain enormously in stature.

Monteiro watched them go. "As you see. Nuns," he stated with unexpected bitterness. "This rascal Durondo sends me everyone who thinks to travel for nothing. He would like to fill my ships with passengers who do not pay. These two are *too* much. I have told them the price of a passage is twice what it is and have said they may go for half fare. It is the best solution, everyone is content. They are unworldly and the Church is very rich, richer than the richest shipowner. But put yourself in the place of this *Interventor.* Yesterday, when he is telling these nuns to come to me, he does not know that today he will have my ships off the river." He turned to the stranger, and a short exchange in their own language left them both wagging their heads.

Bewildered, as I often was by the mix-ups in the scale of things in this country, I asked if it were true, then, that his ships had been ordered interned.

"Yes, that is the order. . . . How did you know?"

I told him about the telephone call his wife had received and its effect upon her, and he turned angrily upon the stranger, who, I now deduced, had come from the *Estado do Norte* with the green envelope and the news of the *Interventor*'s action. The latter protested his ignorance and innocence in a shrug of un-Brazilian exaggeration. It lifted his shoulders and eyebrows so high I looked to see him raise himself clear off the floor.

149

Monteiro took up the telephone and gave his home number. "Here you are seeing the consequences of having no understanding of business," he said to me over the mouthpiece. "Durondo jumps into this rate-war with me at the worst time for him; all it is doing is costing him money, and— *Alô, alô? . . . Sim. . . . João. Sophia—boas novidades!*" Good news! The *Estado* man and I looked at each other with, I am sure, identical expressions. Monteiro's tone was cheerful and assured. I heard several times the name *Aurora*. Of the ships whose specifications I had brought with me from New York, *Aurora* suited him best and he had only been awaiting a "profitable opportunity" to take an option on her. The *Estado* man was listening closely. When Monteiro had finished, there was a colloquy between them. At the end of it both consulted their watches and looked out the window. The street had been hidden since my arrival behind curtains of rain which broke upon the pavement with the crackling of a forest fire, but the downpour was lessening.

Monteiro turned to me. "You are seeing how Durondo is ruining himself. Because his rate-war is only costing him credit, he loses his head and orders my ships to be seized. I think he is forgetting that he is only the governor of a state and not the president of an independent nation. He is forgetting that he and especially his supporters are much in debt to persons who will not like to see me fail. You see? For the banks who hold my notes it would not be good news that I am in bankruptcy. The fear of losses would be very strong if I am liquidated—even in Rio. Now there is this other thing. With these same bankers I have discussed the plan I have for the *Aurora*. They are much impressed. They are much interested. They are wanting me to go ahead. So . . . tomorrow the *Estado do Norte* will carry the notice of the Government's action against me, that is meant to destroy me. *And* on the same page will be another report. It will say how I have registered papers showing intent to purchase the Canadian cargo-ship. It will emphasize how this ship is seagoing but of very shallow draft so she will make possible direct trade between coastal ports and river-towns that are very far up the tributaries. This is something that is never possible in the past, and it is much needed. It will contribute to the prosperity of our whole region because it is an example, and there will be more ships to follow the *Aurora* when she has shown the way. It is something I have dreamed of doing —for the country. Since I am a boy, perhaps. And the name of the ship? Not *Aurora. Massaranduba!*"

150

The round-faced, blasé newspaperman had picked up his hat. There was another conversation between the two. The rain had let up. At the end of the Rua da Industria the river had come into view once more, sullen and muddy-hued beneath the dark, retreating clouds. Water poured from the buildings as if the city had but that moment arisen from the sea.

Monteiro saw his visitor to the anteroom and retired to the washstand that stood half hidden behind a screen in a corner.

Somewhere a ship's deep-toned whistle sounded. Already there were pedestrians abroad. In a parked car on the other side of the street sat a man whose eye I happened to catch, a man in a faded butternut-colored tunic buttoned to the neck in the military style. Heavy-chested, with solid jowls, a fleshy, protuberant chin and a short, thick nose, he seemed familiar to me, but if we had met before he evidently did not remember me, for he looked away without interest.

Monteiro said, "It will now be clear to everyone what is behind this cutting of rates. You will see. My ships will be freed, and in a week, maybe two, the rates will be put back up." He was examining his chin in the glass. "I have much business this afternoon. How do I look?"

"You look fine," I said. "I don't know why. I don't know how you sleep."

"I am letting other persons do the worrying, always. Julian, you will do something for me? No, not worrying. I will see you have no cause for worrying. You will write for me the statement for the press? Then I will have only to put it in Portuguese when I am coming back."

I said I'd do my best. God, I was tired.

As Monteiro left, the sun came out. It burst upon its drenched satellite with the sudden masterful glare of a second, galloping daybreak. The earth, with all its trees, buildings, pavement, glistened like a creation of glass, so new that the excess molten material still poured down every cleft and gutter in sparkling rivulets. What cause could there be for misgiving in such a world?

I sat down before Monteiro's heavy old typewriter. The novelty of reading my own phrases in its familiar purple lettering had worn off. Out of an admiration for American publicity methods and an exaggerated notion of my training in them, about which I had let slip an admission, Monteiro had been getting me to turn out pieces intended for the public—political manifestos heretofore. The fact was that while I had

151

never written a successful line of copy in my life I had in the past few weeks picked up from my intensive course in the public papers of *o Coronel* Achille Durondo a facility in a kind of address that almost translated itself into flowing, hortatory Portuguese, verbal mood-music to put the listener into the desired state of mind. ("Every citizen of the state will acclaim the event in proportion to his imagination and his faith in the destiny of his country, registering by his enthusiasm his confidence in the realization of the promise of the people's legacy," or, "The responsibility for the future rests upon the initiative of men of experience and conscience who, resourceful and progressive, accept its challenge and the obligation to achieve, even in the face of obstacles set in their path by greedy and factitious politicians, the exploitation of the resources of nature, which alone can accomplish the defeat of that one and supreme enemy of the people, Poverty—Poverty in all its cruel manifestations." Monteiro had lingered over that one. Said he, "Well, it will show we are not afraid of the Colonel.")

Inserting a sheet of paper, I commenced to bang away:

STEAMSHIP MASSARANDUBA TO INAUGURATE NEW ERA IN NORTH BRAZILIAN COMMERCE
In an action appropriate to the climax of the Carnival, uniting the spirit of camaraderie and rejoicing that has reigned in the land for the past week with the dedication to exalted ideals to which the approaching season should pledge us, the firm of J. R. de Monteiro today announced . . .

The following day was the last of the Carnival. A newcomer would not have known how long it had been going on. The collective zeal had manifestly not diminished in the least. In the afternoon the crowd in front of the Grande Hotel was as great as ever. I sat down at a table near the one Emile and I had occupied. I was sipping a *cafèzinho* and engaged in the practice, now automatic with me, of surveying the faces around me, looking sharply at every passing girl, when I saw once more the man whose features I thought I had recognized the day before. He was standing back from the crowd, against the front of the *Sapataria Inglêsa*. He wore the same outfit, the color of age-yellowed newspaper, and military cap, which had lost its shape and bore no insignia. I thought him a most unprepossessing figure. His shoulders were too narrow for his chest, which was the size and shape of a barrel, and this, with his short neck, made him look a little apelike. Or perhaps he was more bull-

152

like; he had bulbous eyes, like a bull's. I did not think of the possibility of my being under surveillance. This shows, I said to myself, that if you go about scrutinizing people you find you are seeing some persons repeatedly.

I went back to watching others who were passing by, but later, on looking up from my coffee, I found the man in the yellowed tunic staring at me. As he had the day before, he looked idly away. The visor of his cap cast a shadow like a mask on the upper part of his face and across the thick bridge of his nose. Then as I was preparing to leave I discovered myself once more the object of his attention. This time his gaze lingered, and when he removed it he smiled. It is one thing to have a stranger smile while looking at you and quite another to have him smile to himself after looking away. As the implications rolled in on me, I stood for a moment in a state of mild but accumulating shock.

To lose him in the crowd would be easy enough, I was confident. Yet when I considered how my report of the episode to Monteiro would sound if there were no more to it than this, I hesitated. I thought I had better make sure of my inferences.

Behind the ornately engraved mass of the Grande Hotel the ground fell away to a low-lying area of unpaved streets, deserted sidewalks, empty windows and silence. The few children who played here in the seepage of the gutters were dirtier and more miserable than any others in the city, and they went naked to an older age. The vultures were more cynically audacious. The section slept by day and came awake at sundown. Monteiro soon after my arrival had identified it for me as the district of prostitution, though whether to put me on guard against it or let me know that this was it in case I should be looking for it I was not sure. I headed into it now, walking unhurriedly. When at the foot of the hill I came to the last building of consequence, beyond which there were blocks of single-story, unseparated cells under one long, common roof, each with a single window and door, I stopped to examine the front of this establishment, the name of which was painted in black letters on the globe of an electric light above the door: *Pensão Rosa*. Sure enough, at the head of the street there came with a deliberate and rolling gait, and something of that air of fate that a tank must have for a foot-soldier, the heavy-chested figure I had expected yet was a little stunned to see.

But for a few children we were alone in the street, and beyond the

Pensão Rosa there was no one at all. There loomed ahead of me, as I saw it, the chance to throw my shadower into confusion. I went onto the first side-street, so untraveled that the grass grew in it, turned the corner as if I meant to go on, then when I was out of sight stepped back and took a position against the wattle wall of the corner house. I waited. Up the street the ironwork of the rococo municipal watertank was dusty green in the yellow light of the declining sun. The clamor of the thoroughfare I had left sounded smothered under the hush of the evening skies.

It was a great while, or so it seemed to me, before I heard the sound I was waiting for: the measured *clock-tock* of leather heels on pavement. Even then he was a long time on his way. The moment I noticed that my elongated shadow was cast squarely across the sidewalk down which he was advancing he cleared the corner of the house. Coming to a halt, he thrust his hands into his trousers pockets, looking neither to right nor left. Though my complacency over the disadvantage I meant to catch him at had vanished, I went ahead with my plan to walk straight at and past him. I had not covered half the distance between us, however, when he withdrew his hands from his pockets and made a flinging motion with one of them, with the startling result that a six-inch knife-blade sprang out of it. With that he turned and faced me. I must say I had stopped dead. He dropped his eyes, which were grey with the opacity of china, to his hands. With the knife he began paring flakes from a block of black tobacco. I started to move on when he addressed me. "You got match, mitey?" At first I thought he said "mighty," but I realized the word was "matey" in an Australian or Cockney accent; he also said "gought" for "got."

If I had had time to think—as who ever has?—I should have shaken my head and marched on by. As it was, I stopped and fished out my lighter, and then, cursing myself, had to wait while he put his knife and block of tobacco away, rolled the shavings between his palms, finally stuffed them into a pipe he had extracted from a pocket. Between puffs as powerful as those expelled by the wood-burning engines in the railroad yards he managed to thank me. Returning the lighter, he proceeded on his way.

It seemed preposterous that I should have to make a point with Monteiro of the unlikelihood of the man's having assigned himself to my company for days just to get a light for his pipe, but I did. After an initial sharp reaction to what I had to impart, he grew restless, though my account was brief enough. He nodded, frowned, shifted his eyes, threw a quick glance or two at me. Dona Sophia asked hopefully if I thought the man was English or Australian. No, I thought he was a Brazilian of the *Milícia Estadual* who had perhaps learned English as a seaman or in the West Indies. She thereupon subsided into meditation. Well, yes, Monteiro conceded, it would not be without precedent for the regime to keep watch on a . . . a person of consequence.

"They might think they could make you nervous," said Dona Sophia in a way to suggest that that was all there was to it.

"They might be right," I replied. Anyone would have thought, I reflected, that they had heard my recital before and were concerned to get it over with.

"But you are an American citizen." Dona Sophia spoke with happy emphasis, but her candid eyes, resting on mine, were irresolute.

Feeling that my concurrence was desired, I nodded. I had met the American consul two nights before. A plump young man who looked as if he might be hearing voices inaudible to the rest of us (such, when one came to think of it, being his job), he was sharing a table at the Grande Hotel with Theodore and Margaret Lumkins. The greeting I had received from my ex-shipmates was of the kind that makes one wonder what the matter is, and the consul's manner with me was that of a busy doctor with a hypochondriac; my condition, I was to understand, entitled me to no claim upon him. It soon dawned on me what the trouble was. In the eyes of the American colony I had gone native. I wondered now whether the regime might not have arrived at the same verdict. However, the topic I had introduced was clearly a constraining one with the Monteiros, and, moreover, no one enjoys making an issue of his own apprehensions, so I let the matter drop.

It was, in any case, soon superseded by other concerns. The next day the *Estado do Norte* carried the article about the coming advent of the *vapor* Massaranduba, *née* Aurora, and the day after that came a notice of a *"clarificação"* and *"retificação"* by which the penalties imposed upon the firm of J. R. de Monteiro for *"irregularidades"* had been reduced to a reprimand and warning and its ships, for the sake of the innocent shippers, allowed to proceed with the fulfillment of contracts. This pleasant news was, however, altogether offset by the lead story in the *Gazeta do Pará*.

155

In obedience to Monteiro's summons I had sped to the office to find him with his back to the room, staring out of the window.

"Is something wrong?" I asked.

Although he turned and stared at me, my appearance was not enough to bring him back from wherever his mind was; it did not register upon him; his lower lip remained tucked thoughtfully beneath his teeth. Oliveira, who liked nothing better than to interpose himself between us, came up with some letters to be signed, and these Monteiro took to his desk. I was somewhat reassured to observe that the ritual of the signature was not curtailed. But doubtless it was second nature by now. Thrusting his wrist out from his sleeve, he described circles in the air with his pen. In a descending and narrowing spiral he suffered it to approach the paper and, when it touched, ran trippingly and unhesitatingly through the signature. The signature completed, the pen was then whisked back in an underlying flourish and the flourish crossed—*peck, peck*—with the two neat little vertical marks I had come to know in New York. In snatches between his exertions he said, "I have ordered new stationery. . . . It is to say *J. R. de Monteiro . . . Companhia de Navegação do Brasil do Norte. . . . Vapores: S*anta Sophia, Águia, Monte Alegre . . . Sabiá, Massaranduba." At the end he sat expectantly, as if waiting for the recital, like an incantation, to produce that which would dispel whatever it was that afflicted him. When all that happened was that Oliveira bore the letters away—and perhaps that was all he was waiting for—he picked up a clipping from his desk with an air of reluctance. He said, "Here is not good news. I do not know how serious. It is of course what I have been foreseeing, and I have been warning that Greek. He must be thinking that the Massaranduba is like a girl without attractions, who can be kept waiting forever. Now he will learn that he is wrong—that there can be other suitors."

Though I sent a duplicate to Mr. Willet, I still have today the clipping from which Monteiro now read aloud to me the disturbing news.

"Missão ao Massaranduba," the report is still headed; I don't know why I should expect it to have changed—except that everything else has. It states that a company has been organized through the cooperation of the state to exploit the deposits of gold in the valley of the Massaranduba and that negotiations have been initiated for a concession. The boundaries it describes are just those that our own projected concession claimed. It goes on to say that a Senhor Joaquim Waldo is to visit the

river as soon as conditions permit, further that when the elections shall have demonstrated the ever-growing support given by the people to the present Administration of the state, an expedition under the personal leadership of his Excellency the *Interventor, o Coronel* Achille Durondo, will explore the region. The report goes on to say: *"Os objetivos dessa missão científico-comercial-policial são bem conhecidos dos nossos con-cidadaõs patrióticos, porque sua formação se prende a escandalosa evasão do ouro das nossas regioẽs auríferas, energicamente denunciada pela Gazeta do Pará."* The expedition has in mind the smuggling of gold out of our auriferas regions—gold with which "foreign treasuries are stocked because of our criminal carelessness and unforgivable negligence" *("está abarrotando as árcas dos tesouros estrangeiros pela nossa crimi-nosa incúria e negligência imperdoável").*

We sat for a moment in silence, Monteiro gazing absently at me from beneath elevated eyebrows. I asked who Senhor Joaquim Waldo was.

"I am thinking of the political situation here," he said. "This could give discouragement to the *Frente Única*. . . . Joaquim Waldo? I do not know. He is nobody. The question is, what is the money behind him? Or is there any money? Is it a trick by Durondo? A fairy tale to make trouble for me? It would be very easy—and much more clever than he is usually being. Some of the report I know is bluff. There is no chance at present that they can secure a Federal concession."

I felt too sorry for Monteiro to feel much else, except that I was sorrier still for Dona Sophia. Trying to offer some consolation, I suggested that perhaps the *Interventor* had in one way done us a favor: his action might be just what was needed to put a fire under the New Yorkers. This time it would not be a matter of our simply urging the need for haste before rival interests appeared. The rival interests that had now appeared might be fictitious, but there was the news report. The clip-ping, I said, was bound to be convincing.

As a silver lining, this was pretty minute, but so is a spark thrown into tinder. It was enough to ignite Monteiro. Why did he not think of it first thing? he cried incredulously. It was because he had a mind only for the next meeting of the Faction and what was to be said.

So I was dispatched at once back to the house to work out a letter. This meant adding to one I already had in the works. With information supplied by Monteiro, I had been steadily writing up analyses of every subject related to our enterprise: considerations of its financing, the his-

157

tory of other foreign-owned businesses in the state, the commercial out-look for the Amazon Valley generally, the political situation, the past, present and probable future of mining in the region and the legal posi-tion. The uniform purpose, of course, had been to put Monteiro's prop-osition in the most tempting possible light, and I gathered we had not entirely failed in it. Mr. Willet had written that Dr. Xenides had never before seemed so "keen" and had twice telephoned to inquire about the legal report, an unprecedented action. While counseling Mr. Willet to "place no trust in the professions of your Mr. Monteiro, who will see nothing wrong in defrauding every party to this transaction," he had allowed that he was "greatly interested" and was "refining my plans and bringing all into readiness."

My zeal in this correspondence had, I could tell, amazed my father. That came out in, among others, a letter from him which I had found waiting for me in Monteiro's office and read on the way home. He wrote, "Your reporting is a credit both to you and to the dynamics of the business on which you are engaged. I feel more optimistic than ever before about the prospects of the Concession." He did not add—and did not have to—"and about yours, too." In a postscript he wrote that a letter had just arrived from my aunt Lucy containing the following: "Please tell Julian that in a conversation I had with Emily McIlheny it came back to me about the girl whose gravestone he saw. I don't know how it was that I didn't think of it while he was here except that my mind was so full of Sally Lamar's accident that the name Ellen Jandrey didn't make any impression on me." I put the letter down for a moment before going on. I cannot say how, but I knew what it was going to say. "You probably remember this better than I do, but she was the girl Grandfather was so much in love with and who became ill and died when the false report came that he had been killed in action." To this my father had added, "at Cold Harbor, where, indeed, he lay at death's door for so long that hope was virtually abandoned. He was never the same after this time."

I had hoped that Dona Sophia would not be at home, but she was, and I had to break the news to her and show her the clipping. I explained that her husband thought it might be a bluff, and she took it better than I had expected. I also pointed out that it might give us just the leverage we needed on our cautious customers in New York and said I was going to get a letter on the subject off in time for tomorrow's airmail.

158

"You will make it strong, as strong as you can?" she urged. "You know"—she laid a hand on my arm—"how much we count on you. Because of the hope you have brought of the coming of North American capital and enterprise, the Constitutionalist Party has taken heart. Three days after you came—I wonder if you knew—Constitutionalist posters were everywhere put up overnight." I nodded, my eyes on the tread of the stairs upon which my foot rested. I had not missed them. Neither, it seemed probable, had the *Interventor. Vote com o Partido Constitucional!* they bravely clarioned. "This is very significant," she pursued. "It means the Party has determined to risk all. That is what the Massaranduba Concession has done." She fell silent, but I could tell I had not yet been released. In a troubled and more intense voice she exclaimed, "I wish I could be sure you believed in it!" "Believed in it?" I echoed. "Yes. Believed in it. In a way I feel Colonel Durondo is more one of us, not just as a Brazilian but as a believer in what we are striving for, than you are—though you show that you love Brazil. This news proves he believes in the Concession and what it means. In a way I am glad about it."

"I'm doing the best I can," I said, "considering that I'm only an intermediary. I'll keep on doing my best."

"I know that!" she replied, and the simple affirmation fastened my obligations on me more firmly than ever. *"And,"* she went on with a sudden smile, "you must find your pretty little girl, and because she is Brazilian you will believe too, as we believe!" It was said so lightheartedly I could only laugh, but my feet were heavy as I climbed the stairs to my room. It was no wonder she had doubts about the extent of my commitment. The Concession was to me a device for getting me to Brazil and into the interior. For this I was in honor bound to make repayment as best I could. As for what the Concession would mean in operation—I tried not to think.

I read what I had written of the unfinished letter and found it not unprophetic:

> Important events are afoot in the valley of the Massaranduba. There is now a launch plying on the river. The press is carrying articles on the resources of the valley and the opportunities it offers, and I am enclosing two of them. Prospectors are entering the region in increasing numbers, drawn not only by the celebrated deposits of gold in the streambeds but by stories of emeralds and diamonds to be found there. These are all mere individual adventurers, and the information from the young Bragas at the

159

mines, relayed by their mother, is that only the lower reaches of the river have so far been invaded.

From where I sat I could hear now and again a trolley-car start up and rumble away. It sounded like the soul of the drowsy city rising with a yawning groan in an effort to throw off the torpor of early afternoon—unsuccessfully; it would subside again in a diminuendo of protestations. From the top of the orange tree the *bem-ti-vi,* as the Brazilians called the little flycatcher, shrilled insistently. *Ben-chee-vee!* It evidently expected the universe to snap to attention. It flicked its tail in a pet.

But the point is that the reputed wealth of the Massaranduba has captured the imagination of the commercial class, and it is only a question of time before organized interests take over in the area.

The strains of a hymn from the Protestant meetinghouse were now to be heard—right on schedule. It was to be surmised that the congregation was seeking merit through professions of faith in circumstances discouraging to all but strivers-after-salvation driven by a sense of guilt—among whom I included myself.

The collapse of the rubber boom ruined the thriving commerce of the forest provinces when the present generation of businessmen stood at the outset of their careers. It now seems possible that the long reign of adversity is over. It is argued that the output of the Massaranduba mines will have to be converted into other products for export and thus the river, like a heart pumping blood to the extremities of the body, will infuse the whole economy with a new vitality.

I knew how it had been for my grandfather when he had come back to those scenes that had been theirs together, where he would never see her any more. It was as real to me as if there were a memory that leaped the generations.

I have before me a dossier on the subject of a railroad along the Tocantins River. It was given to me in secret by the Commissioner of Railroads (the plural is complimentary—there is only one) in Durondo's government. This project is the dream of his life. I listened to the plans—he could not help seeing—with the keenest interest. Yes! It was evident that I was impressed, if noncommittal.

160

One person's credulity has worked upon another's. Monteiro, who gave the legend of the Massaranduba its initial impetus, has certainly done nothing to inhibit its growth.

That was as far as I had got. As I finished reading, the Protestants launched into their favorite hymn. Its theme was the tune of "How Dry I Am." The congregation returned to the four-note melody of doleful supplication almost as persistently as the kiskadee flycatcher reiterated its three-note, emphatic cry for action. *Ben-chee-vee!* the little bird insisted, cocking its head to listen. . . . *How dry I am* . . . !

I resumed work on the letter.

Since I wrote the foregoing we have received the news set forth in the third of the enclosed clippings, of which I am appending a translation. It is easy to see what this startling development can do to Monteiro's position.

The ghostly form of the bed behind me, with the mosquito-netting that enshrouded it bunched at the ceiling, the musty fragrance of the city that invaded the room, the atmosphere growing heavier with the gathering potentialities of violence incubated in the skies all seemed in harmony and created a mood of powerful if obscure suggestiveness. I wiped my eyelids with my handkerchief and tried not to let perspiration drip on the paper.

He has built everything upon his promise to make good on the Concession. Should it come to be believed that the *Interventor* is going to be ahead of him, acting through an independent instrument, the opposition parties might well lose heart and Colonel Durondo be enabled to consolidate his power, in which case, Dr. Xenides, in my view, might as well forget his concession.

As I pondered how to bring home to Mr. Willet all that hung on this issue, feeling a little dishonest in passing over my own commitment ("Yes, Dona Sophia, you may count upon me to do my best!"), I thought I could hear the meditative mutter of the approaching storm. Of the first rumble I could never be certain; it might have been the shifting of a piece of furniture in another part of the house. But there were ears sharper than mine to distinguish the warning of what was to come. A piercing scream rent the stillness and was followed by terrified maniac

161

cackling. It was the lunatic woman next door. I could never prepare myself for it. Invariably I froze at the first scream and my scalp crept. A crash could be heard, as of a chair sent flying. *"Mamãe!"* someone shouted—a girl. There came a babble of voices and a sound of running as other members of the family rushed to restrain the frenzied creature.

This was the overture of every cloudburst. The poor woman's dementia would not be allayed until she had worn herself out. The screaming broke out anew every minute or two, while the initial grumblings, as of the heavens mulling over their grievances, grew in ominous purpose, until the bombardment of the city began in earnest.

> The whole intricate and soaring edifice of Monteiro's operations rests upon his reputation, and his reputation now rests upon the Concession. The Concession has come to mean the Future to the responsible citizens of this city—the public-spirited, progressive elements. What is needed now is a concrete witness of interest and decision on the part of Dr. Xenides's syndicate. This is essential if the *Interventor's* move is to be countered.

As the rotundities of thunder fell ever nearer, tumbling with hollow impact beneath the horizon, throwing up the fragments of their explosions, the palpable atmosphere settled ever more closely upon the city. One gulped for air like a fish in stagnant water. But the hymn-singers of the Protestant *igreja,* filled with the fear of the Lord, kept doggedly at it. *How dry I aaaaaam!*

A sullen bluff of cloud had reared itself above the western horizon. You felt you were seeing the approach of night in a material mass, a spectral night dark as a tomb but bleached white as bone on the surface of its rolling contours. *Ben-chee-vee!* shrieked the flycatcher, aquiver. Against the nocturnal shades the foliage stood out in an intense yellow-green; over everything was a preternatural brilliance, like stage-lighting, the sheets of sunlight seeming to flare up from the earth to the canopy of darkness overspreading the sky.

> I feel I must get to the Massaranduba ahead of this Joaquim Waldo— if he is really going there. But Mr. Monteiro wants me to wait here until there has been time to hear from you what response Dr. Xenides's syndicate means to make to Durondo's move and then, if it is prepared to take concrete steps, to go first to Manáos and get a commitment from Senhora Braga.

The wind had not yet arisen, but amid the furious breakers of thunder pitching into the city the fronds of the palms were trembling, vibrating to the mounting tension, voicing their anticipation in a dry whisper. Up and down the street, as the city braced itself, shutters could be heard being shut with a bang. I thought I had better see to my own, and removing my shoes from the windowsill, where they had been sunning, pulled to and fastened all but one of the tall, double-jointed leaves. As always happened, I tingled as if an electric current were passing through me and was almost panting from the stimulus to some sort of drastic action.

I returned to the typewriter.

> The consideration I should like to convey is that I find myself at the point of convergence of powerful pressures. The kind of temporizing which has characterized Dr. Xenides's handling of the situation up to now will, if continued, speedily make my position impossible.

The kiskadee had fled before the fury, and the screams of the mad woman had subsided to an exhausted moaning hardly to be made out through the incessant crackling of lightning. The sky, as black and seemingly solid as the roof of a dungeon, was continuously riven with fissures instantly annealed. The congregation down the street was still singing, but their voices, audible between lightning flashes and thunder, betrayed hurry and anxiety. They called up a picture of passengers in a storm at sea gathered, with hands joined, in song in the saloon of a battered ship. Then, as if one mighty wave had engulfed the vessel, the hymn was extinguished under the roar of an avalanche of sound out of the sky. The side of a mountain ripping loose and toppling upon the city could not have struck with a louder crash. In its wake came a chill blast of wind. The city's walls had been breached, and the ravager stormed through. The trees bent before the charging gusts; their foliage, like tattered clothing, black in the half-night, was strung out horizontally. The palms were different. They seemed to exult in the storm's onslaught. They swayed like dancers, hissing as the wind raked their outstretched arms and cackling like the mad woman next door.

> I cannot continue to go about like a living symbol of all that this country lacks and dreams of having, striving to look always as if there were a great deal more to me than meets the eye.

163

I had never written so candidly. Possibly with the vague thought of making myself heard above the tumult of rain that had now begun, I underlined my next statement:

If the syndicate is not prepared to make a commitment, it would be better for Dr. Xenides to say so and for me to clear out.
Respectfully . . .

Of the city beyond the window the nearer houses alone could now be seen, grey forms standing miraculously stable beneath the tempest. The cohorts of the deluge stampeded down the street in veering silvery masses behind the barrage of cannonading. The volleying, I thought, surpassed any I had heard before. The broadsides pounded into the city with the synchronous flash and boom of point-blank firing. In the fractional intervals of respite could be heard the rush of the rain, the splashing cascades of runnels from the housetops, the gurgling of the rivers pouring down the gutters of the street. The world ran torrents from every slope.

In time came the realization that objects on the other side of the avenue could be distinguished. The rain was falling vertically with a hissing patter steadier than the falsetto wailing of its earlier lashing fury. There were nearby claps of thunder, but not as many. These were the rearguard actions of the storm, the main body of which had moved on to carry the unspent violence of its heart across the River Sea. Its vehemence was reduced by distance to the dull rumbling of submarine explosions.

Light broke through in the west. Beyond the nether edge of the black cloud-roof could be glimpsed a radiant realm of pure enchantment. Like a stage uncovered by a curtain lifted stealthily, lest too sudden a disclosure fatally transfix the soul of the mortal beholder, there came gradually into view a celestial treasureland of airy cloud swirls like a land of dreams blown out of mists of gold, like paradise itself.

Then all at once the scene outside the window burst into light. The earth soared with sunlight, glistened with sun and color and newness; the cool and delicately scented air had the freshness of spring-water. On a cornice across the way three sodden *urubus* presented their half-open wings to the sun's warmth in the pose of heraldic eagles. The kiskadee shrieked with the thrill of what it had wrought; it had not

164

known its own powers! From a score of scattered points came the sound that would forever afterward recall to me my thralldom to that tropical land, the cry that to me is as stirring as the challenge pealed by a knight upon the trumpet hung by the portcullis of a despotic ogre's gloomy castle. From near and far it came—the crowing of the cocks.

Once again the sound of singing was to be heard—but this time of a single voice. Beneath the window a youth in dry shirt and trousers was strolling by, his head back, singing to himself:

"A vitória há de ser tua, tua, tua, moreninha prosa;
La no céu a própria lua, lua, lua não é mais formosa. . . ."

(The victory belongs to you, you, you, little chatty brunette;
There in the sky the moon, moon, moon itself is no more beautiful. . . .)

The song was as devoid of content as a bird's, and I had heard it dozens of times, but one of the times was while I was watching the girl by the entrance to the ballroom of the Grande Hotel; and now, standing by the window from which I had thrown back the shutters, I found myself seized by a shakiness I could not control, and before the spell passed it was as if I had malaria.

8

That evening Monteiro spoke eulogistically about Chapeu Virado, its
serenity, the allure of its beach. As it happened, he was going there tomorrow, to attend to the house. I could go with him and, if I found it
attractive, might perhaps like to stay for a while. There was little to be
done here until we received new advices from New York.

Dona Sophia seconded her husband in all this. When everything was
not quite aboveboard, she could be counted upon to betray it by a certain distinctive tilt of her upturned face and a wistful appeal in her eyes.
The plain fact was that they considered me to be running a risk in remaining where I attracted the attention of the *Interventor*.

The upshot was that the next day I accompanied Monteiro by riverboat to the island and remained in his big, bare house on the beach
when he left the next morning. I went with reluctance. I was under no
illusion about the likelihood of finding the girl in Chapeu Virado, as

Dona Sophia had suggested hopefully in private that I might. At the same time I had almost come to despair of finding her in the city. There seemed to be no alternative but to rely on the fate that had brought her before my eyes in the first place. Moreover, I had to allow for the dreadful possibility that if the *Interventor* became seriously provoked by my presence I could be found an undesirable alien and deported.

However it might have been in the dry season, the resort in "winter," as it was called here, was as far removed from the agitations of the capital city as an island in the South Seas, which, indeed, it somewhat resembled. The houses facing the broad, tawny beach stood tenantless but for caretakers who tended the flowers and any cage-birds there might be. Time was as empty as the house I inhabited. The cloud formations of one day, and the intervals of sunshine and rain, were like those of another. There were no newspapers. The few motorcars were old to the point of agelessness. No one was to be seen working. Nothing apparently had to be done on schedule. No one spoke English. The *pensão* to which I sauntered for my meals, served to me outdoors, beneath a lemon tree, offered an unvarying menu of dishes tasting indiscriminately of fish oil. The only person with whom I conversed, in a manner of speaking, was a pretty, black-haired little schoolteacher, in her early twenties, I judged, who lived in the *pensão* with an older, married sister, but even if I had been vulnerable to distraction from that quarter I should have been preserved from it by the strict system of chaperonage prevailing and the fact that the girl's speech, bubbling up and down the scale in a rain of musical vowel sounds, made my difficulties with Portuguese insurmountable.

I walked for miles on the beach, turning over with a bare foot the seeds as big as oranges or grapefruit that perhaps weeks before in the Mato Grosso had fallen into waters known only to savages. In the expanse of the bay could be seen the curvature of the earth; the filament of distant islands stood clear of the horizon of the water in the refraction of the light. The solitude was immense. One went unobserved except by birds—always the same birds in the same places—and by little fishes in the shallows with heads half out of water, taking in the scene above the surface and below through bifocal eyes. Spending two or three hours a day swimming in the river, which was perfectly neutral in temperature, stretched out in a hammock on the porch at night with the cool breeze off the water on my undersides, I had a sensation of being afloat in existence, of weightlessness. I was possessed by an indescribable exhilaration. I must have been lonely—probably very much so, for I was at a time of life when the capacity for loneliness is great—but in such solitude, in so vast a realm, loneliness can have a quality of universality. It is a property you share with the cosmos itself, which makes you one with it and all it contains, the clouds at sunrise and the trees in the wind. I felt very close to the girl, permeated by her, as if she were all about me. The longing that filled my soul made me know what no one else knew—for my awareness, my apprehension, it seemed to me, had no bounds. I felt an overpowering need to give substance to what filled my mind and heart —in acknowledgment of what she conveyed to me, in testimony to the communication that, now that I was separated from the clamor that had dulled my senses, I was sure passed from her to me. I had a facility— meager enough—in only one form of expression. So I drew. I sat on logs and sketched the vistas of clouds and water, the empty houses behind the dazzling expanse of beach, the palms in the breeze. When the light outdoors was overpowering, I retreated to the house with a collection of objects from the river—seed-pods, driftwood, plants—and sketched them, or a little Caboclo boy who had attached himself to me. I sat at a table in the front room of the house, facing the bay with the blinds drawn on the windward side and no sound to be heard but the inrush and hissing fade-away of the waves, the crackle of palm leaves and the creaking of a pair of blue-and-yellow macaws chained to a perch in the yard. I sketched the little schoolteacher while she sang the sad, ironic *"Canção do Cabóclo."*

As sure as I had felt up to then that I had nothing to lose by remaining on the island, I awoke on the morning of the eighth day with the certain knowledge that I must take the next boat back to the city. There was no question about it in my mind. *The next boat:* the words were actually what waked me up.

As it happened, I should have had to go back whatever my inner counselings. Two letters brought by Emile, one from my father, one from Mr. Willet, which took me with a confusing and disheartening crash back to the world I had succeeded in putting out of my head, saw to that. At first, however, I had put them aside unopened while I prepared to reply at length to Emile's *pro-forma* inquiry as to how I liked living on the island. My casualness was shocking even to Emile.

"Look, Julian," he said, "João says this letter is very urgent."

"Oh." Of course, I recalled that I had written reporting the advent of competitors upon the scene. Monteiro would have taken Mr. Willet's letter to convey Dr. Xenides's response.

That was what I thought at first too, for when I had sufficiently marshaled my wits I saw that it had been written after the arrival of my letter. Proceeding, however—and I forced myself to read it word for word so that I should understand what it said—I saw that Mr. Willet had written it before hearing what Dr. Xenides meant to do about the new development. Mr. Willet seemed to feel there was no cause for worry. Events in New York were moving at last. The tone of his letter, unless I was misreading it, was one of pronounced satisfaction. Dr. Xenides had come forth with the identities of the men composing his syndicate. (I made myself recognize that this was a great and wonderful thing.) They included the officers of the Portalegre Corporation. (This was the company that had been formed to drill for oil in the central Amazon basin and had allowed the concession granted it to lapse.) It was, said Mr. Willet, the company that would take up the Massaranduba Concession, and he was confident from what he had learned from Dr. Xenides that there would be no repetition of the earlier delinquency. If, he wrote, the Concession measured up to my expectations of it—and he had no reason to doubt that it would—the stockholders of the Corporation, who had so far received not a cent on their investment, would have cause for thanksgiving indeed.

I read my father's letter over twice. It gave me the feeling of having been plunged into ice-water. He wrote that, impressed by all I had written about the Massaranduba and by the assurances contained in the documentation I had provided, he had invested heavily in Portalegre stock. He had put into it the proceeds of a mortgage he had taken out on the Georgia property. He had, of course, been able to buy at an extremely favorable price inasmuch as word of the Portalegre Corporation's new interest had not yet got out. What gains the stock might make once production was under way and the potentialities began to be generally grasped there was, of course, no foretelling, but naturally, he had the highest hopes. Mr. Willet was himself taking a bit of a flyer. My father felt that I would be stimulated and encouraged to know of all he and I now had at stake in the undertaking and of the very great credit that would be mine if all worked out as we might trust it would.

When I had had time to think about it, I could see that it was just as well that I was at Chapeu Virado when this letter came. Had Monteiro

169

been present when I read it, he would have perceived at once the measure of my consternation and consequently the extent by which I fell short of whole-souled belief in the Concession, the master-mistress of his fortunes, the vanguard of the future greatness of north Brazil. But . . . My God, I thought, we're in it now! In a dim way I connected this further envelopment of my life by the Concession with the past week's demonstration of how easily I could forget it; an arm had shot out and yanked me back. I could see no escape—other, that is, than in the successful outcome of what we were engaged in. What it was going to take, concretely, to satisfy the terms of my indenture was more than I cared to dwell upon just then; there would be ample occasion for that later.

"Emile," I said, "we've got the rest of the day here. Why don't we go out in *Felicidade?* You remember those big fish you told me about?"

He was conspicuously startled that I should propose such a thing. "Now? At *this* time?" He essayed an indulgent smile. "You should know that *this* time—and that is to say near the end of the winter—that *this* time is of *all* times the worst for fishing. It is the most hopeless! And do you know why? For a very good reason." He tamped his cigarette out in an ashtray, with such gentle taps that it took some time. "For the best possible reason. Simply, the fish are not present! They have gone away. . . . Also, I cannot take responsibility," he added with more resolution. "In this season, as is well known, there are sudden and violent storms."

So I did not get out in the boat.

Emile's concern for my safety was further aroused by my impending return to the city. He saw I had to go, but he mourned over it. The city was on the verge of revolution. As a marked man himself in the eyes of the regime, he could not bring himself to accompany me. By evening, however, as I had anticipated, he was even more unable to bring himself to remain on the island. The bites of the insects and the glare of the sun had given him a very severe headache. This was made known to me when before dinner, which we had together, he produced a bottle of pills and downed two of them with a gulp of water, looking at me supplicatingly over the glass.

To be on hand in case the bus came by on schedule we had to be out of bed at half past four in the morning. The night was still of an impenetrable blackness when we took our position beside the road. The

170

foliage dripped from the night's rain, the drops crashing down through the trees swallowed up in the blackness.

The bus came pushing a feeble patch of illumination ahead of it from its single operative headlamp. Inside it made me think of an old, decrepit, dimly-lighted one-room schoolhouse. It lurched and bounced through the darkness. The driver was totally without a nose and wore glasses fitted with a special band across his forehead to hold them in place above his nostrils.

There was a village at the terminus—Mosqueiro—with streetlamps that cast a dim yellow light upon a single row of plaster houses. A stronger light poured from an open market, where already there was a crowd. The presence of the river was communicated by an aquatic smell in the air, which was cool and damp. In the profundity of the tropical night I was extraordinarily aware of the strangeness of being where I was. There are times when one experiences a hunger of the consciousness, and this was such a time. Walking down the pier, upon which our footfalls had a hollow, muffled report, was a little like walking down the aisle of a darkened theater before the curtain rises—only the theater was the whole pre-dawn world.

The vessel was as large as the *gaiolas* that made voyages of a thousand miles, but no more than fifteen other passengers were to be seen, this being the slack season. The bar from which refreshments were meant to be served was still closed. By the time it had opened and coffee been produced, along with a spherical, glutinous roll as difficult to disengage the teeth from as a piece of caramel candy, the darkness had acquired a hint of translucency, the character of green glass so thick as to be almost black.

The eastern sky began to turn blue while our ship still lay at her berth. It was a shade so deep you were amazed by the amount of light that came from it. The beach stood out white, and against it the vultures standing motionless were very black. I remarked to Emile that I could never understand how it was that, invariably, the vultures went to roost at night in the trees and awoke with first light on the beach. Emile only shook his head; he would, I took it, have expected no better.

By the time our moorings were cast off, the foliage of the trees stood out in its true shade of green, but beneath it, as if the leafy contours were the surface of a pastureland, a subterranean gloom lingered in

171

which the pale houses and puddled streets were like objects laid open to view in a cut-away section of a mine. The progress of the dawn, very nearly as portentous, it seemed to me, as the original process of creation, was to the other passengers routine. Turning their backs upon it, they had settled down indifferently to a wait of several hours.

One of the passengers, to whom Emile called my attention with a nudge, had four or five others grouped around him. A middle-aged man with a rough yellow skin drawn tight over his skull, he sat slightly bent over, his elbows pressed against his sides, never moving and never pausing in his speech, which had a harsh, acid precision. Drawing me aside, Emile told me that years before he had caught his wife in the arms of another man and had driven her out of the house with a horsewhip. Now his one satisfaction was talking. He made the round trip three or four times a week and he talked the entire time. Because he was very rich, Emile explained—if it was an explanation—other people had to listen. Apart from the rest, standing farther forward by the railing, was the village priest, sharp-featured, sunken-cheeked. My eyes strayed past him, but I found that, though the impression created on me was markedly disagreeable, I had to look back. There was a hard glint in the cleric's eye and his lips were pursed in a tight, crooked half-smile denoting, I thought, little merriment. He faced into the wind, stationary as a bird-dog, his black vestments flapping behind him.

Under the light that now soared from beneath the rim of the earth, the river through which we were coursing was beginning to glow with ethereal pinks and blues. The fishing fleet was all around us. The scattered boats, facing all in one direction as they sailed seaward before an exceptional downriver wind, had the air of taking part in observances fitting to the scene's character of a celestial prologue. They cantered dreamily over the waves under their winglike sails. On the foredeck, in most cases, a few dark figures were huddled over a pot of fire while another, cowled, crouched over the tiller in the stern.

Another *gaiola* had appeared upriver of us, end on, directly ahead. Still with her lights on, as ours were too, closing the gap with our combined rates of speed, she bore down upon us fast, gaining rapidly in stature. She was a grey vessel of the Government-owned Amazon Steamship Company, with the characteristic tall, proud, questing appearance of a river-steamer viewed from the fore. One of the smaller vessels of her fleet, she was, I guessed, *Boa Vista,* on the Manáos run . . . and so she

172

proved to be when she came abreast of us and I could read the brass letters of her name.

As she passed at a distance of a hundred feet or so, my eye traveled along her upper deck past the sprinkling of passengers lined up along the rail to watch us go by and wave at acquaintances, as our own passengers were doing. Near the stern my attention was caught by a girl in a white dress separated from the others. She stood pressed against the side of the cabin, her head back, resting upon it. Her dark hair was shoulder-length. With a sensation I now recall as one of sudden, paralyzing constriction, of terror and ecstasy, I saw that it was she. I do not know what my thoughts were in that first instant; what would one's thoughts be if the earth ceased abruptly to revolve, if time stopped? Then I saw—I was sure I saw—that she was looking at me. Her head had come forward, she had made an imperceptible movement, a mere shifting of weight, away from the cabin wall. But the ships were rushing past each other. With a clutch of panic and agony at my heart I took off down the deck, not to be left behind. "Emile!" I yelled as I ran. (Emile had gone to get more coffee.) My sprint carried me behind the backs of the other passengers standing at the edge of the deck, and one of them I almost knocked down; but I could not keep up. Before I had reached the stern, the other ship commenced to swerve away from us. I came to a halt to watch as the girl, her eyes still on me—as again I was sure—her hand raised to her forehead, was taken from view. I had to stand, grasping the rail as one would the bars of a prison, and see *Boa Vista* bear her away. I wheeled upon Emile when I saw his startled face beside me. The words were formed in my throat to tell him to demand of the Captain that we put about and take after the retreating *Boa Vista,* but I realized in time to prevent their tumbling pell-mell out that I should be thought crazy.

A weight of despair sank upon me. At the end of a curved and narrowing wake the tall grey form, already cruelly diminished by distance, was taking her into the limitless reaches of the interior, where a single human being was as a fly in space. I do not know how long it was before I remembered, or seemed to remember, that Emile had asked me what the matter was.

Still straining to see across the water, I said, "I saw someone in the other ship I recognized, and I hoped you could tell me . . ."

Turning to look at him, I saw concern and especially embarrassment

173

in his face. My conduct had been unbelievable. In his country it was impermissible even to raise one's voice.

". . . who it was."

He nodded. A determinedly carefree expression appeared upon his face. He had put my lapse behind us. He said, "I will go and arrange about the coffee—to have it brought to us where we were sitting."

"The ticket office!" I cried joyfully. There was dismay in Emile's face; all was beginning again! I clapped my hand on his shoulder. "Never mind," I said. "Yes, do go! Let's have some coffee." Of course! There would be the passenger manifest at the Amazon Steamship Company's offices! She would be listed on it, along with her destination. I had only to see the list. The problem of knowing which name was hers did not bother me, not simply because there could not be more than two or three unmarried girls aboard (and I believe anyone would have known for certain she was nothing else), but because her name would be intrinsically different from every other on the list; it was unthinkable that in my eyes her name would not stand out from all the rest.

I made my way forward. I can imagine that I was followed by severely disapproving—even if less than astonished—eyes; no one who knew the *Norte-Americanos* either from local examples or from the motion pictures sent down from the United States had cause for surprise at finding one of them drunk at dawn. However, I was not conscious of the other passengers—or of any but one of them. One there was that even in my intense preoccupation I could not be oblivious of. When I got back to the foredeck the priest brought me up with a look that went directly to whatever primitive sixth sense it is we possess. It caused me to turn and confront him. I thought he was going to speak—to spit out a malediction. I had never been stared at with such venom. The eyes in the white face were black with it. It went far beyond the condemnation a mere inebriate would have occasioned. And he could see I was not that. My gaze was as steady as his own, and I doubt that it yielded much to his in malevolence. A warmth that must have meant the blood had rushed to my face had risen up in me. The question of what the issue was between us had no place in my thoughts. Had my soul's salvation depended upon it, my determination not to be the first to disengage from the interlocking of our eyes could not have been greater.

Upon Emile's return the priest looked away. His lips were compressed as they had been when I first saw him, his eyes sharp with a hard and gloating light, as I took it to be. I continued staring until I was satisfied that he had, as it were, quit the field. Yet, though I turned my back upon him, it was not so easy to clear my mind of him. The black of his habit, like a shade impressed upon the retina of my eyes, remained to cast a shadow over the picture I had of the girl and over the light-struck scene itself. Upon this the sun had now come up, striking the ship broadside with such power that the deckhands who had been making the rounds to turn the lights off went straight on to lower canvas shades against its consuming blaze.

A slim figure, set apart, leaning against the side of the cabin, hands behind hips, un-self-conscious, alert, observant—and undemanding. . . . But I could not have known that. And the disturbing quality the figure had for me of being backed against a wall in the full connotation of that image could only have been imagination building impulsively on an accident of posture. I closed my eyes. I saw the brown hair tumbling to break like a wave between the narrow shoulders, the eyes large and dark in the oval of the young face, remembering from our first encounter how they could be as quick as they were soft, and how the delicate modeling of the face brought out the cheekbones. I held onto this impression, confirming the likeness I had of her feature by feature, fixing it in my mind, establishing its reality beyond question. I was jealously, fiercely possessive of it, made so by the threat that the quality of having actually happened would be stolen from it. I knew how that which comes in answer to your heart's desire is by its very nature suspect. The sheer longing to believe it makes you doubt it. Mankind's experience with the supremely desirable puts an axiom in your hands with which to destroy it: *it is too good to be true,* and you talk yourself out of it. Yet I had seen her. And ahead of me, nearer with each revolution of the ship's screws, was the concrete certainty of the passenger manifest. I need not let myself be bothered by the shadow that would not be dispelled from my outlook—a kind of clammy shadow I associated with the sinister figure of that monk. The atmosphere of the bus ride through the dark of the early morning had made me oversusceptible to suggestion. Maybe even going so long without breakfast had something to do with it.

For the first time I was struck by the full oddity of the priest's having glared at me as he had, as by something to be extremely puzzled by. Or had he? Had I, with nerves more overwrought, an imagination more dislocated by the passing of *Boa Vista* than I had realized, read into a look of mere annoyance a virulence that was not there? I turned to have another glance at him and . . . my scalp crawled. There was no priest there! The deck where I had seen him standing was empty.

I stumbled to my feet. There was no such person anywhere to be seen. "That priest!" I cried to Emile. "Didn't you see a priest? Wasn't there a priest here a few minutes ago?"

"Yes! He has just left! He went inside!" Emile spoke as one under dire threat, frantically exonerating himself of guilt. From the look that had leaped to his eyes I could tell what kind of edge my voice must have had.

"Oh. I see." I dropped back into my chair. "Forgive me. I don't know what got into me. . . . I think I dropped off to sleep and had a dream."

"Father Fidelio, that is who it was," said Emile nervously. "He is not well liked." He fiddled with a button on his shirt-front. "He is very severe. I think he is in trouble with the diocese. You could say he is in exile in Mosqueiro."

I pressed my hands to my face in the wake of a second wave of relief. It had not all been my imagination. The priest was a fanatic. He had doubtless marked me for a heretic. There was no more to it than that.

"When I was a child," Emile pursued, settling back in his chair, "it was believed that I was destined for holy orders. I was much by myself. . . ."

I am afraid I soon lost the thread of his reminiscence.

On disembarking I bade Emile a quick good-bye and hurried directly to the office of the Amazon Steamship Company, arriving just as it was opening. The clerk said *certamente* I could see the list of passengers of *Boa Vista.* He walked off to a desk at the back of the room and addressed its occupant, an older man with a plump face and satiny skin. The latter gazed at me momentarily and spoke a few words to the counter-clerk, who thereupon returned empty-handed. The manifest was not available. He was sorry. It was not in the office.

Having to translate what he said and go over it in my mind to make sure I had got it correctly, I was saved from some wild accusation provoked by the chimera—all at once sprung to life again—of a comprehensive plot to keep me from knowledge of the girl.

"Não está aqui?" I repeated under tight self-control. It was not in the office? Where was it, then? *"E onde está, então?"*

It was with the police, he said, looking me directly in the eye. He drummed on the counter with his fingers.

Then could he please tell me, I inquired in my halting way, if among the passengers . . . there was a young girl who—

He interrupted with an energetic reply of which I understood only the words for "no information" and the tone of finality.

I glanced around the office and had the impression, very likely the illusion, of faces quickly averted, work resumed. The clerk waited. I must have shown that I did not mean to be so easily put off, but suddenly I had only a desire to get out of the place, and I left him without another word.

After I had gone a few paces I slowed to a halt, not knowing what direction to take, where to turn. The ordinariness of the concerns that sent others around me on their way struck me with very great force, as something to be marveled at and envied. I was capable of believing that the inhabitants of the city had without need of collusion, as a matter of unwitting instinct, closed ranks to quarantine one in whom they had detected some mark of irregularity of thought or purpose, of intangible traffic in contraband. I was half desperately alarmed, half dangerously belligerent. What was I going to do? What I must not do was go find the priest and seize him by the throat, or the satiny-faced official of the Amazon Steamship Company either. It would only satisfy them that I was insane and that they were right in doing what they did not know they were doing, or at least why they were doing it.

I would go see Monteiro; that was what I was going to do. He would be expecting me impatiently, and there would be difficult explanations if I did not soon appear. But that was not what I had in mind. Monteiro, in a manner of speaking, was a loose end in the skein, one with which a commencement could be made in the unraveling of it. I did not actually reason this way; that was simply the shape things took in my head.

Monteiro was standing by the window looking out when I appeared. It seemed that he had been doing nothing at all, which was unheard of. It occurred to me that he had simply been waiting for me. The smile with which he greeted me, as was characteristic, seemed uneasy and uncomfortable. (Situations in which a degree of demonstrativeness would be in order were likely to embarrass Monteiro.)

"I got the letter," I said, holding it up. It was, I knew, what he was in-

177

terested in, and all he was interested in, at the moment. "I'm sorry to say it was written before Mr. Willet had had a chance to hear from Dr. Xenides about any plans the syndicate might have to meet the new competition. So there's nothing on that score." The delivery of this statement with faultless lucidity struck me, in the circumstances, as an intellectual achievement of the first rank. "However, I think you'll like what it does say." I read aloud, altogether mechanically and—for I had to hear myself above the outcries inside me from what truly and so terribly concerned me—probably sounding like a herald on the stage proclaiming from a scroll, what Mr. Willet had written about the projected revival of the Portalegre Corporation as the concessionaire in the Massaranduba.

Monteiro attempted no concealment of his surprise at this disclosure. "I see," he said slowly. "The Portalegre Corporation! And with the same officers! So we at last know who these illustrious gentlemen are!" His eyes grew round, he drew in his underlip.

I gathered that he wished to mull this over before hearing any more. We sat in silence for a time, Monteiro unblinkingly.

I was wondering whether I should come right out and ask him if anyone with whom he stood in well among the police could gain access to that passenger manifest when he put to me a question that utterly dumbfounded me.

"Do you know who embarked this morning on the *Boa Vista?*"

I had to tell myself that I had surely not been deceived, that it was actually he and not I who had spoken. I was too stunned even to gape.

"Joaquim Waldo!" he pronounced.

"Who?"

"Joaquim Waldo. Who represents the new interests in the Massaranduba! With whom Durondo is dealing! The Government is keeping his departure very quiet. I do not know why. I have heard only because I make it my business to be informed of such things." If there was anything out of the ordinary in my face, he did not appear to notice it. I had suffered in quick succession a crashing disappointment and a soaring relief. "It is very peculiar about this secrecy," he went on. "I put myself in the place of Durondo, and I think if I am sending Senhor Waldo to the Massaranduba, I would like to have this known, to embarrass Dr. Monteiro. Or perhaps I would not. Perhaps I would prefer to keep back the information, to announce it later for effect."

178

"Is there," I asked, "any way by which you could have *Boa Vista*'s passenger manifest examined?" I was almost lighthearted at having learned the mundane reason for my having been refused access to it.

Monteiro shook his head. "If Durondo does not wish it known where he is going, there can be no such easy way to find out. The Captain of the *Boa Vista* himself does not know where Senhor Waldo is going. He is the source of my information—through Comandante Soldano of the *Sabiá*. I have asked myself if it could be he is going to Manáos. The purpose would perhaps be to obtain a commitment from Senhora Braga." He looked at me as if he expected me to offer my opinion, but I knew from experience that he did not. "I am wondering if we have not waited long enough for you to go to Manáos, Julian."

I had already made up my mind about that, but I deemed it prudent to appear to weigh carefully the alternatives. In due course I signified my concurrence, and we turned to the practical aspects.

Sabiá would be leaving in two or three days. Mr. Willet would be apprized at once of what we were planning, and the hope was that by the time I arrived in Manáos, I should have received authorization by radio telegram to offer Senhora Braga an attractive sum for an option to buy. In any case, my purpose would be to obtain a power of attorney from her—and later one from her sons—enabling Monteiro to sell their property. Monteiro would notify her that I was on my way, to prevent her from coming to any precipitate agreement with Joaquim Waldo.

At the end of our discussion, which was very one-sided, Monteiro reverted to the subject of the Portalegre Corporation's re-entry into the scene. The concern did not have a good name here because of its performance in Amazonas, but its having once been so remiss, the reasonable assumption would be that it would make amends and this time carry out its purposes. Certainly the development could be presented in that light. Moreover, there was the advantage of having an existing organization ready to operate. It argued a disposition to action. Such was Monteiro's reasoning, and he professed himself very satisfied.

I said I was glad to hear it and told him, somewhat offhandedly, that which I had been so dismayed to hear of twenty-four hours earlier and had been ready to lay at his door, however unfairly: to wit, that as of the past week the Tates were into Portalegre up to their necks—though that was not quite how I put it.

For the second time Monteiro betrayed surprise, and a good deal more

179

than I had expected. This time, I could tell, he was displeased with himself for doing so. Clearly uncertain what face to put upon it until he had had a chance to think it over, he dropped his eyes and, frowning, nodded brusquely: of course, of course; busy as he was, he had been able to foresee this. He said, "I was informed by your father in the past that this was his plan. To invest substantially in this enterprise when it had reached a certain stage." He could not resist cutting his eyes over at me, or keep from them a telltale glitter. Quite as if he had put it into words, I knew that the Concession had gained prestige in his eyes—and the Tates had lost.

When, an hour later, I opened the door of the house on the Avenida da Independência, I found myself face to face with Dona Sophia. She had seen the taxicab arrive and was meeting me halfway. Emile had been there with an alarming report of my behavior. She had, however, reached her own conclusions.

"You saw the girl of yours on the ship that was passing."

"Yes, I did."

Over a six-hour-late breakfast I told her how it had been. To be able to explain it to an attentive and sympathetic listener with whom I was not self-conscious was like being given a chance to defend oneself against charges of indefinable wrongdoing brought by an array of denunciatory witnesses. I do not know why it should have seemed like that to me, but it did. And once started talking I could not stop. For a week I had lived virtually incommunicado, but it appeared that the sound of the voice for which I most hungered was the sound of my own. Dona Sophia had to remind me to eat. I was a gusher that could not be capped. Everything came out that had happened since I left.

"This is heroic," she said simply when I told her about the pledging of our family's future to the Massaranduba, and the spare characterization, like the inscription on a battlefield monument to valor beyond words, caused me for just that one time to falter in my speech. Moved by her presence, I had, as it were, dropped the information at her feet in passing, with a casualness bespeaking modesty, as a disclosure of something than which the Tates could do no less. Remembering, again, the consternation and anger with which I had received the information myself the day before, I moved on quickly to another subject.

For the rest, she listened gravely, the only change in her expression being that it grew a shade more troubled as I proceeded. I tried not to sound too deeply involved in what I was narrating where it concerned the girl, but I seemed unable fully to control the words that poured from me. When I came to my visit to the steamship office, I made no bones about my concern. I told her I was worried in view of the construction I now realized the authorities were likely to put upon it.

She said she did not see that it could do much harm. When I had finished, having come up to the present, and fell silent, suddenly abashed at how much I had made of my concerns, she asked what I was going to do. What *was* I going to do? I repeated. I meant to make inquiries at every port of call up the river on my way to Manáos, but it was doubtful how far they would get me.

"Comandante Soldano of the *Sabiá* might have heard something about her as well as about Senhor . . . that man—Waldo," she said. "Why don't you ask João to speak to him? Also to consider if there is someone who could have a chance to see the list of passengers, if anything could be learned about *her* from it."

"It's a subject I can't talk about with anyone but you."

Dropping her eyes, she composed her features and made a small throat-clearing sound. "I know João loves to tease about affairs of the heart. It is his great sport. He could not help making a little fun with you after the dance, when I . . . when I 'let the cat out of the bag' by asking about the girl's father, whether he could recognize him from what you said. It was because he likes you. But this time I think he would not tease." She stood up, and as I made to follow her she motioned me back. "You stay here. I have not finished with you."

She was gone from the room for a moment, and when she returned it was with a thermometer.

"All women are the same. They—"

Having dealt me a silencing thrust with the instrument, she contemplated me with clinical impersonality. "Every man needs to be in love. By himself he is very inadequate, only half finished. But I do not know why you have to make it so difficult for yourself. There are so many appetizing little girls! I do not know whether to hope that you find this girl or to hope that you do not." She moved to the window and stood looking out. After a space she consulted her watch, came back and removed the thermometer. Returning to the window with it, she reported, "Thirty-eight degrees."

"At that temperature I ought to keep indefinitely."

"You have exactly one degree of fever—in Centigrade. This may mean nothing, but it may also mean trouble. You are to stay in the house and be watched."

It was a welcome sentence. At noon I was to have left to attend a Rotary Club lunch at the Commercial Club with Monteiro.

Early in the evening (which found me with my temperature back at a wholesome thirty-seven degrees) Dona Sophia raised with her husband the questions she had suggested I ask—not sparing my presence. "Truly, João," she finished, "we must—" She seemed to cast about for the right words. These, I judged, he supplied with a phrase in Portuguese. "Yes, get to the bottom of it," she said.

A protracted shaking of the head greeted this. "I was placing my hope on the schoolteacher in Chapeu Virado," he said lugubriously. "I was telling Julian he must explain he has learned to love her only from hearing what I have said about her. In that way he is improving the opportunity for both of us."

In part relieved at the tack Monteiro had taken, I reminded him of the barriers of language and chaperonage, but he waved them away. "These things only make it more interesting. Once when a young man I had this problem of the chaperone, and do you know? She is also the older sister—but a widow. I tell her she is really the one I love—in her own hearing only, of course—and we arrange an assignation. Then when she is going to it, I meet the younger sister by arrangement, and we are alone together at last."

"João, this is serious."

"*Of* course! Only I am wondering how far on the way to Manáos Julian will go if he is learning that the girl lives on a *fazenda* out from Monte Alegre or Itacoatiara. But I will discover what is to be known." Turning to me, he said, "And about the language. You have forgotten what I have told you about the opportunity for accidentally saying very daring things—without knowing what you are saying? You remember. There is the expression when you are saying good-bye to a girl in the evening, *Sonha de mim,* dream of me. So you would say by mistake, *Sonha comigo,* dream *with* [*wiss*] me, that is, sleeping with me! There is nothing so advantageous with a girl as talking to her in a language you are imperfectly understanding."

What inquiries Monteiro made the next day, and with what success, I did not have a chance to hear.

182

I spent most of the morning transcribing into more authoritative English, for New York, a collection of notes Monteiro had made on a variety of considerations. By eleven o'clock I had come to the end of them and to the end, too, of my ability to sit still any longer, and I set out for a walk.

I took a direction out the Avenida da Independência. I passed the end of the trolley-car line and turned into a dirt road. This led, I found, to a quadrangle of yellow buildings, of plaster, rather imposing to be so set apart, secreted, as it were, in a wooded area. There was no one to be seen among them, and the quiet was disturbing. Then I recalled having heard that the leprosery was out this way. I quickened my pace, disliking myself for my haste, ashamed of myself, but hurrying nonetheless to get past it. Behind me, at some distance, a motorcar headed toward the hospital had pulled up, apparently waiting for me to pass before entering the grounds. It brought relatives of an inmate, I surmised, who because of the shame associated with the disease sought to avoid being seen, and this diffidence made me feel all the worse on the score of my good fortune in life, my health and my callousness.

I turned a bend in the road with relief. Then before long I found myself back on the outskirts of the city and in front of a tiny café over the door of which, across the façade of the building that housed it, was the surprisingly pious legend in decorative lettering, DEUS TE GUARDE. I went in and sat at one of the two tables for a thimble of coffee. After bringing it the proprietor lingered and in a manner markedly cautious and sly, leading me to wonder if the house were prepared to cater to other appetites ("God help you" could be read in more than once sense), put a direct question to me: was I a Protestant? Very uncertain as to what this was leading, I said I was. (I was not a Catholic, anyhow.) Thereupon he strode to the door, cupped his hands and yelled down the block of mud-walled houses, *"Vem par' aqui! Um Protestante!"* He stood there a moment to judge the effect of his words and then, evidently satisfied, returned with a smiling and eager face—I was very glad to observe. In a trice a crowd had formed in the café around the proprietor and his prize. It gave me an idea of the isolation of an outlying section such as this that a Protestant should have excited so much curiosity. There was no sound in the crowd apart from some jostling for front-line positions as the proprietor engaged me boldly in conversation. From what country did I come? Did I like Brazil? Had I a wife and children? Was I going to remain in Brazil? Was it a camera I was carrying? Mouths ajar, the bystanders followed the interlocutory ball back and forth like spectators at a tennis match. My host, it was plain to see, was establishing a lifelong reputation for *savoir-faire*.

I became aware that the attention of the crowd and even of the proprietor was being distracted by events in progress behind their backs. It seemed surprising that another sensation, equal to that which I had created, should follow so hard upon the first, and I may even have been a bit piqued. The sound of a motor could be heard from the street. The proprietor rose and went forward, while those who stood in the way fell back. Through the opening I recognized the car as the one that had been behind me at the leprosery. I also recognized the uniformed figure descending heavily from the back seat as the bull-proportioned agent of the regime who had shown such interest in me in the past. It was one of those moments at which, as when the first chill wind of autumn raises the specter of winter, the climate of existence is transformed.

Declining to notice the ready, attentive host in the doorway, the new arrival stood beside the car, leaning against it and gazing indifferently up the street. Since nothing in my direction seemed to interest him, I managed to hope briefly that a mission unconnected with me had brought him to this precinct. Reason reasserting itself, and with it coming the decision that there was no point in delaying the encounter, I stood up, deposited a coin on the table for my coffee and pressed forward through the crowd, which had closed in again.

He was smartly attired, this time, in the uniform of a noncommissioned officer of the *Milícia Estadual,* with black patent-leather belt, holster and automatic. He brought his heavy-lidded, protuberant eyes around to rest on me without much change of expression and placed his hand on the open door of the car.

"*O Sargento está me esperando?*" I asked coldly, put on my mettle as an American in the presence of a foreign audience.

"*'Sou enviado de sua Excelência, o Interventor.*"

A groan, half gasp, of ecstasy, escaped the ring of onlookers. They were beholding one in whom the *Interventor êle mesmo* interested himself.

I waited.

Laboriously and distastefully he said in English, "You are expected at the Palace." It was evidently a memorized phrase. His eyes were fixed upon my throat.

"Agora?" Now?

"Agora." He spoke as if with contempt for the function of speech.

In the silence that followed, the chauffeur shifted his position and looked sidewise at me. The movement might have been the first step in reaching for his gun or debouching from the car. His small, bony head and big ears, and the bagginess of his uniform on his scrawny frame, could have been pathetically comic, but in the circumstances called up a picture of a mental defective unaccountable for his actions. The crowd was in a state of intense anticipation. Across from me a young woman with eyes sparkling pressed up against her man, as if she were watching a motion-picture thriller.

Unless I were prepared to make a break for it, I could see that there was but one thing for me to do. I got in the car.

We took off with a lurch and a rush. I supposed because speed was a prerogative of an official car the reason for our speeding was that prestige required it. However, it made me feel like a long-wanted criminal whose captors could not wait to turn him in. Worse than that, it made me apprehensive for my life. The monkey at the wheel was too small to handle the machine and was incompetent on top of that. I grimaced at the thought of the pointlessness of dying as an incident to the self-gratification of an undersized degenerate.

I took out a pack of cigarettes, started automatically to pass it to my fellow passenger and as quickly thought better of it. To my annoyance, I could see that neither the impulse nor the reconsideration had been missed. While I crouched to light my cigarette, he leaned toward the side of the car and spat.

"I wonder why you didn't pick me up when you first saw me, by the leper hospital," I said in English, crossly.

With his habitual deliberateness he reached around and scratched himself behind the shoulder. *"Não entendo nada,"* he said, evincing no great desire to comprehend. He had evidently forgotten his English.

"You probably regard speech as an activity suitable only for women and children." I did not bother to address the remark in his direction, or he to acknowledge it.

It seemed highly unlikely that I should be thrown in jail or anything like that. What I foresaw—if we arrived alive at our destination—was humiliation and ignominy. To the charges that could legitimately be brought against me there was simply no defense. . . . Or was there per-

185

haps something? I tried telling myself that what I had done, all my deep embroilment in opposition politics, was for the sole and noble object of helping restore parliamentary government to a long-suffering people. I saw myself standing erect and essentially invulnerable in the dock, but the picture was instantly eradicated by another stab of nausea, like an injection of poison in my middle. To be made to look like a chastised schoolboy, then to be hustled out of the country—that was what I had to look forward to. Damn Monteiro, I thought.

The driver slackened speed a little on the Avenida da Independência, into which we had turned—for reasons of policy or delicacy or by chance —only after we had passed the block on which the Monteiros lived. How well I knew the vista, with its still rivers of shade from which rose the lines of mangoes with whitewashed trunks, the white glare of sunshine, the rich shades of blue, red, yellow and pink of the houses, all contrasting and conflicting to give the panorama the vibrant but static vitality of a painting! What happiness it had been to walk along here! I grasped fleetingly and rejected the scene my imagination contrived for me, in which the next time the car slowed down I vaulted over the side and took to my heels, to hide out in a vessel bound upriver. There would surely be a better occasion for that—if deportation was in fact to be my lot—before the last chance at the pilot station at Salinas.

We reached the Palace without being wrecked, and with that I felt I had escaped the worst that might befall me.

At the gate of the grounds I had to submit to having my pockets tapped for weapons. The sentry was very gingerly in going about his job, apologizing to me with the widespread eyes of a woodcock. He saved till last the leather case strung by a strap over my shoulder. *"Máquina fotográfica?"* he asked. I shook my head, not knowing the word for binocular. His fingers trembled on the catch with anticipatory agitation.

"Apressa-te!" the sergeant barked.

"Look out!" I cried, snatching up the binocular, which the affrighted sentry was on the point of letting drop to the pavement.

The sergeant thrust the now thoroughly unnerved little private aside and led the way briskly and in silence toward the building. At the doorway two more soldiers standing guard in greatly oversized caps eyed my escort timidly, but received no recognition as we passed through.

186

Our pace scarcely diminished, and I had only an indistinct impression of darkly furnished reception rooms and a scattering of petitioners, as I took them to be—men standing about by themselves who looked at us with melancholy resignation as we passed, as if we confirmed a hapless conclusion they had reached about life. Ahead of us, from behind a massive closed door, could be heard a voice harsh, commanding, unmodulated. I should have known it as that of Colonel Achille Durondo quite apart from the fact that no one else would have dared so violate the tense hush of that building.

Here was another two-man guard, and several civilians at desks looking as if they had not smiled since childhood. One of the latter closest to the door, evidently in apprehension of seeing the sergeant barge straight on through, sprang to his feet with a sharp interrogation on his lips. The sergeant vouchsafed a terse reply, which I could not understand, whereupon, with an interested glance at me, the functionary took hold of the doorknob and stood listening like a dancer in the wings awaiting his cue to sweep onstage. Catching the precise moment, he soundlessly swung the great portal open a foot and, inclining his head, glided through. The voice from within, briefly amplified, halted after a moment, then resumed just as the functionary re-emerged sideways through the same minimally-calculated aperture. Pulling the door to but not closing it behind him, he motioned us forward. I looked at the sergeant to see whether he meant to precede me or follow me into the *Interventor*'s presence, whether, in other words, I was being brought in as a prize or ushered in as a person of consequence. The sergeant unhesitatingly took the lead.

The Colonel was at his desk. To one who had seen him close up only in official pictures, he presented an unexpectedly scholarly appearance. This was owing to the steel-rimmed glasses he was wearing. His head, bent over some papers in front of him, had an incipient bald spot on the crown. He was reading aloud to a scribe in a black alpaca jacket seated at a distance from him with a pencil poised above a pad on his knee. Evidently the text was a composition of his own which he knew by heart, for he kept right on with it, without faltering, while slowly raising his head from the papers and fixing his eyes upon the sergeant. From where we were standing by the door, as I recalled having stood when called to the principal's office in elementary school, he looked more than ever (discounting the glasses) like a carnivore on the order of a weasel

187

or ferret. His face came to a rounded point at the tip of his nose. His eyes were velvety brown, of so dense a dye that the whites, when I saw them, seemed to have taken a stain from them.

Colonel Durondo kept us standing where we were while he finished reviewing his statement, making a few changes of wording as he went along, which the secretary busily transcribed. At the end the secretary rose to depart; with his shaggy hair, fatigued eyes and drooping countenance he looked like one who had just got up from a sleepless bed. However, his superior detained him and turned his attention to other papers on his desk, reading and signing them. He had his desk so placed, I was interested to note, that he sat almost a prisoner of it with his back in a corner. Placed haphazardly in the vicinity of the desk were a half dozen straight-backed chairs. At the farther end of the office was a conference table with other chairs around it. For all decoration there were a number of signed photographs on the wall, probably of visiting foreign or south Brazilian, and hence noncompetitive, personages. One looked for a team of moving-men to come in with, or for, more furniture. Either the Colonel had ascetic military tastes or wished to have it appear so.

"Olha!"

The face thrust at me across the desk was that of a striking adder, the eyes so fixed and dilate as to appear lidless. I could hardly have been more shocked if a forked tongue had flickered at me from between the rows of teeth exposed by the drawing back of the lips. I must have recoiled. The other two had started, even the sergeant, who had been standing beside me, scornfully withdrawn from the scene, his hands clasped behind his back. It was the second time in two days that I had looked into eyes burning with malevolence. He began to speak almost at once, and it took no special discernment to grasp that the performance he had sustained of a busy chief of state with more important things to think about than an imprudent transgressor from another country—a performance he must have decided was yielding diminishing returns as he observed my attention wandering—had been paid for in prodigies of self-control. Now he could give vent to the fury that had been mounting under pressure. Not for the past ten minutes only but for weeks on end he had denied himself this satisfaction. He was a man who had an adversary where he wanted him at last. I was aghast at what I saw. The spectacle produced by an ungovernable human emotion of any kind is unnerving, like the hint of an underlying chaos in the universe. My being able to understand nothing of what he said made it in a way worse, for it turned the performance into a horrible pantomime. There was the whine of a whip in the envenomed ejaculations of speech which he expelled with the whole force of his body, in spasms. He gripped the desk. He had snatched off his glasses with his first word, and in his eyes, as I looked into them, I saw only blackness. Perspiration glistened on his forehead and upper lip, and the skin over his cheekbones was blotched with color. The words, the blistering denunciations, fell in lash-strokes. The eyes into which I was looking, which showed the jaundiced whites all around, were, I thought, like bullet holes.

Of course he knew I could not understand what he was saying, and with the spending of his accumulated fury this realization perhaps became insistent. He broke off. He drew himself up with a deep breath through nostrils expanded like a horse's, his eyes half closed. His hands were flat, palms down, upon the desk. All four of us in the room were silent. A voice on the other side of the door could be heard, and street sounds—the clatter of a trolly-car—came through the windows.

Colonel Durondo, without moving, opened his eyes fully again and looked at me. I looked at him.

I was thinking that I could see his temperature rising once more when, dropping his eyes to glare at his wristwatch, he exclaimed between bared teeth, *"Êste Jorge Almeida!"* With an exasperated imprecation he rose from his chair, precipitately enough to send it with a bang against the wall. *"Sente-se,"* he commanded me.

I sat. I knew that he was self-conscious about his short stature and did not like to expose it to unfavorable comparisons.

Exiting from his sanctuary, he took a turn up and down the room. He stopped by a window, not boldly fronting it, but standing sideways, his shoulder to the folded shutter, and looked out. His mood, to my acutely watchful gaze, seemed to be smoldering, wary and speculative. Turning back, he regarded me with one eye, the upper wall with the other. I had heard of this occasional cocking of an eye. The effect was frightening.

"O que tem na mão?" he demanded.

"Como . . . Excelência?"

"Na mão! Na mão!"

I had unslung the binocular before entering the room and was holding it behind my hat.

"Máquina fotográfica?" he asked.

"Não, Excelência," I replied, put out with myself for my unaccountable failure to have learned the Portuguese for binocular.

"Pode me deixar ver?" He extended his hand.

Half rising, I moved a step toward him, handed him the binocular and retreated backward to my chair. He weighed the instrument in his hand and with nervous, sensitive fingers operated the hinge, bending the two parts back and forth, and twiddled the focusing wheel. Turning to the window, he picked an object across the grounds and in a swift, supple movement had the glasses at his eyes. There flashed before me a picture of him in a fight, tossing a rifle to his shoulder—as I have seen a marksman do—with the same quick sureness.

Addressing himself to me once more, he gesticulated rapidly between me and the binocular, asking, *"Porque, porque?"*

The question having been predictable, I had prepared an answer of sorts. I wrote for scientific magazines. (*"Escrevo para algumas revistas científicas."*)

He grunted, weighing the binocular again. *"Caro?"* he inquired shrewdly.

I made a motion with my shoulders. *"Bastante caro."*

He considered the proposition as if it held the clue to matters of great import. *"Os Americanos são ricos."*

"Alguns," I conceded. I was not very sure of the word, but apparently it was all right. Some Americans were rich.

Durondo strode up to me and thrust the glasses at me with resolution. *"Muito ricos!"* he declared in what I now recognized as his public or official voice. *"'Te logo, Doutor Ta-te."* He struck the crystal of his wristwatch repeatedly with his forefinger and said again, as if he were admonishing a refractory and obtuse child, *"A-té lo-go!"* Until soon. With that he picked up a paper from his desk and became profoundly absorbed in its contents.

190

For the rest of the afternoon I was left alone with my thoughts. I was taken to quarters at the end of the Palace furnished much like a room in an hotel. There was a bed swathed in mosquito netting, small tables with dark varnish becoming vermiculated with age, a very big chest of drawers and an adjoining bathroom with a marble washstand and heavy fixtures bespeaking an era when bathrooms were not to be taken for granted.

In quitting the *Interventor*'s office the sergeant had stood back to allow me to precede him, and so had the private secretary, whose bowed head, I could tell, contained but the one idea of shooing us out and getting out himself. Evidently I had gained status, though I could not see from what. In the antechamber I had balked. I demanded to know where we were going (*"Aonde vamos?"*). Unenlightened by the voluble Portuguese of the secretary, who had straightened up but seemed as anxious to move us on as ever, and by the sergeant's briefer effort, disdainfully abandoned, I simply stood. A person was summoned who spoke English. Through him I learned that I was expected to remain in the *quarto* assigned to me until his Excellency the *Interventor* would be free to see me later in the afternoon for further consideration of my case. "Expected to remain?" I had repeated. "Does that mean I am not permitted to leave?" I do not remember the English-speaking intermediary at all. Perhaps a negative personality was part of his professional equipment as a translator. But I can still hear distinctly the tone of voice, as if he were the happy bearer of pleasant tidings, in which he answered me after taking counsel with the secretary: "His Excellency expects you to remain." I asked if I might make a telephone call and was told in the same cheerful, helpful accents that no provision had been made for my doing so and that the subject could appropriately be raised at my next meeting with the *Interventor*. Then could someone please notify Doutor J. R. de Monteiro of my whereabouts in order to spare my friends needless alarm ("needless" was what I said, anyhow) over my nonappearance? That had already been attended to.

A lunch of *feijoada*—kidney beans and *farinha*—was served me in my *quarto,* following which I was brought some American magazines of chiefly antiquarian interest. Otherwise my solitude was unbroken. I brought a fair appetite to the repast and found it quite good, but I must own I had little stomach for reading. Behind me I saw only folly, steppingstones of folly over which we had all—Monteiro, Mr. Willet, my father, I myself—credulously stepped. ("One little item we seem not to have bothered our heads about," I saw myself writing Mr. Willet, "is that Colonel Durondo has an army on the spot and Monteiro has not.") Ahead I could see only the ruination of our hopes, barring the early overthrow of the regime, which from the point of vantage of a guarded room in the Palace did not impress one as easy of accomplishment. It seemed probable that I had now been through the most acutely distasteful part of the treatment I was likely to receive from Durondo, little relish though I had for a session with Jorge Almeida, which I took to be in the books. However, it could be taken for granted that whatever else the *Interventor* had in store for me would be bad. How bad, I could not guess. Indeed, I had given up trying to figure out where I might be headed with him; I hardly knew where we had been. But nothing other than bad could possibly come of my being where I was. And there it was.

I had already taken off my coat and tie, and I now took off my shoes and stretched out on the bed. I sank into it like so much dead weight. For the present there was nothing to be done, nothing I could do. When one has been on a strain there is something to be said for having the power of decision out of one's hands—for a space, anyhow.

I wondered if Monteiro were managing to obtain the information about the girl's identity and destination.

I lay there a long time, my hands under my head, without moving or caring to move. If only I knew her name! Not even necessarily her whole name, not her name as a means of tracing her; that would be asking too much of fortune. Only a name by which to call her, to bring her closer, to voice in the hope of reaching out to her by the power of thought and longing! As I lay quietly thus, the lines of past, present and future became blurred, the distinctions unreal. Fragments of my life floated in on a tide of consciousness that came from as far away as Sheldon Bluff. There was a launch—I could not have thought of it in years—mired and slowly rotting on a tidal flat, but still mostly intact, with much of its hardware remaining, still pert of bow. As a child I took imaginary voyages standing at the helm in its wheelhouse. Outside on the mudflats the little fiddler crabs would marvel, each standing at the entrance to its burrow, rearing up and raising its great claw jerkily, like a diminutive medicine-man hailing a manifestation of the Great Spirit. I thought of those times —those much later times—when near the end of a daylong hike I had stopped to rest on a hilltop or at the edge of a wood and the hush that came with the lengthening shadows, deepening as I waited, unstirring, took on the character of great distances, became thoughtful and expectant, and the grey squirrel barking and flirting its tail on a horizontal branch, the crow at the top of an oak peering from one side to the other down through the foliage, seemed to confirm the presence of that which I could not see though I felt my whole being respond to it, as to the chime of a bell pure beyond human hearing. She was now part of all that had gone before.

I was sitting by the window having a cigarette when I was sent for. I had been sitting there while the light faded and the Praça da Independência and the room in which I sat were swallowed up in the soft dark-

193

ness. The last of the birds had fallen silent and the insects and lizards had struck up, turning the night into a machineshop of fairies. I had made no reply to the knock on the door. When it was repeated and still brought no reply, the door was flung open. In the light from the hall a uniformed soldier could be seen to hurry in and then cast about, feeling his way in some agitation, for a lamp switch, obviously alarmed by the evidence that the bird had managed to fly. The light when it came on was jarring.

The *Interventor* was waiting for me in his office, seated at his desk as he had been the first time. To my surprise, he was in uniform, in dress whites with loops of gold braid caught up at the shoulder. In a chair beside him was Jorge Almeida, sitting with one leg flung over the other, quite relaxed; I had not been prepared to find him appearing so much so in the *Interventor*'s presence. The two men watched me enter like judges at a horse show taking cognizance of a new entry brought before them. There was nothing about my advent to arouse them; one expects to see a horse at a horse show. Likewise, since it would be wasted on a horse, no show of recognition was called for. I had time to think all this, standing—pretty truculently, I suppose—before them.

Jorge Almeida turned to the Colonel. He did not speak, but his eyebrows were raised interrogatively. The Colonel, his expression now acknowledging the possibility of communication between us, signified with a nod at a chair in front of his desk that I was to be seated in it and with a move of the hand turned the proceedings over to his coadjutor. He slumped down a notch, sinking lower in his heavily-starched uniform, a sort of drugged look in his eyes, as if a stupor of weariness had come over him.

Jorge Almeida studied his large hands, of which, with his elbows on the arms of his chair, he had formed a cage in front of his chest, the fingertips pressed together. The stage was his. He arranged his thoughts. He directed a level look at me and commenced to speak in a didactic manner. "His Excellency tells me that he has set forth your many guilty actions. All you have done to take advantage of the hospitality of the state. Your interference from the day of your arrival in the internal political activities. Your efforts to assist the enemies of the legally-created government of the state. Your participation in plots and conspiracies." I thought I could detect in his eye as his very ample mouth closed on these words a mocking gleam more in character than the spirit of the solemnly intoned recital. "Your pursuit of aims that threaten the order and security of the country. I must regret that I was not here to . . . to"—he paused while this time his lips twitched visibly in the direction of a grin—"*translate*. However, it is surely not necessary to specify to *you* your offenses, by which you have placed yourself beyond reach of his Excellency's enlightened good will—and the phrase is his Excellency's own. What you are to understand is this." He spoke as if from the bench. "First, the full extent of your misconduct is well known. Second, the Government takes the most serious view of it. I trust this was made unmistakable to you?"

I cleared my throat. One never knows how one's voice will first come forth on an occasion of stress. "His Excellency has been entirely misinformed. His charges against me are groundless. The Government has been misled by appearances. I consider that I am being held here without warrant."

I was aware that I had spoken without much conviction, largely for the record. But Almeida, who had heard me with a frown, spoke with even less when he replied, in a mere mutter addressed to the floor, "Well, you can consider what you like. What counts is what the Government says. You'd do much better just to accept—"

"And," I put in, emboldened by his evident, quite unexpected, lack of liking for the subject, "I should appreciate it if you would convey what I have said to the *Interventor*."

I saw vexation in his face.

"*Como?*" demanded Colonel Durondo suspiciously, but still heavy-eyed.

"*Excelência,*" Almeida began. His tone was deferential and placating.

I soon saw why. As Almeida proceeded, Colonel Durondo heaved himself up in his chair. His brow was knotted, his eyes were such that even in my swift dismay at what I had touched off I had a flash of recall that in youth he had trained for the priesthood, for they were those of an Inquisitor in whose hearing anathema had been voiced. I braced myself for another outburst of the kind I had endured earlier in the day. It must have been apparent in my face that I quailed at the prospect, and this may have gone some way toward mollifying the Colonel. The breath he had gathered he now let escape. He placed his hand over his heart and rubbed his chest. With the corners of his mouth drawn down and eyes by some physiological peculiarity grown suddenly puffy, he looked

195

me contemptuously up and down. When he spoke, it was in a voice well enough under control but with a bite of scorn and anger, and with one eye fastened on me and the other again scrutinizing the space above my shoulder, which, with the crazy air it gave him, did more to shake me than violent imprecations would have. Since his gaze remained fixed just so, it was not apparent when he had finished until he commanded, *"Traduz!"*

Almeida murmured quickly, *"Certamente, Excelência."* To me he said, "Your impertinence will not be tolerated. It is not for you to question the Government's sources of information. You have engaged in the smuggling of arms. You have engaged in the writing of political tracts."

The *Interventor* interrupted here with another command. Evidently the manner of the translator's delivery did not satisfy him, for when Almeida resumed it was in a louder voice and with a harsh tone more like the *Interventor's* own. I had imported large sums of money illegally. I had made studies of the terrain from the point of view of military operations. I had allied myself with traitors.

"Com os inimigos do povo!" the Colonel interjected.

"You are acquainted with the phrase, I believe," Almeida stated, setting the observation apart as his own by the slightest change in inflection. "You have surrendered all claim upon our consideration. You have placed yourself beyond your Government's . . . beyond the point where your Government may legitimately represent you. It would be . . . in keeping with the seriousness of your offenses if you were brought to trial for conspiring against the security and peace of the state. It would be an instance of true Brazilian mercifulness if you were merely placed in the next ship bound for your own country."

Evidently the next move was mine. I wondered if I were expected to ask for clemency. The day, I suppose, was beginning to tell on me; I had a feeling of psychic debilitation. I said I was indeed sorry to learn that the authorities had received such an unfavorable impression of me and regretted that my motives had not been more clearly apparent: doubtless I should have taken more pains to see that they were better understood. I wished nothing for Brazil but tranquillity and prosperity—*ordem e progresso*—I went on. The sound of my voice gave me the peculiar illusion that I was speaking inside a barrel or tunnel. "My interests," I continued, "are solely in the field of business, not in politics at all. And the undertaking I am engaged in, that I came down here in the hope of helping to advance, is one that . . . one from which north Brazil could only be the gainer." I am afraid I had the tone of one forcing himself to go on to the end. "In the United States it could hardly be imagined that a person with the kind of purposes that brought me to Brazil would find himself in my present unhappy position."

"Very, very fine, Mr. Tate." Still a little subdued, Jorge Almeida had nevertheless largely recovered his personality. "That's a beautiful spirit, truly beautiful. I don't see why any government should be resentful if its downfall is plotted by such idealists." How I detested his elastic lips, especially when he grinned. It seemed to me he allowed himself a good deal of liberty in the presence of the *Interventor*.

Aided by the degree of heat I now felt, I requested him with formality to translate what I had said to the *Interventor* and what I now wished to add, namely, that it seemed to me a government concerned with the welfare of the people would be sympathetic with plans for developing the country's resources. Was it not enough, I asked, warming a little more to the theme, that capital was short in north Brazil, the *mato* such an obstacle, transportation so difficult? Should there not therefore at least be cooperation among those seeking to develop the country? A rumble reverberating in the darkness beyond the windows foretold an evening thunderstorm. It made me, I did not know why, more dismally conscious of the bleakness of the bare, overlighted office. It also put out of my mind anything further I might have been going to say. What was I talking about, anyway?

Almeida opened his eyes. He had been listening with them closed, and his lower lip extruded. He went in for making faces. "Is that all?"

"Is that all? What am I expected to say?"

In the meeting of our eyes I was sure I read in his a cynical and correct appraisal of my qualifications for the role in which I had been presented to the local community. "What are you expected to say? Oh, come, Mr. Tate!"

"*Bastante!*" The *Interventor* had raised his fists to his ears. His set teeth were bared. He cut his eyes from one to the other of us. Satisfied that we were turned to stone, he lowered his hands to the desk. His face relaxed. In the silence another salvo of thunder could be heard. "*Então,*" he said precisely. "*Que diz?*"

197

Colonel Durondo and I observed each other while Almeida translated what I had said. The Colonel responded with a question. "Do you," said Almeida, "believe that the country of the Massaranduba is as rich in gold and other minerals as it is reputed to be?" I must have looked blank, caught unprepared as I was, for the Colonel said dryly, *"Tem uma opinião, não é verdade?"*

"Well, I . . . have no special information about it, your Excellency," I replied, not knowing what kind of water I was being navigated toward. "There are those who have had a good deal of experience in these things—they seem to have great expectations of the area. However . . ." I stopped in order to phrase to myself the point I now knew I wished to make and to let Almeida dispose of what I had already said. "It should be understood that I am merely an agent of the legal firm which represents Dr. Monteiro in New York. I am here merely to assist, if I can, in negotiations with certain parties in the United States, for whom Dr. Monteiro seeks to obtain a concession in the Massaranduba."

Almeida, as I spoke, put on a performance just marked enough for me to notice of a person listening to an improbable tale with an ironical show of going along with it. He settled himself in his chair, folded his arms across his chest and with eyebrows raised and lips pursed paid exaggerated attention, giving a little bob of the head with my every phrase.

"Will you be good enough to translate?" I inquired, as he seemed disposed to remain exactly as he was.

"But of course!"

Colonel Durondo had slumped down in his chair again with his chin nearly resting on his chest, his eyes dull. When not exceptionally stirred he seemed to be overtaken by fatigue. It had probably been a hard day— like all other days, I imagined. However, in response to the translation he shifted his weight forward with something like a smile—the nearest approximation to one I had seen on his face. The two exchanged looks in which a mutual sardonic satisfaction was to be read. *"Diga-lhe . . ."* Durondo directed the other in a brief expression of which I missed the rest.

Said Almeida, "If you expect us to believe than an *estadunidense* would come here and go to all this trouble without expectation of proportionate rewards, you hold our intelligence in small account. Moreover, we know that your father is a stockholder in the Portalegre Corporation and that there is talk that Portalegre will be the concessionaire in the Massaranduba."

"You are speaking in terms of possibilities, conjectures," I said rather lamely. "I am speaking in terms of facts."

I saw that the two men were looking beyond me. The windows, when I turned, were vibrating with light, shivering with the cold fire of lightning. The thunder rumbled like a locomotive hurtling down upon us.

Durondo, when I looked around again, was on his feet, drawn up imperiously. He threw his arm out at the region of the desk in front of me, as if—some inner spring touched—he had been precipitated into action by the thunder. *"Leia!"* he commanded.

I looked at him uncertainly and with apprehension.

"He means for you to pick up that sheet of paper and read what it says on the other side," said Almeida. He was evidently displeased.

"Você vê?"—you see?—the *Interventor* demanded when I had taken up the paper and stared at it for a space.

It was a telegram, on an outgoing form. It was addressed to CONWILL NEW YORK, which was Mr. Willet's firm. The message read: MONTEIRO POWERLESS DELIVER CONCESSION STOP RECOMMEND YOU AUTHORIZE ME NEGOTIATE WITH GOVERNMENT STOP WIRE ME CARE GOVERNOR. It was signed with my name, ready to be dispatched.

I was bewildered, then horrified. My mind rejected the situation altogether—that is to say, the alternatives I could see were now before me. But there the alternatives were. The choice offered was what kind of abyss I preferred to cast myself into. At the same time, I obscurely realized that the position had been altered to my advantage: I had been made overtures to, I was sought after. I thought, Well, let one of them say something. I could sit as long as necessary. . . . The thunder was like wagonloads of explosives being dumped out of the sky.

"Pôde ler," said the Colonel.

Yes, I agreed. *"Posso."* I could read.

Durondo made a statement which Almeida translated as, "We propose to have it transmitted."

I bent over the telegram again. Some course of action, some means of extricating myself, would have to suggest itself! None did. Instead various irrelevancies passed through my mind. I pictured what the Colonel's way with young women schoolteachers must be, how the ultimatum

199

must be delivered, brutally and without preliminaries. The faces of friends came and went, some I had not seen since high school, all so remote from me in my present extremity.

I could say I refused to go along with the telegram. I could ask what would happen if I refused to go along with it. To these responses replies were of course ready and waiting for me. I was sure I did not wish to hear them. I was also sure I did not wish to hear how pleasant things would be for me if I were cooperative.

The sky-splitting slashes of lightning were followed more closely by ever louder thunderclaps. I cast a look over my shoulder again, as at a source of distraction to my thought.

Colonel Durondo, whose attention had also been momentarily diverted to the approaching storm, was still standing. He was leaning slightly forward, hands on the desk, knuckles down. He was pale and his eyes had that burned-out look again. He stood there, as it was suddenly given to me to perceive, the point upon which bore forces far beyond my experiences and beyond my comprehension, forces grinding, inexorable, unremitting, known only to the head of a government. Unlike Almeida, whose eyes were dancing with appreciation of my inward castings-about of mind, he did not see me as a person at all. He turned his wrist so that he could see his watch.

"If this were sent—" I began. I was cut short by a near bolt of lightning and a violent crash of thunder. The sounds of running feet could be heard from without. "If this were sent, the recipients in New York would think I was out of my mind." I addressed the *Interventor* and meant not to look at Almeida, but I did so inadvertently. His cynical estimate had been confirmed, I read in his face, as I had expected to. He as good as said, "I knew it. You'll accept the terms, or seem to, thinking you can slip out from under somewhere along the line."

When he had translated my sentence he added another, no doubt an observation of his own in very much the sense of what I had been sure he was thinking. The *Interventor* nodded. There was a further exchange between them, during which I had the impression that the *Interventor* was hardly able to keep his mind on it, so harassing was the crackle of lightning and the jarring concussions that followed it—though no rain had yet fallen. Our proceedings, against this kind of competition, had a hurried, furtive, almost inconsequential air.

"His Excellency brought up the telegram a bit more abruptly than might have been expected," said Almeida. I stole a glance at his Excellency and found him looking over my head at the window with a strange light in his eyes. "Obviously a full and detailed explanation of the position to your principals will be required of you. His Excellency agrees that it would be well to add 'Letter follows' to the telegram. This you will be able to write—"

The universe seemed to explode in light. Upon the instant, with the sound of a cannon discharged in the room, it was plunged into complete darkness. There had been a direct hit on the Palace, and every light in sight had gone off.

Almeida's voice spoke in Portuguese, softly and in an offhand and conversational tone. In the same tone—which delayed for a moment the impact of his words—he went on in English. "Mr. Tate. Don't move, Mr. Tate. You may be killed if you do."

There was another brilliant shivering of lightning, revealing the figure of the *Interventor* standing, white of face, horribly staring, like Death risen from the battlefield of war, a pistol in his hand pointed straight out from him.

From the darkness where Colonel Durondo was standing came a sepulchral cry: *"Luz! Luz!"* It came again, a voice, an appeal, from the grave: *"Loooooooosh!"*

My hands hurt—from gripping the arms of my chair.

The rain was suddenly upon us. Through its roar Almeida could be heard speaking to the Colonel in the same ordinary voice as before. I thought of him with admiration and with what I suppose could be called fervent moral support. The lightning, dimmed by rain and increasing distance, barely picked the Colonel out of the blackness, standing as before.

The sounds of voices and confused movements elsewhere in the Palace had been almost drowned out by the downpour, but now above the medley arose a clear, reiterated cry: *"Comandante da guarda!"* It grew louder. *"Comandante da guarda!"*

There was a knock on the door.

"Entre! Entre!" shouted Colonel Durondo.

Following the grunt of a door being pushed open, the beam of a flashlight swept the room, blinding me in passing, then struck Durondo, whose pistol, still clutched, was lowered with its muzzle resting on the desk. Instantly, as if recoiling from a profanation, the beam dropped to

201

the floor. There was staccato talk back and forth, amid which the flash-light was transferred to the Colonel, in whose hands it illuminated successively the figures of the officer and soldiers of the guard, blinking in its rays. While it rested upon him like a spotlight in a theater, the officer delivered himself of more breathless phrases, leaned forward stiffly in a semaphorelike salute, spun about and marched his squad off on the double, their heels ringing on the floor. Two other soldiers came in with lanterns, like trainmen. These, at a command from the Colonel, were placed upon the desk. Lighted from below, his visage had a masklike inhumanness. The atmosphere was still one of crisis. Almeida had got to his feet, as had I. He now went up to his superior and murmured a question.

"Sim, sim, sim, sim!" said Durondo, then, addressing the room in general, cried, *"Saiam! Todos. Vão, vão!* Get out! All of you!"

As we filed out, Almeida impelling me forward from the rear, though I was not tarrying, he sank into his chair.

With the flashlights and lanterns there it was relatively bright in the anteroom. On the other side of the door we came through, there stood, alone among a score of men, a woman with a pale silk scarf over her head, largely shielding her face. She turned a little just as I passed, and glancing over my shoulder, I caught an exchange of looks between her and Almeida. I had also a glimpse of handsome black eyes beneath low but finely drawn brows, a nose with curled oriental nostrils, and full, firm lips—a face of character and sensuality. Pride, I deduced, which caused her to draw a veil between her and the world caused her also to disdain drawing it altogether over her features. I was so struck by the circumstances of her being there, with all the implications, that I did not recognize her in the uncertain light and realized only much later who she was: Cora's haughty sister-in-law, Jorge's sister.

With a "Pssst!" and a toss of the head Almeida hailed a soldier across the room and commandeered the soldier's flashlight. To me he said, "Uraga has been told to expect us. That's Dr. Eduardo Uraga, in case you don't know. He's the *Interventor's* special man on economic and financial problems. The question is, when do we eat? It's nearly half past eight. Can you wait a little longer? I doubt if we can expect anything much with the current off."

"If I have any choice in the matter I'd choose to get out of here right now and go home. If I can't do that I don't care what we do."

"Then we'll see Uraga."

We set off through the dark internals of the Palace. So many others were going back and forth with lights that we might have been part of an outdoor pageant at night or a special number in a musical review. A veritable fairyland, I thought wryly. The soldier whose light Almeida had taken kept close behind us. Almeida had a slouching but long-legged stride and swung his head to right and left as we walked; his physical looseness was repugnant to me. . . . The wash of the rain was loud outside the shuttered windows we passed and the rumble of the thunder sent delicate tremors through the building. The sounds were comforting, reassuring me of the continued existence of the familiar world.

Dr. Uraga was not in his office but would be back directly, we were told by a man typewriting by candlelight in an outer room. We sat down in the inner office to wait. There was a kerosene lamp on the desk.

Almeida inhaled to the bottom of his lungs from a cigarette he had lighted over the chimney of the lamp, keeping his head down expertly. Leaning back with his mouth open, he let the smoke drift upward of its own accord. "It can be trying, being with his Excellency," he remarked.

"I see what you mean," I said.

"I mean smoking is not permitted in his presence."

It had not occurred to me to smoke there, but I lighted a cigarette now, preparing myself for more of the ironic raillery with which Almeida had learned to make himself objectionable—prepared myself as I might for being wrapped, fold after fold, in an offensive kind of integument. But he seemed listless and did not even look at me. His was one of those personalities, I decided, that do not function person-to-person but require the stimulation and cover provided by an audience of at least one other.

When Dr. Uraga arrived I thought he could well have passed for a medical doctor. Short of stature, briskly professional of manner, adorned with black-rimmed glasses, he came into the room with rapid little steps, feet turned out, carrying a small bag, not quite a briefcase, and looked alternately between us, as if he expected one of us to be sick or injured. He was clothed in mourner's black: suit, tie, shoes, socks and the straw hat he carried, everything was black but the shirt; when Brazilians go into mourning they are likely to go all the way in. . . . Years later, when I was an official of the United States Government, I was to see him across a conference table at Montevideo and derive a faint, unhappy amusement from the puzzled glances he threw me.

Dr. Uraga rubbed his hands together with professional satisfaction as Almeida made a dry recital of the facts in my case, or such as were not already known to him, I supposed. Yes, he recognized the symptoms. Precisely. They were right out of the book. . . . The rounded lenses of his glasses caught the light, so that he appeared to have two little lamps for eyes. When the case history had been completed, he cleared his throat and undertook a direct examination of the patient.

Was it then true that the Portalegre Corporation was likely to be constituted the concessionaire? Was I acquainted with its record in respect of the oil-drilling concession granted it several years ago? Were we aware that the United States Departments of State and Commerce would take a very unfavorable view of a repetition of this performance? Would the syndicate of officers of the Portalegre Corporation be in a position to abandon the projected concession before local investments were made without loss to themselves? (Almeida, cast in the subordinate role of translator, swung himself about in the swivel chair he had possessed himself of, putting himself at odd angles to the line of conversation as he rendered his offices, so that we were constantly conscious of him.) Was it possible that the syndicate was waiting for a further depreciation of Brazilian currency in its favor? What was the syndicate's attitude with respect to the Braga property? What, exactly, had held the syndicate back from any concrete moves to obtain the Braga property or secure the concession?

I answered these questions slowly and indifferently, in a manner to suggest that I was answering them at all only because I had no particular objection to doing so, not because I felt I had to. However, the last question brought forth from me a strong statement on the evident suspicion of foreign capital to be encountered in Brazil and on the extreme hostility to foreign investors of any stripe expressed by the *Interventor*.

At this, Dr. Uraga removed and fell to rubbing his glasses, revealing small, weak eyes. Squinting at me, he made a huffy-sounding speech which, as Almeida translated it, was not greatly different from what might have been expected, to wit, that the welfare of the state was and had to be the first consideration of its chosen administrators, and so forth, that foreign capital, however necessary, must not be allowed to exploit the people and alienate from them their birthright, and so forth, but that under conditions ensuring that the rights of the nation and the state and of the citizens thereof would be secured, foreign investors would find an honorable and profitable place. . . . The importance these ideas held for the speaker had to be surmised from his very positive tone of voice; it did not come through in any emphasis given them by the translator. When I had been adjudged to have absorbed them, the speaker went on, dealing out one sentence at a time and waiting for the translation in between. It had been signified to me, he understood, that in his deep concern for the material progress of the state his Excellency the *Interventor* was willing even to overlook the past association between those I represented and certain notorious elements here in Pará. . . . The syndicate in New York would be offered the opportunity to participate in the economic development of the country on mutually advantageous terms. . . . The Administration was ready to examine on its merits a plan for a jointly-organized instrumentality to the realization of our complementary interests.

"Is what you have in mind," I asked doubtfully, "a company jointly owned by the Americans and by Brazilians, to mine for gold in the valley of the Massaranduba?"

As if *Massaranduba* were the magic word for which it had been waiting, light burst upon us. The current had been restored. Small cries of triumph were heard in the corridors and rooms outside our own. We blinked and, forgetting for an instant the mutual suspicion which was all we had in common, smiled.

It appeared that my interpretation of the economist's meaning was precisely correct. He was going to say more, but Almeida interrupted him. Dr. Uraga resettled his glasses on his nose in an irritated way while seeming to give begrudging assent to what Almeida had proposed.

"It's getting late," Almeida said to me. "I told Dr. Uraga that the way to do business with a North American of executive capacity is to come to the point. Right? What you'd like to know is exactly what we expect of you. Right again? Right as right can be? So here is the plan. If I forget to put in the 'pleases,' kindly consider them said. First, there is the telegram."

205

"I was coming to that," I said. "You can forget the telegram. I won't agree to it. It's true I can't prevent your sending it, but if you do you'll get nothing further out of me." In the past half hour I had had a chance to come to an estimate of the strength of my bargaining position. "To save time I suggest that you listen to what *I* have to say." The hurt look that crossed Almeida's face might at another time have struck me as funny.

An ability I have always envied in others is that of speaking coolly in argument, without betrayal of emotion, on issues about which they are in fact greatly exercised. I tried now to emulate one of these admirable beings, but with diminishing success as I proceeded.

On no account (I said) was I going to suggest throwing over the client of the firm I represented. If it was impossible to realize the aims of a gold-mining concession in the Massaranduba except by means of a company in which men appointed by Colonel Durondo would participate on a profit-sharing basis—and I took it that that was what Dr. Uraga's proposal for "a jointly-organized instrumentality" came down to—then Dr. Monteiro and the syndicate in New York would have to face that condition. There was nothing I could do one way or another. What I proposed to do was to point that out to them—if my understanding was correct. Actually, it seemed to me, from what I had heard about the Massaranduba, that there should be plenty to go around, while it stood to reason that the more effort that was put into the Concession, whether by Brazilians or Americans, the greater the returns that could be expected. Whether Colonel Durondo and Dr. Monteiro could cooperate was another matter, about which there was nothing I could say. At the time of my arrest earlier in the day my plan had been to go on up the river as soon as possible, to take care of necessary business in Manáos and visit the Massaranduba, and I ventured to say that that was still the thing for me to do.

"Hold on a minute!" said Almeida. He was flushed and his eyes were bright. With the meeting having gone awry following his intervention, he had doubtless lost face. "Cooperate, you say? That is what you said, isn't it? Cooperate? Hand in hand? Do you see the *Interventor* ignoring everything that has happened, forgiving all and embracing Raimo Monteiro?"

"I didn't say what I saw. I said it's up to them. What I can't see is the American syndicate moving an inch in this business if Dr. Monteiro is cast adrift," I said recklessly. "This whole project is the joint offspring of Dr. Monteiro and a petroleum engineer in New York upon whom the syndicate depends absolutely for advice."

"We know about Dr. Alekos Xenides."

"Good. Then you will appreciate what I say about Dr. Monteiro's indispensability." I was by no means sure myself how one followed from the other, but I hurried on. "Perhaps the *Interventor* can get along without the New York syndicate. But I rather fancy"—I was speaking more excitedly—"that such is not the case. We have read of plans of the *Interventor's* own for exploiting the Massaranduba—about a coming expedition—and about foreign interests he is in touch with. There is even a Senhor Joaquim Waldo, I believe. Yet you are finding it worth while to spend time on me. If the *Interventor* needs the syndicate, as I suspect, he will not hinder me from going ahead as I indicated I had planned to. That means going to Manáos to get assurances from officials of the state government there and going to the Massaranduba to make the necessary investigations there—to get all that the syndicate feels it has to have before it can make final decisions. The rest will be up to others." I was trembling slightly from physical tension and feared that my voice sounded a little choked.

Almeida was trying to pull his long upper lip down into his mouth with his lower teeth. He reached across to the desk beside him and laid his hand on the telephone there. Speaking half across his shoulder, he made known to Dr. Uraga what had been said. His colleague looked distressed and discomfited; the patient was uncooperative. Less than to Dr. Uraga, however, my attention was given to the hand on the telephone. When Almeida lifted the handset and spoke into it, it was, as I anticipated, the *Interventor* whom he called. The *Interventor* was evidently not available, however. He asked to be informed when he might speak to him.

The moment he hung up, I said that *Sabiá,* the vessel in which I had planned to go to Manáos, would be sailing within two days.

"Monteiro's boat?" Almeida evidently found the proposition too fanciful even to be very amusing. His laugh was brief and almost soundless.

Said Dr. Uraga, *"O vapôr Tocantins parte amanhã."*

"All right," I said, controlling my temper, "if the *vapôr* Tocantins leaves a day earlier, so much the better. Make it *Tocantins*. And speaking of voyaging up the river, what about Senhor Joaquim Waldo—if I am permitted to ask?"

"What about him?"

"When I get up the river I may run into him. Isn't that so?"

"And what if you should?"

I saw too late that I was headed into a *cul-de-sac*. "I was wondering what my relations with him would be."

"Well now, Mr. Tate, that would be up to you, wouldn't it?" said Almeida with satisfaction. "You seem to be the one who's laying down the terms of your participation."

I decided to go ahead, ignoring his rejoinder, and ask the question that was in my mind and was too important to me not to ask. "I think I may have met him. Has he a daughter, seventeen or eighteen, perhaps, with whom he travels?"

I thought Almeida, after puzzling an instant over the question, was going to shrug it off, but he reconsidered and scratched his scalp reflectively. "If he has, she's down in the south somewhere, probably Rio."

So that was that. "One more thing," I said. "May I ask how much longer I am to be held here, incommunicado?"

"You may ask, but I can't tell you. You heard me put in the call to the *Interventor*. Until I've talked to him and informed him of your . . . your *analysis of the situation,* I can't tell you what to expect." He looked at his wristwatch and again addressed Dr. Uraga. The latter responded with expostulations and gestures, jerkily and indignantly. Transferring his offended gaze to me, he readjusted his position in his chair in the manner of one preparing to be heard from. There followed an interminable quarter hour of interrogation further plumbing my knowledge of what was going on in New York, then of disquisition on Dr. Uraga's part. Sternly, ticking them off on his fingers, he set forth the particulars of the operating company as he visualized it. Almeida translated with growing restlessness, obviously having other things to think about. The organizational arrangements to pertain someday in the valley of the Massaranduba seemed to me, no less, to be of remote interest, and I merely looked attentive while my mind grappled ineffectually with the grotesque and extremely unpleasant situation I was in.

The session was concluded by Almeida's seizing a pause to stand up. It occurred to me that it must have been a proposal by him to make an end before Dr. Uraga had had his say that had aroused the little man.

Almeida said he trusted that I could put up with the discomforts of my quarters while he waited to hear from the *Interventor* and receive new instructions. I shrugged. After the polite but unsmiling ceremony of my leave-taking from Dr. Uraga, he accompanied me back through the building, our one-man soldier-escort falling in behind again. He seemed to like to walk a half pace ahead of me. When we had gone nearly as far as we had to go, he said that he would arrange to have my dinner sent to me and that he was pretty sure I'd find writing supplies waiting for me. "And let's assume his Excellency would be interested in seeing whatever you write to New York and to Monteiro, hm?"

"Why should I write to Monteiro," I asked, "when I'll be talking to him?"

We had reached my door. Almeida looked up and down the corridor as if he could not account for the absence there of something he had expected to find. "Hunh? Oh—it's just a suggestion, if you have anything to say to him. If you're going to get away on the *Tocantins* there may not be much time in the morning—wouldn't you say? See you later."

I watched him go, wondering whether to call him back or whether to go after him until it was too late to do either. The soldier remained standing by the door, and we looked at each other briefly before I went in.

Forlornly bunched together in the middle of the room were my suitcases and portable typewriter. I stood staring at them while the meaning sank in. In its chill wake came a jet of alarm. How incriminating would my papers be in the eyes of the regime? In great haste I riffled through the contents of the suitcases. There was not a single sheet of paper there with writing on it. Of course, all of it—all the letters from New York— might at that moment have been on the *Interventor*'s desk. But I thought not. I felt sure the Monteiros had got to them ahead of the police. That wily old hand had probably got them out of sight as soon as it was clear that something unusual was detaining me.

I heard not another word from anyone that evening—except the waiter who brought my dinner and would have liked to remain talking to such an unusual customer had he been able to make himself understood. The dinner included a serving of beef ample for three, but hungry as I was, and not one to be put off my feed by anxiety—quite the contrary—

I ate it all. Being dog-tired, I consumed an equally immoderate amount of coffee in order to stay awake. Even so, it was all I could do to get through a long letter to Mr. Willet and a shorter one to Monteiro, enclosing a carbon copy of the former. What I wrote was a strictly circumstantial account of the day's events, as colorless as a police inspector's report. Everything was left out that might provoke Colonel Durondo when it came under his scrutiny. I set forth candidly the charges made against me, without commenting on them, and the penalties the *Interventor* had declared would be warranted. I reported in detail the meeting in Dr. Uraga's office, repeating meticulously what I had said about going ahead with plans I had already made and about the upshot's being strictly in the province of others. I left the closing off both letters so I could add to them what the *Interventor's* response was when I should have heard it. I prepared telegrams to Senhora Braga and the two sons, telling them I was en route and about when I expected to arrive.

Shortly after one o'clock, having already fallen asleep twice in my chair, I gave up and went to bed. I wondered why I had heard nothing from Almeida. Perhaps Durondo, being indisposed or still preoccupied with the brunette charmer I had seen at his door, could not be reached. Or possibly I was being kept in the dark as a matter of premeditation. Drifting off to sleep, I was greatly taken by the aptness of the phrase "kept in the dark." He would like to *keep me in the dark,* I said to myself. My last conscious thought was what a clever fellow I was to have realized how it would appeal to Durondo to visit just such a fate upon me.

As it turned out, there was very little to add to the letters in the morning—only the gist of a brief note brought me by the sergeant of the day before and of other days before that. The sentry admitted him just as I was finishing my breakfast. He looked all around him with an eye versed in the practices of detention. He was obviously curious as to the accommodations provided a foreign political prisoner, and gave me to feel that I had done very well for myself indeed. Then, without hurry, he produced the note from beneath the crown of his hat.

It was from Almeida, and read:

I was prevented from communicating with you last night. His Excellency has graciously accepted your analysis of the situation. The sergeant

210

who brings this note will escort you to the customs office (be sure you have your passport) and then to the *Tocantins*. He will remain with you until the moment of sailing to protect you from those who may misinterpret your association with the Palace and not realize that you are superior to the little political differences of our people—all things to all men. Right? If you want to pack any suitcases with possessions you will not need on your trip, you may leave them in the room and care will be taken of them. Any letters you want mailed should be left with the sentry at your door. I will see you aboard the *Tocantins* before departure.

We drove to the harbor in the same car that had brought me to the Palace the day before, with the same stringy chauffeur. The city was shrouded by one of the grey, dripping skies beneath which its population periodically shivered. The rain kept most of the inhabitants off the streets, and for this I was grateful since it diminished the chances of my being seen and recognized by anyone I knew—any of Monteiro's friends, that was. It also, however, lowered my resistance to depression. The day before, I had been carried along by the novelty and strangeness of the happenings and by a certain excitement. Now, like someone on the morning after a party, I was back with myself, with a great untidiness and with disturbing recollections of how I had acted. I meant all to work out to Monteiro's advantage. But would he know it? Would Dona Sophia know it? And *would* it work out to his advantage? I went over the reasoning that had led me to the present position and asked myself if there were any other course I might have taken, if I could have made a better bargain with the *Interventor* if I had used to the full, as leverage, my value to the *Interventor* or could have pressed for a chance to see Monteiro without pushing Durondo—an uncertain quantity—too far and jeopardizing the privileges I had gained. And having asked myself such questions, I felt a need to go ask them of someone else—of Dona Sophia—to explain myself, to face judgment, to reattain a solid footing, even if only upon a finding of my unalloyed culpability.

How did it happen that the way in which I had decided I could best serve my friends in the pass I had reached coincided exactly with my besetting desire, which was to start up the river with the least possible delay? Had I in fact any "friends" in this business? There was Dona Sophia. And Dona Sophia would see that my going on as planned, this very day, actually promised the best results for the Concession—and for her husband. If only there were some way to see her, to make sure she

211

understood. . . . At that point in my reflections we drew up before the *Alfândega,* where I had to be fingerprinted for a visa, required for entering another state.

I had been wondering whether the *Interventor* imagined that when *Tocantins* pulled away from the wharf my movements would no longer need to be watched or confined by a guard. I began to see that it probably did not matter. Beyond the confines of the state there was little I could do. Within them I could be picked up at any time my actions gave offense. I could write Monteiro professing my unalterable adherence to his interests, as I meant to—write him as fully and ardently as I liked—but if he used the letter to show publicly that his party still held a monopoly over the future of the Massaranduba, my fate would be sealed.

It was not pleasant to think of the political embarrassment for Monteiro in my being no longer on exhibit as his party's particular property. But for the tenth time I told myself that he was the victim—as I was too—of his own actions, specifically of his having overreached himself. In any case, there was nothing I could do more than I was going to do. That there was nothing at all I could do until *Tocantins* reached her destination I could not help, and again the realization that everything was out of my hands for the present produced in me a sense of liberation; and this sense merged with and was fortified by the effect upon me of the sight of the vessel in which I was to sail.

The tide being out, nothing of *Tocantins* showed above the embankment but her bridge and top deck—her roof, as I thought of it—and her funnel with its scarlet band. But this was enough. It was brought home to me that I was about to embark on an ascent of the Amazon. Everything else became part of a past out of which I had stepped.

The rain had ceased. The canopy of cloud had slid back, exposing, as if grudgingly, like evil giving place to good, almost half of a blue sky. The sun was still concealed but had ignited the nether edge of the canopy, setting it on fire with gold and silver flame. A crowd was milling about and streaming in both directions across the gangplank, which sloped from the quay down to the ship. One would have thought that half the city, drawn by the promise of the pure, topless blue sky, bright with hope, had assembled on the wharf to seek passage to a land of dreams come true.

Almeida, though not so tall as his long face made him appear, was tall enough to be distinguishable standing just aboard the ship. The sergeant pushed a way through the crowd for himself and me and a porter with my suitcases. He did not sidle along down the gangplank as others did, but sauntered forward as if alone in the world, with the characteristic rolling gait of a man with a gun on his hip. I took a tolerant and faraway view of him and of his tunic damp with sweat between the shoulder blades and across the small of the back. He belonged to what I had already left behind.

And so did Almeida, who, after his initial greeting, took a sharper look at my face, as if he perceived a change in it. "Ah. Dr. Tate! Delivered safe and sound!" he was saying. He resumed. "I felt sure no harm could befall you under the protection of Sergeant ———" I did not catch the name. "I do believe you've positively grown to enjoy having a bodyguard."

"You were able to get a reservation?" I asked.

"The company was glad to be of service. Your name worked wonders —not to mention the *Interventor*'s. Not to mention the milreis, either. I even have a note for you from the owner." He gave a number to the porter, who went aft with my bags.

I took the papers thinking that Almeida and I were perhaps beginning to take pleasure in each other's company, it was so easy to deal with a person with whom the amenities could be ignored.

"I'm going to leave you for a bit," Almeida said. "I have some business to take care of ashore. I won't be long. And the *Tocantins,* whatever you may think, is not on the point of departure."

The sun just then came out theatrically. It was like the dawn, mellower than when it arrived on time, hurrying to make up for its tardiness. Out on the river the sails of the fishing fleet, homeward bound from the expedition I had seen begun three days before, took color. They were red, buff, blue, white. The boats advanced on the incoming tide without motion, as if drawn by invisible strings.

"If you have any traveler's checks you'd like cashed, I'd be glad to oblige. That way we could settle the matter of the cost of the ticket. I trust you are not looking to the Government to pay your passage?" He spoke irritably, and now that I noticed him, seemed to be keyed up, uncomfortably—certainly untouched by the refulgence in which the earth stood beatified.

213

I said I had just been going to raise this question and signed several of the checks on the rail as quickly as I could. He took them and went off without another word.

The owner of *Tocantins* had a humorous turn of mind. His note said that the ship would be honored to have me among her passengers but that owing to the lateness of the notice I should have to share the cabin of a Japanese spy for the first few days. All the Japanese in Brazil were spies, he wrote, but this one was the arch-spy of all those in the north. However, he was a very pleasant gentleman, and fat, and moreover, the Comandante was being instructed that I was to have complete freedom of the topmost deck for my special enjoyment.

Apart from this roof *Tocantins* had two decks. The lower, for steerage passengers and cargo, was only a few feet above the water and was entirely open in the after section. The staterooms of the first-class passengers lined the after half of the upper deck, being flush with the sides of the vessel. They opened off of a broad central areaway, or lounge, which narrowed toward the stern. Forward of the staterooms the areaway opened into the dining-saloon, a portion of the deck containing five tables and open from one side of the ship to the other. Forward of this the officers' cabins extended up the center of the ship with open promenade decks on either side of them leading to the bow.

Riverboats of this class were the next things to yachts. Just now, however, *Tocantins* looked more like a holiday excursion boat crowded to capacity. She was rising inch by inch with the tide. The end of the gangplank on her deck had already come even with the end of the wharf, beside which the sergeant had so far dropped at least half a dozen cigarette butts. But the throng of visitors meandered unhurriedly and the officers and crew stood about idly, as if they had forgotten what one did with a ship at this juncture and were insufficiently curious to find out. Almeida had been right. We had not been on the point of departure.

I went back to my quarters. There I met my cabin-mate, who, if a sinister oriental, disguised the fact very well. He was plump, as had been foretold, with cheeks like the halves of an apple when he smiled. That we were in the cabin together he seemed to regard as a great joke, as he did also, I felt certain, that the cabin was in the ship, the ship on the river, the river in South America. We shook hands warmly.

214

When I left the stateroom I found myself face-to-face with Almeida—and with Cora.

"Oh . . . hello," I said. Confused and embarrassed, I looked from one to the other. Just at the start I caught her eyes, and in the instant before she turned away I thought I saw in them the look of a creature trapped but too proud to show fear of the expected blow. She appeared excessively fatigued, even unwell. I did not take it in then that I was seeing her for the first time without make-up. I was gripped by an awful misgiving.

"An explanation, eh, Mr. Tate?" said Almeida. "That's it, is it? What brings us all together here, eh? Well, it's simple enough. Come along—I have some other last-minute things to say too and there's not much time." Taking his wife by the arm and placing his other hand offensively against my back, he propelled us toward the stern of the vessel, which was open upon the river and unoccupied.

"First . . . First things first, always, right? First, then—Mrs. Almeida. You can imagine my surprise, Mr. Tate, when you fell in with Dr. Uraga's suggestion about sailing on the *Tocantins*." He swallowed and moistened his lips. In the better light I could see that his lower eyelids were drawn up, betraying his tension. He took out a pack of Souza Cruzes, held it out to his wife, who paid no attention whatever, then to me—who declined with a slight shake of the head. He lighted one himself and drew in a lungful of the smoke. Expelling it, he went on. "By a striking coincidence, the *Tocantins* was the ship on which I had booked passage to Manáos for my wife."

My eyes shot over to her. She stood where he had released her arm and was looking at nothing.

Said Almeida, "You may wonder why I should be sending her to Manáos, and I will tell you. I will tell you straight out, without fear or favor, fur or feathers. It will not surprise you, you being a man who sees things as they are. I may remind you that we have in this state certain diehards, politically speaking. And these diehards may be planning to contest the election—in a word, to thwart the will of the people by resort to force. In my view, the bullets could start flying at just about any time. Did I promise a simple explanation? Here you have it! I did not want my wife in the path of any of those bullets. So what was the alternative? To send her out of the state! I decided to do so. Last

215

night, after we had left our friend Uraga, I asked myself if there was any reason to change the plan. There was none that I could see!"

He had taken a stance with one arm, on which he was leaning, against the side of the cabin. The physical exercise of speech, I had noticed before, was salubrious for Almeida. He now seemed to be at ease and enjoying himself. "None at all! I could even see advantages in the present arrangements. It will keep you in communication with the Palace—in a manner of speaking, that is to say. Mrs. Almeida will know how to reach me should need arise. She also understands me. She can enlighten you as to what may be expected of me in various circumstances. So much for that. I must get on." He straightened up, removing his arm from the side of the cabin. "I have your cash. You'll find on the envelope the amount of dollars converted, the rate of exchange, the product, the deduction of the cost of the round-trip passage, the remainder." He handed me the envelope. "One more thing."

"May I go now?" Cora asked. It was her first word.

"If you please! A moment more! May I just get this last item of business off my mind before I have to face our parting?" He interrupted himself with a cunning smile. "Do you know, anyone seeing you two standing together here would think you *brother and sister*. Remember that. I said there was one thing more. This is it." He drew a final time on the cigarette and flicked it overboard, watching it strike the water and die. "I reported your—what did I call it?—your 'analysis of the situation' to the *Interventor*. He accepted it. As far as it went. Nothing beyond it. You may go ahead with his sanction to obtain the information the financial interests in New York—and I bow to them—think they need. The object is to persuade them that they may proceed in the matter of the Concession in the expectation of very attractive profits. When that object is accomplished, you will have done your part. The rest—the arrangements here—can be left to the natives to settle in our own quaint way. You understand me?"

"Yes, I understand you," I said.

Despite myself I kept stealing glances at Cora. I could not help it, any more than a man, although of high principles, could keep his eyes altogether to himself in the presence of a woman divested of her clothing. "Is that all?" I asked.

Almeida had his hands in his pockets. His brown eyes were sharp, missing nothing, a quick light of satisfaction in their depths. "That is all—except that his Excellency *would appreciate* being informed of your movements by mail, at frequent intervals." Turning to his wife, he said, "And now, my dear, the time has come!"

Looking out the stern with my back to them, I heard their retreating footsteps. When I turned, they had disappeared, Cora presumably into her stateroom. Her husband I saw crossing the plaza with his loose stride when I went forward to see if there were any signs of our getting under way.

Evidently this was imminent. The exchange of farewells between passengers and visitors, who presumably had their own way of knowing that these would be timely, had begun. The drifting, amorphous throng, like a coagulating fluid, had broken up into families and these had divided into pairs. The partners met, embraced, then broke apart and formed new pairs, and all without show of emotion or change of expression even as, clutched to each other's bosoms, they looked over each other's shoulders. Finally the seers-off were all ashore, forming a body on the wharf, and the voyagers crowding the rail, as decorous as before. There was no laughter, no audible lamentation, there were no cries, no shouted final admonitions. Only, on the part of the wharfside contingent, there was a forest of raised arms ending in raised forefingers and a chorus of *pssst*-ing. . . . It was as if, I thought vaguely, they were afraid of jarring something loose in the universe.

I was conscious of having been putting off the satisfaction of an unfilled want. What was it? It was desire for a cigarette. I took out the pack—Cigarros Hollywood (pronounced "Awly-ode")—and shook one loose. As I was doing so, the stevedores laid hold of the gangplank, now sloping toward the land. I watched it hauled ashore.

Tocantins trembled as her power was suddenly thrown against the mass of the resistant water. The stone-faced quay backed away from us. A coastal steamer and a British freighter moored downstream of our berth came slowly into broadside view. The crowd ashore had fanned out, homeward bound; I could not see the sergeant at all.

The ship sounded her deep-throated whistle. I had heard that invocation many many times in the booming of other riverboats that reverberated through the city, reaching me as I sat before the typewriter or lay in bed hearing the cocks crowing in the moonlight, and now at last it was for me.

By the time the last blast had died away we were in midstream.

Surely I could be in no hurry to see Cora! Yet, standing at the corner of a cabin, leaning against it, I could not help recognizing that I was alert to the possibility of her re-emerging. I started forward, to go up to the bow and have a look at the river ahead of us, and in so doing deliberately acted to close my mind; I was not going to think about it, I said to myself, with the picture in my mind of pressing down the lid on a box in which were things I was disquieted to think were going to have to be reckoned with.

10

Before reaching the sea the Amazon divides and flows on either side of an island—Marajó—about the size of Denmark. Ships ascending the river from Belém, situated on the southern estuary behind a chain of islands, first go downstream to clear the end of this protective barrier. With that they emerge upon a formidable body of water. While the estuary here is still sixty miles from its mouth, it is fifteen miles across and unshielded from the waves that roll in from the sea. There is likely to be rough going for several hours before the sea's influence is left behind. Riverboats of *Tocantins*'s class often have to await a spell of comparative calm before venturing forth upon the Bay of Marajó, as it is called, turning upstream and making a run for it.

Tocantins decided not to delay. It was late afternoon when we rounded the tip of the last small island and breasted the open waters. The bay was very much as I had seen it first from *Boadicea*. Again a static pageantry of weather filled the heavens. Perhaps it is ordained that it shall always be so at the river's mouth, that there may be effected in the newcomer's mind at the start that changed perspective that sets the realm of the Amazon apart. The grey rain-squalls that veered earthward as before, connecting sky and river, could have stood for so many marching phalanxes—shadow ranks—in the inconceivably vast courtyard extending to the throne-room of the Supreme Splendor itself, a courtyard domed in silver. Pale, luminous, rayless sunlight glazed the colorless sky between the phantom grey armies and burnished the edges of the strand of cloud overhead.

It was nearly dusk before we came directly into the path of the swells riding in from the ocean. Then our lights were turned on, and this had the effect of plunging the outer world into night. The palely illuminated, watery horizons were snuffed out, and with that, blind as we had become, it was as if we had soared altogether off the earth into the darkness of the clouds. Every time the seas struck her *Tocantins* lay back on her haunches and a shudder ran the length of her. I thought with growing awe of her maiden voyage; for like all her kind, she had been built abroad (a brass plate at the head of her saloon deck bore the name of a Glasgow shipwright) and had crossed the Atlantic under her own power.

The evening was as eerie as any I had ever passed. I might almost have been alone aboard that celestial caravan rolling and pitching through the spume of the clouds beneath her hull. The other passengers had withdrawn from the scene utterly. Some—mostly women and children—had retired behind closed doors. The majority had lost no time in stringing their hammocks up in the broad areaway between the rows of staterooms. And there they hung, like so many pendant cocoons. When the vessel dipped to the troughs, they would all sway forward in unison. There they would hesitate, then, as *Tocantins* heeled, all swing back as one. It was a ballet of the mummies, ludicrous and very weird. Two sailors in blue denim jackets had let down tarpaulins on the windward side, for now and again in our course through the turbulent heavens we passed through one of the rain-squalls we had seen, and it was like being sandblasted. My Japanese cabin-mate, who seemed not to be a very dedicated spy, was stretched out in his bunk like a recumbent porcelain Buddha with closed eyes and parted lips, emitting soft, exotic sounds, either moans or snores. In the areaway there was no surcease from a reedy and agonized wailing. This was traceable to a hamper hung on the doorknob of one of the staterooms, later revealed to contain a little girl's pet marmoset.

The evening meal had to be postponed until the seas had subsided and the ship steadied. When the time came, everyone turned out—the shrouds gave up their dead. The transition from the bizarre, even macabre, to the humdrum was bewildering. From being alone in an aerial ghost-ship I found myself in a crowded restaurant. Twoscore diners ringing the tables went after the platters loaded with beef and vegetables as if fearful that at any instant the provisions might be snatched from them. They were mostly small merchants, small-plantation-owners and assistant managers of small mills, of a class of Brazilians I had not heretofore had much to do with. Assuredly the scene was down-to-earth. The ship, moreover, was plowing now through solid-seeming water, no longer floated on the vapors of clouds. Yet I did not quite feel we had come down out of the sky until a nimbus of light ahead of us was resolved into swinging electric lights above a wooden wharf.

That the pilot had been able to make this particular, ill-lighted landfall out of the boundless, watery night was to me incredible. But undeniably it was what he meant to do. *Tocantins* eased up to the wharf, then backwatered strenuously. Several hooded figures on the wharf laid hold of the hawsers thrown to them, made them fast and ran a gangplank aboard.

Tocantins let loose with a prodigious sigh. I kept expecting it to stop, but it did not. It went on and on, loud and inexhaustible, with no regard for the quiet of the night.

A handcart stacked with cordwood stood on the narrowest-gauged of railway tracks leading back to a row of open sheds similarly stacked. The wood was evidently to be our fuel. The hooded figures began laying it stick by stick on their shoulders, which the hoods protected, and carrying it into the ship. Anyone could see that this was going to be a lengthy process. I decided to go ashore.

Having been cooped up since my arrest the day before, I needed exercise, but there seemed to be nowhere to walk. The forest rose up behind the sheds, velvet-black against the sky, and the ground, as far as the light of the lamps carried, was mud.

Sauntering toward me from the direction of the ship was a figure in a white dress. That was what met my eye when I turned to go back.

221

None of the women at dinner had presented a figure in the least like it, and it was Cora's. Her head was bent, a shock of hair over her forehead, and a white handbag she was carrying by the strap banged against her leg at each step. She was walking very slowly, in a kind of careless way, resting her weight on each leg in turn. She might have been unaware that I was coming toward her until I was directly in front of her. She threw her head back then and, letting it fall to the side, regarded me with raised eyebrows.

"That was my streetwalker walk," she said, clasping with her free hand the elbow of the arm with which she was holding the bag. "I couldn't resist the stage-set. The waterfront. The two sordid-looking streetlights. The mysterious cowled figures going back and forth. They represent Fate, you know. The director thinks he's a genius for having had *that* inspired idea."

I responded with exactly what was in my mind. "I didn't expect to see you again today." The statement sounded disapproving, so I added, "I thought . . . I was afraid you weren't well."

"I wasn't. I'm not." The light being behind her, I could see her face only indistinctly. "My head felt as if someone were hammering a spike into the top of it. Two railroad presidents. What am I thinking of?"

"Is it any better now?"

"It's better in the dark. If I can keep out of the bright light for the next few days, I'll be all right. The worst thing now—I'm a little shaky. May we move over to that car there so I can have something to lean against?"

There was an empty, open-topped boxcar on a siding in front of the sheds. On our way to it I had to grasp her arm when she stumbled, but she recovered at once and I let my hand fall. I wondered if her idea was that we should proceed with complete casualness, as if we were back in the days of *Boadicea*. I asked if it were not going to be difficult to avoid the light on such a trip.

Tocantins's hissing exhalation of steam was cut off. The night might have silenced it in order to listen.

She stumbled again, this time catching my arm herself. Her heels were too high for the rough going.

"It'll mean keeping mostly to my stateroom till sunset. I'll do my sleeping during the day, or a lot of it. I've been through this before."

We came up to the little railroad car. She leaned over its side, resting her arms on the edge of the planking, her handbag in the crook of her elbow.

"There's one advantage in turning night and day around," she said. "It's a lot better to wake up from a nightmare when it's bright and sunny, with people around."

"Do you often have nightmares?"

"Often enough. I sometimes wonder where they come from. *I* could never think of such things, and I'm sure I wouldn't want to."

At the end of the pier *Tocantins,* lighted up from within, looked very big, very massive and dependable. I had a sense of transcendent security, such as a devout person might have on the eve of a religious communion—a sublime trust.

"Yet there's only one place they could come from—inside your own mind." I was gratified and surprised that Cora had not caused any significant dislocation in my state of being. It was like having been fearful of using a certain muscle in expectation of pain, then doing so inadvertently and finding that the dreaded complications did not come to pass. "You ought to find out what causes them and do something about it." It was a facile remark, and in the circumstances smug and callous. But I was preoccupied with what lay ahead, rapt in it.

She straightened up and turned her head partly toward me, the light glinting momentarily on her eyes before she turned the other way again.

"What kind of life did you want to have originally, Cora? What kind of life appealed to you? I don't suppose you could have foreseen that you'd be living on the equator, between a sea of ocean and a sea of forest." I had got out a pack of cigarettes, feeling as if I were making a big operation of it, and this I now held out to her.

"Thank you." As it had at other times, the sight of her slim white hand in the light of the match, with the fingers bent back to a degree somehow expressive of a woman's delicacy and vulnerability, touched my compassion. She had turned around, toward the river, leaning back with her handbag clutched to her breast. In the wan light of the lamp her face had the pallor and tightness of skin of one who is thoroughly chilled. Her hand had indeed been like ice when she had grasped my wrist.

"I wanted to be an actress," she said. "I wonder if you can understand what it's like to be an actress. I mean to feel yourself an actress, through

223

and through. It's different from being an actor, I think. Men and women are different. . . . Have you ever watched a cat stretch, or a leopard? How it thrusts out its forelegs, to the very limit, so that all its toes stand out, and its claws, too? So that every sinew is taut?" She drew on the cigarette and with eyes closed blew out the smoke.

"That's what it's like in a part when you're truly *it*. You can feel yourself in every part of you, the way a cat can—the way a cat can even when it's just walking across the floor. Hundreds of people are watching you, forgetting themselves. What they are conscious of is you, every intonation of your speech, every gesture, every part of your body as you move—everything the character feels. The character lives, not just with what you've put into it but with the lives of everyone in the theater. It's like the glow of a fire on you—*in* you. Everyone in the theater is endowing that character with life, and you are that character—and yet you're standing entirely apart, too. You're the creator and the—the created?— yes, the creator and the created, both!"

"You must have been a very good actress." I had almost become lost in what she was saying and had to remind myself how she stood in the scheme of things, why she was here.

She did not answer, only seemed to clutch the big white bag more tightly to her.

"What happened? Why didn't you go on with it?"

"I had an appointment for a tryout for a really good part in a Broadway production—Sarah in *Under the Sun,* in case you remember it; it ran for seven months. I'd been told I could act by those who knew. On my way from the rooming-house where I lived I stopped in a drugstore for a cup of coffee and a cigarette. I had time enough, and at the counter there was a clock facing me, to remind me. I watched the hand of the clock get nearer the time of my appointment. I watched it get there— four o'clock. It was as if I were someone else. Then I watched it go beyond. At quarter past four I had another cup of coffee and another cigarette. Then I went home."

"And that was all?"

"That was all."

"It must have been that in your heart you didn't want to go on the stage." I knew this sounded insincere and, even in the circumstances, felt small.

"I wanted to very much. I was stage-struck, and more. The stage was my only hope for life, as I saw it. I had had an operation and couldn't have children. I was sure no man, knowing that, would want to marry me. So later, when one did, I was so grateful . . ." She paused, breathing in a deep draught of air. She held the handbag out to me. "Take this. I think I'm going to do something silly."

The cigarette fell from her hand, her eyelids drooped, and as she sagged I had just time to catch her.

Lifting her bodily with one arm beneath her knees, the other behind her back, I managed to carry her more or less in a sitting position, so that her head, instead of falling back, rested on my shoulder. I had never seen anyone faint. I was in a panic. I thought she might be dying. I believe I called her aloud, by name, and shook her, to bring her back. She was very light. I did not understand how a complete human being, with a mature person's freight of experiences, could be so light. The surprised faces of the Coboclos loading firewood, arrested, slid by like faces in a photograph, as did first one, then the other lamppost. The rail of *Tocantins* ahead of me was crowded; it had been deserted a moment before. Everyone was craning forward, and in the faces, like massed balloons, were curiosity and, I thought, relish. In the glance I gave them I saw in them the inhumanity of which I had been guilty. During my gingerly ascent of the narrow, insecure gangplank I could feel her uneven breathing. Risking loss of balance, I looked into her face and could see the quiver of her eyelids. She was completely limp.

People seemed to me to be packed like cattle at the end of the gangplank. As I stepped on deck, my mind filled with the atmosphere of disaster, those in the front rank tried to give me room while those behind pressed forward. But it was not as I had thought; there was solicitude in their regard. *"Pobrezinha!"* I heard, and other sounds of commiseration. The expressions I saw in the faces around me brought to my mind a remembered scene I was too agitated to think of trying to place. (The adoration of the Holy Infant, it came to me later.) The Comandante appeared in front of me—a distinguished-looking gentleman of fine figure and carriage—and cleared a way, I following. At the door of what was evidently Cora's stateroom stood a middle-aged, large-bosomed woman who immediately took charge. I had noticed her with disapproval at dinner; she had lumpy features, a gritty voice and a way of looking around with self-conscious complacency, and the material of her tulle blouse strained at the buttons running down her broad back. My feel-

225

ing about her now underwent a total change. She raised the voice I had disliked to disperse the crowd at the door, and when at her direction I had borne Cora inside and placed her on her bunk, she felt her pulse and forehead and studied her face with every sign of confidence and competence. She then addressed herself in a direct and reassuring manner to the Comandante and me. Cora's lips were moving. The middle-aged woman was saying, "*A sua irmã . . . nada grava . . . tudo . . . bem. . . .*" She smiled, and I was so thankful for what she said that the identification of Cora as my sister, with what it implied, made no impression on me. In a grimly amiable way she moved forward to steer us out of the stateroom when, looking over my shoulder, I saw Cora open her eyes.

Without moving she looked around her in a puzzled way. Her gaze alighted on me and her puzzlement seemed to grow greater. Then her eyes slowly cleared; the pucker was smoothed out between her brows.

"I'm afraid I disgraced myself—and you," she said weakly. "Forgive—"

"Don't think any such thing!"

"I simply fainted."

"*Cái fora!*" said the matron—Out!—bringing the authority of her solid bulk to bear upon us.

When the door had closed behind us, I turned to the Captain. "*Café? Cachaça?*" I knew the word for rum, but not for brandy.

He nodded once, in a manner to suggest that I had voiced his own intention, and promptly after he had gone a steward arrived with a tray bearing a bottle and glass and a cup, which he delivered to Cora's stateroom.

Word spread at once among the other passengers that the young American woman had recovered. It had been *nada grava* and now all was *bem*. The episode was concluded. I was left alone on the saloon deck, among the dining tables. My relief, when I measured it against the extreme alarm which had so recently gripped me, became all the greater.

The Caboclos were now loading roofing tile instead of firewood.

I had not finished a cigarette before the door of Cora's stateroom opened upon the broad back of the succoring senhora. This woman of sterling worth, with a grating, full-voiced, motherly admonishment of her patient, stepped clear of the doorway. She was replaced there by Cora herself. After responding in murmured, grateful accents to the senhora's leave-taking, Cora looked around the deck until she saw me, whom she had evidently expected to find there. I hurried forward.

Before I was close enough to speak, she assumed a pose—shoulders contracted, hands offered helplessly, eyebrows raised, the corners of her tightly-closed mouth drawn back—so expressive of an impudent, resigned, exasperated well-there-you-are! that I had to smile before I could ask how she was.

"Poor Julian!" She put her hand to the doorframe—whether to steady herself or just to rest her arm I could not tell. "I feel so sorry for the male when confronted with the femaleness of the female. Just as I do for the female when confronted with—well, you get it. You even managed to bring my handbag . . . ! Oh, I'm all right now. I've had this happen before."

"I'd never have dreamed half an hour ago I'd be seeing you like this!"

The slight smile with which she had dismissed her attack lingered there, abandoned as it were, and I could tell from a certain vagueness about them that though her eyes were still on my face she was not seeing me. Then, just as clearly, their focus returned. She resumed her smile—slipped back into it—and it became rueful.

"Did you have to carry me all that way?"

"You're very light. Ordinarily I'd have enjoyed it."

"You've been very kind. I suppose I'd better turn in. It's been a long day. But I did want to thank you."

She held out her hand. Expecting her from past experience to withdraw it almost as soon as I had touched it, I dropped it before she in fact did so and felt a little awkward as I said good night. Her hand was as cold as ever.

Her door clicked as I turned, and I walked slowly off, troubled in my mind.

A chute had been placed between the wharf and the lower deck of the ship, and down it straw baskets full of *farinha* were being slid. Two voices counted them off in monotone, in slightly different pitch. From my bunk it sounded like an interminable argument of katydids. It was the last thing I heard before I dropped off, almost immediately, to sleep, thinking I should not be able to, so much was Cora in my mind. *"Trinta e quatro. Trinta e quatro. . . . Trinta e cinco. Trinta e cinco . . ."* My last sensation, I think, was that with which I had borne her across the dipping gangplank, unable to help her, unable to put her down, with nothing but a void around us.

It was five o'clock when I awoke and still dark even after I had taken a shower of warm Amazon River water and climbed to the bridge, which stood tenantless. (The officers chose to navigate from a secondary helm below the bridge, at the forward end of the main deck, possibly because the bridge was too isolated for Brazilian temperaments.) Dawn, grey with streamers of cloud like soiled linen, hung along the horizons, found us on a side-channel of the river approaching another tiny clearing with a large but decrepit pier and several houses. Three blasts of our whistle, unexpectedly high-pitched, like the voice of an overgrown twelve-year-old (the cylinder must have been half full of water), announced our arrival and ensured that no one on board would sleep through it.

From the first these settlements fascinated me. They represented the frontier. So far had Western civilization come in the course of a millennium (or two, or three), always pushing back the wilderness. The line that had once stood along the River Rhine and the wall the Romans had built across Britain stood now behind the three houses at the edge of the settlement called Paquetá—one house of boards, the other two of palm-thatch, I was now able to see. Though the interest the scene held for me was not diminished by their absence, the externals of drama were missing, and so was any sign that the inhabitants were aware of the historic confrontation of which they were a part. The settlement remained subdued even after day had fully arrived, even after we had been there long enough to have endured two or three fine northern drizzles and the tide had gone out, leaving the houses standing up above the mud on stilts. The men, in faded denim trousers and faded shirts hanging over them, patched and with the patches patched, were dark but evidently more Portuguese than Indian and went about their work silently, without talk or laughter. As the clearing awoke, women in shapeless one-piece dresses appeared, along with their numerous progeny, the younger ones naked. In the women's faces was to be read a chronic bitterness at having been dealt with so harshly by life. Gaunt, long-legged chickens came out as the water receded and fell with transports of joy upon morsels left behind it.

What a day it was! I saw my first true parrots. Soon after we put in at Paquetá, they began to burst out of the trees behind the clearing in small flocks. They had long, tapering tails and flew as large teal would fly, with quick, decisive wingbeats and heads up. They wheeled and emitted short screams, full of vitality. With them awoke the black vultures, which heaved themselves out of the palm trees, flapping strenuously to gain momentum. As if to show them how it should be done, a turkey vulture sailed by over the treetops on majestic pinions, light as a shadow—on reconnaissance, one would have thought, for some hawk-faced Indian god reigning over the remote interior. Just before we departed there plopped down out of the trees into the mangroves lining the shore an astonishing fowl, something like a pheasant with a heavy, chocolate-colored, white-striped body and a long neck with several plumes standing up from its reddish-buff head, which was like a hawk's. It perched erect like a hawk, too. It was the nearest thing to my idea of a phoenix likely to be found on earth, I thought. Said one of the passengers who had observed my interest, a plump little river-trader named Anjinho whom I came to know because he spoke some English, "It is a *cigana*. It is not good to eat."

The shores of the estuary seemed to be almost entirely forested, but of the forest itself little could be seen when we moved out from the side-channels onto the main body of the river. The enormous distances reduced it to the narrowest of green ribbons, then to a blue thread. Sea and sky—these were what made up the world. You could not think of the Rio Mar as a river. Shoreless ahead of us and astern, it formed the sharp edge of the horizon, beyond which was only the sky. It gave you the same sense of boundlessness as the ocean. With its sandy color and the islets of water-hyacinths floating on its surface, gaily green, it made you think of a vast, barren plain dotted with patches of vegetation by the mudholes. It extended to lengths that stunned the imagination—but the sky was greater still. It was not a dome, as one had known it in lands of circumscribed horizons, but an illimitable ceiling of blue high above the flat-bottomed white puff-clouds, high even above the filmy mists which shaded them, stretching out forever. As the afternoon advanced, compressed grey clouds filled the heavens, forming a level but still endless expanse which, as we crept microscopically beneath it, seemed to revolve slowly above us, like a millwheel.

To return to the interior of the ship from the panorama outside always rocked me a little; I could not quite believe it. What existed within bore no relationship to what lay without, and this—the world through which we were voyaging—was of no interest to the voyagers. Between meals they generally kept to their hammocks. The lounge between the ranks of staterooms, unnaturally illuminated through little green and purple skylights, was so crowded with hammocks it could scarcely be traversed. Under a pall of cigarette smoke the sounds of unhurried conversations were almost as continuous as the drone of the ship's engines and the rustle of the water, and not very different from them. Seldom, almost never, by any chance, did anyone's attention stray beyond the *gaiola's* railings.

A boatload of refugees, I thought, safe and secure at last, might similarly be interested exclusively in resting, talking and eating, and not in contemplating the floodwaters that had made them homeless; I continued to imagine something refugeelike about Brazilians en masse. Moreover, we had an assortment of animals on board just such as might be rescued from an inundation. Pigs, sheep, chickens, ducks, turkeys were loaded daily, and their scufflings, gruntings, quackings and cluckings, not to mention their smells, emanated from below and were soon to be aggravated as we began to fill up the lower deck with steers. On the upper deck the marmoset would sometimes scream for an hour, seemingly without drawing breath. So, in briefer snatches, would a parrot tied to the meat larder, beneath which also were tied, through holes in the edge of their shells, three turtles. A pet oriole had the run of the ship and was apt to drop on your shoulder when you were not expecting it, but he spent much of his time asleep in a sock hung up for him, like a good *Brasileiro*.

What brought the passengers out of their torpor was food. The food was good and also plentiful; five meals a day were served. Where hunger is known only too well and may be anticipated, eating all one can, when one can, is probably a matter of common prudence, of good husbandry, a concern of the deepest instincts. Moreover, the meals were included in the price of the passage and our passengers were of a class to which a good bargain is what life is for.

Cora, though I kept watching for her, did not put in an appearance all day, until the evening meal, after dark. Until then the seat at the Comandante's right, between him and me, was empty. Senhor Anjinho, the bespectacled little trader, who was able to combine talking with eating and spoke a little French as well as a little English, sat across from me.

His wife, who had tawny hair, a protruding mouth and a greyness about her complexion, was at the Comandante's left.

The Comandante's deportment was invariably that of an attentive, if somewhat withdrawn, and well-bred host. His fine lips were characteristically compressed. He looked rather British. A singular aspect of his appearance was that his complexion was swarthy up to an irregular line across the top of his forehead and nakedly pink above this line. His hair was thin and grey, prematurely, I was told, because of past misfortune. He stood in the first rank of his profession, which was saying a great deal.

To pilot a ship on the Amazon, as I was beginning to perceive, meant not only reckoning with the ebb and flow of tides through awkward passages, the current of the river, the shifting contours of the riverbed and sudden storms of wind and rain, but dealing with the problem—one would suppose insoluble—of ever knowing one's location. The panorama from the expanse of the estuary was devoid of landmarks. The land itself, consisting of islands lying flush with the surface of the water, seemed to have the merest foothold and to be in danger of being carried out to sea, along with the mats of nodding green lilies. The islands in some cases bristled with treetrunks, resembling clothes-brushes on their backs and nearly submerged. In others mangroves formed the shore and gave the impression that a flow of foliage like lava had poured across the land to be solidified and arrested by the water. In any case, the shore was featureless. Part of the time we sailed among islands, inshore from the main body of the river, through a web of seemingly indistinguishable channels, themselves giant rivers. They would open up ahead of us or alongside. Half a dozen times an hour the officer on watch was offered monumental opportunities for error. Yet he simply stood gazing ahead, from time to time issuing an instruction to the helmsman in a low voice, and the demonstration of quiet competence in the handling of finite problems had a magnetism for me. It was an antidote to the residuum of the preceding two days, which now and again, despite my absorption in what was passing before my eyes, sent a small, debilitating spasm though me. It caused me to speculate that a happy person would be one whose problems could all be dealt with by adequate technical skill.

With a manner of which she was mistress—more truly an absence of manner—which precluded comment and even any show of curiosity

231

about her, Cora took her seat beside me for the evening meal. In the confusion of the general convergence upon the dining-saloon I had not even known she was there until the Comandante's graceful inclination of the head and courtly presentation of the chair at his right caused me to turn. She was in white, in a dress with a ruffled collar held below the throat by a moonstone pin. She had beautiful carriage; having learned that she had trained for the stage, I realized that I had been aware of this all along. She responded to the attention I paid her with a slight movement of her body toward me, which had the intimacy of a touch and might also have meant nothing. Only when the Comandante had performed introductions all around did she look at me. "And my brother I know," she said. Evidently the Comandante had made a pleasantry of her needing to be reminded of her acquaintance with her brother. Her smile could have been in accord with that droll notion or a sign of amusement at the assumed relationship. I essayed one of a similar nature, but I knew I had flushed. That morning Senhor Anjinho, expressing the solicitude of the table, had inquired of my sister, and for reasons which I did not seek to plumb but was aware were devious, I did not at once correct the error, and it was soon too late to do so naturally.

During the day I had been telling myself that I was going to take the first opportunity for a talk with Cora to see to it that the situation with her was "cleared up." By that I meant having it acknowledged between us that she had been placed aboard *Tocantins* as an agent of Monteiro's enemies, out of mistrust of me, for whatever specific purpose. It was important to me to have this established as the footing upon which we stood with each other so that nothing would be expected of me beyond what was consistent with it. There was also the object of having my own mind swept clear of ambiguities, which opened the way to thoughts I had believed dead some time ago but evidently were not, seeming to have a vitality of their own, independent of the consciousness that had produced them.

By the end of dinner I was no less bent upon bringing about a clarification, but I could see that it was not going to be as easy as I had thought. From the beginning of the meal Cora surprised me. Of her illness nothing was discernible except in the ivory of her complexion, not a pallor so much as a suggestion of translucency, like the moonstone in her brooch, which was perhaps what made one conscious of it. I was used to Cora's propensity for abrupt ebbs and flows, which were likely to put her in dissonance with the tenor of others; she was constitutionally, I had come to realize, an outsider. But there was none of that in her this evening. I could not usually follow the conversation, and when I could, or when Cora explained it to me ("We're talking about the *paludismo* on the river," or, "Senhora Anjinho does not think the carnival music was as good this year as last"), it concerned what did not matter much. What I could not be in any doubt about was that everything that was said was said to her or for her hearing, and I was convinced that this would have been so had the company been a far more dashing one. At the far end of our table were two diners who could scarcely take their eyes away from her, one a young man with a high-bridged nose, like a caricature of a classic Greek, the other, older and starved-looking even after an enormous meal, with a strand of hair combed over his bald scalp which he nervously fingered—a professor, I learned later. Occupants of adjoining tables swiveled their chairs around to take part—especially when the urgent business of eating was concluded and *cafèzinhos* were being taken. Cora herself spoke only a few words now and again. She listened. She was attentive. And she was charmingly pretty, cool as a lily, yet interested, she was friendly yet with a pensiveness bespeaking a nature removed from the commonplace. Her swift, soft laughter, when her eyes would partly close, was a little different from any I had heard from her, and her dusty-sweet fragrance, when she leaned toward me to translate unobtrusively, was also new to me. At the next table the masculine-voiced grey-haired woman who had taken Cora under her wing the night before beamed and cast her eyes about with pride of authorship, and although it was the last sensation I was ready to welcome as a prelude to what I had planned, I could not help feeling proud, too, not only as a fellow American and an evidently favored acquaintance, but as if I were actually her brother.

When, the coffee-period having been done justice to, Cora got up to go, I caught a questioning glance in her eyes as I followed her in rising. I excused myself and accompanied her down the deck. Out of earshot of the others, she halted and, looking at me with eyes that were bright even in the dimmer light, said, "I'm going to be in my cabin for a bit. If you feel you may be in the mood for a chat later on, wait for me. I won't be very long." She spoke with a naturalness I could not have be-

233

gun to emulate in addressing her, gave me a quick smile of the same character and left me gazing after her, not knowing what to think.

The exodus from the dining area proceeded rapidly. I sat down at an empty table, turning the chair to face the side of the ship. It was drizzling again, and nothing could be seen beyond the screen of droplets glistening with our reflected lights, though the grating and chirping of insects indicated that the forest was close at hand. I found myself in the mental maze into which my thoughts inevitably took me when I was turned in upon myself, to be drawn in conflicting directions at the same time by concern for the Monteiros and what they must be thinking, anxiety over the insatiable business of the Concession and what it had come to mean to those who were important to me, awe and exaltation at the knowledge that I was going deeper by the moment into the realm of the great river, the murky waters of which sopped up the lights that fell upon them from throbbing, on-gliding *Tocantins*—always the consciousness, as of the key to life, of the girl I had but glimpsed twice, the quest for whom I regarded simultaneously, or in the swiftest alternation, with the certain confidence of a faith and a realistic, crushing appreciation of the obstacles in its way. What inquiries could I make, and of whom? When I probed the confidence I felt, I fond that insofar as it was rational at all it derived from a conviction that the girl was somehow, in some way, caught up in the skein of the Massaranduba Concession.

I had begun to wonder if Cora were going to come back after all when the door of her stateroom clicked and opened and with deliberate care she stepped out over the high sill, a shock of her fine taffy-colored hair falling across her face; she was still doing it in the new way in which she had had it the evening before. I went to meet her. The hard chairs of the dining-saloon had been entirely vacated by then and half the lights had been turned off, though the flow of talk from the lounge, sounding a little like one's notion of Chinese with all its resonant, nasal *āo*'s had not yet subsided.

When she had led the way back to the place I had been occupying and we had sat down, she said, "I never seem to have cigarettes with me when we're together."

"And I seem to smoke too many when I'm with you." The words were rather roughly spoken, but as I offered her my pack I realized that it was an admission I had done better not to have made. She squinted a little in the light I held up to her and I added, "I'm glad it's not the last time I did this—twenty-four hours ago."

She leaned back with her elbows on the table behind her. "We seem to be fated to smoke cigarettes together on a succession of boats."

I was a little surprised that she would so readily bring up the subject of our being together again in a way that must raise the question of why we were—a question I should naturally be concerned to have the answer to. I was going to raise it then and there, but the somber cast of her features made me hesitate.

"You want to reproach me for being here," she said, surprising me more and also disconcerting me. "You resent it. Considering how it came about, you naturally would." She leaned forward, her elbows on her knees, which were pressed together, her forearms crossing each other, in an attitude suggestive of conserving bodily warmth in the chill air. Her face was again concealed by her hair. "You know of course why I was installed aboard the boat with you?"

"Well, I . . . in a general way, I suppose I do."

"In a specific way, the idea is for me to seduce you."

"I can imagine!" The uncomfortable, mocking ejaculation, startled out of the mists of a vanished, inept, self-conscious adolescence, had no relevance to anything in my head. There is a sensation, which must be known to everyone, of being impaled on a moment, transfixed by it, unable to go on to anything else or to see beyond it.

She straightened up, her face perceptibly shiny in the meager light; evidently she had flushed. Sitting as far back from me as her chair would permit, and regarding me measuringly, she said quickly, "Were you happy back in the States?"

"I don't know. What's that got to do with it?"

Her expression grew reflective. "I was wondering why you had to come down here. I don't mean this personally. You know I like you—very much. But everything has been complicated horribly since your arrival. As it used to be, nothing was terribly serious. It would all have passed over, with a few people killed, that's all—people are always going to be killed. Now everyone is in way over their depth."

I showed, I am certain, that I heard this with amazement. "What are you talking about? I'm the one who's had everything complicated for him—and beyond recognition. Have you any idea of the sort of thing

235

that's been happening to me since I've been here? Can you imagine what I went through at the Palace? Do you know what my situation now is? Do you suppose this is my normal way of life?"

She did not immediately answer, but her eyes allowed me to believe that she was taking account in her train of thought of what I had said.

"I don't know," she murmured. "I suppose you're only the instrument of . . . There's all that money in New York. At least they tell me there's a lot, though they probably exaggerate. Anyhow, this affair you've come down about—this Massaranduba thing—is no joke in these parts, now that it's got money behind it and you're here to prove it. You inspire belief, it seems. I guess that's what I mean. You don't get boozed up and go reeling after women. Things might be different if you did. As it is, you've supplied just what it took. A fever's been started, and everyone's caught the contagion. And coming in the middle of the political campaign, everyone's lost all sense of proportion."

"You're telling me? Do you think I haven't watched it grow? And why has it? Because of me? I can't even speak the language! A wax figure could have done as much as I. No, it's because the people here want to believe, without exception, wholeheartedly. Do you know what's given Dona Sophia doubts about me? She's suspected I don't believe in the Massaranduba. And you blame me!" Reminding myself to keep my voice low, I decided that now was the time to take the bit in my teeth. As if I had literally done just that, I had a metallic taste in my mouth as I proceeded. "You say there's a fever, that it's no joke, and *that* I believe, with you posted here to . . . to . . . what? Make sure I've sold out our client—my friends—completely and without mental reservation or afterthought? People are out of their depths, you say? I should think so! I should say that was putting it mildly, when a man makes such use of his wife, and his wife falls in with it." I am afraid my indignant outpouring sounded more like a rehearsal than the real thing, and its effect must have been further diminished when I added anticlimactically, "Not, of course, that I take what you said a moment ago literally, about the specific reason for your being here."

"As for the 'man' making use of his 'wife,'" she said, leaning forward on her arms, holding onto the edge of her seat, "I'm his wife only in the most limited legal sense, I can assure you. I am not . . . I am not one of his women." She spoke with the strained calm of a principal in a court trial required to put reticence aside. She stood up and crossed the two or three yards between the table and the railing. "Another cigarette, please?" When I went up to her she held out her hand and took the cigarette I offered and lighted it from the stub of the other without looking around. "I think he made plain enough yesterday how he regards me. You should have no difficulty believing that I was speaking literally in what I said. I meant with lights out, a bed at hand—the complete program. My husband wants to be in solid with the boss, and the boss wants to make as sure as he can—or as sure as I can—of your reliability. And how else could I be of help? They'd hardly expect a woman to be able to follow you ashore and make sure you don't send any telegrams you shouldn't or talk to any strangers. I'm supposed to see that you won't *want* to misbehave. You'll notice I have a stateroom by myself; another woman passenger had to be bought off. Since it's understood that we're brother and sister, no tongues will wag if we keep rather close company. Then there are hotels in Manáos. The arrangements are left to me."

"Why would you be telling me this?"

She raised her hand, blew on the back of it, rubbed a place on it with her forefinger and blew on it again. "You were obviously going to demand an explanation of what, exactly, I was here for. So I thought I'd tell you. There was no reason not to unmask this melodramatic scheme in view of another fact of the matter I'm now going to let you in on. I am that unique being—a person who has got a lungful of the intoxicating aroma of the Massaranduba and hasn't been affected. I couldn't care less what happens to the Massaranduba or who gets rich from it or who doesn't, or if anybody doesn't, or if I never hear of it again."

"Why did you come on this trip? Why didn't you refuse?"

"Oh don't be foolish." She looked down the side of the ship toward the stern, turning the back of her head toward me. With the high heel of her shoe as a pivot she twisted her foot this way and that, as if it had gone to sleep.

There was a moment's silence.

"Cora, what are you looking for out of life?"

"Peace," she replied instantly. She addressed the word to the night, out of which the leafy limbs of trees loomed in dusky form near at hand, as if reaching out toward us as we passed, as if they would detain us. It had stopped raining.

"I wish I could tell you how to find it."

237

She said nothing for an interval.

"O-o-o-o-o-oh . . . If I had it I'd probably find it boring and crave excitement." She spoke in a tone that dismissed the subject, then turned to give me, I thought, her full attention, studying my eyes.

"I'll tell you what you *could* do."

"What's that?" There had come back to me as she spoke an item on the bill of particulars I had been nursing against her which I had been in danger of forgetting: her cool underhandedness in apprizing herself, by whatever means she had employed, of the contents of my cabin in *Boadicea.*

From her unchanging expression I surmised that she was still resolving a possibility in her mind.

"You could teach me to see whatever it is you see in—what I'd call scenery. I hear you spent the whole day looking out from the side of the boat. And I know from the reports that were made that you used to go on walks out from town constantly. I never did believe that twaddle about your studying the geography for military purposes."

"I'm glad you didn't." For the rest, I did not know what to say. I was surprised and embarrassed. "I don't see anything mysterious. I just see what's there. And not even that, I'm afraid. Not by a long shot."

She leaned over sideways, raising her foot and reaching down to it. She frequently had trouble with her shoe. I think she would slip her foot out of it and not be able to slip it back in. Perhaps because of their deliberateness, her movements had the effect of bringing her closer to one, even when they did not actually do so—as in this case they did. When she straightened up, our proximity was such that if I breathed deeply my arm touched hers.

"But you see what's there in a way that makes it mean a great deal to you," she said. "I don't think you were telling little Cora a complete fib when you gave out that the purpose of your trip was study and travel. I really believe what chiefly brought you here was your wanting to see —whatever it is you do see. Not that you'd have got very far with the boss if you'd tried to convince *him* of that."

"Oh yes," I said without enthusiasm. "I remember telling you that. It wasn't that I wanted to prevaricate." I met her arch sidewise gaze. "I wasn't a free agent."

"And I haven't been a free agent either," she said without a pause. "I

238

could perhaps tell you something about unfreedom, but . . . never mind."

"No, I suppose you haven't been," I said slowly. "When you got those papers out of my cabin in *Boadicea,* it was Manoel you used, wasn't it?" Manoel was the cabin steward, yellow-skinned and harassed.

She seemed not to have heard. When I had decided she was not going to reply and was feeling ashamed of my crassness, she said, "You must have been very kind to him. I had to raise my price twice and remind him of his wife and children. Incidentally, just before I left the ship he said something about a visitor you had—that would have been Monty —who got a package of some sort surreptitiously from one of the crew and later shut himself in your cabin and came out without it. But I ignored this information. I felt I'd already got my money's worth from Manoel."

I had the sensation of my skin contracting. It was not easy for me to swallow the knowledge she had imparted. But the hot feeling of my ignominiousness did not prevent my being much moved. "I appreciate that, Cora. I owe you a great deal." Impulsively I had put my hand on her shoulder, but with the impression that it had met a negative response I took it quickly away—though how the character of a shoulder's response could be assayed I could not have said. "I didn't know anything at the time about what was going on."

"I was sure you didn't." She drew herself up. "But maybe we could forget about the past. Here we are in the present. Here is this great big river, and the *mato,* and *fazendas* and such. And now you have your assignment. As we go along you're to tell me what you see and make me feel what you feel."

A vain injunction! I was already past being able to convey any part of what I felt, for by then I had had my first sight of the rain-forest— the true rain-forest—to which years of anticipation had led up without preparing me for it.

The southern estuary of the Amazon communicates with the northern through a network of narrow waterways known as the Breves channels, and it is upon entering one of these passages that one enters also the domain of the forest. There is, below one, the water-road upon which the ship has ventured and, above, like a mirror image of the waterway, the strip of sky, and these are the floor and ceiling of a canyon in the forest. Between its sheer and mighty walls of green, rising like thunder-heads to the height of buildings twelve to fifteen stories tall, human history has been left behind, as if it were a dream. There is a sense of having been cut loose from mankind and engulfed in a timelessness in which civilization in its swift passage has left no echo. You understand the fantasy that the rain-forest invariably instills in the minds of the impressionable, that here is a dawn-world inhabited by creatures of eons past, alive as ever behind the miles of forest, in the ancient swamps, il-luminated by the eerie, universal, sourceless light of the beginning of things.

The chasm walls of vegetation when we steered between them were flooded with the ethereal watery-yellow sunlight of late afternoon. It was not enough to imagine that we had been transported back in time. This was a different planet. We were traversing the floor of an ocean, be-tween mountain-ranges of seaweed, in a mysterious other world where water was light as air. The illusion was not impaired by the reddish-breasted toucan that in the manner of its kind dove head-first from a high branch into the lower growth; by the giant black-and-white musk-duck that lumbered off ahead of the vessel, its face scarlet seemingly from its exertions; by the swallow-tailed kite that swooped into the crown of a tree overtopping the forest and pitched up again on its momentum carry-ing a long-tailed prey, presumably a lizard, which it devoured on the wing. These could have been the fishes of this aerial sea.

Tocantins advanced with an alert and, I thought, wary yet peculiarly knowing air, as befitted a guide with great responsibilities who alone had a previous acquaintance with this alien world, with its perils and its paths. Her high-browed mastiff's head would lean to the outside as she rounded a bend and tried to see around it, past the jutting wing of the forest. The officer by the helm would bear down upon the whistle rope and *Tocantins* gave forth with her cavern-lunged bray. Ostensibly the purpose was to warn a possible other craft approaching from around the bend (a craft which was of course never there). Actually, it was to re-assure us of our identity. We were no mirage, no evanescent anomaly; we were Man, Man the conqueror.

The front of the forest was a static waterfall of leaves so dense that individual trees were impossible to distinguish except where one, with foliage yellower or bluer than its neighbors', had managed to thrust a limb free of the conglomeration. But here and there above the roof of

240

this mass there towered a tree so immense that its flat crown, standing out against the sky, was like a forested table-land in itself. These colossi of the forest rose on boles like limestone columns so titanic that between the flanges that buttressed them at the base teams of horses could have been stalled. Such prodigies of nature were to the common run of trees— even of rain-forest trees—as gods are to men, and as long as one of them was in sight it exerted a power over my will, so that I could scarcely wrest my gaze from it.

The scene was one of stupendous and all-encompassing struggle, of mighty trunk against mighty trunk, tendril against tendril. Like a host of frantic supplicants pressed together, mute, blind, all striving to win the attention and favor of an omnipotent monarch, rising on tiptoe, stretching upward, reaching out with their arms, climbing up one another, clawing at one another, trampling one another underfoot, the plants in their inconceivable multitudes were fighting to the death for sunlight, the trees locked in one another's embrace, straining every sinew for space while burdened, half buried, by the network of the creepers. Only exceptionally could the ropes of the creepers' stems be discerned, only where some had won a fingerhold in the celestial domes of the *sumáumas* and their kind and hung down like the cordage of a sailing vessel, or when the configuration permitted a view beneath the branches that thrust out plates of foliage over the water—foliage packed so tight the branches appeared to have been tarred-and-feathered with leaves. The palm that had broken through to the open air to lift its handfuls of dagger-leaves to the sun, as a drowning man raises his hand above the deep, would support such a throng of vines that its trunk would be lost in the barrel of foliage they formed around it. The creepers' leaves blanketed the face of the forest in such close-woven curtains it seemed probable that one could slide down them with no danger of falling through.

Nothing moved. That was perhaps more awesome than anything else; for the immobility of the contestants in their fearful exertions was, you felt, only momentary. Through senses undisclosed to man the plant-consciousnesses had been signaled to the presence of a trespasser, and all were fixed upon him. As long as he was in sight, they would be held in motionless attention. The writhing, heaving, stretching, wrestling struggle would be resumed when the ship had rounded the next bend.

Even here in the alluvial basin where the forest stood at its most formidable, the margins of the river were not uninhabited. Now and again

241

the day after we entered the Breves there were clearings. Some afforded scope for an essay at agriculture. Maize or sugarcane standing among great grey treestumps would be lapping avidly at the strong sunshine with forked tongues of green, but there seemed to be something not quite right about these plantations, which were never visibly being worked, something of ill omen in the miasma of heat and silence holding sway over them. And all around there would be the forest banked up tier behind tier, the trees seeming to be looking over one another's shoulders at the unguarded plot. At other clearings there would be habitations of a sort, a huddle of two or three palm-thatched huts staked up over the mud behind a racquet-shaped jetty in a hollow scooped out of the forest. The inhabitants would stand still as statues as we passed. A boy walking with a basket when *Tocantins* thrust her nose into view would be arrested just as he was, one foot advanced, mouth open. A few men and women would be in evidence, the women in their habitual sacks of cheap dyed stuff, the men in their worn blue jeans displaying inordinately long, bare stomachs, unaccountable even with allowance made for how low they wore their trousers. The naked children were so potbellied they made one think of baby centaurs lacking forelegs. All eyed us unwaveringly as we passed, and surely it was no wonder. Our dazzling white vessel, in which the officers changed into snowy fresh uniforms daily and the passengers lolled in indolence in gay-hued pajama coats—pajama coats over street trousers being for men the standard off-duty garb in north Brazil —could have been a fragment of the Riviera shunted out to the raggedest edge of civilization. No one on board took any more notice of the river-folk than of the flocks of yellow-faced or scarlet-rumped parrots literally blasted out of the trees by the sounding of *Tocantins*'s whistle.

When we intended to put in at a settlement we could count on finding a crowd from the surrounding forest awaiting us. This mystery was never explained. I should not have put it beyond the Caboclos—the "copper-colored ones"—to have instincts capable of forewarning them. These descendants of the Indians, who chiefly peopled the lower river, were an attractive lot to look at, or they were when they did not have so much white blood that they had an unshaved and cadaverous appearance or so much Negro that their clear-cut, somewhat Mongoloid features were thickened. Foxy was the term for their style of physiognomy I had decided at first sight. Their high cheekbones, pushing up, slightly narrowed their eyes, which were closer together than the corners of their wide mouths—these being, moreover, generally set in a broad grin besides. They had black eyes, shining and full of zest for what they encompassed. One was made especially conscious of this by the eyes of our passengers, which were those of slumberous ruminants. Their bodies were slight, supple and muscular, and appeared to be as hard and polished as the finely-finished mahogany they resembled in color.

I went ashore wherever it was possible to get about. Santa Cruz do Buisso's four or five houses and little sugar-mill were connected across the mud by causeways of canestalks, as springy underfoot as a mattress. Behind the settlement there was a mountain of the stuff, with half a dozen humped, plaster-colored zebu steers standing up to their knees in it, glumly contemplating the pile, upon which they were evidently expected to forage. The whole of Saint Michael of the Monkeys (*São Miguel dos Macacos*)—a lumberyard with sheds full of machinery and planks—rested upon a plateau of sawdust. On this it was possible to walk for a couple of hundred feet in any direction, sending blue-tailed lizards the size of small alligators scurrying before you; and walk you had to, for to have stood still in that heat would have been to be picked up by the scalp and dematerialized. Behind a few rows of tattered banana-plants, as around all these settlements, there stood the forest— second-growth as impenetrable as a picket fence and larger trees which, with arms stretched high under their cloak of foliage, put one in mind of sorcerers casting a spell upon the habitations below them.

At places like these we unloaded some tools, boxes of canned goods or a piece of crated machinery and picked up more firewood or baskets of *farinha* or sugar or demijohns of raw rum—a draught of which would make you feel you could expel a sheet of flame from your mouth simply by exhaling, like a dragon. Once nothing at all happened. Each side perhaps thought the other would recollect why we were there if given time. The Caboclos remained seated on the pierhead with their legs hanging over the side, running their fingers through their damp locks of black hair and making gleeful signals at one another. Others paddled up in boats made of hollowed logs with a bit of plank at each end evidently affixed with clay. Sometimes they would jump up from the pier and chase one another around or tussle playfully. They were like an audience of children waiting for the curtain to go up. In a pockmarked rubber tree a black vulture sunned its wings, adjusting its position stiffly and jerkily, like a figure in a marionette show. In the

243

sheen of the noon air the far bank of the river was like a blue fog settled upon the water. The atmosphere rippled. The metalwork of the ship in the sun could not be touched. At length the patience of the Caboclos was rewarded by the serving of our midday meal. It seemed heavy fodder to me, impossible to put away in the circumstances, but the other passengers were clearly of a different mind. The Caboclos, who had perhaps never in their lives sat down to such a meal, looked on at the scene of its ingestion with delight and no trace of envy or resentment, craning their necks not to miss any part of it. I felt so much like an exhibit in a zoo that when the meal was over—dispatched to the last pastry, incredible as it was to me—I joined the spectators on the pier and passed a pack of cigarettes among them, warning them apologetically that they would find *éstes cigarros muitos fracos*—very weak. The Caboclos' own smoking tobacco came in six-foot rods and was black as coal, with an odor like a tarpit when burning. But they were delighted with the cigarettes, too, which they handled as if they were lace.

In a last effort to give the occasion a businesslike air, but to little avail, *Tocantins* as she drew away filled the forest valley with her bellows.

"You like the Caboclos," said Cora.

"Very much. They seem to belong here. Don't they appeal to you?"

We had climbed up to the deserted bridge. It was late afternoon and she was wearing the dark glasses she had on when she came aboard, and these large, black, impenetrable orbs gave one the feeling—evidently shared by the other passengers when she appeared at teatime—that she had been essentially vacated by herself. I had a sense that I was more present at our conversation than she was.

"Oh yes," she replied. "They do. I like the quickness about them. But when a woman looks back on a state of society when men were carefree hunters and left most of the real work to their wives, she doesn't feel quite the same nostalgia as a man."

It was on the tip of my tongue to ask if she would rather have a husband who was a traveling merchant, when I realized that that was very nearly what she had. I could imagine I had turned red and was grateful for those glasses.

"Tell me more about the halberds," she said.

I laughed. The "halberds"—that was what the plants looked like, with their several big leaves at the top of a bare stalk of a stem—grew out in the river in military ranks when the slope of the shore was gradual.

Where we were just then it was steep and the banks, with the tide low, were tangles of driftwood above which the foliage was white with dried mud up to high-water mark.

"I'm serious," she said. "They've made an impression on you." She took off her glasses. The sun, toward which the vessel was headed, had sunk behind a cloud.

"They've stolen a march on their rivals," I said. "They've gone offshore, where they haven't any competition. Of course the conditions are tough and they don't seem to grow more than six or eight feet tall. But at least they have their own niche. They have it all to themselves and they seem to be quite jaunty."

"And you care about them."

"Well . . . It's interesting their being what they are—everything's being what it is."

She seemed to be looking at me with close attention, but it was more like watching me, I thought.

"That's what makes it so absorbing," I went on. "That there's such infinite variety, and within it everything so exactly what it is—being itself." I could have told her that that was why I was driven to drawing, but this was a resort to which I had recourse only when I was alone.

"And is this true of people, too?"

"Not as true of people, I'd say."

The day was fading rapidly. In the forest, slipping by us, it was already dusk. Cora had withdrawn her gaze, as if an object that had passed between us and gone off beyond the side of the ship had attracted it away. We sat in silence for a space. There began that transformation of the atmosphere that comes with the failing of the light, when the day's associations—a brightly-colored, clearly-defined and ordinary-seeming throng—have trooped away and vague and shadowy potentialities of unlimited proportions are being disclosed. The thoughts that had occupied my mind the night before were putting forth their feelers. . . . She had said, "I meant with lights out, a bed at hand—the complete program." Until, with the suddenness of being hit over the head, I had fallen asleep, the words had given me no peace. It was not so much what they called up in my mind as the knowledge of what they must have called up in hers. The possibility had been visualized. She could not have said that without having visualized the possibility, however fleetingly, in concrete terms: the complete program.

245

"It may be true of the Caboclos," I said, "that they are altogether themselves. Or more so than others, anyway."

Perhaps most human beings, other than the simplest, were made up of several persons. It did not seem reasonable to believe that the condition was unique with me. But to go on being, concurrently and intensely, several persons who were strangers to one another—to go on being them indefinitely—I was quite sure was not possible, though in my own case I could not see where there was going to be any give.

11

At five o'clock in the morning could be heard the rumbling intonations of two outstandingly fat passengers—brothers who appeared possessed of a prestige among their fellows derived solely from their prowess as trenchermen. The *conversação* thus commenced signalized the start of the day, though it still lacked an hour of sunrise. I was already returning to get dressed from a showerbath of tepid yet robust Amazon River water, to which I attributed therapeutic qualities. Whatever had troubled me the evening before now seemed of no more consequence than the cigarette ends littering the floor of the lounge, where the lights above the sleepers lying flank to flank in their hammocks appeared sordid now that morning was imminent.

Beyond reach of those lights, up on the forward deck, where the swabbing had not yet begun, it was still dark as midnight. The mists, which when I went to bed had shrouded river, sky and forest, as if these had been erased like a charcoal drawing from a sheet of paper, had condensed into streamers illumined from some mysterious source beyond the surrounding blackness. Suspended without motion in that universal stillness between night and day, they were like phantom vessels afloat in the air. On all sides the forest reared a blacker mass against the darkness, distinct and sharp. Its presence affected one like that of another living creature crouched on the other side of a darkened room, visible only in silhouette, its nature impossible to divine. The air was as thin and pure as the ether of outer space. The earth could have been awaiting its first experience of light.

While you wondered if you were seeing it or imagining it, the blue-black of the eastern sky acquired a jewel-like depth of color. Its fathomless shades of ultramarine brightened to a peacock hue, to turquoise. The radiance spread. The rest of the sky was converted to a deep, translucent blue, itself aglow but imparting no light to the earth below. The ragged tufts of the taller palms were lacquered black above the dark sea of the forest-top. All around, from behind the clouds rimming the small, night-filled saucer of the earth, day stole upward as if from footlights, soaring higher, the sky paling through cobalt to azure until the last shadow of night was lifted finally from the infinite loftiness of its zenith.

Over the sullen summits of the forest the first pairs of parrots had already flown, large-headed and fat, having to exert themselves to make it, while below them a fast-winging flock of olive-green dwarf macaws with bare white faces—beak-nosed little monks in the bodies of falcons—had wheeled close to our funnel, screaming. At the first touch of light the watchful, waiting entity of the forest had been shattered into its myriad components. White-rumped tree swallows wove back and forth, up and down the river—and barn swallows, too, which in eight weeks would be darting elegantly over Connecticut's pastures. Kingfishers, tiny and giant, whirruped from bank to bank with wild velocity. There were satiny black toucans with white, orange or red-and-yellow breasts, or with white rumps and beaks that caught the light like rubies. One, dropping from a limb, was almost swept away by a flock of yellow-winged parakeets which raked by like grapeshot, their grating shrieks such as might be heard from a charge of chariots. From the forest came cries raucous and clear, chirps, whistles, screams, rolling tattoos, gurgles. A tree abeam of us erupted with a geyser of liquid notes, as from a mad

248

musician with a flute. In the distance, like a hurricane gathering force, could be heard a howling monkey's lilting moan.

There was, in fact, a monkey to be seen, a large, heavy-jowled brute less like a zoo-monkey than a black jaguar, picking his footing along the limb of a tree a hundred feet up. He was, to my surprise, spotted by one of the stewards setting the tables for six-o'clock coffee and buns. *"Macaco!"* he called out, flourishing a handful of knives. *"Guaruba!"* The report he would make of the incident would afford general satisfaction at breakfast; the American, who had gusto of creatures (*quem gosta dos bichos*), had been promised monkeys.

There were macaws resplendent in their plumage as generals in the dress uniforms of guards regiments: green macaws with wings blue on the outer surface and red beneath which screamed from the bare tops of the higher trees; macaws aflame with prismatic scarlet, blue and yellow winging majestically upriver to be overtaken by a flock of gooselike tree-ducks, which remained conspicuous in the preternatural clarity of the distance while dwindling in size to a string of jet pinheads. There were hawks on bare branches which paid no attention to us, their numbers testifying to the abundance of life. There were large, stolid red hawks; dapper, slate-colored kites with orange talons; ospreys; nervous, lanky, black-and-white *chimachima* hawks. Birds constantly crossed and re-crossed the *paraná*—black-and-yellow orioles, wax-plumaged *japims,* tanagers, anis, tiger-bitterns and herons of every size and sort cutting beneath our bows with a panicky, galloping flight, crests erected.

In the grey cold of the New England winters I had known that I should recognize paradise when I saw it by the palm-trees. Here there were multitudes of them, palms as far as the eye could reach, and they were like skyrockets projected out of the dim interior of the forest. One could believe that the earth was turgid with fertility of which explosive concentrates had shot through its pores. Some had exploded the instant of breaking ground, others only after a dramatic ascent, the trunks that carried the shower of leaf-rays high above the earth marking, as it were, their graceful trajectories. In some the first force was already spent; the beams of foliage drooped. Others carried such a charge that, like the cabbage palmettos at home, but vastly greater, they had twice exploded, the shafts shot from the crown bursting at the tips into fans of green dagger-rays.

249

But the sun, which had cleared the tallest trees, continued to climb. It bore down ever more concentratedly with its enervating and anesthetizing glare. Before midmorning the last dumpy parrot had been stilled. The vessel slipped along the palisade of the forest, clinging as close to shore as she dared to escape the force of the outgoing tide. Not a leaf trembled. The exploding sprays of the palmettos and the long fronds of the ground-bursting palms stood fixedly as if cut out of tin, flashing with sunlight. Life was suspended. Only an occasional turkey vulture, policing the conquered province, coasted above the forest and a great grey eagle escaped the suffocating heat by soaring above it.

With the turning of the tide we moved out into midstream. Once more the river presented a sealike expanse. Astern, no land at all was visible, only an odd line of little tufts extending partway across the horizon, formed of the taller trees on a protruding portion of the shore elongated by the refraction of the light and lifted clear of the earth. Before us a headland drew back as we passed to unfold the unexpected sight of a village on a bluff—the first high land yet seen. By midday the disc of the visible earth was a frying pan full of boiling grease. Over its entire surface the waves were shot with white-hot light—not just in a path beneath the sun, as it would have been in the higher latitudes, but all around, for here the sun, blazing down from overhead, pre-empted the whole upper sky. The heavens were pale and glistening, glazed over. There was always the shimmer of a haze overhead in the heat of the day. Without it we should probably have been turned into squills of charred leather in the sheer consuming luminosity.

At every phase of the great, slowly revolving wheel of night and day the bounds of creation as I had known them were surpassed. The black clouds that in midafternoon rose in the south were of continental mass. They would come craning up over the sharp edge of the earth, leaning forward from the horizons as they grew. Miraculously, and ominously, as if they might descend upon the world and extinguish it, their stupendous, solid shapes would detach themselves from their pediments below the edge of the earth and pass overhead, blotting out the sun. While their margins danced with electric fire, the world below them would be plunged into twilight. The distant forest, which a moment before had been a representation in watercolor on a pane of glass, would stand black and solid and the river be transformed into an agitated prairie

250

of mud, seeming by a trick of perspective to slope upward to meet the inked line of the horizon.

With the passing of the cloud the light, overpowering in its brilliance, reasserted itself. Blue-white, it seemed to oscillate between the mirrors of the river and the sky. Every wavelet sparkled, the river glowed with the tans, blues and lavenders of an iridescent fish. Life on earth would seem to have perished in the radiance. The very air would be parched—cauterized. Had it not been for the continued rasping of the engines, one could have thought oneself deaf—turned to wood. Yet the black-and-white terns still dipped to the bursting blisters that formed our wake and above the viscous surface of that river of molten glass came the flash of a dolphin's pink flank.

The passengers in their hammocks would be totally inert and the Caboclo sailor at the helm have a fascinated glaze on his eyes, as if he could not close them. The officer standing beside him, his face gleaming milky in the blue shadow beneath the bridge, not infrequently would shade his eyes to peer at the mirage of the shore and silently point a change in course. The land was of forested islands that seemed to repose upon the surface of the water like wafers upon a metal plate. It was still a world of water; a few hours above Gurupá, where the Xingu pours in from the south, and even at places considerably farther inland, the river is twenty miles across. Slowly, hardly more noticeably than the movements of the hands of a clock, immense channels would open ahead and close behind. *Tocantins,* with her raking funnel, her jaunty bridge just behind the snub-nosed bow and her busy, water-beetle gait, was like a child's plaything accidentally propelled into an amphitheater designed for a convocation of the gods.

Between the two hemispheres of sky and water forming the radiant globe of creation, the forest, which divided them, would be compressed to a narrow black frill in the cloud-shadows and an irregular filmy green tape under the sun. But it was always there, day after day, and as the push of the incoming tide grew continually feebler, to fail altogether four hundred miles from the sea, we increasingly skirted its edge to avoid the river's four-knot current. Often its outstretched limbs could almost be touched.

At noon, over the forest's entire front, each leaf stood out sharply above the black shadow it cast. But the sun's rays, for all their power, did not

251

achieve an inch-deep penetration of the gloom within. The forest stood unyielding too, under an assault that seemed certain to tear it to shreds. When thunder rumbled in the south and the black storm clouds built up dome upon dome and the lightning flickered among them, like the flash of cannon fired from the fortresses of giants, and the rain swept in, it was possible to imagine that the jealous heavens, having failed to blind the world permanently with their incandescence or strike it forever immobile with the awful spectacle of their immeasurable cloud-formations, had set themselves to drown it outright. The sheets of rain would come lashing across the water, rampaging furies. The river would be beaten flat, its surface transformed to sandpaper. Against the green canvas shades let down to protect our decks the roar was wild and intimidating. But through all the cataracts the forest loomed unyielding and indestructible as a precipice of granite, and as grey, and when the storm had passed no marks of the visitation could be seen.

"Are you getting a fever from this?" Cora asked. "No—I mean it. Do you know what your eyes are like? I've never seen them this way. They're so bright they're frightening."

"That's just the way they get from an afternoon out in the equatorial sun. It means nothing."

"Are you sure? Your friend Louis the Sixteenth is very concerned. He says you came down from the roof in the middle of the afternoon absolutely steaming." I had observed that one of the obese merchant brothers recalled a representation of the Bourbon monarch I had seen on a coin.

"I know," I said. "He shamed me with his solicitude—after the hard thoughts I've had about him! It never does to forget the kindness of the Brazilians. He patted my shoulder and said I would get the *paludismo*. 'Then,' he told me, 'you will go back to the States and say that our country is not healthful, instead of having homesickness for Brazil.' I'd been skipping rope."

"What on earth for?"

"For exercise. I had a predecessor who set the example. He was a geologist who went up the river in connection with the oil-drilling concession. You've probably heard of the Portalegre Corporation. Somehow it got recorded in the files I had to read before coming down here—that he'd skipped rope every day on top of the riverboat that took him where he was going. It made an impression on me. There was a human reality about it unique in the files on Portalegre. Let's just hope that— But we won't think about that. Don't you feel the need for exercise?"

"I stretch," she replied. "When I'm by myself I'm always stretching. I live by stretching. You should try it."

"I don't think I'd find it enough right now. I feel like an engine that's been having a fuel poured into it a great deal more potent than any it's used to. I have to run it off or I'll explode."

"What kind of fuel?"

"All this," I replied with a sweep of the arm. "You can't look forward to something all your life, then when you realize it find it exceeds all your expectations and not be carried away by it."

"Then you aren't disappointed?"

"Oh God, no!"

"Let me tell you something!" she exclaimed with the air of one about to impart a gratifying secret. "I've become very observant. I've been studying the riverbanks. And I've found that your halberds no longer have their little world all to themselves. Have you been noticing the beds of floating grass and water-lilies or whatever they are, growing out from shore too? And I think they've done even better for themselves than your halberds. They don't have to waste any energy growing long stems to keep their heads above water. They're always right at the surface, rising and falling with the tides—often right among the halberds, too."

"All the same, I'd rather be a halberd. . . . You know," I declared, "I think that one offhand remark I made about the halberds impressed you more than anything else I've ever said. I can't imagine why. . . . The beds of grass and water-hyacinths—I think that's what they are— are always getting detached and being carried down the river to their doom."

"Yes, but what a lovely way to go! I like the little islets going nodding along over the waves. They're so green and gay. And they don't know anything's amiss. They're like Ophelia when she floated away down the stream singing to herself—even to the little lavender flowers they're carrying."

"But in the end there's the grey, remorseless sea."

She bent her head, opened her handbag and rummaged in its contents

253

for something she did not find, then closed it with a click. When I had nearly forgotten what I had said, she murmured, "Yes, there's that in the end." Her eyes could not be seen behind her dark glasses.

The waters of the river, shimmering and glistening, were now of saffron and pellucid blue, and flowed by the ship like oils. We were sitting again on the bridge in the late afternoon. The character of the forest had changed, as indeed it changed every day. It was now of two distinct planes, a lower of dense scrub-growth, its surface in some places as compact and smooth as a golf green leading back from the river's edge, and an upper of billowy, rolling contours supported on pale, bare limbs like livid witches' arms tapering to scraggly fingers interlocked and twisted, with foliage of varied shades of green as concentrated in hue as chemical pigments. In the airy corridors between the two levels beams from the declining sun here and there turned sprays of leaves into heaps of gold coins, but for the rest one looked down tunnels into the primordial and changeless night of the forest's depths. From afar the screams of parrots in the upper tier sounded like the stridulation of crickets. Sometimes a hoarse cry issued from the hidden depths or a large, shadowy bird took wing and was swallowed up in the deeper shadow.

"But what I brought the subject up for," said Cora, "was to show you that I take in what you point out to me. Do you remember what I told you?"

"It hasn't been out of my mind. But how to explain? I try to explain it to myself—for my own sake. I climb up here before dawn and watch the earth come to life, and it is sheer intoxication. I am in a state of bliss. I know how it feels, but I can't say what it is or what it springs from."

I told her as well as I could all there was to be seen at daybreak, all the profusion of life, its vitality, the gemlike perfection of its forms. But it could not, I said, be just the visual spectacle. "There is a feeling—this is what I can't account for—that the pieces all fit together. Yes, that's it. It's like an orchestra with all the instruments playing together, in a single composition. And you are carried along by it. It's like being floated on music you can't hear. You breathe in the air that's never been breathed before and you're exultant in it. All the tangle and confusion of your mind—all are miraculously straightened out. It is incredible that this could happen, so swiftly, of itself. It is like having a tangled head of hair: if you'd never heard of a comb, you'd despair of its ever being put in order. It would be unthinkable, separating each hair in turn and laying it in its place. But if a comb is passed through it, it's done in an instant—all is in place."

"But it doesn't last—this feeling—after the early morning is over?"

"Well, no. . . . Things haven't the same clarity. There's not the same unison. You feel more left out of it. More thrown back on your old self, with the complications and misgivings. But it does return during the day. It's so tremendous what you see here—all of it. Look at it now. Look at this river! Can you see it like this, shot with the colors of an opal, stretching away to the source of all things—you'd think—and not be lost in awe and wonder? Look at those stupendous clouds there in the west, ringed with silver. And the leaves of the forest, how they stand out in the sunlight against the darkness within. It's as if the forest had been dusted over with powdered sunshine."

She had taken off her glasses while I was speaking. "It *is* beautiful. It's all you say."

"Why don't you get up when I do tomorrow morning and watch the dawn come with me?"

The proposal seemed to startle her. After a moment's thought she said, "That's a generous invitation. I know how generous."

"Generous? Any *man* would say it was purely selfish!"

With head bent a little she looked for a space in the direction of the riverbank from under her brows. "No!" she said with emphasis, placing her hand momentarily on my arm. "It's better for you to be here alone at that time—and tell me about it later."

"I don't see why."

She closed her eyes, hardly more than blinking, just as I spoke, as if excluding some consideration.

"Tell me," she said, "when you were a child, did you ever make an exception to what you knew you ought not to do by saying that just this once wouldn't count?"

"Yes . . . I did," I said in a noncommittal tone of voice, not knowing what was coming.

"It's a privilege everyone should have from time to time." She leaned forward a little, clutching her arms to her breast and regarding me over her shoulder. "Not to have something count. Just as this moment I've been thinking I'd like to have your arm around me—if we could have it not count."

255

I had to grope my way from such a great distance to reach the point of taking in what she had said that it seemed to me—though I suppose it was exaggerated in my mind—that an awkward space of time had elapsed before I responded. When I did, moving my chair closer to hers with my foot, she leaned back; my arms just cleared the back of her chair.

"I had a chill," she said. "Not a physical one, though, really."

"We say in Georgia when that happens that a rabbit has run over your grave." The observation had been sprung loose out of my unconscious mind; I had left Georgia too young ever to speak or think of what "we" did there.

She had closed her eyes again. A pucker appeared between her brows. "Do you," she said. "That's exactly what it felt like." After an instant she added, "I didn't know, though, that you came from Georgia."

"It was a long time ago." The scent of her hair, the actuality of her tangible feminine being in the enclosure of my arm, the closeness of her living presence, wholly there, invested with the totality of her personality, shut everything else from my mind. I was overcome by her desirability, permeated by it. It had the power of a promise limited only by what one had it in one to ask. I fought to keep myself from making a move, from speaking an untoward word. I knew how tenuous a lease I held on this moment, relaxed and unguarded as she appeared to be, her mind seemingly emptied of thought.

As the seconds passed I became a little more relaxed too. I put myself off with the self-induced illusion that I could not move if I wished to. Immobility conduced to a kind of trance. My consciousness became confined to the warmth generated in me at the area of contact between us, as if she exerted the same kind of pull on my bloodstream that the moon exerts on the ocean.

She said, "You're a vital young man. Maybe it's true, what you said, and you really have been filled up with some powerful kind of fuel."

I wondered if she were aware of the process going on in me. I said slowly, "I have been during the last few minutes." The statement came out sounding somber.

She drew herself up a little. "There's something I've been meaning to ask you. How do you see the future, I mean your own future? Are you going back to the States soon—once you've come back from this trip?"

The question—an unusual one, for she had never shown much curiosity about the circumstances of my life—sent a chilling sense of guilt through me. I had a picture of myself I should gladly have disowned but was powerless to rise above. I could not, I said to myself. Not right now.

"The future?" I repeated. My God, did the girl really exist, after all? "Yes, I suppose I'll go back to New York for a couple of weeks. Not much longer. This is where I want to be—have to be."

"Will you get a job here?"

"A job? I've been thinking there'd probably be one with the Concession."

She leaned forward, and I followed. We sat shoulder to shoulder. "So you've been bitten by the Massaranduba bug too?" She gave me a sidelong, quizzical look.

"No! I abominate the Concession and what it stands for. . . . I shouldn't have said that. And I mustn't be quoted. But—if the Concession's going to provide jobs, I may as well have one. In addition to having been the means of bringing me here, it could be the means of enabling me to stay. That's all there is to it. . . . No, that's not entirely true." With my thoughts in conflict, torn as they were, the situation as it was between us seemed more ordinary, though my senses were still swimming. "I suppose I do look to it for riches. About everything the Tate family has seems to have been put into it. And there are others—the Monteiros. To that extent you could say I'm hooked, I suppose." Yes, I repeated to myself, if it has to be faced, I suppose you could.

A bird of prey sailing over the plateau of the forest veered off as it caught sight of the ship. It had a pale head set forward on a neck longer than a typical hawk's, heavy, reddish-brown wings and a stubby tail.

"What kind of bird was that?" she asked.

"Some kind of eagle."

She stood up, then sauntered to the rail. She turned and seemed about to speak.

I said, "Am I to be privileged again—sometime?" There was an edge of bitterness in the way I spoke that I had not intended, and I could see by her eyes before they glanced off mine that it surprised her.

Her gaze fell, but she looked up again almost immediately. With her hand over her throat and her head tilted back, so that her eyes as she regarded me were half closed, she said, "I'm afraid I was thinking only

257

of myself." Then, perhaps being struck, as I was, by the negative force of her reply, she added more warmly, and letting her hand fall, "But it's good to know you wouldn't mind coming to my aid again." After the briefest pause she went on, "And I'm glad you're not planning to disappear into the wilds, or the unwilds, of *os Estados Unidos*. If it depends upon the Massaranduba Concession and its providing a job, maybe Cora had better take more interest in it."

The remark was made offhandedly, but the silence that followed it began to develop in an uncomfortable way.

"I'm sure it couldn't fail then," I said in her own half-bantering tone.

"Only think how much more help you'll get in Portuguese when the word goes around that you intend to settle in Brazil!"

"God forbid!"

It was evident that we were not going to get back to that which alone interested me just then. Until Cora went below to dress for dinner we chatted about our fellow passengers and the pleasure they took in expositions of the Portuguese language. My inadequacy in it was a phenomenon outside their experience, and they were unable to accept it. They liked nothing better than to corner me and attempt to remedy the deficiency, which they evidently ascribed to whimsical perversity of forgetfulness on my part, to be corrected by shouted injunctions. At the table it afforded a field for the display of virtuosity by the more articulate men, stimulated by Cora's presence. After Almeirim it was to be further stimulated by the addition of a striking young woman of formidable allure whose dark red cheeks, narrow nose and smooth, black bobbed hair gave her the appearance of a Parisian type depicted on mildly lubricious French postcards; she had a solid, well-built figure, a wardrobe of gay-colored frocks and a direct gaze that penetrated to whatever potentialities of carnality you harbored, then quitted you victoriously.

Anjinho, the bouncy little trader in *farinha* and hides who was said to do very well for himself in a business way, partly by virtue of a fixed scales and a tape-measure that ran nine centimeters to ten, had the advantage of sitting next to Cora and across from me. His first interest, however, was in stuffing himself. He gripped his fork in his left hand like a hatchet and scooped the food in with no self-consciousness whatever about his noisy gluttony. His wife, who was a schoolteacher, had a protruding mouth and chewed her food at the very front of it, between her outward-sloping teeth and her incarnadined lips, and her leopard-yellow hair was already dark at the roots, with the voyage only a few days old.

At dinner the evening I had come down from the bridge with Cora, Anjinho set about to explain the derivation of the comparative and superlative forms of adjectives in Portuguese, about which I had asked some question, trying to distract myself with conversation. *"Doce, mais doce, mais doce de que,"* he illustrated. Sweet, more sweet, more sweet of that. He conceded that a true superlative was lacking in Portuguese. At this the professor at the adjoining table wheeled about with what proved to be an objection. There ensued a lengthy and earnest discussion between the two, at the end of which a flushed and crestfallen Anjinho admitted that he stood corrected. Yes, there was another superlative form, *dulcìssimo*. He had lost face. Later, after explaining to me some nicety of the language, he turned, and to get his own back called out ironically to the professor, "Is that right, Master?" But the professor was busy with his own conversation and did not hear, so the deflation of the little trader was compounded.

That night, unbelievable as it was, the professor gave a lecture. To his fellow countrymen he was an even greater freak than I, I suspected. Yet they were astonishingly polite and deferential to him, and this he seemed to accept as his rightful portion, not out of personal vanity, but as a clergyman might, as the respect due his calling. Tall and bony, with a massive cranium, a protruding forehead over small, overstrained eyes, a narrow jaw and long, knobby, useless hands, he spent the day moving from passenger to passenger for little talks, dividing his time evenly among them lest any feel slighted. It was presumably his innocent certainty that others must share his own conviction of the supreme importance of the things of the mind that enabled him to stand up after dinner at the forward end of the dining deck, his pear-shaped head under the dim light of the lamp, and read and enact a formal lecture from typewritten pages, as if doing so before a crowd of unlettered traveling salesmen in a floating stockyard were the most natural thing in the world. And having no doubts about it, he got away with it. The audience seemed to take it as natural too. Professors gave lectures and this was a professor. His voice rising and falling, his delivery running the gamut from the rapid fire of an automatic weapon to the solemn cannonading of a ceremonial salute, the words issuing now trippingly from the roof of his mouth, now with oratorical volume from the full

259

throat, now with organ rumble from the depths of his chest, he discoursed upon, I gathered, his native state—Ceará. In Ceará there was a bird (so I understood from his panegyric) that sang all night. An effort was made at our table to get me to appreciate the strength of pride in state and loyalty to state in Brazil. (*O estado e o Brasil.*)

The rest of the talk seemed to have to do with Caboclo folklore. Nothing mattered to me just then but the question of whether Cora would be disposed to going back up to the bridge that night and the dilemma, which sent currents of weakness through me, of what I was going to do if we did go.

The issue was postponed. After the lecture the professor came to our table and remained until Anjinho proposed our going up to the top deck, the better to enjoy the night. His wife's hesitations before the ladder gave me some hope that the project would have to be abandoned, but her difficulty, which took the form of a pretty confusion, was found to be only that of explaining why modesty forbade the ladies to precede the men on the ascent, and she followed readily enough when her husband and I took the lead (the professor having chosen to remain with the larger company). That it was to be a lost evening became more evident when Senhora Anjinho was prevailed upon to sing for us. It was her husband who recalled that the treat had been promised since the start of the trip, our anticipations having been whetted by the exhibition of her diploma from the Ruy Gomez School of Music. His policy on the trip was evidently to placate her; it was said that his surname, which meant Little Angel, was not the most descriptive possible.

Senhora Anjinho, as was demonstrated with the first note of her opening selection—*Un bel di,* from *Madame Butterfly*—had a voice of extraordinary power. Even after one's initial shock had passed, a sense of alarm persisted, as if one were witnessing, by the light of the cold moon overhead, before the shadowy forest rising in menacing proportions beside us, a wanton and reckless tempting of fate. But retribution, swift and terrible, did not descend upon the woman. The heavens, as Joseph Conrad remarked in a somewhat different context, do not fall for such a trifle.

When we finally went below, there was already quiet in the lounge. The victim of malaria whom we were taking to a hospital was still awake, a little man insubstantial as a white shadow in his hammock,

260

whose eyes, glittering with fever, with tears, with fright, bored into one's own, as if he sought there the author of his misery. But the others were asleep. The merchant brothers were lying on their backs like twin monster babies, knees apart, tips of tongues protruding daintily between parted lips. One of them twitched in his slumber as I passed. I waited up until it was evident that Cora was not going to re-emerge.

We put tidewater behind us and entered a province of woods lower, more open and much less imposing than the rain-forest of the alluvial shores with its giant, buttressed trees, its concentrated silence, its awful immensity. The trees of the *igapó,* as the forest was called where the land was inundated by the Amazon's annual floods, were scraggly—it was even possible to see sky through their branches—but often their scanty foliage was borne on trunks of enormous girth, giving the effect of monumental ruins taken over by plants. Sometimes there were mile-long marshes of so intense a hue it hurt to look at them and you imagined you were beholding a sea of green flame; they were the home of golden-winged, mahogany jacanas, of white egrets and of a small yellow bird with a black head and a song of a single repeated note that fell upon the ear like drops of the purest honeyed tone. Sometimes the forest would be bright and airy, like magic gardens suspended weightless in an ocean of sunlight. Sometimes you would be startled by what appeared to be a landscaped park of ornamental clumps of trees set back behind luxuriant lawns of flawless texture—only no human hand had been at work there, and the lawns were of floating grass and undulated to our waves. Sometimes the channel would be bordered by weedy growth of a man's height of swampy grassland in which, possibly, red or putty-colored cattle showed their backs and a shack of thatch was buried to its eaves.

Where low ridges first slightly raised the horizon, beyond Gurupá in the north, you had the feeling that the earth was trying to heave itself up under the weight of the forest—a premature effort, for the land was quickly flattened out again. But thereafter it exerted itself to more effect. The next day there were long, forest-smothered hills in the north, flat as boxcars, crowned by little cumulus clouds floating on an ocean of heat. They were blue in the distance, the nearer vegetation being by contrast of a yellow-green almost virulent. There began to be occasional hills back from the river with grassy slopes on which sheep grazed, a house on the crest and a patch of corn in a nook in the woods below.

261

Farms became commoner where the land stood above flood-level, and every sixty or seventy miles on the average there appeared a village of several thousand inhabitants.

Yet for all the assaults upon the forest it was still a world of trees. From the giants of the lower river whose crowns were forests in themselves—survivors of the age of the Titans, before the coming of the gods—the trees ran the gamut to little species farther up the river which clung to the water's edge: forlorn and puny willows crowded on sandspits and ugly, emaciated trees with brittle white trunks resembling the umbrellalike laundry-trees of suburban backyards hung with inert Paris-green leaves. There were squatty trees with a single canopy of foliage through which the grey branches wove like the veins of a single leaf; trees that bore solid spheres of leaves on trunks like tubs; trees like hundred-foot-tall goldenrod plumed with down-drooping sprays; trees that were all one mass of leaf-rosettes packed airtight; trees with sky-high branches that carried only isolated black bouquets of leaves; trees like giant octopuses with bodies flat on the ground and gaunt, leaf-plastered limbs writhing upward like tentacles; towering bulbous trees with iron muscles in their boles and lacy, pealike foliage in myriad airy balls; trees that crouched on distended trunks and trees that shot skyward on trunks of drawn wire; trees with foliage of lemon-yellow and yellow-green, purple-green, black-green and grey-green, emerald, pistachio, malachite and jade; trees from the temperate zone and oriental trees, trees that gloried in the sun and trees that surely grew by stealth in the light of the moon; trees from Arcady and trees from nightmares. Trees, wherever you were, entirely encircled the horizon, closing in the vista of the river before and behind. Woods stood behind the largest of the towns, behind the marshes, behind every farm. Around a cleared space the trees in the front rank seemed to hold back against the press of those behind, like their fellows along the riverbanks, which were braced with splayed roots gripping the mud to keep from being pushed into the water. Where rising land reached the river and the red soil was exposed in gashed cliffs, the trees, as if they had slipped down from the summit, clung to the eroded banks with roots as tenacious as talons fastened into living flesh.

I asked Cora how she thought those who lived here regarded their lot —not the Caboclos but the Europeans.

"They regard it as exile," she said.

262

The departure of one of the passengers, which we were watching, gave the impression that she was right. His destination was a tidy settlement of white frame houses on stilts beneath feathery mimosas and stocky, glossy-green bacaba palms. The ship had been unable to go alongside and a boat had come out, battling the current, to take him away. He stood amid his hampers, a lanky figure, monkey-faced and with skin puckered as a walnut, his back to the trading post to which he was being borne, holding on to the last, in the only way he could, to the companionship of the vessel—by shouted farewells. *"Boa viagem!"* he called. And again, *"Boa viagem!"* as the Caboclo boatmen bent to their paddles. *"Boa esperança!"* the passengers yelled in return. *" 'Te logo,* Tocantins!" came the shout as the ship got under way. So long, *Tocantins!* The passengers cupped their hands. *"Felicidade! Felicidade!"* The exchanges went on to the end. *" 'Te logo,* To-caaan-teeeeeeeensh!" And *"Fay-leee-ceee-daaaaaaadjy!"* the passengers screamed. The last we saw of him, he was waving his arms at us against the background of the shore, at which he had so far not even glanced.

"I have some friends at Topacindo I'm going to see," said Cora. "They'd be glad to see you—they speak English. You could get an idea what an Amazon town looks like from the inside. Would you care to go with me?"

I said I should very much. It was at Topacindo that I was to transship for the Massaranduba on the way back from Manáos.

To an outsider the towns along the river had the quality of being mere postulates, placed there provisionally and experimentally. Because distance had no blurring effect, buildings a mile across the water were as sharp in detail as diminutive scale-models at arm's length. Flanking a grey-and-white church with cupolas (as it was at Almeirim), the row of variegated houses drawn up in military formation, at strict attention, determinedly disregardful of the ebullient vegetation half concealing them, seemed fit abodes for gaily-painted wooden soldiers.

It must have been the practice for those with merchandise to buy or sell to come down to the wharf (along with everybody else) when a ship put in, for Anjinho would always descend into the crowd to press a deal, throwing an arm across the shoulders of a sullen, suspicious European or a self-conscious, nervously grinning Caboclo. Other Caboclos in their worn blue trousers would swarm aboard. Several soldiers would be standing by, so thin and clad in such wide-flaring breeches that they

263

might have been paper dolls. There were always, also, one or two portly personages to whom we brought bundles of newspapers and who, even though their pajama coats might be indistinguishable from the common run, were unmistakably magnates of the community.

Those bundles of papers had a meaning for me. At Almeirim and again at Prainha their bulk showed that they represented a considerable accumulation. I deduced that no vessel from the capital had called there in a week at the very least, and, inquiring of the recipients, I found that this was so. *Boa Vista* specifically had not been seen.

When making these inquiries I took care to keep my back to the river and affect a casual air so that it would not be seen from the ship what I was up to. (I also made a point of not being out of sight of the ship lest it be supposed that I was dispatching a letter or telegram to Monteiro, which left it an open question how I was going to mail the letter I had in fact written him letting him know that no consideration would prevail upon me to betray his interests.) My inquiries about *Boa Vista* made it harder than ever for me to face myself. I could find no excuse for giving in as I was to irreconcilable emotions and urges, except the ignominious and threadbare one of not being able to help myself. By day when I was alone, as I usually was, lost in contemplation of the river, I was transported to a different plane, out of reach of these grinding contradictions. In Cora's company or in my bunk at night it was a different matter. I fought the infiltration of my senses and apprehensions by her being—or thought I did. But the malarial sufferer in the lounge could as well have been expected to purge his blood by an act of will as I to have accomplished a similar end by such a means.

Cora was real and present. More than by the price of the emotion I felt for her—and how much of myself I was pledging to its satisfaction I was in no state of mind to consider—I was concerned, gnawed at, by its frustration. I seemed to be unable to get through to her. What I planned and rehearsed in privacy, when I was able to speak to her of anything at all, of anguish and joy, and could count on her understanding, could not be uttered when I was face-to-face with her. In her company I was held back as by the force of a will superior to mine, or by my own will unaccountably suborned to gainsay my desires. I could no more have gone ahead than I could have lifted a weight beyond my strength.

That was how it had been, and that was how it would be again, I thought as, the night after Senhora Anjinho's performance, we climbed up to the bridge together, alone this time. Mists had formed after sunset, and sky and river were of an identical milkiness, separable only because the forest stood between them like a curtain of black lace. Red sparks poured inexhaustibly from the funnel, a brilliant and cheerful swarm, more fiery than rubies, against the dead-white aura of the hidden moon. The pulsing of the engines and gentle swish of the waters were too familiar to reach the consciousness, but from behind the screen of foliage on which our deck lights fell came the jingling of crickets and the plunking of frogs, like the notes of plucked cello strings.

"You're very silent," said Cora. "I have a feeling that this is especially to your taste and that you ought to be alone up here."

"No, no," I said. "It's especially to my taste just as it is." And, the quality of the night being what it was, I added, "Actually, I was thinking about you."

"Oh? And what were you thinking?" In the way she asked the question, tacitly acknowledging that she had no choice but to ask it, I thought I could identify the barrier between us.

"I was wondering how you can always be so self-possessed."

"Self-possessed?"

"Yes. You always have yourself in hand. You always hold yourself back—and apart. You never act or speak impulsively, in a way that would give you away, or give another person an advantage. Even when you faint, it's with reserve."

She considered this a moment. I was sitting askew in my chair so as to face her. As usual, however, when we were sitting side by side, she faced forward, only cutting her eyes over at me when I spoke. She said, "Maybe there's nothing to give away. Maybe there's nothing there."

"There you are!" I exclaimed. "Exactly what I mean. Could anything offer another person less to go on?"

"But it may be the truth."

"I'll believe it when I find it out for myself—if then." She was drawing on her cigarette—a process which always held an attraction for me, I did not know why. "Cora, I should think you'd be lonely sometimes."

"I don't know. . . . No, I'm not *parrying* the statement or being coy. I just can't tell. When you're one thing or the other all the time, and have never known anything very different, you don't know what it is. I'm just Cora, the way she is, lonely or not lonely. . . . It's a ghostly world out there, isn't it?"

265

There were mists lying on the water itself now. In places they stretched out toward us like snow-covered shores, creating a scene of witchery in which the actual banks of the river formed by the black front of the forest now advanced upon us, now fell back behind a sheet of silvered water.

She leaned down to snuff out her cigarette on the sole of her shoe. I put out my hand, staying hers, and took it from her.

"There's still a lot of good left in it," I said. The cigarette held a slight fragrance of her lipstick when I put it to my mouth.

"I'm afraid I'm wasteful." She watched me inhale. "You make it *look* as if what's left in it were good."

"What *I'm* afraid of is that I get too much out of the blasted things. The trouble is that cigarettes reach what nothing else quite does. A craving for something. A kind of universal craving. Do you know what I mean?"

"Yes. No, I'm not sure. Do they satisfy it—the craving?"

"No, they only quiet it for the moment. But that's a good deal. Why do you smoke?"

"Oh . . . I suppose because cigarettes help you detach yourself."

"Which you of all people don't need any help in!"

She contemplated the pack of cigarettes she was turning around and around in her hand. "Too much could be made of it, I guess, but . . . there are things about the situation I'm in that require considerable detachment. Sometimes I think if it weren't for that I'd be a different kind of person, a little. And sometimes I think if I'd been a different kind of person there wouldn't be the situation. It's the kind of thing you never know, isn't it? But you can always turn things into smoke."

Abashed and contrite, I said, "I'd be the last to think the situation could be easy for you. But I forget! I don't associate you with it. What it is . . . is so foreign to what you are."

We spoke in low tones out of deference to the quiet of the night and also to avoid being heard. From below came the subdued tinkle of a coffee cup and a soft *"A direita"* from the officer on watch.

"Cora, can't you put an end to it?"

The pack of cigarettes stopped revolving. "I have to do it in my own way." From the tone in which she spoke I understood that she had come to a decision which was hard-won, final and uncommunicable.

266

A faint chippering came to us across the water from some terns whose slumbers on the bough of a floating tree the ship had disturbed.

I said, "It's your husband's sister who is Colonel Durondo's mistress, isn't it?" It had suddenly dawned upon me whom I had seen waiting to go in to the Colonel as Almeida and I took our departure. "Your mother-in-law thought it was you when she attacked you. She'd heard a rumor and leaped to the wrong conclusion."

"How did you happen to think of that?" she asked.

I told her about the encounter at the door of Durondo's office. "I'm right, am I not?"

"More or less. But how did you happen to think of it just now?"

How had I? I went back through the concatenation that had led to it. "I'm not sure you'd care to hear." I took quick stock of my daring. "You're not a person it's always easy to talk to—to say things to. . . . There you are," I added with a smile as she turned her head in a way she had, just enough to enable her to let her see what was in my face. "You're apprehensive of what I might say."

Evidently grasping what lay behind this observation, she turned all the way. "Am I then very different from other women?"

"I don't know much about 'other women,'" I replied, feeling I had been caught in pretentiousness. "I mean I've never known any very well who—I've never known any in circumstances like these."

She dropped her eyes to the pack of cigarettes she was holding and picked one out with her long fingers. The hand performed the action, I thought, much as a long-billed bird might have. "Why don't you pretend I'm a different kind of person from the one you think I am? Maybe that would make it easier to say what you were going to. How you happened to be reminded of my sister-in-law's liaison. Was it by something so scandalous?"

It seemed to me that she was forcing herself to look steadily at me, as I was myself to look at her while I answered her. "When I was thinking of how it was that you appeared to be able to stand apart from things, I remembered how you had been able to lower your dress to show me the scars on your back, from what your mother-in-law had done." Inexplicably I felt both that I was having to put forth an enormous effort to say what I was saying and that I was being impelled to do so by an irresistible force. "That made me think of what she had accused you of,

267

and of the woman I'd seen who was in fact the one. But that was just incidental to what was chiefly in my mind, which was what *you*'re like." The huskiness of my voice defeated all my efforts to clear it. "There were other times in *Boadicea* when you brought up subjects sure to give a certain direction and impetus to a man's thoughts. With any other girl it would—would have signified something. But with you—you didn't give it a second thought. It's a matter, again, as I say, of your being able to stand apart from circumstances."

"Were you going to light my cigarette?" she asked.

"I shouldn't have said what I did," I declared when I had done so.

"No. There's no reason why you shouldn't tell me anything you want to. . . . Why don't you have a cigarette?"

"I'll wait and finish yours."

"Tell me," she said. "Perhaps I shouldn't ask, but . . . When I made those thoughtless provocations, did you—did it matter to you?" From her scrutiny of the red coal of the cigarette she might have been appraising a gem.

"Did it matter to me? Did it come back to me while I lay awake at night? Did it set my imagination to work? Do you know what I mean by imagination? I sound like Captain Byram, don't I? Sometimes I've thought that when you awoke in the morning it would come to you, like the memory of an abnormally vivid dream, what you had been through in my mind, what we'd experienced together."

When I brought myself to raise my eyes, it seemed to me that her face before she turned away expressed neither embarrassment nor resentment, but simply the attention one might give to a recital of a friend's unsettling adventure in which one was not directly involved.

"I haven't been good for you," she said. "It can't have been good for you, what you were describing. But I don't think it's been me, as an individual, particularly. I'd be flattering myself if I thought it was." She was speaking, and *her* voice, too, was giving a little trouble, I thought, deciding that I had misjudged the effect I had had on her. "I know how it is with men." She uncrossed and recrossed her legs, dropping her hand to her knee to keep her skirt in place. I waited, perceiving that she had not finished, while she puffed briefly at the cigarette, then reset her lips to begin again.

"I know about the need men have and what it can do to them," she said. "If it goes a long time without being met, and if there's a woman around who isn't repulsive, they do, as you say, imagine all kinds of things. Isn't that what we're talking about?"

I shook my head; she had glanced at me to discover my response. I did not wish by speaking to risk deflecting her from adding to what she had said, as she appeared to be going to. However, she said nothing more, but only smoked industriously, swinging her leg, apparently thinking.

"It's true what you say, but that's not the explanation in this case," I said, my voice sounding false. "There's vastly more to it."

"Still," she replied, moistening her lips, finding a bit of tobacco or paper on one and removing it from the tip of her tongue, "there is this biological process in men. And you must think it would be so easy for me to provide what you need—only a matter of minutes. And then you wouldn't be on this strain. You wouldn't have that trouble with your imagination at night."

I stared at her uncomprehendingly, or unbelievingly. However, I could not see what was in her face, or she what was in mine.

"But with a woman it's not so simple," she pursued. "If it's only physical, it's abhorrent to her. If it's more—then it's much more. She becomes deeply engaged."

"I should think so," I said, perplexed. "So does a man. But is there anything dreadful in that? When you're"—I could not say "in love"—"powerfully drawn to another person, you *are* deeply engaged. Necessarily. You don't resent it. It's what it's all about."

"What do you feel when . . . ?" She glanced up at me almost timidly.

While I understood her question, incomplete as she had left it, I did not know how to take hold of it. "What do I feel *when?*" I echoed. A matter that was intensely immediate was being verbalized and generalized and thus put at arm's length from us. I could not answer in her terms. "You know what it is to desire someone terribly and then . . . then have your desire satisfied."

She straightened up, leaning back against the arm of her chair and gazing directly at my eyes although she seemed at the same time to be shrinking from them. "Suppose I told you that the two things had never happened to me together—desire, love and . . . the other thing. . . . But when I imagine—yes, I have an imagination too. And I've imagined that if a man and a woman are truly sympathetic, he'll make her feel what he's feeling and she'll make him feel what she's feeling. Don't you think that's the way it might be?"

269

"Yes." If we were still on the bridge of a riverboat shared with two-score others, I had no sense of it. "Yes, without question."

"That was why I asked you what I did—what it makes you feel." With that she did finally give way and lower her eyes. "But I suppose you'd find it very hard to tell me."

I passed my hand over my brow. The palm and my forehead, too, were wet with perspiration. "Yes. I'd find it impossible—in the abstract. There's no such thing as what it *makes* me feel. Do you mean—what *would* it make me feel?"

She replied in a small and low voice, "Yes, that's what I meant."

An overwhelming desire to seize her by the shoulders came over me. I might have done so had she not raised her eyes again. Despite everything I felt myself confronted still by that barrier across which I could not reach.

"*What,* precisely, was it you meant?" I could read in her eyes, after an initial uncertainty, a comprehension of my drift.

"What it would make you feel," she said dutifully in the same low voice.

"What *what* would make me feel?"

She hesitated. As if the atmosphere had grown dense and heavy, I felt a pressure on my eyes and on my chest; I had to lift a burden with my lungs to breathe.

She said almost inaudibly, "What it would make you feel to have me."

"I'll tell you what it would make me feel—"

She pressed the palm of her hand hastily, and momentarily, to my mouth, a look of apprehension in her eyes. "Speak softly."

The scent of her hand and a slight taste of salt remained. I said, "I've had you in my arms dancing with you. I've felt your breast against me"—my tongue felt thick—"your thigh against mine." She winced but did not look away. "Everything I contained was concentrated there where we touched. Does that tell you what it would be like? For me it would be to feel through you what life is. It would be like having our nerve-ends laid bare and joined together, so fused I think it would be impossible ever to feel wholly alone again. Do you understand?"

She drew in a breath as if at that instant freed of a suffocating constriction. She was suddenly standing by the railing, her back to me, her head bent low, her hair falling free. She remained thus only briefly, then turned back and with hands pressed to the sides of her face took a few paces back and forth, coming to a stop by my chair just in time to lay a detaining hand on my shoulder as I started to get to my feet.

"No, stay there," she said. She moved behind the chair, where I could not see her, and simultaneously I felt the pressure of her hands on both my shoulders. "Just stay." The back of my head rested against her just above the buckle of the belt she was wearing. I could feel her warmth through my damp hair, and her deep breathing.

"You must leave everything to me," she said in a voice grown calm. "Try to put it out of your mind. Everything will be all right if you'll leave it to me."

She left the pause open, and queerly enough, as far as I could take in things so comparatively extraneous, I had the feeling that all the time when she had for once seemed shaken and at a loss she had not been so but that now when she seemed to have recovered command of herself she was in fact unsure, so divided in her thoughts that she was unable to speak whatever it was that was in her mind to say further. I remained silent, as her grip on my shoulders enjoined me to.

I had asked if she understood, but the question, I thought, was whether *I* understood. It was believable that she had been right, more or less, and that I had only voiced the universal craving of mankind, that I was merely the bearer of a charge more powerful than I could contain and she a lightning rod. But what did it matter? I was pierced through by desire, exhausted by confusion.

"Will you agree to that?" she asked finally, settling—it was evident to me—for less than she had wished to say.

"I have no choice."

I must have seemed sullen as we went below. I was in a state of mind to have thrown myself with abandon into a fight with a rival male as an escape from perplexity and frustration. At parting she held my hand, looking at me encouragingly, in a way that made her appear to be another person, until I reassured her with a smile.

During the night I was waked up by my Japanese cabin-mate, who had sprung out of his bunk shouting *"Su! Su!"* or something like that. I thought at first he was having a nightmare, but discovered he was under the impression that we had run onto a sandbank. I looked out the port and saw the riverbank close by, dully illuminated by our lights. There was that silence when a ship has shut off her engines which is so momentous. The Japanese began smiling and chuckling. We went out

271

on deck and found ourselves to be bang up against what I took to be a brightly lighted pier. But no, it was a sister ship of *Tocantins*. The two vessels had met in the dark of the Amazon night, and each overjoyed to be so unexpectedly delivered of its solitude, they had rushed into each other's arms, like good *brasileiros,* and were now in a fast embrace, while officers from the two met and clasped each other like friends who had thought each other dead these many years. I felt dizzy, and was about to go back to bed when I recalled my letter to Monteiro and the fact that the owner of the two ships was a good *Constitucionalista.* I got the letter out and, while the two staffs were crosssing excitedly from deck to deck, picking up a bite to eat here and there, took it to the Captain of the other vessel with the request that it be delivered at Monteiro's office.

12

While the condition in which Cora had left me did not keep me from sleeping, I awoke in the morning with the memory of having, toward dawn, been assailed by a different kind of doubt having to do with her, a specific and disagreeable doubt. I had countered it by reminding myself that she had disavowed any interest in what befell the Massaranduba Concession. She had freely confessed why she had been put aboard *Tocantins;* she had not had to do so. She had virtually admitted she meant to leave her husband; she would hardly be apt to sacrifice much for his interests. Not only, by the morning's light, was the evidence conclusive, but I felt ashamed of having even for a moment suspected her motives of the evening before.

I anticipated that she would not put in an appearance until after the midday meal and that whenever thereafter she might find herself alone with me would skillfully avoid any situation and skirt any topic of conversation that would give recognition to what had passed between us. For the first time on the trip, however, she took her place at breakfast, and when not long afterward we were standing together by the rail watching a village come into view she let me know she was aware of what had happened and stood by it. Such, at least, was how I interpreted it when she turned to face me and with eyes that sought candidly to learn what they could from mine asked in a significant tone of voice, "All right?"

Though not prepared for a question that evidently went to the heart of things, I replied, "All right."

"You don't sound very convinced."

"I meant to. Only . . . don't forget I'm human," I added without having intended to.

"I won't. I won't forget anything," she said. "Do you know what place this is?"

She would not forget. But, remembering, what then? What, after all, was she giving me warrant to believe? I tried to discover in her face more than I could tell from her words.

"The place we're approaching, Mr. Tate?" she inquired gravely, having colored a little.

"Monte Alegre." I transferred my gaze to it. We could make out the usual crowd already assembling on the wharf, on which was a yellow frame building trimmed in white. For the rest, the village offered to view only a dozen red-tiled roofs resembling rafts floating in the troughs of a leaping sea of treetops.

Anjinho came up in tie, coat and hat. He was ready to go ashore. Until *Tocantins* was made fast, he remained with us, entertaining us—which I had to admit he succeeded in doing—with a demonstration of how a practiced trader operated, specifically how he ran down the value of a piece of merchandise offered to him for sale. Getting me to hold my pocket knife out on my open hand, he poked at it disdainfully, held it up with a winked invitation to Cora to share his amusement that anyone could be simple enough to put such an article on the market, opened his hand with a shrug and let the knife fall back into my palm, was indifferent, mocking, contemptuous, humorous, oblivious, incredulous, and though his Portuguese was too rapid for me to follow I understood everything he was saying and knew everything that I as the seller was saying too,

274

even experienced the seller's angry impotence and shame at the inferiority of the offering. It was an uncanny performance.

I waved good-bye to my Japanese cabin-mate as he descended the gangplank. He was followed directly by one of the officers carrying the usual two or three bundles of newspapers, for the portly persons who came out of the crowd to receive them. The bundles were much slimmer than those we had previously delivered.

"What's the matter?" Cora asked. "What's come over you?"

I was once more contemplating the picture of myself. Clearly *Boa Vista* had put in at Monte Alegre. Was I going ashore and make my inquiries as if I were innocent of any other interest? If I had ever been able to exchange a word with the girl, ever been able to find out who or what she was, to discover that she was real to someone else— I cut myself off. I could have ground myself under my heel. Only human, I had said I was. Only human! *That* was the truth.

"Oh—just the complicatedness of things, I suppose. I didn't know I showed it. The problem of the Massaranduba. What's going to happen to it, and to everybody who has his hopes pinned on it." The answer came almost of itself, springing from what was seldom far beneath the surface of my mind.

Tocantins was blasting off from her boiler, and the roaring hiss of steam in her funnel rendered the activity around us nearly soundless.

"The Massaranduba!" said Cora. "There's no getting away from it. It wouldn't surprise me to hear that even the monte-alegrenses out there are aroused about it. But I wouldn't have thought it would bring quite such a look to your eyes. . . . I'd like a chocolate, it's so soon after breakfast. Wouldn't you?"

She said she had some in her stateroom. I went with her and, thinking the skies were not likely to fall if I did so, followed her in. She did not object or even take any special note of it. Dresses I had seen her wear and a slip hung on a rack at the end of a bunk. On the other side, on a hook by the washstand, was a peach-colored dressing-gown and under it were silk pajamas of a lighter shade, slightly rumpled. A dressing-table set of what I believed to be called cloisonné, in blue, was by the side of the basin. The room was delicately redolent of scented talcum powder. It breathed that compound of poignancy and suggestiveness that makes femininity, for men, the sovereign potion it is. Cora had taken a

275

small box from a drawer. If pressed to it, she would have to admit, I thought, that she had purposely made herself attractive and desirable, consciously inviting desire; else why the soft hair combed and set, why the lips colored a coral red? I watched her, conscious of all that was inherent in that slight figure clad in a cotton dress of alternating stripes of light green shades, and conscious of little else. She had picked out one of the pieces of candy and now delicately bit off a corner of it.

The blowoff of steam was abruptly silenced. Sounds of movements outside the stateroom became audible.

Said Cora, "This is the specially good kind." She placed it in my mouth, her fingers just touching my lips as she did so.

"Let me ask you this," she said as she took a piece of candy for herself, her voice so matter-of-fact it arrested my impulsive move toward her. She had fallen back a step. "Do you think anyone is worrying about how the Massaranduba will affect *your* life? Can you see João de Monteiro eating his heart out about it? If an assortment of gamblers have leaped in over their heads they've only themselves to thank for it. You're certainly in no way to blame."

I was, though, I thought; I and my glowing reports! At least I was surely not blameless. And while I had not been reproaching myself on that score just then or in fact thinking about the Massaranduba at all—I had even forgotten we had been talking about it—I was reminded that I had cause to.

She had moved back against the far wall of the cabin and stood there with an arm across her chest, the elbow of the other in her cupped hand. The light of the port at her shoulder was so bright that her face was in semidarkness. "I don't remember what it was," she continued, "but I was just a kid when I heard a line in a play—I seem to see a debonair character in a Norfolk jacket and plus-fours with a knapsack. The line was, 'The experienced traveler travels light.' That was *it*, I thought. That was what you needed to keep in mind. And I've never thought differently. You don't do anyone any good taking on a load of other people's troubles. Them or yourself." She leaned forward to rinse her fingers at the basin. "If you take on responsibility for other people, the chances are you'll end up being a responsibility of someone else's." She had straightened up, and an odd intensity, unusual for her, seemed to grip her. "The best you can do for others is to look after yourself. It's hard enough to keep afloat—even if you travel light."

276

"I know," I said. A feeling of fellowship with her had flooded me—of simple friendship for her, as for another being with a full allotment of troubles. She was leaning against the wall with her arms folded across her. I saw her as being—as to the best of my knowledge she was—very much alone in the world, with little with which to fend for herself but what was in view around her: a few cosmetics, a brush and comb, a collection of dresses.

"You look better," she said, and smiled. "Come. It's too hot in here. Let's go back on deck." She took my arm and held it as far as the door.

Our stay in Monte Alegre was brief, and Cora was with me during all of it, so I did not get ashore.

All the afternoon before, the side-channels of the river had been widely margined with the floating grass and the coves completely covered. As we forged on past Monte Alegre, the fields of grass extended ever farther out from the channel's banks. Finally the open water dwindled to a narrow path between them. Our progress grew slower. *Tocantins* was soon laboring to keep going at all. Even the passengers began to take notice, and in the bow the officer on duty was banging repeatedly on the engine-room telegraph, whether for more power or to vent his spleen there was no way to know. If it was the former, it was to no avail. Before our astonished eyes *Tocantins* was brought to a complete standstill. Their churning vain, the engines were cut. And there the vessel stood in the middle of what was ostensibly a cow pasture. From the trees alongside came the drowsy bucolic droning of cicadas.

For the past few minutes, from near the helm, where I was standing with Cora, I had been watching a flight of egrets the like of which I had never seen. Squadron upon squadron was passing from horizon to horizon before us, the birds flying in an unhurried and courtly unison. So striking was the spectacle that the Comandante, on his way forward to deal with the impasse the vessel had arrived at, stopped to share with Cora and me his *admiração*. In mellifluous Portuguese, in delicate and precise accents, holding up a hand with thumb and forefinger joined, like the conductor of an orchestra enticing subtleties from the strings while suppressing the tympani, he extolled the beauties of the *garças—brancas e graciosas, bem feitas na sua beleza oriental*. More or less concurrently, with the assistance of the other hand, he directed the operation designed to restore his command to the world of ships. In obedience to his orders the anchor was let go, but apparently the results

277

were not satisfactory, for the Comandante was called forward. Excusing himself, he joined the officer on watch and several sailors who were looking over the side at the bow. He returned wearing an expression in which could be seen a bubbling amusement stoppered with difficulty.

The anchor, it appeared, floated. The Comandante illustrated how it rested in the grass by placing one cupped hand upon the other. "He says," Cora reported, "that he will never be believed when he tells this story."

Unable to turn the ship by pivoting her about the anchor, as I took it had been the plan, they finally brought her around by dint of little forward and backward lunges, though for a time, when she had her bow very nearly in one bank and her stern in the other, it appeared we might be there for good.

Ten minutes later we were back in Monte Alegre. We steamed by at full speed, head high and bellowing, but our trains of grass, though we bore them regally, gave us away. There were still loiterers on the wharf, and these regarded our return passage with mild, incurious gaze.

"They probably could have told us the river was clogged up ahead," said Cora. "There's been something awfully Brazilian about this whole episode."

There were disconcerting aspects of travel on the Amazon above tidewater. When quitting the main river after crossing from shore to shore and navigating the narrow strip of open water between the borders of floating grass lining the shores of the *paraná,* you exchanged the impression of voyaging on the open sea in a launch for that of steaming up a country road in an ocean liner. There was a real jolt in coming out of your cabin to find yourself looking out upon a rural landscape with no water at all in sight over the side, and it was especially so if the ship happened to be passing a farmyard. For the shade of an instant it was exactly as if you had been walking down a meandering country lane and had rounded a bend to discover a steamship placidly bearing down upon you with the pilot—like ours—lolling against a stanchion, nonchalantly rolling a cigarette around between his tongue and upper lip.

After the awesome alluvial forest the country here often looked pastoral even when it was not, which was most of the time. The growth of weeds along the banks, their height not apparent, was what you would expect along a country road, and there were stretches of grey and desiccated woods that resembled—again in the absence of an indication of scale—an old and overgrown orchard. That such it was would seem, when there was an opening in the woods, to be confirmed by the presence of a couple of turkeys in the lower branches of one of the trees and of a crop of green pears in another. Then, when upon your nearer approach no sign of human life was to be seen and the turkeys turned into vultures and the pears took wings with the harsh screams of a flock of conures, all suddenly seemed the more wild and irretrievably lost. But another time two cow faces might be thrust at you out of the weeds, the turkeys prove to be turkeys and the pears, if not pears, at least an unripened crop of cocoa-pods, and the opening to contain a human habitation. This might be only a mud hovel looking furtively out between fountains of banana-plants, or it might be a neat structure of palm-thatch enveloped in a crimson-flowering bougainvillea in the middle of a clearing as bare and smooth as a hardwood floor, set about with sprigs of rose-bushes, shaded by an ivy-green mango tree with a plantation of manioc in the background. These more prosperous establishments would communicate with open water through a channel cut in the floating grass. At the head of it, just under the bank of the riverbed, the family boat would be moored, a gaily-painted dinghy with truncated ends, the after one bearing the name—*Boa Esperança* or *Santa Catarina*. Beside the boat, standing in the water, would be a little thatch structure built like an outhouse but open on the riverside. It was a bathhouse, providing privacy for ablutions—and, said Anjinho, for effect, a chance for crocodiles to make off with an occasional child.

The family would be lined up to watch us pass. The men would stare at us with their arms hanging at their sides, stolidly and, I imagined, sullenly, resenting and envying our great white ship, suddenly materialized before them like a vision of a resort hotel sent to try the faith of an anchorite. They had the stocky build, square head, swarthy coloring and wavy black hair of the Portuguese (I assumed) and were quite unlike the lithe, clean-limbed, graceful, largely-Indian Caboclos of the darting, close-set eyes. There was generally a complete progression of naked children; any gaps in the series owing to the depredations of crocodiles or other hazards were not apparent. The younger women were often attractive; the hard life was kind to the figure where urban ease on a diet of sour bread was ruinous. And the women had their admirers in *Tocantins*. These were the Louis Seize merchant and the young man with forehead and nose all of a piece, like a horse's, wide-spaced eyes

279

with droopy lower lids and shoes with built-up heels. The two now spent much time on deck, and when we passed a *sítio* (little farm) or a *fazenda* (big farm) would examine the wife and daughters of the family with a shared binocular and exchange observations, the fat merchant with a hand on the other's shoulder, the stub of a cigarette dandled on the end of his tongue.

Finding it somehow disconcerting not to know, until we were right on top of it, whether what we were passing was desolate wilderness without even a voice to cry in it or someone's backyard, I thought that those whose solitude we swept through must be even more disconcerted. I asked Cora if she could imagine how it would have struck an American pioneer woman on a homestead in the wilderness to look up from her corn-pounding to the stream where the panthers drank and find herself being ogled by dandies from a passing excursion boat.

"I can imagine," she said, "that it would have done more for her morale than a visit by an itinerant preacher. But I see your point. It *is* an odd embellishment of frontier life."

At the confluence of the Amazon and the Tapajós lay Santarém, but well before the town came into view there were large dark patches in the tawny Amazon which were of Tapajós water, the last unassimilated pools of the great tributary. As we proceeded, following the southern side of the river, on which the Tapajós entered, the expanses of dark water grew ever greater until the water was all dark except where there were upwellings of the Amazon resembling yellow clouds in a deep olive-drab sky. Even when these disappeared, however, the Amazon could still be seen farther offshore, sharply divided from its new bed-fellow. The combination was reminiscent of yellow custard with a burnt-caramel sauce.

The forest below Santarém was distinctive—gossamer in texture, it appeared, and radiant, almost like a long, low cloud of sulphur dust hugging the riverbank. As we approached the town, day was ending, but the long white beach, which was another of Santarém's distinctions, was still conspicuous. A flotilla of *canoas* had put out to intercept us. Caboclos by the dozen clambered aboard, and we were brought in as by a crew of lighthearted Moro pirates. The main boarding party waited on the wharf, a milling mass of bodies on which, in the dusk, the heads appeared to be bobbing independently about, like coconuts in a white, choppy sea. The usual chorus of *pssst*-ing across the narrowing stretch of water preceded the onrush from ashore. I cast my eye over the crowd on the lookout for soldiers with an air of having important business aboard the ship, but saw none. I had it on my mind that Santarém was the next-to-last military post under the authority of Colonel Durondo, who could at any moment, I kept thinking, change his mind about leaving me at large. After Topacindo, I should be in the clear, at least until I got back to Topacindo on my way to the Massaranduba.

In the throng that swept aboard there were many vendors, some offering cakes, some articles of deer and alligator hide, some bundles of aromatic fibers of a kind that supplied one of the components of the characteristic scent of the country, for the north Brazilians kept them with their clothes. What were particularly in evidence and apparently peculiar to Santarém were shiny black bowls fashioned of the gourdlike *cuia* and incised with romantic scenes the inscribers could never have beheld, of Alpine peaks, chalets, mountain lakes and spruce trees. Some, like souvenirs at home, bore the name of the town of issuance; others, more Latin, such tender aphorisms as *Love Makes Adventure.*

The view from the ship was terminated by a row of two-story plaster buildings, the bottom floors of which were occupied by shuttered shops. Crowning the façade of each building was an urn between two wavelike ornaments curling in toward it, a familiar stylized design. It gave the block, Cora observed, the appearance of being composed of the upper sections of so many Sheraton secretaries.

In the crowd on the dock was a fair-skinned, stoutish man about forty years old who stood out not only by reason of his complexion but because he was a head taller than the others and surrounded by a band of laughing young girls with whom he was evidently having sport.

"An Englishman, you can be sure," said Cora. "Wherever you go in this country you'll run into an Englishman. Often a lone Englishman. Usually doing something prosaic, like representing a bunch of British exporters or managing the local electric company, but at bottom probably a romantic, though. Like you. They'd die rather than let on to it, however. They never become any less British, no matter how long they stay. Look at this one. He's 'joshing' the girls, as he'd call it, or 'having them on' or 'pulling their legs,' just as if they were his daughter's friends at an English boarding-school. And strangely enough, it's made to order.

281

The girls love it, as you can see. It's such a relief for them, after the young men they're used to, who look at them with eyes full of lugubrious poetry and mussed-up bedclothes."

The Englishman—I took her word for it that that was what he was—had held my attention from my first sight of him. As we stood there, I watched him with an increasing nervousness; I caught myself tapping a tattoo on the railing with my hand. I was afraid of his going away before I had a chance to get ashore alone to speak to him. If there were anything to be learned from anyone along the river, he was obviously a man to question, an English-speaking person who came down when a ship was in and was, I felt sure, observant.

My ingenuity paralyzed by my appraisal of my behavior—ashamed of myself but unable to do other than as I was doing—I said baldly that I thought I might go ashore for a quick turn around the town—for exercise before dinner—and asked Cora if she would care to join me. I added, deprecating the expedition, that perhaps I could find a shop selling cigarettes that was still open. I had no notion of what I should do if she chose to accompany me, but she did not. She said, "If *you* say it's going to be a quick turn, I'd better let you go by yourself."

I walked the length of the commercial quarter and back—a matter of a few minutes—and then returned to the dock, from which the Englishman and his little friends had not stirred. They were still watching what was going on around them and teasing one another.

As he saw me approaching him purposefully, his features took on a neutral set. I introduced myself as a passenger in *Tocantins* and said I hoped I could get some information from him. Clearly the advent of another Anglo-Saxon did not strike him as a presage of the millennium, but he awaited my interrogation with a receptive and not unfriendly countenance. The lines that fanned out from the corners of his eyes were pale in his red-burned face; evidently he squinted in the sun, and one could see why, for his eyes were a pure, bright blue. The girls had fallen back in the expectation, their alertness seemed to say, of witnessing an historic meeting.

"Do you happen to know," I asked, "whether the riverboat *Boa Vista* put in here during the past week?"

He answered without hesitation, in an indubitably English voice, "Yes, she did. Three or four days ago. Four, I sh'd think."

"I wonder if by any chance . . . I should say, if you were down

282

here when she was in, whether you happened to notice a particular passenger." I looked for a quickening of interest in the clear blue eyes that would make it easier for me to go on, but saw none. "I was wondering whether you'd seen a young girl among the passengers."

As I stared at him, the notion grew in my mind that he was going to boycott the question as being in violation of the code of an Englishman.

"About seventeen years old?" I hazarded, brazening it out.

"Yes, I rather think I did."

Without breathing I went on. "Slim, with brown eyes and brown hair reaching nearly to her shoulders?"

"Ummm." He turned and put a question to his little flock. There were shakes of the head, accompanied by tossing locks. "I can't answer for the eyes. I do seem to recall the hair as you describe it."

"Was she with anyone, do you remember? *Did she get off here?*"

Again there was an interminable wait, during which I could perceive no change in the blue eyes, no recollection forming.

"Actually, when I saw her, she was getting on. Whether there was anyone with her, I couldn't say."

"Getting *on?* But is it possible that she'd got off before then? I mean, had the ship been in for a while?"

"Quite possible. The ship had been in an hour or two, I expect."

"Did you notice anything special about her?"

"How d'you mean?"

"Anything out of the ordinary about her? Anything at all?"

"I'm afraid I've told you all I can."

"I see. Well, I'm very much obliged to you."

I had gone a few paces back the way I had come when I heard him call, "Ahoy there, *Tocantins!*"

I turned, and finding that his eyes were on me, walked back to him.

He said, "It did seem to me that perhaps I'd seen her before. Where, I couldn't say. And she was quite pretty." He nodded in farewell and looked around at the little belle beside him. *"Muita linda. Não feia, como aquela pequena feiticeira."* As he spoke he drew back from the girl with an expression of exaggerated disapproval. I left them with his "ugly little witch," her face scrunched up, raining blows upon him, which he caught, grinning, on his upraised arm.

I went back to where I could walk, and walking, weigh, rehearse, dissect, analyze and build conjectures upon what I had heard. After

283

once more pacing the length of the waterfront and back again, I kept on going. The street turned into a country road of loose, well-churned earth pitted with footprints. The dark water of the Tapajós lay behind a grassy bank on one side, the dim shapes of houses set back from the road behind gardens on the other. I found myself stopping and peering at these houses and staring at the other persons who were abroad, mostly men in twos and threes who strolled into the feeble light of the streetlamps as I passed. I seemed to think that I was looking for something, and had to remind myself that I was not. I realized I must have appeared to be when for the second time a figure stepped from the shadows beside the road to ask if I needed directions. This one was a tiny Negro clad only in white trousers rolled up into the semblance of a loin cloth, a little Nubian in onyx, scarcely visible but for his trousers of ivory. I hardly knew how long I had been walking before it occurred to me that I had better get back to *Tocantins*.

I found everyone at dinner and the meal half over.

After offering the Comandante my apologies I explained to Cora that once I started walking I could not bring myself to stop.

"I saw you in discourse with *nosso inglês*," she commented. "Did you find out anything of interest?"

"He wasn't a very garrulous type. I had a feeling he could make shift without me. You probably noticed that the conversation didn't last long."

"Maybe he had the idea you were interested more in his little bevy than in him. You weren't, were you?"

"I'm not as easily diverted as that." I noticed that for once she had not changed for dinner but was wearing the same dress with the vertical green stripes she had had on that morning.

I asked, "What put such a thought in your head?" She was stirring her coffee. She appeared to be unwitting of the sidelong glances she was receiving from the professor and Anjinho, who were having a spirited conversation unmistakably for her benefit. Anjinho was expansive. His wife was indisposed and had been confined to her cabin all day.

"Oh . . . I had the feeling you'd been diverted," she replied.

Her voice had a teasing inflection, but I had the impression immediately afterward that she had already put the subject from her mind. There was no opportunity, or need, for me to respond, for Anjinho had addressed her directly with one of his sallies and she laughed. She joined the conversation of the others. After a space she looked at me

284

over her shoulder and asked with a smile if I were getting along all right. I said I was but was afraid I was poor company that evening. "I must be sleepy," I added. She nodded. "You must get to bed early," she declared. Then, replying to a question from the professor, she was drawn back into the general conversation. When I had finished dessert I told her I was going to duck back into the cabin for a bit and try to catch up on correspondence and would see her again presently.

Closing the door behind me, I dropped onto the bunk and fell once more to turning over in my mind what the Englishman had said, testing its impregnability to doubt. I told myself I must keep my hopes under control. The girl he had said he had seen had been of the right age, slim, with—he thought—hair such as I had described. But in all of this he had only been concurring in what I had said about her. He had volunteered nothing except that she was pretty; and maybe to a man of forty all slim seventeen-year-old girls were pretty. This one seemed to have a leaning toward that view.

There was no good lying down. I sat up and looked out the port. The Englishman and his consorts had disappeared before I had returned to the ship and most of the others on the dock had now dispersed. The dining-deck had been cleared of interlopers for the serving of dinner, but now some of the vendors were returning.

Against the electrifying evidence—if it could be trusted—that someone else had seen her at last and that she was still ahead of us on the river, there was an insistent voice from some grotto within me where primitive superstition still held out, and this voice, which heretofore had been ready to speak of conspiracies to keep me from knowledge of the girl, now urged that I was being baited by forces it alone could identify, being doled out scraps just sufficient to keep hope from starving, and no more. I told myself that this was absurd, but there was always the galling knowledge of my powerlessness. If it had not been purposely contrived that I should be chronically the dependent of events, able only to await what might come, never able to take the lead, it might just as well have been.

After an hour the sounds began to be heard that foretold departure. I went out on deck. The friends and relations of a passenger we had acquired and the remaining few vendors were taking their leave. The very last of the latter was one of those with a tray of the black *cuia* bowls suspended by a strap around his neck. I glanced at them as our paths

285

crossed and one caught my eye that, when it had registered on me, caused me to turn about and take after the seller. I overtook him in a few steps and bought the bowl. Among all those depictions of Swiss scenery and legends apealing to sentiment was a design of crossed flags, nearly furled, which to my astounded eyes were those of the Confederacy —the early form, called the Stars and Bars. It was not possible, yet there it was—an arc of stars in the upper inside corner of the union, the field divided by a horizontal line. Beneath them were carved in undulating rank the letters forming not "Conquer We Must for Our Cause It Is Just" but TAPOJÓS-AMAZONAS.

I stood with the object in my hands, mystified, and looking back up at the darkened façades of the Santarém waterfront, which, far from suggesting an explanation, seemed only to rule out the possibility of there being one. I was still standing there when, as the ship trembled to the churning engines, Cora appeared beside me.

"Look," I said, "Confederate flags!"

She peered at the bowl. "What are *they?* Oh—you mean the South in the Civil War?"

"Yes. How on earth do you account for them?"

"Well, I don't see how you can tell what they are. But it's a mixed-up world down here. Odd individuals drift in from almost anywhere, and many of them don't get any farther."

She did not appreciate the singularity of what I held in my hand. I said, "This flag hasn't been flown since 1861. It's unfamiliar even in the South."

"I don't know. I still don't see how you can tell much about it, there's so little showing."

The whistle spluttered and droned in what sounded like a solemn warning of eternity. While we watched, Santarém's halfhearted lights shrank back into the dark, damp, soft night, and once more *Tocantins* had a lonely world of overcast sky and inexhaustible black waters to herself.

"There's something about Santarém you can't shake off, isn't there?" Cora observed.

"I can't understand those flags."

"Let's ask the Comandante if he can throw any light on them." The Comandante had just put in an appearance. He was at that moment taking his seat at the dining table. The last serving of coffee for the night was being made. "He's had more experience of these river-towns than anyone," Cora added.

The Comandante, along with his hospitable friendliness, had a physical aloofness, a way of holding himself erect and compressed, albeit gracefully, as if to avoid any sullying contacts. When he put his long-fingered, preternaturally clean hand to an object, you felt that it acquired virtue from the touch. The little black *cuia* bowl, supported on his fingertips, became momentous, the central object of rites. However, he handed it back to me almost at once, at the same time delivering his opinion to Cora.

"He says the flags are actually those of the—*Como se chama, esta companhia?*"

"*Companhia Fluvial de Santarém e Óbidos.*"

"Yes. A small riverboat company sailing mostly on the Tapajós. It's a blue, white and green flag. The stars are from the national flag—the Brazilian flag, that is. He says you could have seen one on the launch that was tied up at the edge of the dock near us if it had been daytime."

I laughed, shamefaced. Looking at my trove again, I wondered how I could have been so sure of what I thought I saw when there was so little to go on.

Evidently extending his explanation, the Comandante resumed in the beautifully enunciated speech I had learned that he reserved for topics he held worthy of cultivated address. With lips and gestures both he caressed the language.

"Hm! This will interest you," said Cora in an aside to me.

The Comandante finished. Said Cora, "The strange thing is, he says, that at the end of the American Civil War a great many from the Southern side came to Brazil to escape the rule of the North."

I nodded. I was right in thinking I had remembered that.

"Most of them went to the south, as far as São Paulo, but some—he thinks about a hundred—came to Santarém and settled. They brought very little with them, and he thinks they had a very difficult time. They expected to practice agriculture, but at that time there was very little agriculture along the river and the *mato* was hard to overcome. They hoped to grow cotton, but the country was not suited to it. What happened to them all, he does not know. Some must have given up and gone away, perhaps down the coast, perhaps to Rio. The children of those who

287

remained probably married, many of them, with the people already there, and this has gone on for three or four generations, so you would not see any difference between them and others at Santarém. The Comandante says he has met only one who says he is a descendant of one of the settlers from the South and who speaks English. He's a young man who's working now on the Fordlandia rubber plantation up the Tapajós."

"An employee of the Ford Motor Company," I ruminated. "And that's the end of it."

I saw the Comandante, who had been listening to Cora's translation with his sensitive immobility of countenance, stiffen with a cup of coffee halfway to his lips. In the silence that fell upon the ship as swiftly as if he had raised a hand to command it, a scraping sound could be heard, coming as if from the bowels of the earth. It traveled the length of the ship and stopped.

"*Uma árvore,*" the Comandante murmured, and raised his cup the rest of the way.

It sometimes happened that a riverboat ran afoul of a barely-submerged floating tree, always with the possibility that her rudder would be disabled or a propeller knocked off, or even that she would be rent open. (It was an accident of this kind that had befallen Monteiro's *Aguia.*) The conversation of the scattering of coffee-drinkers resumed more gradually than it had been arrested.

I said to Cora that I was going to turn in, as she had suggested. I did not think that my attempt at casualness was successful, but she appeared not to notice. She was drumming softly on the table with the pads of her fingers. "I'm tired too," she said. "I think I'll do the same." There was, I thought, a look of strain about her, a little as if she were listening for a sound just beyond range of audibility. Now that I came to think of it, she had seemed to become a bit tense as the day progressed, either keeping silent or talking more rapidly than usual.

In the morning, before daybreak, we nosed up alongside a small clearing in the forest to take on firewood. A few Caboclos were already sitting on the stack of wood awaiting us. Others, in answer to our trumpeting, paddled up in their *canoas,* sunk to the gunwales, and, disembarking, shook hands all around. As usual, they were grinning and their eyes shone like the eyes of toy animals, and they moved with light-footed and perfect balance. Each of them had the kind of assurance you would look for in a divine-right monarch. The homeliest of the lot, an undersized Indian-Negro specimen with Mongoloid features and small eyes beneath a straight black brow, had no less of it than the others.

Anjinho told me that they received one or two tokens upon depositing an armload of wood in the ship, depending upon whether the load contained five sticks or ten, the quantity in turn depending upon how recently the bearer had had malaria. None of them looked as if he had ever had a day's illness. All the same, it took four hours to load the ship, and it seemed like more.

We stopped again interminably during the morning, this time for a shipment of cattle. There was a stretch of open country lying in a stupor of sunlight along the *paraná* and a corral beside which we pulled up, pretty much like a bus. We were able to come within ten feet of the bank, so sheer was the slope. Fifty-some steers and a sprinkling of heifers were in the corral and a dozen Caboclo cowboys sitting on the fence. These had the keen eyes, lanky and hipless build, high spirits, tousled hair and addiction to falsetto yippings that apparently go with cowboys of whatever nationality. They were soon, in addition, black with mud from head to foot. The hooves of the animals had turned the wet soil of the corral into soup, and into this the cowboys were forever slipping and falling or pitching headlong as they dashed about after the stampeding cattle.

The method of loading was a grisly one, requiring each animal to be lassoed, prodded and pulled off the bank into the river, drawn swimming to the side of the ship, then hauled up with the derrick by a line looped around his horns. The beast would kick violently, the whites of his eyes showing behind the irises, until, clear of the water, he would give up and go limp. Hanging like a gourd, he would be swung inboard, a section of the deck having been removed to allow for this. For a moment he would remain suspended there, face to face with the passengers who had gathered to watch the proceedings and wore expressions as impassive as the seemingly lifeless steer's. Pained distaste was stamped upon the Comandante's face. Cora refused to be present at all. I looked on because I could not seem to help it.

Lowered to the deck below us, the wretched creature would be pounced upon by a contingent of cowboys and, buffeted with kicks, his tail brutally twisted, be spurred to his feet. Going down again once or twice, splay-legged, on the mud-slick surface, he would lunge off out of sight into the bowels of the ship, bellowing with despair. We would hear the rumble of hooves, the crash of a board and fiendish yells.

"*Uma tourada em baixo*"—a bullfight down below—the Comandante murmured, forcing a smile.

After the midday meal we moved onto the main river. The water was glassy and heavy. The forest, dimmed by intervening sheets of sunlight, was a mere mood bounding the vista. The world was formed of light and heat, and what appeared substantial was only light and heat in the form of jelly. The heartbeats of toiling *Tocantins* made her structure tingle; otherwise there was virtually no movement anywhere. A mother and child lying together at the bottom of a hammock were a knot of limbs glistening with perspiration.

Cora was in her cabin, probably lying down; she had said she could at least take off her dress there. Her tenor was as even and deliberate as ever that day, but as during the previous evening, I suspected it was costing her an effort to maintain it. Because my conscience about her was bad, I was sensitive to her mood and ready to blame the difference she may have found in me for the difference I saw in her. But twice she seemed to have to rally her attention to take in a remark I had made, and I decided that what was troubling her must be something else—what, I could not tell.

Despite the weight of the atmosphere I could not settle down.

The worst of the heat had passed when Topacindo sidled into view. Cora had come out a short while before to remind me, as if she had not done so at lunch, that we were going ashore to see friends of hers, and I had taken a shower and donned a clean white suit.

Topacindo, for all its special relationship with the Massaranduba, made a disagreeable impression. Like other river-towns, it occupied a bluff above the water, but its gaunt plaster buildings seemed moldier than those elsewhere. They looked to me, I do not quite know why, like painted skulls, horribly weathered, and their barrel-tiled roofs like red hair dampened and carefully combed down over their brows, above their sightless eye sockets. Some corrugated sheet-iron sheds were clustered at the bottom of a dip in the bluff as if they might have slid there. The hulks of two wrecked riverboats, red with rust, stood offshore, their bows in submerged mudflats. The turnout of visitors on the dock was smaller than we were accustomed to and less animated.

Cora explained as we went ashore that she had telegraphed ahead to her friends, who would be expecting us. The Coutinhos lived out of town, however, and having no way of knowing the exact time of *To-cantins's* arrival, would not have been able to come in and meet us. We should have to hire a carriage to take us out to their *fazenda.*

We found one at the foot of the dock. It was an ancient open Victoria, I suppose it would be called, of cracked leather and tarnished brass. It had a disreputable-looking driver and was drawn by two of the little starveling horses of the country, one chestnut, the other colorless, both with ribs and hipbones that stood out like a skeleton's. I asked Cora if she were sure we had time for this expedition, and she said the Comandante had assured her that we should be here even longer than at Santarém. The more impatient I was to press on, I thought, the more *To-cantins* dawdled.

The market, sheltered in an open-sided building in a square by the dock, displayed a good stock of local produce—fruits and fish, dried and fresh, from the river. However, the shops along the main street, above the high, ugly sidewalks, seemed through their doorless doorways to have hardly enough merchandise to be worth staying in business to sell. There were some coils of rope, dingy drygoods, straw hats, wooden-soled sandals, skimpy rows of canned and bottled edibles and potables that looked as if they had been around a long time, a launch's propeller, two rusty machetes—*facões,* as they were called here—an antiquated firearm partially wrapped in newspaper. As we ambled down the alternately sandy and muddy street, men and women walking slowly along turned to stare at us, somewhat like somnambulists, and vultures skipped out of the way, tails up, heads lowered, one sinister eye cocked back at us.

"This is not, somehow, the way I pictured the gateway to the Massaranduba," I said. "I suppose riches that are still underground don't do much for a community. I don't know why I should have thought they would."

"That's right. Give them time." Her expression as she surveyed the scene around us did not add anything to her laconic retort. "How exactly do you intend to arrange about getting to the fabulous Massaranduba?"

I told her about the Braga family and what I knew about the situation of the sons. "When I see the mother in Manáos, I'll find out from her how her sons get up there from here. You can go practically the whole way by launch, I know."

"We've been talking about those who've gone in over their heads in this Massaranduba business. I'm not sure you realize what deep water *you*'re in. I think we'd better have a talk about it before long."

"I'll give it my full attention."

The masonry buildings of the town had given way to houses of palm-thatch with the family washing drying on the grass, the customary parrot in a window, and here and there a pair of domesticated tree-ducks in the yard. The road was for the most part grass-grown and swampy. As the little horses minced along, the driver would sometimes pivot all the way around in his seat to look at us. His face was puffy and reddish, and he was between badly needing a shave and having a beard. He might have been an old London cabby too well acquainted with pubs but for his melting Mediterranean eyes, which besought our commiseration with him in the injustice of his lot and accused us of complicity in it. He must at some time have lived where motion pictures were shown and have seen some of the Old West in which stagecoaches careened as they took the curves at a gallop, for whenever we had a corner to go around he lashed the horses into a show of cantering. They would then throw back their large hungry heads and send up a splatter of mud. He made so free with the whip that we had to order him to stop. Goats, brown and black, made way for us. We came, most astonishingly, upon a thoroughfare that was nothing less than an esplanade. It was formed of two broad roadways, going straight through the country, separated by an elevated section designed for the safety of the promenaders and to divide the two streams of vehicular traffic. Only there was not another human being in sight or another carriage, let alone a motorcar—the nearest of which was four hundred miles away, in Manáos. Shade-trees and palms had been planted at regular intervals bordering the avenue, but there was nothing else alongside but brush-grown grazing land.

"Here's your gateway after all," said Cora.

"It's headed in the wrong direction."

When we turned off the esplanade, the sun was setting, causing the white trunks of the trees across the rangeland to stand out like golden veining in the orange-washed, dusky green of the foliage. Cora was wearing an ice-blue dress with square neck, one I particularly liked, as I may have told her. Sitting beside her, my shoulder touching hers when the carriage lurched, I could feel her nearness in a prickly sensation along my side, as one may feel the sun's rays through clothing; I could not pretend to myself that I did not. I could not extinguish the feeling, I could not put it out of my mind. There was a sweet taste in my mouth.

The silence that fell upon us after one of us had spoken almost had body to it. There is a kind of being alone with a woman in which an awareness of what is possible between the sexes, indeed what the sexes are for, is shared, is reverberant in the air, like harmonics between you, like a soundless, fluttering concussion. You stand together upon the brink of a vortex, the downward-funneling current pulling at you, as when, upon a beach, the waters of a receding wave flow past your feet. With the sun going down on that remote pastureland, with Topacindo, the last outpost, behind us and the dissolute coachman hunched over his reins like a figure summoned up from the Underworld to bear us across some final divide, we were as alone together as if we had been on a desert island in an empty sea. I asked myself what difference it made what instinctive response the situation called up in me. I was not in fact alone with Cora and was not going to be.

"I never knew Margarita Coutinho very well," said Cora for the second time that afternoon. "I only thought of coming out here because I feel sorry for her. They had to move up here because of some failure of her husband's. It may not be very gay. You'll enjoy the Valdestes more, I think. I thought we might drop in on them for a few minutes on the way back to the boat—as I said. They live in Topacindo itself. Incidentally, it might be just as well not to say anything to the Coutinhos about our seeing the Valdestes. I think there's bad feeling between them."

I told her—also for the second time—that I was grateful to her for the chance to have a glimpse of life in an Amazon settlement and that I was agreeable to anything, just so long as we did not miss the boat.

"We could hear it blow from the Valdestes' and be there in five minutes. It wouldn't leave without us. This isn't an impersonal country like the States." She slipped her hand under the shoulder of her dress and in an inattentive way made some adjustment of her clothing.

The house to which we drove up was of the same construction as those in town, of stucco with high, arched windows, though its tiled roof sloped to the four sides. It looked stark, however, standing in the

293

dusk alone but for a few trees and a long, low shed beside it, among a number of cattle enclosures fenced with thin saplings. Inside it was a little more cheerful, though the chair cushions were threadbare and the bindings of the few books worn and the general effect was one of meagerness. We sat at a table on which was a brass kerosene lamp with a shade of green plates of glass and had cookies with *mate,* which tasted as if brewed of tea-leaves adulterated with straw. In addition to Senhora Coutinho there were two elderly women and an elderly man who, when one looked at them, nodded genially like the toy figures made by the Chinese with their heads balanced against a weight on a fulcrum; so in order to avoid animating them unnecessarily one looked at them as little as possible. Senhor Coutinho was in another part of the house, with a high malarial fever.

Senhora Coutinho was in her early thirties, dark and with an aquiline nose. Cora had said she had been a beauty in her youth, and I could believe this, though her face was wasted and lined. Her still fine eyes looked at you with forlorn and disabused hope that you would see her as otherwise than she was.

Senhora Coutinho having been educated in the United States, the conversation was in English. Cora explained that I was on my way to Manáos in connection with a business in which her husband was also interested and touched lightly on the pleasant surprise it had been, after we had come to know each other on the trip down from the States, to find me aboard *Tocantins.* Whether our hostess was satisfied that this was the whole story, it was hard to say. Perhaps nothing outside the pool of her unhappiness was very real to her. While Cora was talking, she looked at her with the expression of a woman window-shopping before a display of finery far beyond her means.

She said she had had another child since she had last seen Cora, a little girl, but it had died. She tried to console herself by thinking of the suffering the child had been spared, though it was useless to tell oneself this. But who knew? Perhaps one was better off to be out of this world. She had not meant to have so many children when she married. One or two, perhaps. But six had arrived. In addition to the five of her own, she now had to care for two of her brother-in-law's and his wife's. Her brother-in-law had lost his reason and had to be taken away to the asylum. His wife had gone too, to be near him, leaving the children

294

with her. Had Cora known about the brother-in-law? Yes, that had happened to him. Quite suddenly. She rolled in Cora's direction eyes that spoke volumes, or intimated that volumes could be spoken were it not that her lips were sealed.

Senhora Coutinho sat with the quiet heaviness of the exhausted. She was neither apologetic nor self-conscious as she went on speaking exclusively and at length about the misfortunes that had befallen her, especially the misfortune that was Topacindo itself. It was as if, simply, there were nothing else in the world to talk about—as if there could be no question in our minds but that everything else was trivial by contrast.

There had been two big mistakes, she said. The first had been marrying too young. Her parents had been ambitious for her, that was why they had sent her abroad for her education. But at nineteen she had lost her head and rushed into matrimony. The result had been the succession of children. The second mistake was that her husband had gone into politics. He had had a good business, with his brother, a cigarette factory, and they had been well off. But the two men had not been able to resist the lure of politics. It had been fatal. They had made more powerful enemies than they had made friends. To save what they had put into their party they had put in more, and still more, until everything was gone—except this *fazenda*. So they had moved up here to Topacindo. They ran a dairy farm, and she taught school in addition.

Various children had come out of hiding and formed a shifting, squirming audience on the fringe of the lamplight. Such generalized considerations as the state of the family's fortunes meaning nothing to children, they were playful and seemed gay enough. The oldest, a girl of about twelve, wound up a big, old cabinet-phonograph and put on a record. It was the quartet from *Rigoletto*. The faint, honking voices wavered like a wobbly wheel.

Senhora Coutinho said she worked from five in the morning until nine at night, but nothing seemed to bring in any money. They could not afford to buy feed for the twenty cows and hence were able to have them milked only once a day. I was so astonished by this non sequitur I got her to repeat it. Yes, once a day—at three o'clock in the morning! And anyway, the milk did not pay. Half a milreis a liter—three cents a quart—was all it brought, although it was the best milk in town and the leading families would drink no other. However, the cows were usually dry, and when they freshened they had so little milk the calves took most of it. "It's the same with cows as with women," she said. "The bigger the baby, the less the milk."

The quartet scratched to a halt. The daughter turned the platter over and *La Donna e Mobile* was heard. Senhora Coutinho looked vaguely around the table as if she had lost something, then seemed to recollect what it was she had in mind and took our *mate* cups in turn and refilled them.

"And we can't get anyone to work for us," she resumed. "When you see how poor everyone is here, and how little they have to occupy themselves with, you'd think they'd be glad of a chance to do a little work and improve their condition. But if you can persuade a girl or young man to come and work for you, they won't stay. Why should they? They've made a few milreis, and that's all they need for the moment. They don't want to work, and they can get all they want out of life without working. All they want is to sit around without doing anything and have enough to eat and a little *cachaça* now and then.

"They won't even work for themselves. All along the river there is no real agriculture. Why should anyone try to introduce food-plants and cultivate them when he can make enough to keep himself alive by picking up *castanhas* and cocoa in the forest?

"It is a terrible life here. So lonely. You can't even have friends. You see Mrs. Cobral in the morning and mention Mrs. Moura to her, and as soon as you have gone she hurries over to see Mrs. Moura and tells her hateful things she says you said about her. There's nothing else to talk about. No one is doing anything that is interesting, there's nothing outside of people's personal lives. When Mrs. Moura has heard what you are accused of having said about her, she is angry and won't speak to you. And so you lose all your friends, and everyone envies and mistrusts and dislikes everyone else.

"Apart from my husband and my children I have no life, except my flower garden. But it is thankless, too, to try to grow flowers. Did you notice the roses when you came in?"

"The light wasn't very good, but as well as I could see them I thought they looked lovely," said Cora.

"Yes, the roses are pretty enough, but did you see how they were? Each plant has to be grown in a can with a larger can around it and

296

water between them, so the *saúbas* won't get them. And then mosquitoes breed in the water!"

Neither Cora nor I could find anything to say to that. After pause I ventured to ask if riverboats often called at Topacindo, though I recognized that the Valdestes would be more likely to have the information I was fishing for.

She delayed replying while she spoke to one of the old women, who thereupon, working her lips poutingly, rose with a groan and withdrew, shunting two of the smaller children before her.

"Not as often as at Santarém and Parintins. But it may be different before long. Topacindo may become much more important. They say the Massaranduba development will transform it. I don't know. Everyone says it's the hope. The newspapers that reach us have a lot about it these days. But you'd know more about that than we do. Do you know if it's true that wealthy American interests are going to have a huge concession there? My husband is very excited about it."

"I don't know. A lot depends on the state government, I imagine. Would you know if anyone has arrived at Topacindo recently on the way to the Massaranduba?"

She shook her head. "It's all in the future. There are a few traders who go up in that direction. And some prospectors. But no one else from the outside. Except of course the young men who've got a mining camp up there. One of them came through last month on his way back from Manáos."

I should have liked to learn more about the Bragas, but she seemed to know little about them other than that they were "exceptional boys, very idealistic," and I did not feel I should keep the conversation cornered for my private purposes.

When we took our departure shortly afterward, the two women embraced with evident feeling. The older clung blindly for a moment to the younger before recovering herself and smiling—I think for the first time since our arrival.

When we had settled once more in our carriage, I said I felt as if we were turning our backs on a drowning person.

Cora had sat back in the corner of the seat. I could not tell whether she was separating herself from me or turning to face me. She was pale in the moonlight.

297

"We are," she said. "What the Coutinhos need is a friend with influence. In a poor country, where there isn't enough to go around, if you haven't got either influence or money, drowning is about all you can expect. Did you notice the almost beatific look that came over Margarita when she was smoking the cigarette you gave her? Even an ordinary brand of cigarette is a luxury for them. But I guess you did notice. I saw you hide the pack behind your cup and leave it there. That was thoughtful of you. Let's have one of mine now."

The carriage was moving so slowly and the night was so still that the flame of the lighter hardly needed shielding. The horses plodded with heads nodding as if in sleep. The driver was half asleep himself, not having fully awakened from the nap we had found him taking, sitting on the floor of the carriage with his head in his arm on the seat.

The coal of the cigarette, when she drew upon it, cast a warm glow upon Cora's face, and the sight was a pleasant one. Like the sparks from *Tocantins*'s funnel against the curdled sky, the coal contained in its red brilliance the very principle of fire, the flame of hearth and altar, in that blanched landscape.

"Money and success—wonderful to be superior to, when you've got them," Cora pursued. "It's not hard to imagine how blissfully the Coutinhos must have been in love to begin with, what a rosy picture they had of life. They could hardly wait to get on with living it. Who would have been so heartless as to tell them their little paradise was built on money? But—no money, no paradise. Isn't it a dreadful thought? You can't do everything with money, but you can't do much without it, can you?" She gave a sweeping glance at the fields frozen in the moonlight around us. "We're a long way from anywhere. What are you thinking about?"

"What you've been saying. How much comes down to money. I can hardly remember a time when the fear that that was so wasn't stalking me—always with a companion, which was the corollary that I wasn't going to have any. As long as you have the money you can think fine thoughts. You can cultivate the higher values. You can travel. You can absorb elevated impressions. But the grim reckoner is always there. If you keep paying him off, he'll let you alone. He'll let you cut your little capers. He'll even keep still while you pretend he isn't there. There's a gentleman's agreement among us all. If you won't notice the grim reckoner standing behind me with a rope around my neck, I won't notice him standing behind you. But he has to have his daily ransom. Fail to meet your payments and he'll gather you in. It's Topacindo for you then, boys!"

"But you have nothing to worry about. Not with the position you're in." Though I could not see her eyes except to know that they were unmoving, the steadiness of her regard as a zephyr fanned a wisp of hair across her cheek made me ponder the statement a moment.

"The position I'm in with respect to the Massaranduba Concession, you mean. Well, my importance has been inflated to the bursting point, I can tell you that."

"I don't think you know how strong your position is," she interrupted.

I shrugged. "In any case, what's to come of it? I'm no businessman, and I don't know. I'd have had no faith in the beginning of any great industrial enterprise. It would be impossible, I'd have said. I'd have said any big city would be impossible. Yet they've been built, by the hundreds. So I shouldn't worry if the Massaranduba sometimes seems a fantasy to me, especially at the end of a day like today. Yet today has been just such a day. You've seen Topacindo. You've made a joke about it. That esplanade—the gateway to empire . . ." I paused, trying to sort things out in my mind. "What you were saying a few minutes ago—it touched on what's been in the back of my head all day, I suppose. If the Confederacy had had what the Massaranduba promises to produce— money—it wouldn't have lost the war, and there'd have been no need for any emigration to Brazil. And if the emigrants had had money, they wouldn't have disappeared, as they have at Santarém. Or have they disappeared? I walked up and down the riverside. Shouldn't I have felt their presences? Do human personalities disappear completely?"

I knew I was speaking irrelevantly and wildly, and the contraction of her brows as she stared at me, which I could see even by moonlight, brought me back to myself. "Excuse me, I'm not making sense. It's just that we can never get altogether away from that war, you know. It's still trying to collect from us, or we're still trying to puzzle it out. But never mind. What I was thinking about was the Bragas—the 'exceptional boys, very idealistic,' as Senhora Coutinho called them. While she was talking, I was thinking—not for the first time—that they might make me feel differently about the Concession. They're not a hypothesis

299

of the future. They're flesh and blood, real persons actually living there and producing something. Wouldn't that make you believe in it? That is, if you wanted to believe in it?"

"If I wanted to believe in it?"

"Yes. Don't you have to want to believe in it? Or do you prefer to believe in poverty, failure, defeat? I have to believe in the Concession, for reasons you know. Surely the Bragas will help? They're making the Massaranduba pay. What they're producing is gold. Gold! How could anyone fail to respect that? Gold is what keeps nations from going under. Gold is the antidote to Topacindo, isn't it? It's what the grim reckoner demands, to allow you the privilege of living and feeding a family and having fine thoughts. So it must follow that tearing the country apart to get at the gold and bringing in more steamboats and railroads to burn up the forests for fuel are admirable and wonderful too."

"What they'd tear apart would be comparatively small, wouldn't it? This is an immense country."

"Yes, as immense as the wilderness was behind the thirteen colonies."

"And you'd hate to see it go the same way. It's more important to you than mankind."

"No. But no matter how important mankind was to me, I'd still feel as I do about this. No matter how much more important than night I consider day to be, I still think unending day would be a horror. I've had a belief I cannot explain that mankind doesn't exist independently of— No, I'll be honest. I've responded to what I've seen from the deck of *Tocantins* with the part of me where I feel my life is. It's always been that way, in the presence of such subdued equivalents of the Amazon wilderness as still persist at home—forests and mountains and marshes, a peregrine falcon among the buildings of Manhattan. They've given me a sense of portals swinging open—how much more dramatically here!—on realms beyond my encompassing, but which I've always felt I belonged to, which I've felt had an unlimited potentiality. It's difficult for me to explain—as I've said before. But what of it all? If I feel I can't live without spinach, am I justified in arguing that without spinach the human race will perish of malnutrition? Shall I spend my life preaching the virtues of spinach while I'm driven back with my dependents on some Topacindo somewhere—for want of that which the Massaranduba Concession promises to provide if I serve it loyally?"

300

She said, "I'm afraid it hasn't turned out to be a very happy idea—bringing you to Topacindo."

"No, Topacindos have to be faced. This one should never have existed, I know in my heart. . . . No, ignore that observation. It's part of what I have to get away from. This Topacindo must exist, with the prospect of being elevated to the level of that esplanade by the gold of the Massaranduba—and beyond, far beyond. Anyhow, it does exist, along with all the others, and as I say, better they be faced. I haven't grown to this age without some suspicion of what the facts of life are. . . . *You're* the one on whom things have been tough today, for some reason, I'm afraid."

"No. No, you're mistaken. It's been a day like any other," she replied as if fending off an invidious allegation.

We sat for a time without talking, and as it had had off and on during the day, the silence between us had the quality of a policeman with pencil poised to take down and possibly use against us anything we might say. The phantom fields and trees stretched away on either side. Cora spoke to the coachman, who started. He cracked his whip, and the horses—wraiths in the moonlight—lurched into an accelerated shuffle. Cora half rose, smoothed her skirt beneath her and sat down again facing forward, so that we were side by side. Her hand rested on her leg beside mine. I placed my hand on hers, enclosing it, and thus we rode along. Her thigh was firm and presently warm beneath my fingers. In the intensification of the being-alone-in-the-world-with-her feeling, the pull of the downward-spiraling current grew very strong, and with it the sense that it was necessary only to surrender one's grip on the complexities of life to be floated free of them, to be drawn in ever-quickening descent to the ultimate simplification in the consuming flux.

"The Valdestes are definitely expecting you?" I asked, not trying to exclude from my voice the hope that the visit could be omitted.

"Yes, they are," she said.

13

The house before which we drew up, on a street running at right angles to the waterfront, seemed larger than its neighbors and had a balustrade along the roof. Only enough light came from the windows between the slats of the shutters to show that the shutters were drawn. As I was paying the cabby, two soldiers appeared, walking abreast. They came to a halt some distance off, stared at us, then came forward again, passing us without another glance.

We were met at the door by a maid. Cora and she exchanged a few words, after which Cora led the way into the living-room. The Valdestes were out, she said, taking stock of the appurtenances of the room; they had been expected back some time ago from a trip they had taken in their launch to a *fazenda* up a nearby river.

The room had a floor like that of the Monteiros' living-room, of broad, alternating, nearly black and white boards, appearing to have been designed for some kind of game to be played with life-sized men. There were the usual massive Victorian articles of furniture assembled of heavy pieces of dark wood: a sideboard; a library table along one side of the room, supported on deeply-turned pediments, with some books and magazines on it; big chairs seemingly as permanently placed as park benches; a couch with an India-print spread; some smaller tables, two with lamps with shades of red cloth and with weak bulbs. The room was shadowy. I stood in the center of it, uncomfortable both from the sudden disruption of our proximity during the ride and from the sense one has in someone else's home, in the absence of the owner, of prying.

"What are the Valdestes like?" I asked. "You haven't told me much about them."

"They're quite ordinary, really, but they're better off than the Coutinhos—as you can see—and not as depressing. As I told you, he has a business here, lumber, I think." She had lifted the cover from a rosewood box on one of the tables. "Cigarettes," she said. "Piedmonts, too, of all things. And look there. It's a well-appointed home, isn't it?" She nodded at the sideboard, where, among other glassware, stood a bottle and some tumblers, the bottle proving to be of Scotch, three-quarters full. "The maid is going to bring us something to eat," she pursued, continuing her tour of inspection. The house and street were quiet. A rattling, rumbling noise from the distance, the only sound to be heard, was recognizable as that of *Tocantins*'s winch. Topacindo was at dinner.

I said, "This is the farthest apart from other human beings we've ever been together, at least since the afterdeck of *Boadicea*." I had not meant to say it.

"I suppose it is," she said, gazing up at a painting of a harlequin on the wall.

She came back to the table with the rosewood box and took a cigarette from it. "Have one?" While holding out the box she looked back down at the cigarette she had taken. Her head bent, she stood in an oddly stiff way, her feet apart, toes turned in a little. I went over to her, relieving her of the box and taking a cigarette for myself, and picked up a box of matches from the table. But she did not move, only continued to regard the cigarette in her hand, so there was no point in my lighting a match.

Suddenly it came over me that she was expecting me to make an overt move toward her—came over me with a knocking of the heart I could

303

almost hear. But the moment passed while I stood frozen. Tilting her head, she looked up at me, then put her cigarette in her mouth so that I could light it.

When I had done so, she asked, "Do you feel any less depressed now? From the way you felt in the buggy . . . Don't look so anxious!" She smiled.

The sharp, resounding tread of approaching steps on the sidewalk reminded me that at any moment the Valdestes might return and that I had no decision to make because there was nothing I could do. "I don't mean to," I said.

It did not feel natural to be standing as we were, together in the middle of the room, as if we were forming part of an invisible crowd. The natural thing would have been to sit down, but we remained as we were, as if our shoes were nailed to the floor, Cora half turned away from me, my eyes fixed upon the curve of her cheek.

"Or rather," I went on, "if I do look anxious, you must know the reason."

She said, "I remember I told you that you were to leave everything to me. I haven't forgotten it." Her head dropped a fraction of an inch. "When I put on a dress . . . when I put on this dress this afternoon I thought of . . . of taking it off for you."

At first I did not believe she had said what I had thought I heard her say. Then, hearing it over again in my head, unsteady on my feet, I felt as if I were standing in an onrush of dreams. I glanced, probably with an expression of desperation, at the door. Cora, who had intercepted and followed my glance, spoke again, in a murmur. "Yes, we can't be sure how near the nearest other human being may be, can we?"

"There's your stateroom in *Tocantins*—or mine." My voice had a thickly suggestive quality, like a leer—perhaps inevitable—that made me recoil from it.

She looked away with a slight frown and spoke as if carrying on a hurried argument, though not, necessarily, with me. "I don't know what would come of it. No, I don't mean that as naïvely as it sounds. I know what would come of it, naturally, but I don't know what would come of *that*—the further consequences. There's such an awful lot involved."

What she said baffled me. Had my mental processes not been so slug-

304

gish, I should probably have thrown up my arms in a wild remonstrance. By the time I had got around to that impulse, the time for it had passed. Also, the maid had come in, carrying a tray of food. We had both looked around at her guiltily. I watched her with eyes that only gradually took in what they were seeing. She unloaded the contents of the tray on the library table. There were beef sandwiches, papaya (here called *mamão*), the little bananas known as *inajas,* and coffee.

The maid was dark and chunky and probably very young, and she seemed frightened at being alone with such exotic and abnormally-complexioned human animals, under their silent observation. The dishes clattered in her hands, and contracting into her black dress, she escaped as quickly as she could.

"Would you like a drink?" Cora asked. Her voice had the flatness that voices have when a subject of mundane concern is spoken of in an emotionally charged atmosphere

"No, I don't think so—unless you'd care for one," I replied in the same kind of voice, like an amateur actor reciting his lines—but one in the dark as to what the script called for next.

She shook her head. "Not right now. I think we'd better eat something, though, when we've washed up."

I nodded, without having given the proposition any thought or knowing why we should eat anything. While she was in the bathroom, which she had asked the maid about, I was wracking my brains to know how to deal with the problem of her—her what? That was the problem!

The bathroom was down the hall. When I had come back from washing, there was more sound of movement in the street, I realized as, just then, a woman's voice, full-throated and comfortable, spoke from directly outside the window, startling in its nearness. "Every time there's a noise I'm going to think it's the Valdestes," I said.

We methodically, like proper guests at a buffet dinner, took up plates and filled them.

In a tone of voice that took us back to the point at which the maid had entered, I said, "I can't fathom you at all. If I didn't know you well enough to know it's not true, I'd think you were trying to see how much havoc you could create inside me. No, I know it's not that," I put in quickly in response to the look she turned upon me, "but it's as bad as if it were. You stir up—you let me imagine things and at the same time you draw back. I suppose there's a reason—something behind it, an obscure set of contradictory impulses. But, Cora, you've got to know what you want!"

"I'm not sure you know what *you* want."

I replied in the only way I could have replied—without thinking. "I told you what I wanted!" It is improbable that the lights had actually grown dimmer, but the atmosphere seemed murky, as it had once before on the bridge of *Tocantins*. I wondered if she were going to respond skeptically. With teeth on edge, I thought she had warrant for saying what she had; if her impulses are contradictory, what in God's name are mine?

"I'll tell you what I want," she said, and from her voice it was evident that she was not speculating about what was in my mind but was absorbed by what was in her own. "But sit down. Let's talk calmly. If you don't eat, I'll know we're not talking calmly enough."

We sat in opposite chairs, facing each other, and while I waited for her to begin we chewed resolutely on our sandwiches.

"May I bring you some coffee?" she asked presently, standing up.

"Yes, thank you." I could have got the coffee, but I gave in to the desire I recognized to watch her cross the room, to observe the shape of her legs. I was finding it hard to swallow what I was eating, though I was sure I was chewing it immoderately. As she stood by the table, filling the cups, I said, "It seems a very strange thing to be here—with you —in an unknown town, halfway up the Amazon River, in the house of someone I've never met. It's a little like having had a drink on an empty stomach; it cuts one loose from everything. If you feel at all as I do you shouldn't have any difficulty telling me what you were going to." But I doubted that there would be time for it, with our host and hostess likely to come in at any moment. "It's nice being waited on, by such a waitress."

She had brought the coffee to me. "Is that the way you feel? I mean, cut loose from everything? Do you feel you could speak without . . . being embarrassed?"

"Yes." I took the cup from her. "For example: I like it when you bend over toward me in that dress."

I could not tell, as it became clear to her what I meant, whether she were trying to smile or trying not to, but in either case she was having scant success. There was a sheen on her face.

"Do you think cups will be safe on the chair arms?" she asked, though

I doubted that she would have heard my answer had I given one. I could see as she sat down, still holding her cup and neglecting to arrange her skirt about her, that she was getting her thoughts in order, and I did not speak. "It's very simple, really," she said finally, after making a slight gesture with her hand and shoulder, like a shrug. "What I want is just"—her voice fell—"two things. One is to avoid suffering. I don't like tragedy. I don't want it to happen to either of us."

"But why should it?" I was struck by the hard light in her eyes when she looked up at my question.

She said, "I'm thinking of very concrete eventualities. I'm thinking of Colonel Durondo."

"What's he got to do with it?"

"You've seen him. You know about him. You must be aware that he's a violent and ruthless man. He's not going to let himself be done out of power if he can help it. And he can do a *very great deal* to help it. There's very little he can't or won't do. Politics are life-and-death matters here, as I've tried to tell you. You must have learned from João Monteiro. Doesn't the fact that I'm being used as I am—or was meant to be used as I told you—with the connivance of the man who is legally my husband, give you an idea of how Durondo's mind works, and how he goes about getting what he wants?"

I was almost ready to smile, though manifestly she was very serious indeed; I had never seen this kind of earnestness about her. Yet what she said was so obviously altogether extraneous to what was pushing us both to the extreme of agitation. I said, "I didn't know this kind of thing—the struggle for political power, and all—interested you very much. But supposing what you say is true—and I don't for a moment doubt it—it's nothing new. Why should you suddenly be concerned about it?"

She seemed disappointed in my reply, as if she had failed in her endeavor. "It doesn't interest me," she said. "I'm only concerned about it because it doesn't intend to let us alone. If I'm ever free of it . . . Why don't you eat?"

While she stabbed at her fruit with her fork, blinking her eyes, I took the last two mouthfuls of my sandwich and looked at her once more in bafflement. Surely she was not having to keep the tears out of her eyes! No, that was not possible. In the silence the *tocking* of leather-soled shoes approached the door again, but as I stiffened anticipatorily again passed

307

on, accompanied by the mutter of a man's voice. Cora paid no attention.

"The point is this," she stated with renewed emphasis. "I think you mean to remain loyal to João Monteiro and his party. That is, you intend before the political showdown is reached to let him claim that you and the men in New York with the money are going to stick with him in the Massaranduba business—which will give the *Constitucionalistas* a great advantage. And that is just what Colonel Durondo is determined you shan't do."

I stared at her without finding any additional illumination of what this was all about. "I feel as if I were hearing someone else talking," I said. "Even when I'm closest to the political goings-on, they don't seem entirely real to me. Even when I was a prisoner in the Palace, they didn't. For the rest, I'll tell you how it is, if you really want to know. I told Colonel Durondo it was not up to me to decide whom the syndicate in New York would work through in Brazil. All I could do was collect the information the syndicate seems to want and pass it along. They'll make up their own minds as to how they wish to proceed. But Monteiro's still our client. When I get back from the Massaranduba, I'm going straight to his house and resume where I left off when I was picked up by the *Milícia Estadual*. I never said I shouldn't. I'll go on reporting Monteiro's side of things to New York. . . . I declare, Cora, I don't know why we're getting into all this."

"Because the political goings-on *are* real. They're real to me. They must be real to you. If I sound like someone else, it's because I *am* someone else. I'm trying to be you, to be your judgment. I want you to remember that. I'm speaking as you ought to be speaking to yourself." She looked at me in a way that reminded me of teachers I had had as a child. "Do you intend to be back and take up with João Monteiro again before the elections?" She was sitting erect, whereas I had slumped down in my chair.

"Yes," I said.

"You mustn't!" she exclaimed almost before the word was out of my mouth. "You don't know what you'd be risking!"

I hitched myself up and reached for a banana. My slow stripping back of the peeling may have seemed to connote languid bravado, but in fact the subject made me uncomfortable. "I'm an American citizen. They might throw me in jail or deport me. But I don't see how they could do much worse."

"Much worse!" She had not moved. "Oh don't be naïve! *Any*thing could happen to you. Do you suppose the *Interventor* doesn't know how to conceal the official hand?"

"If that's the case, I should have thought of it before I took on the job."

"Look, Julian. You don't owe João a thing," she said with patient firmness. "The moment he involved you in the political situation he . . . put you in jeopardy. And I know something about it. I've heard. Believe me, that freed you of any possible obligation to him. All I'm asking is that you don't come back before the elections and don't make any declarations in João's favor. Send your reports back by riverboat if you want to, but don't come down yourself. Send word back that you've got malaria—you probably will have—if that'll make it easier to face Monty later. But stay where you are. Let the best man win, as between Durondo and Monteiro—without your getting in the mangle. Whoever comes out on top can go ahead with the Massaranduba Concession— and you'll be able to stay with it, you won't have ruined yourself with either side."

There was only one explanation of these speeches. "You've been put up to this, haven't you?" I asked, feeling a tightness inside.

"Of course I have!" she said impatiently. "I was honest with you about that to begin with. But what difference does it make? What I've said I'd say anyway. I want you to save us."

"Us?"

"Yes, me too. I want to have done with all this! I want to leave Jorge. I told you that. And having left him, I want to be able to forget him. Forget him, forget him!"

She sounded and appeared more shaken than I had ever seen her, and I could feel in myself the physical repercussions of her emotion. "But what's to prevent your leaving him at any time? You've only to go down to the docks and get on a foreign ship. You'd be perfectly safe. If it's a question of money, I have enough to meet the expense and you could—"

"No, it's not a question of money—or safety, either. It's just not as easy as you think. Far from it, far from it!" She shook her head in tight little shakes, and I could tell that it was not primarily with me she was disputing but with a voice inside which had been counseling her as I had, probably over a long period of time. Since it had apparently done so in vain, there was no use in my persisting in doing so. We fell silent. The stillness seemed to echo with the vigorous voices in which we had been talking.

"Would you care for more coffee?" I asked.

"Perhaps so." She rose and we walked together to the table. We filled our cups, lighted cigarettes and returned to our places.

After seating herself she opened her mouth to speak, hesitated, then said, "I'm asking you to consider not only yourself but also the future of the Massaranduba Concession. Colonel Durondo is the one who has the power. The *Constitucionalistas* have only expectations."

She was going on, but I interrupted. "I didn't know you cared about what happened to the Massaranduba."

She was sitting well forward in her chair, as she had been before. "It isn't a question of what I care about. It's a question of what you care about." She gave her cigarette a series of hard taps on the edge of the saucer. "No one I care about is going to be affected one way or another by what happens there—except you," she added in a voice at once softer and wryer. "You say you have a nightmare fear sometimes that everything depends on money. It's a nightmare to be without it, I can believe that. Let anyone who doubts pay a visit to Margarita Coutinho."

"You'd have me also invest everything in the Massaranduba, like the rest. You'd have me deliver myself up to it, body and spirit." I sprang to my feet in a sudden burst of feeling and strode a few steps back and forth. "There are two things I can be thankful for. One is that *you*'re not dependent on the Concession—that the Concession isn't all that stands between you and a fate like Senhora Coutinho's. The other is that I can't feel that faith in the Concession everyone else feels. If I did, and if I thought Durondo alone was the man who could deliver the goods—and he may be—my God, what mightn't I end by doing? From the very noblest motives, of course! Who can be sure of himself? But as it is, I can keep my head. I can remember that my first duty is to Monteiro. If he embroiled me in the struggle for political power, I at least didn't hold out. I've only my own weakness to blame for my being in so deep now. I can remember that if it hadn't been for Mon-

310

teiro I shouldn't even be here now, I shouldn't even have heard of the Massaranduba—let alone of you. For me to leave him in the lurch to ingratiate myself with Durondo would be beneath anything. How could you expect me to be able to live with myself if I did that?"

"If João could win the Concession by washing his hands of you, even with all that your father has put into it, he'd do it like a shot. He certainly wouldn't risk—certainly wouldn't run the risks for you that you seem determined to run for him."

"I'm not answerable for him—only for myself. What I wish I understood is why it's so important in your life—other than because of your generous concern for me."

She had been holding her cup and saucer while I was speaking, and now she lowered them to her lap. While she had not changed her position, a certain heaviness seemed to come over her, her expression to become a little withdrawn even though, after a moment, she smiled.

"I'd better let the maid know she can clear away—if you've finished?" she ended inquiringly.

When I nodded, she left the room and I remained pondering what I had told her I did not understand.

She returned with the maid, who brought with her a glass pitcher containing pieces of ice and water. We all three took a hand in loading the plates and cups back on the tray, and this the maid bore off as if she were carrying a dishpan of water to put out a fire.

"There was something else you said you wanted," I reminded Cora. "There were two things."

"I'd like a drink first. You'll have one, won't you? You can't let me drink all by myself. I don't ordinarily think of having a drink, but now I thought I'd like one. So I asked the maid for some ice. I'd like mine with just a little more water than whisky, if you don't mind fixing it."

She spoke a little breathlessly, so I regarded her more critically. "You do look as if you might need one," I said. "A little pale—the way you did when you came ashore the first night out in *Tocantins*. You don't feel that way, do you?"

"No, I'm not going to faint."

She walked across the room away from me as I set about preparing the drinks. I was generous with the Scotch, feeling more than a little in need of some myself. With my pocketknife I chopped off chunks of the ice. When I turned, Cora was sitting on the sofa, leaning forward on her

311

arms, gripping its edge. I joined her there. Without ceremony we raised the glasses to our lips together and drank, a good draught each.

"The Valdestes couldn't have set things up more hospitably for us even if they'd known we were going to be entertaining ourselves here," I said.

"They couldn't."

"I'd been hoping to find out more about things here from them than I could from Senhora Coutinho. A place where I could put up on my way back through here, for instance. But it doesn't look as if there were going to be much time. Perhaps I'll have a chance on the return trip."

"Probably so," she said, taking another substantial drink.

Feeling an obscure need to keep up, I did likewise. "And the other thing?" I asked. "What was the second thing you said you wanted?"

Looking down into her glass, she said, "I want you to make love to me. Here. Tonight."

The sensation I had was one I have had otherwise at rare times of fright when the blood has left my skin, leaving me feeling as a hand does in a glove. It must be the result of the nervous organism's jarring to a complete halt. I know I stared at her, however, for the picture of her sitting beside me with head bent, her pretty face looking almost swollen, as if she had been crying—I suppose the blood had suffused it— her shoulders rounded beneath the dress I had said I liked, was not to fade with time.

"The Valdestes," I said against the force that gripped my throat.

"They won't be back tonight. The maid has had word. The launch broke down at the place they were visiting. I've told the maid she won't be needed any more."

I had not taken my eyes off her, and I saw her now plainly—indescribably plainly—in the ways she had permitted and incited me to see her. Yet I could not put out a hand to her! That barrier, like a pane of indestructible glass, was still there. . . . No, it was not just that. Something was wrong. I felt that just as strongly when she turned her head and looked up at me, and for an instant I had the sensation one has when for a long time one has been alone with a girl in the darkness and the light is turned on and one seems to be seeing a stranger, a stranger with whom one has been sharing prolonged intimacies.

When it came to me what was wrong it threw a pitiless light over all that had passed between us before this moment, revealing the full extent

312

of her calculation, the full scope and life-history of my fatuousness. "But
the two things are related, aren't they, Cora? My not going back to Monteiro and our making love. One is the price of the other."

Her eyes once more on her glass, she said, "Yes."

"In other words, the plan is being carried out to the letter. You are offering yourself just as your husband and Durondo have arranged, as a
move to ensure my reliability. It seems unbelievable, doesn't it, that I
could have been so naïve as not to have seen all along that the plan
was being followed. As a matter of fact, you found me naïve about
something a little while ago." While the words expressed a wholly
justified bitterness, they were just words. Inexplicably I could not work
myself up to the indignation the circumstances cried out for. Again
something was wrong. The heart of the situation was not where I was
looking.

"I've asked myself how I could keep you from jumping to that conclusion. I thought by being open with you at the start I might prevent it."
She was looking me full in the face, but I knew from the angle at which
her head lay back and from her eyes, which were narrowed self-
protectively, that she was willing herself to confront me as she was. "I'll
be more honest still. Appearances are even more damaging to me than
you yet know. The Valdestes were never going to be here. This is all set
up for us. The *Tocantins* is being held here overnight on the pretense
of being searched by the *Milícia Estadual* for documents destined for
an anti-Government organization across the state line. But what I
told you was true, Julian. I care nothing for Durondo or for Jorge or
for the Massaranduba." Though her position had not changed, it struck
me then as being one of pride as much as of forced courage.

"I do care for you and for me," she went on. "I want both things—
both the two things I said I wanted—for your sake and for mine. If it
will help you believe it, think that I'm considering myself only. For myself, then, for what it would mean to me, I want you to promise me
you'll stay clear of Monteiro, and the political contest in general, until
the fight's over. I want the other thing, too. I'd like to make you
happy. Notice I say *I'd like*. It would make *me* happy if I made you happy.
I'm still thinking of myself, if my saying so makes me seem more honest,
I know what's between us. I haven't forgotten a word you uttered on the
bridge that night. I know how tension's been building up in you. I'd
like to help you get over it. I'd like to hold you and give you the kind

313

of release you need so badly. That would give me pleasure, and . . . you'd make me feel what you were feeling, wouldn't you?"

"But the one . . . the one is still conditional on the other, isn't it?" I asked desperately.

"Yes, it is," she said in a low but natural voice, as if there were nothing out of the ordinary in such a proposition. "What other means of inducement have I got? If I were a gun-moll I could draw a pistol and put you in captivity till the elections were over, and make love with you behind locked doors—with a pistol at your head, if it helped you with your conscience. But I can't do that. This is the only way I've got."

"But, Cora, this isn't a thing you can bargain over!" I cried. She sat there within arm's length of me, a warm, breathing presence, meltingly feminine, like a rosy glow in the sky at dawn, a being holding the key to endless corridors of feeling, a woman clad in a thin dress and a slip, which I could see under her knee where her skirt was drawn back, and little else. She gazed at me unwitting of the impassable bars she had rung down before me, her eyes dark—so dark I realized she had turned white, perhaps because of my scrutiny.

"Is self-preservation so shameful?" she demanded between breaths. "I'm asking only that you have no more regard for others than they have for you. No more than twice as much, I might say. Look at me. It's nothing remarkable for women to be willing to do things for men. It's easier for them to do things than to admit what they're doing. To speak of what they're doing. But I'm doing that. Does that mean nothing to you?" She was clutching her glass with both hands. The color had mounted to her face again, giving it the glow it always did. "Shall I be more particular? I could specify what I have in my mind when I say I've thought what the consequences would be of my taking off my dress for you. Would that help you understand how much I want to give?" She sat rigid, and while the light was not strong enough for me to see clearly, her face must have been burning.

A force within me was fighting to break through bonds that felt like iron bands across my chest. "I don't need help. I understand," I said. But I did not understand. At least I did not understand what was driving her to a course that made such demands on her it changed her personality. I could not face her, neither could I keep my eyes away from her. I was still holding the glass, and I took another drink from it. The

314

mere performance of a routine act helped a little. "If I weren't going to live past tonight, good God, I wouldn't hesitate, Cora. It would be almost worth not living past tonight if I could be sure it was what you—"

She broke in here. I had not meant to be taken quite literally, though the desire pressing so hard upon me was such that I could at least conceive such a solution, but she took me literally. She cried out with real horror, "No, no! That's just what you can't think of!" There were both dismay and appeal in her face. "Don't dream of such a thing! You're confusing opposites. It would be to live, to hold onto life!"

"All right," I said placatingly. "I only meant to show that . . . how almost anything . . . You see what I mean."

She seemed reassured. Some of the stiffness left her, though she remained looking doubtfully at me, nibbling her lower lip. The strength of her reaction had startled me. "What were you going to say?" she asked. "If you were sure I what?"

"Only that it would be almost worth not living if I were sure it wasn't just an inducement you were offering," I said with a shrug. "But it doesn't matter—since I must expect to go on living and having to face the consequences of what I do."

"Do I mean it just as an inducement?" A glitter came into her eyes. Her breast rose as she drew a deep breath and held it for an instant before letting it escape. "It *is* that. You *don't* understand."

"It doesn't matter! You've made it impossible, so what does it matter?"

"If I were different, if I were more experienced, it wouldn't be like this," she said, her gaze falling from my eyes to my chest. "I could make you know." With the hand holding her glass resting on her lap, she had slid forward on the sofa and was leaning on her arm, held stiff at her side. Her skirt had pulled up over her knees, but I took it that she was as unaware of that as she was of what I had just said to her.

"Why don't we finish these drinks?" I interjected. I had seen from the abstract but alert look in her eyes that she was pursuing a train of thought, and while I did not know whether I had the strength of will to bring it about, a voice told me, cutting through the tangle of my feelings, that my one hope was to get us out of here and back to the ship.

While she gave no other sign of having heard, she obediently raised

315

her glass to her lips. After taking a swallow she raised it again and finished the drink. Having also finished mine, I took the two glasses back to the table.

"I told you I could be specific and describe . . . what I thought and felt when I thought of . . . us, together," she said. "But it would be easier—at least I'd rather . . . There's a poem. I made a copy of it, and I have it here." Her face was still flushed as she looked across the room at me, anxiously. Her hair was damp on her forehead, and from her speech I knew she was breathing rapidly. Whatever her emotion was, the symptoms of it, like her legs, heedlessly bared, intensified mine. Now was the time to go, that instant, I told myself.

"Would you bring me my handbag? I want to read it to you," she said in a voice with hardly enough power to carry to me. She rubbed the back of her hand across her eyes, as if they were watering.

Now, this instant, I repeated. But I went and got the handbag, thinking as I did so, with a sense that it had just been given to me to see it all, that we were caught up in words. Everything was words! It was not a question of whether we were going to have an affair. We were having one—in the realm of words. A spell had been cast upon us so that whatever we tried to do we turned it into words.

When she had taken the bag from me she put her hand palm down on the couch beside her, meaning for me to be seated there. She had pulled her skirt down. I sat down while she searched through the bag and took from it a piece of paper, which she unfolded and spread on her lap. Bending low over it, she passed her hands over her eyes again. "I'm not crying," she said in a straitened voice. "It's just that my eyes keep misting over." She threw me an appealing glance, then looked down at the paper again.

"This is really the middle of it," she said. She began to read, in an even and steady voice:

"With still unwilling eyes, she read in his,
That which, were she untutored and unlearned,
A child in knowledge of desire's wants,
Must yet have made her woman, knowing well
The fierce imperative she woke in him,
That, fired by what it claimed of her, and what
It would not be gainsaid—her lips, her breasts,
Her nakedness—would seek her out, would give

No quarter and concede no reticence,
Until it carried all before it, and,
Achieving her, would bend her to contain,
Subdue, a storm past either's bearing. This
Was what awaited, what must be, if she
Gave way to what their beings jointly urged.
All this each saw within the other's eyes;
A knowledge so avowed in his as faith
In paradise might burn within the gaze
Of one condemned to death, in hers half veiled,
Confessed by shyness cornered at the last.
Unnerved, in sudden panic on the brink
Of that from which she saw no turning back,
From which no part of her could be withheld,
She struggled, pinioned in his quick embrace,
Vainly to deny her mouth to his;
Weakness, like a traitor, had its way,
Stole through her veins and opened to his quest,
The access to her she had striven to bar.
Mouth pressed to mouth, lost to the world and time,
One soul's two halves that, yearning to rejoin,
Clung each to each and did not stir but for
The satisfaction of their mutual thirst
In the prolonged enactment that prepared
The flesh for what the prelude symbolized.
Then . . . No! Her mind cried out but no word came,
As on her thigh she felt the hand, cool, warm,
Possessive. Drugged with kisses interchanged,
She could not wrest her mouth away, but held
Yet tighter in his arm, of strength deprived,
Felt all she was, had been, could ever be,
United in one longing singleness
To grasp eternity, to live forever
In but a moment, give to him she loved,
The sweet torment of self from self set free,
The rapture of release from loneliness
In close conjunction of those parts wherein
Two pulsing bloodstreams all but merge as one.
And so, while still her inborn fears cried out
In warning of her self's loss to herself,
Depicting starkly, forcing her to see,

317

As if she stood apart, the literal acts,
To shock her into shame, the hand she placed
On his to stay it, rather by its powerlessness,
Gave license where it would have given check,
Her body, now self-willed, beyond command,
Made move, advantaged the invader's aim.
Its eagerness would be betrayed to him,
She knew, were he to touch her breast, and straight
Her faintness grew, to think what purposes
His learning of it might incite . . ."

The full awareness of what I was about did not come to me until after the act, until it had happened and was over. I had clasped Cora in my arm and with my free hand turned her face toward me, for me to take her kiss, and she had started violently away, her eyes round with shock. My arm had fallen. We stared at each other, and both our faces doubtless mirrored the astonishment, consternation, confusion and humiliation stamped upon the other. Our minds both lay open to the other, and the pain I read in hers and she assuredly in mine caused us to avert our eyes.

"I'm terribly sorry," she said. She had let her head fall. "You took me so by surprise. I wasn't expecting it. I didn't mean what I did. It wasn't what you think." She looked up beseechingly.

I had got to my feet and moved a few paces off. From where I stood, leaning against the wall, I could see her over my shoulder. "It doesn't matter what it was," I said. "I lost my head. I can stand just so much." It was as if I were having to lift a heavy blanket with my voice. There was an ache in my stomach. The knowledge that I had been saved from a monstrous faithlessness by a mere unreflecting response of hers made me see myself, in the midst of my life, as surrounded by a wasteland. Apprehensively I watched her rise and come toward me. I straightened up and turned to face her.

She stood before me without speaking, regarding me calmly, and the mere fact of her doing so was challenging, representing—as I felt sure it did—a feat of self-mastery. No trace was to be seen in her, except for her heightened color, of the emotions of a moment before. After a time that could not have been as long as it seemed, she said, "But I don't want you to have to stand so much. I don't want you to have to stand anything at all. You don't have to. What I want is for you to give it—give me—another chance."

"I'm not going to throw over Monteiro—close as I may have come to it just now. I'm not going to sell out my friends."

A subtle transformation seemed to take place in her. Still standing very nearly as erect as before, she appeared to become limp. "You can forget that part of it," she said in a low voice, her eyes downcast, as it were submissively. "Do what you like about Monteiro—all of it."

"No, but I wouldn't!" I cried. "I'd do what *you* liked! You wanted me to think how it would be: making love with you and possessing you altogether. And I did think how it would be. You saw! And I knew if it would be like that, I'd have no will apart from yours. I'd bring you John Monteiro's head on a charger—anybody's!—not because you'd demand it but just to please you, to get you to keep on. And you know this. You couldn't help knowing it. But there's the other fact, too." She listened with an alert, curious interest to the words that poured out of me. "My making love to you is *not* what you want. I could tell, Cora! It was automatic, it was your instinctive reaction, the way you wrenched yourself free. And the look in your eyes! It wasn't just that I startled you. It was that you hadn't had time to prepare yourself. It needed preparation. Do you know what you're asking? I'll tell you. It sounds insane, but it's what I think. You're asking me"—I had to fight to bring the words out—"you're asking me to rape you with your connivance. You are! And the reasons I have for saying that—" I was driven to keep on talking, to keep her from replying while she was as angry as I knew she would be, but she broke in anyway, with a gasp.

"That's horrible! It *is* insane!" She reached out for the back of the chair beside her. "You can't believe such a perverted thing!" Her eyes were almost as they had been when she had felt herself suddenly in my arms.

"I don't know what I believe," I said, my momentum having altogether gone. "I suppose I was wrong. It's not an easy thing to understand." The pain in my stomach was particularly sharp. I had to pull in on the muscles to contain it.

"You can't have it both ways!" she exclaimed, still aroused. "You can't have it that I'm so . . . passionate you'd be lost if you made love to me, and at the same time . . . at the same time, cold."

319

There was no contradiction in it to me, but I was not in condition to find words for what I felt: that it was her very ability to stand apart and thus to be capable of perception, of contrivance, of knowing what, when and how, that, with her talents as an actress, made me believe that with Cora it would not be an affair satisfying the need that led to it but a narcotic leading to an addiction. I said, "All I know is the effect you have on me," and with a minor hope of lightening the atmosphere, "I feel as if I'd been spitted and turned before a very hot fire." I managed a smile. "I can feel right where the spit goes through me."

She did not return the smile. "It's your own choice," she said in a low voice. "You know I could help it."

I shook my head. "Not now you couldn't. I've been on the spit too long." My renewed smile did not feel any more natural than before. She searched my face, her brows puckered for a moment.

"It won't last. We have all night."

Her statement reminded me of where we were, which I had lost sight of, and as I thought of the outside world a cock crowed in the distance and was answered by one closer by. Though it was still far short of midnight, the sound brought the feeling of dawn and of the spaciousness of the sky above the still-dark earth.

"We've got to go, Cora."

I was not sure what her response would be, but I expected something more than the expression of reserve, even inattentiveness, that greeted this.

After a space she said, "I was hoping this wasn't going to have to come up." She was twisting the gold band on her third finger, presumably her wedding ring. "We can't go. You particularly can't. The *Interventor* has arranged for soldiers to be posted in front of the house and behind. They have orders to arrest you if you leave before daybreak." She turned swiftly and walked to the long table. With her back to me she continued. "You see how his mind works. If you stay the night, he'll take it you've been bought and feel safe—or safer—about you. If you don't, he'll surmise you're holding out on him and are a danger to him. I suppose you feel degraded by all this. Perhaps you can imagine how I feel, having had it put up to me by the man I stood beside in a church five years ago and was married to. . . . Put up to me with an alternative that—" She broke off. I could not see her face. *"Come here."* These words were uttered in a tone not of command but of entreaty.

I stood where I was until I felt heartless. Durondo's presence seemed to me to fill the room, his black eyes with their tobacco-stained whites to be fixed upon me with cynical appraisal as I went across to her.

"I don't know why," she said, still with her back to me, "he should feel so very much safer about you only because you'd spent a night here."

"I do."

"It needn't make any difference, what he's done!" She swung around to face me, her back to the table, to which she held. "Achille Durondo is five hundred miles from here," she declared, from which I understood that she also had a picture of his looking on. "There's no one here but you and me." I was watching her steadily, and the hopelessness she saw in my regard must have bothered her. She passed the tip of her tongue over her lips, drew a breath to resume and thought better of it. Then, with an effect of plunging ahead, she said. "Only you and I, wanting the same thing. Only the trouble is, I don't know much about men, about you. Isn't it? I'd learn as we . . . as we went along, I promise you, but—"

"*Yes,*" I could have said, "*I know, I know.*"

"—but now I don't. I don't know what would attract and excite you and what repel you, and I'm afraid to take a chance. You said you liked it when I leaned over toward you—in this dress. You meant you liked to see . . . though with what else I wear, you couldn't. . . . But I don't have to wear this dress, or the other. And then if you were sitting there, I could . . . Only, it might repel you. Even my saying so may."

I pressed my hands to my face. But the floor was unstable beneath my feet and I had to uncover my eyes to keep from losing my balance. Before letting my arms drop I turned aside to hide my expression. I strode with uncertain steps to the sideboard, where the Scotch was. With my back toward her so she would not know fully what I was doing, I filled a glass from the bottle. Taking a deep breath, I began to drink. Big gulps would get it over faster, I told myself, but with the first one I felt that the whisky was burning the flesh from my throat. With my eyes shut tight and with tears from the smarting fluid welling up in them, I went on, but with smaller swallows. My insides rose, contracted. I saw my entrails as a fist doubled up against the incursion. Halfway through the glass I had to stop. *I'll never make it,* I thought. My stomach was in spasms. That, I thought, was going to defeat me. I should not be able to keep the stuff down. Even before I could finish, it would come up.

321

"I don't think I like this," said Cora, articulating each word. "Am I such a monster that it takes all that to anesthetize your conscience?"

By taking a breath between swallows I got most of the rest down. The last ounce was beyond me.

"What makes you think you can hold—" At this point she must have realized what was afoot.

Nausea and cramps had me bent over the table. I made myself straighten up and I filled my lungs with deep gasps. Already the first signs of a relaxing effect were noticeable. My vision followed slightly in arrears of the movement of my eyes. I was winning the battle with that accursed whisky. In a few moments, even if I subsequently threw up, I should be out of commission for the rest of the night.

"I had as much as this once before, at a New Year's Eve party," I said. "Of course I took it more gradually. Even so, I thought it was going to kill me before I went under. I mean literally. Naturally, I had quite a period of gaiety before I felt the full effect. This time I don't think there'll be more than five or ten minutes. Just about time for a cigarette."

I walked over to the table on which was the rosewood box as steadily as an ocean liner; the image was one that struck me forcefully at the time. Cora, I could see from the corner of my eye, was watching me. To avoid having to face her for the moment I did not offer her a cigarette as I lighted one for myself. "You might keep your eye on this," I said, holding the cigarette up and speaking to it. "I might not have time to make safe disposition of it before the curtain is rung down."

I essayed a glance at her as, with that characteristic saunter of hers, she came up to the table and took a cigarette for herself. I struck a match and held it out for her. "While follow eyes the steady keel," I said. "As a vessel I am perhaps more grim than daring."

She said, lowering her cigarette, "When I recited that on February twelfth—let's see—oh, I don't know how long ago, I was eleven or twelve—I'd have been surprised to know the circumstances of my next hearing it. Not that I'd have understood them. I suppose if we knew what kind of goodies life was going to put in our stockings we'd never hang them up."

"If I knew what kind of goodies were going to be found in *your* stockings I'd certainly hang them up." My satisfaction in the achievement of what I considered a high-water mark of wit and gallantry was cut

322

short by a griping seizure and more nausea. I could not keep from grimacing.

Cora, wincing, expelled the smoke she had held in her lungs while I was in the throes of the attack. When my face had cleared and I had raised the cigarette to my lips, she said, "I don't know whether you're a fool or a hero. And I don't know whether I'm a fool or a witch—or something that rhymes with 'witch.'" She inhaled again from her cigarette and reflected. "I have nightmares sometimes in which I'm standing in a lake of icy air, my legs numb and the numbness rising. It's not invariably at night, either. In fact, the nightmare's always there, never very far away—that lake of air as cold as death. And do you know what? I thought you might inject me with life. That's what I wanted. For you to make me proof against that nightmare. To inject me with life. But it might just as well have worked the other way around, mightn't it? I might have infected you, the chill might have seeped into you from me."

"A hazard of the lists against which I am now proof, my pet. The only risk I run at this hallowed moment is that of combustion. *Vide* my cigarette. A live spark, the fumes of alcohol which I exhale and . . . modesty forbids me to describe the full glory of the ensuing pyrotechnics. Suffice it to say that having illuminated your skies, I should nevermore darken your doorstep, nevermore perch like a pallid bust of Pallas above your chamber door. A plaster bust of Pallas? Or just a bust of Pallas? I am a bust myself, a plastered bust. Never mind. Nevermore, like *Corvus corax principalis*. . . . You start, my dear, you look amazed. You had not guessed it was the subspecific form, had you? I assure you it was. Chief Inspector Murdock was no less dumbfounded, though he tried not to show it. 'But it was *principalis,* my boy,' I cried, clapping him on the shoulder. The police mentality! 'How did you know? You weren't there,' he growled. 'Surely you did not suppose it to have been *C. c. corax,* the Mexican form!' I crowed. Cora Braun as was, you look puzzled. It is to the raven that I had reverence. Or should I say to the raven that I had reference? But mistake me not! I am second to none in my reverence for ravens. I revere life in all its forms. In college I was known as a veritable Paul Reverer. 'Though I speak with the tongue of men and of angels, I cannot awaken the Middlesex villagers and farmers to the beauty of life in all its forms.' So said Paul the Reverer. My experience was even more

323

thankless. There was a girl in Lexington I could not even awaken to a reverence for sex. Perhaps she was listening out for the British. What do you think? As for me, I revere sex in all its forms too. Middlesex, Essex, Wessex, Sussex. Is there no Norsex? Is there no sex in the North? Probably not. Very little, comparatively. Senhor Anjinho says that where there is snow there can be no love. But then of course there's Norfolk. Oh-oh! What am I *saying*? Why don't you have a drink? Do wonders for you! A little, little drink. No more. Ah, but in that drink of Scotch what dreams may come, when we have shuffled off this mortal coil! To answer the question: lovely dreams! Do you know what a coil was? A garment worn by ladies of the court. 'S a fact! Worn with a coif. Come, a little drink?"

"Shut up."

"Have to get it yourself, though." I held onto a chair as another spasm brought me to the verge of retching. "Go ahead. Plenty of it there. You're being . . . You know what I think? I think you're being standoffish. Not stand-stillish, I regret to say. You're like everything else. A little wavyish. I'm going to sit down. Come on, you sit down with me. You think I'm drunk? I've just been pretending. You know what's making me the way I am? You are. I haven't got alcohol in the blood. I have you in the blood. You're the most beautiful woman I've ever seen. You're whipped cream and marshmallow and strawberry sauce. You remember what we were going to do, only you didn't really want to? You will now. It'll be different. Everything wonderful. Everything warm and lovely, lighter than air. You'll see. It just so happens that I'm about to die, but that's all right. What a way to go, in the arms of lovely woman! A consummation devoutly to be wished! I'll help you off with your coil."

I lurched toward her. The room reeled. I found myself clinging to her, more for support than to embrace her. But then as the swirling subsided and I felt her back in the grasp of my hands—she was as stationary as a pillar—and my hand moved down her back, and there was a trickle as of molten silver inside me, a ray of clarity, of clear purpose, penetrated the steamy murk of my mind. My hold on her tightened, and I moved to find her mouth with mine.

She must have pushed free. I felt a stinging blow on the side of my face as the room tipped on end—*She smacked me, good and hard,* I thought—and then a harder blow on my hip and shoulder. I found myself looking up from the floor. I had fallen. The sound of laughter filled the room, which was swinging eccentrically, Cora always at right angles to the floor, like a blue icicle. The laughter was mine, and stopped as a great ball of heat seemed to break in my stomach. As soon as I could move I hitched myself a few feet to the couch and pulled myself onto it, as a man overboard in a stormy sea might pull himself into a bucking lifeboat.

Lying there, I had to close my eyes so as not to see the crazy gyrations of the room. It was not much better, however, when I could not see them. The couch was pitching wildly, sloshing my brains from side to side like water in a bowl. I lay on my side, holding my stomach tight. A sensation of something happening to my feet caused me to open my eyes. Cora was taking off my shoes. She next took off my tie. "Thanks," I said, then gripped my stomach even harder. I did not seem to be drunk any more. I was simply ill beyond belief, I was simply dying; such sufferings as I was enduring must necessarily be a prelude to death. If only I could arrest the motions of the couch a little, I thought, I could die more peacefully. Its violent oscillations were rocking me back and forth. I rolled over to the edge and put my leg over the side to brace the unmanageable contraption. But prey as I was to the writhing of my insides, I could not stay long in one position. I found my eyes open when I had believed them closed, for everything was dark, and the discovery that I was blind horrified without surprising me. Then I noticed that the windows were perceptibly banded with light—by the moon beyond the shutters. Cora had turned off the lights. I thought I heard her voice at the door, but the sound belonged to another life. After that I do not seem to have been much aware of anything.

When I came to, awakening in the dark from a persistent and tortured dream that my head was a great iron ball in a foundry and finding that awake it felt just as it had asleep, the past caught up with me in a rush, like an avalanche. My stomach was beginning to buck, which was doubtless what had waked me up, and rolling out of bed, holding on while I got my feet beneath me, I staggered off, reeling, to find the bathroom. I crashed into furniture, finally got myself oriented by the long library table and, with the floor tipping before me like the deck of a ship, pitched across the dark room to fetch up against the doorjamb. That took me to the hall. All I had to do then—and the emergency was upon me—was to stumble along, my hand against the wall, catching myself with each step as I nearly fell, to the second door on the left. The light-cord in the bathroom was above the basin. Holding my stomach down from one second to another, I swept the air with my hands till I caught it. The light came on like the muzzle flash of a cannon in my face, but covering my eyes with my hand, I managed to reach the toilet just before I erupted. On my knees before the bowl, I was wrung out as by iron talons, such as those, gripping iron spheres, that formed the feet of the bathtub beside me; repeatedly they wrenched my vitals. It went on until there was nothing left, then went on some more. Eventually a blessed weakness of purification spread through me. I got to my feet, and returning to the basin, held onto it while I tested my command of my breathing. I was alive. On the other hand, my headache was savage and my insides felt as if they had been hung on a butcher's hook.

After dousing my face time after time with water and tucking my shirt back into my trousers, I went back to find the light on in the living-room. Cora was standing there. She was clad in a dressing-gown—the same peach-colored garment I had seen hanging in her stateroom—and beneath it silk pajamas of a lighter shade.

"How are you feeling?" she said. "Or need I ask?"

I tried out my organs of speech before committing myself to replying. My tongue was as if it were in a woolen mitten. I sat down on the edge of the couch. "I have a lot to, er . . ." I could not think of the word "expiate." "I had it coming to me—and it has." I could not even raise my brows without a throb of more violent pain in my head. My nausea was like vertigo, as if I were teetering on a tightrope. "What time is it?" I was perishing for water, but knew I should not drink any.

"About four-thirty. I've put the remains of last night's coffee on the stove. Such as it is, it'll be ready in a minute."

I tried with a gesture to indicate my inability to find words for my gratitude. "I'm sorry I waked you," I said. I threw up my hands. "Sorry I *waked* you! Of all the things I have to be sorry for!"

"You have nothing to be sorry for. On the contrary, I'm . . . I tried to take advantage of you. Wait, I think I hear the coffee simmering." She walked from the room, lowering her head a little, her dressing-gown swishing. Her hair had been combed—hastily, I thought—but she had no make-up on.

When she had gone, I tried, with my head in my hands, to piece together what I could recollect of the evening before, which is to say unscramble from the dementia the evening had merged into. I was still at it when she returned carrying a tray with the coffee pot and cups on it.

"I certainly wouldn't call it taking advantage," I began. "Far from it."

"I was thinking of something else," she interrupted brusquely, putting the tray down on the table. Her setting out of the articles occupied her attention and gripped mine. I watched her with the wonder and slight sensation of adoration of a patient in a hospital watching the ordered and compassionate procedures of a nurse.

Taking a chance on betraying my oblivion of a whole chapter of events in which I had participated the evening before, I asked her how she had come by her sleeping clothes.

She said, "After you had . . . retired, I sent one of the guards to the boat for my things. I had already packed them. I thought there was a chance I wouldn't be going beyond here."

"What do you mean?"

"I'll wait in Topacindo for the next boat going back. Why don't you come and sit by the table here?"

I tried to fit her disclosure into my scheme of things, but discovered that I really had no scheme of things. I eased myself into the chair and received the cup of coffee as if it were the sacrament. It was too hot to drink.

"No, what I meant by taking advantage of you—or trying to—has to do with something quite different," she said. She had remained standing and was stirring sugar into her coffee as if she were preparing a medicine for herself. "I wanted to use you to buy my freedom from my husband. I was going to say to him, 'There you are. I've given you what you want. The slate's clean, I owe you nothing. Good-bye.' So you see. My motives with you have been very mixed, I'm afraid, a strange assortment."

It was hard to mobilize my mental equipment, bruised as it was. I was too sick to take in anything very clearly but that I was very sick indeed. The coffee could only be sipped, but it helped my morale. "I don't know why that should be necessary," I said. "What do you owe him? Why don't you just walk out? I've never understood."

"I want to be able to forget him!" She sat down and shook her head. "I can't explain. He's had bad luck ever since he married me; things have all gone wrong for him. So much so it's changed him—made him even more . . . Oh well."

327

My eyes were like leaden balls in their aching sockets. She could not have understood how sick I was, I thought, or she would not have looked to me for any lucidity of mind at all. I clung to the echo of what she had said lest I become lost in my mental disorder. With an effort I declared, "It was no fault of yours. Monteiro says he's a rotten businessman, with a genius for making the wrong decisions." The coffee was threatening to start my stomach into motion again, making clear what would happen if I had the glass of water I so craved.

"Marrying me was one of them," she said.

"That's preposterous! You're infinitely too good for him. If there was any mistake at all from his point of view, that was it." I wanted to say more, to be more effective, but I felt as if I were the focal point of all the soreness and sickishness in the universe. I hoped she realized it. "I want to talk to you again about it," I said, "when I'm more able to think clearly and can make you see. Maybe you'll still be here when I get back from Manáos. If not, we'll meet when I return from the Massaranduba. The point is, you owe him nothing. If he ever had a claim on you, he's forfeited it a thousand times over. There's nothing for you to feel despairing about. I could show you that. All that's required of you is a simple decision."

"All right," she said. Her gaze shifted irresolutely. She passed her hand over her forehead in a gesture expressive of weariness. She took a drink of coffee and bent over the cup. "I hope I haven't hurt you. If I have I'll be punished for it. I didn't think I would. I did want to save you from danger. That was one of the things."

"You haven't hurt me," I said. I was suddenly overwhelmed by regret and remorse that all had come to nothing. They were like a grey, choking fog welling up around me. It was incredible that what was not there one moment could be so devastating the next. But what was past was past, and it was irremediable.

I had, I thought, better get back to the ship.

"Why don't you come on to Manáos?" I said. "Give up the idea of staying on and going back from here?"

She shook her head.

"Can't I persuade you?"

"No. Go on your way. It's *your* way. You shouldn't have any trouble with the guards outside now." She added in a sudden hurried tone, "We'll meet when you come back. As you said."

328

I found my shoes, tie and coat and went to the bathroom for a final ablution and attempted grooming. When I returned she had put on lipstick and done something further to her hair.

She walked with me to the door and held out her hand. "I'm not all bad," she said. "For what it's worth, I wish you luck. More important: think hard about what I said about the risks you'll run if you provoke Durondo."

Her hand was so cold that I raised it and pressed it against my chest. I tried to convey, by looking into her eyes, what, I did not know. Whatever it was, I felt, though she smiled a little, that it was incommunicable. When I released the pressure on her hand, she withdrew it, and she dropped her eyes just before I turned to go.

There were, right enough, two soldiers keeping watch on the front door. They peeled themselves away from the wall against which they had been affixed and one rid himself unobtrusively of a cigarette. They did not, I judged, know whether to salute or exert their authority in some way, and in their indecision I walked past them.

The houses were dark, the streets deserted, and in the light of the gibbous moon in the west Topacindo had a fungoid appearance, without color, without solidity. Leaving the high sidewalk for the roadbed, I stumbled along. Regret and remorse! I knew myself and I could foresee all the occasions when, incited unendurably by imagination, I should hold myself mad not to have taken advantage of what Cora offered, should torment myself with wild schemes for recovering what I had rejected. The reasons I had had for fleeing it even after her withdrawal of the condition she had set would be forgotten in those hours, and I should remember only what could have been and how, wounding her, I had spurned it. In time the memory would lose its sharpness and be overlaid. But that other! I could not see how anything would ever efface or dull the recollection of how close I had come to, how little credit I could take for not having gone all the way to committing, an unforgivable betrayal of a human trust.

A soldier with chevrons on his sleeve and an air of being in charge stood on the deck of *Tocantins* at the head of the gangplank. Staring at him boldly, I said, *"Agora, você pode partir."* He could leave now. He must have been astonished by my effrontery if he had not already been so by such a figure as mine appearing there at all at that hour.

My thirst had become insupportable. I picked up a glass from a table

329

and took it to the red-clay urn in which the drinking water stood. I held myself to a single glass, but that was too much. I had to hurry to the toilet, where I vomited again.

And now what? I asked myself. I was sitting, a few minutes later, on the edge of my bunk, taking off my shoes. How was I going to live with myself? A romantic, Cora had called me, and see what it had brought me to! A dreamer of never-never beings, unequal to the requirements of this world, unequal to the temptation Cora had put in my way—unable to resist it—then unequal to the opportunity. Why unequal to the temptation? Because I could not control my thoughts. And why unequal to the opportunity? Because, having found I was unequal to the temptation, I knew I could not trust myself with the opportunity!

Or was there something more? Was it because the windows were open and the cocks crowed, evoking the dawn and the property of its freshness and spaciousness of unburdening the heart—that and the being who was inseparable in my mind from all the dawn stood for?

Was it one or both?

No matter. I was sick, horribly sick, sick with liquor, sick with self-revulsion. Senhor Coutinho was sick too, sick with malaria and doubtless also with self-revulsion. He was probably a romantic, too, throwing good money after bad in pursuit of the will-o'-the-wisp of political glory. The only safeguard was to confine oneself to what was concrete and real, to attend to business. And my business for the present was the Massaranduba Concession.

Lying down in my bunk, I fell into a half stupor. Without knowing how long I had been there I heard the blast of *Tocantins's* whistle and felt her engines kick off once more.

14

A few hours later I got up to shave and do what else I could about my appearance. I had been aroused by a knock on the door and a loud, official-sounding admonition from the other side, repeated, diminuendo, down the length of the lounge. It was, I deduced, a warning of our approach to the state border. So it proved to be. The border was formed by a high ridge running down the river's edge. On both sides little soldiers in tan cotton and patent leather came aboard to go through the ship examining documents. One, who had been through *Boa Vista,* could recall no girl aboard; I had not been able to help asking. For the time being I was out of Durondo's reach. I had a glass of water, survived the test, had another, and brought a cup of coffee back with me to my stateroom. Propping myself up on my bunk, I settled down to read, picking out a book I had too long put off studying—a guide to prospecting issued by the United States Bureau of Mines. Though my mind kept breaking away from the subject and had to be brought back, I felt sustained by the book's premise, which was that the problems to be solved in this world were finite and concrete and would yield to a businesslike and methodical approach. By remaining still and avoiding the slightest movement of the head, I found I could preserve the illusion of being on the right side of incapacitating illness. I put out of my mind any thought of going ashore at the town of Parintins, which from the port above my washstand resembled Santarém. It was built upon a high, grassy embankment behind a row of mangoes. The thoroughfare bordering the embankment was thronged with promenaders in white, the day, I recalled, being Sunday. There seemed to be a legion of little girls, like gulls on a beach, all in white too. The starched loose-ends grimness of Sunday was evidently inescapable even five hundred miles up the Amazon and invaded the cabin, or else it was my imagination. What was it the weathered tile roofs here reminded me of? Something very close to them in appearance. . . .

Mildewed corduroy.

The resolution I had formed, to engage in no more futile quests, was not even tested in Parintins. The picture I had of myself making my usual inquiries there, when I imagined it, called up another of myself completely demoralized in consequence. I do not know whether it was in part the town's condition or altogether my own that made me so sure the inquiries would be fruitless, but that they would be was evident to me, and oppressed by my thoughts, I went back to my reading, determined to keep my mind on it.

In the middle of the afternoon, well after we had left Parintins, I ventured out. The Anjinhos, man and wife, were sitting at a table, the husband with his usual bottle of red *vinho nacional,* entering the details of the latest scalping in their ledger. They expressed regret that my sister had decided—so they had heard—to stop off at Topacindo with friends. At another table the professor from Ceará, his cranium more skull-like, his eyes more guileless than ever, was scribbling away, no doubt preparing a lecture. A curious and revolting red-haired child, whose sex I was never able to make up my mind about, was wandering around with vacant face dragging behind it our last uneaten turtle, on a string. The mammoth merchant brothers reposed in their hammocks, heaving, the wet brown ends of the cigarettes they nursed on the tips of their tongues kept magically alight. Behind the open door of his

332

quarters the Comandante reclined in his bunk, looking up through half-closed eyes at the curls of blue cigarette-smoke above his head. Before adversity struck northern Brazil, he had commanded oceangoing vessels and been a respected figure in every port south to Santos, I had learned, and perhaps it was the ghosts of those days he saw in the smoke.

That night I was able to eat a full meal, and the next morning I was physically almost back to normal.

As we drew nearer Manáos, man appeared to be doing progressively better in his contest with the forest. There were more and larger clearings along the *paranás,* mostly the rangeland of cattle *fazendas.* The house stood in the distance, freshly calcimined in white or pale blue, men and women watching us from the veranda. Horses and cows grazed in the meadows. In the limpid air the effect was of a bucolic idyl. One had almost the sense of observing, from a darkened museum corridor, a brilliantly illuminated diorama done in perfect miniature. Tall, bare trees stood about in the fields, their naked limbs, bleached white, still stretched to the sun as if they had not been told that they were dead and the leaves all gone from their groping fingers. On all sides the forest had drawn back, one would have thought of its own accord, like living tissue from a gangrenous infection.

In other places the issue of the contest seemed more doubtful. Santa Maria de—I never quite caught its name—was one. *Tocantins* put into it for firewood, and I went ashore with the Anjinhos, Senhor Anjinho and I together helping his wife up the bank over rotting piles of cornshucks and papaya rinds. The two- or threescore inhabitants lived in a haggard chain of broken-backed frame-and-thatch dwellings strung out along the bluff on stilts, grey as driftwood and hollow-eyed in the glare of light from the tireless and ferocious Amazon. Children made up fully two-thirds of the population. Those who were white put me in mind, to my horror, of a collection of stuffed monkeys of such execrable taxidermy the hair had all fallen out, leaving bare, clay-colored, erupted skin. An embalmed-looking infant in its mother's arms had a growth on its scalp resembling chicken-droppings. The mother herself, apparently the first lady of the settlement, retained some remnants of good looks, but was pathetically thin and beginning to be twisted from overwork and deprivation, and her upper jaw was toothless but for two yellow fangs. The husband, however, was a fine-looking fellow with firm features and a head carved out of bully-beef. The woman proceeded to tell Senhora

333

Anjinho about their life here. We had sat down on some wooden benches, surrounded by Caboclos who, having deposited themselves on the ground, stared at the sky over our heads or winked at one another. About all I understood was that the husband had been a Portuguese immigrant, that they had come here upon their marriage eight years before and—like the Coutinhos—had had six children, of whom two had died. With this confession the woman smiled timidly, apparently not sure that we should not think it funny. The husband was withdrawn and uncommunicative, ready to resent any inference about his worth as a man that we might draw from his circumstances.

Behind the village were forest and scrub-growth so dense they could not be penetrated except via the tunnels made by steers which were too dangerous on that account to be ventured upon, we were warned. Along the bluff, down which we were conducted, were *cuia* trees with green fruit as big as soccer-balls growing directly from the largest branches, such as you might expect to find in a child's drawing. And, serving as the chief source of currency, there was a grove of cocoa trees. It was pleasantly dark in the grove, for the foliage completely shut out the sky. The sunlit scrub-growth in the distance resembled panes of bright blue glass set at the end of dim green aisles with the cocoa pods hanging palely green and yellow, like lanterns, overhead. But the oval, pointed leaves of the cocoas were yellowish and evidently diseased, and these and the cur dog that came sniffing apprehensively at our heels, looking as if it had been partially cooked and then rejected, made one wonder why, where everything wild was the incarnation of vitality, each plant and animal the white man took under his protection fell heir to sickness, like the white man himself.

At the end of the settlement was the schoolhouse. It had a roof and one side of lath and clay before which stood the teacher, a white woman with a flat, round face, dark complexion and the familiar, faintly squinting north Brazilian eyes. At a sign from her the pupils rose. There were about twenty-five of them, perhaps from six to twenty in age. A few were white with unhealthy, blotchy-pink skin, and two with crinkly hair were evidently part Negro. The rest were predominantly or wholly Indian, wax-clear in complexion, prognathous and with large black eyes a trifle tilted above low-bridged noses. Putting myself in the teacher's place and imagining myself having daily, all morning long, to address those rows of opaque black eyes, before which it was certain that the cultural acquisitions of twenty-five hundred years of Western civilization could be paraded without eliciting a flicker of response, I shuddered. Perhaps it was to sustain the teacher's morale, for reassurance that Western civilization did in fact exist, that two advertisements were affixed to the wall behind her. I cannot think why else they would have been there. One was for some confection that came in a can and was a source of rapturous content to a young woman who beamed coquettishly from it, the other, picturing a white egret, was for Garça brand butter, *"a melhor manteiga"*—the best butter.

The pupils had gone into a trance at our advent. They stared straight ahead and waited. Not an eye in the room was turned to us. I felt awkward, like one more testimonial to an exotic luxury.

"Canta!" the teacher directed. The injunction came out of a clear blue sky, but the children melted dutifully into song. Their voices were murmurous and vagrant as the sounds of the wind in the trees. Then without warning the contralto of Senhora Anjinho broke forth beside me. It was as if a Valkyrie had risen like a skylark in our midst. The sibilations of the student body were of course buried under the sound. But Senhora Anjinho, herself a schoolteacher, knew what she was doing. The chorus, after the initial recoil, took heart under the protective cover she afforded and swelled audibly. The girls, in straight bobbed hair, some with a rich brown gloss, sang primly, but the boys were still unreconciled. I understood little of the song, but three words I did understand were enough: *America, Brasil* and *Liberdade.* The words could have meant nothing to the children. *Libertaaaaaaadjy! A Melhor Manteiga!* At the precise end of the song the children stopped and Senhora Anjinho was left alone in a sustained note which she wound up with a triumphant toss of the head.

On our return through the cocoa orchard a large red squirrel fled in chattering terror, showing that whatever else might be wanting in the settlement, firearms were not. In the trees were large nests of ants. One of the biggest had the appearance of a brain-coral, its surface covered with white ants whose waving limbs gave them the appearance of coral polyps. In their ingenuity they had constructed a covered runway like a tube leading from the nest down the trunk and off across the ground; perhaps they were termites. The tube crumbled easily when it was heed-

335

lessly stepped on, but the workers seemed not to mind or even to apprehend the catastrophe, but flowed on over the debris like a stream of white corpuscles.

I had fallen behind the conducted tour. When I turned to follow it I found in my path the most beautiful snake, and one of the most beautiful living creatures, I had ever seen. About twenty inches long, very thin, of a consummate delicacy and refinement of form, it was colored a burnished and incredibly brilliant green with each scale edged with black. On its underparts the scales were a pure grey suede in hue evenly edged with light green. Its eyes were jewels of gold, black-pupiled, protruding lidless and alert from its long, narrow head. Coiling to strike was clearly the last thing in its mind. I picked it up gently by the neck. It made no attempt to resist or escape—it was, it seemed, too guileless for that—and after a few experimental movements of its sinuous body it lay quite still, its eyes brilliant as ever, and wide with innocence. The little creature was perfection.

I was still carrying the snake when I re-emerged into the open and rejoined the others, who were gathered about near where we had come ashore. The first chance encounter of a pair of eyes with the snake produced an outcry. In a moment everyone had taken it up: *"Venenosa! Venenosa!"*—the Caboclos in their rags, the woman with the yellow fangs, the burly husband. Cried Anjinho, "Poisonous!" Gesticulations were made for me to throw the reptile on the ground, and the Portuguese husband and one of the Caboclos picked up sticks to be ready to dispatch it. There was no use pointing to the evidence of its whiplike lines that it was nonvenomous. I walked to the river and after one more look at the delicate creature's pert and perpetually astonished eyes dropped it in and sadly watched it swim flowingly away through the water, the embodiment of grace, its head a full six inches above the surface.

I had had enough of the settlement. "Maybe we ought to go back and deal with the chiggers before they dig in," I said to Anjinho. (The treatment was to rub one's legs with rum.) "We don't want to hold the ship up. . . ."

As you passed the mouths of its great contributory streams you expected to find the Amazon itself, unendowed as yet by their flow, conspicuously smaller on the other side; but eight hundred miles from the sea, where the Madeira came in, bringing tribute all the way from

Bolivia, the river had still the dimensions of an inland sea, and the dolphins arching through its surface and the cormorants skimming its waves gave it the character of one.

I was ready to crawl into a dark hole. I was played out; there had been nine days of it, of the columnar steam clouds ascending from the horizon to inconceivable altitudes, of the boiling contours of the forest that went on and on forever, of the time-annihilating, space-devouring river, so awful in its extent that to encompass it the plane of the earth and the vision of the beholder had to be stretched out of all proportion to familiar reality. Sleep seemed to bring no rest. I struggled for what felt like the better part of a night with the illusion that I was being spread over the screen of the immense panorama, so thin I was reduced to translucency. All night long, brilliantly lighted images seemed to flood through me—the same that in the daytime I felt at sea among, with nothing underfoot. I awoke once saying to myself, I'm a roll of light-struck film.

I would find myself thinking of the opera troupes from Paris and Milan who in the heyday of Brazilian rubber twenty years before had made this same trip in vessels like *Tocantins* to sing in one of the great opera houses of the world—in Manáos. What could they have thought? Must the suspicion not have crept upon them that the expedition was an unaccountable and monstrous hoax, which could end only with their abandonment to the trackless jungle and the knowledge that someone, somewhere, was laughing? I found it as hard to believe as they must have that at the end of this voyage was a modern city with streetcars and automobiles. But their credulity must have been taxed more than mine. They had to picture Manáos as a principal legatee of the New World's promise, the capital of a booming empire where fortunes were being made by penniless immigrants and lowly rubber-tappers being metamorphosed into patrons of the arts, the site of a new opera house for which the best was none too good. I could picture the opera house as having stood empty for most of my life and the city itself as a relic of a burst bubble, a monument to the vanity of greed. At least, that is how I did picture the city, as partly in ruins, as having gained in dignity from adversity and sorrow, its tragedy giving tone and a quality of depth to the parvenu civilization of which it had been so flamboyant an outpost. It seemed an odd place in which to be transacting the business of the

337

Massaranduba Concession. Not knowing how I was going to proceed in that, driven by desire to plunge into the Massaranduba itself, I chafed under the necessity of having to go through with it.

Had I been even more bankrupt of responsiveness than I was I should still have been stirred by the spectacle of the Amazon's meeting with the Rio Negro, on which Manáos is situated. The juncture was far more dramatic than that of the Amazon and Tapajós, the contrast in color being much greater and the Negro—a river of pure, intense, glistening, unclouded black—bringing in a comparatively greater volume of water. Those who have seen it have made it world-famous.

We came up hugging the south bank, on the Amazon side, turning toward the mouth of the Negro only when we were nearly abreast of the promontory separating them and cutting across the division between the two at right angles. Seeing them flowing side by side without admixture was like seeing day and night dividing the firmament along a clean line before you, was as if you were witnessing the interaction of two fundamental laws of the universe made visible. The persisting division between the two rivers was so sharp you could have sliced them apart with your hand, having the Amazon against the palm and the Negro against the back of it, and so it continued as far as you could see. The Negro appeared to push the Amazon back, as if it were the more powerful river, but evidently the Amazon simply flowed beneath it, for downstream huge bubbles of the tawny water could be seen welling up through the black and mushrooming out with an infinite and ponderous slowness. It was by such upheavals that it gradually obliterated the Negro. That such a tide of black water could merge with the Amazon without darkening it in the slightest perceptible degree seemed outside of nature. The explanation was, I supposed, that the Amazon's color came from sediment, the Negro's from a dye. One was opaque, the other transparent. The water of the Negro, like that of the cypress swamps at home, was crystal-clear in a tumbler, golden at six inches, claret at a foot and a half, black only beyond a yard.

With its unruffled surface of black marble mirroring every leaf of the bright green forests of its rolling banks, mirroring the heavens in indescribable shades of blue and grey, dull, remote and strange, like the sky at the predawn of life, the Negro must be, I thought, the most beautiful river in the world. After the savage, leonine Amazon that ripped forests from its shores and toyed kittenishly with the writhing trees it floated to the sea, the still and silent Negro was like a river in the realm of the dead, if death could be imagined without its finality and gruesomeness, as a longed-for release from time.

The Negro could not have been better conceived to lead to the Manáos of my preconceptions or to render the Manáos of actuality more shattering on first impact. Manáos was not New York, but on the tenth day of isolation on the Amazon its waterfront was the Machine Age personified.

The city from a distance resembled a vast, bare limestone slope rising gently from the river. Only as we drove nearer did the expanse break up into blocks of buildings, then into separate structures. *Tocantins* seemed to shrink in size as she beat her way into the harbor and up to the iron docks for which it was renowned, and justifiably so. The docks were veritable freight-yards floated on enormous iron cylinders, like boilers; at the crest of the Negro's annual flood they had to stand over thirty feet higher than they did in the period of low water. Everything was in action—in pandemonium, it seemed to me. Steam-derricks gasped and ground as they disemboweled the ships moored beside them. Cars on rails shuttled back and forth across the docks. From the distance came the all-but-forgotten sounds of blaring automobile-horns and crescendo screams of accelerating trolley-cars. *Gaiolas* crowded the harbor. Alongside the docks lay oceangoing freighters, two flying the red ensign, one the black-white-and-red, with swastika, of the new Germany, the fourth the flag of Brazil. They were so huge, so immovable, they might have been lofty outcroppings of the bedrock, excavated by tiny troglodytes. Bleating, *Tocantins* sidled toward a berth aft of *Ardenhall, West Hartlepool,* and tossed a hawser ashore well under the stern of that impervious giant with the hope that someone would pick it up and make it fast, which someone did, though that was about all the notice that was taken of us.

I was impatient to get ashore; while I was going to have to remain in Manáos for forty-eight hours in any event, until *Tocantins* set out on the return trip, the sooner I could make a start on what I had to do the sooner I could expect to have it behind me. I was eager, too, for a respite from the ship, in which I could not light a cigarette without evoking occasions on which I had lighted one with Cora. What had first priority, however, was getting in touch with Senhora Braga, and with that I needed help. Accordingly, I waited until I could accompany the Englishman who was the local agent of *Tocantins's* parent company and had come aboard with the gangplank. He was distinguished in appearance by bearing himself with a slightly lopsided stoop, presumably from the habit of bending an ear to those of shorter stature, but was chiefly notable in my eyes for seeming to feel entirely at home where he was, in a city that from first to last I thought of as having been, in effect, dropped by parachute into the wilderness.

The demoniac tempo and clangor of industry on the march prevailed in Manáos, I quickly discovered, only over the harbor, though for a time the mood was prolonged by the goggle-eyed American motorcars that careened through the streets unimpeded by traffic congestion. Three-storey buildings had also become novelties, and those that walled in the plaza to which we crossed from the docks were high enough to make me think myself on the floor of a canyon. They were purple in the shade and very still. The plaza was decorated with flowerbeds and statuary and with the inevitable ficus-trees, with their foliage of incendiary luminosity in the blazing sunlight. Here they were sheered into cubes as well as the conventional cones and paired to form archways, which were as smooth and regular as masonry. The Englishman, seeing me examining them, called my attention to their small size. "They never have a chance to grow large," he explained. "They make such perfect ambushes for sharp-shooters that every time there's a revolution both sides systematically rake them with fire at the very start, just as a precaution."

The chief of police in Manáos was a particular friend of Monteiro's whom I had been planning to visit, and I thought now of asking where I might expect to find him. I added that I could not seem to remember his name.

With a glance over his shoulder the Englishman said, "It's just as well. He's hiding out in the *mato*. There was a kind of by-revolution a few days ago."

"It wasn't anything caused from outside the state, was it?" I asked anxiously, thinking of the chief's connection with the *Constitucionalistas*.

"Oh no. It was purely local and without political significance. It was the result of a set-to between the army and the police. It seems some soldiers were cutting up in a café and someone complained to the police. The police sent a couple of chaps on horseback, one of whom ordered the ranking army officer to make his fellows behave. There were some words and two of the soldiers seized the policeman's horse by the bridle.

The fat was in the fire then. The policeman whacked at them to no avail and thereupon shot one, and then, as the other did not desist, him also. In the ensuing scramble the second policeman was killed, also a longshoreman, and a civilian was badly wounded. The civvy fell back behind the counter, on top of two of your blokes—two officials of an American company—who had taken shelter there. They escaped as soon as they could and went straightaway to the club, arriving all covered with gore and creating something of a sensation."

I said I could see how this might have made some trouble for the chief of police but that it seemed to me excessive for him to have to flee.

"They don't do things by half-measures here," he said. "The army went after the entire police force. They rounded up half and put them in jail. The others got away to the woods. I'm told that when the captured police were paraded to their cells the jail's inmates gave them a very rousing welcome."

"And who's taking care of the policemen's duties now?" I asked.

"The firemen—pending the inauguration of a brand-new force."

The office to which we drove was very like Monteiro's, though the proprietor's manner of entry, set apart by the sailing of his panama hat across the room to the dextrous hands of an office-boy, would have startled the foot-faced Oliveira. Senhora Braga was not listed in the telephone directory, but the Englishman found the number of the *pensão* where she lived and soon had her on the telephone. The transmittal of my message provoked an explosive response. While he held the receiver a little apart from his ear with an expressive look at me, the diaphragm rattled to what sounded like the barking of a fox. "She had your telegram. Will eleven tomorrow morning at her place be all right?" he asked me. I nodded. When he hung up he observed, "She seems to feel you've been a long time on the way. I gather she'll be primed for you tomorrow."

The Manáos of my anticipations, haunted by its history, preoccupied by the desperate anomaly it presented at the heart of the Amazon's wild realm, proved to be hard to find. The Manáos that came piecemeal into my view was not easy to take seriously at all. It struck me as a clown among cities. If a good deal of heartache was to be inferred beneath the greasepaint—and it was—well, that was in the great tradition of the circus. The shops into which I wandered after taking leave of the English agent—it was too late to call at any of the Government offices that

341

day—were touching in that they offered little but trinkets for sale. The size of the shops, which were on the scale of department stores, only made more evident the meagerness of the wares displayed on the great counters, in the glass cases: a few American alarm-clocks, pens, faucets, cheap neckties, empty perfume-bottles, bolts of inferior cotton-prints, little brown birds and reptiles carved from blocks of *guaraná* (the same substance that made the delicious tonic-water), wooden ashtrays and "novelties" of various kinds. So did the size of the sales-force that converged upon the customer smiling the smiles of the chronically disappointed. . . . There was, too, the depressing spectacle of a grand mansion, deserted, that brooded above the muddy inlet to which *Tocantins* moved that evening—sent to Coventry, it would seem, along with several others of her kind—there to lie up, lightless and waterless, for the duration of her stay. The mansion had been the residence of a former governor of the state who had made and lost a fortune in rubber and was now a storekeeper.

But it was Manáos's greasepaint that caught the eye—transfixed it, amazed it. Nothing I had seen so far—and I thought I had seen the ultimate—had prepared me for the houses of Manáos. The colors—rich, deep, glossy, brilliant, of every known pigment—were such as squirt unalloyed from an artist's tubes of oils, and in the façades of chromatic fantasy the tall windows topped with Gothic arches were outlined in white, like the elongated rings that clowns paint around their eyes to give them expressions of startled wonderment at life. Design had run wild. For miles each house was a rival, entirely individual in its embellishments, of the witch's cottage of gingerbread in *Hänsel and Gretel*. What was especially puzzling was that the colors were uniformly bright, with no trace of weathering, which was the more remarkable in that—and this was more remarkable still—the shade trees had been shorn of their outer branches, which left the houses exposed to the sun; for block after block the gaunt, black, truncated skeletons of once-splendid mangoes, now leafless, gave the scene an incongruous element of wintriness. The houses looked as if they had all been painted the day before.

And that, I learned, was just about the case. The mayor, oppressed by the city's shabby appearance, had promulgated an ordinance: all houses to be repainted forthwith. I was seeing the results. This explanation was given to me by a high Government official. He also told me the story behind the denuding of the trees. Half the citizens wished to have the trees cut down on the grounds that they kept the streets from drying out after a rain. The other half wished to keep the trees regardless. So the mayor compromised. He left the trees but eliminated their foliage! The wet streets beneath them, which were of the reddest of all red clays, resembled canals of congealing arterial blood.

Manáos's crowning glory was of course her opera house. If it was not another Hagia Sophia it was only because Manáos was not another Constantinople. Relatively it may have been even more imposing. Basically an edifice in the form of a cube with cornices separating its three or four floors (the number was difficult to determine), its front, thrust out from the cube somewhat like the partially-extended front of a bellows-camera, had the shape of a slice of bread and was composed of three loggias of differing heights, designs and pillars, one upon the other, topped by a frieze under a barrel roof. Behind it, upon the cube proper, rested the mighty dome, shingled in round-tipped glass scales, blue, green, red and gold in color, dazzling beyond mortal description. One approached the intimidating pile across a broad, empty plaza entirely paved in tiles forming sharply wavy bands—*S*'s that kept on *S*-ing, like snakes—each band broadening and narrowing rhythmically, pulsatingly, white bands alternating with black. With the sun on it the whole opera square appeared to be rising slowly like a magic carpet with the wiggly motion, though in reverse, of a flat shell sinking in water, bearing with it the few casually-clad passersby and a squad of schoolgirls in baggy uniforms of white shirtwaists and dark skirts. Entering the building, one found oneself in a large foyer decorated to represent Night, with lotus pillars supporting a dark blue ceiling in which a round lamp served as the moon. Passing on, one came into a circular gallery. From this various subsidiary rooms led off, each owing something to the Pharaohs, the Doges, the later Bourbons or the court of Napoleon. The auditorium itself was not very different from an American temple of the cinema in its marbles, red plush and purple velvet, gold leaf and creamy curlicues. Encircling the interior was a row of shields on which the names of Brazilian composers and writers (Ruy Gomez being the only one I recognized) kept somewhat incongruous company with those of Shakespeare, Beethoven, Wagner, Verdi, Goethe and other giants. The capstone of the entire design, inside and out, was for me a large blue enameled

343

sign occupying a conspicuous position behind the principal and most elegant box, which bore in white letters the legend: TOILET OF THE GOVERNOR.

It was in the afternoon of my second day in Manáos that I was shown the opera house. By then I was prepared to take a cheerful view of Manáos and its excesses—even the terrifying ride it gave one on the "Circular" trolley-car route; not that one could, in any case, be very critical of a city with other car-lines running to "Flowers," "Keepsake," and "Poor Devil" (an abbreviation of the name of a church: Saint Anthony of the Poor Devil). I had had rare good luck. The business I had to transact, which had been preying so on my mind, had all been dispatched with miraculous ease and swiftness. For this, thanks were owing to the Minister of Transportation. The service, valuable as it was, was not what I was chiefly to remember Dr. Salomão Mendoça for in the long run, however.

At breakfast that morning, to my astonishment, a messenger had brought me a note on the stationery of the *Chefia de Transporte,* in English. It was signed by the *Chefe,* Dr. Mendoça, and suggested that I call upon him at his office; he had heard of my arrival and knew of my business. He said he would be free at ten o'clock if that would be convenient for me.

Gratified and flattered, I was on hand promptly at the appointed hour. However, for the first few minutes of my interview with the Minister appearances were that I had been summoned not as a token of the Government's favor but to be put upon the carpet.

Superficially Dr. Mendoça had the appearance of a Spanish—or Portuguese—grandee, with saturnine or Mephistophelean overtones. He had the swarthy complexion, the hawk nose, the commanding brows over dark eyes full of vigor, the Vandyke beard. However, his neck was short and when standing he appeared a little hunched and was not as tall as I had expected, and his eyes, as I discovered when they ceased to be narrowed at me accusingly, were not piercing and disregardful, like the haughty hidalgo's, but inclined to be watchful for the other person's opinion and were quick to fill with sympathy. Later, catching him at a revealing angle in a strong light, I observed that the beard covered what appeared to be a severe burn on the side of his chin, which was perhaps why he wore it. He was of an age to have been my father—a rather obvious deduction from his having informed me at one point that he had a son of my years.

After motioning me to a chair beside his desk he told me, speaking fluent English almost without an accent, that he had heard from several sources, not omitting the press, that I had come to Manáos to seek assurances of the Government's sympathetic attitude toward plans to develop the Massaranduba basin and willingness to extend such facilities as might be required. He had been prepared for this by communications from Dr. Monteiro some time ago. He had understood that I was an associate of Dr. Monteiro's. Now, however, came a dispatch from the *Gazeta do Pará* reporting that I was visiting Manáos and proceeding on to the Massaranduba under the commission of the *Interventor*. At the same time, it was true, dispatches from the *Estado do Norte* had it that I was doing so as the representative of Dr. Monteiro. Would I have the goodness to explain?

I set forth the terms on which I was operating in accordance with my understanding with Colonel Durondo. However, the inflection he had put upon the word *"Interventor"* and his expression when I pronounced the *Interventor's* name emboldened me to let slip an inkling of the state of my feelings and be a little more explicit than I should otherwise have been about what had led up to the agreement. A glint of amusement in his eyes became unmistakable. Noticing, too, the curl of his moist red lips beneath the moustache, I let myself go a little further in retailing the particulars of my arrest and detention. His questions, revealing an accurate insight into the effect all this would have had upon me, further abetted me, and soon he was undisguisedly relishing the narrative, while his relish spurred me on. He kept his profile toward me—a practice he continued—but cut his eyes over at me frequently. At the end he laughed briefly and shook his head.

We talked at length. Dr. Mendoça, it came out, knew a good deal about me—not only what was on my passport but my background, the evolution of my political activities, my mode of life. He explained that he had a number of friends who knew me: Dr. da Lima, Dr. Goês, Dr. Moura, and others, and he was always interested in people. However, he pointed out, news was a little slow in reaching Manáos unless it came by telegraph. Soon, in the field of conflicting interests over the Massaranduba, we had marked out a kind of private enclave for ourselves in

345

which I felt perfectly secure in whatever I chose to say and he allowed himself all the latitude a high public official could possibly be expected to. I learned that Joaquim Waldo, of whom Dr. Mendoça knew, had almost certainly not come to Manáos.

The physical atmosphere of the office, very different from that of the rest of the gloomy building, which was too big for the visible staff, as Manáos itself was too big for its shrunken population, was soothing. The sunlight, evidently reflected through the shutters from a large puddle or pool of water outside, cast a rippling illumination on the ceiling and far wall of the darkened room, as it might within an underwater grotto. The delicate porcelains displayed in brackets on the wall in lieu of pictures and the bronze urns, dark with antiquity, on the tables—all evidently of oriental origin—fell in with the image in suggesting seashells and sunken treasure. All this, in turn, inspired me to associate Dr. Mendoça himself, who had moved out from behind his desk to sit in a chair half facing my own—all the chairs were of rattan—and cushioned— with the figure of a merman, an undersea king, depicted on a map of the world I had had on the wall as a boy. He not only looked like the merman but he wielded authority over a realm to me scarcely less exotic.

There was no doubt in my mind that the Minister was a busy man. It was not only that his secretary—a stoop-shouldered clerk who looked over the top of steel-rimmed glasses grey with fingerprints and bristled with pencils—came in from time to time with muttered messages and went out with clarion-voiced instructions—but that, long as our meeting was, Dr. Mendoça had the air of compressing much into the space of time. Perhaps much of what went into it was going on in his head. His gaze was restless, he twirled a yellow pencil end over end in his hands and kept the proceedings at a quick tempo. He was anything but reposeful. Yet he seemed far from desiring to conclude the meeting, and I felt encouraged to talk. In the circumstances I hardly needed to be. All I could think of was myself and the Massaranduba Concession, which in my eyes rose like a mountain range between me and what I felt life had to offer, whatever that might be.

Watching the clock, I had been telling him about the Bragas, of whom he had heard, and as the time neared eleven and we still had not come to my business with him I informed him of my appointment, asking if his secretary could call Senhora Braga and tell her I was going to be late.

I added that I really ought to take a translator with me and asked if he could put me on to one.

"I do not wish to intrude in your affairs," said Dr. Mendoça, "but if it would be of service to you I shall be very glad to have her here. Of course, if you have private matters to discuss—"

I broke in to assure him that I had not. I was truly overwhelmed by his generosity, I added.

"It is the earnest desire of the Government of the State of Amazonas to encourage the rational development of the Massaranduba basin. That is official policy," said Dr. Mendoça.

The upshot was that Senhora Braga was asked to come at twelve and said she would do so.

I was far less sanguine than Monteiro about the prospects of obtaining powers of attorney from the Bragas to sell their property since it seemed to me we had little to offer by way of inducement. Dr. Mendoça, when I had enlightened him on the subject, thought I was in a better position than I believed. It was a matter, he said, of making the most of what I had on my side, namely that I myself was putting up a good deal in the form of the time and comfort sacrificed in all these travels; further, that our being in a position to conclude the transaction at once would certainly weigh with the syndicate in New York. Would it, I said hesitantly, be an intolerable imposition if I asked if he could have the proper instrument typed up for me so that it would be ready for Senhora Braga? Not at all, he said. The price agreed upon between the Bragas and Monteiro, I added, was twelve hundred contos, which I was sure he would regard as confidential. He said of course he would.

"I must succeed in this!" It was as if a charge had gone off beneath me, both propelling me to my feet and releasing the words. "I've got to do everything I possibly can—without fail. It's enormously important." When I had a chance to think of it I was astonished that I should have presumed on our brief acquaintance to explode in such fashion, regardless of what was fermenting inside me.

If he thought it odd he did not allow me to know it. "Yes, I can believe that there is much at issue in it for you." He snipped off the end of a cigar he had taken out and, holding a match to it, caused it to puff like a blast furnace. "But am I right in deducing that there is more in it than meets the eye—more than, ah, what would affect the circumstances of

347

the . . . interested parties, yourself included? What I am saying is this: has it become a necessity to you to prove yourself in the complex of this problem?"

"No. . . . Yes. It is for everyone in the context of every problem, isn't it? Isn't life a matter of succeeding? Only think," I exclaimed in a suddenly louder voice, with the transparent impulse to drown out what I had just said, "all that hinges on the outcome of this project, and for how many! Surely that is a tremendously important consideration— enough in itself."

"Of course," he said, and in his analytical brown eyes, regarding me sidewise with a certain heaviness, I felt I stood revealed beyond my own ability to recognize myself, related to bench-marks of human behavior established by experience far beyond mine. "This is a decision you have made only recently, about the identity of life and success?" he asked. "You are a late convert to this doctrine?"

"You're a success," I replied. "It didn't come about by accident." I imagine I colored up over what sounded like an impertinence. What he did not know, I was thinking, what I myself could never forget, was how close I had come to betraying everyone who trusted me in the business we were talking about, how much I had to make up for.

He looked at me quizzically over his cigar. The quality of his regard had changed—had lightened. He knocked the ash off in a bowl at the corner of his desk. "Oh, I am never minimizing the importance of money. For a Jew to do so would be ungrateful. For Jews especially it has been indispensable for many, many centuries. Armadillos must have their armor, porcupines their needles, insects their protecting colors, deers their speed of running and Jews—if at all possible—money. German Jews at this moment preferably in foreign accounts. . . . Let us have some coffee. You would like some?"

He tapped the bell on his desk, and when his secretary came took occasion to dictate the power of attorney.

"What I can do to help you is limited," he resumed. "The laws of the State of Amazonas relating to foreign-owned enterprises are no more or less restrictive than those of our sister states. What I am able to do is write you a letter in my official position expressing the Government's satisfaction in principle with the development of the Massaranduba region for the common advantage of the foreign investors and of the state and federation. Also its readiness to explore and cooperate in the full degree possible in the realization of plans for the improvement of in-strumentalities of transportation in and in the surroundings of the Massa-randuba Valley. That is not a great deal, but I do not see how your syndicate could expect more—particularly after the affair of the Portale-gre Corporation, which has left a bad taste here. But I may give you my private assurance that the Government will meet you halfway. We are suffering here from severe economic depression, as you know. There has even been talk that Manáos might cease to exist. We will be very cooperative to attract capital into the state."

As I sought to express my thanks, he held up his hand with the cigar between two fingers and raised his voice a little. "There is one other private assurance I can give you. If it transpires that Colonel Durondo is to have an effective influence in the Massaranduba Concession, then the other assurances I have given you will be reconsidered." With a change of voice but almost without pause he said, "Young man, I understand why you decided to proceed as you have. As events had happened, you had not a very wide possibility of choice. You have so far evaded the issue. But each of the two political parties is determined to make a show of you as a token of the capital it can bring to the state. They cannot both have you as an exclusive possession. I cannot see that they will let you go on very long without being clearly on one side or the other. Have you considered what you are going to do?"

"Well," I replied, dropping my eyes to my coffee cup, "at least I don't have to face the question immediately—or as long as I am out of com-munication. Or so I've been telling myself. Various things could hap-pen." I was wondering how far I could describe the spot I was actually in as a consequence of the *Interventor*'s contrivings when the secretary returned to announce the arrival of Senhora Braga.

Dr. Mendoça glanced at the clock. "She must have left her house the moment she put down the telephone," he commented. "However, I sup-pose we may as well have her in at once?" He drained the last of his coffee.

I doubt if she could have been kept out. She came in like the interven-tion of fate—tall, dark, gaunt, portentous. She carried, and appeared ready to wield, a black cotton umbrella, man-sized, and wore a dress of much the same material, which hung upon a frame scarcely less wiry and stiff. She stood just inside the doorway looking from one to the other of us with the grim smile of a matron in an orphanage who—

349

her suspicions confirmed!—had caught two boys at the cookie jar. Even had convention not prescribed it, I'm sure we should have got to our feet as we did.

Dr. Mendoça looked sidewise at me with amusement concealed in the corners of his eyes and mouth, reminding me that it was my show.

"Senhora Braga," I said, *"muito praser."* I introduced myself and then presented my host, *sua Excelência, o Chefe do Transporte, Dr. Mendoça.*

She made a stiff little bow, closing her eyes as she did so, and Dr. Mendoça returned it with gravity and a murmured period or two in Portuguese.

In what followed I was primarily a spectator. Dr. Mendoça himself, though having to carry most of my end of it, was chiefly a listener to, and a translator of, his visitor's outpouring. Senhora Braga did, however, hold her fire—and it was evident that this was what she was doing— while he explained to her, and repeated to me in English, that he had invited her to his office in order to be helpful to a friend and foreigner who was without connections in Manáos or adequate familiarity with the language, and that he was not to be considered as having any official capacity for the occasion. She also listened, looking first at me, then at Dr. Mendoça with close-set black eyes of a sharpness accentuated by her narrow, high-bridged nose while I explained for Dr. Mendoça to translate what I thought she ought to know and did not already know about my reasons for being in Manáos.

No whit relaxed for having sat down, she scarcely gave the Minister a chance to finish before she broke into what sounded like the case for the prosecution. Her tone was so strident, her emphasis so strong, her expression so bitter-gloating that I looked to see Dr. Mendoça wince or recoil under the stream of evident invective, and I grew more and more troubled, wondering what on earth kind of obstacles were going to have to be overcome. He listened calmly enough, however, tapping his lips in slow beat with his pencil—he had extinguished his cigar upon Senhora Braga's arrival—and in just such a manner as a psychiatrist might listen to a patient's recital of her dreams or childhood experiences as a routine part of therapy. From time to time he nodded. It would have been in character had he taken notes. Finally he leaned forward and held up his hand. *"Fas favor, senhora; fas favor!"* he begged. Even with that she could not be brought to a halt for several more sentences.

"Do you understand nothing of Dr. Tate's language?" he asked her.

She looked uncomprehending.

"This is quite interesting," he said to me. "I am sorry you cannot have understood it. We have here a woman—surely a lonely and pathetic woman!—whose life has been emptied of most of its content by widowhood, by the absence of near relations and—let us be realistic—by the passing of the years. She is evidently of distinguished birth, or she is of that belief, but all her adult life she has had to accommodate herself to circumstances—er—beneath her. Her life has become centered in her two sons. She is living very much in them. She is violently impatient of those who do not see the world in terms of her sons' deservings. She does not say so, but I think she imagines a conspiracy against them. She has a conflict within herself about them. Being a woman of strong and ill-nourished ego, she is passionately desirous for their success. This would be her vindication. She would triumph in their great achievement. However, she also suffers anguish from their absence and would greatly like to have them by her. And she is very worried about their health at the Massaranduba and the lack of regularity in their lives. About that, I think we shall now hear more."

"Yes, but what did she say?" I asked.

I daresay he had been going to tell me anyway, and he did so, though briefly. She had extolled her sons' dedication to the progress of their country. Others talked of great plans, but her sons were giving up their lives to toil and sacrifice to obtain for their country the wealth of the Massaranduba. It was of the future of the people of Brazil that they were thinking—though no one seemed to care. It seemed that the world would be content to abandon them there. But their courage and fortitude would never fail, however cruel the trials. They were carrying forward civilization. They were bringing a land possessed by the *mato* into commerce with the world. But two young men could not be expected to do alone the work for which an army was required. They were showing the way, but money was needed. Only money could bring dependable labor and machinery and medicines. Her sons were building a dredge. They were bringing it in and building it part by part. This was an example to the world. But the world must appreciate this example. It must be worthy of it. Money was needed, much more money than they had. And the world was indifferent. Foreign capitalists were greedy and unwilling to exert themselves, and Brazilian officials were thinking only of their own advantage and their ease.

351

Senhora Braga listened with evident impatience, even dark misgivings, to the recapitulation, and when Dr. Mendoça paused, though he may not have finished, she recommenced with vigor.

She was terser this time, and Dr. Mendoça translated her pronouncement without comment. Her sons' mission was to show the way. They were willing to sell their property to bring others into the Massaranduba who would have the means they lacked to bring their dreams to reality. It was not that they were abandoning the dreams. They would be willing to stay and work for the Concessionaire and of course the Concessionaire would wish to have them, for they had expert knowledge of the Massaranduba, and not only that, but they were young men of the most remarkable qualities and destined for high honor in whatever work they undertook. She, too, wished the property to be sold—so that all would be provided that was necessary in the Massaranduba. Her sons had been ill and were exhausted. It was not right to expect them to go on like this. A big company was needed—like the Ford Company on the Rio Tapajós, to have modern white buildings and offices— and a hospital, with doctors and nurses in uniform. Just like North America: a company with a large staff, a great many officials and specialists, and the employees living well-ordered lives, on regular salaries, with regular working hours. There would be a commissary, and quarters for married employees. Also vacations, regular vacations. Being a North American company, like Ford, there would probably be an airplane, too, of the kind that could come down on the water.

I wondered what things were like there as it was. "Could we see now if she's prepared to sign the power of attorney?" I asked.

Dr. Mendoça had his secretary bring the paper in. It provoked considerable discussion when she had read it. The problem in persuading her to sign it was, of course, our inability to give anything concrete in return. I depended upon Dr. Mendoça to play up the sacrifices I was making with no surety whatever of any recompense. He spoke with warmth and evidently with effect, for I gathered from the way she began to look at me that I had come alive in her eyes as a human being. At length she put her name to the paper, signing in a large, scrawling hand with such force that the nib, catching in a flaw in the paper in passing, flicked a fine spray of ink in its path. A subsidiary problem during the discussion had been to prevent the lady from charging off tangentially with the conversation. Her dead-black, not very long hair, was partly shaken loose by the energy with which she launched these digressions. As it was, I had to pledge myself to require the purchaser to agree to apply the name "Braga" on maps to the site of her sons' mines and to follow her sons' instructions in the matter of attaching conditions with respect to their future employment by the Concessionaire.

As she stood up to go she made an observation that caused a flicker of surprise in the Minister's eyes. She thought, he reported, that the life of her sons would provide material for a dramatic and inspirational motion picture, and one that would be very popular and would acquaint the world with what her sons were doing. She was sure I would agree when I had come to see what kind of men they were and how much they had done. She hoped I would do what I could to interest the producers of Hollywood in making this motion picture. . . . I could only nod in a solemn way—a cowardly device giving latitude to her hopes, guaranteeing only that I had heard.

At the last she stood with unexpected irresolution in the doorway, then spoke directly to me in a tone of unmistakable appeal. Finishing, she drew from her black beaded handbag a crumpled handkerchief which she held to her mouth, watching me with watered-over eyes while Dr. Mendoça translated.

"She thanks you for coming. She knows you will do all you can to bring about the sale of the property. There is no time to be lost if her sons are to be extricated from the hold the Massaranduba has upon them."

"Ferei o possivel," I declared with earnest conviction. I would do all I could. It was not enough, but I did not know what else to say.

She left behind her an atmosphere I found very uncomfortable. However, I reminded myself, I was at least going to the Massaranduba, and from her point of view especially there was some merit in that. To Dr. Mendoça, I said promptly, "It's obvious that I'd have been at a total loss without you, sir."

He had gone over to his desk and was examining a calendar on it. "I can very well believe that it is time for her sons to be brought back to civilization. I would judge that they have undertaken too much for their resources. Yet they cannot readily abandon what they have invested. I hope that the syndicate in New York does not let them down."

"You couldn't hope it any more than I do."

"No, I am sure that is right." He had remained beside his desk and was working at relighting his cigar. "I am naturally very eager to see this development in the Massaranduba take place. The Deputies would wonder what kind of minister I am if I did not think it important to the country. . . . If you have nothing better to do, would you care to take *jantar* with me? . . . Good. Our army has just conducted a war against the police—a successful war. You have heard? But all is normal in the city. Entirely and altogether normal." He had got his cigar going again, puffing at it between sentences. "Everyone must hope the Massaranduba Concession will be a success—everyone who is a humanitarian. And who cannot be a humanitarian? How can we not be ruled by considerations of what will happen to individual human beings—whether they will have a little more money and live a little longer and more comfortably?" He had moved to the window behind his desk and opened the shutter a few inches to look out. His strong profile was lighted by the sun, the forward thrust of his head accentuated by the short, assertive beard. "In the past it was thought that we served the human race best by serving God. Now it is thought that we serve God best by serving the human race. So I spend much time here thinking how we can extend navigation on our rivers and how we may finance railroads where the land is not under water part of the year. And now"—he closed the shutter again—"we have the letter to write for you to send to New York to show our friendliness to North American capital."

15

In the end I not only had the midday meal with Dr. Mendoça at Manáos's leading hotel but spent most of the afternoon in his company seeing something of the city.

Of the restaurant I retained no impression but of the conventional dark Brazilian woodwork, filtered light, heavy cutlery and yards of white cloth on the table and in my lap. I talked at length about myself and with unpremeditated frankness—the consequence of having been bottled up in myself under pressure and of having an attentive listener who seemed always to be ahead of one in understanding and with whom, therefore, it seemed as natural to talk as to oneself. Moreover, I was stimulated by having my problems in Manáos so satisfactorily disposed of and by the knowledge that on the morrow I should be on my way to the Massaranduba at last. Then there was the bottle of red wine we consumed. I even went so far as to confide to him in general terms the nature of the trap laid for me by Colonel Durondo at Topacindo.

Dr. Mendoça said that he was trying to understand precisely how affairs stood with the proposed Massaranduba Concession. He took it for granted that Colonel Durondo would have been in communication by some means with Dr. Alekos Xenides, whom he knew to be shrewd and capable. Colonel Durondo would wish to cut Dr. Monteiro out of the business and have all arrangements carried on between him and Dr. Xenides. Presumably this did not suit Dr. Xenides, either because he felt ethically bound to deal through Dr. Monteiro, whose idea the Massaranduba Concession had been in the first place, or because he anticipated that Colonel Durondo might shortly be out of office, replaced by the *Constitucionalistas*. If the second consideration had weight with Dr. Xenides, so also would the opposite—that the *Constitucionalistas* might fail. Unless he thought that a commitment by the New York interests would ensure the *Constitucionalistas'* success, he would probably avoid any more associating himself irrevocably with Dr. Monteiro before the election—which would surely be a great disappointment to Dr. Monteiro.

Dr. Mendoça followed with his eyes the movements of the waiter as the latter set the beef course before us, as if they held an unusual interest for him. Resuming, he said that he found very striking the importance that I had come to acquire. I was, of course, a hopeful presage from the States that was concrete, which surely gave me novelty. . . . He left the thought unfinished. If, he went on, he was correct in supposing that Colonel Durondo had been in communication with Dr. Xenides, presumably through an intermediary in New York, it must follow that Dr. Xenides wished to have it understood that he set great store by my reports—for surely Colonel Durondo had been very attentive to me.

He raised a forkful of food, then set it down. I had indicated, had I not, he asked, that Colonel Durondo would believe that his stratagem in placing temptation in my way had proved successful? I nodded. (I was certain that Cora would remain totally silent on the subject, permitting the logical inferences to be drawn from the circumstances.) Then, said Dr. Mendoça, he thought that Colonel Durondo might well claim publicly that I had come over to his side, since he would feel safe in doing so, and this would surely alarm Dr. Monteiro. I told Dr. Mendoça of the

356

letter I had sent Monteiro and of my intention to send him another by the hand of the Captain of *Tocantins* with further reassurances.

Said Dr. Mendoça, "If Dr. Monteiro feels impelled because of the claims of Colonel Durondo to make these letters public, and Colonel Durondo believes you are deceiving him, you could be in grave danger. . . . I have the suspicion that this aspect of the situation is not of great concern to you?"

"Oh no, I'm deeply concerned by it," I said, having been jacked up in my chair. "If I don't appear to be, it's because . . . just now . . . I can't see much beyond the fact that in a week I'll be face-to-face with the Massaranduba at last." I felt the wine sufficiently to be aware of a need to speak with deliberation. "The prospect of some sort of action—physical action, anyhow—has just about pushed everything else out of my mind." I could only hope the ardor that I could tell had crept into my voice despite me did not betray the vision that now—far from the plexus of the complications—danced before me: I pictured myself, though without much clarity of detail, crashing through obstacles by sheer desperate energy and carrying the Concession through to success. "I'm sure Dr. Monteiro wouldn't do anything to put me in any danger. In time I know there's bound to be a day of reckoning—and I know I'll be worried enough as it approaches."

"I hope you will be." He refilled my wine-glass. "I am curious," he said, "about the phrase 'face-to-face at last with the Massaranduba.' You will not mind if I pry? We Jews are in-corri-gible askers of questions. It is no wonder we are frequently in bad with our fellows. Recall what happened to Socrates! I would hazard the guess that it is not the passion for the mining of gold that has brought you to Brazil. Perhaps you would tell me what it was?"

I looked at him, although as if from a distance, with fascination not untinged with amused exasperation. He met my gaze with eyes as bland as could be. He had put a bit of roll in his mouth and was munching it with vigorous little movements of the jaw. One would have thought I had made an appointment with him for treatment of my case. And I told him—told him how, and for how long, I had dreamed of coming here, and when I had done and he wished to know whether the actuality had lived up to my anticipations I told him about that, too, how it had exceeded them, how for weeks on end I had been filled with excitement.

357

He exchanged nods with a table of diners across the floor who had been staring at him for his attention, then turned on me once more the kind of regard one might direct at a book. He said, "I detect a reservation in your voice."

"Because I have to be concerned with other things." As he said nothing and his continued silence made me nervous, I added, "There's the concrete reality of the world of Massaranduba Concessions to be dealt with. As we were saying."

"True. But there is the inner reality of oneself—to be ignored at our peril—and our dreams may be our clue to it." He helped me to a further serving of a vegetable compote, then himself. "I have had a country of heart's desire, one known to neither geography books nor histories, I fear, and of the long, long ago. This country came to my knowledge because of a visitor from it, a girl who had in her something of Hadassah —Esther—the beautiful Jewish girl who became the wife of Xerxes and the Queen of Persia and saved the Jews; something of the accomplished Zubaida, who was Harun al-Rashid's queen; something of the lovely Shirin, the Armenian who became a Persian princess. I saw her portrait once—a Persian painting of the eighteenth century, of the school of Shiraz, called only, 'Young Girl with a Fan.' She was of exquisite beauty —naturally; how else would I have imagined her? And I am afraid she was only in my imagination. She was a princess of the court, with the lightness and grace of a dancing girl. She spoke of her native land, of palaces in the sun with tree-shaded courtyards where the splash of water was ever heard . . . palaces containing treasures of all the arts, painting and sculpture, masterpieces of the craft of goldsmith and silversmith and lapidary, where honors were given for the composition of poetry and music, and to astronomers and mathematicians. She was to be my guide to this land, and to be the comfort and refreshment of my spirit there —when the time should come. Surely we all have experiences of this kind? Perhaps you think that at my age it should be forgotten—for dealing more successfully with reality. Those were your words? Yet I have not forgotten. It has given me a glimpse of the homeland of my spirit. And perhaps of something more. In this fantasy I have described, there was a quality always of the *remembered*. There was a sense that I was calling up from the distant past—what? A reality of the past? A dream of the past? But this is taking us beyond the limits of profitable speculation.

358

. . . It is interesting that from very different beginnings we have been brought to a crossing of paths here in Manáos."

I had had a prickly sensation during his reminiscence, as if an invisible web were being spun around me, and was glad of, as well as surprised by, the abrupt change of subject. Pointing out that he knew all about what had brought me here, I asked what the circumstances were in his case, whether he had always lived here—which seemed to me unlikely. He told me that he had come to Manáos from Recife as a young man in pursuit of his own Massaranduba Concession—the rubber boom. He had come to make money, and he had made it. He had also seen the handwriting on the wall. With the start of the rubber plantations in the East Indies it was clearly only a matter of time before wild Brazilian rubber was priced out of the market. He had got out of rubber, but to take advantage of the experience he had gained in upper Amazon trade and the low shipping rates he foresaw when rubber exports should have fallen off, he had gone into lumber and hides. He had divided his time between Manáos and Recife—and travels abroad—until a friend of his had become Governor of Amazonas and asked him to take a post in the administration. He had accepted the portfolio of Transportation, believing it to be an important one and finding a challenge in the problems involved.

Yes, it was a sacrifice to live in Manáos, more even for his wife than for himself. But he felt that those who had prospered in Brazil, as his family had, had a debt to pay. Moreover, he sometimes nourished a hope that a home could be found in Amazonas for Jewish victims of persecution in Germany, ultimately for hundreds of thousands. But the difficulties were of course immense: lawyers, doctors, merchants, tailors and storekeepers from Europe were hardly suited to settling an equatorial wilderness. And there was division in his own family on the issue. His elder son was a Zionist.

He was interrupted here by a diner from another table, who came up to speak to him and was introduced to me as the Minister of Agriculture —a tall, robust personage who might have been a motion-picture idol when younger, of the kind that reigned in the period when he would have been the right age, with prominent eyes, a warm, bold gaze, a curved, sensual mouth and a strong heel to his chin. He grinned in the manner of a man of chronic good spirits habituated to eliciting a response in kind from others; it was as if we were enjoying a joke to-gether. Scarcely anyone entered or left the restaurant without exchang-ing signs of recognition with Dr. Mendoça.

When we were alone again, Dr. Mendoça said, "When a man is domi-nated by a hatred, it must be something in himself which he is hating."

"Do you mean it? That's the last impression I'd have had of him. He looks as if he'd never hated anything."

Dr. Mendoça stared at me. "No, no. I mean Herr Hitler. Were we not speaking of Hitler? Well, I was thinking of him. The reason why he hates the Jewish people is because unconsciously he sees the German peo-ple—I may say all Western peoples—going in the same direction as the Jews have gone. I give Hitler credit for prescience. What a tragedy for mankind that this prescience, which awakes a response in so many, should be given to a paranoid monster!

"We Jews have the characteristics which are causing Herr Hitler his obsessions and which have made tranquillity difficult for us to attain because we were driven from our country—nearly two thousand years ago—and in Europe were prevented from having part in the life of the land. We were denied the possibility of being a people with a home, which is only possible to a people with roots in the soil. We became essen-tially nomads, although nomads confined to the ghetto. Now the same thing is happening to the Christian peoples of the West—only not under force by a conqueror. They are losing their identity with the soil by the progress of civilization. They are becoming estranged from the land and are choosing to live in ghettos—very elaborate ghettos, but still ghettos. And so they are becoming as we Jews are—intellectually alert, articulate, witty, satirical, self-conscious, moneymaking, worldly, humanitarian, even obsessively humanitarian, lucid in thought, analytical, in the arts skillful, clever, proficient at performance and entertainment, but no longer creative in the great sense. They are becoming like us, with the gift of 'success,' but unhappy, neurotic, seeking and not finding.

"My son says that it would not answer the need to have provision for a place of refuge in Amazonas. Or it is part of the reason. I think I have been talking too much in his presence when he is growing up. He applies to the problem the merciless logic of youth and is not afraid where it may lead. To settle the Jewish refugees in Amazonas, however many of them, he says, would be only an expedient. Or as he expresses it, 'There is more to having roots in the land than owning a plot of ground

360

on which to hoe mandioca. It would make no difference how much mandioca they produced, they would still be out of place here. They—we—would still be homeless. All the mandioca in the world and everything you can buy with it will not give meaning to life.' That is what my son says.

"I tell him he is not talking about the problem of the Jews, he is talking about the problem of modern man. He shrugs. He can only prescribe for his own small part of the human race. Others will have to worry about the rest of it. And the solution he prescribes is for the Jews the return to Palestine. A people cannot be at home but in its own country, in the land of its origin, where its roots truly are, in the soil of its ancestral gods. The essentially Jewish creation, our religion, our philosophy, our literature, our music, our conception of life, is the outcome of our experience in Palestine. It is the flowers of the Palestinian soil. That is his argument. It is impossible for us to resume the Jewish tradition and make it live except in Palestine. There only can we be part of the land and therefore at one with our gods. He is agnostic, and it is easier for him to say 'gods' than 'God.' It was not just *a* god who made our people what we are, or what we were. It was a god whose seat is Palestine and a god whom we can experience . . . *intimamente*—intimately—only in Palestine.

"You English-speaking peoples have an expression, 'The chickens are coming home to roost.' I can recognize these chickens, and it is difficult for me to argue with my son. Judaism is monotheistic. That is true. But in our hearts we think always of Yahweh not as everyone's god but as a god whose home is Palestine, a god of our people. That is why Judaism is not a missionary religion. If you told me you had read our sacred books and wished to become a Jew, you would only astonish and embarrass me. I could think of nothing but to suggest that we go to the Club Inglês for a Scotch-and-soda.

"There is in the land a spirit or genius, I think, that makes it truly the motherland, or fatherland, of those whose home it is. I said the peoples of Europe were becoming separated from their lands by material progress, as the Jews were separated from theirs by force. But the peoples of the Americas are far ahead in this. When they crossed the ocean they left behind the lands which nurtured them and gave them their culture—shall I say the lands of their gods? In the New World they are strangers to the lands in which they live. They are Europeans without Europe.

361

In north Brazil, more than anywhere I have been, one is conscious of this. It is painfully evident here that the people and the country are alien to each other. When you see Manáos you are seeing the . . . *umm* . . . I do not know whether there is a word for what I mean, in either Portuguese or English. *A cristalização?* The crystallization? *O resumo.* . . . The epitome, perhaps?—of New World civilizations. Like a sad joke about them. Did you feel as you arrived that it was astonishing to find the city here at all? The truth about Manáos is that it will flourish or disappear according to economics. In its veins, in place of blood, there is commerce. If the commerce flows, Manáos will conquer the *mato;* if not, the *mato* will conquer Manáos. One or the other. You cannot think of a marriage, can you? A *fusão,* a fusion? An integration of the land and the people, to create a new culture, with its own personality? I go before the chamber to defend my request for appropriations and this little devil in the back of my head whispers, 'Would it really make any difference if Manáos vanished? Is there anything *here?* Beneath the surface is there anything?' I answer that *on* the surface, anyway, there are fifty thousand human beings who may or may not eat, who may or may not have education, and that is reason enough for working for the prosperity of Amazonas. But all the time the question is in my mind whether any gods would weep for us here if our city fell, as surely there were gods who wept when Jerusalem fell, and Athens, and Rome. Or had the gods gone first—back into the hills?

"I think it would be different if the Europeans had come to the Americas in their infancy as peoples, when they were barbarian Gauls and barbarian Goths. If they had been in the . . . their *formative* time, the essential spirit of the land, its genius, would have shaped them after its own character. They would then be North Americans and Brazilians and Argentinos today, truly so, not orphans of Europe—although very rich orphans, some of them. There would not be constant warfare between them and the land, but harmony. They would feel themselves part of the land, like the rocks and the trees, beside the native hearth and the native altar. There would have been a flowering of the arts, as in Europe, as in all the great cultures. Or so it may be. . . . Were you very young when you left your birthplace in Georgia?"

I was caught unprepared by the question. It took me an instant to recover. I told him I had been ten years old.

"Do you ever feel homesickness for it—enough to think of going back to live there?" After a pause, during which I remained oddly tongue-tied, he said, "The question disturbs you?"

"No," I replied. "There's no reason why it should." I thought for a moment. "The answer is perhaps that I feel more homesick when I'm there. Or more unhappy and restless, anyhow."

"And why is this?"

"Probably because it's changed, or because I have. You know how it is when you go back to a house you've once lived in."

"And find strangers living in it? Or find it empty?"

"Yes," I said. "With a billboard, an advertisement, in the yard. And a big concrete highway swooping by in front of it, with a dead possum on the highway, run over by a car."

Dr. Mendoça lighted a cigar. We had finished the main course, and he remained thoughtful in his turn. The movement of his eyes and the tilt of his pouted lips made me think that he was going over in his mind what he had said and finding it good. My mind was blurry from the wine I had drunk in the heat, much of it on an empty stomach, and I drew on the cigarette I had lighted as if it were a bottle of smelling-salts.

Dr. Mendoça had taken an envelope from his pocket and scribbled on it. Replacing it, he resumed in the confident voice in which he always spoke. "When I have visited in the Southern United States, I have detected the semblance of this kind of *personality* of culture I am speaking about. It is like an echo. The people of the South are like a people who have a home together, or the memory of such a home. Perhaps the presence of the Negroes has contributed to this. They came as primitives and they composed a peasantry, providing the society with roots in the soil. They were much a part of the Southern soul, as the Russian peasants were so much a part of the Russian soul—as I think a peasantry may be indispensable to the soul of a people. And perhaps that is what we are talking about—whether a people has a soul. Also, there was the long and terrible war. This took away from the people everything. It was the reverse of material progress and industrialization. The people were brought close to the soil and close to one another because nothing else was left.

"I have noticed that among the people of the South there is a kind of homesickness. It is the same among the Irish. And it is most strong, I think, among the Jews. With the homesickness is a feeling of guilt which

363

will not let them alone. It is the feeling of the defeated who accuse them-selves, of course unconsciously, of being not worthy of their heritage."

"I was brought up in the North. I know the North better than the South."

"Yes," he declared without giving me a chance to say anything. "You were brought up in the country of the conqueror, like a Jew. And when you return to the birthplace, the conqueror is there, too. The house is empty. *Cartazes* are affixed to it, and there is a slaughtered opossum on the new concrete highway. So you come to where the dead opossum is a live *tigre* and there is not yet the clearing in the jungle for a house to which *cartazes* may be affixed. And where the Ministry of Transporta-tion cannot obtain the appropriation for even a few miles of macadam road."

He paused again while he took a drink of coffee and touched his napkin to the undersides of his moustache, but this time I did not speak.

"You and my older son are the same age," he said, not noticing a de-parting diner endeavoring to catch his eye. "While you have come to the Amazon River, he has gone to London. He is in the struggle to have more Jews permitted entry to Palestine. It has become his life!" He looked at me as if he thought something in my appearance might cast a light on his son's behavior. "I have expounded all the reasons why Zion-ism cannot succeed, but he is not moved. And I point out that even if it will succeed only a small fraction of the Jews of the world could be accommodated in Palestine. 'More than you think,' he replies, 'but even if what you say is true, the small fraction will provide roots for all Jewry in the soil of Zion. It will place us in touch with our God at his own altar. Every Jew in the world will feel different for it.' I ask him if he really believes in a God—he who has read so much in science. His an-swer is: 'The nature of God is a matter beyond the possibility of human comprehension. It lies outside the reach of human thought. Therefore for human beings the question of whether God exists is irrelevant and without meaning.' I make one final argument: 'You will go back think-ing to find God and you will be fully occupied searching for oil.' 'We shall find both,' he says.

"I do not believe it. I know better. If the Jews have someday their own country in Palestine, the best that can be hoped for is that it will be-come a Belgium of Asia Minor—one more industrial country, one more among others which are growing more alike all the time, with a prosperous urban people no different from what they would have been in Europe or the Americas."

His eyes continued to rest on me, and while I knew he was pursuing his own thoughts, his expression was that of a man receiving a report that was no more encouraging than he had anticipated. Uncomfortable under his gaze, I could still think of nothing to say, and was relieved when he turned his attention to his cigar, knocking the ash off into a saucer, and again picked up the thread of his discourse.

Everyone, he said, had to seek his spiritual home. This was the deepest need of the human personality. Everyone had to seek this home himself. No one could do it for him. That, he, Dr. Mendoça, had to remember. Palestine had no attraction for him. It could be admitted that Brazil was not truly a nation, not a homeland to which one could wholly belong, but was like other countries of the New World still a colony of Europe, out of place and without integration. Yet there were seven generations of Mendoças buried in Recife. Who was more Brazilian than the Mendoças? The Indians! He believed his son would discover that. But youth was entitled to its own mistakes—if to nothing else. It did not matter that his own ties of affection were with his fellow Brazilians, that the gods of Palestine were in his conviction irrecoverable. It mattered no more than that the great wild interior of Brazil, where the gods had yet to be created, or perhaps he should say yet to be invoked, and to which I was so drawn, also had no attraction for him, because he was too old—not so much too old in himself as too old as a Mendoça. Perhaps the quest for Zion, though fruitless, would lead his son to the discovery of truths. If there were no hope for a people wedded to twentieth-century civilization to regain a lost identity with a homeland, perhaps the individual, by the very reason that today he was not part of a people, of a tribe, might be able to see farther, to have a clearer vision, perhaps in moments of inspiration to have communication with what is behind it all. And if this failed him—his son and me—there was a next-best that was not altogether to be spurned. He himself had found that he could make do with it. He, Dr. Mendoça, consoled himself with the rewards of thought and reason. He was modern man—one who had been modern a long time. And typically enough he was in Manáos, without gods and without a country. His home—*faute de mieux*—was the field of knowledge, especially knowledge of man.

I had, by asking, elicited this explanation of what the next-best was,

365

which he could make do with—as of course he must have expected me to. I was clear enough in my head only to rue dully that I was not more so. It would never fully come back to me what he had said, I thought, and such, I fear, has proved to be the case.

He was sitting sidewise to the table and to me, one leg stretched out, his head turned so that he faced me. Said he, "I pay for the privilege of devoting myself to knowledge and to the enjoyment of aesthetics by improving transportation in the State of Amazonas, or trying to. Also by kindness to concessions for the extraction of minerals. I hardly count the bits of writing I have done on oriental arts and Brazilian history. . . . Come, let us finish this purple *sorvete*. Then we may go on a ride around the city on the *bonde*."

Dr. Mendoça walked with short, rapid steps and seemed to have a slight limp, which may have been only chronic nervous haste pressing against the limitations of the physical apparatus.

Cars on the Circular route ran only one an hour, but he had timed it so we had a wait of only a few minutes. It was an elegant conveyance into which we mounted, flashing green and yellow, redolent of fresh paint and—the line being narrow-gauge—exceptionally long and slender. The land on which Manáos was built was hilly, being cut by ravines ("Much of it had to be filled," said Dr. Mendoça, "as if real estate were as scarce in the upper Amazon basin as on Manhattan Island"), and the cars were operated like roller-coasters. At the top of a hill the motorman would release the brake-handle, causing it to spin dramatically, and push the throttle up to full speed and hold it there. Gathering momentum, the car seemed to touch the rails only at lengthening intervals. The descent was like riding a cannonball. The branch-ends of the trees tossed wildly in our wake and ahead of us horses and cows, misjudging the car's velocity, sprang terror-stricken when it was upon them, all but brushing it with their tails. Clutching the back of the seat in front of him as unashamedly as I, Dr. Mendoça cried above the roar of the onrush, "This is the last time I bring a *Norte-Americano* on the Circular. You see the effect." In the rear of the car a dozen soldiers were whooping with laughter and egging the motorman on with wild yells.

I had seen Brazilian streets that marched grandly past stately mansions to fetch up in a few yards at a swamp on the edge of the forest, but here the city not only came to abrupt halts but had afterthoughts and would crop up again. The trolley line took off into the wilderness with the air of a transcontinental railroad. The red clay of a road that crossed the tracks, in conjunction with the untropically-uniform bright green of vegetation-matted hills, reminded me of north Georgia in a season of good rains. There was no reason to suspect the existence of a city within two miles or two hundred. Then suddenly a clearing would round into view and, standing cheek by jowl with the utmost ordinariness, a huddle of three-story apartment-buildings. "The end came here almost as suddenly as at Pompeii," said Dr. Mendoça. "And here we are, just as we were at that moment. Except that we have been invaded by vegetation instead of by ash and lava."

When we had completed the circle and he had, insisting that he had time for it, showed me the opera house with sardonic relish of my astonishment, we said our farewells, I with the vow, which time was to corroborate far more than it usually does such vows, that I should never forget his generosity, company and discourse.

At the very last I asked the question I had been putting off from moment to moment. Could he, as Minister of Transportation, find out without too much trouble if a young girl, unmarried, probably accompanying her father, had arrived a few days before in the S.S. *Boa Vista,* and if so her name? Dr. Mendoça allowed the question to hang for the briefest moment while he regarded me in an inquiring, kindly fashion, then with a nod that was more of a grave bow said that he could find out without any trouble at all. And, no, it would not be necessary for me to telephone him. Someone from his department would be going down to the docks before evening and could take a message to me.

The message arrived at *Tocantins* little more than an hour after my return. Written on plain paper, it said: "1. There was no such young lady as you described aboard the *Boa Vista* upon her arrival here, I am sorry that I must report. 2. There are some peculiarities about the conduct of your Dr. A. X. that I do not understand. 3. You should act as if you had need to be careful, I think, beginning soon." It wished me good fortune in all things and was signed "S.M."

In the morning I expressed my further gratitude in a note which I was able to drop off at his bureau, thanks to *Tocantins*'s English agent, who drove by there on the way to taking me out to the Club Inglês. The Club, or *Cloob,* where the local British with the instinctual sureness of bowerbirds had constructed a swimming pool, tennis courts and a bungalow with deep verandas on which to have drinks and exchange shorthand references to the country's offerings in the way of riding, shooting and boating on the Rio Negro, might equally well have been in Ceylon or Uganda, or so I found myself thinking in the light of a remembered observation of Dr. Mendoça's: "The English conceive, perhaps correctly, that there was created with the universe a spirit of Englishness for them in time to appear and embody, and that this spirit will remain, substantially unalterable, until the end of everything. There is no such thing as an individual Englishman, as you and I are individuals, somewhat luckless individuals. They are all bits of England. It makes no difference how eccentric they are—and they may be very eccentric—they are still bits of England."

As the time of her departure drew near and passed unheeded, *Tocantins* presented the appearance of a stage at the finale of a musical melodrama of exceptionally heterogeneous cast. There were three-generation family groups, one all in black, without a white thread in the entire collection, one including a young girl of guileless brown eyes and face so painfully sweet and naïve it hurt to see her. There were fat men all about, grave and important fat men staring down at their bellies. There was a debauched-looking boulevardier with a pencil-lined moustache, the complexion of a mushroom and red-edged eyelids. There was a Negro (a doctor, it transpired) with close-cropped, evenly-grey hair, a flat, chieftain's face dominated by enormous eyes, which rolled as if by means of a concealed mechanism; he bore himself with the dignity of a statue but with an acute consciousness of the impression he was creating in his bulky sporting cap of mottled orange and black. There was a Corsican bandit with a squat treetrunk of a body and a tight mass of black hair rising from his scalp and matched by another curtaining his mouth. There were families with the slanted Indian physiognomy, out of their element and as inert as abandoned marionettes. All but these sat at tables and talked or stood in groups and talked or surrounded the officers and talked. Gamins with grinning faces and thin limbs with knobby joints darted in and about the forest of legs *psst*-ing at one another.

The passengers and their relatives remaining behind were on the point of being torn from one another's bosoms by the imminence of the ship's departure when they were put to the necessity, before which professional actors might have quailed, of protracting their tender farewells for as long as it took a late-arriving passenger, a female, to surge up the gangplank, sweaty but in no whit discomposed, and be meticulously processed by the document-examiners. Being Brazilian, they were able to carry it off without visible constraint or flagging of conviction, but an ordeal was created for my English acquaintance. *Tocantins's* agent had kindly made a point of seeing me off. There had been a firm hand-clasp. "Yes, good trip. Cheerio. Yes, of course. You must buy me an ice cream when I come up to—where was it? Never mind, I'll find out from . . . Thank you. Yes, I shall. So lahng!" Then he was off, mercifully finished with it. But then there was the delay and—horrors!—he was called back on the ship's business. He did not see me, of course. Only a faint redness below the eyes betrayed his distress. Minutes went by while he waited for the Comandante to do something about a piece of paper, and still he did not see me.

The veritable stir of departure was spreading. A moment earlier emotional displays were forbidden; now they were compulsory; emotion must sweep all before it. Voices were tense, words urgent. The gang-plank was down and all were ashore who were going ashore, including the Englishman—except one visitor who had missed the summons; for him the gangplank was hauled back and held patiently until he had negotiated it.

The ship was moving. Hands were wrenched from hands, voices became an octave shriller. The Englishman was standing by, prevented by stern convention from departing ahead of the guest. He did not see me, of course—had not once seen me since the official good-bye. The vessel was ten yards offshore before he looked in my direction—and by Jove! there I was! He had been looking everywhere for me! He saluted, smiled, dropped his eyes. Without raising them again he somehow knew the instant I looked away and—presto!—though I looked back immediately he was gone.

The sun had sunk without my noticing it. From the center of the river Manáos lay in deep shadow. Behind it the sky was stained with sunset colors such as might have come from another than the ordinary spectrum or have belonged to another and vaster and exotic firmament revealed through rents in the envelope of the earth's atmosphere. There were streaks of wild, weird yellows and eerie, glass-clear greens, and against these *Eisenach, Bremerhaven,* as she swung slowly around at anchor—the breeze, as it often will, had dropped with the sun, leaving the ship to respond to the current of the river—was like the hulk of a vessel beneath the surface of the sea.

369

Before quitting *Tocantins* at Topacindo, I wrote three letters for the Comandante to take on to his destination: a factual report to the *Interventor* of what I had done; a more expansive account, with protestations of fealty and a promise to be back before the elections, to Monteiro; and, enclosed in the envelope to Monteiro for him to get safely into the mails, a letter to Mr. Willet full of confidence and reasons even more urgent than before for Dr. Xenides to persuade his syndicate to act without delay.

Shortly after we docked at Topacindo there was a knock on my stateroom door, which, in response to my *"Pode entrar,"* was pulled back just sufficiently for a young man with slicked-down hair and tortoiseshell glasses to stand in the opening. "Senhor Santos?" he asked in a loud voice, looking at me observantly. I shook my head, whereupon, with a whispered, *"Para você, Senhor Tate,"* he flicked an envelope onto my bunk and withdrew, closing the door as he did so.

It was a letter from Monteiro—at last. While I had been telling myself that he had hardly had a chance to communicate with me safely, I had fretted exceedingly over the utter silence in his quarter. I skimmed through the letter, then, reassured, read it carefully. He had had the letter I had sent him. He thought I had done just right—from the beginning. They had been very worried, but I had proved myself a good Brazilian. His wife, Sophia, had said so. (That conjured up an engaging picture for me.) He hoped I should be able to get the powers of attorney and all the information at the Urubu mines that Dr. Xenides could desire. He wished I could return soon, to communicate the information to Dr. Xenides, but he feared that in any case it could not be expected that the syndicate would apply for a concession before the election. Considering all things, he thought I must not return until just before the election. The greatest mistake would be for me to be in the wrong hands at that time. Also, by staying where I was I would have more chance to make myself an expert on the Massaranduba. *Sabiá* would be in Topacindo in six weeks' time, on the first of the month; he would see to that. I must be sure to be in time to embark upon her. He would arrange for the vessel to remain overnight in case it seemed advisable for me to go aboard inconspicuously in the dark. With the Captain I could arrange for the method of my disembarkation on arrival so that I should not attract notice. The regime would have no reason to suspect me of dangerous intentions and thus would not be watching for me.

That was the gist of it. There were also good wishes for my well-being and safe return and a characteristic expression of confidence that after the storm would come the calm, or prosperity. (*"Depois do temporal vem a bonança."*) I could imagine that he was under considerable tension. Anyway, we were in complete agreement on my staying at the Urubu mines as long as possible.

I had three days in Topacindo. This was no treat, but I might have had to wait much longer, and when *Tocantins* pulled out I felt the new phase of life had already begun, that I had in fact entered the magnetic field of the Massaranduba. I walked around the village and out into the range-land, once and only once passing the house where I had said good-bye to Cora. Part of the time I read. The inn's meager accommodations were public. There was a communal dining-table and several communal area-ways in which hammocks were slung, these dormitories, like the dining-room, opening off an interior patio. But privacy was not very important in a country where the absolutes of being in bed and being altogether up did not prevail. The realm of the hammock was a crepuscular realm, of which the denizens, uniformed day and night in pajama coats and trousers which either were or resembled pajama-trousers, were never committed to either condition and slipped from one to the other on the spur of the moment.

On the first day I had a visitor. He was a middle-aged man with a thin growth of hair on his scalp, a face that narrowed to a pointed jaw and a skin that appeared to be a size too large for him; very possibly he had lost weight. He did not disguise the official nature of the call. The card he handed me, carefully bending the corner in the prescribed manner (so the recipient could not later palm the card off as a fresh one, and his own), had under his name *Chefe do Escritório das Licenças,* or something of the sort; I was too apprehensive to take close note of it. At his suggestion we had coffee together in the dining-room. I soon decided he was harmless, though I had no doubt he was acting under the instructions of the *Interventor* in interviewing me. He had a manner both shy and forward, keeping the handle of his umbrella over his mouth and using his eyes and eyebrows expressively as he talked, giving me a vivid picture of how a stage-door masher of a generation past might have gone about propositioning a chorus girl. He spoke no English, and his soft, insinuating Portuguese, impeded by the umbrella handle, was all but incomprehensible to me, so there was little communication between us. This did not seem to trouble him, however, and my offerings, more or less random, apparently contented him. He left me thoroughly mystified. I was going to have to grow years older and more experienced before I recognized that he had been simply a bureaucrat carrying out the letter of an assignment preparatory to the drafting of a report.

On the third day I haunted the dock where the riverboat I was to take on the next leg, a kind of miniature, shabby *Tocantins,* lay up making ready to depart. Before daylight the next day we sailed.

From Topacindo we steamed for three days up a broad river with forested banks and intermittent stretches of cleared land such as I had seen along the *paranás* of the Amazon. The sun beat down, the waves broke like glass beneath the bow, the forest slipped by and drowsiness hung upon the riverboat like a malady. When we put in at a cattle ranch or village of the familiar driftwood-grey stilted houses to pick up or drop off a passenger or a bit of cargo, the feeling was as if the episode were taking place in one of those dreams you know is a dream but is so vivid you almost believe in it. A grumpy priest in a discolored cassock gave me up as a bad job over the language difficulty. I watched the banks pass and at night, in a hammock slung with a dozen others amidships, slept the deep sleep of one with nothing awaiting his attention. I had a sense of biding my time.

I had never evolved a consistent picture in my mind of how the Massaranduba might look. The images that flashed before my inner eye when its name was mentioned were derived from nothing on earth, unless it were a city of clustered towers across the plain, dazzling in the sunlight, or a palace with the ascending forms and golden magnificence of the pipe-organ of a cathedral. When, as we approached a fork in the river, the Captain and owner of the vessel, standing behind the helmsman, as he often did, like an opera tenor who has just composed himself for an aria, looked over his shoulder at me and announced perfunctorily, *"O Rio Massaranduba,"* it may have come as a shock to me to find it not greatly different from the river we were on. But I doubt that it did. A god making a first appearance to a mortal habituated to his worship would doubtless have an awesome presence however unexceptional his features, and so it was as I beheld the legendary river opening up before us. Among the singular properties claimed for the Massaranduba Valley, a distinctive appearance on the part of the river had never been one, so the beauty it turned out to possess was an extra. All rivers with forested banks are beautiful, but the Massaranduba was a small Rio Negro with black water reflecting the colors of sky and foliage, though in agitated mosaic owing to its swifter current.

The forest had become a black wall of night and the sky been drained of the last colors of the sunset when we drew up at the settlement of Baracurú, which was as far up the Massaranduba as the riverboat went. For anyone going farther there was the gas-powered launch, a craft about twenty-five feet overall, lying alongside the pier to which we tied up.

I had been told that the launch's schedule conformed to that of the boat from Topacindo, but on the whole it seemed remarkable that this should prove to be the case. I should not have been surprised to learn that it was days away. I should not have been surprised to find Baracurú a nest of savages with the shrunken heads of my predecessors strung from its eaves; and, indeed, lighted by kerosene lamps which picked out the myriad chinks in the thatched walls and cast grotesque shadows as silhouetted figures were framed momentarily in the doorways, it had the air of a clandestine and illicit encampment. If you come to where you know nothing about anything and have no control over circumstances, being unable even to discuss their intricacies with anyone, it comes unexpectedly when events follow not only an orderly sequence but an advantageous one. When I tried to find out before disembarking what arangements would be possible for me pending the departure of the launch, I was told to wait. A conference was held in the riverboat, over coffee, between the riverboat's owner and the owner of the launch, who wore a frayed, stained, knitted shirt, like an undershirt, barred with dark blue bands and had a long, glistening, inexpressive face, smudged with oil and stubble. Insects swarmed around the overhead light. I sat by under the self-oblivious scrutiny of a throng of spectators on the pier, a throng which, except for the slapping of legs and arms, was hushed and still. As any exotic stranger will in a like situation, I had become a charge upon the country, to be looked out for by the habitués. At length I was given to understand that the Topacindo boat, which had to take on a load of firewood, would remain through the night, so I could sleep aboard and in the morning would need only to step across the pier to the launch, and that the launch would carry me on to my destination, or as near it as the depth of water in the Rio Urubu would permit. Whether the riverboat was staying over or the launch leaving early on my account, I did not know. I did learn that carrying passengers, cargo and mail to and from the Urubu mines was the launch's chief business.

In the morning I swung out of my hammock in the dark. There was a faint stirring of air from up the unseen river and a smell of wood-smoke from a fire being made ready for coffee. The boat's superstructure and the nearby trees were dripping from a night shower, and across the wharf the launch could be heard bumping gently against a piling. There was that quality of the first beginnings when all is potential in the black nebula of the night, when objects are dark suggestions of themselves waiting to be realized and the air that will breathe life into living things is fragrant and full of hope. Many hundreds of miles from all that was known to me and all to which I was known, I stood on the narrow deck holding onto a guy-wire and drank very deep of it. The Massaranduba River was a voice of persisting cajolery from beneath the stern of the launch, against which its waters struck with the sound of softly applauding hands. The alert quiet of the gathering but still invisible day was such as to release and give wing to one's most boundless expectations. Those which had been taking form within me were ambitious—too ambitious for me yet to admit to myself in so many words. I was going to become the one who knew the territory of the Massaranduba Concession, what it looked like, what it felt like, what it was; and I, alone of all its suitors from New York to Brazil, would be able to speak in its name —the name that exercised such authority over the minds of men wherever it was uttered. I felt this with a force that had an almost vindictive intensity—I could not have said why even if I had recognized it.

For three days and nights—half the time it took God to create heaven and earth, I remember thinking, though with no great impatience—we pushed upstream against the river's current. The engine ground away, the exhaust kept up a rapid, steady drumroll and often the blue cloud of our burnt gasoline enveloped us, keeping even with us as if it were tied to us, like ectoplasm. It must have been extremely uncomfortable traveling. In addition to the crew of three there were as many as eight passengers at a time—all Caboclos—and of course there was no place where a hammock could be hung and one slept wherever one could among the lumps of cargo in their basket-woven containers, cushioning oneself with whatever part of one's gear lent itself to the purpose. However, I was

374

bothered by the discomfort no more than by the tedium, and no more than a river is bothered by incidentals as it flows to its certain appointment with the sea. I was prepared to welcome far worse hardships as being, for reasons ill-defined in my mind, likely to improve the prospects of my achieving what I was bent upon. I ate the fish we carried with us, supplemented by a few eggs and bananas we picked up at the rare riverside communities of a few shacks, and tapped the store of canned provisions I had laid in at Topacindo only twice, when I could no longer resist the thought of the food in the sack against which I was leaning. There was little variety apart from the occasional regal macaws flying with their easy grace up the river ahead of us or toucans sartorially elegant in black and white, with brilliant spectra on their bills or breasts, which took cover at our approach. Occasionally the face of an alligator, like that of a submerged horse, could be discerned awash in the river. Unbroken forest formed the banks, and morning and afternoon went on without change. There were times when it seemed that we were navigating the same stretch of river over and over again. Once when we hit what appeared to be precisely the same rain-squall every half hour there was on the other side of it each time the same kite perched round-shouldered on the same bare branch. It was slate-grey with orange talons. The first time its face and beak were also orange. It was a relief to note the next time that they were black.

There were two series of rapids before we reached the mouth of the Urubu River. In the first the boulders barely broke the surface. There was little white water, and we were able to make sufficient headway against the current to creep past the landmarks on the power of the motor alone. The second series, *As Queixadas do Massaranduba,* the Jaws of the Massaranduba, were more formidable. They could be heard from afar like the roar of a railroad train on a trestle. You saw at a glance the reason for the name. Rocks like the stubs of dirty grey teeth stood up in the river's course, though as you approached you saw there was more than one row. Around them and over them and between them the river surged and leaped, an entirely different river, stampeding and murderous. It gave us no chance at all to beat a way upstream against the waters pouring through the gaps—as well expect to take wing—but we headed close inshore and there, it transpired, there was a less turbulent stretch. Finding that everyone else other than the proprietor-engineer was dropping over the side into thigh-deep water to take hold of a towline from the bow, I did likewise. Close to the bank, where the water came only to our knees, we leaned against the rope while the motor and rudder held the boat offshore, and thus, step by step, we pulled her through. I was excited and uplifted by the physical contest.

The Urubu, which led off from the Massaranduba but diverged from it only gradually, was a small river with somewhat more flow. Its watershed in its lower reaches must have been very confined, for during the first day of our ascent it received only insignificant tributaries and thus retained its width; only on the second did the trees on its two sides meet overhead. If there were any living creatures in the shadowy woods, they took flight at the sound of our motor before we could see them. There was nothing else to remind one that this was wilderness. Our placid progress along the watercourse, with the four remaining other passengers—all laborers bound for the mines—chatting off and on through the hours, made me think myself in a great woodland preserve laid out with an artificial stream by a noble lord for pleasure-seekers surfeited with civilized refinements.

As time passed, another fancy took hold of me—that the goat we had acquired before leaving the Massaranduba had the office of a guide. A brown billy-goat, hard and firm of body, extremely self-sufficient, he stood resolutely like a figurehead at the very peak of the launch's bow. His eyes, placed on the sides of his face near the top of his head, at the base of his polished, curved black horns, were golden with horizontal slit pupils and were kept fixed on the river ahead. When he tossed his head or wagged his little tail or stamped his small black hoofs, it was with the smartness of a military bandmaster. He was not in the least shy and accepted without to-do the leaves I managed to snag for him.

I spent much time sitting with the goat. I wondered if the dwellers on Attic hillsides three thousand years ago whose world was inhabited by creatures of the fields and woods and mountains that were half caprine and half human would have perceived what was concealed from me in those remote and brilliant eyes, and what it was they would have perceived.

We spent the night ashore at a spot where the ground stood well above the level of the river and there were no mosquitoes, evidently a regular stopping-place, for there were open structures with thatched roofs, under which to swing a hammock, and a fireplace of rocks. The next day the river grew even narrower, until it seemed to me incredible that the

376

launch could go any farther. Yet it did, and for some hours. I have never seen such nagivation. The stream became so straitened that the launch's propeller sucked the water away from its banks with the rushing, gurgling sound of a receding wave well ahead of the bow—a most extraordinary sight. Frequently all hands had to tumble over the side to lighten the craft and, pushing and lifting, maneuver her over a shallow stretch. It was grueling work, and pursuing the launch into hip-deep water, it was all we could do to scramble back over the gunwales to sprawl panting on the boards. Again I thought with exhilaration that this was more like it! My muscles craved resistance, seemed to have a thirst of their own to be pitted against obstacles.

At dusk the helmsman throttled down the motor, we glided toward the shore, one of the crewmen jumped in ahead of us to ease the vessel in and we were there. Or we were as near there as the launch could take us, which left eight kilometers to be covered on foot, so I understood when the craft's owner pointed into the woods, held up eight fingers in front of my face and barked, *"Kilometresh!"* I nodded, but he looked doubtfully at me, and when he had organized the party, arranging for the Caboclo laborers to carry my duffelbag in turn—a considerable load for one man though I had left most of my belongings in Topacindo, where I had bought the bag—and had picked up a lantern preparatory to leading the march, he did so again, holding up the lantern so that the light fell on my face and on his own, which glistened as ever with perspiration and oil.

I had come in a short time to feel pretty doubtful myself. The swift onset of dusk had brought home to me, perhaps not inexplicably, the magnitude of the distances in this country. I asked myself what there would be to take hold of in the vast tracts of woods making up the proposed concession. The confidence with which I had embarked from Baracurú had so far ebbed that had there been, the moment before we set off into the darkness, a way for me to have gone back in time to the point before I had taken on any responsibility for accomplishing anything in this aloof, interminable and doubtless intractable domain, before I had committed my self-esteem to it and my hope of earthly salvation, I might have taken it. As there was not, I undertook to persuade myself that it was always with a sinking heart that one approached a journey's destination and unprecedented demands upon one's resources.

The track we followed—I directly behind the launch-owner, the goat bringing up the rear—was often steep, and when level was muddy. My expectations of the amenities likely to be found at the end of it—never high—had to be revised downward; to transport anything along the way we were traversing beyond the bare necessities was clearly out of the question. That consideration made me feel better. It rendered what lay ahead at the mining-camp less intimidating and evoked before me that which I knew I could triumph over: discomforts. The physical act of walking did something for my spirits too, and so did the soft shower of rain that soaked us. The feeling of belligerency just under the surface of my mind, which had buoyed them up for the past week or so, was stirring again.

16

The site of the mining-camp was distinguished in the darkness by nothing more than a few dim lights glimpsed here and there through openings in the trees as we walked along and by some sounds of voices in broken exclamations coming from their direction. No voice at all was to be heard from the more brightly-lighted structure for which we headed, a bungalow with a steeply-pitched gable roof, as could be seen from the light that filtered through its slotted walls. However, the launch-owner's halloa was answered from within. We entered and found two men sitting at opposite ends of a table in the room from which most of the light was issuing. One had a scattering of papers before him, the other a machine-part of some kind and a file in his hand. They were white men —very white. I stood, arrested by their pallor, the exhaustion in their faces, the wildness of their gaze. The one with the papers before him, over which he was still bent protectively though he had looked up from them at our entrance, was a contemporary of mine, I should have guessed, and by his appearance might have been a poet, in a poet's conventionally impoverished surroundings, surprised with eyes filled with the torment of an elusive vision. He had the regularity of feature usually found only in artists' idealizations, and his face had been refined by suffering, which brought out his cheekbones, wide mouth and burning eyes. It was a face one felt had beauty in it. The other, who was smaller and perhaps ten years older, made a rather ferocious first impression with his dilated, slightly bloodshot grey eyes and his thatch of brown hair, his eyebrows and moustache—all lighter in color than was common with Brazilians—bristling menacingly, but the impression was altered when almost at once he turned to stare inquiringly at his junior, as if awaiting a cue. The two had got to their feet and extended their hands in turn with something of the incredulity of castaways to whom a visitor appears, though it turned out that they knew well enough who I was, my telegram having arrived by the launch on its previous trip. The younger man identified himself as Tonio Braga and the other as Manoel, with a last name I did not catch and never learned; we called one another by first names from the start.

Tonio set about to make me at home with a nervous impulsiveness and a rather lost air. I soon saw that he was not quite steady on his feet and seemed to have a little difficulty focusing his vision. His eyes looked feverish because, obviously, he had a fever; not much, probably, but some. I left him with the mail the launch-owner had brought while I changed into dry clothes in the room to which he had had my bag carried. On my return he offered me some rum, but as the bottle was nearly empty and there was no other in sight I took very little—only enough to make a long-delayed cigarette taste even better. We communicated as well as we could in a mixture of elementary Portuguese, English and French. I had to concentrate, and this was not made easier by a sound of moaning, not loud but reiterant, that came from another room. I resisted the thought that the sound explained the absence of the other brother because I did not like to think that if it did Tonio's disregard of it—which in truth was even more upsetting than the sound itself—could be so complete.

Assuming that Tonio would be impatient to learn all I could tell him of the course of events revolving upon his family's property and the proposed concession, I set about the laborious task of making this known

380

to him. Although the outward, factual position was that I was doing him and his relatives a favor in coming to the mines, I found I was speaking almost in a tone of self-justification, as if I had to give an account of my stewardship. It was the effect, I was aware, of the plain indications of what the young men at the mines had been enduring. I knew I must appear to be bursting with health, ill-gotten from a soft and protected life, and was reminded of Senhora Braga's complaint of the world's abandonment of her sons.

The moaning that had distracted me had subsided, but only to resume after a space and rise through a crescendo to a weak outcry. This was enough to impinge upon Tonio's notice, though not, apparently, to disturb him. *"O meu irmão,"* he said, getting up and murmuring an apology at having to leave. He was gone only a few moments. Jacques had the *paludismo,* he explained on his return. By gesturing in turn at the source of the moaning and at himself and pantomiming a man dropping into bed, he indicated that he and his brother had attacks alternately. With a nod at Manoel he turned down the corners of his mouth and, arching his brows half comically, wagged his head. I was to understand that with the hirsute little engineer it was *comme ci, comme ça;* he contracted malaria, but only occasionally—*às vezes*—not to excess. Manoel seemed charmed by what he heard. His upper lip drew back in a grin. As I floundered along in my recitation I noticed that he watched Tonio, snatching only glances at me, as if it were only in Tonio's face that the significance of what I was saying could be discerned. I was no less observant of Tonio's expression. I was trying to tell what impression was being made on him. I seemed to have his attention. His gaze never strayed, though occasionally he grimaced, screwing up his face or elongating it, stretching his eyelids and eyebrows, as if he needed to ensure or restore its mobility. But he asked no questions. Often he nodded and sometimes he helped me out with a word, proposing it interrogatively, but when at length I took to asking him if he understood, it turned out several times that he had not, though he was going to let me proceed as if he had. I concluded that he had reached the end of his endurance for the day and was struggling to keep from showing it. *"Por hoje basta?"* I suggested. *"Amanha eu continuo?"*

His reply, if it was a reply, was not immediately forthcoming. He cast his eyes on the papers on the table and, without speaking or changing his position, reached out and began slowly and meticulously rearranging

381

them. I watched the process for what seemed a long time, wondering if it were possible that all the while I had been struggling to elucidate what so vitally concerned him his mind had been on those papers. Evening up the edges of a stack, he explained what they were: *"Os relatórios de producção,"* reports of production.

He rose and, holding momentarily to the back of the homemade chair, gave me a smile that could have been shy or confidential or both. *"Vem par' aqui,"* he said, taking up the lamp.

I followed him into an adjoining room. It was a small room, a cubicle. On one side were shelves stacked with boxes, cardboard and wooden, and some books, evidently reference works. On the other was a small safe. Kneeling before it, Tonio opened it and brought forth a sack about as big as his fist and of silk, it appeared. With the sack between his knees on the floor he untied the fastenings with fingers as delicate as a seamstress's, then took from the safe a sheet of stiff paper. Forming a trough of the paper with one hand, and as if he were going to roll a giant cigarette, he emptied part of the contents of the sack into it with the other. I found I was holding my breath. In the half-light of the kerosene lamp the gold glittered as if it were in full sun. It was mostly in the form of tiny flakes, but there was a scattering of larger pieces up to the size of a raisin. It was beautiful, and more, no question about it, with the smooth, oiled look that gold has. It was hard to withdraw one's eyes from. It might have had a life of its own, with a consciousness of what men would do for it. *"Muitos,"* Tonio murmured with a sweep of the arm to encompass our surroundings. *"Muitos!"* He spoke not as a vendor talking up the value of his wares but as the sharer of a solemn secret concerned lest its portent not be grasped. His face purified by privations, like a saint's, I could have believed as we knelt there side by side that he was pledging us to some exalted purpose. I stood up, and after restoring the little bag of gold to the safe, Tonio did so too. *"Temos os planos,"* he said.

After we had separated for the night, I stood by the window in my room for a spell looking out, though I was tired. The night was very dark. Only a few stars were visible; the rest were obscured by clouds, against which the demarcation of sky and woods was lost. Tonio's invocation echoed in my ears. "Much . . . Much!" Even more alarming than the first appearance of the two men—and the sound of the third—was my dawning realization that they did not themselves know how far gone they were.

They had plans. I think I already suspected that unless he were carried out Tonio would never leave the Urubu mines until those plans had been achieved and that they never could be until an organization came in behind him with copious resources; Senhora Braga, erratic as she might be, had not been wrong about that.

The plague of doubts that had fastened upon me when I stepped off the launch had quit me entirely. What had happened to bring about the change I could not tell, but I had a feeling of the strongest kind that the country lying under the shroud of the night around me was waiting for me. Much, much gold was there; it was surely true. The expectation that had excited me earlier returned now with renewed force. I would master the Massaranduba through knowledge of it and make its compelling power felt as far away as New York—especially in New York. In pursuit of that knowledge I would not rest. I was going to show them! The more I drove myself, the more I had to endure, the more I risked, the more I could count on the favor of fortune; that conviction, still unthought-out, had returned too. It was a matter of propitiating destiny. The spectacle of the debility of the poor wretches I had just left gave me a more overweening sense of my own strength. It was for others to be sick and weary. I was—I felt it—invulnerable to ills, indefatigable, watched over by a special providence.

If I had to identify the first tremor of mental derangement in me, I should perhaps single out that moment as the beginning.

In the morning, by daylight, amid the stir of the camp, such as it was, what had seemed clear the night before seemed perhaps a little less clear. But my resolution was as strong as ever, and at breakfast, even before daybreak, I discovered that for one way of acquiring merit of the kind I had had in mind I should not have to look very far. I could starve. Tonio did murmur that new (and I assumed fresher) provisions were being fetched that morning from the launch. I could not see from the next or from subsequent meals, however, that they made much difference. There was mildewed rice with boiled weevils in it, and rolls made of moldy flour with centers of fetid beef. And that was what there was to eat. There were also tea and coffee, with *rapadura,* and these made life possible. The Bragas seemed not to care for *farinha* and no other

383

vegetable could be grown in this part of the Massaranduba Valley, I was told, because the *saúba* ants would defoliate the plants. (The manioc, or cassava, the source of *farinha,* was immune because the hydrocyanic acid it contained was deadly to ants, as to human beings, who could eat the roots only after the juice had been extracted and they had been cooked.) Observing no *saúba* ants in the area, I thought it would be worth while trying to grow something at the camp, such as bananas, but it appeared that there was a further obstacle. Even if the plants escaped the ants they would be eaten by the two bullocks kept for hauling supplies from the launch, and it was impossible to fence in an enclosure for the bullocks for the same reason that it was impossible to locate better, even if more distant, sources of provisions. The reason, which soon seemed to me a natural one, was that nobody had any thought or energy to spare from the mining of gold. So the fare was rice and rolls, and both tasted like a hole in the dank earth. For years to come any suggestion of their odor would turn my stomach, would put me for the briefest instant back where I had known it with a verisimilitude that would cause my heart to falter.

The scattered structures of the camp were made of roughhewn slats and had steeply-pitched roofs thatched with palm leaves, like the bungalow. The place resembled a collection of remote backwoods farms of the southern Appalachians except that the clearings were confined mostly to small yards and strips around which were still-standing arms or islands of the forest. Muddy paths led off to the workings. The camp had been sited to take advantage of the streams that fed through the vicinity into the Urubu. Along these, gangs worked at placer mining. At each location sluices had been constructed of a series of wooden troughs, called boxes, which carried water down from a high point of the stream, like a millrace. Gravel from the streambed was shoveled into the sluice and worked with spades so that it washed gradually away, leaving exposed any particles of the heavier gold or trapping them in grooved cleats filled with mercury. There were a dozen or so men to a sluice, all dark-skinned Caboclos in straw sombreros and loose-fitting white jackets and trousers, resembling conventional representations of Mexican peasants. All told, about a hundred were on hand at the moment, but Tonio informed me that the number fluctuated wildly and uncontrollably as the laborers came to make a little money and went off to live on it while it lasted—and to get back to their women. Few women

384

were to be seen in the camp. There were several, however, who seemed to lead a kind of shadow life at the bungalow, remaining in the background. Indeterminate in status, they were of an Indian type, small, rather squat, with straight bobbed hair, and eyes that I could make nothing of whatever. They appeared neither to shun notice, particularly, nor to expect to receive any.

There was a tank raised on wooden scaffolding to supply water for household use by gravity feed. There was a little store with a sleepy half-Chinese shopkeeper and a stock comprising two clusters of dippers made of tin cans, six fancy, stiff straw hats, two striped neckties, a few shirts, some chinaware cups, half a dozen firearms, a shelf of bottled condiments, matches and a few other comparable items. And there was the machineshop where Manoel and three young Caboclo assistants operated a big drill press, a forge and some power-tools, which worked off a gasoline motor.

The machineshop was where the future was being hatched, and if there was a question as to what kept the young owners holding doggedly on here with no comforts much above the minimum requirements of existence while their health failed and the mines, hand-worked by irresponsible, undependable labor, were surely not making them rich, the answer was doubtless to be found in the machineshop. For this was where the dredge was being fabricated. On the ground were lined up some twenty heavy, reinforced iron buckets, each about a cubic foot in shape and capacity. These were being joined with strips of iron at foot-long intervals, bottom of one to the top of the next, to form an endless chain which would revolve about two vertical sprocket-wheels, like a bicycle-chain, and be turned by an engine. The whole contrivance, of which part of the framework had been constructed, would be mounted on a scow and would dig its way up a stream, scooping up the gold-bearing gravel and dumping it on deck for washing, and creating a channel deep and wide enough for it to float itself in. There was a drawing of the completed machine on the wall and others of various parts. Manoel and his crew worked on it when they were not repairing tools or the sluice-boxes or one of the water-pumps, and Tonio, and later Jacques, would usually during the day find an hour away from the supervision of the gangs to take a hand in some part of it.

The pile of iron at the end of the shed from which the dredge was to arise looked to me more like the wreckage of a high endeavor than the matrix of one. I did not have the heart to ask how long the dredge had been under construction and how much longer its completion was expected to take. Everything was done at a retarded tempo, as if the medium of the air were as resistant to movement as water, and simple tasks required a marshaling and concentration of forces. Until I grew accustomed to the sight I had the feeling of watching inebriates coordinating with difficulty. Of the three white men Manoel seemed to be the steadiest, no doubt because he was the most simply organized. In machinery he evidently found a complete life, a total fulfillment. It did not matter whether he was building a dredge or straightening a nail, he gave himself up to it as single-mindedly as a dog with a bone to bury or a scent to investigate—as indeed the terrier he resembled. Outside the realm of machinery he referred all uncertainties to his employers with confident, unquestioning mien.

Did they see themselves, I wondered, investing all the pitiful scrapings of their energies in that dredge only to have it thrust aside, disregarded, by the abundantly-equipped American engineers? What did they think would befall when the Corporation took control? The truth was that any change in the present dispositions other than their having equipment they now lacked and the ordinary amenities was beyond their apprehension. The outside world had lost reality for them. The politeness with which they gave ear to what I tried, at the beginning, to tell them about the turbulent political currents swirling about the Massaranduba and about the complications in New York only concealed—or emphasized— the difficulty they experienced in keeping their minds on it. Tonio went about giving his attention to what required it with an air of one remote from the sordid commonplace, so that one expected from him utterances of an elevated or metaphysical nature, though what he said concerned almost invariably the problems and prospects of the Urubu mines. Jacques, when he emerged, was not much different. He was a few years older than Tonio, with heavier-lidded eyes and a less finely-formed face and perhaps given over more to the day's business and less to a hypothetical future. Tonio, anyhow, seemed to be the curator of the collection they had of clippings, mostly from trade journals in the heavy-equipment field, illustrated with photographs of steam-shovels and clamshell diggers, ore-crushing stamps, ten-ton trucks, monitors menacing as coast-artillery guns, which they visualized as being someday at work in their surroundings. However, Jacques as well as Tonio liked to mull over

386

them in the evening when we were not going over the records of production and various assay reports. They seemed to believe they had only to excite my enthusiasm for the equipment and it would be as good as on its way.

How, I asked myself, did I know they were not mad? They looked mad, though in a holy or ascetic way, and they sounded mad when one or the other was in delirium, babbling and sometimes sobbing or crying out excitedly, and their expectations of being handsomely seconded but left on the whole undisturbed by the American mining concern that would buy them out (*"Tu vois, mon vieux, que nous connaissons le territoire et les problèmes"*) seemed to me mad too; indeed, I was forced to conclude that I should be betraying them if I got them to sign the power of attorney and condemning them to death if I did not. . . . But they were producing gold. Maybe that was as good a test of sanity as any. There were three of the little silk bags in the safe waiting for one of the brothers to take to Topacindo on the next trip of the launch, and a couple of dozen small lumps of amalgam of gold and mercury to go with him also to have the mercury distilled off and the gold recovered.

While I was engaged in fixing the topography of the camp in my mind and on paper, I came upon a sight that left me feeling sick. Two vultures rose from a mound in a cleared space on the outskirts of the camp, which proved to be a refuse dump. On it I found the head, legs and some offal from the goat that had stood gazing ahead with gem-bright eyes from the prow of the launch.

It took me less than two days to cover the ground at the Urubu mines as well as I needed to, roughly mapping the streams, locating the workings on the map, photographing them, correlating the production records with them. That left me free for the operation I was in a fever of impatience to begin, which was to explore all I could of the area of the Concession. The map I had of it was back with the papers Monteiro had sequestered, but the Bragas had one of equivalent coverage, though if anything it was even sketchier, and I made a copy of this.

When Tonio heard my plan, which was to trace the main streams and exposed reefs as far as I was able, he insisted that one of the Caboclos of the camp accompany me throughout for safety's sake. I saw his point well enough but I wanted no one with me growing tired or bored or watching me teach myself to apply what I had learned of the principles of prospecting—or intruding in what was a matter between me and the

387

country of the Massaranduba. I circumvented the injunction as one may circumvent nearly any—by progressive minor violations, presenting no clear-cut occasion for making an issue of it. I began by announcing that I was going only *um pouco* up the Iguarapé das Vacas, which ran through the camp. That afternoon it was *um pouco mais*. It was no time at all before I was off on daylong expeditions with only short-lived objections from Tonio. I was always very particular, however, to draw on the map the route I meant to take, and keep to it, so they would know what direction to follow in looking for me if I failed to return. I also agreed to carry a weapon from the camp's arsenal. A short-barreled rifle, it was a nuisance to lug along, burdened as I already was with a machete and a mineralogist's hammer from the camp's stores, stuck in my belt, and a pack, but even if I did not take seriously the notion of using it to defend myself if I were threatened by any of the wild Indians who came occasionally into the area from up the river (usually minding their own business, it appeared), I was well aware of the value it would have for signaling if I broke my leg. To begin with, my pack was only a little sack containing some meat-centered rolls, tea and sugar, a tin cup for boiling water, a pan for washing gold and a hand-sized washing-trough, slung over my shoulder. Later I carried on my back the rubberized duffelbag from Topacindo loaded with my hammock, a sheet of light duck to spread as a shelter from the rain, a change of clothes for when I got soaked and food for two or three days. It was not long after Jacques was on his feet again, frightening as well as pathetic in appearance with his tangle of hair, stubble of whiskers and sepulchral eyes, that I started going off for distances too great for me to be able to make it both ways in a day. That was one reason why I never got to see very much of him. The other was that he left on the next trip of the launch to take the output of the mines to Topacindo. To put aboard the riverboat there along with his box of gold-dust and amalgam, he took also three letters I had written. One was the usual periodic report to the *Interventor,* another a note to Monteiro in which, since the letters were going into the open mail, I could say only what I was prepared for the *Interventor* to know I was telling his enemy—little more than that I was well and proceeding with my investigations. The third was to Mr. Willet giving a detailed report of all I had so far learned that made the Massaranduba a glowing prospect. This last, I should have been upset to learn, was to impress its readers as much by its extravagance and eccentricity of expression and occasional incoherence, even indecipherability, as by the information it contained.

By that time I was well on the way to dementia. It was a gradual process, a slow erosion of all the faculties but those that bore upon my quest. I did not become wholly irrational. It was only that my rationality became narrowed to my obsession. Outside its narrow focus everything merged into obscurity, like objects in the darkness outside the concentrated beam of a light; I did not even remark upon their loss. I was achieving what I had said I was going to achieve.

The Bragas had ceased to question my comings and goings. It would hardly have occurred to them to do so. I was beginning to know more about the country than anyone else at the camp. I had been where nobody but Indians, so far as was known, had ever been before. And that was only part of it. I had gold to show, gold enough to silence anyone it was shown to. I had gold-dust, gold nuggets in rocks from streambeds, buds of gold in fragments of quartz hacked from reefs. In the end I was to have gold from the headwaters of the Urubu, from the Rio dos Tigres, from the Rio Tabará, from the Rio da Mulher da Tristeza, from streams I named myself. All the specimens were properly segregated and labeled as to origin. (I was neat and precise and methodical, not at all as might be expected of a person so far out of his mind.) I had, said Tonio, an *afinidade* for gold, and I believed him. He had looked up with searching eyes from the spoils of my first notably fruitful foray when I had laid them in front of him and before speaking had passed his tongue over his dry lips.

It never occurred to me any longer to wonder if Tonio and Jacques were insane. Their mode of life, if I thought about it at all, seemed to me conservative and confined, in every respect a necessary concession to their state of health. I was constantly on the move. It was beyond my power to stop. I was driven to it by a machine inside me that never rested. Whenever inaction was forced on me—while I lay awake at night in the bungalow after having had to come back for provisions, while I waited for a turn in the weather during a heavy rain—there came continually before my eyes the rippling of water over sparkling sands where the gold grains lay and the gleam of pyrites in a pale quartz reef leading how far no one knew, containing no one knew what quantities of the sovereign metal. I had taken my belt up two notches and the seat of my trousers hung baggily, as I noticed when I reached for my knife in my hip pocket. I must have looked like a fugitive from a posse when I came in from the woods showing the cumulative effects of constant exposure to the elements, unshaved for three days, famished. Most of the time I think I was running a low fever. It was nothing to compare with the Bragas' when they were having one of their bouts, but it had me talking incoherently in my sleep, or so they maintained.

Said Tonio one morning after Jacques's departure, when I had been there several weeks, *"Qui est cette Elaine? Une charmante fille? T'amie?"* I asked him what he was talking about. *"Tu as crié ce nom pendant la nuit,"* he said. I replied, *"Eu não conheço nenhuma Elaine. Cela va montrer que tu as écouté le bon Manoel—tôdas as noites."* He wagged his head. *"C'était toi, mon ami. Demands a Manoel s'il n'avait pas tu écouté. Um grito do coração."* Tonio spoke mildly, as indeed he always did, and his brother, too, and merely teasingly, but it irritated me to be accused of uttering in my sleep—and as a "cry of the heart," no less—a name that meant nothing to me, associated with no one I could remember. *"Du café, s'il vous plaît,"* I said. We were sitting at the breakfast table, which was covered with a white cloth; all meals were served on a tablecloth. I was aware of the danger that my irritation would flare up. He accepted a cigarette I offered him from my dwindling supply, and I lighted one myself with my coffee. I said to myself that I was annoyed because I had been having bad dreams and did not like to be reminded of it, especially since they were beginning to seep through into my waking consciousness, too. *"Como?"* said Tonio. I looked up at him inquiringly. He was regarding me as one who has been addressed but has failed to hear. I had evidently spoken my thought aloud. I smiled. "I'm beginning to talk to myself," I said. *"Começo a falar comigo,"* I repeated in a louder voice.

It was at the end of this conversation or during the next that I learned that the mysterious Joaquim Waldo had preceded me at the Urubu mines. I wondered why I had not heard of it before. Nothing in my position gave me a right to interrogate Tonio on the subject, but I suppose he could see that I was interested. He volunteered that the visitor had come in his own launch with four men in his party, two from Topacindo, one from a village on the lower Massaranduba, one from the upper river, a civilized Indian; that he had stayed only three days, asking questions and looking; that he had been curious about the time of my expected arrival; that he was a big man and blond, "like a German," though he was Brazilian, and not talkative. Tonio's interest in the matter seemed to wane at this point. I was standing at the window. I could just distinguish the outline of the forest against a sky that looked as if it were going to be grey. As for Joaquim Waldo . . . I turned back to Tonio and said I had heard that he was very close to the *Interventor*. Oh yes, he replied with evident surprise that there could be any question of it; it was with a mission from the *Interventor* that he had come. Monteiro, I went on to say, had never heard of him, and we had wondered what his *environs* were. Yes, yes, said Tonio; well, he came from Minas Gerais, he worked there for a Canadian company—the Toronto and Rio Grande Mining Company. Tonio had picked up his coffee cup, found there was nothing more to drink in it and was sloshing the dregs around in it. His mouth was half open to speak; he evidently had more on his mind. He then came out with it. I could comprehend little of what he said, although, after commencing with reluctance, as I thought, he finished by seeming anxious for me to understand. I had to get him to go over parts of it several times. At length I believed I had it straight. The Canadian company had been watching the news about the Massaranduba. Senhor Waldo, with the cooperation of the *Interventor,* was reporting to the company all the information he could obtain. He believed the company would apply for a concession covering about the same territory that my principals were considering. The *Interventor* was very desirous of their doing so. However, he wished not to have a public disclosure of their interest made until a time when it would be of greatest effect, which would be at the end of the month. Tonio and his brother had had to respect Senhor Waldo's confidence and say nothing of it until it was certain that I should not be returning until the next trip of the launch, which would not put me in Topacindo before the twenty-eighth.

This was important, I said to myself, more important than the question of whether it was going to rain. I asked Tonio if the Canadian company were also interested in purchasing his family's property. He replied that Senhor Waldo said it was. I had noticed that he and Jacques had seemed not very keen to pursue the subject when I had brought up the matter of their signing the power of attorney.

The full relevance of all this rolled in upon me. This could affect very much my prospects in the Massaranduba. This was serious. What I thought was: first, Senhora Braga's signature on the power of attorney

391

would preclude the sale of the property through anyone but Monteiro for three months; second, I must on no account fail to return with the launch when finally it got back here or to make connections with *Sabiá* at Topacindo; third, I must keep going as hard as ever in order to make the province of the Concession, in a way that made sense to me at the time, mine. I decided I had better encircle on the calendar the date of the launch's expected return, but when I went to do so I found I had already done it.

Tonio had picked up his notebook in preparation for starting out on his rounds, but he paused. *"Je n'aime pas beaucoup ce Monsieur Waldo,"* he said.

"J'espère," I replied after a moment, *"je suis confiant . . . qu'il ne sera pas nécessaire . . . pour vous depender sur la companie canadienne."*

That is my recollection of a scene I know took place. But my memory of those days is hazy, groping and uncertain. A very long time was to elapse before I had the slightest desire to remember them. And then, if what one reads is true, a concussion of the brain will efface the memory of the past precedent to it, the principle being that the worse the concussion, the longer will be the period effaced; and perhaps the blow need not be physical to produce that effect. I close my eyes and I see little but what I saw when, at the Urubu mines themselves, I was prevented momentarily from obeying the monitor inside me that goaded me to be afield. There comes back to me the sight of those clear streams and the sound of their murmuring, as of secret, barely audible voices, and the sight of the ridge-crests disappearing into the trees, leading ever on, and the sparse spatterings of sunlight, like gold, on the forest floor. It is no wonder. Day after day for weeks, apart from brief stopovers at the mines, I saw little else.

Branches of leaves reached out always over the stream, like hands held out over a warming fire. Where the vegetation was not too thick I walked beside the stream. Sometimes, when it was not too deep, I walked up the stream itself, which the tennis-shoes I wore made practical. When following the stream was impossible, I took to the ridge. Walking was usually easy through the dry upland forest, and getting back to flowing water was only a matter of going far enough straight downhill. I had good excuses to follow the ridges. The ridges went straighter than the streams and were easier to walk at a steady pace, which made estimates of distance more accurate. This in turn simplified the task of following my progress on the map and filling in topographic details and the locations of my finds. Moreover, to discover the extent of the reefs was important, and my object was to take with me when I left the mines as full a collection of samples as I could transport, to which end I brought back with me from every expedition as many as I could. In all this I was as meticulous as a miser. But the reefs were less exciting than the streams. Even quartz rock rich in gold usually reveals none to the naked eye, and there is no easy test for the presence of the metal; pyrites may make it appear that gold should be there and may look like gold themselves, but they prove nothing. I did, however, find visible gold in the reefs far oftener than I had any right to expect. I found it, I was convinced, by clairvoyance. As I explored a reef I would seem to see gold; a warmth of expectation would be kindled in me. I would drop to my knees and pore over the rocks around me, combing them, scratching away detritus and leaf-mold, avid and possessed as a dog on a freshening scent. I should put the sense of premonition down to imagination overstimulated by fever, hunger and monomania were it not that I did find gold—not always but often enough, remarkably often. Perhaps the explanation was that gold in detectable concentrates occurred in certain formations which, with heightened faculties, I came to recognize unconsciously. Perhaps the quantities of alluvial gold I turned up could be similarly accounted for. Alluvial gold occurred simply wherever the flowing water had let it come to rest, for the time being at any rate. But it may be that the character of the bottom, its configuration, was a determining factor. Even in my conscious mind I was aware that my scourings were likely to be much more profitable where the stream poured over a shelf of rock, probably because where the gravel was deep most of the gold must lie buried, accessible only by dredge. The presence of gold in the streams was important not only in itself; it was evidence that reefs in the watershed were gold-bearing, for these were the origin of the alluvial gold. Gold-dust and free nuggets or nuggets in smooth pebbles could have come a long way, tumbling down the watercourse in the eons of geological time, but gold in bits of rock not yet rounded with wear was likely not to have come far, for the crystalline rock yielded to the abrasive and fragmenting action of the stream where the dense, malleable gold did not.

The process of panning tried my patience. A double operation of swishing out the coarser material with the big pan, then more carefully washing the finer pay-dirt in the small wooden trough was necessary to the salvage of gold-dust, and it was time-consuming and tedious. I relied mostly on finding nuggets that came to light earlier in the procedure or, where panning had showed a section of streambed to be promising, might be located without panning, by quartering the site on hands and knees and scrutinizing the bottom, raking over the pockets of sand and gravel and trying by urgency of desire to detect the presence of the metal. I had a habit of crying out—actually it was more a grunting exclamation—when I saw the glint of a small bean of gold. I tried to control the habit, for the sound, breaking in on the stillness, affected me disagreeably, but I was always so intent on the search and so pierced with exultation by discovery that the cry broke from me unaware, jarring on my nerves and giving me a repugnant picture of myself grubbing naked in the streambed like a rooting animal.

The consequences could have been far worse than mere unpleasantness. Once in response to my unwelcome exclamation I heard a sound from the forest nearby, or must have, for I looked up and beheld an Indian standing perhaps seventy-five feet away, arrested in the tense, knee-flexed position of one suddenly and powerfully startled. He stared at me in wide-eyed astonishment, as I must have been staring at him. He was almost as naked as I, wearing only a short apron, probably of woven fibers, and, on a cord around his neck, carrying a quiver of arrows for the dark brown bow he held, which was a third again his own height. He was of a beautiful color, the color of tawny autumn leaves with the sun on them. He had black hair that fell around his shoulders, a lithe build proportioned to his small height and fine features. He looked more like a figure from an ancient Egyptian tomb than the type of Amazonian Indian usually represented. But the picture I have of him is one that was left on my retina. While he was there I was numb to all but the peril I saw myself in; I took it for granted that he was not alone, though my quick glance to right and left disclosed no others. My eyes went to my rifle, lying by my clothes on the bank. So did his. We returned to staring at each other. Slowly I rose to my knees, and from motives that I suppose may best be described as those of an anomalous self-consciousness, grinned. He must have figured that I could reach the rifle before he could fit an arrow to the bow and let fly with it, or else his intentions were as unbelligerent as mine, for he took a step or two backward into the mottled shade and simply disappeared, so uncannily that until I crept forward, rifle in hand, every nerve protesting that a pack of whooping savages was about to fall upon me, and examined the place, I could hardly believe he was not still there. I dragged my clothes under the shelter of a bush and, sitting down just as I was, smoked the stub of a cigarette I had forced myself to extinguish in the middle two hours earlier.

As I looked back on it, the encounter, beginning without preliminary, terminated without aftermath, might have been an accident of time, bringing me into juxtaposition with a figure of a thousand years ago or a thousand years hence. I told myself that of course this could not be so and that I must be more cautious hereafter and watchful for more than the gleam of the master-metal, but the resolution proved difficult to maintain in the face of the seeming emptiness of those woods which, whether real or imagined, impressed me to the point of preying on my mind so that at times the sight even of an Indian or a boa constrictor would have been welcome as showing that the emptiness was not a purposed one.

I knew, without dwelling on it, that the passion I had contracted for turning up proof of the quantities of gold in the area had transformed me into a person whose ways I should not have recognized. It seemed entirely reasonable to me that I should be as I was, however. I was making the most of the time I had. It was for the Massaranduba Concession that I was doing it, for all those whose fortunes hung upon it. It was for my own future, which I saw as destined to be here—where I was successful. I was one who *"tem tido sorte nas suas descobertas,"* as Manoel said, curling his upper lip under his moustache in his terrier-grin and looking to Tonio for confirmation; I was fortunate in the search for gold. I hunted gold *"com absoluto succeso."* That was it. My qualifications would be indisputable, concrete—solid as gold. I was achieving a success in a way the world could understand, could not disparage. I was proving myself a success in the primal meaning of the term. There could be no doubt of it. There was the gold! I could have conceded that anyone whose quest for gold was rewarded as mine was could not help coming under the metal's sway and yet not have granted that this was what counted in my case. The gold, I said, was only incidental to my object, which was to be able to speak for the territory as no one else could.

There was surely no question about the driving incentive I felt to encompass as much of it as I could. I could think only of going on and on,

395

hurrying in order to give myself time to ferret for gold; I chafed under the necessity of returning so frequently to the camp. It was not the need for replenishing provisions that brought me back; I had become fairly adept at spearing fish, using a trident-head Manoel had forged for me, modeled on one I remembered from the American Museum of Natural History; this I could carry in my tin cup and fit on the end of a pole when I needed it. (The fillets I cut from the fish and stewed with rice in the cup were not very tasty but they were nourishing.) I had to touch base at intervals if I were to be sure of not having to wait till I starved in the event of an accident before someone set out to look for me.

The craving to keep pressing the quest was hardly touched by fatigue. It would be stirring in me even while I sat leaning against a tree, tired out, stiffness settling in my limbs, and the rain roared in the trees and pelted the duck canopy over my head.

I would erect the sheet in the form of a lean-to when it seemed that a downpour was coming up and gather some firewood. If dry kindling was lacking I used the emergency supply I carried in my pack, drying out some more pieces over the fire before I went on. Hot tea and a rationed cigarette were all the solace I could have asked for. The tea seemed to steam out my chronic fever, so that for a while I no longer felt my heartbeats at the back of my eyes, and I had found a kind of aromatic foliage that on smoldering embers drove off mosquitoes and *pium* flies. But I suffered from the inaction and the thoughts that came with it.

Even while I told myself that I was only proceeding very sensibly to cover the ground as well as I could and accumulate evidence of what they were looking for in New York, I could not hide from myself my expectation that if I kept on going I would find something, something special, something I had not found so far. And what would it be? Was I looking for some monumental accumulation of gold which I could scoop up in my hands and let trickle through my fingers, bouncing with ecstasy like a baby in its bath? The diamonds and emeralds there was reason to believe lurked in these streambeds? Or was it that I thought if I kept on going in deeper I should somewhere come upon what lay behind the silence and emptiness that oppressed me, at times put my nerves on edge—something that withdrew before me?

I went all the way to the Massaranduba River on a trail from the mines, setting out so early I had to carry a lantern to begin with, caching it later—the first person known to have walked it in a day. The banks of the Massaranduba, on which I spent the next day, were not lifeless. There were flocks of *maracanas*—green conures with red patches under their wings—tanagers, *japims,* kiskadee flycatchers, and in one place butterflies in such numbers, variety and brilliance that they seemed explicable only as a supernatural visitation. There was also—what ordinarily would have enchanted me—a procession of twenty or thirty monkeys, pale brown in color, which flung themselves from tree to tree and scampered up the limbs, barely touching them in their flight. Where the trail ended at the broad river a clayey bank formed the shore, and from this the vegetation had been cleared, for a Caboclo village occupied the site, and the open view that burst upon one, the sudden spaciousness of the vista, the ocean of light and sweep of sky and water alike aflame with the colors of the sunset, was staggering. I had emerged from the fastnesses of the country, I thought, instead of penetrating farther into them, as I was always set upon doing. But while this was true enough, I was not sure that it explained the sense I had of something lacking when I looked at the birds and animals to be seen on the river. It was as if they, too, were touched with the emptiness I had come to be so conscious of around me.

I had been followed to the river's edge by most of the settlement, which consisted of about five families. My initial appearance had stunned the inhabitants. Another person of my coloring had been through here, I understood when they pointed to my hair and made gestures of a man coming from the river—Joaquim Waldo, no doubt—but to have such a phenomenon appear from the landward side, on foot, passed belief. Another fact I grasped was that men looking for gold and diamonds sometimes put in here and that the settlement supplied paddlers for their *montarias.* Very likely it was because of the consequent neglect of the settlement that fire-ants were taking over the place. In most of the weed-grown manioc fields the ground was upheaved by nests of the pests and rotted with their tunnels. The little demons looked much like our common red ants, but their stings were like injections of vitriol and in the vicinity of their fortresses they attacked without provocation. No kind of footstuff could be kept in the settlement except in baskets suspended on cords treated with some kind of repellent. I had to hang my pack on one of the cords, for I was prevailed upon to spend the night

397

there—a mistake I did not make a second time. I was told the settlement might have to be abandoned.

At the evening meal a rain of litter descended gently from the palm-thatch overhead where the roosting bats were being aroused to activity. The *pirarucú*—the giant fish of the Amazon basin—which with *farinha* made up the fare, was so rank that even I found it unappetizing, and long after dinner I was kept in audience, a sovereign imprisoned by the attentions of his subjects, who sat all around me, plying me with questions most of which I could not understand no matter how insistently repeated and discussing me among themselves with sparkling eyes. The session went on and on, and while having to preserve a polite demeanor I grew more and more frantic. Mixed up in my frenzy, boosted along and accentuated by it, was my concern that I had had no time that day to pan for gold; there was always a conflict between my impulse to find gold and my impulse to explore farther. Before I was freed I was hanging on by my teeth to keep from bursting from the house.

Having ascertained that it was possible to proceed up the river on foot, I escaped with first light in the morning. I marched along the river for four hours but saw very little of it, for the trees that bordered it were shrouded in the leaf-shingled skeins of creepers, impenetrable to vision as to light. Behind them I walked in a gloom even more sunless than the forests I was used to. The largest break in the wall of foliage came where a broad, shallow stream tumbled into the river. It was by this stream that I saw the butterflies. Myriads were thronging the sandy banks of the stream, alighting daintily and showing patterns of colors beyond human ingenuity to have devised. I wondered what had drawn them there. Then I had one of my sudden insights. I rushed forward heavily, scattering the dancing host, and flung off my pack. In a half hour's panning I had a respectable pinch of large-grained dust. It was apparently a rich site, and I was able to make a notation on an otherwise blank section of my map. My hands were trembling.

I decided I had gone as far as time allowed when I came to a place where the Massaranduba ran through a gorge. On either side upthrust rocks raised above the squat palms at their bases had the air of ruins, as if here had been an ancient city of the jungle, its walls long since breached by the wild, dark flood of the river and its inhabitants fled. The rocks commanded a view of the river, and on a shelf giving protection from the breeze I laid a fire for tea and prepared to have something to eat. I was about to touch a match to the shavings under the kindling when my eye was caught by a movement in a tree upriver. What looked like the shadow of crisscrossing branches was a spider monkey, an unbelievably attenuated fellow, like a child's stick drawing. With arms outstretched, clasping the branch overhead, tailtip wrapped around another branch and one leg dangling, he squatted on a limb of a tree, regarding me with eyes that even at fifty yards were mirror-bright. I blew out my match to watch him. Abruptly he switched his attention to the ground below him—hidden from me by the rocks—craning his neck. Then he was off, sailing pell-mell through the treetops. I peered over the rock just as a dugout canoe shot out into the open water. It was propelled by three Indians, men with lank black hair falling forward as they bent to their paddles. Their faces were painted or tattooed with black lines and squares, and their naked, smooth, chunky torsos were almost terra-cotta-colored. And the strength they had! The paddles of the Caboclo rivermen, whom I thought of as semi-aquatic, were toys compared with those wielded by these Indians, which for size could have been made from the tops of oil drums. The heavy dugout flew forward, slicing across the swift current; it seemed not impossible that those rhythmically straining paddlers would lift it right out of the water.

It came to me, with the impact of a thought which had been clamoring unsuccessfully for attention, that this was actually happening, and to a flesh-and-blood me. Perceiving that those fierce-looking boatmen might turn downstream and round the promontory which hid me, I made a dash for the forest, bent double. They did not turn, however, and I saw them no more.

As nearly as I could tell at the distance, they had had the same rather flattish features, narrow, slightly tilted eyes and short-limbed, stocky figures as the young women who led an unobtrusive existence at the bungalow. I was reminded of the similarity when next I was at the mines and was accorded a kind of recognition by one of the three I had not had before, and should as soon not have had again.

I had come in after dark the following day by the light of the lantern I had hidden on my way out. Tonio was down with malaria. He looked up from his hammock at anyone who came in, his eyes full of the horrors they told you he had been witnessing and with fear and pleading in them lest the newcomer prove to be another one. He threshed about and did not at once recognize either Manoel or me when we went in to him. We took turns applying damp cloths to his brow, wetting them from the urn in which drinking water was cooled by evaporation through the porous clay.

While Manoel was with Tonio late in the evening and I was sitting at the dining-table trying to clear my head of irrelevancies and overcome my weariness enough to write down some facts about the last trip, one of the three girls came in, approaching quite close to where I was sitting and surprising me; none of them had ever before been so forward when I was around. She stood for a moment in her waistless, pullover dress, which hung down from her breasts, and listened to the groans and mutterings wrung from Tonio by his delirium. Then she turned to me and smiled. Any smile occasioned by the wretchedness of another would surely seem to qualify as cruel, but this smile, which was to stay with me, was not that. The tormented sounds were simply, to her, funny—funny noises. She invited me to share the joke. There was no harm in it, any more than in a small child's pulling the legs off an insect. She expected me to grin in mirth over it, along with her—we two. Assuming an expression meant to be vague, I went back to the writing I had been doing. I raised my eyes again only when I heard her bare feet padding across the floor. She paused in the doorway leading to Tonio's room, looked back over her shoulder and smiled again. It was a different smile, but once more it was just for us.

No one could have missed the implication of her changed bearing: I had a tidy stock of gold in the safe; I was unprovided for as a man; Tonio was flat on his back and Jacques was away. My grasping it, however, seemed to me another instance of the uncommon lucidity of perception I was convinced I was possessed of at that time, must have been possessed of, I argued, to account for my success in detecting gold. (I fancied I was catching things by surprise at the edge of my vision. They came to me with preternatural vividness "from around corners," I told myself, and was so struck by the astuteness of the observation that I kept repeating the words to myself, like a monk telling his beads.) This new element in the situation made me even more than ordinarily anxious to get away the next day, but I doubted that I should go at all with Tonio as bad as he was and his brother away. By morning, however, the quinine Tonio had wolfed when he felt the attack coming

400

on had sent his temperature down and it seemed that he was recovering, as he vowed he was. So I set off as usual, only a little later.

I had gone less than a hundred feet in the woods when, hearing the scuffing of leaves behind me, I turned and saw her—the girl of the evening before. She was hurrying up the trail toward me. Finding that I had stopped to look at her, she slowed her pace. She advanced in an unhurried, idling way, walking from the hips, her eyes fixed upon me.

Clearly, I thought, it would be better for me to be off while it could still be imagined that I had not understood that her purpose was to overtake me. I turned again and walked on in the direction I had been going in, more rapidly, but with a distinct sensation of itching between my shoulder blades. Before I came to a bend in the trail that would take me out of sight of her, I could not help snatching another glance behind me. She was standing where I had last seen her, unmoving, stony-faced. Again I hastened on.

But I was not able to leave her altogether behind. A disagreeable flavor had been added to the medium in which I had my existence, which was not unlike a fluid in the way the visible world often swam in it and objects sometimes were difficult to pin down and I myself occasionally seemed to be in danger of floating. Also, the crudely-cast figure of the young woman kept coming back to me during the day, with a dogged vividness, as things would against the neutral and receptive background of that changeless and uncommunicative forest. I saw her stalking up the trail, conscious of the commodity she had to offer, sure of her ground. Repelled but unable to escape, I watched her approach with matter-of-fact and businesslike suggestiveness. Gross images came before me in which she inspected the gold she was earning even as she earned it. These were followed by others in which she had been sent to me as the embodiment of the emptiness around me, her embrace its instrumentality—that same emptiness that at the end of the day, after dark, made me sometimes feel unbearably alone, so that I would have to remind myself with the sight and touch of the gold I had garnered of what I was purchasing at this price. And I would build up the fire at such times, though at night, when it was burning bright, I liked to sit well back from it, out of the illumination it cast, watching it from a distance. A cup of tea never tasted better than then, or a cigarette either, smoked to the halfway mark in small drafts inhaled so deeply the smoke disappeared for good.

Heavy woods, so lightless the ground was largely clear of under-

401

growth, were notoriously poor in animal life, I told myself. It was apparently true even of equatorial woods. That was all there was to it.

There was not a complete dearth of living creatures. The buzz or jangling of insects was to be heard at intervals, and snatches of birdsong, especially where a body of water or a great fallen tree created a break in the forest. Or there would be scurrying sounds in the dead leaves, at a distance. But all would fall silent at my approach. However cautiously I crept up to the marshy fringe of a pool which the sunlight reached through a gap in the forest roof, the plunkings and gruntings of the frogs would cease. I was permitted to see almost no living things—except insects, and there were fewer of them than I should have expected. Birds fled before me. I ran after the sounds of four-footed creatures scampering from me, but I could not overtake them. Defeated, humiliated, I would stand looking after the animal, muttering a curse. The rustling would die in the distance and the silence close in again. If a cicada grinding away through the heat of the day failed to desist at the sound of my footfalls it was only because it was so high in a tree. I could heave a stick up into the branches to show it that it was not so far as it thought—*would* heave a stick at it—but my stick falling short, it would continue unperturbed, proving that it had calculated correctly the distance at which I would be harmless.

Then one day I was walking up a stream when a creature leaped from the water's edge into a growth of tall, fernlike plants that bordered it; I caught the merest glimpse of a tawny form. I could tell by the thrashing of the foliage that it was trying to scale the high bank beyond it. "Oh no you don't!" I cried, shaken with anger. With fumbling hand I snatched back the bolt of the rifle and slammed it home. "Not this time!" I threw the weapon to my shoulder and fired at the commotion. The crash was blinding, and faint repercussions sounded in the distance. Then all was still. I rushed forward. A small deer, no larger than a dog, lay on its side on the broken fronds, motionless, bleeding from a hole in its back. Its neck was extended and its eyes were open. It was alive. As I bent over it, it stretched its neck even farther, trying to turn its head away from me. One would have thought I had affronted it—only that— and it was averting its eyes, refusing to see me, concealing its wounded feelings. Then its uncomplaining brown eyes, half closed, were vacant, and it was dead.

I lay by the edge of the stream with my head in my hands, in horror and despair. *It shouldn't have fled,* I said over and over again. It was the creature's own fault! It shouldn't have behaved with me as if I were dangerous! If it hadn't acted as if it had cause for fear, it would be alive and well now. I would have poured affection on it, I would have shared my rice with it. I did not look up. I knew what I could expect to see if I did. The girl of *Boa Vista* would be standing there, regarding me as if she knew I was there but could not see me. She would be as real as the Indian had been who had appeared so suddenly and vanished so uncannily.

When I finally let my hands drop from my face, my eyes fell upon the largest nugget I yet had found. It was basking in a single arrow of sunshine beneath the wavelets of the stream. I lowered myself to my knees, that repugnant "Ugh!" of discovery still loud in my ears, and extended my hands to trap it, fearing, I suppose, either that the current or its own powers of transposition would carry it away. Neither did. It was irregular in shape, like a lump of chewing-gum, but bigger than any lump of gum I had ever seen. It was heavy in my hand. I was amazed at the gift of divination I seemed to have. I marveled at it, wondering if I had always had it unaware, if I could count on having it always.

I thought of staying and working the section of stream beside me; to be deterred by the presence of the little dead deer would be stupid. But I had in mind an area I had planned to reach by nightfall, so I picked up my gear and moved on, singing in a raucous, winded voice. It was better to sing, I felt, than to talk aloud to myself, though I had to brace myself not to feel shock at the sound of the first few notes. The practice made an advertisement of my presence, but in the vast extent of those woods the chance of meeting another trespasser was virtually nil, I was satisfied, having seen how little there was to bring anyone but a prospector to their depths. So I sang, though neither loud nor musically.

"*A vitoria há de ser tua, tua, tua, moreninha prosa!*
Lá no céu a própria lua, lua, lua não é mais formosa.
Rainha, da cabeça aos pes,
Morena, eu te dou grau dez!"

It was a way to keep my thoughts channeled.

The worst of it was that the solitude of the forest was a mirror to one's thoughts, a wall against which they rebounded upon one. The woods were alive with the contents of one's mind, like a moving tapestry of figures fading, looming . . . advancing, withdrawing. One was the prisoner of one's thoughts, physically enclosed by them. All around there was nothing but oneself. In the emptiness, as in a vault of amplified echoes, one's slightest product of mind was grotesquely magnified, was made to resound through the void.

Scenes of my childhood would come before me again and again. They were of episodes that hung isolated in my memory, unrelated to anything before or since, pictures of times when I had got out beside a train and walked along the tracks through grass and brush-growth loud with grasshoppers and had picked blackberries and smelled the hot, resinous needles of the long-leaved pines in the sun; when I had rowed out by myself across the river in front of our house to a tidal flat and the grunts of a croaker beneath the boat mingled with the slapping of the water against the bottom and the creaking of the oars in the locks; when with another youngster, a boon companion, I had bicycled to the end of the oystershell road that skirted the bluff and looked for Blackbeard's treasure where the wind-driven seas had exposed timbers long buried in the sand. These fragments of the past came back with an excruciating completeness of atmosphere, of sound and scent, and stirred an overwhelming nostalgia as for something lost. In some mysterious way she, the girl of *Boa Vista,* was associated with them. There would be the fragrance of pine needles or blackberry bushes hot in the sun or of the salt marshes, and I would see her. . . .

There were other things which I could only pray I should never see as I lay dying.

I sometimes thought of Dr. Salomão Mendoça.

The time when I was going to have to depart drew near. I had it in mind, as fixed and absolute, that I had to leave with the launch on its next call. The decision had been made for me by the imperatives of the situation. I doubt that I could have made it on my own, even at those times when all I should have been leaving was hateful to me and frightening. I could not imagine what quality existence would have when I was away from the territory of the Concession, no longer searching the streams for gold and tracing the reefs. Even the time I tarried in the camp, when I could not help it, I felt was being charged against me somewhere in an unforgiving ledger. There were the farther distances to

404

be gained. The thought of them kept some part of me awake even while I slept at night and preyed on my conscience like a commission only half discharged. All would remain unresolved at my departure, I thought vaguely, but compellingly.

It was almost dark when I returned from the next-to-last trip I had time for. The lamps were lighted in the bungalow. Knowing I could not find my way back by night, I had walked the last three hours without stopping, and I slipped my pack off as I entered the bungalow, dropping it just inside the door.

Sitting there near the table, which was already set for dinner, was someone who was neither Tonio nor Manoel. A stranger. A greater shock could hardly be imagined. There was nowhere for a stranger to come from—at least this kind of stranger. He was big, and he astonished me with his robustness. Of course there was Tonio for contrast, across the room. Tonio's growth of whiskers, though probably only two days old, stood out black against his clammy complexion. The man was fairish-haired but tan-skinned. He stared at me with as much surprise as I at him. What business had he, I wished to know, looking so damned mystified? Anyone would have thought that he was at home here and I the interloper.

Tonio, whose khaki shirt was dark-streaked either from ablutions or from perspiration or from both, made us known to each other. The newcomer, as of course I had realized by then, was Senhor Joaquim Waldo. He had evidently not been as perspicacious about me, however, for upon being informed who I was he looked more astonished than ever. A moment passed before he heaved up out of his chair. We stood facing each other, separated by the width of the room, neither being moved to step forward to clasp the other's hand. He spoke first—I suppose he felt he had to explain the way he had been looking at me—saying in a distant way, in English, that he had not known who I was, having expected a person more like the kind to be seen in a law-office; something of the sort. He smiled as if to make a joke of a comment that sounded invidious, but the smile was brief and unwilling, and disagreeable. His voice had an even tenor, and he spoke with a strong accent and much hissing of s's. I replied that I had not been in a law-office in a long time. We each turned aside from the other, with a conspicuous unanimity of impulse. I asked Tonio if he were feeling any better. He appeared surprised by the

405

question, and displeased. *"Assim bem,"* he said shortly, picking up from the table a small wrench of Manoel's. Excusing myself, I went off to clean up.

Joaquim Waldo was a man in his early thirties, powerful but not hard; he would turn corpulent in another ten years. He had a broad face, a nose short and curved, like a falcon's beak, and opaque, slightly protruding grey eyes. He peered as if he did not see well, but did not wear glasses. The idiosyncrasy may have been part of his slowness of movement. The impressions I received being chronically exaggerated, I saw him as an overgrown sloth and was repelled, even outraged. I suppose our aversion for each other would have been apparent to anyone. The circumstances that had brought us together would alone have set us at odds, but the difficulty I had in tolerating his presence, as if I were being cut off from the source of light and air, and he, I suspected, in tolerating mine, went beyond that. An animosity having an existence independent of us both might have been present like a slumbering dog ready to be provoked at a word. Perhaps it was a common awareness of this danger that kept us within the bounds of civility with each other. When during the evening I forgot his presence, as happened several times, my mind being suddenly elsewhere, and then again discovered him there, firmly and self-assuredly ensconced, as if it had been ordained so, I was irritated all over again. Discoordinate as my thoughts were, it penetrated to me that his return, given the kind of man he seemed to be, signified that he meant business. Well, let him, I thought, very satisfied with my magisterial philosophicality. Let him.

One compensation there was: we ate a great deal better than usual. Our visitor, who had arrived two days earlier, had brought supplies of food with him which he had been sharing; he could hardly have sat up eating his delicacies by himself. He rubbed his hands together when the houseboy spread canned beef, potatoes and beans on the table and brought in a small stalk of bananas, nearly gone. Pouting, he examined the display to see if any item might be missing. One was. After he had sent the houseboy back for it, it developed that there was even butter, canned butter. *Hi-diddle-um-cum, tarrum-tum-cum; through the town of Raaaaaamsey!* The nursery song kept bobbing up in my thoughts. As in a Wagnerian opera, it was the leitmotiv in my thoughts for Joaquim Waldo, wholly imappropriate.

I was sure Senhor Waldo would not have chosen to victual a competitor from his stores, and I did not enjoy taking his bounty, but neither of us could have refrained from doing as we did without making an open issue of our differences. However, I ate the minimum consistent with not making one—my capacity was limited at that time anyhow— and when, after dinner, he took some bottles of beer, *"tipo Pilsener,"* from one of several boxes he had called for his crew to bring in, I declined his offer of a glassful, which was harder than forgoing more food. He himself ate and drank more than the rest of us combined. Tonio constitutionally had little interest in food, and Manoel, whom Senhor Waldo ignored as if he were a menial, would have been prevented by his grinning diffidence from taking much of anything had not Tonio directed him to serve himself more generously and given him his own glass of beer, forcing the provider of it to open a second bottle. *"Come!"* —Eat!—the latter said several times to Tonio, leaning across the table at him, and later, *"Bébé!"*—Drink! Each time I could see a movement of Tonio's Adam's-apple, as if his throat were closing. He seemed slighter than ever under the visitor's brooding bulk, and ate with manifest effort. Said Senhor Waldo in one of his infrequent remarks to me—it was as if, in speaking to me, he had forgotten himself for the moment—"We have to bring some strength back to Mister Braga." He pronounced this dictum with satisfaction and translated it for Tonio, letting his gaze continue to rest upon him, as if he expected something to happen. Tonio flushed.

Another time he addressed me to ask if it were the case that I was leaving with the regular launch on the next trip, in four days. I replied that it was. He said that he would be leaving before me, then. He was, he added, going to "go up the river a little way" before returning to Topacindo. From his conversation with Tonio, I had gleaned the information that since his last appearance at the mines he had already been once up the river—the Massaranduba, it was to be assumed—and back to Belém. In connection with the latter there was some mention of the *Interventor,* at which Senhor Waldo could not help cutting his eyes at me. He looked at me so seldom I could only conclude that he was consciously avoiding doing so more often. When, my thoughts having strayed off to the scenes that had come so largely to comprise my world, a word spoken by one of the other two would bring me around, as if I had fallen asleep without knowing it and been dreaming, I would catch Senhor Waldo looking away just as my eyes would have met his. I could tell

407

that he was puzzled about me and curious, and that while he talked to Tonio it was I he was seeing; something in the corner of his eye betrayed him. He drummed on the table with his blunt fingers. All this made me more watchful of him. He had thin lips which turned in upon his small teeth, and their set indicated, I thought, that he was self-conscious and on edge—not as self-assured as I had thought.

I was very much aware that he had come up to Topacindo the first time in *Boa Vista,* but the question he could have answered for me I could not bring myself to ask. Once, though, during a silence at the table, it did actually come to my lips. "I didn't realize you were coming back here," I said instead, since he had noticed I had been on the verge of speaking. He looked from me to the doorway before replying; it was at this moment that the men came in with the boxes. He said then, with one of his smiles which looked as if they tasted sour to him, "The place has attractions for me. As it has for you."

Hi-diddle-um-cum, tarrum-tum-cum. . . . There was nothing joyful in the reiteration of the inherently sprightly little refrain. It was sinister.

The man described as the civilized Indian resembled the young women now in a back room and also the Indians I had seen in the canoe, having the same face sloping outward to the mouth. However, he had short hair and his face was unmarked, except for two vertical lines down each cheek, black but seemingly faded, and he wore a shirt and calf-length, ragged trousers. He looked at me—I could not conceive why— as one who thinks he has seen another person before and cannot remember where. His eyes were dull black, like a bear's.

With Senhor Waldo's pouring of the warm beer there comes a lapse in my memory. The impressions I had brought in with me from the forest, of scenes actual and illusory, were so indelible that what went on in the bungalow had the quality of objects glimpsed uncertainly at the bottom of a stream beneath the sharper, more brilliant images reflected on its surface. My recollections resume with Senhor Waldo's interrupting me with a question as I sat after dinner writing in my notebook. I had explored much of the country while I was here, was it not so? He spoke with a false, patronizing brightness such as an adult might muster up in dutifully engaging in conversation a child he disliked, in the presence of its parents. Although I had not been able to understand what he was saying to Tonio—had not even been listening—I had had the impression that he had taken a slighting tone with him, too. I could tell, moreover, that he had been boasting about the scale of operations of the firm he was working for in Minas Gerais. My eye caught by a sweeping gesture of his arm, he had turned to me and, slouching down in his chair and tilting back so that it creaked, said, "They don't play. When mountains are in the way, they move them." He had let his gaze sweep the room we were sitting in, a look of faint amusement on his face, and his voice, as he spoke again to Tonio, had been even flatter and more didactic than usual, unmistakably disdainful. Tonio had glanced at me as if to ascertain whether his humiliation had had a witness. Doubtless it was Senhor Waldo's policy to run down the value of the property.

That was why, when I had replied to his question by saying that I had been around a good deal, I added that I had been recompensed for my time, on the whole, and then, after having remained motionless for an interval under his speculative gaze, reached in my pocket and took out my prize nugget, which I carried as a talisman, and tossed it to him. It hit the table with the thud of a boulder. It was not in my interest to whet the acquisitiveness of rivals, but I felt a common cause with Tonio in the face of an outsider like this one. Tonio threw me a warm look.

It could be seen that Senhor Waldo, as he turned the nugget over and around in his hand, was engaged in a reappraisal. He asked in a voice calculated not to give the question too much weight whether I had found others like it. I told him that it was the largest but that the collection I had in the safe certainly— The end of the sentence I had embarked on went clean out of my mind before I could reach it.

"You have found much gold, you were going to say?"

"I've been fortunate."

He handed me back the piece. "Tell me this, Mr. Tate," he said. "Have you found much because there is so much here it cannot be overlooked, or because you have a secret of finding it?"

"*Como?*" Tonio demanded. "*Qual foi a pergunta?*"

They spoke briefly to each other. Said Senhor Waldo, "His opinion is that the country is rich in gold but that no one could find what you have found unless he had a special sense for gold. Is that true? Have you special sensory equipment?"

"I couldn't say," I answered. "I've been lucky. I don't know why." The uneasiness had gone from his manner. He looked over my shoulder, absently, into the distance, the corners of his mouth turned down. His eyes rolling over at me, he asked if I were going out again before I left, and as I replied nodded as if he had asked the question only as a matter of form and knew what the answer would be. I said I was, and had been about to tell Tonio what my plans were.

"Please go ahead."

There was a river of considerable size on the border of the Concession, flowing away from the Massaranduba, about which the Bragas had no information and which I thought I could just reach in the time available. I drew on the map the route I proposed to follow, which was not a complicated one. Senhor Waldo looked on. He asked how I could tell where I should be able to walk if I had never been there. "Well, it's like this," I began. Without remembering how I put it I pointed out that it was characteristic of the country that the terrain sloped up between the streams to a low ridge which one could count on being able to follow and that in this case the main possibility of going astray would be in crossing the divide between the Massaranduba system and that of the river I was seeking to reach—the Rio Ipaituba—but that there a compass would keep one on course, and the route would lie over high ground presumably easy to traverse. I had not been unaffected by his show of respectful interest.

"Are you not afraid, out there by yourself?" he asked.

"What of?"

"Indians . . . tigers . . . snakes . . . becoming lost?"

His delivery reminded me of what Cora had told me of theatrical agents and directors who test an aspirant by taking one side of a dialogue and throwing lines to him in a toneless voice.

"I carry a rifle. And the farther I go safely, the safer I feel in going farther," I said in accents approximating his own. I stood up. "I have to make an early start."

Back in my room, having told Tonio I should see him in the morning, including Senhor Waldo with a glance, I stood by the window smoking the half-finished cigarette I had brought with me—a Player's, from the same source as the dinner I had eaten. Afraid of what? I had asked. My bravado did not impress me. I would have to face it. That man, for reasons that were immaterial, confronted me with it. The truth was that behind everything I saw on my marches I saw also the juggernauts from Tonio's thumbed-over portfolio of machine-age marvels—the steamshovels, the hydraulic monitors. Had I not known long before I came here that the more I succeeded in what I should be trying to do, the

410

more certain it would be that the country of my exploration would be stripped to the bone, chewed up, pulverized, washed into the rivers and thence into the sea—league upon league of it? And that would only be the beginning. I could see the army of machines that had laid it waste, fueled by the profits, spreading out on all sides of it, engorging the lumber, rooting for minerals, leveling the forest for rangeland, for towns, for cities. On and on they would go, insatiable, never-ending. That was the specter that walked beside me as I strode the pathways of the forest, my urge to press on in pursuit of an ever-receding something that could free me of the logic of my actions serving only to implicate me ever more deeply in the enormity.

I felt hot and as if my head were not on firmly. The vision conjured for me was so real that for an instant I thought I was in it—again as if I had fallen asleep and were having a dream.

I took a last, deep, hungry draw on my cigarette and made an effort to collect myself. I had a return of greater lucidity—like a breath of cooler air coming in the window. Perhaps, somehow, it all might yet be taken out of my hands.

There was a knock on the door and Tonio entered. He came directly to my side and laid his hand on my shoulder. *"Tu tens visto! Tu tens visto!"* he said in a tense murmur. *"Que porco! Jacques e eu—nós assinaremos o teu papel."*

They would sign my power of attorney. The grip of the hand on my shoulder tightened.

411

17

There are times of reckoning when an event impossible to misconstrue opens one's eyes to all the little antecedent signs one has had of what was coming and seemingly has willfully ignored, these now tumbling into place like pieces of a picture puzzle to form a design of inescapable import. One sees it all—and it may even be that what one sees will suggest that it will be the last thing one shall ever see.

By dint of hard walking, by taking advantage of every moment of light, I reached the Ipaituba by noon of the second day, spurred on for the last half-mile by the sound of its waters and by an excitement that went beyond even the anticipation of discovery. Then, when I hastened out to its rocky bank and saw from beneath the overhanging boughs of the trees, fifteen or twenty feet below me, its black pools and rapids blinding white in the sunlight, I had a sense of my expectations being confirmed that was as unaccountable as the expectations themselves had been. Yes, this was it, I thought; and I had a sensation—I do not think it was something I imagined at a later time—of being led to go downstream, as it were by a gentle tugging at a psychic sleeve.

I had stood looking at the river only a short time when, for whatever reason, certainly not because I had heard any movement above the rush of the rapids, I swung around. The recoil of the heart at what I saw came before there was time for fear, was merely the shock of surprise. One after another I saw them: three Indians—three, but no more. They had been coming toward me, but now were halted. They were spread out, like game-beaters, perhaps a hundred feet away from me, not hard to spot in the open woods. They were of the terra-cotta-colored, face-painted kind—or two were, who were nearly naked. The other . . . the other was the Indian of the evening before, with the marked cheeks, the shirt and frayed trousers—Joaquim Waldo's Indian. I was ready to hail him. The cry was formed in my throat, it rang in my head. I almost thought it had escaped me. "Hey! You remember! *Amigo de Senhor Waldo!*" But the menace of the half-crouching, motionless figures, each with bow in hand, the enormously long bow of the small Amazonian Indian, had struck home.

Without moving their places the savages had relaxed, had straightened up. There had been a motion of the hand by Joaquim Waldo's man. The thought sprang to my mind that I had been recognized as not the enemy they had taken me to be. It was quickly dispelled. One of the naked ones slowly—ever so slowly, eyes on me, as if he were testing me out—raised his hand and reached over his shoulder toward the sheaf of arrows that just topped it. I thought, This is it. My mind had the bleak clarity of a whitewashed cell and the same chill of the ultimate pass in it. Its clarity extended back to Joaquim Waldo, and behind him to Colonel Durondo. I was to be murdered here, the American was to fall victim to an attack by Indians—a hazard of the *mato* beyond the Government's control. I slipped the rifle off my shoulder and, holding it tight in my left hand, took hold of the bolt with my right. My movements were as deliberate as the Indian's. As the Indian withdrew an arrow from the quiver, I drew back the bolt, slowly, as silently as I could. The others were waiting. I felt little but a constriction of the throat and skin; there was no time for more. I glanced down as I shoved the bolt forward to make sure the cartridge was going in true. . . . The clip was empty.

No! Protest surged up in me. The clip had been full the evening be-

413

fore I left, and I had not touched it since then. Natural laws had been subverted by a monstrously malignant power. It was a doom that had been passed upon me from a source beyond appeal.

The Indian, seemingly more confident, fitted arrow to bow. I saw other bows brought into position and I bolted for the cover of a tree. There was another clip in my pack—or had been. I snatched the pack from my back. There was a *whack* close to my ear, and a soft whine. An arrow had struck and glanced off the tree. I could see two of my assailants; the treetrunk was no protection. Abandoning pack and rifle, I made a sprint down the riverbank. At about the same distance from me as the Indians, I had noticed a projection of the bank extending out toward one of the river's pools. The slope of the projection, however, was a mass of rocks, and as I ran for it, picking my path ahead of me, my stomach was tight in apprehension of the consequences if my final leap fell short and failed to carry me across them or if the pool were shallow and I were dashed from a fall two or three times my height on rocks just below the surface.

I saw Waldo's Indian running to head me off. He had dropped his bow and had a knife in his hand, its long blade slicing the air as he swung his arms. He was fast, but had not the cue for speed I had. There was an expiring whisper and a blurred streak before my eyes—another arrow. Without slipping where a slip would have been the finish, I made the turn for the promontory well in the lead. The jump-off was a few feet from me. A slash of pain ripped my left shoulder, and I almost stumbled under the impact of the blow. An arrow, its force spent, tumbled end-over-end toward the water below me as with all my force I sprang from the brink. My eyes were closed as I fell, a sickening void where my stomach had been.

The knell of finality struck within me as a scalding pain shot up my leg; I had landed on the rocks! No—I went under. The leg was not shattered; it kicked for me as I struck out. I came to the surface already headed downstream with arms thrashing. The hurt in my left shoulder was like a tiger's claws holding me back. The arm was heavy and felt as if it belonged to someone else, but it operated as I swam with all my strength.

Then a force far mightier than any I could exert took hold of me— the river. I was snatched, spinning, into a chaos without up or down, and I knew nothing but the choking, blinding water which was racing off with me in demoniac triumph, plunging me into depths, tossing me into the white of frantic spray and, while I struggled to swim, foolishly as a bug in a maelstrom, speeding me toward terrifying black boulders. I was hurled upon them, warding myself off with my arms and striking them glancingly. I lost the sense of its being a mindless and mechanical river. I was being dashed to destruction in a stampede of raging fiends. Every second was my last; I went through death with each one. Down I went, in horror and panic, hysterical for air, my soul frozen in a silent shriek, rejected by whatever mercy was in the universe.

I was ejected out of the depths, reprievd for another doom, shot toward a cleft in the rocks in which a tree was lodged. I took the shock on my arms, and then, as they instantly crumpled, on my chest, had just strength enough, with the wind knocked out of me, to grab and hold on, to stay above water and get my breath. But the tree came gruesomely and obscenely to life beneath me, rearing up, and was pitched through the gap; I had dislodged it. Still I clung to it, my right arm around the trunk. It rolled over in the plunging current, but I came up beside it and held on. For the moment I could keep my head mostly above water and could breathe.

From what I could see of it as the log rose on the undulations of the water, the river was like a giant millrace, its current swift but with no obstacles to crash against or overleap. I held on. It took all my strength to do that. Whatever existed beyond the log was becoming as remote as myth. Only the pain I was in, the pain that I felt radiated from my entire body, was real. Even my body, apart from the pain, was unreal. It was like the shell of a cicada in which I constituted a single excruciating ache.

I had nearly lost sense of where I was when the log was checked in its course. The water was flowing past me. My feet touched bottom. A limb of the tree had gone aground. I was in a kind of bay or backwash, on the other side of the river from the one on which I had started. I set about the grim labor of plodding ashore. I thought of Frankenstein's monster essaying its first steps. I clenched my teeth and my fists and intensified my gaze to hold onto consciousness. I was tempted to faint as by an eiderdown bed. . . . There was a dark den of foliage when I came heavily out of the water. Into this I dropped. I was afraid to look at my shoulder, but made myself do so. I could not see it well, even when I had further ripped apart the rent in my shirt. What I saw was like a slice

415

in a piece of meat, however. The wet cloth around it was stained an anemic red. There was nothing I could do about the cut. The thigh of my right leg was raw on the outside. My body was in a vice of pain. I feebly wiped away with my arm the tickliness on my cheek and forehead. The sleeve came away smeared with blood. I raised my hand to my scalp, wincing at the touch of my fingers, cringing at what they encountered. Nausea knotted my stomach. I rolled over and lay prone on the ground.

My limbs were leaden. I was turning to wood.

I thought of the arrow and of the poison that would have been on the arrowhead: curare, or the infinitely worse, legendary secretion of a toad. That was why my muscles were freezing up. The paralysis would extend to my lungs and that would be the end. This was what it had all come to, all the wealth of possibilities, all the days and years warmed by love given and received, all trickling out in a corner of an inhuman wilderness where my weathering corpse would probably never even be seen, unless those assassins were at that moment hunting me down.

I remember no more until dusk except a sailboat on a choppy sea rocking lightly in a tempo rapid as march time, with sails bellying shallowly and collapsing to the same rhythm as it strained interminably and futilely to outdistance a pall of darkness overspreading the sky behind it.

Just before nightfall I came sufficiently out of a ferment of anguished dreams to know where I was and to take in the significance of being still alive. Among the swollen shapes of pain that pressed on my eyes there was, off somewhere, an elusive panorama of actuality in which objects had their true value, though it must have soon faded for good. While it lingered I managed to get up and move a few paces on my hands and knees down to the river's edge. In lowering my mouth to the water I fell forward, soaking myself again. Water to put out the fire, I thought; I was burning up inside. It took my utmost to regain my shelter before I was struck down by weakness, dizziness, stiffness and hideous pain, now pounding in my shoulder and head.

After that I am sure of nothing but pain and heat. I did not know when the night ended. The torturous delusions I suffered while stretched unconscious on the ground merged with those that pursued my later halting progress down the river, which itself was like the defeated wanderings I had endured in my head. Pain dominated both equally, pain which took the form chronically of machinery or transformed me myself into machinery; I was an engine of coiled and twisted pipes and

416

plunging piston-rods, of steel-hooped cylinders near the bursting point from pressure of steam in them.

As bad as the heat and hammering of the machinery was the goading, relentless, maddening reiteration of images and sounds. As I lay unconscious but with the illusion of hyperconsciousness, I was hounded by such things as gold-braided frogs on epaulettes that swung in on me like planets in their orbits, the hulls of ships that passed over me, faces I recognized or did not recognize that re-enacted the same play of expressions, phrases dinned over and over again into my ear out of invisible boxes—*Codfish eyes with red rims,* soon modified (it struck me as a tremendous but thankless improvement) into *Bloodshot codfish eyes.* . . . *Bloodshot codfish eyes.* And, *"In that case, the subterfuges would be superfluous."* This was uttered in a trial at law by one of counsel, but it was I who had originated it. It was intoned in a voice that, while not unduly loud, filled the universe, and it was repeated again and again. Like all the other things, it was devoid of meaning but freighted with portent, as thunder is. I was in a torture chamber being broken down by these repetitions, yet I was also being taken by them to the central meaning of life, as by the pronunciations of a jealous and loving God. With them were prolonged and cruelly frustrating ordeals in which I sought to accomplish some quite ordinary purpose, like keeping an appointment in an hotel or collecting a motorcar from a repair-shop in a gloomy factory district before closing-time. In each case successive trivial obstacles—a misplaced hat, the difficulty of putting through a telephone call—prevented my making any headway, balked me at every turn so that I grew frantic. Perhaps these interminable episodes were the signalings of an irrepressible memory of the importance of getting back to where I ought to be, back to the mining-camp, before it was too late. The realization even broke through to my consciousness. It may have been what aroused me, got me on my feet and set me lurching forward when I thought myself only just come out of the forge and off the anvil of my fabricator, heavy and stiff as ironware, burning-hot from the flames, head throbbing. But the direction I took was downstream. I do not know whether I was aware of it.

It was daylight. I could see where I was going as I limped to the water's edge to drink again, crouching painfully.

An absurdly-drawn butterfly was passing before me without movement of its parts. It was actually a little fairy with a wand and wings

417

ending in curlicues. (It was a figure, I think, from a screen or theater-curtain I was familiar with as a boy.) It swam before me for hours, it seemed; nothing could sweep it out of the way. Its triviality made its persistence a taunt. It was a spy, an agent of those who were trying to convince me that I had lost my mind. It sat in judgment and was the monitor of the penance I was performing.

I drank frequently from the river, easing myself down to it. The ground always tilted like the deck of a ship and threatened to pitch me into the water. But generally when I was thirsty I found I could not get to the river through the latticework of branches, or else when I did the bank proved to be too steep for me to risk descending it. These obstacles, I shrewdly perceived, were not fortuitous. I penetrated to their purpose. They were all part of a stratagem designed to deceive my understanding. But I was not to be taken in. I was gifted with all-seeing vision. I could see the pulse in the sky. It was only a person born under . . . under the something of the moon who could see the pulse in the sky, of which the poets made so much. It was an unusual sight. But it was not deeply impressive. It was like the heartbeat of a frog, as you see it when the frog is on its back. The sky was just the color of a frog's belly, and not much bigger, really. And there was the pulse, just a kind of squeezing and twisting, then relaxing, of a small area of the sky. My head throbbed in time to it.

I grasped at branches to steady myself and help myself along. Sometimes I caught hold of leaves—or what I thought were leaves, rough-textured leaves. But it turned out that I had stripped the skin from the member of some living creature and I dropped them and rubbed my hand on my trousers with disgust. . . . The sky had become a frosted blue bowl through which poured waves of light in a sinuous and unwholesome rhythm.

I was not alone in the forest. The treetrunks were living beings. There was a special name for them that would come to me. It would come to me. . . . Caryatids. One had only to look closely to see them. They stood there happily, murmuring to one another. They took no note of me, except that their eyes, as they swept past me, may have hesitated thoughtfully.

A grove of caryatids. That was what this was, and presumably it was the same elsewhere. It was strange that no one had ever noticed them, especially as the katydids had all along been insistently crying their pres-

418

ence. And what a different light our recognition of the handsome creatures in the treetrunks would throw upon everything! My discovery justified the trial by pain and fire I was going through. I was bringing truth back from the outer confines of human endurance. As a result of it everything would have to be reappraised. Hardly a branch of human knowledge would remain unaffected. A clamorous band of grey-haired scientists, many with grey beards, too, were demanding proof of the revolutionary claim I had made. They were not actually there, I knew, but it was the same as if they were. Then when I went to display triumphantly the truth of what I had announced, the caryatids refused to let themselves be seen. Only treetrunks were visible, and when I went from one to another, clasping them in my hands, I could feel only the unyielding wood. The caryatids were in there, I knew, but were disdaining me, abandoning me. "You'll have to come back another time," I said to the scientists with a wheedling smile. The nearest one sank his fingers vindictively, like a claw, into my left shoulder, and the pain bursting through me forced me to my knees. I could see myself from the outside through all this, standing back from it like a theatrical director and watching myself go from tree to tree patting the trunks imploringly. The scientist was like a gryphon.

Then a kind of knowledge struck me like an autumn wind, bending my thoughts over like trees. The knowledge was that I must get back to—where? It would come to me presently.

A hideous and monstrous despair and terror fastened on me in the depths of an illimitable thicket in which my entire life, past, present and future, was engulfed. Palm-fronds and vines, knife-edged, saw-toothed, bristling with thorns, barred the way in every direction. I sidled between them and crawled beneath them. Blood trickled down my forehead from the cut in my scalp that had been reopened. I was on the threshold of hysteria. The muddy ground beneath me and for as far off as I could see was sundered, and a loathesome and horrifying *sucurujú,* a water-boa, as big around as I, slithered away like a one-piece rubber train on a curving track. It was a relief, at first, when I beheld a procession of mourners in white cowls, with shepherds' crooks, passing in procession beyond the convolutions of vegetation in which I was being driven to frenzy but could not make a rash move without impaling myself. But the mourners only drove home to me the extremity of my plight. I called out to them but no words issued forth, only the guttural sounds of a

419

mute. Then I knew why they passed without a sign. It was I whom they were mourning. I was condemned; it had been decreed that I should be mourned.

The sun hung directly overhead, just above the leafy tops of the brush-growth, and it followed me, always immediately overhead, as I groped my way through the network of plant-stems. The air was overripe, too heavy to breathe. Although the earth was damp and oozing, there was no water to drink. Down on my hands and knees as I tried to scrape under a tangle of branches, it seemed suddenly easier just to let go, and so I did. The ground struck me, and I was jabbed in the chest. . . .

I was being worried, chivvied by wranglers who would not let me rest. They were preparing branding-irons before a fire. The heat of it was intolerable. I had to have water, I had to be dowsed with water. The flames were playing over me and my skin was dry as parchment.

My thirst, aggravated by the burning pain that was trying to wring me out, was more compelling than my weakness. I hitched myself up from where I had been lying with my cheek against the rank, damp earth. I saw that the sun had moved.

I was lighter than air but could not escape my body, which was heavier than ever. I was like a balloon weighted down by sandbags. There had to be a way to break loose, if only I knew what it was. If I could sever the bonds I should float up through the strangling vegetation and sail across the sky with the Aeolian beings, the echoes of whose cries filled my ears. But I was imprisoned in a body as ponderous as a diving suit. "I am suffering the penalties of death and being cheated of its peace," I protested. "Look into your heart," came the reply. Enigmatic, it yet filled me with contrition and foreboding.

Before me there was a field of dancing silver beyond the screen of leaves. Then I was standing on the bank of the river, I was dropping to my knees in the water, I was letting myself fall forward into it, gulping it, stumbling farther out into it and sinking myself in the poultice of its coolness.

There was a long walk when I had had my fill of the river, a succession of steps in sand and gravel, among boulders. I found it important to watch my feet, seem to have scrutinized them interminably, held by their resemblance to a pair of small animals leaping forth in alternate bounds, always there just in time to catch me before I fell.

I saw without surprise a white launch at a distance from me, close in-

420

shore. Sagaciously, as I viewed the evenly lighted pictorial scene, I said to myself, It's a cover of a magazine. If I knew which magazine . . . The all-important advantages I should derive from that information were so self-evident that the task of defining them would not be worth the effort. It would save me . . . from all this, I said. But in my throat was a lump of knowledge, big and heavy as one of the boulders around me, that that could never be.

The launch, growing larger, became the center of the scene as, weak-kneed and shaky, I was drawn toward it. There she is, I said. I felt in the last stages of drunkenness. The craft was wedged between rocks. Around the bow, which was sunk in the sand, water eddied. The free-board must have been quite low, for I found myself on board almost spontaneously. I deduced that the artist must be around here somewhere himself since this was clearly the model for the painting he was going to do rather than the painting itself. I walked along the narrow strip of deck past the cabin and found the door of the cabin, in the rear, standing open. In it I saw the man I expected to find. His eyes were as round as the peculiar steel-rimmed black button on the tip of his finger that he was pointing at me. I could see that I had appeared at the very moment that something had startled him but, looking behind me, saw nothing to account for it.

In my mind there appeared with the effect of a signal clarification, like lettering on the glass pane of an office door, the statement: "I am on my way to the Urubu mines. I have to get to Topacindo. Back to *Boa Vista*." There, it was out, I thought. It is quite possible that I said it aloud. But I was confused. And the validity of the scene had become questionable, for I could see that the grey-haired artist was a man I recognized. Yes, he was a man I had seen before. But how was that possible? A college professor of mine, if that was who he was, could not be in this place.

He had lowered his hand, in which I saw a revolver clasped. I lurched forward into the doorway and grasped the jamb, awash in a sea of weakness. There was a cry, not loud, though as delivered with all the crier's strength.

"He has come!"

And she was there!

In a corner of the cabin she was seated among some cushions, her bare legs drawn up beneath her. As I had seen her in my mind so many times, she had her hand at her forehead, holding back her hair, which

421

touched her shoulders. I gazed, lost, upon her slim, oval face, gazed incredulously, starved for the reality after all the endless vain imaginings. It was the face, at that moment, of one just awakened, the eyes dark and blurred with sleep not yet wholly dissipated by the light of surprise and recognition, a face open and eager but still a little veiled with remoteness. I was conscious of an extraordinary change of atmosphere, as if she had behind her not the narrow wall of the cabin but a landscape such as a portrait might have for a background, with a perspective of great distances and with wooded hills and meadows in the evening, as when the notes of a singing thrush carry across a quiet valley. The illusion told me the vision of her was unreal, as time and again it had been in the past, but I would not believe it, and started forward to grasp it before it faded. Even as I did so it was being borne away from me as on a platter. The scene tilted so that I lost my balance and fell, and was jarred savagely as I struck the side of a rocky cliff in falling. End-over-end I fell, recognizing myself as Lucifer tumbled from paradise in a picture I had once known.

The darkness was thronged with people, who jostled me. I was an obscenely distended figure, in appearance a structure of sausages, in actuality inflated with superheated air. It was a busy street-corner, but the crowd evaporated, and I knew it was much later than when I had last been aware of anything. A rumble, like the rolling of stones under a surf, was to be heard. It resolved itself into a human voice, a man's voice. I was prone on a floor of some kind, my head on some soft material, in an enclosure like an oven. There was a light in the place as of flame coming through a furnace-door, but steady, unflickering.

Then I saw the girl again. The orange radiance made a picture of her. She was reclining, half sitting, a few feet from me, her shoulders wedged in a corner for support. Her gaze was fixed upon a point at some remove from my head and above it. The rich light that fell upon her came somehow, I guessed, from a setting sun. From beneath lids lowered a little dreamily her eyes gave back the radiance from their hazel depths. Her skin glowed with a deep color, and the waves of her dark brown hair were lustrous with the fiery light. Her face was turned a little from the direction in which she was looking, as if she were somewhat withheld from that to which she was giving attention. I did not believe I had an existence in the scene, any more than a reader has an existence in a story, though the story may be more absorbing than anything he is

422

part of. The perfect being to whom my eyes clung was just such as the imagination might be led by art to create out of its own limitless longings, the quintessence of young girlhood, as intimately realized as a creature of the mind and as unattainable, as yearned for as immortality might be. She was just as I remembered her. Again there was that atmosphere about her of far distances illumined by the level rays of a newly-risen or sinking sun, and freshness in the air, as of dew, and the earth's fragrance. I only wanted not to be banished from it again, to have it go on, and into that yearning went all my soul.

"It is for his own good, too. It may be his only chance." The words issued distinctly from the direction in which the girl was gazing.

"Ellen!" I said the name aloud. I pronounced it as if I had hit upon the secret of everything, the answer to everything. She looked quickly at me, and this small action was to me tremendous in its import, as much so as a demonstration of the validity of a religious faith. We existed in sufficiently related worlds to communicate. As I raised myself to my elbow, then pushed on up to a sitting position, she followed my movements with, I thought, a little of the expression of a young mother watching a child essay its first step. Raising her eyes to mine, she gave a little smile. It was a smile of sympathy and reassurance, and more—the kind of smile that might be given across a crowded room, setting the giver and the recipient apart from all others on earth. Yes, it was a smile of *recognition*. But there was a sadness in it, or in its lingering disappearance. I noticed that the focus of her gaze seemed uncertain and that her head lay back against the wall as if it were heavy for her—then also that her hands, slim and tapering, were inert beside her, as if they, too, were too heavy to be moved.

"Something is the matter, you're not well," I said, though I could not be sure that I had spoken aloud. And she did not reply. She only let her gaze fall for an instant before raising it to the point at which she had been looking when I had regained consciousness. The reason was—the realization came to me—that the man was talking. I turned so that I could see him, swiveling from the waist to avoid stretching the skin around my throbbing shoulder. He had the dense, rather short, tweedy grey hair and the strong face of bold features I remembered having seen before, the brooding, ranging eyes under low brows, the straight, jutting nose, the wide mouth like a cleft, drawn down with pain or suffering when he closed it on a word. The Grande Hotel in Belém—that was

423

where I had seen him. But having taken this in, I began to be less clear in my head again. There was the blurring and recession of images, the hot feeling behind the eyes, the metallic taste in my mouth. Yet I heard him talking, and myself, too. "You're her father," I broke in at one time, my voice sounding in my ears no less than his to be independent of me, foreign to me. "I knew I had seen you before," I said triumphantly.

She was ill. She had a fever. There was something about the medicines he had; they were not helping, or had run out. She had to be taken to a doctor. The launch's motor had failed, her bow was stove in and she was aground as well. The men had deserted or had otherwise somehow disappeared; I did not try to get it clear. He needed my help to carry her to the nearest village. I must have avowed that I was ready and lurched partway to my feet, for the cabin commenced to gyrate, and he had hold of me and was easing me back down.

"I would rather die," the girl said, her head fallen forward. Her hand was on a stone, a grey stone veined with white, about the size of a brick, which I had not seen before.

What did she mean? I had to work my way back to what her father had said after helping me back to the floor. He had said he would have to cauterize the wound in my shoulder. There was no other way. It would have to be done with a hot iron. He had asked me some things about myself, and it was in replying that I had been conscious of my voice carrying on, sounding like a recording of itself. He had appeared already to know what I was telling him.

"What?" I asked. Oh. Was I prepared? Did I think I could stand it? "Yes, go ahead—if you have a way of doing it."

Having, from an unexpected twinge of self-consciousness, fastened my eyes upon the floor, I almost missed her tense, faintly murmured "Thank you!" It was nothing, I assured her, and reminded her that I was the one who would be helped in the first place. The formality of this utterance made me see myself as a large beetle standing on its hind legs. When I looked up she raised her eyes instantly, returning my gaze receptively. I felt I had been lifted to a new and altogether different standing in life, from inconsequentiality and obscurity to the glory and responsibilities of an emperor. I cursed the fates that now when she needed the one thing that ordinarily I could have counted upon giving her—my physical strength—I could not stand without reeling or even command my mental processes or see accurately. I hitched myself across the floor to her side. She shifted her position, as if to make a place for me beside her. Her head, held upright and unsupported by the wall, wavered, and I wondered if her thoughts toppled into confusion as uncontrollably as mine.

All would be well, I told her, fetching my words up from a great depth, it seemed to me. I tried, with what I said, to throw a protective mantle over her. In the morning we could start downriver—with a litter or even by raft. A village with a boat could not be very far away. Soon, before she could believe it, we would be where there were those who would have the drugs to make her well. I did not know how closely she was listening. Our knees were touching. She was real. The lovely face, proportioned to her slim, long-limbed build, its delicate modeling accentuated by her fever, made me want to worship the god that formed it. Her eyes, shadowed by their lashes, seemed, I thought, not quite able to confront what was in mine or to let them go either. I was wracked by inability to contain or convey the devotion that overflowed in me. "I'd die to make you well and consider myself the happiest man on earth." At my words the struggle in her eyes seemed to become more acute. I had a feeling that something that was looking out of them at me was fearful of being crushed. "But you know," I said, all the while ready to break down from the agonizing fear that all that was happening would crumble into nothingness. "You must know. You knew the instant you saw me!" Knew what? "Knew . . . knew that I have always loved you, as far back as I can remember, and before. God, don't you know how I've looked for you?"

She stared at me as if hypnotized. I was aware of the passage of her breath between her dry lips as her breast rose and fell. Then her gaze softened and was withdrawn, and shifted to her father. Following it unwillingly, I saw that he had his back toward us and was silhouetted in the darkening cabin by the bluish light of a gasoline stove. She said, still with her eyes on him, "I am lame. You did not know that. And . . . people treat me differently. They do not like to have me near." I shook my head emphatically as she was speaking. I told her I did not believe it about people, and if there were any such they were people I did not like to have near me. I told her I would make everything up to her. I talked of the places we would travel to—the headwaters of the Rio Mar, the Andes, the far reaches of the blue Pacific, the Spice Islands, the seafowl colonies of the grey Antarctic. I talked until, as on the slow,

425

enormous exhalation of a volcano, I was floated away from the earth and my thoughts feathered off into incoherence. But still, I believe, I spoke; the words were as round as marbles in my mouth, and were inexhaustible.

"It is only sometimes that I am lame!" she cried. "And I can ride, I can ride! I am not lame on horseback!"

I bent my will to clear and stabilize my vision, and saw excitement and pleading in her face. I knew, I knew, I said; when she rode, the horse was a kingfisher on the wing! I saw gladness spring to her eyes and lips. She knew the wild, headlong joy of the kingfisher's flight, but what counted was that she knew I knew it. . . . Only why was I so sick? What curse was it that at this time my thoughts should be disembodied from me, borne on undulating vapors of sickness?

Did I ride? She was holding the grey rock in front of her in her two hands, like a bridesmaid with a bouquet. There was continuity in what was happening between us. Question and answer followed upon one another! She swayed a little toward me. I could tell how much hung on her question. We were talking about riding, and I avowed I could (I was surely going to take the first opportunity to master the art, anyhow), crying that with her at my side I could outride the Valkyries through the clouds. And so we should, I said: up the snowy passes, through the dazzling valleys, raising behind us a dust of raindrops and snowflakes.

"Our hoofbeats will be the thunder!" she exclaimed. "We will surprise the eagles and give them greetings!"

"And when we reach the summits colored crimson and gold—then we shall swoop back to earth on our winged steeds in a long glide, like the eagles, through the twilight."

"Then we will have a feast of *ananás* and *castanhas* and goat's milk and cakes. Then we will have another ride by the light of the moon. Right through São Francisco and through the Chefe's *fazenda* so that he will say that it was we who made his cows go dry! And there is a place where we can leave the horses, and I will show you where to go and wait and if you are very quiet and not afraid, to see an *onça*, almost to touch! He is very proud and rather crazy, and dangerous even for me. He goes slouching along the trail, swinging his head, with his mouth open, like this." She did an imitation of the jaguar, thrusting out her jaw and displaying her teeth. I listened enchanted, as God might have upon creating heaven and earth and finding that that which was sup-

426

posed to have life *had* life and was living! "Oh, I can show you lots of things! A place where a man and a girl go and hide, the man to lie on the girl—if you would be curious. All you can see in the dark is the girl's legs in the air, but the things you can hear are very amusing."

I did not have time to think of being startled by these observations when her father spoke. He said he was nearly ready.

She looked quickly between us, like a wild creature whose two sole means of egress from a trap are barred. I told her she was not to think about it; it would be quickly over.

"You may hold the stone," she said, offering it to me.

Taking it, puzzled, I said, "Is it a very special stone? Has it got unusual powers?"

She seemed surprised by my questions, but she heard them, that was the point! She looked down at the stone. "It is like all stones. Oh—it has perhaps come a long way, down the river. You see how it is worn smooth. I like smooth stones better than rough ones with sharp edges."

I nodded and thanked her. She straightened up a little and placed her hands on my shoulders. My eyes closed; anything I could have done to prolong her touch I would have done.

"Think that it is for my sake only," she said. "Then it will not hurt so much." To my rapture, she began to unfasten the buttons of my shirt. She worked with a frowning seriousness. From the concentration of her gaze I knew she was having trouble with the same dizziness and instability of vision as I. Everything that happened, now and all the time, seemed in a most peculiar way to come from a distance.

"What are you thinking?" she asked.

"Thinking? I . . . ?" I was thinking of something a while back that I was going to ask her. "I have been wondering how it is that you and your father speak English—not only to me, but between yourselves." (Their accent was not Brazilian, and they spoke fluently, but with odd inflections and slightly unusual vowel sounds.)

"It is so we will not forget how to speak it."

I was going to ask more, but she set about slipping the shirt off my shoulders, and her gentle touch around the gash from the arrow sent such shivers of ecstasy through me I forgot everything else. When the shirt was off she caressed the inflamed skin around the wound with a touch as light as falling flower petals. "You know what I like," I said. "Have you the courage to look in my eyes and read my thoughts as well?"

427

As she did so I thought surely there was in her eyes something of what she must be seeing in mine, which caused her lids to contract perceptibly, as if in the presence of a too-bright light. She had opened her mouth to reply when from behind me her father spoke. She said, "Did you hear what he asked you? He thinks it will be best for you to drink some *cachaça*. Would you like some?"

I shook my head. Over my shoulder I said, "I would like to marry your daughter."

The silence behind me grew freighted—outraged, perhaps. I turned. The father was standing with a soldering iron in his hand, the head of which was dusty white with a suggestion of a dull red glow within it, like current jelly covered with powdered sugar. The expression on his face, which floated at a distance before me, seemed to be such as one may wear when doing a complicated calculation.

He said, "You think this has never happened before, never in the history of the world. You think it is all what you have done—that you have all by yourself come here and found my daughter." His lips formed a tight half smile of bitter unhappiness.

The tips of the girl's fingers rested motionless, barely palpably, on my shoulder. She said in a low, straitened voice, "He is thinking of my mother. He has never recovered from losing her. And during all the years since she died I have reminded him of her. It would have been better for him if I had died with her."

He had restored the iron to the flame. Her last sentence had been spoken so softly I had scarcely heard, but he had not missed it. "No," he said in a voice as loud and clear as the stroke of a bell. "No. Better for her to have died? It would have been better only if it would have been better for me to have died too. I was deaf and blind but for her, and would have been deaf and blind but for one like her." He turned his head aside, the cords in his neck standing out, as if it would not do for his face to be seen—not that there was much danger of that in the darkening cabin—but his carriage was aloof and proud. After a moment I saw that he had picked up a splint and was lighting it from the flame in the stove. When he had done so he held it to the wick of a lantern beside him, and this he carried to a hook in the center of the ceiling.

"Perhaps it will be given to the young senhor from North America," he said, "to be able to imagine how it would be to lose the power of sight and hearing when he has been given them. . . . From North America, did I say? Yes, and from the South, too." He was still standing by the lamp. His mouth opened in laughter, but no sound came forth. The lamp, cutting the cabin up into patterns of light and shadow, had the effect of materializing us out of a nebulous condition of being and, appalled as I was, too, by the sight of the man, I had for the first time a recognition of the utter strangeness, in all its dimensions, of what seemed to have come to pass; and this, together with the man's inexplicable address to me, caused to flare up in my mind with more force than ever the possibility that delirium had run away with me. "Wait a minute!" I cried, pressing my hand to my eyes. Wildly I conceived that all might disappear—the man, the girl, the launch—and leave me back in the tangle of plants beside the river. I must have tipped forward, for I felt the girl's hands on my shoulders brace me. Reassured by that, I dropped my hand from my face and saw that nothing had changed. *Nothing had changed!* I had won another reprieve!

"Are you ready?" the man asked from behind me, at the stove.

There was an imprint on my mind of the girl looking at him with compassion and wonder as he had been speaking of her mother. I knew for certain that he had lifted a corner of the curtain on what to her was mystery.

"Yes, go ahead," I said.

The girl's air of anxious and frightened proprietorship as she rose to her knees, her hands still on my shoulders, filled me with a warmth wholly unlike that of the fever. Speaking over my head, she said, "Please leave us alone for a minute, Papái." There was no response. "Please. You want him to be well? Is that not true? To help carry me?"

"Be quick, then," he said. His footfalls went the length of the cabin and up the companionway.

I had not taken my eyes from the girl's face. Looking down at me, she said, "I think I may be able to keep it from hurting you very badly. If you do as I say, I will try to draw your soul into me so that you will not feel so much the pain." Her high color and the brightness of her eyes showed she had fever enough to account for any delusion, but what she proposed as possible I did not think of as one. I asked how it could be done. She leaned forward so that I could not see her and with her lips just above my ear said, "I will put my mouth on yours and you will let me draw your breath in with mine, and if everything is right your soul will come with it."

429

In the midst of the faintness of rapture this utterance produced in me I was brought up sharply by the crudest jealousy. I held her a little away from me. Had she done this with . . . others? She shook her head. "No. How could that have been?" She seemed surprised that I should have asked. It was the second time she had shown surprise at my ignorance of a matter that was one of intimate knowledge to her. But I still looked questioning, and she explained further. "My mother told me about it and how it could be done."

I heard her father's footsteps again and knew by them as well as by the movement of the girl's eyes when he had crossed to the other end of the cabin and had taken a position behind me. "Now," she said, look-ing back at me. We were in each other's arms, and her warm, soft lips came, open, against mine. Her hands pressed against my back compel-lingly. I yielded to the gentle demand of her young mouth as gladly as if I were delivering myself up to paradise. . . . And I was! I was swept to an Arcady where the fulfillment and intensification of an all-encom-passing yearning progressed together. All the premonitions I had ever had from mornings in spring, from mountains tranquil above the cloud-shadows, from poetry, music, art, of a triumphant knowledge outside the register of human apprehension were combined in her embrace, as in a sunburst after an eternity of grey skies, and I thought my heart must explode. I felt a heavy pressure on my shoulder as a cry, smothered by my mouth, broke from the girl. She contracted convulsively, stiffening, her hands digging into my back, and as I heard the sizzling of burning flesh I knew with horror that she was bearing the entire pain of it. I sought to wrench free, to put her from me, but she clung to me, her mouth crushed against mine. Then suddenly she slumped, collapsing inert in my arms. An instant later an agony stabbed me like an ax brought down on my shoulder. "Almost done!" The words came as a gasp from behind me. I held the unconscious form of the girl to my chest, matching the force of my worship of her against the tearing, ma-niac torrent of pain.

"There!" A noise of stumbling and clattering followed, and then he was kneeling beside me, taking the girl from my arms. I could have held her no longer; strength had left me. When he had laid her down, I fell forward upon her and buried my face between her legs to shut out the torture and the image of scorched flesh, the odor of which was

430

overpowering. Consciousness was receding like a train pulling out of a station.

"You must sit up. I have something to put on your shoulder."

I fought against the outflow of will. I had to hold on or all would disappear—*as it had not yet!* While I tried with the resolution of desperation to obey the summons back to the pit of torment, I was grasped from beneath the shoulders and lifted. I was propped up against a vertical surface.

"She fainted. Her breathing is all right. It may help her to rest."

The words—a reply, I realized, to a question I had asked—came as from one exhausted by physical exertion.

I said, "How could—"

He interrupted. "She has a power of hypnotism. Common enough, would you not say? As soon as I saw, I lifted the iron. This is a powder I am going to put on you. It will not hurt."

But it did—like a rain of fire on the raw flesh. I heard his voice going on, issuing in my mind from a figure like a preacher's in a rural pulpit, though I was not deceived by that. I see through the disguise, I said to myself, my eyes closed from exhaustion. I did not hear what he was saying.

Yet the pain, overmastering the fever, soon seemed to bring increased lucidity. The scene, when I opened my eyes on it, was clear and sharp, like a reflection in a convex mirror. My love, the possessor of my soul, was lying on her back, one arm across her eyes, her breathing regular, but too rapid and shallow. I took her other hand and placed it on the stone, which I had released, I was not sure when.

Her father put a cup of coffee in my hand. "Would you like this, too?" He crouched beside me, long enough to light a cigarette and hold it out to me. He had big biceps and sturdy shoulders; he was a strong man for all his grey hair. He did not return my look, and his face was impassive. It appeared a little swollen beneath the eyes.

The act of swallowing coffee and of drawing smoke from a cigarette gave me a little of the sense of being I, as I had always been I, and consequently I held the girl in my gaze with determined fixity, in terrible fear that as I became myself she would lose substance. Yet she did not. She was made to seem excruciatingly real to me and at the same time a matter of pure, intense, solely subjective knowledge by the discernible

431

shape of her breasts beneath the thin material of her shirt, reviving the memory of their pressing warmly against me, like an outgoing, an unreserved gift of herself. The curve of her cheek imparted to her lips the faintest curl of a smile. The lower, so softly rounded, bore the dark mark of a cut; she had left the taste of blood with me when she had fainted. Hard as I stared at her, she grew blurred; tears that, spent as I was, I could not repress, came stinging to my eyes. An unbearable contrition and compassion for her overcame me. But tomorrow . . . tomorrow I would have a chance, and I would carry her to help if I had to do it single-handedly, if I dropped dead at the end. The pain in my head was like a physical substance about to burst through the forehead. I wiped my eyes and looked around upon the scene. I must hold it with my will!

"When is this to be taken away from me?" I cried in a menacing voice.

"What do you mean?" he asked.

"When is it to be taken away from me?"

"You're not dreaming, if that is what you mean."

I subsided, panting, to get my breath back. I had not imagined that torment of pain. *That* was true. I had to have been fully conscious then. But everything remained to be explained. Everything was inexplicable! I was shaking my head. No, no, it could not be. With a bitter shrewdness I exclaimed, "I couldn't have found her! Can't you see that? Not like this—stumbling on her, in this place, this nowhere. The odds—impossible. I'm not here, or you and she aren't here. I'm being taunted."

"You can think whatever you please," he replied. "But you are here and I am here. And," he added, "she is here." He said something about there being nothing very surprising in it, that it was certain I was coming to the Massaranduba, and that he should have expected me here, though it was farther than—farther than what I did not hear. His words were making no sense to me. But something had brought me down the river. That I recalled.

I asked, "Who is she?"

"She is my daughter."

"I know that. It's not what I meant."

There was no answer. I screwed myself around so that I could see him over my bad shoulder. He was sitting on a box pouring from a bottle into a tin cup like the one on the floor beside me, containing the coffee.

432

I saw him plainly then—or perhaps it was only later, in distant retrospect—as a man caught between the strength that was in his jaw and mouth and the sadness that gave a stunned look to his eyes. But I was not concerned with that.

"What are you doing here, on this river?" I asked. He again ignored my question, only sat tipping the cup this way and that, and unable to stand the added pain of my twisted position, I turned back. My weakness was a drug; I must not give in to it! I said, "You resent—hate—my being here. You'd throw me out—shoot me, maybe—except that I can help you move her."

I knew he was drinking. I could hear the panted exhalation with which he set the cup down.

He said, "It does not matter. It had to be. There is no avoiding what has to be. In any case, I believe I have not much longer. For one reason or another, there will be no need of me. I can read the signs! All goes remorselessly on, as it must. I thought I was bringing her here against her will. And now? Was it she who willed it from the beginning? Was it she who sent the launch on the rocks?"

As the silence drew out, I thought, He cannot, he must not, stop there!

I had nearly given up when his voice resumed. "Of course not! Yet we were finding gold. Gold enough to move mountains when they got wind of it in the right quarters. Gold enough to take her away to North America, to a Northern city where there are long winters and people live indoors. Where birds and animals, plants . . . trees . . . the sky . . . do not matter so greatly . . . do not make such strong claims. I would have taken her and protected her through it! It is with people —in the world of people—that those who live must live, even if it is on a ranch. It is not possible to go always across the current, to have a fever when a forest is cut down.

"And here you see what it comes to. The launch is lost. The prospecting, the mapping, is finished. And you are here. So it has worked out, and it would be easy to misunderstand if you did not know that life must keep repeating itself until . . . until some end is reached. I do not know."

The girl turned on her side, so that her head rested on the arm that had shielded her face. The skin over her closed eyes was so delicate it had a faintly bluish cast, like a shadow lying on it. Her eyelids stirred,

433

twitched, though the long lashes did not lift from her cheeks. Her brows contracted, and she moved her head again. I thought, I was sure, that her lips formed my name and that I heard her breathe it.

"Do not wake her!" said her father sharply, though quietly.

"I was not going to," I murmured. "How did I know her name was Ellen?"

"It is not Ellen. It is Feicita."

I did not know what to make of it. I tried to puzzle through the steam swirling around in my brain, but I did not know what I was looking for and had to give up. I said, "You wanted to keep her away from me." I ruminated on that. "You want to keep her for yourself."

"I want to keep her from harm."

"Why should she come to harm through me?" But the words sounded so glib and callous to me as to warrant his apprehension, and a cold fright came over me. I wanted to cry, "I love her! More than I love life! As I love life!" But it was impossible.

"Are you so different from anyone else?" he replied.

I would be, I could be. But I did not say it. It would have been of no interest to him in any case. The pain was like flames on my shoulder. A thought broke upon me like a comber of the surf. "You're saying she's real, aren't you?" I asked softly, shrewdly—trapping him.

He did not reply. "Aren't you?" I repeated sharply, rallying my reserves of strength to get to my feet. But I could not make it.

"Stop fretting yourself. I have told you. Nothing seems real to one who has a fever like yours."

I asked, "What did she mean when she said people treated her differently?"

"They cross themselves when she comes by!" He waited, then when he resumed spoke in a different, more willing voice. "Perhaps you do not know how small and cruel people are—most people. At the *fazenda* she is adored—though there have been more than a few who have not stayed, or whom I have discharged. Elsewhere, in São Francisco, she is always the subject of malicious and hateful talk. She is accused of immorality. But with no one of the countryside. With unidentified, mysterious persons. Accidents and misfortunes of nature are blamed on her. The cattle sicken. A wild animal is killing the calves. And she is to blame. She has been seen in the vicinity on her horse acting in strange fashion. A man is bitten by a snake. Or one cuts his foot open with an

434

ax. It is because he provoked her enmity by speaking freely of her or driving her from his property when she was riding there. It was this way with her mother. And in São Francisco they have not forgotten! The daughter is like the mother, they say. A widow is found to be pregnant. She has an attack of hysteria and tells how one night she is awakened suddenly. She finds a strange, hairy man from the forest by her. Feicita is there and she is under Feicita's spell. She cannot move or cry out to prevent the wild man from having carnal knowledge of her. That is the kind of thing that is told of her."

The lantern was burning lower. The girl stirred frequently, evidently unable either to find comfort in her position or shift it substantially without worse pain. I could hardly breathe, I had so tightened up in an unconscious effort to diffuse my love out over her and shield her from suffering. I thought of swabbing her brow with a damp cloth to cool her, but decided that the risk of waking her was too great.

Rain was drumming on the deck above. I did not try to understand why her father had become talkative. Every sentence sounded as if he were grinding it out of himself. I had a picture of a hand twisting a resistant handle.

"They are afraid of me in São Francisco, and with reason. But once when I was away they came and took her off. To a convent school. She escaped. She made her way home—a hundred miles. I do not know how. They paid for it when I returned, one with a smashed jaw, one with a broken arm. The priest I merely tossed into the river.

"They cannot forgive her for the good she has done for them. She has a healing power in her hands. There are those who have. It is a power of causing the muscles to relax, I think. Those whose pain Feicita has relieved are the most spiteful behind her back, the first to speak of witchcraft. That is human nature. They change the syllables of her name around. *Feitiça,* they call her—from the word for witch.

"There was a man half crushed beneath a tree he had felled. They could not get him out. And the tree so big it would take an hour to cut through! He begged to be put out of his agony, but no would do this. Then Feicita came, and . . . and she put her hand on his head, and sang, and the man . . ."

The speaker came to a halt and there was a pause before he resumed in a rough, peremptory tone. "It was a simple song, a lullaby, '*O Murucututú.*' But the man stopped crying and moaning. Before the end he

435

had died at peace. There were none there who could restrain their tears. But later . . . later they began to talk. How was it that she could send a soul on its way? It was sorcery! They remember that she can find lost jewelry and money. They do not understand that she has intuition, that she can find in the memory of the person the record of the movements that led to the loss. To most people it is a sign of alliance with evil powers. People's souls are filled with fears, and fear makes them hate. They are afraid of her because she is natural. She does not understand proprieties. She speaks her thoughts directly and truthfully because she is without guilt. Those who love her love her the more for it. But the others . . . You had better know these things.

"When the widow who had conceived made the charges against her, a deputation called at the *fazenda*. This was when I was away. They made their accusations. Feicita cannot understand the kind of enmity they had. She was quite cheerful. She said she thought probably the woman had had a possession. Probably she had gone at night out to the stables and submitted to a goat. This sometimes occurred with widows, she explained. She has ideas, or knowledge, of extraordinary kinds. Matings between human beings and animals were the origin of satyrs and centaurs, she said. Or they were the origin of the legends; she was not sure which. She said the woman was mistaken about her being there. Then she said—and I can imagine how it was, she speaks in a way always friendly and innocent—she said she was sorry, she would have been curious to see it. She is so young, and she has not learned to disguise. Then was when an order was obtained to remove her to the convent school.

"When Feicita enters a room or if you meet her suddenly, it is like coming before an open window. It was so with her mother. No, it is more like a blind man in a confined room who comes before an open window. He is aware suddenly of great depth. The air is fresh, of great spaces. Everyone feels this, in one way or another. I see it happen. People know something is different. They begin to talk importantly and excitably about their concerns. They talk about their occupations, their crops, their livestock, their work in the office, their houses, their politics, their friends in high places. Feicita sits there watching them with her bright eyes telling nothing. *I* do not know what she is thinking. Or forgetting them if a butterfly goes by the window.

"If you let her take you where she will . . . if you follow beside her

436

through forest and fields, letting her show you and speak of what she sees . . . flowers and trees and rocks, the living things that inhabit them —all that makes up the world that man was born into—you will know how it was when man *was* born into it. You will see it as a man might who had been condemned to die . . . who had thought never to have seen it any more, and had then the gift of life restored to him. And yet you will miss something. What, I do not know. Feicita used to look to me for something more, as her mother had. And I could only look dumbly back, not knowing what she wanted. In time she ceased to expect more. In time her mother had ceased to expect more too. But the way she had looked at me when expecting that which I did not know how to give—*that* never left me. No, God, it did not! Not even after *she* left me, when Feicita was born. Least of all then! The eagerness, the joy, the love, then the wonder, the puzzlement—but with no less love. When I saw it last . . . when I saw it last was in a dream—at the end, as the end was coming near. It was not only once. It was several times —may the heavens be merciful! Several times I had this dream!"

There was a scraping sound, resonating, as, I supposed, he pushed from him the box on which he had been sitting. It was like a bellow in the darkened space we shared, in which I sat in a stupor of exhaustion, gripped, held fast to consciousness by his discourse, being dragged behind him by what I visualized as a hawser, to which I clung for my life's sake, feeling at the same time, as I sat, the iron weight of my aching limbs.

He went on in a voice that strained hoarsely against the restraint he kept on it. "In it, in this dream, I was plowing under a dark sky, plowing an immense field . . . a field that curved over the horizon, so. The end of the furrows could not be seen. And in the traces . . ." He stopped, and I heard him drink. "In the traces there was an old man with white hair and a white beard, in a white garment. An old man, but tall and strong —my God, how strong! He turned and motioned me on with his head. He commanded me. She was standing there looking at me. I looked back at her over my shoulder. My tongue was turned to stone. I looked at her dumbly as I followed the plow. I had to plow; my hands were frozen around the handles. The old man pulled the plow with terrible strides. And we went over the hill, leaving her standing there."

My skin like ice, I looked up and beheld him looming over me. I did not know what to expect. I struggled to my feet, managing to do so this

437

time by holding onto an abutment of the launch's side I had been leaning against.

He said, "The walls of the room that opened when she came near . . ." His face was only a foot from mine. "They were the walls of time! That is my hope, my only hope. That she is apart from time. You understand? Do you see what I mean?"

He was out of his mind, I thought, still thrilling eerily to the timbre of his voice. "Yes, of course I see. But there's tomorrow we have to think of. Tomorrow we have to carry Feicita down the river."

"Tomorrow," he repeated like a mechanical echo. He moved off. "Do you think you will be able?"

"I'll have to."

His hand was at his head. "You must get some sleep. On deck. That is the place for you."

"You're from Santarém. Or were once. From the Confederate colony." The obvious truth had penetrated my mind, turbid as it was, sometime back.

"That has nothing to do with it!" He only just remembered to keep his voice down. "The deck is the place for you!" His voice was higher-pitched than usual. "The rain has stopped. There is a canopy over the stern. There are some sacks there." As I sought to engage my faculties with this proposition I must have seemed resistant to it, for in the tone of one answering back he snapped, "There's no room in here for you. And it is my launch!"

Sleep was what she needed, I said to myself as I paused at the steps for a last look at her. Let nothing happen to her! I spoke the words silently in tones of dire warning, gripping the doorjamb, as one with a mandate to put the Almighty Powers on notice. . . . She seemed to have quieted down. Or perhaps it was just that in the darkness her small stirrings were not detectable. Her father was wandering in his mind. I was not going to let my hold on sanity be imperiled by contagion.

I shivered; the air on deck was cool to the skin. In tomorrow's daylight all would seem normal, with only the practical problems of moving her to be dealt with. I was going to be better. Already, I thought, the pain had greatly lessened—though it may only have been that I had become remote from it. I heard the rushing of the water, and must then have had a relapse, for at first I believed it to be the sound of fountains in a palatial garden with matched, curved stairways of stone descending from a balustraded terrace; the picture of this garden swung in upon me with a blast of heat and an aching of the teeth. But the rapids above the launch were discernible; I made them out in their spectral pallor against the black current as I clutched a stanchion in the stern.

The sacks had a rough texture, but their dusty scent, as of dried grass, was not unpleasant. My head ached, my heart pounded and I could not find a position of tolerable discomfort. I had no hope of sleeping. Yet I must have fallen almost at once into unconsciousness, for I remembered nothing later but opening my eyes, with the moon full in them, and finding them fixed upon a statue, a being of lunar light and lunar shadows —a girl, Feicita.

She dropped to her knees beside me and sat back on her heels. Her face was held in a V formed by her hands, like a flower bud in its sepals. After a time, while I existed only in the compass of what my eyes took in, she lowered her hands and spread them on her thighs. "I wanted to see you," she said. "I did not mean to faint. It was because I am sick."

"Feicita!"

Her head went back a little, her eyelids descended, as if in speaking her name I had passed my hand across her brow.

I sat up. "I am sorry I called you Ellen. I don't know why I did. Or rather I do—but it goes back a long way."

"I liked it. It did not surprise me. You may call me Ellen if you wish."

"I like Feicita better."

I remember that as I gazed at her, her eyes lost in shadow but for the glint of reflected moonlight in them, it seemed to me that all—all there could be—was contained in the here and now between us, that there could be nothing more, nothing beyond it to move on to. An indescribable clarity seemed to extend to the horizon of all possible experience imbued with the sweetness of her being, with her fragrance, which evoked the images that had floated beside me in the days before this, scented with sun-warmed fruit and pine woods.

She looked aside, and I saw that her attention had been caught by a tern perched on the railing a few feet away. It had evidently just alighted, for it was settling itself on one of its small feet. She snapped her fingers and the drowsy bird, without extending itself, opened its bill in soundless protest. The scene touched a familial feeling in me; I felt a little like a father with wife and child. I must have made some sound of amusement, for Feicita looked a little startled, then glanced back at the bird

439

and smiled. I think it had not really impinged on her consciousness until then; her mind had been elsewhere. She reached out toward it as if to pet it and still it took no alarm, only watched her hand come above it, its head cradled between its shoulders, its bill still open. She said, "You probably had a bad dream, which disturbed you. I must not tease you."

My fever was rising again. My head, I thought, was full of sand. When I moved it I could feel the contents shift with a squealy crunch, like the sound of a footfall on a hard-packed beach.

"I don't know how to tell you," I began, "what it did to me—your doing as you did, in the cabin." I felt as gross as if I were walking in rubber boots through a flowerbed, but did not know how to do better. "I could have killed myself for letting you take on yourself what you did. There was no way I could have foreseen . . . I still don't know how it was possible."

"It was nothing." She was sitting, leaning on her arm, her legs drawn up beside her. "There is something I am going to ask you." She stared straight ahead. Then her head sank and she seemed to contract within herself. "I am not used to being sick."

"Here—lie down," I said.

I arranged the sacks quickly on the deck, a horrible fear once more at my vitals, and she stretched out on them, her head on her arm. Even in the moonlight a feverish flush showed dark on her cheeks, and her eyes, after she had momentarily closed them, appeared dilated with darkness. She raised her hand and with it set about to fasten a button at my neck; I had my shirt drawn around me under my bad shoulder, with my other arm through the sleeve.

"Why did you say to my father that you wanted to marry his daughter?" she asked, her attention taken up with the difficulties she was having with the button.

"Because I do. Because you're all I want in life. Wasn't it settled before I came?"

She gave up trying to fasten the buttons. She slipped her hand up under the bottom of my shirt and drew a line down my chest with her finger, then another. "I would not be a wife like other wifes—other wives."

"I don't want a wife like other wives. Tell me how you are feeling."

"I am feeling only a little sick. Tell me what kind of wife you do want."

440

I was thinking that I had a fire under my mind—my eyes and throat were hot from it—and that she and I were somehow, with no derogation of reality, creatures of the flames. "There are flames," I said, and checked myself. I looked up at the sky for deliverance from my confusion, but had to close my eyes for dizziness. It seemed that another tern had joined the first one on the railing. I took her hand and held it until the illusion of the fire licking at my imagination passed. I let myself down beside her. She was regarding me questioningly; I had propped myself up on my elbow so that I could look into her face. "A wife who will go with me to the ends of experience," I said. "Who will stand beside me before the ultimate beauty and wonder. Whose breast I can lay my hand on to make the beauty and the wonder bearable. With whom it will be as it was in the cabin." Her eyes, so close to mine, so limpid, seemed free of all reserve.

"It is only for times when there is a great need," she said softly, having divined my intention. "It is dangerous. I know that from my mother."

"How could she have told you these things when she died when you were born?"

I watched her lips as she replied. It was as if I had lived apart from humankind until that moment and had never seen the movement of a girl's lips, the way they met over her teeth and parted again. She said she did not know, she could not explain.

"Why is it dangerous?"

Her lips forming the words as beguilingly as before, she replied, "Maybe if I had your soul in keeping with me too long I would not be able to let it go."

"My soul is yours anyway."

She sat up, after one false start, as if she had found her slight body of an unaccustomed heaviness. Her hair shaped the contour of the back of her head but in front hung free, and would have hidden her face had she not held it back with her hand.

"Are you afraid?" I asked.

"I am afraid I will never be happy again when I am alone."

"Only if you don't want to *be* alone again. And if you don't want to be you won't have to be."

Her wide eyes, looking askance at nothing over my head, were those of a person who hears, or almost hears, a far-off sound. Instinctively, to

441

stay her, though without thinking, I put my hand on her leg at her knee.

Her attention returning, she said, "The terns have gone! And I did not even notice when they went! You see, that is because you are here."

She put her hand lightly on mine. "Whatever I do is thought strange," she said, tapping on my chest with her finger and scrutinizing it. "Ordinary things, like going out at night. And how many creatures would you ever know if you went out only in the daylight? Not the *onça!* And there is an *anta,* a tapir, an old fellow, he is not really bothered by me any more. But you will see him, he is not very intelligent. And it is only at night that I can ride without some of all the clothes my father makes me wear and not have anyone find out. Another thing. It is thought strange to go out in the rain. It is all right to take a bath in a tub of dirty water, but not in the clean rain. Is it not they who are strange, to go through their lives with another person asleep in them who will only wake up and be alive if there is rain falling all around, and everything dripping?"

The rain. . . . I was jolted and sickened by a visitation I had by myself as I had sat beneath the tarpaulin while the rain fell, my teeth set with an impatience I was trying to subdue with a cigarette while the thought of all the gold yet to be discovered gripped me. "Yes, it is surely they who are strange."

"I thought of you very often in the rain," she said. "Especially often then—when it was grey for a long time, with a chill. It made me think of other . . . of another land, where you were. And my heart would cry out in the wet woods. I wondered if you would hear, wherever you were. The cold rain would make me think of my desire for you."

She leaned over and, as she had done in the cabin, gently touched the skin around the lesion on my shoulder. "It does not hurt so much now?" I shook my head. She went on. "It was for me. It was because you were coming here that this happened. It is part of life for the male to suffer injuries on account of the female. I do not know why, but there is something about it. Stallions are sometimes badly injured. That is from fighting over the mares. That is how I learned about males and females. I was riding on the range when I was a little girl. There was a great battle between two stallions. They stood up on their hind legs and struck out with their forefeet, and they laid back their ears and bit. Before one of them was beaten and ran away, they were both cut and bleeding. There were two mares standing by, and the stallion that won the

442

fight—I thought he was going to fight with one of the mares next, on account of the way he acted. But that was not it. The most amazing thing happened to him. . . ."

Her account of the episode was as complete in detail as it was matter-of-fact in delivery. At the end she said, "I had known before that that was how it was with people—I mean I had always known—but it was only then that I knew I had known."

"You don't mind—about people?"

"Oh no." With a quick movement she bent down and, almost impalpably, touched her cheek to the seared place on my shoulder. "It is something I have often thought about, imagining how you would be when someday you would come. The next time you are cut and bleeding from fighting Indians, you will see that I do not mind."

"Must I wait till then?"

"No, only until I am a little well again."

In her candid, troubled eyes there was a sudden question, as if I had started to speak.

I said, "With a kiss, perhaps this time I could transfer strength to you, instead of pain." I made a move to sit up, but she pressed me back lightly with the hand that reposed on my chest.

She sat without speaking, looking down while she varied the pressure of her fingers on me, now pushing down firmly, now scarcely touching, in a mysteriously intelligible, unutterably moving communication. Then, as she had done in the cabin, she commenced to unbutton my shirt. I froze with the joy of her touch, with the lacerating tenderness of her application to the task. With a sense of overstepping a dizzy chasm I reached up to her and unfastened one, then another, of the buttons of her shirt, a leaden weight of suspense on my heart, which I thought would crush it, until all were undone. Sitting half sideways, as she was, leaning toward me, one side of her shirt hung open, and I touched the warm little breast that stood exposed, pendant, roundly conical from her bending over. The smoothness of the skin drew my fingers over it in an incredulous and fearful reverence. I was contained in their touch, as she in the flesh's yielding firmness; my hand enclosed the all in all of her. My heart was laid waste, more so still when with an enchanting un-self-consciousness she looked down with interest at what I was about.

"I like that. It does to me just what the rain does, but in a very different way."

443

With my hand on her back beneath her shirt I drew her down beside me. Her mouth against mine was warmly submissive, softly inducive. . . .

I thought my soul must burst from me. The shackles struck from it, its hunger was on the instant greater than I could believe the universe had power to satisfy. We clung to each other, our breaths commingled, melting together, imbued, pervaded each by each. I was charged with her in every cell. Her past was mine and mine hers. I knew how that could be and how what was between us was equal to eternity. All experience was contained in it, as all the heavens may be concentrated by a lens in a pinpoint of burning luminosity. Everything came to me at once, in a flood of random sights, grand or simple, but all with a force of revelation. I saw the great river at dawn as I had seen it before, with parrots like big bumblebees taking wing from the still dark woods, and as she must have seen it, with a harpy eagle presenting its war mask from a dead limb; saw palmettos leaning over a yellow strand and heard the poignant cries of the shorebirds and the dirge of the receding surf; saw flowering trees against a blue sky where white clouds reposed like sleeping swans and trees before the dawn biding their time behind the mists of the night; saw a Negro field-hand bent with years scattering grain to a flock of hens as in a ritual of priesthood; saw a Caboclo boy with a marmoset like a surprised little old white-haired man on his hand; saw the stallions battle and the dust rise from the savage thudding of their hoofs and the mounting of the mare and the home thrust like a lightning bolt sunk in the earth; saw the sensitive visage, sharp and clean, of a grey fox I had once surprised over a hilltop; saw the procession of broad-winged hawks strung out on bent wings before a northwest wind sending summer southward; saw a trogon of plumage brilliant as the armor of an Eastern prince poised watchful on the loop of a liana; saw flowers that burst like suns above the meadowgrass and flowers like sculptures of luminous wax in the darkness of the forest—all these things and more, severally and altogether, instantaneously or spread over long minutes—I do not know—and in all of them the secret proclaimed . . . a secret I never since, never since then, have known. Yet it was there! The knowledge that was beyond knowledge! I cried within myself, *Yes, that is it!* It was a secret I had time and again almost surprised, almost grasped at those moments that in her embrace had come crowding back to me. The knowledge of it had eluded me so narrowly I had caught its very echo in the golden cascades of the veery's song spilling

444

from the moss-grown temple of a hemlock grove, in the Chopin étude sounded from an unseen piano in a house mellow with silence.

To impart my life and heart to her, to possess hers in return, to be united with her beyond the bounds set by human limitations—I strove to convey to her by message of lips and hands the desire that was so compelling it seemed impossible my life and heart should not, as desire willed, flow into her through our bodies' contacts.

"Wait." She had separated her mouth from mine, and the air was cold on my face where hers had been. Her injunction sounded as if she had barely breath enough for the one word. I could feel her lungs laboring. She raised herself up, for a moment resting upon my chest, her breasts pressed against me, our hearts hammering madly against each other. Then, pushing herself up from me, she managed—only just managed— to sit up. Clasping her arms in front of her while I felt as if we had been sundered by a knife and tingled with the onset of foreboding, she said, "Promise me something. Promise me that you will never come back here for the men in New York. Promise me that you will not be one of them the way you were in Belém. Promise me you will not work for that gold-mining business."

A reeling astonishment brought me upright. She was talking about the Massaranduba Concession. There was a crashing in my mind as of breaking glass, a world of glass tumbling and shattering. I knew what she meant, all she meant—though I did not know how she knew. The Massaranduba. . . . The name was enough to bring them all before me, all who looked to it for their fortunes. And as they pressed their claims, did Feicita see irresolution in my eyes? Did I hesitate to throw them all over and purge myself of their dreams of plenty?

Did I hesitate? No, God help me, I do not think I did! For a moment I had been bewildered, and bewilderment might have looked like doubt —but not to her who could read my mind. And the words came tumbling fast from me. Yes, I promised! I would not be one of them again. From this moment the Massaranduba Concession would mean nothing to me. I would never work for it.

And then, merciless heavens—then I knew that nothing we do or are can ever be effaced, that there is no escaping the evils we embrace, ever, ever, ever; for there came before me, real as anything that ever happened, the picture of myself grubbing in the streams for gold. I was there on my knees, working over the gravel like a man possessed. I could not

445

exorcise the damned presentment, but must stare at it transfixed as my excesses in the grip of that monomania were re-enacted before my eyes and thus before hers, which were fixed upon mine. The light in my face was like a crazy man's—my God, had I looked like that?—and there was that detestable and avid grunt as my hand closed on a cursed nugget.

"Julian . . . !" A spasm seemed to take her, cutting off her exclamation. Her eyes tight shut, her shoulders hunched together, she rocked as if in pain, then cast herself forward into my arms. She lay huddled against me, her face buried between my head and chest. She was trembling, and the trembling grew more violent, so that her breath came shudderingly. Extending her arm around me, she pressed closer into me. "It is so cold," she said, her voice muffled. "All of a sudden I am so cold."

Numb with terror, I tried to encompass her in my arms. "Forgive me, Feicita!" I moaned. "I didn't know, I didn't mean it. Forgive me! I'll be everything you want. Only show me how!"

She shook her head. "It is nothing you have done. It is my illness. I have never been ill like this. I am frightened, Julian. . . . No, do not leave. Stay!" In my alarm I had cried that I would bring her more clothes to keep her warm, but she clung more tightly, and she remained clinging to me as, with my heart in a grip of ice, I lowered her to the deck and stretched out above her, lying over her to keep her warm. She was still shaking and spasmodically contracting. I said, "It's a chill. It comes with fever. It will pass. Very soon." The instinct to harbor her, to draw the cold and sickness from her into me, was so fierce I thought it must prevail over everything. And in a faint voice, echoing my yearning, she said, "I wish I could crawl inside you."

"You have, that's where you are, that's where you'll stay!" I talked reassuringly—not babblingly, I implored the Almighty—about her getting well. My excess of fear was unreasoning, I tried to believe, unreasonable; there could not have been a change so sudden and drastic as it seemed. I was hysterical, I told myself; intangibles could not poison. But through me as I held her there poured without hindrance waves of the bitter and frightening darkness that engulfed us.

"Talk to me about yourself," she said in a quick, inflectionless voice. "I cannot know it all unless you tell me."

Talk about myself? To be able to see her I moved so that I was resting on my side, on my elbow, but still protecting her. But she kept her face pressed against my shoulder. She tried to button her shirt but could

446

not, so I did it for her. She said, "You were going to tell me . . ." So, although I did not think I could, although the seizures of shivering she had, when she drew even closer to me, caused me to falter and lose the thread of what I was saying, I talked and talked on. I told her all about the two times I had seen her before this and how afterward I had tried to find her, and about the premonitions I had had of her in the past. When I flagged, she prompted me with a question between breaths. What did I think she would look like before I saw her? Was I not disappointed? Did I know that the first time, in the Grande Hotel, she had known that it was I she had been waiting for, though her father had taken her away? That she had made her father learn about me—the things she did not already know in her heart? That she knew when she saw me on the other riverboat that I would come after her? Did I think I would ever find her—as she knew I would? Was I going to take her to visit the country of my birth, where she had heard that her ancestors had lived? Finally the spells of shivering ceased, but then when I stopped talking she lay without speaking, silent except for her breathing, which was like that of one who has been crying.

I was about to ask again how she was feeling when, turning her head from my shoulder, she said in a whisper, "What is it I hear?"

I listened. "Thunder," I said. The rumblings were almost continuous in the far distance up the river.

"No, not that. Do you not hear the owl?"

I listened again. There were the thunder and the rustle and gurgle of the river and the sounds of insects. "No, I hear nothing like an owl," I said.

She looked up at me with eyes distraught. I could feel her gathering her strength to rise, but the effort required was too great for her. She said, "You do not hear the owl that I hear?"

To still the pity and terror that would sound in my voice I bit hard on the back of my wrist. I said, "Yes, I hear it now. An owl of some kind."

She seemed to want to stretch her head back as far as it would go. Her neck was arched, her eyes pressed shut. She looked as if she were going to cry out, but she made no sound until suddenly she collapsed and threw her head against me. "Hot." She expelled the word as if against an obstruction. "I am hot." Her forehead and cheeks shone dark in the moonlight.

447

"I'll get some cool water." I hardly dared speak for fear of communicating my terror.

"No." She grasped my arm. "Not just this minute."

My panic was conjuring up visible forms before me which I could not face, which my thoughts flew wildly from.

"Feicita, Feicita!" My throat, down my chest, was scalding. The moon had disappeared as she had spoken and I could hardly see her, only enough to know that her lips were moving. I bent to listen as she felt her way down my arm to my hand and clasped it. "I never knew how much alone I used to be," I heard.

"You'll never be alone again!"

I saw that a light had gone on in the cabin. On my knees, I picked her up, then rose to my feet. The darkness was the enemy, I thought with a rallying of hope. It was in the darkness that malevolence held sway, in the sinister darkness. The dawn could not be far off, to put the hideous black night to flight, to bring wholesome day! She was curled against my chest.

That is how I think it was—up to then. But I do not know, I cannot be sure of particulars. My brain was a sack of hot BB shot, I thought at that juncture. It concerned me only as it made me fear toppling and falling with her as I carried her down the steps.

The lamplight showed the father standing in the middle of the cabin. He looked like a crude kind of statue, his legs apart, arms hanging, eyes staring at me from under furrowed brows, as if he were stupefied.

"A wet cloth," I said. I laid her down on the cushions.

Then—everything began to go. In my mind it was like a ship that was going to sink. The scene departed from the concrete, swung haphazardly in space. Sitting back on my heels, I had to close my eyes to keep from toppling over, while the place rotated, as in a vortex. Going down, I thought. And where would I come out of it? Again I thought, It will be in those bushes by the river; I have imagined everything else. After that I could tell by the behavior of my head that things were being stabilized, and when I opened my eyes I saw I was still in the launch and Feicita was lying where I had placed her. Her eyes were large and, I saw with sinking dread, seemed empty or sightless, or filled with the namelessly remote. But as I looked they returned to me with a light of perception and interrogation. I forced my features into some kind of comforting response. Then, as her father handed me a damp cloth, she turned to him and a faint smile appeared on her lips. I glanced up at him too and was stunned. He was grinning—with the aimless grin of a baby which has just discovered its facial muscles. Then it was clear. I thought, Oh, he has lost his mind, he has been let off of it.

Applying the cool cloth to her forehead and chest, I was in less danger of breaking down. I was able to smile at her with a shade more of conviction. Perhaps it was only because I was doing something. She gazed steadily at me with eyes hazy and glistening with the fever, but intensely speculative, as if she were coming out of a coma and were not sure of what she was seeing. I thought, She wants me not to let her go! The knowledge crashed into my mind, throwing into tumult my already frantic fears. I dropped my head momentarily to command my face into order. Beneath her shirt the small, low dome of her breast was hot to the touch, and taut. I saw in her eyes that I had understood.

Then her face grew blurred. I had time for only one drowning man's thought: Is it happening to her or to me? My mind was stricken blank, as if a stroke of lightning had effaced everything there, leaving it white and glaring as a cinema-screen when the film has flickered out. Down the long length of a white corridor, as in a hospital, the words grew as they hurtled toward me: "She is dead."

The blasphemous, hellish sentence, aimed at her like a rock-slide, would kill her if I did not throw myself in its path. I clasped her to me, rocked with her, heard myself hysterically imploring her love. "No, Feicita! *No!*" The cabin rang with my voice.

She would not listen, she would not hear. She lay limp, her eyes closed. The strength was struck from my arms, and I fell forward with her. The universe flew apart in madness.

I did it, I did it.

I was yanked away, yanked to my feet with maniac violence and slammed back against the wall.

"You did not kill her! You did not kill her!" The father was shouting at me. "You are lying!" His insane, contorted face was before me. "You are saying I killed her mother! That is what you are saying! That is why you say you killed her. You want me to think I killed her mother! But you are wrong! I did not! There was no place for her in the world —for either. They could not live. There was no hope. Now it is over! All is over!"

I would not live, I could not be made to live. God would strike me down. No one could curse God as I cursed Him and live. I called on the man before me, whose face was in his hands. "Where is that gun—that pistol? Get it. It's God's will—God's will not to have me live another minute. I don't have to. Get the gun, do you hear? *Get it!*"

He lowered his hands. A look of cruel secretiveness appeared on his face. "You have not earned it," he whispered exultantly. As I lurched toward him he leaned back like a ballet dancer. *Insane as ever,* I thought. The next thing was that I saw his fist coming at me, as big as the end of a freight car. And that was all.

Heat and cold, heat and cold—and bright light. I tried to put them together, but was incapable of it. . . . Heat and cold, and orange light—and the feeling of having been run over by a truck. I opened my eyes. There was a great conflagration near me and I was lying on the ground. My legs were in water—in the river.

Oh no!

It all came back to me, roaring down upon me like a thundering express-train. I staggered to my feet, falling once in the process, unable to stand up straight. The launch was a roaring, crackling forest of flame. I made to rush to it, but the heat blasted me back before I had gone three steps. I fell on my knees, harrowed beyond the soul's enduring, riven by agony, frantic for oblivion. I watched, seeing in the inferno the hell I would carry inside me till death released me—if it could.

And then—oh, God, no, let it not be so! I cried—and then, horror piled on horror, the launch began to move. I saw, in my recoiling mind, standing to the helm— No, I would not see! But the vessel was moving, the stern swinging slowly around. There came the hollow scraping of the keel on gravel. It was floated.

The river—the river had risen. Burning savagely as ever, roaring and crackling, an island of fire, the launch drifted offshore and with quickening speed, hissing as it sank by the bow, moved down the river.

18

Day was breaking when I finally gave way. I went down like a crumpled paper bag. There was no more stumbling, sometimes half running, through the forest; no more casting myself against the trees to drive out thought; no more flight from the merciless juxtaposition in my mind of her eyes at the end and the eyes—as the light faded from them—of the deer I had slain; no more hoarsely cried pleas to the heavenly powers to destroy my reason, to grant insanity; no more likelihood that my brain would indeed be unhinged by the panting, bleating, sobbing sounds that issued from me. There was nothing left in me. Nothing was left.

The scene on which I opened my eyes when consciousness returned was such as I have known on cool grey summer days at home when a breeze turns up the silver undersides of the leaves and a steely light is over all and there is no color but a frosted green. The river was like a river in an engraving; that it should be in motion seemed a trick of advanced technology. "A world of mathematics," I mumbled. "There is nothing in it but symbols of what are taken to be real things." Here where the river was navigable the current was not swift or broken by rapids. I waded in, let the water lift me off my feet and struck out for the other shore. I swam on my side, using only my right arm, unconcerned whether any stroke prove to be my last, rather surprised finally to find ground under my feet. I felt as if my jaw and half the bones in my body were broken.

It was not as far back to the spot where the Indians had caught me as I expected. There was no sign that they had ever been there or that I had: no pack, no rifle.

I walked all day, retracing the way I had come—so long, long ago, it seemed. Unconscious observations unconsciously acted upon must have guided me. I had no fever left. I was as cool as . . . The image of a chicken in aspic, white and with its bones showing through, crossed my mind.

Constantly I was repossessed by what had passed. I was back in it as one will be back in a fevered dream one has had, in a flash, totally pre-empted by it. I was condemned to live it again by instants, over and over. It lay in wait for me on every side, exploding soundlessly in my mind—and there it was again, and the delirium, and I with it, just as it had been the first time. I thought I could not support the impact, I thought I would go down. Yet I did not go down. I kept on living, I kept on walking. And the only reason was, I think, that I was empty, that there was not enough left of me with which my destruction could be wrought.

I slept the night through on a bed of leaves in exhaustion. In the morning I was as stiff as if crippled with rheumatism, but the stiffness passed during the day as I trudged on. I had recovered enough to be aware, without any sense of deep involvement, that I was weak and light-headed from hunger. I walked as one might recite by rote a narrative of the march of another. I had a second night in the forest during which I dreamed of food.

The first person to see me when I emerged at the camp in the afternoon was the young Indian woman who had once followed me up the trail. She stood paralyzed, then gave a scream of terror and fled.

The Bragas and Manoel came hastening from the bungalow. My consciousness had been brought to a focus by the woman's scream, and it

452

was brought to a focus again by what I saw in their faces. With utter disbelief there was fright, if not panic.

I learned that I had come back from the dead. Two Indians had come in from the forest with my belongings and a story of having found my dead body on the shore of the Ipaituba, where it had been washed up. I guessed from the way they stared while they were telling me this that they not only had my being alive to get used to but also my appearance. They ceased staring when they saw that I was noticing it.

One of them said my hair appeared to be *queimado*—burned.

"Does it? Does it?" I cried, and they looked frightened again. "My cooking fire flared up," I mumbled. It had not been a dream, I said to myself, even the ultimate horror.

I had to suppose my appearance extraordinarily changed. When I saw my face in the mirror I screwed it up and tried several other expressions to see if it responded, if it were mine. The hair in front did seem to be short and noticeably frizzled on the ends, which only the near proximity of a fire could have accounted for.

They found the wound on my shoulder also, when they came to dress it, to have been *queimado,* badly *queimado.* I twisted my head around to see it as well as I could, then made a movement of my fingers illustrative of skin being drawn together. "Arrow," I said, *"venenoso."* Miraculously, as it seemed, my various cuts and abrasions elsewhere were healing, and I was without major infection.

Joaquim Waldo had left the camp as soon as the report of my death had come in.

The best of the stores was produced for me, and since the launch had been in just two days before—and left again—it was better than barely edible. I fed to satiety the ravenous animal inside me.

My account of what had happened to me must have seemed to the Bragas sparse to the point of imbecility. I explained that I had been attacked by Indians, had escaped by swimming down the river and had been in delirium for I did not know how long—nothing more. They must have decided I was in no condition to deal with an interrogation, even in English, which they were struggling along in, and they quickly ceased to press it. During supper and afterward they carried on an active, commonplace conversation among themselves. I was able to understand that they were covering up for me, as it were, so that there would

453

seem nothing unusual, nothing significant, about my silence. I was able, too, to feel grateful for it. I sat watching them after the meal, remembering to sip my beer as they sipped theirs. It was difficult for me to take in fully that the ordinary life I associated with a remote past had been going on right up to the present and was still going on.

We had finished our beer when someone mentioned Joaquim Waldo.

"Joaquim Waldo . . ." I repeated, seeing before me a blond incarnation of grossness and avarice, of what was most despicable in human beings—a murderer. "I have to kill him."

I had had a certain kind of knowledge that there was something for me to do, something that justified all that exertion, all that walking. Now I knew what it was. It was plain to me the next morning as I marched the long trail to the Massaranduba River behind two young Caboclos provided by the Bragas to carry my pack in relays. I had a mission, a purpose in going on, such as a ghost has, that causes it to walk the night until it has acquitted itself of its task. I had only to kill Joaquim Waldo to escape what I could not endure. My mind was quite clear on this point. Senhor Waldo intended to catch the next riverboat from Topacindo, I had been told. He had a three-day start on me, and a launch besides, but sooner or later I should come up with him, and then I should kill him. The Bragas had appeared greatly concerned about my declaration and had talked of the police and the militia, but had also been sympathetic and had agreed that justice must be done. I had told them, of course, what I had originally neglected to point out, that my attackers had been led by Senhor Waldo's man. In the morning they let me know that the question of how the cartridges had been removed from my rifle before I had left camp had been answered; the girl who had screamed as I had walked out of the forest had not been seen since. They doubtless thought there was no chance of my overtaking Senhor Waldo before he left Topacindo. They tried, in vain, to keep me at the camp for a few days.

The Bragas had signed the power of attorney, which had once been so important to me. They had placed in my sack the gold I had collected. Along with the gold, Alfredo had taken from the safe the tobacco pouch that served me as a wallet and held it up in front of me. "Your monee," he had said, putting it in one of my breast pockets. I nodded. "And cigarettes." He had put a pack in the other. There was something about sending my rock samples by the next launch. It had been impossible for me to tell them good-bye—quite as impossible as if I had forgotten the words—but I waved as I walked away, and again as they called " '*Te logo!*" after me.

The walking was different from any heretofore, for my canvas shoes had fallen apart and I was wearing the high-cut leather pair I had brought to the mines but had not yet used. These were heavy and chafed my feet, and I felt like dropping and sprawling out on the ground. But there was no danger of my doing so. I set a fast pace, leaving it up to the Caboclos with the pack to keep up as best they could. The time to rest would be when Joaquim Waldo had been disposed of. I would be able to rest then as never before. The event was prepared. It was like a letter dropped into a mailbox. It was on its way. Only the time and the circumstances of its delivery remained uncertain. My release was a foregone conclusion. All I had to do was to keep going, to hang on, until the inevitable worked itself out. The knife was on my belt, fastened to its holster. It had remained there through all that had happened.

I had assumed that I could engage a crew with a *montaria* at the village of the fire-ants to take me down the river, and I found I could. By waving milreis I prevailed upon the men to set forth that very evening, taking advantage of a nearly-full moon and sleeping in the craft by turns. Once we had skirted the rapids we held to the center of the river to take full advantage of the current, so we must have made good time. I think we spent only one other night en route, and for it we pulled in at a river village—one which was a bit superior to the paddlers' own. In the *montaria* I lay amidships beneath a half-barrel canopy of palm-fronds and gazed ahead past the backs and straw hats of the two peddlers sitting side by side. Beyond them the waters of the Massaranduba River flashed back the sunlight, nearly dispelling the shadow beneath the canopy. I was as sore and as inert as if I had been dropped from a great height. Sometimes I fell asleep, but as often as not only to be grasped by the leg and shaken good-naturedly back to consciousness by one of the Caboclos. From the imitations they gave of the sounds I emitted while sleeping, I could not blame them for wishing to be spared them. I was glad enough to be awakened. The confusion of my mind while I was conscious, in which my fragmented thoughts were like pieces of pictures being worked around in a sack, with objects unbearable to contemplate continually coming uppermost, was worse than anything likely to afflict me while asleep, but awake I was able to some extent to contend with it. I had an antidote: the prospect of closing in on Joaquim Waldo. The effect of

455

cigarettes on a depleted physique and the routine performance of smoking were sedative. Conserving my supply, I chewed on some sugarcane while it lasted and then on the handle of my knife.

I had no expectation of finding the riverboat still in Baracurú. It had, in fact, departed. It had done so only two days before, however. I had planned on taking the overland route to Topacindo. This being so much shorter than the route by water, it seemed to me, though I was not up to working out the calculations, that if I pushed myself hard enough I might still make it to Topacindo before *Sabiá* departed and thus intercept Senhor Waldo there—unless there were another vessel bound downriver calling at Topacindo just ahead of *Sabiá,* which was very unlikely. I tried to remember whether Monteiro had said that *Sabiá* would wait at all for me, but I could not.

When I close my eyes I see Baracurú as a tableau of stylized figures, white-clothed with brown heads and arms, representing, as in the contemporary ballet, something not quite clear, but vivid and insistent. I see them as motionless, however, maybe as struck dumb with amazement that I intended to walk to Topacindo. I know they found it hard to believe. They tried to dissuade me, then insisted on providing me with a horse and with a boy to bring the horse back at the end of the first day. I have no memory of where I spent the night, but I recall graphically enough the first few hours of the next day and the difficulties I had with the horse. It was one of the usual small, meager animals, and such spirit as it had was contrary. When, moved by pity for the frail creature, I would get off and walk where the trail was steep with loose gravel underfoot and then try to remount, the ingrate would shy away, and once I was back in the saddle would balk or start treading to the rear. At best its mincing gait was so slow I railed inside at it. Soon I put the guide on the horse and took the lead myself on foot, the horse in the rear having to trot to keep up. A couple of hours of this had it in a panting sweat and its rider in a state of anxiety, so I sent them both back with suitable compensation, strapped the pack on my back and set off on my own for Topacindo, then about eighty miles away.

The eventuality I dared not contemplate was that the agony lodged in my heart would surpass what I could endure and bring me down before I could reach my goal and, through expiation, be relieved of the incubus. I had to hurry.

It was hot. I had never suffered from the heat in Brazil, but I did so

456

now. The sun appeared to have singled out the particular spot of country I was traversing to bear down upon, and I had no protection from its fiery pressure. I had no hat, and it seems that there was little shade along the way. I have often wondered about that country. It lingers in my mind as hilly and rather open, with stands of trees rising above the brush-growth—a gnarled sort of country, lost and forlorn, the vegetation lifeless in the heat, no birds stirring but an occasional turkey vulture gliding above the trees. Was it a country of thin soil and chronic drought, remote and wild, or was its gauntness the consequence of a working-over by man? I cannot say—or see that it matters, actually, though even at the time I was touched with some puzzlement about it, as once I had been disconcerted by similar uncertainties about the littoral to be seen from *Tocantins*. I did not know as I plodded along whether jaguars and dart-blowing Indians were observing me from the hot shadows or whether on the other side of the next hill I might come upon a great ranch-house with scattered outbuildings and the lord of the manor and his lady greeting guests on the porch. I visualized this hypothetical *fazenda* —I do not know why—as very grand, in terms of a conventional vignette of the Old South.

Once in a while I did come upon a habitation of sorts, depressed in character, of wattle. Such shabbily-clad denizens as were in evidence, and with whom I exchanged vague salutations, stared at me dumbly, either debilitated by their prostrate surroundings or, more likely, stupefied by the oddity stalking past their front yards. Infrequently the habitations were of stucco, a few together—except that I think that was only on the second day, or the third.

I spent the first night, too tired for anything but sleep, in what could have been an abandoned cattle shelter, but one still sound enough to support my weight in a hammock from its uprights and give shelter from the night's rain. For food I had bananas and hard-boiled eggs with which I must have been provided in Baracurú.

The terrain all along the route had the configuration of a washboard, with the ridges and valleys respectively a few hundred yards apart. The troughs between them might be a few inches deep in water or hip-deep, but none could be crossed dry-shod. Unused, to begin with, to leather boots (originally acquired for the trip out of misplaced respect for the Massaranduba's reputation as snake-infested) and now alternately baked and soaked in these heavy casings, my already blistered feet became

457

spongy and the skin began to split and peel off. To hold them together I bound them with adhesive I had left from a first-aid kit and put on all my socks—four pairs. This helped, but not much, and the nails in the heels of the boots were starting to come through, though I did not realize that was what it was. With half the distance yet to go, I estimated, every step had become painful. My pack bore me down and cut into my good shoulder (the other having to be spared altogether). I felt as if I were crucified on that pack. In addition to the hammock, the gold and the ordinary necessities, it was weighted down with part of my collection of rock-samples the Bragas had loaded into it, probably not imagining I should ever have to carry it any distance, and under these, unquestioningly, I dragged myself along. I drank immoderately from the water I waded through. The heat was so perishing it was impossible not to. I was still thirsty even when I had drunk my fill, and I felt as if bubbles were eddying up through my stomach as they do in a swamp, and it was of swamp-gas that my exhalations tasted. At all costs I had to keep going.

In midafternoon I came to a sort of trading post with three or four men inside passing the time of day. Their faces registered the usual blankness on seeing me. I could perceive no food on the shelves, but a bunch of bananas hung in a corner. "How much?" I asked, holding out some money. One of the men replied in words I could not understand and they exchanged looks, but no one made a move toward the fruit. They asked if I were English or German, and seemed not to know what a *Norte-Americano* was. I tried again with the bananas, but with no other result than that eyes dropped. So I turned and walked from the shop. Out under the sun again, I remembered having seen a stack of straw hats on a shelf, but I could not bring myself to go back for one and perhaps meet with another mysterious rejection. "Topacindo!" I said aloud.

As the day advanced I decided that I had better keep going all night. I was afraid that if I stopped I might find myself in the morning too stiff and too intimidated by the pain of walking to continue.

The one remaining edible in my pack was a jar of little wieners, part of the provisions I had bought in Topacindo and saved for the final extremity. I ate them by the last of the daylight, sitting on a bank of earth with my feet turned inward, on their sides, to spare the soles. I looked around at the clumps of trees growing black against the deepening blue of the sky and felt my face, my hand lingering over my open mouth.

I was rational enough to question the sense in which I was present here. The concrete way in which I had once lived on Eighty-sixth Street in New York recurred to me as being different from this. I had a dim perception of having become separated from the continuity and coherence of mankind's collective experience and cast adrift where the rules of causality did not pertain. It was evident that I had not died or I should not have been suffering this physical ordeal, but I thought that the experience of one who had might be of this kind. I extricated the pack of cigarettes and with a hasty, probing finger found one more left. This I lighted and drew avidly upon, as upon a specific against the threat of uncontrollable disorder within. Tomorrow there would be Topacindo; I had no thought of anything beyond that.

As I reached the end of the cigarette I was startled by a little voice that called from a nearby wood. *"Hai!"* it said at intervals, with an uncanny clarity and human quality. I told myself it must be a bird, probably a kind of nightjar. But the intonation was terribly human. *"Hai!"* It was sad, gay, knowing, innocent, gently mocking, timidly inquisitive.

I got to my feet, wincing at the pangs that shot up from them. "I must get on," I said, addressing myself aloud, as I had fallen into the habit of doing. The black tide at the bottom of my mind had been stirred into motion, was showing signs of rising. I dreaded the darkness that was rapidly taking over the earth.

As the light drained from the sky, the trail descended. It wound among clumps of vegetation which grew higher and higher the farther downhill I went, and closer together. I found I could no longer be sure of the trail, and had to trust I was going in the right direction. At length I could progress only by forcing a way through the tangle, caught repeatedly by my clothes and pack-straps. There were tremors running through my nerves. I talked to myself in what were intended as calming tones. To my immense relief, I broke through the brush-growth and found myself looking out into the open upon the newly-risen moon. Only—the open area was an expanse of black water, the surface of an impassable river.

"Hai!" said the little voice. Although I had been walking away from the woods from which it had first called, it was closer now than before. *"Hai!"*

The forbidden images were thrusting themselves forward. The ground was beginning to quake beneath me. One little push would send

459

me off through the woods again, blind and gagging with torment of soul. I concentrated on breathing deeply and regularly. "I'll go back the way I came," I said. "The moon is up. I can probably pick up the trail where I missed it."

So I fought my way back through the brush-growth. When I came upon what appeared to be a path leading off to the side, I followed it. Almost immediately I was hopelessly lost in an utterly black forest, standing in water. As I shifted the weight of my pack and tried to see something, anything, the intractability of externals doubtless steadied me by drawing my thoughts outward. "Regardless of this," I said, "I'll be in Topacindo tomorrow." I went sloshing off through the woods, constrained largely to feel, or bump, my way along. There was nothing else to do but go on, and it made no difference that I could tell what direction I walked in, except that when the water became deeper I veered away from where I took the river to be.

I finally spied a point of dim light and, bearing on it, came out on dry land and to a cabin. The family of Caboclos to whom it belonged must have been shocked nearly out of their wits to have me present myself in their doorway inquiring dully about a way to cross the river and find the road to Topacindo, but if so they rallied promptly. They became very voluble, too. I understood at least that they were telling me I must spend the night with them. Since the alternative of pressing on no longer seemed practical, I thanked them and hung my hammock in a space they made for me by kicking a sow and her brood out of the way. Heaven knows where they thought I had dropped from. I was touched by their hospitality.

It was not all that, however. I was an acquisition. I had hardly fallen asleep before another couple arrived and set about to engage me in conversation. No doubt they had to establish to their own satisfaction that the outlandish stranger, albeit fully grown, could speak no better than a two-year-old child. Word about me must have spread up and down the river for miles. Not a half hour passed without more men and women coming in to prod me into wakefulness and see how I spoke and behaved. They were in a state of great good nature. All night long they filled the cabin with the sounds of talk, *cachaça*-drinking and spitting, especially spitting. Nearby a dance (I supposed) was started, and the drums kept up a complicated rhythm until daybreak. I was having a return of fever and was somewhat delirious, but how much so I could not tell since the hubbub around me was so like the fantasy of a fevered brain anyway. Bubbles of swamp-water kept breaking inside me. The hawking and expectorating went on ceaselessly.

At dawn my hosts, who could not have closed their eyes all night long, gave me a little fish and a banana and, refusing all payment, led me to where a footbridge of planks spanned a narrow part of the river. They were happy to the last, waving gaily.

I reckoned I still had about twenty-five more miles to go.

Every step now felt like a step barefoot on broken glass. The bottoms of my feet were raw flesh. Putting one foot before the other had become an act of will. I paid no heed to where I was. It took everything to keep the mechanism going.

As the day wore on and the trail became a road, there were more frequent farms, with a man or woman working in a plot of mandioca. At each I had the same question: *"Por favor, a que distancia fica Topacindo?"*

"Vinte e quartro quilómetros."

Twenty-four kilometers! No, I would think. It was impossible! I knew I should come to the end of it, but I did not see how.

I exhorted myself with the name of my destination. "Topacindo!" I had no thought now for any reason for my being in such a hurry to reach it or for my being there at all, or anywhere else. It was simply that reaching Topacindo before nightfall was all that my mind could contain. Whenever the chance offered, I asked my question—how far was Topacindo?—and always when the answer came I recoiled from it, the distance being beyond all hope. My socks would heal to my feet, and then a stumble would rip them loose. The kilometers diminished, but the pack was like a mountain on my back, I was weakening from exhaustion and hunger, my saliva tasted of stagnant water.

Topacindo!

I set one pulpy, palpitating foot before the other, trying to walk without putting my weight on either. The countryside unwound with infinite slowness. The kilometers grew fewer. I felt that I was wearing down an enemy.

The sun set prematurely behind spreading black clouds. A downpour was on its way. Thunder growled from afar. As I hobbled faster, the

461

black mantle advanced out of the West and serpent's-tongue-flickering of lightning with it. Soon the thunder was almost as unremitting as the rumbling of an oxcart on cobblestones.

I entered Topacindo at a run. It was a shambling run, but a run nonetheless. I made it to the central market with the first few heavy drops on my shoulders. As I came beneath its sheltering roof, the skies opened and Topacindo with its brave lights disappeared in the deluge—but not before I had marked a riverboat at the wharf.

"*Sabiá?*"

"*Sim.*"

I bought a half dozen bananas from the stallkeeper who supplied the answer. Sitting down on a crate, I sent a boy off for coffee and cigarettes and, my head against a post, watched the vacillating curtains of rain. The vessel would not put out during a downpour. I ate halfway through a banana, then underwent the sensations of an internal collapse, as of inner fortress walls falling to a besieger. Because I had been thinking only of reaching Topacindo, the goal had come to seem possessed of an importance in itself. It had none. I was there and was no better for it—was worse for it. I was flooded with dread and anguish more merciless than ever for their having been held at bay by the physical demands of that agonizing march. I looked around in a panic for the reassurance of human faces. There was none to be found in them, any more than if I were being borne to the hangman without their knowing or caring, invisible to them—to the people with those faces, safe and secure in their ordinary concerns.

But Topacindo was Joaquim Waldo. At the realization of how near he must be, my heart thumped madly for a half dozen beats—I could not tell with what emotion beyond knowing that it left the palms of my hands clammy. I sent the boy who brought my cigarettes and coffee to buy a straw hat for me. I wanted it to pull down over my face.

I ate another two bananas without tasting them, hurrying to get to the coffee and a smoke. While I was having these, and waiting for the rain to let up, I was steadied somewhat by a resurgence of the conviction that no latitude was given to or imposed upon me, that I was being borne along on the current of the foreordained. That I had made it to Topacindo before the departure of *Sabiá* was proof enough. I was an instrument directed at a certain purpose. It was out of my hands. Events would proceed as they do in a dream, on their own impetus.

462

When the rain stopped I shouldered my pack and with my new hat low on my brow moved toward the wharf, walking like an old man on the wreckage of my feet and keeping as far as possible in the shadows. Near the ship but shielded from its lights by a shed, I waited until the neighborhood of the railing was clear of passengers, crossed quickly to the gangplank leading to the cargo deck and went aboard. Now that I was in action I felt as sure of what I was doing as a musician must in following a well-known score. The after half of the deck was lined with cattle, pressed side to side. Taking my notebook out of my pack, I wrote on a page of it, *"Estou em baxio,"*—I was below—signed my name, tore it out, folded it and addressed it on the outside to Comandante Soldano, *Sabiá*'s master. I found and tipped a porter to deliver it. Events were moving. There could not be a great deal longer now to wait, I thought, not much more necessity (I felt obscurely) to live from moment to moment with eyes fixed straight ahead, afraid to let the gaze stray, like a man walking a narrow plank above a pit of venomous reptiles.

Comandante Soldano came tripping hurriedly, and very lightly for a portly man, down the companionway followed by one of his officers who, it turned out, spoke fair English. Their snowy uniforms had almost a halo in the half-light. The Comandante seized and gripped my hand in both of his, peering into my face with a hastily-masked expression of shock and disbelief, which I was to see re-enacted more than once thereafter. I had been reported dead, I was told. I nodded, and asked if a Senhor Joaquim Waldo were aboard. He was. The Comandante, when I explained that Waldo had tried to engineer my assassination for the *Interventor,* understood readily that I must be kept out of sight; we had already moved to a sheltered spot. He was eager to tell me—speaking of the *Interventor*—of the crisis that affairs had reached in the capital, but I was interested only in what arrangements could be made for me on board. The upshot of the discussion of this subject was that I was installed in a storage enclosure at the very stern of the lower deck, no more than half full of freight, and that the presence of a passenger in such unusual accommodations—which was bound to be known from the food and water brought me, if from nothing else—would be explained as necessitated by my being under quarantine for communicable disease. The Comandante said he would have my belongings at the inn sent for.

The compartment bore a resemblance to an attic in an old house. It was redolent of rosewood oil, not to be regretted in consideration of the odor of the cattle outside. It was barely large enough to take a fully extended hammock, but it had a port on either side and a single electric light. A chair, a box for a table and a washbasin and earthenware jug of water were brought in. So was a large dinner (any chance observer would surely have deduced that the invalid was convalescent), and some disinfectant and dressings for my feet. So, a little later, was the suitcase fetched from the inn. Consideration of what my next move should be would have to wait till the morrow. I could no longer think beyond dumping my aching body into the hammock. In the morning the next sheet of the score would doubtless be disclosed to me.

One item of guidance was vouchsafed to me that evening. Obedient to it, I forced myself to climb out of the hammock and, having already ascertained that the door had no lock, to stack some crated cans of rosewood oil in front of it.

It would have seemed that nothing short of an explosion at close range could have aroused me that night. In fact, the click of the latch was sufficient to do so. I awakened so instantaneously and completely that I imagined I had already been lying awake, or had not been to sleep at all. Even above the muffled racket of the engines in the stern I could hear the knob turned and the creak of wood on wood as the door was pressed inward against the crates. This was what the score called for, clearly. In an unrealized way I conceived of it as having been unwinding while I slept like the roller of a player-piano. Noiselessly I hoisted myself out of the hammock, found my trousers and took the knife from its sheath on their belt. Holding it between my teeth, I lifted the three crates with the utmost gingerliness one by one and put them aside. There was no further sound from the door. My premonition that this was it— what everything had been leading up to—was so strong I never thought to doubt it. (. . . *through the town of Ramsey; Hi diddle um-cum over the lea, hi diddle um-cum feeeeedle!*) I was surprised that he had found out so quickly that I was aboard, but having done so he had, I could see, no choice but to put me out of the way as soon as possible, and as quietly. It was one thing to arrange the killing of an American citizen by savages in the remote wilderness, another to shoot him down openly in a populous steamship. Gripping the knife in my right hand, I took the knob of the door in my left and snatched it open, stepping backward as I did so, behind the protection of the doorframe.

The dark figure of a man stood a few paces away, in my eyes like an

464

extrusion of a nether world. The big torso, broad head with feminine mass of hair light-colored around the edges in the rays of the lamp behind him were those of the one I expected. Senhor Waldo had a background of cattle, beyond which there was black night. One arm was held crooked in front of him, and there was a strip of steel, on which the light glinted, at right angles to the hand. It was a blade, not a gun. I sidled around the edge of the doorway to get into the open and gain room for maneuver, clutching my knife more firmly.

He said in a low voice, deep in his chest, "It would be interesting to know how you have managed to be still alive, and how you are here. Unfortunately, there is no time to find out before I rectify the mistake that was made." The words were braver than the tone of voice in which he spoke, or at least that in which he finished. Half turned to face me, as he was, the light striking him from the side fell upon the knots of his forehead, the turtle-beak nose, one pale, swollen eye. The critical instant at hand, he stood irresolute. He had been expecting to dispatch a sleeping victim with a quick thrust and instead found himself facing an armed adversary who was circling around him as if knife-battles were an everyday affair with him. I was moving to get the light full on him. Invincibility had been bestowed upon me. My certainty of it, my total lack of doubt, must have been apparent. I felt no stimulus of excitement, but only a sense of an inexorable power working through me and a preemptive volition to eliminate the man in front of me as the cause of all my wrongdoing, the instigator of my evil, the barrier to my reprieve from the sentence of madness. I could tell from the way his lips were drawn back as he came squarely around into the light that the sight of me was unnerving to him. My face, I imagine, was that of a cold-blooded killer. He was giving ground as, holding myself tense and a little bent—and probably putting my weight on the outside edges of my feet, like an ape—I moved in toward him. He was backing in the direction of the stern, toward a corner formed by the open side of the vessel and my storage enclosure. When he had only a step left for retreat before he would have his back to the wall, his face, to my amazement, was suddenly transformed. It lighted up as if he had tasted a delicious, stolen joy, with an expression of desperate exultation. I crouched, expecting a berserk charge. Instead he slapped his knife into his other hand and with the one freed dug into his trouser pocket. His fist caught as he was pulling it out again. Springs released inside me.

465

The pistol he held was halfway to firing position when I struck, parrying his knife-wielding arm, throwing myself sideways against him and driving the blade of my knife into his chest with demoniac force. I could hear the hoarse gathering in of breath for the cry that never came. Over the knee-high bulwark he toppled backward out of the ship into the darkness, and but for my catching at the last instant with my left hand at an iron stanchion I should have followed him.

I pulled myself precariously back in board, stood panting, getting my breath and strength back, then, on a wild alarm of the nerves, swept the deck with my eyes expecting to behold a crowd there gazing at me with horror. But there was no one, no one at all. There were only the steers with their backs turned. I groped about in my mind seeking facts to which to cling. Had it really happened? Had anything really happened? My hands, my pajama coat and trousers, were—unmarked. The deck was placid, the engines beat their stern, hurried rhythm. What had happened? Was there any difference betwen happening and nonhappening?

The planking at my feet was unmarked too. But a long-bladed knife—not mine—lay there. I overcame repugnance, picked it up by the warm hilt and tossed it instantly overboard. As it struck the water I saw as vividly as if it were before my eyes a body sinking to the dark depths, protruding grey eyes staring sightless, a knife-hilt stuck out of its chest, a dilute red stain in the water—to signal the piranhas.

Bent double, my clasped hands pressed against my stomach, I staggered back to my door and into the lightless interior. God in heaven, I had killed the wrong man! Joaquim Waldo's death could do me no good. The only one whose death could help me was my own. I saw it now with cruel clarity. Some mechanism of the mind, in the depths where life is clung to at all costs, had tricked me, switching images, foisting upon me the illusion that by slaying that other I should be eradicating all that was intolerable to me in myself. In setting myself to do away with Joaquim Waldo, it was my own removal I had counted on.

I fell across the hammock. *"Feicita!"* I cried. *"Feicita!"*

But there was no refuge, none in all the world. From all sides the black shapes of remorse and despair closed in.

I was waked up. "Yes? What?" I said. It was the steward with coffee and rolls. Light, dull and grey, came in through the open door in which he

466

stood with his tray. There was quiet; this was a riverboat and she was alongside somewhere. *"Muit' obrigado."* All this I had time for before the jaws of realization closed on me with a crunch and the horror of the night rose up before me like a ghoul on the dank air of an open grave, blotting out the day. It had been inconceivable to me that I could get to sleep that night, or any other; yet I must have or I could not have waked up—unless the skinned lump on my forehead could possibly have meant that I had knocked myself out when I had banged my head over and over against a wooden upright to numb my thoughts. No, that was not possible.

I craved light. For most of the morning I sat on a box by the port. Light was the antidote to darkness. It was the element of a world that was ordinary, commonplace, sedative. I felt I could endure anything I had to provided there were light around me, and calm, with the stir of people going prosaically about their business. It was being condemned, alone, to the night, that caused panic, being drawn into the tomb of the darkness, beyond reach of human help—like a body to the unspeakable solitude of a river's depths. The taking of a man's life, whatever the act might once have done to me, could not menace much further a mind and heart already ravaged to their capacity for feeling, but the horrifying circumstances of it had their effect in denying me escape from the agony of pity, of loss, of self-loathing by the avenue down which I had sent that man's life. I could not kill myself. Not now. To have plunged myself into the darkness that had closed over that corpse as it sank beneath the water with the image of death in its eyes was no more possible for me than climbing into a coffin, there to await the thud of earth shoveled onto the lid and the progressive muffling of voices around the grave. I should have done it when I could, I thought—as I had meant to. . . . I sat at the port like a prisoner at his cell window, watching but not seeing the inhabitants of the settlement pass to and fro (the ship was loading firewood) and extracting all the good I could from the light.

When the sun was overhead and we had been under way for several hours the Comandante and his second officer appeared at the door, refraining from entering in deference to the fiction of my infectious ailment. After rather abbreviated inquiries about my condition and needs they told me that Joaquim Waldo had vanished. There was a pause before the Comandante said (as it was translated to me) that it was neces-

467

sary to presume that Senhor Waldo had gone ashore at—— (whatever the name of the place was) and been prevented from returning, had perhaps strayed and become lost, although it would be a peculiar thing to have happened. They thought I should like to know.

I said, "He came down here during the night to put a knife in me, but I got in ahead of him—I struck first—just as he pulled out a gun. He went over the side."

"Que diz?" the Comandante demanded as the other stood speechless.

It must have been my perfunctory account that took them aback. The facts, more or less, I think they had suspected before coming. I had decided some time back that if I were to have their help I had better let them know what there was to tell.

Heedless of appearances, the Comandante strode forward and, nearly wrecking my fragile self-control, clasped me to him in a proud embrace. Taking his turn respectfully, the second officer held my hand warmly in his, his eyes shining. My God! I was a person to be felicitated! I was one who had proved his manhood!

The Comandante said he would have to report Waldo missing at Obidos that afternoon, presumed left behind. If the police inspected the ship, I was to be identified as a German unable to speak Portuguese, put on board without papers as an emergency case, and was to be only semi-conscious, unequal to interrogation in any language.

Before leaving, the Comandante asked if I should like to have him send me a bottle of something. Wondering why I had failed to think of it for myself, I told him I should like it very much, that a bottle of *cachaça* would do, if one could be bought for me at Obidos. I also put it to him that Dr. Monteiro would unquestionably approve if *Sabiá* made the best possible time in delivering me at our destination.

The police did not come aboard.

A drink of rum as stiff as I could take it had little effect except that the corrosive action was so strong it provided a temporary distraction. A second drink and a third, when I was able to get them down, did more. My thoughts lost continuity and definition, the alarms of my imagination became less harrowing and more aimless and sluggish.

For three nights the rum enabled me to get through the period from sundown till I lost consciousness.

By day I hobbled around a little in my confined quarters, worked at reading until I could keep my mind on it for two or three sentences at a time, and made a discovery. I found that in sketching I could escape the more destructive part of myself, as one might escape from a cage in which fending off a savage animal was the height of each moment's achievement. To determine precisely what it was that I saw when I looked at sunshine and shadow penetrating translucent water or at clouds heavy as battleships, sustained on wings of light, was exacting. It was a task I was able to give myself to for appreciable intervals of time because, as by a divine clemency, it softened the sense of intolerable separation from that which I had lost. But I did not take in that this was how it was—I was conscious only of a diminution of pain when I had been sitting with pencil and notebook—and after the first sight of familiar island shores which told me that *Sabiá* was about to disembark me into the clutch of inescapable demands on my faculties I did not for some time to come think again of what I had learned.

It was midafternoon when the vessel circled into the wharfside. The city, sloping back from the river, was glistening from a rain we had passed through shortly before. The impression it conveyed of spanking newness was to be accounted for not solely by its appearance of having been just sprayed with lacquer; it had not yet been peopled. The waterfront crowd was only just beginning to straggle out from under cover. Along with the stevedores and the flock converging upon the place to which *Sabiá* was heading, the military came much into evidence. I recalled the Comandante's telling me that several Constitutionalist deputies had been arrested and that a thoroughgoing intimidation of the Party was in progress, with tension mounting.

I had arranged with Comandante Soldano that I should remain in my hiding place while he sent an officer ashore at once to let Monteiro know that I was alive and aboard, unless Monteiro should be on hand.

He was not to be seen on the dock. But among the faces upturned to the approaching *Sabiá* was one that sprang out at me. It was Jorge Almeida's. I drew back from the port, bewildered. How could he have known I was not dead and was in *Sabiá?* Standing well back in the darkness, I looked out again. I was not so much fearful as sickened by the complications that were awaiting, like octopuses ready to get me in their tentacles. Perhaps the image was concrete enough in my mind to call up another more horrible one never far from it. At any rate, it occurred to me that Almeida must have come down to meet Joaquim Waldo. I watched cautiously as he scanned the ship's upper deck. He

469

would not for an instant be put off by the story that the *Interventor*'s agent had missed the boat by misadventure at a fuel stop.

There was no chance to consult with the Comandante. Against the possibility of a search, I could not hide. The sick German, of whom Almeida would unquestionably hear if he made any inquiries, would have to be accounted for. I should have to continue in the part.

Whipping myself up with an effort to a sense of an emergency, I got out of my shirt and into a pajama coat, took off my shoes and socks, dropped the nearly empty rum bottle over the side and collected everything out of keeping with my role and put it in my suitcase, which I placed against the wall behind a crate. I thought of darkening my hair with shoe polish, but was doubtful of success and repelled by the ignominy of such a resort; Christ, they could not expect *that* of me! Self-respect was going to have to be compromised severely enough at best. Inasmuch as Almeida could have no suspicion that I was still alive, I was unlikely to be betrayed by a detail like color of hair if I could keep my other features concealed.

When all was ready and I had a chance to look out again, Almeida was not in sight on the dock. After one more careful scrutiny of my quarters for cigarette ashes or other signs that the patient was not as badly off as described, feeling like a sick and exhausted adult forced to play a game with children, I climbed into my hammock and lay there, face down. My having heard nothing from the Comandante showed that something was amiss, as something was bound to be with the disappearance of an important servant of the regime.

At length it came. Abrupt voices were heard, and the military thud of feet above the sounds of the cattle. I heard the door flung open, the voices, after a moment's silence, suddenly distinct. Feeling goaded, impatient, sour, I lay without moving. Fear of contagion or the lack of a clear idea of what was being sought may have kept them from coming in. At any rate, I heard no further sound of movement until the door was closed. I waited a few minutes before getting up.

An hour must have passed with only ordinary shipboard and dockside noises. Then the engines commenced to pound and I could see to my surprise that the vista framed in the port was beginning to slip by; *Sabiá* was pulling out. When she was well offshore, the Comandante and his second officer entered after identifying themselves. He confessed he had found it difficult not to betray his nervousness as they approached my compartment, and congratulated me on my *perspicácia* in having foreseen the danger and prepared for it. The news that Senhor Waldo had vanished from the ship had, he said, created a stupefying effect upon Senhor Almeida and the officer accompanying him. They had summoned several soldiers, and had not only searched the ship but questioned the crew and all passengers who had not yet left the ship and taken the names of those who had. It was interesting, the Comandante observed, that Senhor Waldo's precautions not to be seen when he went below to kill me had served so well to cover the circumstances of his own fate. It was *muito irônico*. The ship was now on the way to the *açougue*—the slaughterhouse—down the river to discharge the cattle. Dr. Monteiro would drive down there to meet me.

He was waiting when we arrived, and hurried aboard as soon as a plank had been laid from ship to shore. It was not so much impatience to see me that accounted for his haste, I imagined, as anxiety to shorten the time when he would stand exposed to view, knowing that I was probably looking at him. Inasmuch as we were both disposed not to make a to-do over it, our reunion was got over with quickly, with the briefest possible acknowledgment of the occasion for emotion it presented. However, there was no mistaking Monteiro's jubilation at my return, severely checked in its outward show though it was by self-consciousness. Observing it, I wondered what mattered so much. The mere fact that I was alive? Relief at being able to inform my family of it after having notified them of my reported death while engaged in his affairs? Ulterior advantage from my reappearance? What expectations of life could anyone entertain that would cause him to be so pleased about anything at all?

After I had given him a compressed account of what had befallen me, filling in the outline he had had in the message from the Comandante, and we were driving along the gravel road, flanked by tangled woods, I saw that his elation had waned. The reason was, I thought, that I could not match it, I could not show excitement at being back. I tried, but felt I was only making matters worse. I was a wet blanket, a drag on the occasion. There were signs that he was nervous. He stole glances at me while I gazed at the road ahead through the dark glasses he had brought for me. (With these, and my hat covering my hair, and my loss of weight, he was confident of my not being recognized.)

Without my knowing when, exactly, the subject was introduced, he

471

was talking about the letters I had written him. "The men I have trusted betrayed my trust. Or rather [razzer] one of them has done this," he said. "I believe I know his name." From what he went on to relate, it appeared that my reported defection to the side of the *Interventor* had so depressed and alarmed the *Constitucionalistas* that Monteiro felt he had no choice but to show the Party leaders my pledges of unswerving loyalty, and this information one of them had passed on to the press. It had been published, and my life consequently been put in forfeit. All had been as Dr. Mendoça had foreseen it would be. Monteiro's relief at having got across this awkward matter without stirring me to wrath, or even provoking any show of concern on my part, could not have been missed.

After a sidelong study of my face, quickly terminated by his having to address himself to the road again, he said, "I, too, have had to kill in self-defense. It is sometimes a necessary action. It is not pleasant, but it is better than being killed oneself. It is nothing to . . ."

As he was having difficulty finding the words, I said, "I know. I'm not letting it . . ." Seemingly unable to find words myself, I signaled the matter away with my hand.

Again I wished futilely I could be less torpid and negative in the face of his recovered zest, barely concealed. "Tell me," I said, "what is going on here?"

That was what he wished to talk about. He went over more fully what I had heard from Comandante Soldano. There was demoralization among the *Constitucionalistas*. Durondo had been pressing his advantage very hard. In addition to arrests and harassments there had been an effort to link the Party with revolutionary opposition to the Federal Government. By seeming to put the Massaranduba Concession off again into an indefinite future, my reported death had undone the good that had been accomplished by the disclosure of my letters. The news that I had returned alive after circumventing an attempt by an agent of the regime to murder me would create a sensation extending even to Rio. The regime would be revealed in all its brutality, immorality and perfidy. And inefficiency. The Constitutionalists would be "electrified to action!"

"If my story is believed," I said.

"It will be believed. Was it not Waldo himself who brought the report of your death? And there is a scar from the arrow, is there not? A se-

472

vere one? Then in your deposition you will say what you know that the Bragas—"

I cast my eyes over at him in mild curiosity to learn what had arrested his speech in mid-course. He was turning something over in his mind.

"The failure of Waldo to return," he said, "may be taken as a confession of guilt. It could be thought that he has heard of your escape and has fled."

It did seem that that welcome construction might be put upon it. I asked if the regime might not try to do a second time what it had failed to do the first. Monteiro shook his head. Durondo would never have an American citizen attacked if he thought there were danger of exposure. And now if anything happened to me, he would be blamed even if it were not his doing. Monteiro's purpose now was to arrange the disclosure of my return in such a way as to make it most effective and to keep it from being known that I had come back in *Sabiá;* he did not wish me to be arrested on suspicion of complicity in the disappearance of Joaquim Waldo. I was responding with a sense of desperate hopelessness to my first taste of the renewed requirements of ordinary life.

Monteiro went on to question me about the Massaranduba—cautiously and elliptically, probably being leery of turning up facts not in keeping with its now proverbial attributes. However, when I remembered to tell him that I had the power of attorney signed by both the mother and the sons and had given him an idea of the extent of the area I had explored without finding anything more adverse to report than the dismal living conditions at the mines, he took heart and delved more energetically into the store of information I had brought back. When he had drawn enough out of me to appreciate how much gold I had with me, not to mention rock-samples, maps and reports, all available for display at the political meeting he had called for the evening immediately upon receiving the message from *Sabiá,* he became withdrawn, as a dog coming into possession of a well-fleshed bone will slip unobtrusively away with it, mistrustful even of the donor; I had forgotten that propensity of his. We drove for a time in silence.

I was afraid he might remember that the last time we had seen each other he had been going to find out for me about the passengers in *Boa Vista,* and I dreaded having to listen to what he had learned, whatever it might be. But he never brought it up.

473

After we had entered the city he called my attention to the unnaturally quiet streets, which I should not have noticed on my own, the impact of the city after weeks of isolation was so powerful, so confusing, so discordant. The population could feel that a crisis was at hand and was inclined to keep out of the way, he explained. Thinking that I had never passed through scenes more aggressively cheerful, I was not sure that he was not romanticizing. He said he had sent Sophia with the children to Chapeu Virado. I asked him if he himself were safe in remaining. He replied that he was not a deputy, only a private citizen, and asserted what I had heard him claim before, that Durondo was afraid of him. He also said that if he fled the psychological effect on the opposition to Durondo would be of the worst possible.

The Avenida da Independência, as we drove up to his house, did seem underinhabited compared with my recollection of it. Returned to, the remembered vistas seemed quaint and innocent, as a preceding generation does to its heirs. The Monteiros' house resembled a boudoir turned inside out.

Monteiro got out ahead of me to unlock the door and send the boy out for my suitcase. I had collected the sack from the Massaranduba, which had been on the back seat, and was opening the door when I noticed that a car which had come up on the other side of the avenue, from the opposite direction, was slowing down. My back was already turned to it, and I averted my face to reduce the possibility of being recognized.

There was a shocking, all-obliterating *bang!*—loud as the explosion of one's own brain. I jerked around. The car—a black touring-car—was passing slowly, the driver bent over with head almost touching the wheel and a man in the shadow of the back seat concealed behind the skirt of the canvas top but for one arm and shoulder, and a hand with a pistol in it. I had just time to take that in and to have the thought, What does the fool think he's doing? when he fired again. I saw the smoke start from the pistol's mouth and simultaneously with the detonation heard the bullet smack into the windshield column. I dove out into the shelter of the car, and as I did so three or four more blasts came in quick succession— but from my other side. At the same time, from the street behind me, came the loud protest of a strained motor, then the crescendo roar of a car taking off at top acceleration. The black touring-car was a half block away when I raised up. Monteiro was crouched at his doorstep facing the fleeing car, a pistol in his hand, his teeth bared. He was a puma at its deadliest. He looked around at me at once, his expression transformed.

"'Stá bem?" he cried, rushing forward. "Are you all right?"

"Yes, I'm all right." I was more concerned for him. I had so far felt only the initial quiver of shock, not the great, sickening return wave. "Are *you* all right? What was it? Were they trying to kill me again?"

Satisfied that I was unscathed, he looked up the avenue after the vanished car, then down it. Windows and doorways had filled with staring spectators, who looked ready to duck in again. "They must have been waiting around the corner. Come, let us go in." He picked up my sack from the sidewalk, and as I limped along beside him took my arm, gripping it so hard it tingled. He was darkly flushed.

Inside, while he closed the shutters, I lowered myself into a chair. My strength seemed to have dissolved. I could not believe it was the simple narrowness of my third escape from assassination that was doing this to me. That would argue an infatuation with life I could not recognize in myself—though doubtless the body had its own hysteria in the face of extinction. I was feeling the effect, I thought, of the repeated encounter with Death itself as a crêpe-hung figure of unspeakable features one could come face-to-face with around any corner. In the back of my mind was an icy emptiness. I stood up and tried walking around, automatically setting my weight down easily on my feet.

Monteiro had left the room. I heard him talking on the telephone, and at considerable length. When he returned he brought two glasses of what resembled iced tea but turned out to be Scotch and water. Handing me one, he said, "We can drink this [dzis] *to* our healths or *for* our healths [helts]. Either [eezer] way, it will do *us* good." He explained that he had communicated with the police.

While I poured some of the drink down, not relishing its dank taste, he set his glass on the arm of a chair, took off his coat, loosened his tie and unbuttoned his collar. He had beaten off a homicidal attack and was confident he could deal with any other situation; that, I perceived. There was a dangerousness about his carriage such as I had seen in a bull which had bested a rival and was not going to get out of the way for anybody.

I said, "They must have guessed I'd come back after all."

"They may have thought more about that mysterious passenger in the

475

stern compartment," he observed. Evidently anticipating what I was going to say next, he added, "This was not the doing of Durondo. Of that I am sure." He was working his hands together, one inside the other, the knuckles cracking. "This is the doing of a man who is acting only by himself. And who would this be? Who would have *private* cause to seek your death? I think—the man whose plan about you Durondo has been following, without success. The man who would be blamed. What we have seen is the act of a man who has lost his head, from anger and fear."

"Do you know whether you hit him?" I asked, thinking of the sergeant of my repeated encounters and wondering whether he was likely to try it again. I had got over somewhat the feeling of swimming among phantasms. Monteiro's solid presence helped tie things down.

"I know I hit him, and I think I killed him. Also I think I recognized him. I think he was Jorge Almeida."

"You think . . ." While I gaped at Monteiro, it was Almeida I saw, as vividly as in life, with his wide, grinning mouth rubbery as a horse's, his insinuating posturings, his sloping walk. I saw him in the back of that black touring-car, concentrated on murder, firing that pistol at me, meaning to kill me. And now he might well be dead. Sprawled without life in a sordid mess of blood.

It was a moment before I could speak. "Poor . . ." I began, and hesitated.

"For Cora it will be better if he is dead—after the first news, when she is used to it." He sat down and stared at his watch.

Impulsively, the words coming almost at the same instant as the thought, I said, "You saved my life out there. I'm very slow in thanking you."

He looked at me as if he had heard me speak but had not taken in what I had said. I repeated something about how grateful I was—more than I could say—but he had looked away again and was staring at a corner of the floor.

"It is my fault," he said, "that you have so nearly lost your life—all these times."

"We've been in it together all along. I knew the risks I was running. I don't blame you in the slightest." This was the statement I had prepared against the contingency of his reproaching himself, but the signs that a fissure might appear in his reserve and emotion get the upper hand of him were so disturbing to me that I had almost forgotten it. "What matters is," I declared, "that you've saved my life. That, and the question of what's going to happen now, what we're going to do next."

He rubbed his eyes with his thumb and forefinger. "For one thing," he said, "I must make sure that when it is all over you have no cause for regret. I must make you rich." He picked up his glass and took a sip. "That I am going to do. We are going to make each other rich."

As he put his glass down and bent forward to rise, there came a knocking on the front door, causing me to start.

"This will be the police at last," he said. "You go upstairs. I will say you are too sick to be interviewed and that I will bring you to the station tomorrow."

The police were not there long. Monteiro called me when they had gone, but before I got downstairs was again on the telephone. When he had finished he came into the living-room, where I was waiting, and said that since he had had to inform the police who I was the news of my miraculous return would soon be spreading, and to make the most capital out of it he had been reporting it to the press, together with the full account of the attempt on my life in the Massaranduba by Joaquim Waldo's agents and the second attempt this afternoon by an unidentified person; who that person was, he observed, would soon become known. The police, as he had expected, were making no trouble. They had gone now to question others in the vicinity, whose testimony would of a certainty support his account of the occurrence.

While I was in my room with the police downstairs, I had composed a telegram to New York and had had occasion to think about the situation we were in. Giving Monteiro the message to have sent, I asked him what he thought Durondo would do when he heard the news and learned that Almeida had been shot, perhaps killed.

"He will disclaim him. He will know very well that the actions of Almeida and Waldo can be fatal to his future. And you will see that they will be. *We* will make sure of that. You have been very unlucky for Durondo. Fortunately for Brazil, you are a man of courage. When all that has happened between you and Waldo is known, you will be a hero of the Constitutionalist Party."

I said, "I think I had better have left by that time." I had been

477

seated, but I stood up to get an ashtray, and I remained standing by the table while I lighted a cigarette. "I feel I should return to the States in the very next ship—the sooner the better."

He was not at all put off by this. In fact, it appeared that he had come to the same conclusion. He said that the Lamport and Holt Line had a ship leaving in three or four days and he would make a reservation for me. "I agree it is best for you to return at the earliest possible. To put a fire under them in New York. They must sign for the Concession now! They will have everything for which they can ask—all the information, the evidence of gold you can present, the power in my hands to negotiate for the Bragas, a friendly and cooperative government here in the state. Yes, that I can promise."

I knew without turning around how he would look—like a man with a battery of telegraphs going inside him, absorbed in the rousing messages all coming in over them at once.

"And where had I better be until the ship leaves," I asked, "in case Durondo should take it into his head to bring his unlucky piece down with him when he falls?" To spare my feet, I was leaning, stiff-armed, on the table.

Monteiro was prepared, it transpired, to move me at once to the house of an acquaintance of his where no one would think of looking for me. However, it was quickly apparent that this was by no means his preference, that he considered it extremely important to proceed with his plan to produce me at the evening meeting and felt that moving the meeting at the last minute to another and distant location would seem to make fugitives of us all. So I told him by all means to keep the meeting as planned, that I would stay.

I saw that the resolution of this question was all he had been waiting for before going into action on his various fronts.

"In the morning," he said, "we can think again about what is best. Perhaps Chapeu Virado. . . . You are sure you are not afraid?"

I told him I was sure. It was impossible to explain that what I sought to escape was not danger to life and limb but the exactions of extravagant circumstances, the requirements of situations from which I stood as hopelessly apart as the coldest-sober outsider from the ebulliencies and contentions of intoxicated New Year's revelers.

"Oh—and one thing more," said Monteiro. "The things you have brought back from the Massaranduba."

478

"They're in the bag, in a package done up in canvas. Do what you like with them."

The telephone was never long idle that evening. One of the incoming calls, during dinner, was from Monteiro's friends on the *Estado*. It brought word that Jorge Almeida's body, with two bullet holes in the side of the chest, had been found beside the road in an outlying section of town. "So now," said Monteiro, who I could almost have sworn had gained in physical stature from the news, "it is known to everyone who was your attacker." The driver of the car, as he added, had evidently decided he wanted nothing more to do with the matter and had simply unloaded the remains as quickly as he could.

The meeting that evening was, by Monteiro's later report, a complete success for the Party. Had I sought a hero's or martyr's acclaim, it could have been pronounced one for me, too. Photographs were taken for the press, and then I was called upon for an account of my findings in the Massaranduba region and of my encounter with Joaquim Waldo and the consequences thereof. I could not refuse to go through with it, but with no intention of seeking any longer to promote the fortunes of the Concession, I spoke without animation, as one reporting on matters of no concern to him—which after all, with its seeming approximation of scientific detachment, may have been the manner best calculated to win over an audience. I paused frequently to give Monteiro a chance to translate, and this enabled me to get my thoughts together as I went along. Looking at the ceiling, I strove to empty my mind of what could cause the unthinkable impropriety of a breakdown before this assemblage and induced in myself the condition of one crossing an emotional desert. In this I had to withstand the effect of the disconcerting regard directed at me by an English-speaking writer for the *Estado*, a man I had seen before in Monteiro's office. This person—tall, in his middle thirties, round-faced and skeptical—took notes, looking down his nose at the paper, while I spoke and stared at me the rest of the time. I was not sure whether he suspected I was withholding a good deal that mattered to me or was trying to divine how I had been affected by the episodes I was relating—or both. I brought my account to a close with my arrival at Topacindo. That was by prearrangement with Monteiro, who informed the gathering that I had been transported back to Belém under forced speed in a boat whose owner preferred to remain unnamed for the present. As I had expected and prepared myself for, I was required to submit the raw scar on my shoulder to inspection. Again I recognized that I had no grounds on which to refuse.

Monteiro had my exhibits, as he called them, laid out on a table under a sheet, but, once more by prearrangement, I excused myself at the conclusion of my talk. As at past meetings, my foreign citizenship and the inappropriateness of my being present at a political discussion were cited. As I was about to leave, the *Estado* man inquired if I had any theory to account for Waldo's disappearance. Before my hesitation became noticeable or he had been provoked to explain why he asked the question, which would have made it more pointed, Monteiro intervened. "Roberto," he said, "tomorrow—tomorrow there will be time. Tomorrow he will enter into all the speculation you desire. All right?"

Emile followed me from the meeting. Together we went out onto the side porch, and there, behind the dew-frosted elephant-ears, visible to each other but probably—a point on which Emile took care to satisfy himself—to no other eyes, we had coffee and rolls as in the past, in my first days in the country.

It had been only to see me and tell me of his great relief and joy at my return that he had ventured to come to the meeting, Emile informed me. He was at great peril in doing so, for recently "that monster" had been heard to threaten that an example would be made of him, Emile Beaupérie, as the symbol of cosmopolitan influence endangering the unity of the people. The week that had passed! It had been beyond words. He held his hands up before him, fingers spread, as if he were rendering adoration to a jealous deity or warding off an expected blow. His hands were those of one who has been too long in swimming. "It has been terrible! You would not believe how terrible. Only persons who have experience' the ferocity of political passions in this country would believe. . . . You have come back at the time—" He placed his handkerchief to his lips, reconsidering. "Of course, you have had trouble too, and also danger." He said he had heard my recitation with much compassion for the hardships I had surely suffered and for the near loss of life. He did not know what I would think of this country, of this Brazil. But speaking for himself . . .

I stretched back in my chair with the passivity of a sunbather, hearing the swish of the street-sweeper's palm-frond broom, seeing the scurryings of the innocent gecko lizards on the ceiling, inviting myself to sur-

480

render to the soft night and the tranquillity it seemed to hold out. But it was useless.

I sat up. I wondered if the customs of the country prescribed the removal of a corpse to an institution of some kind or whether it would be carried back to the dead man's home. Would Cora be in the house tonight with a chalk-white cadaver that lay in utter and terrifying aloneness?

Emile, with chair tilted back, was narrating an experience he had had in the *mato*, evidently recalled to him by my own. It seemed to be replete with hazards. When the kitchen-girl appeared with our refreshments on a tray, he brought his chair forward to rest on its four legs and regarded suspiciously the fare set before him. "Of course, I do not mean for you to think it is to me, actually, that these things have happened. It is to a very good friend. I am putting myself in his place. And to speak truth, it is the same—almost—as if it *did* happen to me. Such is my capacity for sympathy, for entering into the condition of another." He had broken off a piece of roll and this he consigned to his mouth, shifting it to the side, so that his ascetic, sensitive face, with its spent eyes, ballooned out at the cheek. "I felt it all. I suffered with it all. It *was happening to me.* You see this? I became sick with it."

"Emile, has Cora any friend she can turn to? Someone she likes who could be with her tonight and help see her through this?" I realized how odd it was that I did not know. "Someone other than Jorge's relatives?"

He held his knife, with its lump of butter, poised above the stub of the roll he was holding. He said, "Sophia was much with her and watched for her before João sent her to Chapeu Virado. Probably, I think, she was making arrangements before she left for Cora not to be alone."

I tried to understand what he meant. "Before she left? But what cause was there for anyone to look out for her before tonight?"

He gazed at me as if he were not sure how to take my question. "Because of— Is it possible that João has not told you?"

"Told me what?"

I could not miss the small signs of restlessness or discomfort in Emile such as he always manifested at the intrusion of someone else's misfortunes. He dusted the crumbs from his fingers. "Well . . . it is that she attempted to . . . put an end to her life."

481

"*What?* How? What did she do?"

"In an automobile. By sitting in the automobile in a closed garage with the motor running."

"And what happened? Is she all right?"

"She was discovered. In time. Yes, she is all right now."

"When did this happen?"

"Oh, let me see. Tuesday . . . Friday. Almost two weeks ago." After a silence he said, "I think it will be much better for her, now, with Jorge gone. I think she will be much happier. He was a very bad husband, without heart. He was cruel. It may surprise you to hear this, but no one has more reason than I . . ." He paused. "Yes, life will be much better for her without him. I am sure she is realizing this. So there is no need for worrying."

I thought with mounting shock and horror of how much it must have taken to drive her to this. Could it have been, I wondered, that she had acted on impulse, on the spur of the moment, under extreme provocation, suddenly seeing her life as intolerable, as hopeless? Or had she been brought to it gradually over the long course of time, amassing drop by drop the despair it would take to overcome the frantic instinct to live, no matter what?

Emile offered me a cigarette from a tortoiseshell case. While holding out his lighter he said, "Tomorrow will be a very bad day here. I think the worst for many years."

I was casting about in my mind for some way of getting in touch with Cora. Nothing I could say would be of any use to her, but the impulse to communicate was perhaps itself important to communicate. As the man her husband had felt he had cause to kill and had died trying to kill, I stood in an ambiguous—to say the least—relationship with her, certainly in the eyes of the world.

"Yes, I suppose so," I said. "In what way particularly?"

He told me. There was something about news of the vessel bringing Federal troops being only three days away, the *Interventor*'s having not much time to frustrate the will of the electorate, the psychological advantage that the Constitutionalists now had and the failure of the attempts on my life which had marked the *Interventor* "a losing man," this being, as he said, all-important. He expected that it would be decided at the meeting tonight to call upon the *Milicia Estadual* to refuse the commands of the Usurper. There could not fail to be a showdown.

A quality of incredulous breathlessness had come into his voice. He had stopped speaking and had his handkerchief at his forehead. He looked as if he were having indigestion. His handkerchief had released a sweet musk on the night air.

"I must not excite myself," he said. "I am under the orders of a physician to avoid excitement. I told him I must remain here where my presence is needed until the issue is settled. But he has obtained my promise to leave the city the very moment when I can be spared. Chapeu Virado is only a few hours away. From there one could return quickly if one were needed." He looked at me as if I had put this idea into his head, rather to his surprise. "Perhaps even tomorrow afternoon would be advisable. What do you say? Will you go with me to Chapeu Virado? Would it not be good to get away from all this? To be subjected like this to this political madness—there is only humiliation in that. It is not worthy. I have a philosophy about these things. It is that the supreme service a man can perform for his country is to make an example of its ideals in his own life. I am thinking now of the ideal of manhood. To be a man—it is to stand fearless before the elements. That is what I am thinking of now. At Chapeu Virado there is the river and the challenge of the wind and the waves. You will see! I have my boat, my *Felicidade*. We shall go out together, you and I, in *Felicidade,* and give battle to the great fish of the Bay of Marajó. You may not have heard this, *amigo,* but I am known for my passion for sport."

"Yes, I know," I said. "I have seen your fishing-tackle. You have shown it to me, Emile. The hooks. The line."

I leaned back, unable to suppress the stifling sorrow that rose within me, my head against the side of the house, my eyes closed against the sudden smarting of the lids.

Presently I felt Emile's hand on my arm. "There is much sadness in life," he said.

19

After he had finished a hurried breakfast, I saw Monteiro only once before the end of the afternoon, when he dropped in at the house to snatch a little lunch and, I think, show that I had not been forgotten. It had already been evident for some time that things were amiss in the city. The trolley-cars had stopped. A few shots in the distance had brought an immediate deadening of sound. From then on the silences were ominous, being filled by the imagination with stealthy preparations for violence. More shots were heard, now one or two together, again a greater sprinkling. They came generally from the direction of the downtown area, but from different sectors, and never in sustained bursts. Ordinary traffic noises had nearly ceased. What motorcars were to be heard were mostly at a distance, and going fast, sometimes with horns blaring. There were no shots in the near vicinity, but for a time I could hear the shouting of many voices, presumably from the Praça da Republica, and once the faint crackling sound of a number of running feet.

I sat upstairs working on a letter to New York, repelled by every word and consequently having difficulty making headway. My attention would stray to the window and I would look out across the red-tiled roofs and the geysers and billows of vegetation that, like the freshness of the earth after a rain or in the springtime, seemed to touch a latent vitality in the blood. There was a fertility in the air, too, as in the atmosphere of a greenhouse; it was alive in the nostrils, rich with the emanations of life in abundance. The sky was a soft, moist blue, and boundless, such as I had known it when one felt weightless in the buoyant atmosphere. But waiting to depart, I had already as good as left it—though that was the least part of the separation I felt from it. The estrangement was not that of impending physical alienation merely, and it was not only from Brazil that I was estranged. The electric calling of the kiskadee fly-catcher; the tanager diving into an hibiscus with a flutter of wings blue as the heavens; the verve of a flock of parakeets sweeping wildly across the sky; the yearning wail of a riverboat at home in the long, far-distant aisles of the river and the forest; these things came to me from a past I could only believe irretrievably lost, forever inseparable from heart-crushing grief. . . . I would turn from the window back to the type-writer. The letter had to be written.

Monteiro brought home a copy of the *Estado* with my story and photograph under a banner headline. Sitting at the table, he threw off sidelights on the tense situation between mouthfuls, like the incidental flashings of an overloaded electric motor, in deteriorated English. It was difficult to grasp even part of what he was saying. The two sides to the conflict, it seemed, had spent the morning in exhortations of the public and in negotiations with and appeals to the commanders of Durondo's "public force," which comprised the original *Milícia Estadual* and newer, improvised but adequately-armed formations. These had so far temporized on orders to take over control from the civil authorities and make wholesale arrests of his political opponents. The shooting I had heard had come from minor affrays between individual outriders of the embattled factions. The Constitutionalists had overwhelming popular support. By nightfall it should be clear what the outcome was going to be, and Monteiro had little doubt that I should be able to add to my

485

airmail letter the news that our side—the side of progress, of justice, of the Massaranduba Concession—had prevailed. Nothing was said about moving me to another place, and feeling that the time when there might have been some point in doing so had passed, I did not raise the matter. Incredibly, Monteiro had remembered to make a steamship reservation for me.

After he had gone, I tried to call Cora on the telephone. For a long time I could not even get central. When I did and was put through to her house, I ran into the barrier of a Portuguese-speaking voice at the other end from which I could learn only (and without being sure even of that) that the senhora was *na cama,* in bed.

The intermittent firing had ceased by the time the afternoon thunderstorm came trundling in to hose the stage clear of its cast of human actors, but after its rampage, as if the breasts of the belligerents had been stoked with turbulence during its passage, firing broke out again, and in much greater volume, with a machinegun setting the pace. There were more speeding cars. A few came down the Avenida da Independência full of soldiers or of coatless young civilians, some on the running-boards with shirts billowing out behind them and eyes half closed as if in sensuous relish of the wind's caress. Once three men came running down the street, in full flight, it seemed, from the glances they cast back over their shoulders, but no pursuit appeared.

At sunset, while I was wondering how far my feet would carry me if I went out, and feeling I could not stand solitary confinement much longer, especially with darkness coming on, a car was brought to a quick stop in front of the house. Almost before I could make ready to escape down the back stairway, I heard the door yield to a key, the sound of voices and footsteps.

The light went on and through a doorway I saw that it was Monteiro and four or five of his friends. Several were talking at once. Visibly keyed up, they remained standing in the hall, too engrossed in the discussion to come any farther into the house. Only one, the *Estado* man, stood apart, differentiated also by his height. He leaned against the wall, observing the others. Monteiro also was silent, letting the waves of talk beat upon him, holding in reserve the judgment that the others, I suspected, were addressing themselves to. I remained in the background and was not noticed except by Monteiro, who recognized me with a meditative look. Whatever else was implied, it certainly did not appear to be a party facing defeat.

Breaking through the talk as if he had not been listening, Monteiro spoke to the *Estado* man and then, in English, to me. "Julian, you take Roberto—Senhor Ribeiro—upstairs." He had come forward, motioning with his arms to bring us together. "He will tell you what is happening." Lowering his voice, he said, "And you may tell him everything. He has already suspected. It will be safer to tell him all. He is a friend and may be trusted."

Senhor Ribeiro and I climbed the stairs together. I resented Monteiro's having delivered me into the hands of this stranger, this newspaperman, and would have even more, and been alarmed, too, except that, first, I realized he probably had no choice and, second, I had confidence in his ability to deal with any menacing consequences. However, that did not make me look forward to the conversation that was in store.

I said as I tried to ascend the stairs with a normal gait, "I was shocked at the amount of firing there has been. I'm afraid the casualties have been . . . considerable."

"Some people are born to kill and some are born to be killed, and at a time like this it's difficult to keep the two sorts apart," he said coolly. "Actually, I think the two sorts are the same, for the most part." He spoke with an English intonation, and with his appearance of having height to spare and his un-Brazilian habit of keeping his hands in his pockets, might in fact have been English.

As we entered my room, he looked around as if with curiosity, though without being consumed by it, to see how a *Norte-Americano* lived in the home of one of his compatriots.

"Monteiro said you'd tell me what's been going on. I take it things are working out well for his side?" We had sat down facing each other— stiffly, for my part.

"Yes, very well. The professional corps of the *Milícia Estadual* has repudiated the *Interventor*'s orders to round up the opposition deputies and take over the legislature. Even the newer units of the public force are refusing to act. There is great rejoicing throughout the capital, one may presume through the state as the news travels. The *Interventor* has only a few military units to count on. They are holding out around the Palace—of course, with a number of civilians."

487

"I see. Well, it does sound very good," I said, aware that my comment had the ring of mere conversation-making but not much caring. Having finished with an inventory of the books on my table, he was leaning back in his chair with his hands clasped behind his head, giving his attention to me. "What is going to happen now?" I asked.

"This is the question before the meeting," he said with a movement of his eyes to indicate the floor below. "That is what they are discussing. In an hour they are to call upon Dr. Moura. As you know, Dr. Moura is the man to succeed Colonel Durondo." I nodded, and he went on. "The military, of course, does not like to fight with itself. And, of course, no one wishes to see a battle. Meanwhile there is the possibility that reinforcements for Durondo could come from outside the city, before Federal troops can arrive. Or the Communists or the *Integralistas* rally to his side. [The latter were the Brazilian Fascists.] So that is what they are discussing. What to do."

I nodded again, looking sidewise at my writing-table, on which were a pack of cigarettes and the still unfinished letter to New York. I had said all I felt it incumbent upon me to say, and now, I thought, would come the questions about *Sabiá*.

What he asked, however, was whether I had been examined by a *médico* since my return. He was sitting as before. Now fully alert to trouble, I said I had not.

"The reason for my question," he said, "is this: the wound on your shoulder appears to me to have been made not by an arrow, a weapon, but by a burn." I had thought that by now it had healed too far for anyone to tell.

I scrutinized my loosely-tied shoes, noting a scuff-mark on the toe where whitening was needed. "That is because it was cauterized with a hot iron."

He lowered his hands from behind his head to the arms of the chair. "Under an anesthetic?"

I shook my head, hardly enough for him to see.

"I'd like to hear," he said, and added, "Only for my own knowledge, of course." He accented the *"hee*-ah," making light of his wish, as if its satisfaction must rest entirely with me. But obviously it did not. Those who have obtained a piece of information are always in a position to extract more. He waited with head a little back, exposing to view his long nostrils, for he had a sharp nose despite the rotundity of his face.

488

His motionlessness somehow succeeded in conveying the impression that important processes would remain in abeyance until I had spoken.

I said, "After being struck by the arrow and escaping down the river, I lay in a thicket overnight. I was a mass of cuts and bruises, and my temperature was well up. I was delirious. I remained that way while I wandered farther down the river the next day. In the afternoon I came upon a disabled launch belonging to a man who was prospecting and mapping." I found there was actually a feeling of relief in drawing these memories out of the deep abscess in which they lay and being apart from them, if only for a brief moment, as I could have only with an impersonal stranger. "The man treated me—with the effect you saw last night. The treatment worked—or something did, evidently." Beyond the window the trees masked all but a few lights from houses and street-lamps. I felt I was looking out upon a graveyard. Nothing was left of the sunset colors in the now deep blue of the sky. "During the night I lost consciousness and was put ashore. I never learned the man's name. But he set fire to the launch—just before killing himself, I assume. The launch was enveloped in flames when I came to. In the morning I set out to return to the Urubu mines."

"Was there no one else in the launch?"

"There was one other . . . who was ill and . . . did not survive the night."

"You do not wish to say anything more on that subject?" From his quietness and the casualness of his regard I had the idea that he was making himself unobtrusive, and it gave me a different feeling about him.

I had no intention of telling him any more, but even if he had been one to whom I could have opened my heart I had no objective means of determining where the borderline was between what had actually happened and what I might only have imagined. What I was certain of in my mind might by the standards of another, regarding it with skeptical rationality, be suspect, be dubious, and my knowing that I could not establish logically that which I believed, which I knew to be true, was a source of anguish and shame to me. The time would come when I should cease to be troubled on that score, but it had not yet.

I said, "I was irrational much of the time, and subject to hallucinations."

He stood up and walked to the table beside me, where he picked up

489

the cigarettes. "May I?" he asked. "I have run out." I said of course. Lighting the one I had taken and then his own, he blew out the match, tossed it out of the window and remained looking after it.

"Tell me how you managed to dispose of Joaquim Waldo." After a moment's silence, his back still turned to me, he said, "You need feel no anxiety. I do not wish to make trouble for you. More than anything at this time I would like to have the state rid of the presence of that vulgar little ruffian in the *Palácio do Govêrno*. I am not likely to wish harm to the stumbling block over which he has come to grief. I am pretty sure you were aboard the *Sabiá* with Waldo—under quarantine; that was the device of concealment."

"Suppose I admitted to what you suspect. What would you do with the information?"

"Nothing—unless you are accused. If you are, I think it would be to your advantage to have a friendly newspaper ready with your own account of the events. No, I will be truthful. There is more in my mind than that. I am looking for everything that will incriminate Durondo. It has occurred to me that something may have come out in your last encounter with Waldo that could be used—I mean without danger to you. I don't know what. I am only following intuition. As João says, you have been bad luck for Durondo, and maybe there is a consistency in this." As I held back, giving myself time to think but not, in fact, thinking, he added, "Last night you passed quickly over your trip back from the Urubu mines. But the more I thought about it, the more remarkable I thought it was that you had walked a hundred and fifty kilometers in three days, in such a condition. I said to myself, it was not just to be back here quickly. You had a stronger motive. It was to overtake Senhor Waldo. Am I right? I would certainly not blame you. I would admire you." He had perched himself upon the windowsill.

"I meant to kill him. I don't know whether I would have if he hadn't tried to kill me first. I was out of my mind. I thought that by destroying him I would— But that's beside the point. The fact is that he found out somehow that I had come aboard *Sabiá* and the first night out from Topacindo he came below to complete the job Durondo had given him. He didn't get away with it because I'd blocked the door and waked up when he tried to get in. I went out to confront him. We each had a knife, but I was so sure of myself, and looked so wild, I guess, that he faltered and fell back. When I closed in he started to draw a pistol. So I

490

threw myself on him. He fell back overboard with my knife in him. I wish it hadn't happened. But none of this is going to help you. Even if you made it public and involved me in all kinds of mess, it wouldn't do Durondo any special harm. He's already paid the penalties of Joaquim Waldo's effort to do me in."

He appeared to cogitate, looking at me as if there might be something about me he had previously missed. "Why do you so greatly regret giving Senhor Waldo what he deserved? Even if you had had any choice, it is what the law would have done, given the opportunity."

"Because I can't get it out of my mind," I said. "It's always there in the darkness—that body sinking into the river's depths! I had three nights to live it over and over, sitting by myself in that cubicle in *Sabiá,* there where it happened. It made me see the night like the inside of a tomb. Have you ever had the thought that we are all buried alive and don't know it? No, I suppose not. I wasn't myself when— I told you I was out of my mind. None of the things that were the matter could be improved by the killing of Waldo. That could only complicate—" I recalled the cigarette I was holding and raised it to my lips. Blowing out the smoke I had inhaled, I said, feeling what-was-the-use-of-talking, "And now there is Almeida. Another killing, another corpse lying somewhere in the dark—finished, with its hideous private knowledge locked in its heart."

"You should never have had to stay by yourself for so long in that place in the *Sabiá!"*

"Oh—I don't know that that made such a difference. I drank myself into insensibility every evening." Finding him standing above me, looking down at me with concern, I said extravagantly, "If you're looking for a way to neutralize Durondo, maybe you could provoke him into doing likewise. You could shut off the electric power and have bottles of *cachaça* sent in to him! Only, of course, he's a total abstainer." And now, I thought, I was going to have to explain why I had said that. And, naturally enough, that was what he asked me. "Well, I was thinking of the time I was with Durondo in the evening when the lights in the Palace were knocked out during a thunderstorm. The effect on him— I could see it's true that he's on the verge of madness." Being looked-to to continue, I did so. "He kept a grip on himself as long as we were there, but it took all the willpower he had in him to do it. It was clear that he was seeing in the dark the kind of thing he must expect his

491

enemies to see when he maroons them in the forest at night." Having not yet succeeded in disposing of the question in his eyes, I added, "What I meant, when I began, was that if he'd been a drinking man he'd probably have grabbed for a bottle and not let go till he'd drained it." I finished somewhat irritably, "Or so I imagine, putting myself in his place."

Senhor Ribeiro took a stride to the chair he had vacated and swung around into it, thereupon leaning back as if for the purpose of contemplating me from afar. It occurred to me to wonder if the impression he gave of an unshadowed nature—like a nut-man I remembered from a nursery book or an advertisement, a Mr. Filbert, I believed—were not traceable simply to the sparseness of his eyebrows. "The power went off, did it? And the *Interventor* was gripped by terror! The power could go off again, could it not? Let us imagine that the effect upon Durondo was what you said it was the other time. What could we do? How could we take advantage of this?"

"There being no hope that he'd eliminate himself from the contest by drink even if given the means."

"There being no such hope. The question is, how can we take advantage of his weakness to frighten him into submission, to cause him to give up—at least to incapacitate him somehow? You saw how it affected him when suddenly he was without light. And you have some understanding of Durondo. You can write in his own manner."

"Yes, I observed him, and I felt that if anyone around him had made a false move he'd have been shot dead in his tracks." I could feel the force of Senhor Ribeiro's will like a pressure on me. I rubbed my forehead, trying to think. But the exertion of mind that was required was too great. Suppose the Colonel *were* terrified—more than ever. Suppose he were brought to look, in his imagination, into the very pit itself, by some means which did not suggest itself to me. What then? He would probably be more dangerous than ever. He would be, that is, unless he could be offered a way out, an escape, if he came around. But what kind of escape could there be from his nightmares? And why should I be put on the spot by this domineering newspaperman to wrack my brains over such questions? All the same, there was something in my mind that was responsive to what we were talking about, if I could think of it. It went back to a time when I was immersed in the Colonel's speeches

492

and had imagined a verbal duel with him in which his antagonist would use his own weapons.

Senhor Ribeiro leaned forward and snuffed his cigarette out impatiently in the ashtray at the corner of the table. "I fear that my idea was an empty one." He glanced at his wristwatch, his face cold with disappointment. "We may not even have a way to get to him. Any man we could trust would, as you say, risk being shot on sight by him."

I said, "A priest could get through to him, couldn't one?"

"Yes, that is true. And what then—if a priest did get to him?"

The association I had been trying to bring back had come to me. "Durondo studied for holy orders in his youth. Something made him do so—inclined him in that direction. Something later made him become a soldier. I suspect the same thing—the thing we see in his fears. A priest might be able to reach it and . . . use it to . . . bring him around. That is, if a priest would."

"Well. And if a priest would? What would he do?" He had dropped wholly out of the distant and unruffled character of an onlooker. While I was thinking of the demanding task it would be to answer his question, he asked if there were an alcoholic drink in the house. I told him there was a bottle of Scotch on the sideboard in the dining-room.

He made the quickest possible trip to the lower floor and back, returning with the bottle of Scotch and two glasses. He poured out substantial drinks and handed me one of them. "Cheers," he said immediately, raising his glass. It appeared that he had not much time. I dutifully joined him; I was glad enough of a drink, I found. "That will help free your thoughts," he said. He snapped out the lamp on the table so that the only light in the room came from the weak bulb down the hall. "There. You are going to be the priest and I am going to be Colonel Durondo. Drink the drink and then let me hear what you are going to say."

No, thank you, I thought. I had no stomach for it. It was not in me to perform. I reached over to the table and set the glass down on it.

"The man gave orders for your death," Senhor Ribeiro reminded me. "He is quite capable of doing so again. Many others may die unless he yields." He had resumed his seat. The thin light from the hall fell only upon the back and side of his head. "It was your idea. You must have had something in mind."

493

I said, "It wouldn't be feasible. The sort of thing I was thinking of would make great demands on anyone who undertook it. I'm sure you couldn't find a priest who'd do so. It's not much of an idea anyway."

"Nevertheless, I'd like to hear it," he replied in decided tones. "The picture of Colonel Durondo rigid with fear of what he sees in his imagination in a palace plunged into darkness has in my view promise." His voice stopped on a suspended note and I could suppose him holding the picture in his mind while he remained silent. "As for the difficulty of finding a willing priest," he began, giving each word deliberate emphasis, then paused, "perhaps it would not be beyond my resources to assume the part myself."

"*You?*"

It was evidently a proposition to which he had to give further thought. Finally he said in a brusque voice, "Yes, why not?" then added, "Clothes make the man." He spoke in a way to foreclose consideration of that aspect of the problem. "If I'm prepared to go to such lengths, you should at least be willing to tell me what you think I should do when I go there. You brood on the death of Waldo. If you can help save the lives of others far more worth saving than his, you'll be released from that burden."

If only it were merely Waldo's death! I could expiate that a thousand times over and feel no differently. Sitting with my head in my hand, I sought to direct my thoughts to what we had been talking about. Yes, I should like to help save lives—to save them from death—if I had any belief that I could. . . . It was terrible and appalling to perceive (my thoughts had got away from me again) how life kept on going in all its ramifications, its infinity of whirling, squirming, bouncing, grasping, scheming, vociferating, minuscule parts no matter what enormities, what horrors took place in its midst. The Black Knight of Death could wade into it with a broadsword, laying waste around him, and it would close in behind him, and before the last head had stopped rolling the marketplace would be in full operation again, the jousting for position in full tilt.

Senhor Ribeiro had settled back in his chair, once again like a waiting spectator, his hands clasped together in front of him. I tried to imagine him confronting Durondo. I saw the Colonel clearly enough, standing behind his desk with the lamplight picking out the undersurfaces of his face, his eyes dilated with apprehension of those things with which he meant to strike his enemies numb with terror when he abandoned

494

them in the forest at night. . . . I had seen those eyes before, once, in a photograph of a man before a firing-squad in the instant he was struck in the chest by bullets and, wide-eyed, was staring death in the face. How many times had that photograph not appeared before me in the past five days?

Said Senhor Ribeiro, "If you were fluent in Portuguese, I'd say you yourself ought to go and see what you could do with the Colonel." His voice was very soft as he went on. "*You* know what he would be seeing with the lights out, don't you?"

I thought he was telling me I was mad, like Durondo, and was about to make a retort that would probably have only confirmed him in that impression—if it was his impression—when there leaped to my mind a picture so monstrous, so ghoulish, so depraved as to drive even that consideration out of it and leave me shaken to know myself capable of it. I picked up the tumbler of Scotch and had a big gulp from it. Recourse to alcohol was beginning to lose its novelty, I could not help reflecting.

"Tell him," I said, "that you have come to inform him of a scheme conceived by his enemies so diabolical that the Church . . . that the Church must implore his cooperation in . . . in preventing events from coming to such a pass." My God, did Ribeiro really mean to go through with this crazy interview? I was going to ask him when, though I could scarcely distinguish his expression, I recognized that we had passed the point at which we could go into that again.

"*O Coronel é um homem de maginação, de idea.*" The sentence had popped into my head. "Remind him of that," I added. The words were the product of that earlier occasion when I had given thought to how the propensities and susceptibilities revealed in the Colonel's orations might be exploited to influence his judgment—an operation infinitely easier to execute in the abstract than Ribeiro was likely to find it in reality, if he actually went so far as to attempt it. The notions I had were beginning to come back to me. I took another considerable draft from the tumbler and helped it down with a deep breath.

Haltingly, as I separated out my ideas and groped for words, but with increasing flow as the whisky worked its dissolution of self-consciousness, I put before Senhor Ribeiro the line I thought he might profitably take.

It had been given to the *Interventor* (Senhor Ribeiro was to say) to understand in the full capacity of his soul that which the generality of

495

men perceived only superficially and sporadically, that on this earth we were surrounded by oblivion, an oblivion as total as the darkness of the ocean's floor, where wrecks and dead men lay. He had been singled out to receive this burden of understanding because he had the strength to bear it and the gifts of leadership to show others the way to conquer it. In his youth he had been drawn to Holy Church, for he recognized that the Church transcended death, that being immortal in herself she conveyed immortality. In the true faith, he had seen, there was triumph over darkness.

But the Church could not suffice for the young Achille Durondo. His temperament was too ardent for the cool seminary. He was a warrior. He had come to his decision. He would do battle for the soul of his people—*o povo*—in terms not of the next world but of this! The call to serve his country was to him not to be denied. It was the call he had ever heeded, first as soldier, next as chief of state. As one and as the other he had comprehended and striven to awaken a comprehension in others that the solidarity of man with his fellow man was the safeguard against the all-enveloping extinction. Unity was the fire lighted in the darkness of night. To stand together, to be as one in civil life as in the military—that was how he taught them to know security. Unity through struggle against the enemies that sought to divide us—*os inimigos do povo*—that had been the goal to which he called upon the people to pledge themselves. The Colonel had contended in his own soul with the evil powers—at night, when the stillness of the forest stood beside our beds and we felt we could reach out and touch the darkness, as it were the walls of a catacomb. As *Interventor* he had dedicated himself to fusing the populace into an indivisible whole, with which each individual would be indissolubly united, safe from the malignancy which overtook and extinguished him in isolation. He had sought to inspire the people with his knowledge that in the people itself, marching as one into the future, there was immortality. He had undertaken to transform the state into the weapon of the people. His regime had been a torch in the darkness, throwing back the shadows of the wilderness, of negation.

Though I felt an external force to be operating through me, carrying me along, I had an inkling of knowledge that time was short before I sickened of the enterprise and the words stuck in my throat. Whereas I had so far been speaking to the tabletop, I turned now to Ribeiro and

496

addressed him as the *Interventor,* spurred by a sense of the need to hurry which my finishing the contents of the tumbler did not lessen.

"Excellency! The people—the people who crucified our Savior—have been unworthy of you. The true prophet comes always before his time. You have been betrayed. The people are unschooled, brutish. But do not let them destroy you. You assumed the responsibilities and burdens of the *Interventor*'s office. You have toiled unresting in that office. You have given yourself to the state without reservation. And what has it gained you? Misunderstanding. Malice. Envy. And now, peril to your life. You have done all you can for the people. Someday it will bear fruit, for you have planted the seeds, and you will be remembered as the beginning. But you can do no more for the people now. Think of yourself. Spurn the office of *Interventor.* Save yourself from the terrible fate that awaits you if you are taken alive. Call off the resistance of your followers and no more will be heard of the atrocious design conceived by your enemies. That, I am empowered to promise. And what is it that they have in store for you? If they capture you as they mean to, they plan to take you deep into the *mato,* into the darkest part, at the darkest hour. And with you they will take two corpses—Jorge Almeida's and Joaquim Waldo's, which has been recovered from the river. You are to be handcuffed to them, one wrist to each. And there you are to be left."

There was a grunt of shock from Senhor Ribeiro.

"And how is this to be avoided? By holding on to the end here in the Palace, fighting room by room? Reflect, your Excellency, on the disparity in numbers! No, I say and I ask you to believe that further resistance will only ensure the carrying out of your opponents' unspeakable plan. Do not give them that satisfaction! Do not condemn yourself to die alone with death in the remorseless vaults of the forest. There is another way. . . .

"Excellency! Repudiate death! Reject it! Put it from you, now and forever. You have traveled far from the Church. Return to it! Share with it the burdens impossible for one man to bear alone. Accept its injunctions and receive its reward of eternal life.

"Permit me, Excellency . . . Permit me to report to those who now besiege the Palace that you have offered to lend your qualities of leadership to the Massaranduba Concession. Say that you are willing to assume command of the forces of law and order in the vast region of the Massaranduba, where the future of north Brazil is to be born . . . where

497

the *mato* will be thrust back, where the means will be created to enrich the country and redeem the people from poverty and ignorance, so that they may be worthy of your vision. But give the word and you will be welcomed with handclasps, and those who have been your foes will themselves write up your creed that all Brazil may know of it and be guided by it."

I had made it to the end, but only barely. The facility imparted by the alcohol had deserted me. Revulsion combined with the effect of the drink to make me nauseated. My feet burned—for I had stood up in the course of my exhortations. The objects in the room, including the inert, slumped figure of Senhor Ribeiro, glided into their proper positions only as I looked at them. I needed food. Lowering myself into my chair, I said, "You asked for it. That's what I had in mind."

Tipping forward, he rose to his feet and stepped forward to the table to switch the light on in the lamp. I shielded my eyes from it with my hand. Speaking at last, he said, "I think you may have it." The satisfaction in his voice made me realize I had felt myself on my mettle.

He returned to his chair, half sitting on its arm, and when I dropped my hand was biting his thumbnail and regarding me from under his brows as if he were seeing in me a rerunning of the scene he had asked me to play. Removing his fist an inch or two from his mouth he said, "I must be, myself, entirely convinced that there is a prospect for success before I present the scheme to Monteiro and others. Otherwise . . ." He screwed up his face. "Damnation! If I think about it I will never do it!" He looked at his watch and stood up. There were spots of color on his cheeks.

Whatever it was he was about to do, he stopped and stared down at me. "You know," he said, "I don't think the Colonel's own confessor, if he has one, could have hit the mark more truly." It appeared that he was going to say something further, perhaps more personal, but instead he picked up his glass and drained it. He said, "Would you truly consider recommending Durondo for such a position with the Massaranduba Concession? Do you think there is a chance that João would do so?"

That seemed to me the least refractory part of the problem. "I shouldn't worry about that. There would have to be a Massaranduba Concession before the question could arise, wouldn't there?"

Senhor Ribeiro's inconspicuous eyebrows went up, a gleam of appreciation lighting his eye rather wickedly. He would, I guessed, have liked to pursue the subject, but for this, too, fortunately for me, time was lacking. Already the meeting downstairs was over; a door was opened, a voice—Monteiro's—was to be heard.

"I will have to present this proposal on the way to Dr. Moura," he said. "If I do it satisfactorily, our debt to you may prove to be even greater than we had imagined. Tomorrow, when there is more time—"

"Yes, tomorrow. But now you had better hurry."

He seemed reluctant to leave it like that, but his quick survey of me apparently did not suggest a way of expressing what was in his mind, and I waved him on. I followed him to the head of the stairs, which he descended boundingly, half sideways, to accommodate his length of limb to the narrowness of the tread. The others were waiting in the entrance hall, looking up the stairway—a solemn conclave of figures made stouter by foreshortening. Monteiro was not one to go in for demonstrativeness; his ordinary way of greeting was simply by the nature of his regard of you to include you in his train of thought. I had learned to reply in kind.

I wondered what justification I thought I had for writing off the Concession. That I had put it out of my life was hardly enough to doom it.

The empty house had no more than resounded to the thud of the closed door than I knew I could not remain any longer in it that evening. Unsteady as I was, I put on my tie and coat and wrote a note to leave for Monteiro on the hall table saying that I should be at the Grande Hotel in case he came back before I did. The café would be well populated but with anonymous human souls I should neither have to address nor be addressed by. With taxicabs unlikely to be available, there was the question of how I was to get there, but this was solved when I thought of the houseboy's bicycle in the shed in the backyard. I could press down on the pedals with the only part of my feet that could bear my weight without pain—the insteps.

I spent the whole night in the Grande Hotel, sitting in dark glasses at a table at the rear of the café, not feeling that I was staying up all night because so many others were wide awake all around me. Indeed, the crowd appeared to grow as the night progressed. Although the children had gradually disappeared and women were in a small minority, the Praça da Republica and adjacent streets were nearly as thronged as on the afternoon of a band concert. That the conflict was now localized around the Praça da Independência was evident from the direction of the sporadic firing. The citizenry, which was to be assumed possessed of an ingrained discrimination in such matters, clearly accepted the vicinity of the Grande Hotel as safe. Any sudden noise or movement attracted a disproportionate but not alarmed attention and curiosity—or an attention that would have been disproportionate in other circumstances. Keyed to a pitch of expectation, the crowd was apparently prepared to await events signalized almost anywhere and in any manner. Sipping beer—after I had eaten—and occasionally smoking, I was less at the mercy of my thoughts because of the numbers of those around me, the movement, the hum of talk, the pell-mell of personalities, the clatter of china and glassware.

At an early hour of the morning a wave of shouting, beginning murmurously from the same direction in which the sound of firing had come, swept through the multitude toward the hotel. Only when it was taken up ecstatically by the crowd in the café could I make out what was being cried: *Viva Baptista Moura! Viva Baptista Moura!*

Well, I thought, we're in.

It was dawn before I pedaled my way back to the house. The crowd everywhere had thinned out, but the clamor went on as avidly as ever, if diminutively, in my tintinnabulous ears, like the tumult of the sea captured in a conch shell. Almost as clearly as I could still hear the voices, as of a happy, yelping pack on a fresh spoor, I could still see the lines of snake-dancers and the jigging, much as it had been in the Carnival, the opening and closing of mouths in faces that, animated by the same emotion, all looked alike. In retirement against the wall, behind my dark glasses, I had presented a suspicious figure, I realized from glances cast at me. *"Estrangeiro,"* I had had to explain briefly to one partisan with fierce, close-set black eyes who was clearly of a mind to make an issue of my ostensible failure to share in the rejoicing at the governmental overturn. I wondered how Durondo's defeat had finally been accomplished. I was ashamed to think of the exhibit I had made of myself with my supposition that contrivings of mine could alter events in the heroic arena of a state's political life. And there the performance was, fixed indelibly in Roberto Ribeiro's mind! But it did not matter.

There were lights in the downstairs rooms of the house when I came within view of it. In a quarter of an hour they would not be needed. The sky was already a brilliant blue, filled with the glory of day. From far and near the crowing cocks strove each to reach a higher register of triumph than the rest. The black masses of houses and trees were acquiring color from the clear light of the heavens, and the red of the roofs was distinguishable from the green of foliage. I could make out the yellow blossoms of the bignonia that covered one whole corner of the house. The world was being given another chance, a fresh start, cleansed of the residues of the past. But coming to it from the wrong direction, as part of those residues, I felt I defiled the hour.

Before I had turned into the lane leading to the backyard it had become evident that there was company at the house. Three cars in addition to Monteiro's were parked in front of it, and along with the lights that shone through the shutters there could be heard a sound like that of water flowing underground, such as is made by many excited but solemn voices.

There were about twenty guests distributed through the living-room and dining-room, I found when I had let myself in with my key. They were standing about, all men and most of them holding cups or glasses. It was evidently a victory celebration; good cheer, barely counterbalanced by a proper gravity, shone in every face. I meant merely to signal Monteiro from the doorway as I went by, letting him know that I was not a casualty of the night and conveying my congratulations on the outcome of events, but he called out my name across the room in an unusual departure from decorum and beckoned me to him. He was the center of a group of six or seven others, and made one think of a bride at a wedding reception, except that the heightened color of his complexion, the sparkle of his unseeing eyes, his smile protracted to the aching-point, acknowledged not the imminence but the successful conclusion of hanky-panky of high degree. There could be no question of who, at least among those present, was chief engineer of the happy eventualities.

"You have heard the news?" he said in greeting. Almost before I had a chance to reply that I had he went on. "I have been thinking you must be on your way. I telephoned the Grande Hotel when we came in and I was told that a *Norte-Americano* who had been there all night, and with dark glasses, had just left. I was worried. Also I was wishing you to be here for our rejoicing."

He had clapped his arm around my shoulders as soon as I had reached his side and, since our eyes were too close to meet comfortably, had addressed his remarks as much to the others as to me. He followed them

501

by more, in Portuguese, addressed altogether to the others. It was as it had been on our round of calls the day I arrived in Belém, and I knew I stood before them as the augury of the Massaranduba Concession—a still unrealized, still hypothetical Massaranduba Concession, but one nevertheless capable of toppling a government, as there could be no doubt it had been largely instrumental in doing. I was beamed upon from the semicircle of faces.

When I had a chance I asked Monteiro what finally had brought an end to the resistance at the Palace. I observed that there had not seemed to be much firing after dinner and that all I had heard had been the crowds proclaiming the *Frente Única*'s candidate, Baptista Moura, sometime after midnight. Monteiro pursed his lips, frowned slightly and snatched a quick glance at those around us. "It is a very peculiar occurrence—complicated. Tomorrow I will tell you all about it."

His reply appeared to offer me an opportunity to take my leave and proceed to bed, where there was now little danger of my lying wakeful. When I had shaken hands all around and was departing I remarked to Monteiro, hopefully, that I saw that Senhor Ribeiro had not come back. I was not eager to have our session recalled by his presence, even if only implicitly, and was afraid he might be in the next room. With the same expression as before Monteiro looked down at the floor and shook his head. "He is at the offices of the *Estado* writing his story. He will be here tomorrow."

I awakened shortly after noon, and before I had finished dressing decided I must try to see Cora, regardless of appearances. To leave without a word of farewell would be unthinkably callous, an inexcusable affront to her. I also recognized that I wished to see her. To be blocked from communication with others is to have a pressure build up inside one that must in time become unbearable, or unhinge the mind. I did not think of it that way, or think at all; I only felt the pressure and remembered that Cora was human, was honest, was undemanding and had recently touched bottom, so that I should not have to make any effort with her that would be beyond me.

When I went downstairs I found Monteiro and Ribeiro seated at the dining-room table over coffee and rolls. Their complexions were like dough. It was plain they had not been to bed even yet. Ribeiro, who was holding his cup in his two hands, as if he could not have managed it with one, had not shaved. They looked around at me with exhaustion's economy of emotion and movement.

Said Ribeiro, "Ah, Mr. Tate. The innocent cause of it all." He picked up a folded newspaper beside his plate and let it fall again. "You may read all about it here. The undertaking entered into by his ex-Excellency, Colonel Durondo, respecting his future activities in the state and in connection with the Massaranduba Concession. An undertaking which promises so much for the future welfare of the Amazon basin—it says so here."

"Colonel Durondo is departing this afternoon for the south [dzis afternoon *for* dze souse]," Monteiro put in.

"His priest and his physician have prevailed upon him to seek recuperation from the burdens of office, which have been so great as to cause prostration—and *that* is the truth. He goes with the blessing of a tribute in the *Estado do Norte*—the first in many a month—which is part of the compact. Leading public figures will be on hand to render honors at the sailing."

I asked guardedly how it had come about. Weary as the two men were, there was detectable a kind of sympathetic vibration between them, as there is apt to be between persons who have shared an escapade. I was not sure they were not preparing a joke on me, for reasons I could not guess at.

"Roberto is a very remarkable actor," said Monteiro. "He is being wasted to be writing for a newspaper. If he can make a priest who is able to fool an *Interventor,* then I think he will make an *Interventor* who is able to fool a priest. What do you say, Roberto? The next time you will be our candidate, eh?" He was in his character of sly boyishness, which he generally reserved for social occasions and the company of teasable girls. I was not convinced. "Sit down, Zhulian," he said. "You will take coffee?" I nodded and sat down on the edge of a chair. He pushed his cup away from him. His sleeves were rolled above his forearms, which were as solid-looking as a day-laborer's. "Of course, this must never be mentioned. That is why I could say nothing in the presence of others last night. Roberto can never have credit for this historic performance. A legend has been created for north Brazil—the legend of a mysterious priest who has appeared to save an *Interventor* from himself and from his enemies and then has disappeared forever, before anyone can learn who he is. And that is how it must remain—a mystery. Poor Roberto! And poor Zhulian! Your part can never be known either. But you will have other rewards—more useful ones, yes?"

I turned to Ribeiro and asked if he were telling me that he had actually gone in to Colonel Durondo, and as a priest.

"It is a good question," he replied. He was leaning on his elbows, looking up at me sideways, the rims of his lower eyelids having the appearance of raw meat. "It is one I asked myself as I marched through the ranks of the soldiers in masterful strides in my . . . let us say 'borrowed' raiment. Was I actually doing this? Fortunately I was in semidarkness; we had had the power turned off—throughout the district—so there was not much light at any time." He spoke with even emphasis, didactically. "The things one does for one's country! But men die for their country, I reminded myself. So why not this? That proved to be a good question too. Because finally, when I came to the climax—and you will remember what that was, I trust—I thought I was going to. That is to say, die for my country."

I was embarrassed. His recital, if taken at face value, required a serious and sympathetic reception, and a most admiring one, while I was still uncertain of the spirit in which he was offering it, not because his manner lacked anything in earnestness but because I was plagued by incredulousness. It was beholden on me to meet his reflective regard steadily—I mean I owed him that—but I had to drop my eyes. I did so on the excuse of shaking a cigarette out of a pack I took from my pocket.

He had paused only briefly before going on. "But I shall tell you all about it tomorrow. Now, I am too tired. *Virgem santa,* I am worn out! And that is not all for tomorrow. You will have to start work on the Colonel's creed—*O credo de Durondo*. He is very excited about it. His expectations are high. At the end it was all he could talk about. João, I must go. I promised my wife I would return home an hour ago."

Monteiro, who had been gazing at his friend as if he expected to learn more than he had so far heard, raised his eyebrows—an expression without significance with him, a mere mannerism. "He brought up the *credo* with Dr. Moura, too, in the negotiations. It competes with the Massaranduba Concession for his interest. Well, we will live up to our bargain. . . . I am thinking also to lie down for a little time."

After Ribeiro had forced himself to his feet and picked up his coat from the back of a chair, he relaxed his decision a little. Otherwise I should never have found out anything more from him, for he was to be busy the next day when he was not recouping his sleep and on the day after I was to depart. (If the creed of Durondo was ever written, it must have been Ribeiro who had to write it.) Standing behind the chair from which he had taken his coat, holding to the back of it, he said, "I must tell you that you guessed right about Colonel Durondo—how to reach him. Throughout. Only I had to go further. I had to say more, to improvise, to repeat myself, even. I thought if I stopped talking he would shoot. I felt like a Hindu playing a flute to a cobra. He sat crouched over his desk like a cat, his hands out in front of him, one of them on that automatic. That was after I revealed to him the so-called diabolical plan of his enemies, if they captured him. The expression that came into his eyes then . . ."

Senhor Ribeiro shrugged. Presumably he had no desire to slip back into the atmosphere of that meeting. In lighter tones he said, "I crossed myself. Strange! I should never have thought of doing that if I had not been in that cassock—which I could not forget, as it was buttoned up to the chin, and very uncomfortable. In fact, if the Colonel had not addressed me as 'Father,' I could not have succeeded. As it was, I could not have worked harder for the Colonel's soul if I had been truly a priest."

I made a gesture with my hands of having to give up. "I'm *sorry,*" I said. "I don't know quite . . . I suppose I wasn't thinking of your actually going through with it."

He did not wait for me to finish. "*I* insisted, I have not forgotten. And we must believe it was all worth while. . . . Though knowing my country . . ." He shrugged again. "Perhaps for the Colonel himself the benefits will be lasting. He has rediscovered his piety. I mean he has discovered that he has always been pious, that he has been pious all along. This was made known to me in a passionate declaration of faith, during which his eye went off. I tell you . . . Well, enough of that for the present. Except that—what I forgot to mention—the *credo* is to contain a strong statement of the importance of the Christian discipline. . . . João, you will telephone me before dinner? *Sem falta?*" He inclined his head to us in a bow. *"Fidalgos. Viva o milêno!"*

Said I when he had gone, *"O milêno?* The black man?"

"The millennium," Monteiro replied shortly. More warmly he continued. "The wisdom of the plan that Roberto has carried out is that it was not only terrifying Durondo with the possibilities but it was also giving him a way out with respect. That is why I was in favor of it and urged it to Dr. Moura. Durondo had lost his support and was finished—which he has known. There is no possibility that a man who has lost his mind and is behaving with such irresponsibility can remain long in power here. The time for such men has passed. But surely much blood, many lives, could have been lost, which have been saved. I must say, Zhulian, I did not foresee all that would be the result when I went to meet you in the *Boadicea* that morning!"

Coming from Monteiro, that was a tribute. But sitting over my second cup of coffee after he had retired, I felt no sense of accomplishment or encouragement, only discomfort and disquiet, almost as I might have had the maneuver recoiled upon its perpetrators. I recalled—though I could not see that it was apposite—a puppet-show I had watched as a child, giving it my complete credence, and my shock when at the end one of the operators stepped down upon the stage and the puppets were suddenly revealed as small and mechanical. What, I asked myself, had I wanted? And I gave it up. I saw myself with bitter distaste and self-condemnation as being like a waterlogged hulk in the trough of the seas, never quite foundering yet unable to rise to the waves. The necessity of getting away from myself was more impelling than ever, and more even than before I thought seeing Cora might help.

It had turned into one of those grey, almost chilly days. By the time I had rolled my bicycle through the front gate of the house I used to pass slowly by in the hope that Cora might come out as I was doing so, I felt far less sure of myself. It struck me that the line of reasoning that had brought me to her door had been derived without regard for Cora's probable desires and situation. Its collapse, like that of a trestle too fragile to bear its own weight, left me feeling stranded, as on the far side of a chasm, upon the doorstep. The door itself, crossed diagonally by bands of black and purple cloth, repelled advance, and I might have turned and retreated had I been sure I had not yet been espied by anyone within. The house, on a side street, had struck me on my first sight of it by its drabness and was of a uniform muddy-brown color. In appearance it owned nothing at all to Cora.

The woman who, after a long delay, opened the door a foot in response to my knock, caused an upleap of the sense I had that my presence at this house was in grossest violation of the proprieties. She was clothed all in black, large, severe of face, with a ponderous bosom, the necessity for counterbalancing which gave her a commanding posture. She did acknowledge that Senhora Almeida was at home, admit me and take upstairs a note I hastily scribbled, signed with my initials only. When she came back, stopping at the foot of the stairs, she indicated that I was to follow her. This I did, up the long flight, my eyes on a level with her great, authoritative posterior. She led the way to the back of the house and opened farther a door already ajar.

Cora was in bed, sitting up in a pale blue dressing-gown, holding my note as if she had only just received it. Quite as if she were the last person I expected to see, I experienced a suspension of faculties. She looked different, though I could not tell how. Or perhaps it was that my picture of her had been drifting away from the original, evolving on its own. In an instant I said to myself, No, of course, this is how she looks.

"I didn't know about my coming," I said uncertainly, searching her face for a clue as to whether I should not have come and, since I had, as to how the occasion was to be—how *I* was to be. Until I spoke, her blue eyes appeared mere mirrors of surprise and wonder, fixed upon me —perhaps of apprehension, too. As if my words had released them, they traveled over my face curiously. If she was surprised by the gauntness that I now recollected was there, she did not show it. Turning her head sideways to the door, she evidently listened to the descending footsteps on the stairs. When they had become inaudible she said, "The housekeeper—my wardress."

No—I reversed myself again; she had changed. Her eyes and the structure of her face had become more prominent, and there were fine lines radiating from her eyes where I remembered none.

"She has an evil eye," she went on to say, "and if there's an evil ear she has that, too. I'll be glad to tell *her* good-bye!" She looked down at the note in her hand. "I didn't know whether you'd come." She raised her eyes and gave a smile, a forlorn one, I thought, though maybe a little self-mocking, too. "I didn't believe you'd disappear out of my life without a word. But then I couldn't tell. How does a man act toward a lady whose husband's tried to kill him? And then there was the possibility that *principle* would enter into it. You might be run off with by a *principle,* like the lady on the bull—Europa, I guess she was."

"Cora, are you ill?" I made a gesture to show that I meant her being

507

in bed. "Or is it—" I paused awkwardly. Or was it the effect of carbon monoxide poisoning topped by her husband's sudden slaughter?

"I'm only just ill enough not to be able to go to the funeral mass. Which is to be in about an hour. No!" she interjected before I could speak. "I knew you'd start like a guilty thing. But there's no need to. There's no reason for conster*nation*. You have not done something dreadful by coming here at this time—though Madame Snooperina, there, who idolized Jorge, will undoubtedly think so, and probably suspect the worst. I can't think of a nicer thing to have happened than your coming just now. Providence doesn't fall all over itself to respond to my every need, so let's not question its sense of propriety when it does."

I said, "I couldn't help coming. I had to find out how you were—after everything." She looked very pretty, to me, with her heart-shaped face and features of a porcelain shepherdess, even now when her complexion had lost tone and her golden hair much of its gloss. Only one feature put me off a little—her thin lips and a manner she had, occasionally, of protruding them momentarily.

She raised her hand to her temple, touching her hair with her fingertips, half shielding her face. "Well, before you make up your mind—and before you sit down—will you just hand me my renovating kit? My compact and lipstick. They're on that precious little piece over there." She nodded at a plain, worn little table, like a kitchen table, with a mirror hung on the wall above it, at the foot of the bed. On the table, incongruously, was a handsome, gleaming silver tray for pins, a squat silver jewelry box and the blue cloisonné toilet set I had seen in *Tocantins*. The table itself was in keeping with the room, which was very small and furnished, for the rest, only with the bed, which was of cheap enameled iron, a night table beside it, a shabby straight-backed chair and another, small three-legged table. On the last, however, transfiguring the dismal interior, was a bunch of yellow carnations in a vase set against a splendid fan of feathery foliage.

"The explanation of the room," said Cora as I handed her the articles she had asked for, "is that it's the farthest corner of the house I could find. It's a maid's room. I thought . . . if I owed him anything it was to wait a few days before getting out from under the roof altogether. . . . You'll have to pull the chair up closer. There's only the one ashtray here."

508

"You haven't told me how you are," I said when I had sat down beside her.

She let drop the hand with which she had held the compact open before her, but continued staring in the direction in which it had been, as if she were still looking into the mirror on the inside of its lid. "I don't know," she replied. "I still have to reassemble myself to see what sort of design I form. It's been less than forty-eight hours since Jorge died, though it's hard to believe. . . . You know, the way to have the last word is to die. I guess it's a comfort to know that in the end you have the last word, even if the last word is only the pathos of dying. There were good things about him. Maybe he'd have been a good father. But I think if I let myself I'd feel such relief that he's out of my life that I wouldn't be able to feel anything else. I couldn't wish him still alive unless I wished you dead, and myself, too—though the method he'd chosen of putting an end to me was by a more roundabout route."

"Why did you do what you did?" I asked. "It can't have been altogether to get away from this. There are so much less drastic ways of doing that."

She held the open compact up before her again. "It didn't seem drastic. It seemed less drastic than anything I could do. There wasn't any other solution that required so little of me." Looking into the tiny mirror, she applied the lipstick with as little self-consciousness as an operator in a beauty parlor working on a customer. Having finished, she drew her lips taut over her teeth and rubbed them together, then bending her head, regarded her image from under her brows. It was as in the past: I was unable to converse while Cora was performing some routine action. It simply gripped my attention. "It seemed a way of never having to do anything drastic again." She snapped the compact shut, placed it and the lipstick on the table beside her and, raising her knees, encircled them loosely with her arms. "I think it is time for one of your ever-ready cigarettes," she remarked.

I said, "What I can't get out of my mind, Cora, is how much it takes to drive a person to this extremity, what a nightmare your life must have been to you for you to prefer this alternative."

She cast her eyes at me briefly without moving her head. "Oh, I don't know. I sometimes think things don't seem as good or as bad to me as they do to other people. I probably haven't got a very active imagination.

It didn't seem a very hard decision. Actually, I'm not sure I ever really came to it, all the way."

I asked her what she meant.

"I'm not sure I expected it to be final. And . . . you'll notice that it wasn't. That's always significant in these things. My last thought was that I'd forgotten to go to the bathroom. Would you believe it? That fastidiousness could be more lasting than the desire to live? Or maybe it isn't. Maybe it shows I hadn't really lost the desire to live. Anyway, when I thought of my oversight I tried to rouse myself and to call out. It may have been a mental distress signal I sent out that brought them looking for me. . . . You have got a cigarette, haven't you?"

Taking a pack from my pocket, I shook a cigarette partway out of it. "You're brutally honest with yourself, aren't you?"

She drew the cigarette out with the characteristic bird's beak formed of her thumb and forefinger. "I'll take that as a compliment, though I'm not sure it is one. Sometimes I think that being honest with yourself is the only virtue. I mean that unless you are honest with yourself you don't get full marks for any other virtue, because you don't really know what you're doing. On the other hand—" She dabbed the cigarette on the tabletop, presumably to pack the tobacco in it. When I had lighted it and she had puffed up a fiery coal on the end, she resumed. "On the other hand, I can't help thinking that when you can't be anything else, when you've failed at everything, you can always be honest with yourself. Not kidding yourself seems a kind of negative accomplishment, the last thing you can take pride in."

"You carry it to the point of being hard on yourself."

"Well . . . perhaps it's that if I draw an unattractive enough picture of myself the real me won't look so bad by contrast. . . . I suppose you'll be going back to the States soon?"

"I? Yes. In a couple of days. Cora, why don't you come too?"

She leaned forward, her arms stretched over her knees, which her head nearly touched. She seemed to be smiling, after a fashion. "Together again on shipboard. By popular demand. The orphans of the storm. . . . I can't deny it's tempting—or would be, ordinarily. A woman couldn't ask for an escort for her vanity who'd do more for it. But even if there weren't other reasons, I'd still have to stay here until all kinds of things are settled. Legal things."

"You *will* come home then?"

510

Straightening up, she expelled a cone of smoke over my head, following it with her eyes. "Yes. I'll go then." She tapped the ash off her cigarette. "And by the way, I've been meaning to say ever since you came in that you look as if you'd had some rather bad dreams lately."

"Do I?" I studied her hand, lying on the sheet. She slowly closed it into a fist. I looked up. "Actually, I've been dreaming repeatedly about a sanguinary battle between an orthodont and a thesaurus. But I'll spare you the details."

"Ha. And how do you know I want to be spared? As a matter of fact, I want to hear all that happened to you after I saw you last. Until you decided to come back here ahead of the elections, ignoring my pleas, and nearly got yourself killed. Not just once, but twice. And blew everything here sky-high."

"It might turn out to be a rather long story."

"That's all right. I heard the Little Mother of All the Russias go out the door on her way to . . . where she's going, a minute or two ago. We've got the rest of the afternoon."

In the telling it proved to be briefer than I had led her to expect. Her attention was unflagging, to my surprise, and in fact, she appeared to be awaiting more when I had finished, but—quite apart from all I could not speak of—I found myself hurrying forward as one might in crossing thin ice. I did not wish to get into deep water, as with the opportunity she was giving me, in the subtly enervating insularity of the little room at the far, top corner of the house, and with her receptive femininity, there was danger of my doing.

"So there it is," I concluded.

"You must let me see the place where you were injured."

I protested that I was not a football hero, but she was adamantine. "I have my reasons. If you insist on being bashful you'll make me ashamed of having showed you the scars I've got from the political passions of this country—not that it did any good for me to do so. I should have told you to take your coat off when you came in, by the way. You must be hot in it."

When I gave in and, after removing my coat, slipped my shirt off of my shoulder, my back turned to her, she said nothing. However, upon my starting to put my shirt back on, she laid her hand on my arm to restrain me. I had a curious feeling of being seen through physically. I said I was afraid it was not a very pleasant sight.

511

"It can't have been a very pleasant feeling." She sighed, releasing my arm. As I turned, she lay back against the pillow, her eyes resting indeterminately upon me. "I was trying to—I don't know how you'd say it—get back into the situation when this happened—reinvoke it. I have a feeling of our being—what?—in the same medium, as a brother and sister might be for being in the same family. I don't think I'd have this feeling if we didn't have something unusual in common—a similar experience. As if we'd been on a long journey together. No, not together —independently. But to the same far-off country. It isn't on account of anything you told me happened to you. But perhaps the actual events aren't what count."

I nodded. With my arm over the back of the chair I stared at the cigarette lighter in the palm of my hand. "Do you think you're going to have an appetite for life in the future?"

"Well, as I say, there's going to be a somewhat different sort of me from now on. Exactly what sort, I have yet to discover. But—there'll be lots of small pleasures: Fifth Avenue in October; the feeling of satins and taffetas and furs, and spending money on clothes; being chilled again, and when you're cold and tired, steeping in a hot bath; salads for summer lunches; entertaining novels. No plays, though; too many ashes to be stirred up there. And people. Always people. People in crowds, and people singly. All of them so busily being themselves. All performing with incredible and fascinating consistency. Never being jarred out of character even if the skies fall."

She leaned forward to reach into the breast pocket of my jacket, which I had hung on the back of the chair, for the pack of cigarettes. As she did so, her dressing gown fell a little away from her, and in the lurch of my senses, I thought in a flash of bitter scorn of myself that I had the answer for me. It mattered not at all what you believed you felt about life. Life gave the orders. A word from Life and the dog inside you sprang up whimpering with eagerness to do its bidding.

In replacing the cigarettes in my pocket she held the lapels of her gown together.

"You'll be all right," I declared. "You've nothing to reproach yourself for!"

She desisted from what she was doing to look quickly at me. She returned my gaze as if she were paralyzed by it, or appalled by what she saw. It was such an arresting change that it even broke through the black thoughts of myself which had overwhelmed me. "What is it? Is anything wrong?" I asked in alarm.

She seemed to pull herself together. "That was silly of me," she said in a voice not fully her own. "I thought you were being sarcastic. I see now you couldn't have been. But there was such a look in your eyes. All of a sudden I was back in that garage."

"I'm terribly sorry! I was thinking only of myself. Believe me."

"Of yourself? I'll believe you, if you say so. But I don't know that that makes it any better—if that's the way you look when you think of yourself. You need . . . Look. You'll have to give me another cigarette." She held out her hand, on which lay the one she had taken, snapped and split. She cleared her throat. "Why don't you light one for me?"

When I had done so I said, "I'm not sure I ought to be here. I'm afraid I may bring back the wrong associations."

She shook her head, her attention fixed upon the cigarette. "It's good for me, having you here."

"Couldn't you get out of the house before tonight?"

She shook her head again. "It isn't necessary. I have some sleeping pills. And," she added, almost before the connotations occurred to me, "there's no danger of what you may be thinking."

I felt that anything I might say would probably be unresponsive to her manifestly absorbing train of thought, the nature of which I could not divine.

After we had sat for a time in silence, she raised her head and faced me. Her eyes were hard—with resolution, I surmised. "Did you ever," she asked, "after you left, think of the last time we were together?" She sat stiffly erect.

"Very often."

Without any movement of her head or body she extended her arm, as in a regal gesture, and tapped the cigarette on the ashtray. "I wonder if ever with regret."

I hesitated. My throat had tightened. "To be honest—yes. I thought I had been a fool. Not to mention brutal. I hoped you felt there were extenuating circumstances." Leaning forward, my forearms resting on my legs, I was looking at my hands.

"I made it impossible for you. I owe it to you to make it up to you. I would let you make love to me if you wanted to."

In the pit of my stomach I had that sick-sweet sensation as of falling.

513

I looked swiftly up at her, and while she met my gaze—surprised, intensely questioning as it must have been—unflinchingly her hand went to her throat and she drew closed the neck of her dressing-gown. My eyes dropped momentarily to her hand, taking cognizance of what she had done. I smiled a little wryly. She deliberately removed her hand and squared her shoulders.

I thought it was heroic and very nearly said so. What I did say was that she owed me nothing. "And if you did owe me something, what kind of man would I be to let you settle an account with me on . . . in such currency?"

"It isn't just that. I expressed myself badly. I was trying to avoid saying what . . . it seems I must say. I told you in Topacindo it was what I wanted. It still is."

The contraction of the atmosphere, the narrowing of the apprehensible to the immediately present circumstances, was like that accompanying a severe accident. In our propinquity in that isolated little room the circumstances in their permissiveness were all-inciting, inflammatory. "Cora," I said, once more staring at my hands, "the trouble is that I haven't much emotion left, for anything. Passion—love—wherever they come from, there seems to be emptiness. There seems to be nothing there." Nothing, I thought, but the worm of desire, answerable only to its own needs. If my words sounded callous, I am sure she had a different impression from my face when I looked up.

She handed me the half-smoked cigarette. While I nervously drew upon it, tasting the faint, perfumed flavor of her lipstick, she said, "I know how it is with you. It's not much different with me. It's because of that that I suggested what I did. If it could only be at the cost of a great emotional tangle, it would be impossible for both of us." She spoke softly and hurriedly, as if we were secret agents with only a moment for the imparting of information. "But a man and woman can come together as friends, can't they? For mutual comfort?"

It did not seem right to look at her. I kept my eyes on the cigarette. The pressure of air was like the pressure encountered by a deep-sea diver. "I wouldn't want you to feel cheated," I said, "or feel anything was a rejection—was a reflection on you." But the words were like dead leaves in the wind, my deep misgivings, my resistance, irrelevant in the towering presence of the genie that had been released from the bottle.

"I wouldn't—if you wouldn't either. I only want to have us let go—

let everything go, until there's nothing left but what we started life with. To sink deep down, to the beginning, without being alone there." Her speech had become more anxious and rapid.

I put out the cigarette and with the sense of propelling an ill-balanced and unfamiliar mechanism walked myself to the window and pulled the shutters.

That she should be sitting in bed in the dusk-filled room waiting for me, expecting my return, having invited this, was to me as I looked at her a fact of unassimilable proportions, throwing the universe out of kilter, turning perspectives inside out. I had the feeling that it was no less so to her, though I should have expected her, as an older, married woman, to have a self-possession I was short of. She looked at me as if I were a figure of great but uncertain portent.

I sat down on the edge of the bed. My feeling of unnaturalness was numbing. "We have lots of time, haven't we?" I asked. What if my heart stopped beating? I wondered. I felt a little all over as a limb feels when it has gone to sleep.

She was smoothing her robe out over her thighs and nodded. "I'm sure you've had lots of girls," she said.

"No. Not at all." I was greatly surprised. "Far from it."

She raised her eyes to mine, but as quickly looked back at her hands, pressed together in her lap. Swallowing, she said, speaking in the same strained voice as before, "I suppose they're very different. Or perhaps one is very much like another when the lights are out."

I wanted to tell her that she need not go through with this, but I had said that at the outset and could not well repeat it. Anyhow, I was too close to her, and she was wearing nothing beneath the dressing-gown, as I had seen.

She may have read my mind, for she said, almost without giving me a chance to speak at all, "This was entirely my idea, wasn't it? Maybe I've got you into something against your will."

"You know that's not so!" I moved impulsively toward her, but she intercepted my hand and held it between hers.

"Why don't you get undressed?" she said.

I was a little taken aback. "Do you want me to? Now?"

"Yes."

She watched with restless eyes half veiled by her lowered lids.

Just before I finished I paused. "You, too," I said.

515

"Oh." She flushed in confusion. "Must I?" She raised her hand to the lapel of her robe. "This is just—it isn't anything. It won't be in the way."

"Yes, you must," I replied, hardly able to speak.

With head bowed she put her legs over the side of the bed, holding the robe carefully together across them. Standing before me, she looped her arms over my shoulders and with her face concealed from me said, "The thing is, nude ladies aren't just like statues and paintings. They're not idealized and they're more detailed."

"It would be dreadful if they weren't."

She kept me close to her while she maneuvered out of the robe.

Concerned that the experience not fall short of her expectations of it, I blamed myself that she did not seem to be gaining from it what she sought, was not losing herself in it. It was, I thought, as I had warned her, that I was incapable of the love that would have made the difference. Her demonstrations of ardor were abrupt and brief, and as if prompted by something other than an interplay of emotions between us. My advances encountered either tenseness or a submissiveness that seemed— or would have seemed to me if I had been able to think with such detachment—a matter less of instinctive response than of conscious purpose. Blinded as I was by long-starved urges perhaps made more desperate by unhappiness, I nevertheless found myself continually checked— not thwarted, but reminded of myself and quelled by being made aware of circumstances in an ordinary light. ("Is this what you want?" she asked, making sure of my intent before accommodating herself to it.) Especially was I nonplussed when she murmured, short of breath, "Wait a minute. It's getting to be too much for me." I thought once more of how she had been at Topacindo, but with bafflement, unable to guess at her wishes. There was a virginal quality about her—though again I was incapable of such a specific diagnosis at the time. I wondered if things might be different in total darkness. She was fearful of my seeing her, and when my separating myself from her made it possible, clung to me so that I should not.

"You must be ready now," she said, taking me aback another time. Evidently she herself was not to be considered.

And that was how it was. She became, I thought, as near nonexistent as was possible, a person in suspension of being. But the mechanism of man is contrived to carry through on its own momentum, requiring little more encouragement than does an avalanche—and being as little likely to be impeded, though I exerted all the self-restraint I could, feeling that any pressure might crush her.

Consuming urgencies are vitiating in their aftermath, when they are spent. But what was enervating denouement to me was for Cora the beginning. Stretched out beside me, sitting up or resting on her elbow, she was as one released, made free and heedless, bounden only to her own propensity, flushed, her hair damp at her temples, a beading of perspiration between her breasts disregarded, her eyes ripe with knowledge. First experimentally, then with increasing boldness she gave and invited caresses going beyond those previously passed between us, spurring me on with questions and murmured avowals of satisfaction. These interjections became more broken, then ceased as, holding fast to me, her embrace tightening, she seemed to contract within herself, drawn downward, her grip on me her only hold on the outer world.

Quieted, she lay a long time as she was, her head in the curve of my neck. I could feel the breaths she expelled suddenly as if her lungs could not contain the air they had expanded tiredly to take in. And I felt a trickle of tears, drop after drop running down my shoulder. She did not sob, there was no catch in her breathing. It was simply an overflowing of tears, and from a store that, I thought, must have been a long time in the accumulation. I did not try to bring her out of it or intervene in any way. I knew at last that everything to do with her had to be left up to her.

"We must pull ourselves together," she said in a voice that sounded as if she had come back from a long way off, like a person awakening from sleep. I realized that it had been some moments since I had felt the runnel of a tear down my flesh.

"Yes, I must go," I agreed.

"Then look the other way, please."

Having put on her dressing-gown again, she sat on the chair with her back turned, replacing her make-up, then lighting a cigarette. The back of her head and neck, seeming so defenseless, and her busyness, all by herself, were touching. When I had dressed I stood behind her, my hands on her shoulders. One was what one was; she and I both. She had tried, as well as she was able, to make me happy, I was certain. I should have liked to assure her, in words of warm conviction, that she had succeeded, but I feared that if I tried she would detect in my voice that which would give me away. "Whatever I might say would only point up its inadequacy," I said, "so perhaps it would be better if I said nothing."

She held still. "Yes." Her voice was low. "Let's leave it at that."

I remained standing as I was, looking over her head, seeing not the paneled door beyond her but a landscape in my mind that lay featureless before me, spread flat and exhausted as far as the eye could reach.

"Well," she said in a rallying voice, sitting up straight, "I don't have to worry about what might be going on here." She placed her hand on her abdomen. "That's *one* thing, I suppose, isn't it?" Holding the cigarette in a V of her fingers, she passed it to me over her shoulder with a flippant toss of her hand. "I saw you looking at my carnations. They came without a card, for *me*. They're from João Monteiro, I'm sure. It would be just like him."

I agreed that it would, and was grateful to him. I asked if she would be returning to the States as soon as she could get away. She was looking down at her hands, which she was holding, backs up, side by side. "At the first moment."

"Have you given any thought to what you'll do when you get back— other than let me know?"

"Stop biting my nails, I hope. O-o-o-h, I've often thought of starting an expensive dress shop. I like an atmosphere of means, and as I think I said, I like people. I like especially to be with women who have a surplus of time and money. There's no better way to keep your thoughts from taking on more than they can handle than by being surrounded by people who're tremendously preoccupied with trivialities. That means women of leisure. I mean human, personal trivialities—not motorcars and watching sports. My ambitions aren't very heroic, are they? But . . . you've got to get through it somehow, and with whatever equipment you've got."

"Yes," I said, "you've got to get through it somehow."

When I had put on my coat and picked up my hat, she stood up and took hold of my arms and, squeezing them, laid her cheek for an instant emphatically against mine. She gave a quick smile, almost a nervous grimace, and whispered good-bye. It seemed to go without saying that this was indeed good-bye for the present—until New York. I told her I would write on my arrival. "Yes," she murmured, "do." Holding the door open for me, leaning against its edge, clutching it above her head, she raised her eyes, a question in them, I thought, but before I could tell for sure or know what it might signify, she bent her head to rest her forehead against the door. When I turned at the top of the stairs and raised my hand in farewell, she raised hers in response, but with the door nearly closed on her and the light behind her I could not see her face.

The sailing of S. S. *Coleridge* was advanced a day, to the next afternoon.

Dona Sophia arrived in the morning with the children via the boat from Mosqueiro. I left my packing when I heard treble voices down-stairs happily irreverent of the gravity in which the house had become steeped. The children set off on a round of repossession, as if they were going to sack the place. I met Dona Sophia in the hall as she was standing just within the open door. "Julian, we are so excited!" she exclaimed as I came forward. That I was beaming both with the long-delayed pleasure of seeing her again and with delight at the joyful turn public events had taken, I was confident. Yet, looking full in my face she seemed, as it were, to have run into a stone wall. She appeared dashed. "What's the matter?" I asked. She replied, "That is what I was going to ask you." Her handbag was hanging open—from having paid the taxi-cab driver, no doubt. I told her enthusiastically that nothing at all was the matter, as far as I knew; everything was splendid, the news the best possible. "Perhaps," she said, "it is that you have lost weight. You are very thin."

Despite the best front I could put on, I found her off and on as the day progressed cutting uneasy glances at me. I recognized in myself a contaminant, a skeptical presence, an open door admitting a chill draft, and saw it as a blessing that my removal was only hours away. She filled the house with bustle in solicitude for my anticipated needs during the voyage. Servants had never been busier. My last-minute laundry was done; a hamper of fruits and cakes was packed; the yard-boy was sent on a shopping-trip for shipboard amenities.

As opportunity offered, I described to her the features of the Massaran-duba, especially during a coffee recess. It was, I believe, simply because of her anxiety lest I let drop the veil from some fatal flaw in its promise —an anxiety more overt than her husband's had been—that the strand of amber-colored beads with which she was toying snapped during my recital, cascading the little globes all over the dining-room floor. Her condolences over the misfortunes I had incurred were voiced, as with

519

shame for her country, while she stood before my half-packed suitcase, twisting its straps, her back toward me, and when she swung around at the conclusion her face so entreated my good will that to reassure her I had to laugh—the first time I had done so in many days.

The time available having been reduced, Monteiro devoted the midday meal to an exposition of his final ideas and instructions about the Concession. Obviously local conditions had become dramatically more propitious for the grand project, and this Monteiro naturally urged me to make the most of. But I could tell that the Concession no longer held sole and undisputed sway over his designs. If opportunities had opened up for the Concession, so had they for much else besides. The Concession had already done much of its work, though concretely it had progressed not an inch since I had arrived upon the scene as the tip of the long shadow cast by the financial interests of New York. The evocation of the Massaranduba had toppled the arbitrary and personal despotism under which commerce had been frustrated, had languished. It had won the state for the business elements and made the realities of economics, with their coherence, the guiding force. Monteiro had a great deal on his mind. I knew as he drew in the under part of his lower lip and with eyes luminous in their shadows gazed at his *farinha* and *copu-assu* that his mind was full of the callers expected at his office and of the afternoon appointments he had at the offices of others.

His wife saw it too, I could tell—better than I, no doubt. It was the source, I suspected, of the disquiet she was trying not to acknowledge. The great political victory had ushered in not a breathing-spell, not a chance to collect all the scattered pieces, but a further extension and proliferation of her husband's involvements. She looked at me with a suggestion of panic at the back of her eyes, but I fear found very little in mine to allay it.

Against my protestations Monteiro insisted upon putting off the affairs that vied for his attention to see me aboard the ship. Dona Sophia came too. "This *is* the beginning of a new era," he said, placing a hand on my shoulder with the diffident heartiness of a father essaying an unaccustomed camaraderie with a son. "I wish to tell you the *last* thing that you are to hurry back and share in it *with* [*wiss*] me." He meant it. He would somehow have contrived a place for me in his house of many mansions. It relieved my mind a little that he found a matter to

520

discuss with the ship's agent, who was with the Captain, so that the time was not wholly lost to his working-day.

Left alone with me on deck, Dona Sophia said, "João will not thank you as he should. He is not capable of some things. But he is very, very grateful. I know that, and you must believe me."

"No, no!" I said in real dismay. "He has no reason for gratitude!"

I think she only half heard me. She looked at me with solemn interrogation, pausing before speaking again. "Please tell me truthfully, Julian," she said, "what expectation is there that the men in New York will now at last make application for the Concession, so the suspense will be over?" The candor and trust in her face imputed to me total experience and competence. I was glad we were without witnesses.

"I don't know," I said with a deliberateness and resignation that could have been construed as implying that the matter was beyond even my perspicacity, though what lay behind them was simple sadness for her. "I have no way of knowing. But," I added, "one thing is certain. Your husband will go on being successful—ever more successful, I am sure. You can rely on that. He will be a leading power in north Brazil."

Her face clouded with doubt, she looked over the side, into the murky waters of the river, holding onto the rail. "Yes. But will it bring us calm and peace of mind?"

"I hope so," I replied. "I surely hope so."

20

The Massaranduba Concession! The great project of development of which the Concession was to be the instrument was, I learned when I saw Dr. Xenides in New York, to move on to higher realms, beyond the sphere of those who had seen it along so far. As for the Concession itself, there was to be none, and those who had worked so hard for it and invested so much in it were left empty-handed.

The Tates, not unfamiliar with fortune's second thoughts, weathered the disappointment with a fortitude born of habit. The house at Sheldon Bluff survived the liquidation, but denuded of income-producing land. It was put squarely up to my aunt whether she could devise a means of sustaining herself there. She met the emergency with resourcefulness. With its ante-bellum character artfully recaptured, the place became "Moss Oaks," an inn offering reasonably well-to-do winter visitors, mostly in flight from Northeastern snows, spacious accommodations, an enchanted setting, a superb Southern cuisine and the living traditions of the past. The brochure did not exaggerate. My aunt and the colored help toiled at it to get it going, the latter with next to no pay for the first six months. Thereafter there was seldom an empty room either in the house itself or in the annex (purchased out of profits and a bank loan) between the two sand-fly seasons of October and April. The transformation in my aunt herself was no less remarkable. From lack of leisure her consumption of cigarettes fell off and her voice lost its roughness. She let her dark hair grow and caught the luxuriant tresses up in a bun at the nape of her neck, bringing it to the world's notice that she had a classic profile. She mastered the subtleties of cosmetics and exchanged her masculine gardener's attire for full-skirted dresses with snug bodices, and if she was more of a driver than one pictured the belles of the house's early years to have been, it was at least credible that she was the granddaughter of one of them. It could not be seen that she was much less happy than she had been before; she took things in stride, whatever came, with a resilient and unreflecting spirit—an admirable woman. The libretto of a highly successful stage production caricaturing the less attractive folkways of the poor whites of the nearby mainland was composed by one of a team of musical-comedy writers from New York at Moss Oaks.

Jacques Braga died, and Tonio was brought out in the nick of time. That I learned from a letter Dona Sophia wrote me. The Urubu mines were abandoned before the Massaranduba's new and highly-placed sponsors had begun even to think of doing anything about the territory.

Monteiro's interests and influence were to grow ever more extensive. He was one of a score of Latin Americans written up in an American business magazine as representative of the new, emerging middle class among our southern neighbors upon which the salvation of Latin America from radical and destructive revolutionism depended.

Cora I never saw again. We exchanged letters for a while, but upon returning to the United States she settled in southern California, and if she came to New York at all did not let me know.

I had not the slightest expectation of the Concession's success when I left Brazil, though it had not been vouchsafed to me to know upon what particular reef it would come to grief. Its actual fate I was the first to learn. Dr. Xenides reserved the information for me, and my equanimity in the face of the unhappy tidings he had to impart was patently a surprise to him.

523

Our last interview got under way much in the manner of our first. That is to say, he arrived late for it resembling a Balkan version of an old-time Southern cotton-planter—more so than before, even, by virtue of his having exchanged his dark suit for a light one more in keeping with his broad-brimmed hat.

"My doctor's orders," he said after he had ushered me into his inner office and closed the door behind him. He had evidently detected that I had been—or he had reasoned that I would be—impressed by the forbidding character of his not-youthful secretary, who sat with orthopedic correctness and a disdainful inexpressiveness suggesting that she had come unscathed through years of exposure to men's baser impulses.

He settled himself in his chair and let a stentorian breath escape. "As you see, I am no more agile. But at my age it is praiseworthy only not to become more decrepit." He regarded me with frank interest. "So you are still alive. After all your adventures, of which I have read."

"Yes, for what it's worth," I replied offhandedly.

His eyebrows went up, the corners of his mouth down. "So that is how the wind blows! For what it is worth! Very good! It is the beginning of wisdom to prize life for what it is worth, not for what it is not worth. It is wisdom that most people never achieve. . . . Did Brazil come up to your expectations? The Amazon River?"

"What? Oh, yes. Beyond them."

In contrast with the refulgence that touched all aspects of the Massaranduba Concession in the land I had left a fortnight earlier, the surroundings in which we were met on a critical phase of the Concession's fortunes seemed especially nondescript. An extra-large but well-scarred desk, a table of the same character, plain wooden filing-cabinets and chests of map-drawers and shelves containing yellowed cardboard boxes made up the furnishings of the room. I might have been at a surreptitious rendezvous on a business of shady nature. The man who stood as intermediary between the two sides, the keystone of the arch, as it were, invested by me with and doubtless possessed of power, wealth and richer experience of the world—of two or three worlds—than I would acquire in several lifetimes, seemed, however, quite at home and in no hurry. He had in my eyes the character of a court magician who, able to materialize gold, armed retainers and palaces at will, nonetheless keeps a dusty, cluttered shop in a garret—a preference which, when I had encountered it in fairy tales as a child, used to puzzle me. He was con-

524

templating me as if wondering what kind of creature it might be amusing to transform me into.

"I would give a great deal to have been in your shoes since the last time you were here," he declared.

"To see the Amazon River?"

He laughed silently, the creases in his fleshy face deepening. "I have seen the Amazon River and nearly everything else. I am two thousand years old. More. Did I not tell you? No, it was to be a presentable youth in a foreign country. That is an enviable fate. But you who prize life for what it is worth have full knowledge of that. Of how it is that proper young girls permit themselves the most astonishing freedom with a young man who is a stranger to the country and hardly can speak its language. You would think they believed such a young man to be not real, but a creature of their nighttime fantasies with whom they may indulge themselves as if it were a fiction. There was a time, I could tell you—I was even younger than you—when I was visited in my poor quarters by a young lady of the highest rank, and she was wearing—this came to my attention in due course—only a strand of pearls, silk stockings and an ermine coat. You can imagine what a gesture this permitted—as if she were spreading her wings to fly! But I must not be a garrulous old man in the presence of that which you have taken so much trouble to bring me." He nodded at the small suitcase I had with me. I asked if I should open it on his desk.

"Please," he replied.

While he examined the contents, I wandered to the window and stood looking out. Little was in view but the wall of masonry and glass on the other side of the narrow street, for Dr. Xenides had established himself at the heart of the district where the buildings pressed almost as close upon one another as the upended slabs in an ice jam. However, through the windows across the way fragments of offices could be seen, stocked with men or women at filing-cabinets or typewriters, large brown glass ashtrays, appointment-calendars and wall-calendars, in-boxes and out-boxes full of papers, assorted accessories in brown or green enameled metal: lamps, ashtray stands, a coat-tree, a water-cooler. I looked in vain for a departure from the theme; even the pots of Sansevieria on two of the windowsills looked as if they had been sent by an office-supply house. A few of the offices, I could see, were uncluttered, with green or maroon carpet, a corner of highly polished table, a leather-covered chair or sofa,

525

a print in a narrow frame on the wall. In one, directly across from me, the executive occupant himself was to be seen at a walnut desk with fluted corner posts holding converse with a secretary. Unsullied was how I imagined everything in that office—the man's hands and lean cheeks, his cuffs and somber grey suit, the secretary and her white shirtwaist with modest ruffle down the front, the desk-blotter, the leather-framed photograph on the desk, the black onyx fountain-pen set. Was the secretary with her carefully set blonde hair—femininity-on-ice, I pictured her —another being after hours, I wondered, capable of repairing to a man's apartment for some variant of the performance with the ermine coat? The thought affected me disagreeably, with a sensation of internal disorganization and a whiff of the atmosphere of a street-corner at 3 A.M. The man at the desk was holding a pencil out from him by the tip of the eraser-end. Out from it flowed decisions, like broadcasts from a radio antenna, causing factories to rise in St. Louis and the produce of a thousand farms in the Midwest and the South to change hands. Swim, or sink, that was the rule of the world. This was one of the swimmers.

"You have done extremely well," said Dr. Xenides. "I must confess I am astonished that you have been able to do so well. Would you agree to let me have these and pay you for them?"

Surprised I said, "There is no reason for you to pay me for them. I brought them here to leave with you. They are part of Dr. Monteiro's presentation, to support the case for the Concession."

"Yes." He had pushed himself back from his desk. "That brings us to a rather distressing consideration." He laid his meaty hands, fingers interlaced, across his stomach; they looked as if they were linked by the heavy gold bands of the two rings he wore. Following his gaze, I had the peculiar sensation of a person, expected by him, entering at the door and crossing the room to merge with me in the chair in which I had just sat. Dr. Xenides's lips were set in a sorrowful pout, but I fancied I descried a gleam in the comfortably embedded eyes, over which was that characteristic, faint, oily sheen, such as is sometimes found on coffee. "Mr. Tate," he said, "I must tell you that there is to be no application for a concession. I have done all I can without success."

"A great many persons are going to be terribly disappointed to hear it. What seems to be the trouble?"

He waited, perhaps for some further show of emotion on my part, before resuming abruptly. "It is the Brazilian Government. Its pronouncements and decrees in recent months have convinced my interested parties that the trend in Brazil is strongly against the private foreign investor. They believe the day is not far off when foreigners engaging in the extractive industries in Brazil will face impossible conditions."

"I am sure Dr. Monteiro could set their minds at rest on that point."

"No, the decision is made. I did my best, but it is final. The Massaranduba Concession is no longer under consideration." His immobility of body and countenance as he continued to gaze at me seemed to give the finality of events incontrovertible expression; all was finished, there was nothing left to do.

Nettled by his brusqueness and complacency rather than affected by the Concession's sudden demise, I asked with a gesture at the articles spread out before him, which I avoided seeing, "Then why do you want these things? What will you do with them?"

That restored him to animation. He shifted position, opened a humidor on his desk, offered it to me and upon my excusing myself from his hospitality, took a cigar from it, clipped off the tip with a special gold device in the shape of a razor blade and lighted it with a match that took some rummaging about in a drawer to find. The process struck me as protracted.

"You must try," he said finally, "to put yourself in my place. A difficult task? But try nevertheless. It is possible that I have not many active years remaining. I could not afford to lose time or money through this uncertain business. I had to make the most of my assets in it. You will remember my showing you maps of the Massaranduba and pointing out to you that there were no others like them? All the time I have had several men in the field extending this survey. Ordinary foresight required that I make myself possessed of all the information I could obtain. And then what did I see happen? The Massaranduba became important news. It became an object of great political rivalry in the country. But why am I telling you this? Who knows of this better than you? Who knows better than you, too, of the extreme hopes the Massaranduba has awakened?"

He squirmed backward into a snugger position in his chair. He drew on the cigar and expelled the smoke with sensuous deliberateness, watching it with brimming eyes contentedly narrowed. When he looked back at me and resumed, it was with the comfortable air of picking up the thread of a story involving others. "To my gratification, I find that my maps, and the other information I have obtained, are considered to be

527

of great value. Since this collection is the only one of its kind, we have what is called, I believe, a sellers' market. The Brazilian Government is very interested. There is money in the Massaranduba, eh? Very much money! There are private parties, too, who are interested—in São Paolo. Because they are persons of German race, the Government may be worried. You know about the appeal that the new Reich makes to many of the overseas Germans. The Brazilian Government would not of course wish to have a foreign power like Germany achieve through nominally Brazilian citizens a predominance in a rich area of the country far from Rio. Or perhaps this consideration has no part in its calculations. I really do not know. I can say only that my negotiations with Rio are proceeding satisfactorily. Our remaining differences as to terms are quite narrow, and these exhibits you have brought should help close them. I tell you this frankly as a reason for you to accept payment."

For a while I said nothing. I daresay he felt he at least owed it to me to give me all the time I wanted.

"Did you have one of your surveyors, your explorers, operating on the Rio Ipaituba last month?" I asked.

"The Rio Ipaituba? Hmmm." At first he seemed not to comprehend my question. "I do not think I have heard of this river."

"At the extreme southwest of the territory the Concession was to have incorporated, flowing away from the Massaranduba."

"The extreme southwest. . . ." His eyes, emptied and watchful, did not leave mine. "It is possible. Yes, that area was scheduled next for exploration. Of course, I had no direct dealing with the men who went into the field. It was all managed by an agent of mine in Brazil. Why do you ask? Did you encounter someone on this river who you think may have been working for me?"

"Briefly. I seem to understand things a little more clearly. Mr. Monteiro told me that before I had arrived you had given me the character of an accomplished young go-getter from a law firm world-renowned for its commercial work. I suspect he was telling the truth."

He looked at me in manifest enjoyment of his own impudence. "I thought if I could put you years ahead in your career with the stroke of a pen it would be a pity not to do so!"

"And there's another thing. I remember you were having business in Canada the last time I was here. Were you behind the interest of the Canadian firm in the Massaranduba?"

528

Nothing registered at all in his face. Then, perhaps to hide it, he bent his head to examine his cigar. "Yes, there was a Canadian organization that was interested for a time. One with operations in Minas Gerais." He looked up and smiled disarmingly. "But don't press me too hard, Mr. Tate. You have your little secrets. You must let me have mine. I can tell you this, however. I had nothing to do with that man you had so much trouble with, who was supposed to be acting for the Canadian organization but was procured by the Governor, Mr. Durondo." He held up his hand to forestall an interruption, though I had none in mind. His expression had become serious and matter-of-fact, perhaps wholly so for the only time during our interview. "In actuality, the entrance of the Canadian organization into the affair was in Mr. Monteiro's interest, in prodding the people here in New York—as you yourself foresaw that it would. I can promise you that throughout I have done everything I could to bring this business to consummation." He paused, with a question in his face.

"I am sure you have," I said.

My tone was evidently not entirely satisfying to him. The question in his face remained. I had increasingly the impression that he was a little bothered by my failure to appear particularly affected by the proceedings.

He resumed. "Because you have put so much into the business and undergone so much on account of it, I thought you deserved to be the first to know of the unfortunate outcome. But now I see it is no favor to you because it is you now who must carry the bad news to the others."

"It's no matter," I said. "It will be equally hard on them, wherever it comes from."

He emitted a bearlike noise between a clearing of the throat and a grunt, such as a sleeper might make, and just as unself-consciously. Impatiently, even irritably, he opened one drawer, then another of his desk, finally coming up with a checkbook. "I am trying to think," he said, "how much would be fair payment for the articles you have brought back from Brazil."

"None! I don't want anything for them!" He had been gazing at me with the speculative, quizzical air that goes with the interjection "Don't tell me! Let me guess!" The look of startled surprise he now gave me made me realize how emphatic I must have sounded. In a much moderated voice I added, "As I said, I'm only Dr. Monteiro's representative in

529

this. If there's to be any payment, it would be to him. You can take it up with Mr. Willet if you'd care to."

He snapped the checkbook shut and tossed it on the desk, and I was prepared for a biting response. However, he remained staring at the object as one will at the surface of a pond into which one has cast a stone. He grunted again, but in no way to compare with the previous eruption, and when he raised his eyes again it was with a tolerant expression, even with appreciation or amusement.

"So that is how you get even with the old man!" he exclaimed. "Well, that's all right. It is what I might have done at your age. Youth is the time for gestures. Youth can fling away its substance because all will be replaced. Youth is served in everything. The young can be contemptuous of money because they do not need it. They do not know what they are eating or care what they are wearing, and young men can have freely, for nothing, the enjoyment of girls. They do not even need to provide a meal. The girl will cook the meal and be the dessert herself. I remember when I could afford the gesture of disregard for money. It gave me a fine feeling. What a devil it made me think myself! Yes, I, too, could then hold life to be of small value, having so much of it to look forward to. But the luxury of youth is not one that lasts forever, my friend. You will not believe me now, but you will remember someday what I have told you. That day you will wake up and discover that you are expected to pay. And more and more you will have to pay for less and less."

A draw on his cigar set off a short spell of coughing. He coughed without inhibition, blowing out his heavy lips and moustache, filling the room with his booming. He cleared his throat with the same raucous vigor, looked around as if for a place in which to spit, gave up the search and rolled his attention over at me again, reminding me of a walrus coming up for air, eyes still bleary from the depths.

"You would think life hardly worth living," he resumed hoarsely, stopping to cough and clear his throat once more. "You would think it hardly worth living if it could provide no better than a modest villa in Ramleh—that's Alexandria—and the things that go with it: the southern sun; the most dishonest but efficient and skillful servants in the world; the pleasures of the table, with the rich and savory dishes that a rice staple seems to inspire; the other indulgences of the flesh adapted to the condition of those who are young only in spirit; the presence of

530

antiquity, which is important, for those who cannot look far ahead with surety find the past more congenial than the future. Nothing more stirring than that! Yet the time will come when such an existence will be very acceptable to you. You will be able to find some contentment in it when you consider how much worse it could be." He placed his hands upon his thighs with the evident purpose of assisting himself to his feet, but instead he leaned back in his chair with a sigh.

"You were looking into the windows across the street," he said. "Within blocks of this building are the offices of corporations more powerful than all but half a dozen governments of the world. Their officers are what you would expect. They are . . . *hard-boiled*. But they know who is the master. When money calls the tune, they dance. Fast and faster! They jump up and clap their heels together. They are wise to do so. I danced this jig myself for many years. I learned the steps. I came to dance it well. And now it is my privilege to summon the musician and watch the others dance. Even the *hard-boiled,* superior Americans.

"Yet would I give you all the advantages I have won for what you possess without effort—your youth. I would make the exchange very gladly. This was in my mind before you came, when I was thinking with regret of the disappointment I must cause you. I told myself that the situation was therefore not unfair. Indeed, it was weighted heavily in your favor. And now I find there is no great disappointment. I might have saved myself the sympathy. The matter of the dance of which I have spoken does not touch you."

"If you think that, you are very much mistaken," I said. I wondered if I should be required to accept his check for the loot of the Massaranduba in witness of my total acceptance of the way of the world.

"Am I?" he asked after taking a moment seemingly to assess my response. "So much the better then!" His rumbling voice filled the room, as the sound of a railroad-train fills a station. "Because the dance will be played, and if you do not command the musician, the musician will command you."

Raising my eyes, I found him looking at me like a fond parent.

"You will do!" he declared. "You will come out all right. You are exactly as I was when I was a young man."

"It's good of you to say so. . . . No, please don't get up," I interposed as he appeared again about to make the effort to rise.

"You must visit me in my retirement," he said, having readily aban-

531

doned the effort. "I will try to contrive some amusement, and you will give me the opportunity to see how you are doing."

Replying that I should look forward to it, I took my departure, leaving him to his evident enjoyment of the prospect he had called up.

I telephoned Mr. Willet and my father and gave them the news. That left me with nothing to do and plenty of time for it—by a reasonable estimate, the rest of my life. To distract myself from my thoughts I had an early dinner, but the device was not very successful, for the restaurant, which undoubtedly was packed for the noon meal, was nearly empty for the evening. Afterward, following the drift of my feet, I walked down to the Battery. The ferry for Staten Island was loading, and drawn by the water, I followed the scattering of late, homeward-bound commuters aboard.

The evening was warm, with a light blanket of smoke haze merging in the west with a low bank of cloud. Behind the pall a fiery sun was sinking. A gull the color of black-walnut ice cream—one of the immature summer ones—launched out from a cluster of pilings at the end of the slip as we pulled out, flappingly heavily in the sultry air before it gained momentum and a command of the medium. The unremitting, never-ending drone of the city, drowned out spasmodically by the lurching groans and clangings and clashings of the elevated trains, fell away behind us. Even the yelping of the towboats grew more distant. The waters of the bay appeared heavy and passive, and the cargo-ships moored in the roads with deep shadows gathered in their hollows, seemingly beyond any possibility of ever being under way again, rode as high as they would have in a basin of mercury. Under the languor of the fading summer evening the scene of the bay, into which I had steamed only the day before, with the myriad shifting flavors of Brazil carried in the ship's wake, like fallen autumn leaves which seem to pursue the fleeing motorcar, had the quality of a scene in retrospect and of sharing the present with scenes of the past, indeed with all that was left of bygone days.

The deepening orange light that fell upon the side of the ferryboat, upon the cargo-ships bleeding rust through numerous wounds, upon the distant buildings of Long Island, faded out altogether. The sun had gone. But in its passage the strata of clouds above it were transformed into fields of radiant pink surf matching in intensity the rarefied blue of the sky and then, as the light ebbed from them, stood darkly against a glow in the west of so hot a hue one imagined the earth to have opened up beyond the horizon, uncovering the volcanic fires at its core.

As I stood by the rail watching, I ceased to see the far-off waterfront of New Jersey across the bay and beheld in its place the forested shore of the great waterway of the Amazon as it had appeared at the last from the deck of the ship that was taking me away—before I shut myself off from it.

I had been alone with Dona Sophia until nearly the end, and turning to her, had asked, in as ordinary a voice as I could manage, if she knew of a song called *"Murucututú,"* which I had heard could possibly be sung so as to assuage the pain even of a dying man. *" 'Murucututú'?* Yes," she had said in some surprise. "It is a simple little lullaby. *'Muru-cututú da beira do rio, vem ver meu filhinho que ainda não dormiu.'* 'Owl from the bank of the river, come see my child, who is not yet sleeping.' The mother tells the child to go to sleep, otherwise the owl will come carry it away. *Murucututú* is the sound that the owl makes." I had held myself together; I was not going to give way. And I had prevailed over myself, while the Monteiros departed and even afterward; I had stood immobile on deck as the ship pulled out and headed toward the bay. But finally I could endure no longer the sight of what was before me and had taken refuge in my cabin, throwing myself on the bunk, having barely made it in time.

And now I was back there again, seeing it as I had seen it then, but gripped by it, held fast by it. For however long the illusion may have lasted, I was there on the mighty river with a completeness that left no room even for surprise. There it was, the infinitude of the sky filled with the fires of the earth's forging, the strands of cloud above the vanished sun melting into gold, and behind the vessel, between the black and crenellated walls of the forest—wavering inked lines marking the juncture of sky and water—the stupendous River Sea, a cauldron of color, leading to the secret and mysterious fastnesses of the continent, and in the sublimity of the spectacle it displayed, in the presence of the Unknowable, the Unimaginable, to which it testified, releasing all the flood of awe of which the heart is capable.

I grasped one of the ferryboat's iron posts for support. My flesh crawled with the thrill of a premonitory excitement, as at night in a close room when a stir of air from without billows the curtains and with

533

quickened senses one is made alert to the portent of far distances. My heart was pounding wildly.

Feicita!

I was back once more in the launch, saw her as, with eyes already closed, she held tight my hand and summoned for a last effort her failing strength. "Beyond," I heard her murmur. "Julian! *Beyond!*"